LAMMANA

Lammana

Spiderwize
Remus House
Coltsfoot Drive
Woodston
Peterborough
PE2 9BF

www.spiderwize.com

A CIP catalogue record for this book is available from the British Library.

The views expressed in this work are solely those of the author and
do not necessarily reflect the views of the publisher, and the publisher
hereby disclaims any responsibility for them.

This book is a work of fiction. Apart from places and historical fact, any
resemblance or otherwise to actual persons, living or dead, or events,
establishments and institutions, is purely coincidental.

ISBN: 978-1-911596-19-6

This novel is dedicated to Kathleen Mary Austin, a wonderful and remarkable mother to three children, whose life has been devoted to her family

LAMMANA

PHILIP A. D. AUSTIN

Prologue

Looe 1749

Cornwall is a county steeped in the history of smuggling. It was a way of life for the people of these shores, a livelihood no different from fishing or mining, for these ill-gotten gains meant the difference between subsistence or existence, hunger or starvation, even between life and death itself. And on a cold spring night, high on the cliffs above the town of Looe, near to a deserted and dilapidated stone cottage, this enterprise was unfolding.

Approaching the building along a rough dirt track, slightly wet from a recent light shower and just wide enough for two horses, was an empty dray. The horses were black matching the night sky, for it was a new moon, a new moon just on the cusp of waxing, and darkness was the perfect ally for their nocturnal activity. Both the horses and the drayman didn't need any light; they knew the way all too well, having negotiated it many a time and could navigate the twisting route blindfolded. But noise was the enemy, and on a still night like tonight sound travelled far. So, covering the horses' hooves and tied around their fetlocks were cloth socks to muffle the sound of their progress up the track.

A portly man, wearing a cape, was steering the team slowly towards the cottage. Another man, tall and wiry, was waiting impatiently at the entrance, beckoning the drayman to hurry up. But he didn't see him, or if he did, ignored him and continued at the same pace and rhythm as before, until he finally arrived.

'About time. What took you so long?' came an angry whisper as the watchman grabbed the reins causing the horses to break the silence.

The drayman didn't answer immediately, but got down and removed his cape.

'Had to stop. Thought I heard something in the stitches back there,' pointing in the direction he'd just come. 'Don't like it. Sounds too quiet,' he continued.

'That's what we want, stupid.'

The drayman ignored his comment. 'Even the horses are spooked tonight. They sense something. They're not usually skittish like this.'

'Don't be daft, who'll be out on a night like this, cold and pitch black? Anyways, I've not heard nothing.'

The drayman looked at his companion with suspicion, 'Well, no doubt you've had a few drams. That'll deaden your senses.'

'Needs to keep warm somehow. 'Spect you've had a few yourself, anyways.'

'You know me, I'm a God-fearing man and don't drink on the Sabbath.'

'No,' said the watchman in an unconvincing tone, and went off to signal the all-clear to the smuggling party on the beach below.

The drayman tethered the horses to a post and waited for the men to arrive. He took a quick snort from his hip flask, looked at it and muttered under his breath, 'A bad deed this is, a bad deed. Don't like this one bit.'

He was right to be wary, for back where he had pointed and behind a low bank were Revenue Men, waiting for the moment to make their move. They had been positioned at their posts for a considerable time before the activity they were now witnessing had started. It was a cold night and by now, after two hours, the wet had penetrated their defences and was leaving them numb with anticipation.

In charge of the operation was William Trevellick, a middle aged man, tall, stout and confident of his position as local magistrate and merchant in East Looe, as well as owner of a nearby manorial estate. He knew that smuggling was rife in the town, something that was affecting his trade. He wanted to apprehend the men responsible, particularly the ring leader. Only that morning, he had received information that a smuggling run was on for this very night, bringing contraband across from the nearby St George's Island, a haven for the free traders. And so there he was, with his comrades in arms, waiting for the villains to fall into his trap.

His forces were split in two, one group on the cliff top by the cottage, the other waiting on the beach below. Up on the cliff, behind the bank, Trevellick's new deputy was getting anxious. He was a man in his early twenties, a friend of the family who wanted to make a name for himself on his first operation.

'Can you see the cutter?' he whispered.

Trevellick shook his head in the negative. He had sent word to Cawsand for a revenue cutter to be dispatched to aid his operation, but had received no confirmation. He wasn't even sure if it was being deployed.

'We need that cutter in place before we make our move,' came the young officer again.

Trevellick just nodded and said, 'Aye.'

He knew this of course and could tell that the young officer was feeling the tension just as much as he was, although for an entirely different reason.

Concealed behind the bank, they had a good view of the cottage, the Island, and sea below, although they couldn't see the beach itself. The cottage, where the smugglers were carrying out their illegal activity, was well suited, being empty and isolated except for the occasional vagabond who would use it for a night or two and then move on.

It had been the birthplace of Looe's own pirate, a Captain Colliver, who sailed the Indian Ocean and the Far East plundering ships and becoming a hated figure by both his own crew and the ships he attacked. No one knew when or where he died, but he is reputed, so legend had it, to have returned and buried treasure on St. George's Island, threatening the family that inhabited the place with death should they reveal his cache. The townsfolk considered both the Island and the cottage haunted by his ghost, so that no one dared approach the dwelling, let alone step inside it, and the Island was thought of as an outpost to his spirit, where death would befall the unwary.

The smugglers had now started loading the dray and Trevellick knew it would take some time to carry the contraband up the cliff, but he also knew that time was running out.

'There she is,' said the young officer, 'we can make our move now.'

Trevellick turned around and could see the twin-mast cutter, its white sails piercing the blackness of the night.

'Not yet son, wait 'til it gets closer. Don't want any of them thieves escaping.'

He waited a few minutes and then gave the signal. A dozen men sprang up and out into the gloom, pistols ready, and advanced on the cottage. The watchman was first to capitulate as he had no idea what was happening, the liquor having dulled his senses. He even greeted the Revenue Officers and offered them a swig from his flagon.

The drayman managed to escape in the confusion, but he had lost the horses. Two of the smuggling crew, near the dray and carrying barrels, also surrendered without any resistance. Everything was going as planned, but then shots were fired. Shouting and the sound of fighting could be heard, and then another shot. This time it seemed to have found a target, for a terrifying scream penetrated the night. An Officer was down.

It took a full half hour for the situation to be resolved, but in the end all of the smuggling crew were caught and held by the cottage. There were seven of them.

'Who's the Officer down?' cried Trevellick.

'It's the young recruit,' came a reply from his Deputy.

'What's his injuries?'

'He's dead,' said the officer.

Trevellick looked at the motley crew of smugglers, eyeing them one by one, trying in vain to ascertain, in the dim light of his lantern, which one looked like the leader. They all looked like guilty ruffians to him. So, with a determined tone and showing his anger, he said 'Who's the ring-leader?'

Silence followed.

'If he will not show himself, then you all shall be indicted for murder,' he said, making it plain that he meant it.

A low murmuring came from the smugglers and, after a few glances and protestations, out stepped a tall man.

'I am he. I am the leader of this group. I am responsible for these men.'

Trevellick sized him up.

'What name do you go by?' he demanded.

'Josiah Thomas of Talland.'

'Well Josiah Thomas, you are indicted with smuggling and the unlawful killing of a King's Revenue Officer.'

He was dumbstruck. He knew the risks of smuggling, it was a capital offence and he was willing to accept the consequences and he also knew that no Cornish jury would convict him or any of his compatriots. But murder, that was different.

'I'm no murderer,' he protested, 'I didn't kill the man. Didn't even fire my pistol.'

'You are the leader and as such should take responsibility for what has happened.'

'In the eyes of God, I didn't kill him,' he protested again.

Trevellick was having none of it. He wanted him tried and hanged, on the spot if he had his way. 'I saw you kill him myself,' he said, 'and that is what I shall testify to the court.'

Josiah Thomas was beside himself, beginning to think that the Revenue Officer had some grudge against him.

'No Cornish court will convict me,' he sneered with confidence.

'That may be so, Josiah Thomas, but you will not be tried in a Cornish court. You are to be taken to the Exeter Assizes, and tried there for murder. As for the rest of you...'

Just then another Revenue Officer came over and interrupted, 'We're ready.'

'Good, let the people of Looe see that smuggling doesn't pay. Burn the cottage. Raze it to the ground,' cried Trevellick.

He knew that the townsfolk were superstitious about the cottage, considering it to be venerated ground that had been cursed by the Pirate Captain in an act of treachery, and that by burning the cottage it would touch the souls of the people and resurrect his wrath. That's what Trevellick wanted. He wanted to be feared as the one who defied the curse.

One of his officers, a local man himself, came forward and protested.

'You can't do this. It's sacred ground for those folk in Looe. It's cursed and they fear what might happen. That's why it's been left to rot all these years. For they fear he will return and seek revenge for the way the townsfolk evicted his family and forced them into destitution, only to die one by one of hunger and cold.'

'It's old folk's tales,' interjected Trevellick. 'This is the work of the King and it shall be done.'

At this point he nodded to his men with the torches who set the cottage ablaze. It immediately went up in flames, ignited by the pitch the men had poured over the site. With this, Josiah Thomas, a man enraged by innocence, freed himself from his captors and ran over to Trevellick. The cottage was a burning cauldron, its refulgent glow catching the demonic rage in his face. He took hold of Trevellick by the shoulders, looked into his eyes as though he were demented and uttered the words that would send a man insane.

'Know this William Trevellick, for I know who you are, know this, that the ghost of Captain Colliver will come back to haunt you and your family and your descendants, until justice is done.'

He shook Trevellick and then pronounced, as though invoking the Devil himself, 'I curse you in the name of Captain Colliver.'

With that he shoved Trevellick to the ground and spat on him to seal the deed. William Trevellick looked aghast at Josiah Thomas, a man possessed, as two officers wrestled him to the ground, fettered him in irons and led him away to his impending fate.

1

Looe 1999

It was the vernal equinox, the first day of spring. But the season had yet to attest itself in Cornwall, with winter still holding its icy grip. The county had experienced some frosty days and Looe, a coastal fishing port with its maritime climate, had felt the unseasonably cold blast from the north. Roofs were still coated in a white powder, windows etched in an opaque glaze, and cars, that had yet to be moved, had their windscreens burnished in the same freezing veneer.

To the visitor the town appeared a monochrome of grey, covered with a marbled wintry adornment that matched the hues of a leaden sky. That was the first impression which assaulted one visitor, a middle-aged man, standing on the bridge that spanned Looe harbour. There appeared no colour to the picture, no warmth to the town, which was imparting a message to turn back and not venture forth.

A northerly wind was blowing down the river valley, straight from the Arctic and straight through him, out to sea. People were passing huddled in thick coats and hats with scarves wrapped around their heads like turbans, trying to escape the biting wind. That is except for one brave, or foolhardy, individual who seemed to be ignoring the frigid weather, wearing just shorts and sandals and sporting a coloured shirt as though he were in the tropics.

The onlooker had only known one other time as cold as this and that was many years ago when he was bird-watching on the marshes of the Wash, looking at the tens-of-thousands of migrants that use the mudflats as a wintering ground, feeding on the rich food that it provides. Then, as now, a freezing wind was chilling him to the bone. His mood seemed to mirror the bleak weather. What was he doing here on such a day? He knew the answer. 'Follow your heart,' he heard himself say, and smiled. It was a smile of remembrance.

The man was tall in stature and dressed like most he had observed, providing protection from the biting wind. He was wearing a warm country jacket, gloves, a scarf and a hunter's hat, hiding his facial lines which disguised handsome features. He had hazel eyes, fine cheek bones and a statuesque nose, the sort that adorn Greek deities, that today, however, was suffering the vagaries of a winter chill. He was more used to the milder climes of London with its urban heat-island effect where the temperature can be a good few degrees warmer than the rest of the country.

For the moment he had his back to the wind, looking down across the harbour. To the left of him was the town of East Looe with tiers of houses rising up a steep valley side to Shutta, the oldest part of town, above which were more dwellings until at the top were a line of modern bungalows that created the effect of a crater rim from down below. The harbour itself was a natural divide from neighbouring West Looe which seemed to be a mirror image of tiered houses, but on a smaller scale. Two converging valleys had constricted development to a small bluff of land that was dominated by a bleak row of coastguard cottages keeping watch on the harbour below.

He looked down over the side of the bridge and counted the arches. There were seven. Why he had counted them he did not know. Perhaps it was a subconscious retrospective, a childhood penchant to count objects and bridges had always held a fascination. Their arches, rather than being engineering structures, somehow told tales of warring armies that had used them to defeat an enemy or the people who had crossed them for reasons of trade or discovery, but most of all, they communicated a handshake across a divide once separated by geography. But not all bridges offer mediation and Looe Bridge still spanned a chasm of apathy and distrust, that for some had yet to be appeased.

From four of the bridge piers ran a series of mooring chains that seemed to delineate the muddy grey harbour. They were positioned in straight lines creating the effect of lanes in a swimming pool, except this swimming pool was empty. It was low tide and all the craft in the harbour were beached like giant whales, waiting for the life-giving sea to return. There were vessels of every description, from small dinghies, fishing boats and yachts to a large luxury cruiser, and if the man had looked beyond his achromatic view of the town, he would have seen that they would have provided colour to his mood, albeit camouflaged with a frosty coating.

To his right, on the west side of the harbour just a few yards down from the bridge was a Cornish Lugger, an old twin-mast sardine boat that had been converted from an original flat-decked vessel to one that now had a cabin superstructure. Gulls had peppered it with guano and it conjured in his mind a picture of a Jackson Pollack painting and the thought that it could be transported to the Tate Modern and displayed as another piece of New Art. It was a ridiculous idea and its absurdity raised another smile.

The grin didn't last as another cold blast hit him broadside. He turned and looked up river into the teeth of the wind. He grimaced. At low tide, the river flowed to his right, having cut a narrow channel into the muddy harbour bed, and about one hundred yards away it then branched. To his left from the confluence, the West Looe River can be traced upstream passing the Mill Pool Car Park, where he had left his vehicle only a few minutes ago, before turning north with Trenant Wood on one bank and Kilminorth Wood on the opposite bank, past the quaint hamlet of Watergate before meandering through beautiful Cornish countryside, only to find its source in some obscure industrial estate not far from Liskeard. Ahead flowed the East Looe River, longer and more distinguished than its cousin, with its headwaters springing from hallowed ground on the southern periphery of Bodmin Moor, betwixt the pagan and pious, between an impressive Neolithic chambered tomb and a standing stone dedicated to a ninth century King of Cornwall.

Rising up from the banks of both rivers was thick ancient oak woodland, looking foreboding with its skeletal structure still laid bare at this time of year, covering the slopes all the way up to a filigreed horizon. The man noticed a heronry on the far side at the confluence of the two rivers and nearby, the woodland opened out to reveal a villa-style house with a lawn sloping down to a deserted jetty. Exposed mud flats were populated by wading birds, some redshank and sandpiper, probing for worms and other marine invertebrates, whilst a pair of avocets, beautiful, elegant birds, occupied the shallow water's edge, sifting the mud with their up-turned bills. Under the umbrella of trees hugging the river bank, a lone heron was stealthily hunting for bigger prey watched by numerous gulls, perhaps waiting for an easy meal.

This was a familiar scene to him, one which he would normally become absorbed in, watching the nuances of intertidal relationships, an unrivalled soap opera where the characters are real and the story-line is survival. Yet today, he could not focus on the unfolding episode before him. His mind was elsewhere. Even the woodland, a camouflage of black and white, was lost to his thoughts and with the freezing wind cutting into his face, he could not appreciate any of its beauty.

What was he doing here? He could go back right now to the warmth of his car. But that would be a waste of driving from his sister's home in Devon, where he was staying. More than that, it would be a betrayal. A betrayal of his memory. He had decided to come to Looe when browsing through an old photograph album the previous evening. In it were snapshots of his first holiday, over thirty years ago, and he had come across one of him and his sister standing either side of their mother on the quayside at Looe. He wanted to find that same view again. He wanted that connection on the first anniversary of his mother's death.

The man turned around again to face the harbour. It felt more comfortable. He wondered which way to go. East Looe to his left looked more promising. It had the fishing quay, all the shops, and was busier than its rival across the river which, from what he could ascertain, was almost deserted. Yes, East Looe was more appealing, but the man chose west. 'Follow your heart', his mother used to say and so he proceeded in that direction.

Descending the bridge, the lugger was now directly below him as he walked along the quayside and rather than looking like an expensive piece of art, it was just a vessel in need of a good clean. With the tide out the harbour bed was a good four to five yards below, which, without any railings, looked an ominously long way to fall. He kept his distance from the precipitous edge. Taking advantage of a dry harbour basin a man had his boat careened, cleaning the wooden hull of barnacles and other marine encrusted deposits, whilst further away two men were digging for lug worms, presumably for bait on a later fishing trip. The man was delighted to see a little egret, a smaller cousin of the heron, quite close and below him, paddling a muddy pool with its bright yellow feet in order to agitate prey to the surface. A black-headed gull, still in its winter plumage, was doing the same whilst some juvenile herring gulls, noticeable by their mottled feathers, were tugging at some seaweed, hoping it was a tasty morsel of food.

The wind didn't seem as strong below the bridge and the man was beginning to enjoy himself by guessing the home port of the commercial fishing vessels from their insignia. Most were FY, which he immediately recognised as Fowey, a few miles down the coast. There were a few PZ for Penzance, and it took him a little while to deduce the port of NN on a red trawler, thinking at it must be Newlyn, although he wasn't entirely sure. But SS eluded him. All he could come up with was South Shields but that was on the mouth of the Tyne on the North Sea coast, which was unlikely.

He was still trying to think of a fishing port in the south west when he almost slipped off the side of the quay and onto a small open boat called *Lady Jane*. She looked an elegant craft befitting her name, constructed of wood and by the looks of her, had recently been varnished for the holiday season ahead. Across the harbour more boats were high and dry. This time they were perched on the opposite quayside, yet to be returned to the water after a winter of repairs. The whole scene was a reminder that Looe was a working fishing port as well as a place for tourists, the two industries dovetailing to produce a unique experience for the holiday-maker.

He smiled to himself again, this time because he was remembering those innocent, seemingly halcyon days as a young boy when he would fish for crabs off the quay, eat ice-cream, build sandcastles, collect cuttlefish and build camp fires with his sister on the beach. The family would take boat trips along the coast and out to the Eddystone

Lighthouse, the trip he remembered vividly for being particularly rough, with the boat rolling and tossing in the heavy sea causing most of the party to be violently sick. 'We were in our element' he thought out loud, rather surprised at the outburst. His father always said that the sea was in their blood, he having been an officer in the Navy. Perhaps it was just a desirous fantasy, for they lived nowhere near the coast, but more likely it is deep in the psyche of the people who are an island nation.

Whatever the reason he was captivated by the ocean and the unknown beyond the horizon, and would imagine he was a buccaneer on the high seas battling against tempests and sea monsters from the deep, and raiding Spanish galleons laden with gold. Or he would be an intrepid explorer rounding Cape Horn on a voyage of discovery seeking lands incognito. Later in his youth, he was the commander of a mighty Dreadnought, forging through heavy Atlantic waves, seeking victory at sea. As he reminisced, he realised that perhaps his father was right and the sea was in his blood.

He looked out across the harbour. It was about the right spot and he removed the photograph from his pocket. A few changes were discernable. Across the harbour a new building was evident, the fish market and the crater rim of bungalows that adorned the top had yet to be built. But apart from those changes and a few more modern craft in the harbour basin, he could have been in Looe thirty years ago.

The old church tower across the harbour was visible, so too the same tiers of houses creeping up the east cliff in the background, and down past the fish quay to the harbour entrance was the pier. Not a traditional pier, he remembered, more a breakwater protecting the beach. It had a name, but he couldn't recall it. In fact, he couldn't remember much else about Looe although many of his childhood memories could be witnessed today: children still fish for crabs, build sandcastles and go on boat trips although camp fires had been replaced by portable barbeques and you wouldn't find many cuttlefish nowadays. But the beach itself was still the same perfect arc of sand as it was back then, now flanked by tiers of cubist concrete slabs looking like a giant's set of toy building blocks. Even the town itself hadn't changed much, with a few more cafes, bistros and restaurants, but still possessing an enduring appeal.

The man was now sitting in a blue and white building, rather like a bus shelter, on the quay side above which was a sign proclaiming it to be a 'Fisherman's Berth.' Apart from him, it was empty. It also felt a few degrees warmer, sheltered as it was from the wind. He now watched the water slowly make an entrance to the harbour, inexorably engulfing the muddy bed, an advancing tide that promised rebirth. His gaze was fixed upon a small wooden craft, a gaff-rigged sail boat of pre-war age, he guessed, and imagined himself sailing it in preference to a modern fibreglass yacht moored nearby. The gaffer had a timeless elegance that seemed in harmony with his thoughts and he watched the embryonic flow envelop it in a shallow pool that would soon breathe life into the old whale.

He delved into his pockets once again. This time he pulled out an old tobacco tin. On the lid was the picture of a jolly sailor sporting an iconic white beard and smoking a clay pipe, proclaiming the contents to be a satisfying smoke. His father used to smoke a pipe and may have bought the tin whilst here in Looe. He had found it whilst clearing out his mother's house and had been surprised, almost bewildered, by its contents. He opened the lid. Inside, were a coin and a piece of paper. He unfolded the paper and read.

My dearest Son, Robert

The map you have been bequeathed was given to me by a stranger in Tangiers where my ship was anchored for a while after the war.

I and a fellow officer went ashore and came across this trader in the souk. He told me that it showed the place of buried treasure, taken from a ship that had been plundered, the crew and passengers killed by a notorious pirate. It was worth a pirate's ransom, he said. He wanted too much money for it. I haggled with him, but the man would not come down low enough, telling me it was genuine.

I didn't buy the map. Perhaps he thought I was easy prey, but didn't reckon on my skill at poker nor my intransigence. Then something quite extraordinary occurred. On being formally addressed by my fellow officer, the man then inexplicably shoved the map into my hands and gave me a silver coin, saying it was mine, and that he didn't want any money for it, as though he were glad to be rid of it. He said it was stained with pirate blood and had a curse put upon it.

As you can see, the man gave me an old map of Cornwall, which had a cross on Looe and said that there was buried treasure to be found. This will explain why we went to Cornwall for our holidays. I was interested to discover whether there was anything in the story. I never found out. The coin, I discovered, is a Spanish pieces-of-eight. I'd like to think that the man was indeed convinced of the tale and that you will unearth a cache of treasure yourself.

Maybe you will. But beware of the curse! The man seemed possessed when he foretold it, although it was probably just a good sales pitch - except he never received a penny from me.

Good luck son and remember, the sea is in our blood.

Your loving father.

Robert, for that was the man's name, had never seen the coin or the letter from his father before, nor had he ever recounted the tale to him. His father had died before his formative teenage years and in those days of the mid-sixties, unlike today, boys were slow to mature and his father, who was entrenched in pre-war Edwardian, even Victorian values, probably thought he was too young to be told.

Robert looked at the coin; it was a piece-of-eight, a former silver Spanish coin. He was somewhat sceptical about its provenance, but it was an interesting tale worthy of any good pirate legend. Such imaginations had been left in his childhood and he wasn't about to go off on a wild goose chase looking for buried treasure. In any case, the map was missing. In fact, when he thought about it, there were several items that had mysteriously disappeared from his mother's house. One item in particular, which she had promised him on her death, had captivated him during adolescence as a paragon for his vision of beauty. It was a genuine Art Nouveau table lamp, forged in silver, in which a slim naked woman with outstretched arms was holding aloft a ball-shaped lamp. It was worth, he knew, a small fortune. But more than that, as a teenager he had looked longingly at the naked idol, wondering what delights beheld such exquisite form, and whether one day he would fall in love with his own divine goddess.

If he was honest, he would have preferred the lamp to the map. Both were no longer in his possession, but he had the coin and the letter. The coin was a reminder of those past holidays when they would go to local museums and where he would marvel at the display cases of artefacts from a past maritime world, a world which was made romantic but which he later realised was a harsh, brutal world, where life was cheap. Or he would read about the exploits of smugglers and how they would outwit the revenue men by building ships with false keels or hide barrels of contraband in the most unlikely of places. They would explore caves and venture to remote, inaccessible coves, often scrambling down cliffs to reach the beach below. It was a childhood adventure worthy of any Enid Blyton tale and as Robert gazed at the coin, he realised that his father had left him a priceless legacy of memories, as well as a coin with history, a history he was destined to uncover.

2

ooe is an archetypal Cornish fishing port. It is a place where
the river meets the sea and is blessed with an estuary and
harbour offering protection from the prevailing elements and has,
ever since early medieval times, provided the perfect shelter for the
maritime industry.

The county is studded with these natural havens. They are a result
of fluvial erosion and the consequence of the last glacial period when
vast ice sheets caused global sea levels to fall. Free from ice the rivers
of Cornwall, in order to reach the sea, cut deep clefts into the ground
which resulted in an inundation of these valleys as sea levels rose once
more. It created flooded estuaries, known as rias, and some of the
larger rivers in Cornwall, like the Fal and Fowey, have deep harbour
anchorage, even at low tide, that can accommodate large ocean-going
cruise ships.

Looe estuary, with its relatively small river catchment, has been left
a tidal harbour that is home to a modest day-fishing fleet. Although
influenced by the tides, the vessels are often tied up in the harbour,
unable to venture out into wild open seas because of adverse weather
conditions. An island is situated about half a mile south from the town
and protects the harbour and beach from the prevailing winds, with
a consequence that Looe Bay can often be quite calm, whilst beyond
a strong swell and cresting waves can make for challenging sailing
conditions, even for the larger trawlers.

Looe Island has had a long and chequered history, particularly
for one so small. It dates back to the early days of Christianity in the
county when it was home to a small community of Benedictine monks

who built a monastic order on the summit of the Island. Legend has it that Christianity was first brought to Cornwall in the sixth century by Saint Piran, an Irish abbot who arrived on these shores tied to a millstone, having been cast adrift in stormy seas from his homeland. He established an oratory church in Penhale sands, where he landed, and from that moment the word of God spread throughout the county, most likely at that time in pockets of holiness within a sea of pagan worship.

Documents show that Looe Island was once referred to as St Michael of Lammana, although some residents of the town, those whose roots are deeply buried in the past, call the Island by its old name of St George's. It's a legacy, so it is believed, when a chapel stood on the apex of the Island and housed an image of Saint George, thus becoming a focus for pilgrimage.

Robert couldn't see the Island from where he was sitting, but he remembered it. As a young boy he had waded out to the Island on a low tide but didn't set foot upon its soil, for he and his father had to return before the tide turned and the shallow water became too deep to negotiate. In any case, he was told it was privately owned and that nobody was allowed there, except by invitation. He thought it unfair that he wasn't able to experience being marooned on an island, much like the characters in an Enid Blyton novel he had been reading, and vowed then that one day he would explore his own island of adventure.

He was still in the Fisherman's Berth, watching the water reclaim its territory. The harbour was slowly coming to life with a few of the shallow-draught boats succumbing to the tide. He was still looking at the gaffer beginning to awaken from its enforced slumber. Its hull was now completely surrounded and before long it would be clear of the muddy bed, able to move once again. Soon, with the rising tide, the harbour would be full and all life restored until the next low tide.

It was then he realised that SS stood for St Ives, a similar sized fishing town which he had visited on a day trip to the Land's End peninsula and where his father had explained the tides, telling him that for people who are dependent upon the sea they are vitally important, perhaps more so than time itself.

'Time and tide wait for no man,' he thought, not so much in

reverence to the saying, but in response to rumbles from his stomach. Opposite him, on the corner of a square next to a fire station, was The Quayside Café. It looked inviting, especially on a day like today; not just cold but bitterly cold. At first he thought it was closed but on closer inspection he realised all the windows were steamed up. He ventured to the establishment and with a degree of apprehension opened the door and peered inside, not stepping beyond the threshold lest it be empty.

The interior was small and intimate and he was surprised to see three people inside; a young couple just finishing their lunch and an old man, near the entrance, drinking a mug of tea and looking slightly furtive. Robert looked around for a few moments to decide which table to avail, and selected one in a far corner next to a window and a warm radiator. But before he could take a seat the proprietor, a man in his late thirties with a shaven head, broad smile and somewhat overweight, enquired:

'Are you for Harbour View?'

'No,' replied Robert, with a puzzled look.

The proprietor apologised and explained that the café held the key to the holiday flat by that name and that guests were expected early afternoon. He bid Robert welcome.

Each table had its own Cornish theme and Robert sat down at the one displaying coastal scenes of Bedruthan Steps, St Michael's Mount, Kynance Cove and Land's End. In the centre of the table was an antique vase containing a posy of scented white narcissus, their perfume providing an accompaniment to the homemade soup he had ordered. Whilst he was consuming the delicious and warming broth the young couple, having paid the proprietor, left and he felt a cold breeze from the open door and was glad he wasn't sitting where the old man was. Robert glanced at him, thinking he was still acting secretively. Then he saw the old man top up his mug with some spirit from a hipflask, a clandestine performance which seemed to violate some ancient prophecy that he had himself sanctioned, as he continued to fiddle with the hipflask and look at it as though it were an object he despised, his gaze carved with scorn.

Despite the warming soup, Robert was still cold to the bone and felt like asking the old man for a dash of his secret elixir. It looked to be having a beneficial effect on him since he was only wearing a chequered shirt, unbuttoned at the neck and sleeves rolled up, whilst Robert was still cocooned in jacket and scarf. He had the look of an old sea dog, Robert thought, and was probably used to harsh cold weather, his face swarthy and etched in wrinkles, being a testimony to many a year at sea.

The café was now empty apart from the two men. Robert looked around. The walls were adorned with framed prints, some depicting classic railway posters proclaiming the delights of Cornish seaside towns and others depicting historic maps of the county. One particular map caught his eye. It outlined the South Cornish coast, from Plymouth to Falmouth, and was clearly a reproduction of a Tudor map that highlighted fortifications and other important features in Cornwall in defence of the realm, presumably from Spanish invasion. It looked familiar. Robert was sure he had seen such a map before. As he was studying the map, Robert felt the old man looking at him and, as he glanced in his direction, noticed a look of scrutiny in his demeanour and a face that suggested suspicion. Robert's own suspicion, wondering about him, was interrupted by the proprietor.

'Did you enjoy your meal?'

'Pardon?' replied Robert, now looking at the old map again, but turning round to see the proprietor standing by the table, his frame slightly bent as though wanting an answer.

'Was everything to your satisfaction?' he repeated.

Robert looked at his inquisitor. 'It was. The soup was most delicious.'

'Thank you. We aim to please.' The proprietor hesitated a few seconds and then in an enquiring tone, continued, 'are you visiting Looe?'

'Sorry?' retorted Robert, noticing the old man taking an interest in their conversation. He downed a mouthful of his elixir, with the proprietor's back to him, but in full view of Robert.

'Are you local or just visiting?' rephrased the proprietor.

'Oh, just visiting for the day.'

'Lovely day for it,' he said with a sarcastic smile.

'Could be better,' Robert replied in a deadpan tone wanting to drink his tea in peace.

19

But the proprietor hadn't taken the hint and continued, 'Do you live in Cornwall?'

Robert wondered, rather irritatingly, what he wanted. Finally, the proprietor took the hint saying, 'Sorry, I'm not wanting to pry, but I do like my customers to feel at home. Hopefully they will return.'

'That's okay. Your café is certainly homely.'

Robert considered whether to answer the question which might lead to a conversation he wasn't in the mood to have. But, against his better judgement, he decided to see how far it went. 'No, I don't live here in Cornwall. I'm from London, but visiting my sister who lives the other side of Plymouth.'

'What brings you to Looe on such a day?'

'We, that is, my parents, sister and me, used to come here on holiday when we were young. We stayed in a cottage in the old part of town across the harbour.'

'Ah, East Looe,' the proprietor said with an air of resolute disapproval.

Robert was puzzled by this. He continued though. 'I found some photographs of us here in Looe and wanted to see it again – a trip down memory lane, I guess.'

'That's what brings a lot of folk down here. That and the fact that Looe is a holiday destination for families with young children. It has everything to offer. It's not pretentious like some resorts I could mention.'

By now, Robert was wondering if the proprietor was some sort of tourism representative, trying to put Looe in the spotlight and that all his customers, rather than viewing a poster, had to endure a discourse from him on the merits of the town. Robert took a sip of his tea pulling a face, not at the proprietor but because it was now annoyingly tepid. He hated cold tea. Sensing Robert's irritation, the proprietor proffered a fresh pot and wished him a nice day, hoping to see him again, perhaps when the weather improved. He returned to the kitchen and Robert was relieved to finish his hot beverage in peace.

The old man was still at his table. But with the departure of the proprietor he got up and in a shuffling motion, as though his sea legs were on a pitching deck in a force ten gale, went over to Robert. He lent on the table with what Robert saw were enormous hands, twice the size of his, and in a broad Cornish voice uttered, 'you don't want to go t'other side. Nothing but trouble theys are,' shaking his head as though condemning everybody from that side of Looe.

As he regained his full height, which to Roberts's eyes was little more than five foot, he could see the old sea dog was heavy-set in stature, a man who could no doubt keel-haul a boat with his sheer body strength, but for his bandy legs. He said good afternoon to the proprietor, who was still in the kitchen and out of sight, and departed, leaving an icy blast in the café that enveloped Robert.

'Bye George,' came a muted reply. 'See you tomorrow.'

Robert was left feeling a cold atmosphere and not just from the wind chill from the open door. There was no doubt as to the old man's feelings about the people of East Looe and Robert wondered what his obvious disapproving sentiments were about.

'Sorry about George,' said the proprietor who had emerged from his kitchen, wiping his hands on an apron. 'He's lived here all his life and has never got on with the folk on the other side. There's a history of simmering antagonism between the two towns. It's not really evident today but there are some folks who cannot forget the past. Even I've experienced problems myself and I'm not a Looe man.'

'You have?' responded Robert, with a modicum of interest.

The proprietor took that as his cue to explain the circumstances. 'My wife and family moved here from London about four years ago to open a restaurant specialising in fish and shellfish dishes. I used to be a fisherman so knew the trade and wanted a fresh start, away from the capital. I had heard about the reputation of Looe as one of the best places to source fresh fish. We had the perfect place lined up and were sure there was a market for fresh, locally sourced meals. We just needed approval from the local Town Council. But it was refused on the grounds that there were already many restaurants in the town and another wasn't needed. How can that be when there's a growing demand in the catering trade? We appealed, of course, but to no avail. I have my suspicions that a local family, a sort of institution who seem to own half of Looe as far as I can tell, had council members on the committee and brought pressure to bear. The family obviously didn't want any competition, that's all I can guess. Maybe I'm wrong but there is certainly something fishy about that family, if you will excuse the pun.'

Robert smiled. 'Sorry to hear about that,' he interjected in a sympathetic tone to comfort the proprietor. 'So how did you come by the cafe?'

'We were lucky. The good Lord was looking after us. The café came up for lease and we've never looked back. It's not quite as lucrative as a restaurant, nor as challenging, but we've done well.'

Just then the door opened, followed by another icy blast, and in walked an attractive woman dressed as if for a session on the piste.

'Hi John, just off to pick the kids up from school,' she said, slightly out of breath and closing the door behind her. On noticing Robert she continued, 'Oh, please excuse me, didn't expect to find anybody in here on a day like today.'

The proprietor gestured, 'This is my wife Jane.'

'Pleased to meet you,' replied Robert. There were a few awkward seconds and to break the silence he continued, 'I loved your homemade soup. It was delicious.'

'You must thank John for that. He does a lot of the cooking in the café.'

'Most,' John was quick to say.

Robert empathised with the proprietor and could see antagonism brewing here, let alone between two towns, as Jane gave a telling look towards her husband.

'Just popped in to say we're going into Liskeard so won't be back until later. See you then. Oh yes, the guests for Harbour View won't be arriving until tomorrow now.'

John looked glazed as though he wasn't listening, which seemed to annoy Jane yet again.

'Did you hear?' she barked.

'Yes my lady,' he said in a compliant tone.

Again, she gave another deprecatory look and with that said goodbye to Robert and hoped to see him again. At first, he couldn't understand the proprietor's reply, and then after a few moments it was obvious.

'Is that your boat moored in the harbour called *Lady Jane*?'

'Yes, I bought the craft when we moved down here mainly because of its name, although I wanted to have a small craft to mess around on and take the children out fishing. My wife can be a bit domineering at times, ordering us to do this and to do that and the name seemed appropriate. So it's become a habit of mine to address Jane as such, much to her consternation.'

Robert wanted to get going but had been intrigued by the proprietor's story and wanted to know more about the latent antagonism between East and West Looe.

'You say there's been a history of tension between the two towns. Do you know what?'

The proprietor then gave Robert a brief potted history of Looe. He explained that the two towns gained royal charters in early medieval times and that for centuries the two towns had grown independent of each other, the 'sunny side' of East Looe and the 'money side' of West Looe having no wish to be joined together. But ever since the first bridge was built, in the early fifteenth century, there had been a simmering rivalry which often resulted in fighting between the two clans, even on the bridge itself. It had become a symbol of identity, like crossing the Rubicon, and to wander into enemy territory was tantamount to a declaration of war. Today a friendly rivalry exists, but occasionally tensions bubble to the surface and then the bridge, once again, becomes an advocate of animosity.

'I could go on, but...' continued the proprietor.

Robert wanted to know more but could see the proprietor himself was becoming a bit agitated, wanting to close the café and so quickly interjected, 'that's okay, another time perhaps. In any case, I must be getting on.'

He paid the bill and bid him farewell. Just as he was leaving he noticed a sign above the counter: 'Welcome to The Quayside Café – enter a stranger, leave as a friend.' The proprietor saw Robert gazing at the sign. 'It's our motto,' he said.

'A good one,' replied Robert, 'and so true.'

'Thank you,' he said in appreciation. 'If you have time and want to see the best view of Looe, take the old coast path for a couple of hundred yards. You can't miss it, it's behind the Smugglers Arms. It's steep at first, but soon flattens out.' And with that parting comment, Robert left the warmth of the cafe.

Outside, the weather had improved. Some blue chinks could be seen in the sky, no longer the slate grey of the morning. It didn't seem as cold either although there was still a brisk northerly blowing. Even the early frost had melted, revealing colours that had hitherto been obscured. The tide was now well in and the harbour showed some signs of activity, with a small open boat loaded with empty creels and steered by a man clad in yellow oilskins, returning from an inshore catch of crab and lobster. Beyond that and further down the harbour, near to a lifeboat station, a gig was being launched, whilst another one was already making its way out of the harbour, just clear of the pier.

Despite the improving weather it seemed a rather grim afternoon to be rowing but the world pilot gig championships, which are held on the Isles of Scilly each year, were only just a few weeks hence and training for them is taken very seriously indeed. He watched the crew of six women and coxswain set off in pursuit of the men, their craft struggling against a strong flowing tide.

Robert found the Smugglers Arms just a few yards away and the path the proprietor mentioned. It was not so much a path, more a narrow lane, just wide enough for a small vehicle. On one side were several brightly decorated cottages and on a painted gable-end wall was a plaque declaring the place to be a past floral winner in a best kept village competition, although there were scant signs of blooms from the array of pots and empty hanging baskets.

The lane narrowed after a few yards as he began to ascend. It was steep. Thigh achingly steep. Robert climbed higher and as the gradient eased more and more of Looe revealed itself, occasionally obscured by houses and overgrown shrubs, until finally the view opened out to a superb vista at the top of the climb. Out of breath and limbs in need of a rest, he stopped and leant on a railing. His reward for the effort was a panorama taking in the harbour, bridge and the valley beyond, some of West Looe and most of East Looe, including all the houses rising up the opposite hillside. The pier was now to be seen for what it was, a banjo-shaped breakwater which instantly reminded him of its name: The Banjo Pier. The beach was clearly visible, despite the tide now coming in, and beyond it to the east could be seen the towns of Millendreath and Downderry and the wide arc of Whitsand Bay all the way to Rame Head, beyond which was Plymouth and the coast of Devon.

He was glad he had taken the proprietor's advice and decided to explore just a bit further. The lane contoured round to the right and after a short while he came to a crest where it descended back down to the sea, whilst a switch-back narrow path continued on up. It was quite pleasant now with the sun breaking through the clouds, and being in the lee of the cliff there was very little wind. Even so, Robert was a little out of breath and stopped, looking at the two alternative routes. Which way? His beating heart told him down but he knew full well that he would choose the more demanding route. As his mother used to tell him, 'those that overcome adversity are rewarded in the end.'

The path zigzagged up the cliff and became narrower the higher he climbed, as though he were being channelled into a trap, like birds into a mist net. Tall hedges of furze, hawthorn and blackthorn lined the path, creating a mysterious ambiance, attenuated by the sense of seclusion and silence. Robert couldn't see anything; not the sea, not Looe. But he could hear the sound of the waves below and the screams of gulls above, which seemed to add to the atmosphere as though he was now in another world, where reality is overtaken by fantasy, the mind conjuring noises that didn't exist or shapes in the hedgerow that spoke of the unfamiliar.

He stopped to take in the solitude. The sun was shining premonitory beams of light through the cloud and in the confinement of the path its warmth was delighting him, mixing with the sea air and invading his senses. He closed his eyes, and listened to the natural orchestration of the gulls and breaking waves, accompanied by the sound of bees out in the late afternoon warmth, seeking nectar from the few plants that were flowering. It was intoxicating. He had a feeling of levitation, where his mind tried to see above the hedgerow, to seek a glimpse of the hidden world denied to his vision.

Then a banging noise interrupted his meditation. It sounded above him. He looked up, but could only see some gulls gliding effortlessly on thermals. He walked on a few paces further. A rustle now. He stopped again. Was he imagining things? He was alone and despite his manly frame, felt a little vulnerable. He was never a person for confrontation. His heart began beating a little faster. He crouched down and peered through the hedge to see if anything was there. Nothing? There was the banging noise again, only it seemed louder, more ominous. He turned around and looked back down the path. It was deserted. He tentatively walked on only to be halted by the noise once more. It was close, an irregular yet repetitive sound, a warning knell that was beckoning him to a past life and a future where he would finally have his boyhood wish: his very own Island of Adventure.

3

What is it about love that it can strike when you least expect and at the most unlikely time? And is love, fate? Is the arrow of desire a self-inflicted wound that will consume the body, leaving just broken shards of memories and an unfulfilled life that is to be resurrected once more? That is what Robert thought as he looked at a vision of love, a forlorn love that had blossomed many years ago when he was at university.

It was there he had met Madeleine. She was a beautiful girl from County Kerry in Ireland. He knew as soon as he set eyes upon her, she was the divine goddess he had been waiting for. Although he was a good-looking, intelligent man, she was a few years older, had many admirers and he thought she was beyond him, an unattainable love like the lamp he had coveted in his teenage years. His shyness was a handicap too. He floundered every time an opportunity arose to talk with her, unable to communicate his feelings and his passion, even though she found a great profundity to Robert, a maturity and insight beyond his years. If only Robert had known. He could talk about science and nature, the cosmos and art, but the intimate conversation of desire eluded him, as though a cursed constriction of the throat prevented articulation as soon as they were alone. And so, by the end of the first academic year, although she had unwittingly gilded his idol, because of his reticence he could not seize her radiance.

During the summer vacation, his mood became doleful. He couldn't remove Madeleine from his thoughts; a pre-Raphaelite goddess with flowing red hair, eyes that seemed to entrance, an intellect as sharp as her beauty, and a slim figure that promised delight. Yet despite his ineptitude, she had not spurned Robert's attempts at courting her favour. She had even extolled and enraptured him when describing her home in Ireland, as though it were an invitation into her affections. Perhaps he was deluding himself? That such beauty would deign to acknowledge his presence, for he himself could not see the attraction of his own personality, a teenage frame that lacked adulthood and an experience of love that had yet to be fulfilled.

Rather than succumb to self-pity and melancholy, he decided to take a trip to Kerry. He didn't know where she lived, but she had alluded to the county town of Tralee. In any event, he wasn't expecting to see her. He just wanted to experience some of the countryside mentioned by Madeleine and so provide a springboard for conversation when he returned to campus. She had enthused, often with great passion, about the region, so much so that he imagined them there together sharing the experience of its rugged landscape, the juxtaposition of mountains and coast, the warmth of the people and drinking Guinness whilst listening to traditional Irish music. It was, of course, wishful thoughts, but it provided the catalyst for his journey into her heart.

Tralee is situated at the head of a bay in the shadow of mountains that form a backbone to the Dingle Peninsula, the most northerly promontory in a series that protrude into the Atlantic in South West Ireland. The town itself was unremarkable except that it was the birth place of the fifth century Irish Saint Brendon, who is renowned for his legendary voyage across the Atlantic. But Robert wasn't in Tralee for its aesthetics, or lack of, nor its history, and spent the first few days wandering its streets and frequenting cafes and bars hoping that he might see Madeleine.

He didn't. Having finally exhausted his futile search, he hired a motorbike and set off to explore Madeleine's countryside, towards a high mountain on the Dingle peninsula which she had often eulogised about. The drive was certainly beautiful, with glimpses of the coast to his right and heather clad mountains flanking him to his left until they opened out onto a magnificent vista of Dingle Bay and the high peaks of the Inveragh peninsula beyond. It was all that Madeleine had described and more as he descended from a high pass towards the town of Dingle.

It was a small town with a genuine Irish feel to its character. But Robert didn't stop and continued along the road which hugs the wild Atlantic coast, towards the most westerly tip of mainland Ireland. Every twist and turn seemed to offer more breath-taking views, but none more so than the imposing mass of Mount Brandon, a whale-back colossus that plunged to the sea only a short distance away. This was the peak that Madeleine had lauded, describing its panoramic vista as one of the most stunning in Ireland, a spiritual high which only God could have created. He had to see it for himself, and by doing so he would be close to her, for she had said it had a soul that infused its pilgrims. He wanted to feel her spirit, seek her soul.

He had never attempted a mountain so high before, his record thus far being an assault on Kinder Scout during a school field trip to the Peak District. His trepidation was misplaced, for the route to the summit was an easy climb, following a pilgrim track marked by cairns each displaying a cross, all the way to the top. And there, on a clear warm summer's day, the view was as Madeleine had recounted: a glittering montage of blue and white impasto, a wash that surrounded the emerald peak and the narrow strip of the peninsula. It was magnificent.

Never before had he been so emotional. He could feel Madeleine imbue him with desire. He closed his eyes. He wanted her. Wanted her passion. He imagined the heavens open and his goddess appear as if conceived by the spiritual journey, an angel of heaven taking him. It felt so real, yet he knew it was in his mind. It was always so. Trust in fate, he told himself. His mother would say that. But fate never dealt him a winning hand.

He watched gulls and other seabirds, fulmars and kittiwakes he thought, their cries piercing the silence. It was an idyll. Nothing is permanent in an oscillating life of hope, love, and the daily endeavours of living, only fleeting moments of true happiness. He was with Madeleine, a precious, stationary moment that he had conjured between hope and love. He closed his eyes and felt her presence enter his soul. Only the wind and the birds were audible in his meditative mind, a tranquil place that lifted him above reality to a plane where a faint call touched his senses.

'It's quite exquisite.'

It was, he told himself. But the annotation felt real, not the imagined words of his desire.

'Robert?' it continued.

It was real. The voice, with its familiar Irish intonations, was an aphrodisiac to his heart. He opened his eyes to see a figure standing before him framed in a gilded light, a golden hue that radiated desire.

'Beautiful,' he replied.

Madeleine knew what he meant and went to kiss him. In that moment he lost his inhibitions and they fell into a passionate embrace upon the sacred mountain, as though it were an altar for them to release emotions that had hitherto been hidden by convention.

'So you decided to see my Ireland?' she said, as they surfaced for air.

'I had to. You're so lucky to live in such a beautiful place.'

'You've chosen a lovely day. It's not always quite like this. I've been up here many a time when it's shrouded in cloud. But I can always see through the mist and see the true nature of God's creation.'

Robert immediately grasped her meaning. 'Perhaps God was guiding you here. It's rather fortuitous we should meet up here of all places.'

'He is always with me,' she replied.

'I would like to think it was fate. A divine fate. But whatever, I'm so glad you're here. Perhaps you can point out some of the view? I'm not sure what I'm looking at.'

With hands clasped and shoulders touching, she pointed east to her home town of Tralee and then south to the wide inlet below them.

'That's Dingle Bay with those two long sandy spits either side over there. And beyond, can you see that range of mountains, and the highest one?'

'The one which seems to be glinting in the sun?'

'Yes. It's a reflection from a metal cross that stands on the highest mountain in all of Ireland. It's called Carrauntoohil in the Macgillycuddy's Reeks. It's as high as many Scottish peaks.'

'An Irish Munro?'

'I guess so. It is over three thousand feet, as is this one we're on,' mused Madeleine, realising that Robert wasn't such a novice to mountains after all.

'Have you climbed it,' he asked, knowing that she probably had.

'Of course. Not as often as this one though. It has a special meaning for me.'

'What's that, if you don't mind me asking?'

'I don't mind you asking, but I will not answer just yet. I will one day though. That I promise.'

Robert could see from her expression that it did indeed hold some special meaning, that one day he would be a privileged recipient of Madeleine's secret and it gave him a sense of intimacy with her, a shared understanding that bound them together.

As she continued her panoramic tour of the summit vista pointing out the salient landmarks, Robert looked on with increasing awe, not at the mountain nor the views, but at Madeleine, entranced by her every move, hypnotised by her lips expounding the landscape, wanting to taste her once more, wanting to feel the delights of a slim figure, that had finally awoken a latency he had imagined all those years ago. And as his gaze finally settled upon her special mountain, reflective flashes of light could still be seen from its icon, as though it were signalling the two embraced lovers, communicating an approval of their communion from high above.

*   *   *

Being Irish, Madeleine was a Catholic. She had faith. Not a devout faith but a belief in God, who, to her, was kind and merciful and she would one day be admitted to His Kingdom. Robert had no faith in such transience. His doctrine was science and reason, an existentialist philosophy underpinned by evolution and a love for every creature on this earth and their right to an existence, not a divine right, but a right to life, no more, no less than his own. He would argue that every living creature had an innate spirit, an energy, a will to live, and when death does occur, that energy is released to be consumed by the birth of another living creature.

He loved nature in all its glory, a sort of animism, and had often conjectured whether plants had souls, particularly since many trees, with their contorted forms, gnarled trunks and longevity of life can claim to have a conduit to the past, more so than any animal. So too in the very fabric of the earth; rivers and mountains that are forever in flux, their forms a result of eons of time, bearing witness to the spirit and energy of the planet itself.

It was that spirit and energy that became the foundation of Robert and Madeleine's relationship. They would have amicable arguments on metaphysics and faith, friendly arguments which had no conclusion other than passionate love-making, a symbol, they concluded, of the unity between them and their philosophies. He accepted her faith and she acknowledged his ethics.

For the rest of their time at university Robert became increasingly confident in himself, losing his shyness and stammer. They discovered many common interests, filling their days by devouring culture, going to museums and art galleries, attending the theatre and classical concerts, even developing a mutual love for opera. London sated their appetite for learning and by graduation they had outgrown the metropolis.

Robert moved to Ireland with Madeleine. It was a natural progression and life was good in the Emerald Isle. It was a place with heart and soul, a place where he wanted home to be, a home with Madeleine. And fate played its card again when, on a trip around the Ring of Kerry, a road traversing the Iveragh Peninsula, they stumbled across an empty cottage for sale. It was set in a remote valley looking out to sea towards a pair of rocky islands, the Skelligs, which Madeleine said were a metaphor for their love – the pious and the pagan. They would regularly visit the cottage making plans on how they would renovate it and, once complete, how they would make a life together, have children and grow old in each other's arms. Life was mapped out by them and they were excited about the road to their idyll.

On Madeleine's birthday Robert planned a climb of Carrauntoohil. It would be his first time scaling her special mountain and he wanted it to be a spiritual journey to celebrate her birthday, as well as a declaration of his love. The morning was beautiful, and so was Madeleine with her red hair matching the carmine hues of a summer sunrise. Early morning mists were billowing down from the western ridge of the mountain and settling in the valley, creating an ethereal atmosphere as they made their way up. Down below in the valley, the summit seemed like a majestic cathedral crowned by a mighty cross and they were on a pilgrimage entering its domain to consummate their love. The climb was indeed a pilgrimage. Not a saintly one, but a joyous trek to the high altar, where, kneeling by the cross, Robert proposed to Madeleine. Never could she have imagined a proposal in such an exalted place, one so special where she felt on the edge of heaven, close to her God and to her love.

Robert took out a bottle of champagne and two glasses from his rucksack and he toasted first her birthday and then their engagement. Madeleine looked at Robert and Robert at Madeleine, and in the midday sun, on a deserted summit, they discovered a spiritual love as though God himself was sanctifying their union and that it would last until the end of time itself.

As they lay there atop the mountain, slightly inebriated, taking in the majesty of the landscape across Kerry and lost in their own company, it was Madeleine who broke the contemplative silence.

'Robert.'

'Yes Maddy.'

'I've a confession to make.'

'You have?' he replied with a degree of concern.

'Yes. You remember that time on top of Mount Brandon?'

'Of course. How could I forget?'

'It wasn't pure fortune that we met there. I saw you in the town of Dingle that day. You were on your bike. I shouted, but you didn't hear me. I knew where you were going so I finished my work in the town and went to the base of the mountain. It was a sort of test. If I saw your motorbike then I knew that you were the one for me. So I climbed in your footsteps, to win your heart.'

'But you had already won my heart.'

'I know that now. But back then, I was a naive girl from rural Ireland. I couldn't see past the attention until I realised that all they wanted was my body. You were different. You wanted my mind as well. I only appreciated that towards the end of the first year. So I invited you to visit me. I hoped you would. I would regularly go into Tralee to see if you were there, but to my disappointment, you weren't. It was fate that I should spy you in Dingle and that God was leading me to you.'

Robert was astounded. Of all his inept attempts at procuring Madeleine's affections, fate was indeed playing its hand, for she had already been won and it was he, rather than she, who had been naïve enduring heartache in those early days of courting her.

'I'm so glad you did,' as he leant over to kiss her.

'There's something else I want to tell you.'

'Another confession?'

'No. It's that promise I made on that day to you.'

'About this mountain being special to you?'

'Yes. It's a spiritual place for me. I know it may sound preposterous to you, but I feel on the edge of heaven up here. Close to God. It's a place of sanctity for me, where I can commune with Him.'

'You know I accept your faith.'

'I know. Sometimes I envy your atheism Robert.'

'I too sometimes envy your faith. That there is a merciful God. That there is something else other than this earthly paradise.'

'I admit it is comforting. But it's just a product of birth. If I'd been born in India, then I would most likely be a Hindu with all their gods. Certainly not Catholic. But Catholicism is in my very soul, indoctrinated, I would say, since my first breath. I like its rituals and the peace of the church, with its icons and incense providing a sort of continuity, a framework for belief. Except for the most devout, faith can be superficial. Those that have sinned can seek absolution in the confessional. It's quite ridiculous really. But even I'm a hypocrite of my religion. Sex before marriage is a sin for which I do not apologise for. I have never sought absolution from a priest who is no nearer to God than me. Up here, I feel close to Him and can ask for his forgiveness.'

Madeleine paused for a moment. With a presentiment look, she gazed beyond the horizon towards another world and then with a solemn voice continued. 'But there are some sins which are beyond His covenant. Do you see what I'm trying to say, Robert?'

'I think so,' although he really had no idea at all other than she was admitting to a sin for which her God would not absolve her from. But what it was, he could only guess. Perhaps Madeleine was saying that they shouldn't have made love, especially in her special place. He looked at her. She was, Robert thought, seeking that absolution, with her head bowed in an act of prayer. She motioned the cross, looked at Robert and smiled.

They kissed and returned to their own thoughts, unaware that a thick blanket of cloud was heralding an approaching weather front. Madeleine was the first to spot the dark mass. It looked foreboding. They collected their equipment and made a hasty retreat back the way they had come. With it beginning to rain, Madeleine said that it would be dangerous to be caught on the arête they had traversed in the morning and that there was a quick route down a gully which she had used once before. They carefully picked their way amongst the now slippery boulders, helping each other towards the gully of Hags Glen.

'We have to go down there,' she gestured.

Robert looked at the steep descent she was pointing to and wasn't sure if it was a wise move, then he looked towards the storm that was almost upon them and acquiesced to her better judgement.

'Okay. But take it slowly.'

'Slow and careful,' confirmed Madeleine.

That was their watchword. Madeleine lead, being confident of the terrain. The first few paces down the gully were the most difficult, having to scramble with hands and feet. After a short while, with the ground becoming shallower, it became easier, but just as they thought the worst was over the heavens opened causing the gully, which had been no more than rivulets of water, to instantly fill into a raging torrent. It now became a battle against relentless wind and rain and a gully that had become a death trap.

Madeleine's mountain skills were good. But as she carefully picked her way down, every so often she would miss a step and slip. She stopped and turned to see Robert following slowly a few paces behind, but confident in his progress. She looked up to the summit and the cross and then returned to continue the decent, unsure about herself. She realised the champagne was impairing her judgement and knew alcohol and mountains didn't mix. Mindful of the watchword, she continued, but yet again missed a footing and slipped, only this time she was unable to halt her slide. She cascaded down the gully like a rag doll, hitting her head, finally coming to rest by a large angular boulder some sixty feet away. She lay there motionless staring into the heavens.

Robert looked on horrified as she disappeared down the ravine. He scrambled to her as quickly as he dare, slipping himself a couple of times, bruising his body and scraping his hands. It didn't matter. He needed to reach Madeleine. When he finally did so she was lying drenched and contorted with blood oozing from a wound to her head, staring motionless into the heavens.

'Are you alright?' he anxiously wailed, looking concerned at Madeleine's state.

There was no reply.

'Madeleine!' he shouted, and kissed her several times on the lips in an act of resuscitation.

She stirred and opened her eyes.

'Are you okay, Maddy?'

'Yes.'

'Thank God for that. For a moment...'

He assessed her injury. Despite the blood, it didn't look too bad. From Madeleine's rucksack he located the first-aid kit and bandaged her wound as she, looking towards the summit, thanked God.'

'We can't remain here, Robert.'

'I agree. Are you up to moving on?'

'Think so.'

It was then, as Robert tried to help her onto her feet that she was struck by a sharp pain in her leg. Instantly Madeleine knew it was broken. She couldn't move. With the relentless rain drenching their faces they sat in the gully together, silent, knowing what to do but unwilling to communicate the obvious. Robert was scanning the mountainside hoping to see somebody, whilst Madeleine was drifting in and out of consciousness but trying to hide it from Robert, realising that her head wound was more serious than they had supposed.

'You need to fetch help,' declared Madeleine.

'I won't leave you.'

'You must Robert. I'll be alright. It's just a broken bone,' she replied, trying to reassure him. 'There's a farmhouse about half a mile down the track. It won't take long.'

He was not convinced but knew himself that assistance was required. After several protestations, and with the rain relenting and Madeline being sheltered from the wind, he felt confident enough to leave her and seek help.

Just as he was about to leave, Madeleine grasped Robert's arm.

'We shouldn't have made love in the shadow of the cross. But I'm glad we did. I love you Robert, I love you with all my heart.'

They were the last words Robert heard her say for on his return, having called for assistance, she was lying lifeless on the ground, her face tainted with blood and with a cadaverous gaze looking towards heaven. He collapsed to the ground and kissed her, trying to breathe life into her. But she remained motionless. He felt for a pulse, but there was none. He raised his arms towards the cross and with an inconsolable wail, cried out, 'Why? Why take her? Why take my Maddy?' A kind and merciful God had exacted retribution for her sin.

4

Robert looked at his vision of love. A love so cruelly taken from him, swallowed up in an instant on that fateful day high on the mountain in Ireland. An idyll that was never to be. For in front of him, peering above the hawthorn hedge and partly hidden by a large pampas grass, was a whitewashed cottage that could be mistaken for the one in Kerry, the one that he and Madeleine were to live in for the rest of their lives. In that moment he thought he was on the summit of that mountain, on the edge of heaven, where she was waiting and they were going to live that life they had mapped out. He wished he was. But reality can be a cruel taskmaster. He was not in paradise, but in Looe on a cold spring day.

What fate had brought him to this place, at this moment in time? As he tried to reconcile that day on the mountain, the pain that had left him bereft for months after Madeleine's death returned, and with it the demons that had haunted him for so long. Was he responsible for her death? He should have stayed with her. If only he hadn't taken the champagne: that was to blame. He should have seen the approaching storm. He shouldn't have agreed to take the gully route down. She had died there, alone on the mountain that she loved. Was God punishing her for their sin at a holy site, violating the sanctity of the cross? Madeleine herself had said they shouldn't have. She knew God was going to take her.

He tried to exorcise the demons of that day from his mind but they were taking hold of him again, consuming him once more, this time only to leave an empty shell that would be washed away by the tide. Was it his destiny that he should find love again? And if so, would it be taken from him once more as it had on so many other occasions in his life. Was love to be a curse fated upon him, he thought? Once again, he wondered if he was responsible for Madeleine's death. Or was her death some form of a cruel test played out by her God?

Robert looked transfixed at the cottage. He was struck by a paralysis of memories, of demons which he thought had been tamed. He felt as though he was being pulled between the two worlds of past and present, as if caught in a whirlpool with his head spinning around in the vortex from which he couldn't escape. As he stood there, incapable of moving, unable to rationalise, a cold gust of wind raced around the cliff and hit his senses.

Having surfaced from his drowning, yet wary lest his past took hold again, he carefully walked on a bit further, the high hedge giving way to a cultivated recess, overgrown with ivy which had spread and was now choking a wrought iron gate on which was a nameplate with the letters, LAMMANA. Next to the gate was a 'For Sale' sign. This was fate. How could it not be, Robert thought? He was excited. Perhaps he was going to live his idyll after all, not with Madeleine, but with her memory and she would be with him watching from the edge of heaven. He hadn't seen the cottage properly yet and didn't know the price, but he knew he was going to buy it, whatever the cost.

The cottage looked deserted. He ventured to a wrought-iron gate and opened it but the hinges had rusted solid and it fell to the ground with a clatter, disturbing the silence and startling him in the process. Feeling somewhat guilty, as the gate was now irreparable, he tentatively leant it against an adjacent stone wall and realised it was the same inauspicious start that he and Madeleine had had: this was fate, his mind was now convinced.

There were a few steps up from the gate followed by a sloping path at a right angle with a stone wall, topped by some picket fencing showing signs of neglect on the cottage side, and an overgrown privet hedge on the coastal side. After about ten yards or so, and again at right angles, were some more steps leading up to a terrace in front of the cottage.

Now Robert could see the whole façade. On the ground floor there were two windows either side of a central doorway set in a covered porch, whilst to the first storey were two more windows immediately above the ones below. At either end of the gables were two prominent chimney stacks standing proud of a slate roof, which was slightly bowed in the centre. It was, Robert considered, exactly like the cottage in Ireland. He wanted it to be. It had to be. It was meant to be. Even the porch over the front door, with trellis either side supporting a spider-work of overgrown clematis, not pruned in many a year and now being choked by ivy, was an unerring replica to his recollections.

The cottage had a forgotten ambiance, not lived in for a long time. But what struck him most was a feeling of serenity, the same sentiment he had had with Madeleine when they found their idyll. It was as though the cottage was once a place of sanctity emitting an air of peace and solitude, a place where penance and piety were to be found within its embrace.

Robert went over to one of the windows. The frame was rotten revealing layers of different colour paint, sculpted and weather-beaten by westerly storms. He squinted through the opaque glass but could only see an empty room with a fireplace to one side. The other window was much the same, but it had a broken pane through which a faded curtain was blowing in the wind emitting a musty odour of mildew, a signal to its deserted state. Around the rear of the cottage was a single storey lean-to with a sloping roof containing two skylights to compensate for its north-facing aspect. Peering through a rear door, Robert could see a kitchen of some sorts with a table and chair to one side, but nothing else. An upstairs casement was open and banging in the wind, the source of the noise that had first alerted him. He contemplated scaling the lean-to roof and entering inside, but his better judgement prevented him.

Behind the property was a small slate patio backed by a retaining wall, above which was the sloping bank of the cliff. This was supporting a variety of shrubs and small trees that clung to the slope and had been invaded by bracken that was being strangled by a vine. On the town side of the cottage was a small entrance vestibule with a pitched roof, portholes to the two sides and a solid door which opened onto views towards Rame Head. Further aside was a dilapidated old shed constructed of asbestos, Robert concluded, and a small garden in which there had once been some attempt at stocking it with herbaceous plants that were now overgrown and in need of attention. But it was pretty, and he thought it would be enjoyable to nurture it back to its former glory.

On the other side of the cottage and towards the back, up against exposed rock that looked as though it had been hewn out by hand, was a ramshackled summer house, once painted in sea blue but now faded, augmenting its rustic character. Above the entrance was a piece of driftwood with the name *The Sea Shack* just about legible. Robert liked it, pleased that it faced the Island, and he imagined writing a novel inside, gaining inspiration from such a stunning setting.

Beyond and above the garden, so as not to obscure the sea view, was a small stand of conifers, Scots and Monterey pine, their branches swaying in the wind and making a low droning noise that created an air of menace as though ghosts of past inhabitants were telling him to be wary, depart and never return. Pine needles were scattered everywhere, some in large piles where the wind had collected them, whilst above a hawthorn hedge, interspersed with struggling cultivated shrubs, was the sea and Looe Island, the first sighting that day.

By now it was getting late and with the cloud cover once again heavy in the sky, darkness was descending upon the afternoon. He had seen enough and now wanted to find the estate agent before they closed. He retraced his steps downhill, this time finding it easier. He passed the café which was now closed, the proprietor putting up chairs on the tables for their nightly vigil, and walked briskly along the quayside to the bridge.

A string of lights were shining along either side of the harbour giving a welcome glow to the gloom and reflecting in the ripples of the water. All the vessels had now come to life, bobbing up and down in a small swell created by the wind, and as Robert crossed the bridge thinking of his conversation with the café owner, was he now crossing into enemy territory? It didn't feel like it. But if he bought the cottage, then maybe it would.

The estate agency wasn't difficult to find, being almost opposite the far side of the bridge. He briefly looked in the window to see if he could see the property listed. He couldn't, and so he went in. A woman was sitting at a desk and on the telephone to a client. She smiled at Robert and beckoned him to sit down.

As she was talking, Robert couldn't help but gaze at her. She was very attractive. Sculptured features portrayed a Pre-Raphaelite Madonna, with beautiful eyes and lips that asked to be kissed. Hugging her slim figure was a cream blouse, accentuating her femininity and making her very much desirable, Robert thought. But it was her red hair that transfixed him, long with a thick fringe on the forehead, a reminder of Madeleine and as he stared at her he was looking into a window of the past, his lost love and one that hadn't aged. She looked at Robert, caught his gaze and smiled, upon which he quickly looked away in embarrassment. He wasn't looking for love, although it seemed providential that he should find the cottage and then a beautiful woman who could be mistaken for Madeleine. Was somebody playing with his emotions?

The estate agent put the phone down and looked at Robert with another smile.

'Sorry you had to wait. The trials and tribulations of being an estate agent. My name is Tara. What can I do for you?'

Robert looked at her eyes. They were blue and sparkling and he felt them looking inside his soul as though she knew what he wanted. She had seen his gaze. And as she spoke, he looked at her lips and he did want to kiss them, to feel that connection to a love that was no more. His heart began to race as it told him to seize the moment. But out of decorum Robert remained seated.

'I've come about the property you have for sale over on the cliff in West Looe. It's called Lammana,' he said.

Tara mentally recoiled from his enquiry. She knew the property, knew it only too well. It had been deserted for many years and despite her professional involvement, she had an interest in it herself.

'Yes, I know the property.'

'Have you the details and can I arrange to view the cottage?'

'That will not be possible as it is no longer for sale on the open market.'

Robert's heart missed a beat. Love found and love taken away in an afternoon, he thought and under his breath, told himself that love is indeed a curse. Tara looked at Robert and could see his disappointment.

Her eyes penetrated his exterior and she saw an opportunity, one that she could control.

'It is, though, being sold, by auction, tomorrow,' she added.

He was relieved. But being auctioned tomorrow? At least it wasn't sold, he told himself.

Tara continued. 'As for the details, I can give you them if you're still interested.'

'Yes, if you could please. What's the auction price?'

'It has a guide of fifty-thousand pounds.'

Robert thought for a moment, unsure he heard her correctly.

'That seems rather low, is there something wrong with the property?'

She paused for a second to collect her thoughts and then said, 'Well, it's being sold as probate and the executor now wants a quick sale. It also needs considerable renovation, and access is difficult to say the least.'

'How so?' he asked.

'You cannot get to it except by foot on the old coastal path. It has a rear entrance backing onto the open ground, but again there is no vehicular right of access across it. Indeed, access across this land is only possible by consent from the owner. But...'

'That's no problem,' Robert interjected before she could continue.

'But, it may be a problem, because it's built of mundic brick.'

Robert flinched with a questioning tone, 'mundic brick?'

The estate agent then explained that mundic brick was a peculiar construction material that was used in Cornwall back between the wars. It was like a modern concrete building block except that a mundic block, which would better describe it, is composed of poor quality quarry aggregate which has a tendency to weaken and crumble if moisture attacks it.

'The consequence is that any building constructed of this material is not deemed mortgageable,' she finally added.

'That's no problem either since I've sufficient funds to finance the purchase, assuming I secure it at the auction. But I am concerned about the mundic brick.'

She had been serious whilst telling Robert about the construction material, but now adopted a more encouraging stance.

'In that case, it could be good news for you as it would exclude many potential buyers, particularly developers and the buy-to-let market. And even better news,' she continued as though enjoying lifting Roberts's hopes, 'the cottage has been recently tested and the blocks have been declared sound. That's not to say they won't deteriorate in the future but if the external render is maintained, then there's no reason they shouldn't last.'

Robert now felt encouraged and smiled at her. 'That is good news.'

'If you're still interested the auction is at Webb's Hotel in Liskeard tomorrow morning at 11.30.'

She got up and fetched the details from a filing cabinet and handed them to Robert together with an auction pack.

'Have you ever bought a house at auction before?'

'No,' replied Robert, 'but I have bought a Victorian fire grate at a sale room!'

Tara laughed and said, 'Well, it's the same process, but once the gavel goes down on a sale then it's a legally binding contract, usually to be completed within a month. I advise you to read the auction pack.'

'No problem,' he confidently replied.

Tara could see that Robert was very much interested in buying the property. She had valued it herself and knew the attraction of the place, with its seclusion and views out to sea. But she also knew of its past history and the reputation surrounding it.

She looked at Robert and now, rather than seeing a client, she noticed a handsome man who obviously had money, a combination that she found alluring. She wanted to know if he had a wife or partner and began formulating a strategy that would elicit that information.

'Do you live in Cornwall?' she began.

'No, just visiting for the day. Quite a coincidence that I should find the cottage and it's up for auction on the very next day.'

'Yes, perhaps fate was playing a role.'

'Perhaps,' Robert replied circumspectly.

'If you get it are you going to live there?' she enquired, and then added, 'with your family?'

'Oh, I've no family, just me. But I will renovate it myself and live there. It is quite beautiful.'

'Well if you like it on a day like today, then when the warm weather of spring finally arrives, it will be an idyll.'

Robert was stunned and speechless. Why had she used the word 'idyll'? Was she Madeleine, reincarnate? He was somewhat annoyed that she had stolen their description, but Tara was delighted that he was available. She planned her next move.

'Look, I'll be at the auction tomorrow, in an official capacity of course. I'll look out for you and help you through the process if you like.'

'That would be very kind, thank you,' said Robert, having just about recovered his composure. 'Until tomorrow then Tara,' he said with an expectant tone, smiled, and got up to leave.

'Until tomorrow, Mr...sorry I don't know your name.'

'Colliver, Robert Colliver.'

With that disclosure the estate agent's face turned pale, as though she had seen a ghost, a spirit from the past, and one that she was very much fearful of.

5

That evening, back at his sister's farmhouse in Devon, Robert was lost in a myriad of thoughts. He could not settle. His mind was wandering between the cottage and Madeleine. It was in turmoil, trying to make sense of everything. But uppermost was the image of the estate agent, Tara, and her resemblance to Madeleine. What forces are at play, he thought, and wondered if he was unwittingly being drawn into a game where he was a pawn in other peoples play?

His sister, Ruth, was intrigued by his disclosure of events that day, but thought his judgement was misplaced by his obsession with fate.

'What about Caroline?' she asked.

He had forgotten about her in the maelstrom of his mind.

Robert had met her five years ago whilst on a trip to Morocco. They had fallen in love and travelled together for a year, before moving into Caroline's flat in London, where she worked. Robert didn't have a job, he didn't want one and didn't need one; he was financially independent. But his days of leisure and pleasure, as Caroline put it, began to consume her with jealousy and she resented him not working, not contributing to a future she wanted. Her career was tracking fast. She had become Head of Medieval Archives at the British Library and wanted further progression, to which Robert felt he was excluded. Their relationship had become strained and by mutual agreement he left and moved to his sister's a few months ago. He still had feelings for her, still loved her if he was honest, but seeing the cottage, the memories of Madeleine had surfaced, and with them his demons.

Ruth had hoped her brother and Caroline would get back together and that the separation was just a breathing space in a stifling relationship compounded by being in London: cities and she had never been friends. During his enforced exile, Robert had slowly been won over by the peace and tranquillity of the countryside, renewing his love of wild places, and the fact that the metropolis was so far away, almost irrelevant to life in the West Country.

His sister's farmhouse was situated on the edge of Dartmoor. Robert would seek its rugged beauty and untamed landscape, the granite tors, the megaliths and abundance of bronze age antiquities luring him in as though into a mire itself. They provided a focus for his mind, a natural cure to his mental ferment. But as much as he loved the moor, the sea was always ebbing and flowing in his mind. When it seemed to fill his thoughts, he would wander to a high tor near to the farmhouse and there he could see Plymouth Sound and the coast of the South Hams, and the restless ocean would beckon him. The sea was most definitely in his blood, and no amount of wild moorland transfusion would dilute that feeling.

Ruth didn't think he should rush into buying the cottage and not at an auction when he hadn't seen it properly, nor had time to investigate it. She tried to convince him to return to London.

'Give Caroline another chance,' she begged.

But she couldn't persuade him to abandon the venture.

'It's not going to be like before, running away from your responsibilities,' she remarked, hoping for a reaction that would wake his senses.

After Madeleine's death, it was clear to Robert that if he remained in Ireland his demons would win. So he secured a teaching post at a college in Norfolk, the furthest place away from their idyll he could possibly be. For the first few years he was engrossed in teaching, starting early and working late, to placate his nightmares. It worked. He had tamed the grief and pacified his demons; life was beginning to return to him. He began to socialise more and soon found himself engaged in casual relationships. They satisfied a need, but were unfulfilling. He found himself making comparisons and judgements about the women, which was a mistake, as they could never be a match for Madeleine; she was on a pedestal too high for the ordinary to scale, no matter how much they deserved respect.

He admonished himself for being selfish and became frustrated by the banality of life, missing the intellectual sparring he had had with Madeleine. Teaching became a burden. No longer did he look forward to the classroom but saw it as a punishment, a self-inflicted chastisement that began to hurt. And to amplify his pain, the College wanted more from him, telling him to wave flags and pronounce allegiance to a new order that had arrived, where each student was a cash machine that he had to exploit. Education was sacrificed for the attainment of league tables, he had to work longer hours and his precious holiday time was slowly eroded. The teacher was expendable in the brave new world of the intellectual production line. He loathed it.

To escape his new nightmare, he would wander off into his own world where there was only him and Madeleine, in their idyll by the sea. It was only a temporary escape and the reality of the classroom would soon resurface, reminding him of his responsibilities. So at weekends, and in the term-time breaks, he would seek solitude in the expanse of the Ouse Washes, the North Norfolk coast, or the wide open skies of the Wash, sitting for hours watching birds and the migrating wildfowl; pink-footed and greylag geese and whooper swans. He would watch the vast numbers of knot and dunlin follow the tide as they probed for worms and crustaceans, and then suddenly take to the air in a mass of winged awe, as a hen harrier dived from above. And as dusk fell, he would marvel at a flock of a million or more starlings in their murmuration spellbound at the majesty of their choreographed dance. He wished that he were one of those avian angels and would look up into the sky and see two migrations; the birds' northerly one to their summer breeding grounds, and his own, which would go south and east and west to lands where he was anonymous and where he could find a new meaning to life. And that is what he did. He left teaching, left Norfolk, and went travelling.

Robert knew it was not going to be the same. This time it was different. He wasn't going travelling to escape his demons but face them head on in a new life by the sea, where fate had decreed it.

'But you're making a new life in the shadow of the cross,' Ruth replied.

No, he was getting on with life, by accepting whatever hand was dealt him. That was his mother's mantra and he was now chanting it too.

He went outside to clear his head. It was cold. The raw wind of the day had subsided and a restless mist was beginning to form, a haze hugging the ground which would slowly rise, giving way to another frosty morning. He looked up into the night sky. Stars were shining all around him, and as he circled taking in the majestic constellations of the cosmos, a shooting star crossed his path. He imagined it was Madeleine, conjuring a wave from the edge of heaven and waved back, but the trail had vanished into the ether. That transitory moment made him wonder about life, about relationships. It, they, can so easily be born and die like the meteorite, a black metallic rock that had travelled millions of miles, had survived the intensity of heat as it entered the Earth's atmosphere and had created an evanescent spectacle, yet memories of that journey would be lost.

Sleep that night was hard to find. Rather than clearing his head, the evening observations were still playing accompanied by Greek mythological stories his mother used to tell him: of Orion, the hunter, and close by the Pleiades, daughters of Atlas, or Cassiopeia who vainly declared 'no woman is more beautiful than I', and Andromeda, her daughter, who was tied to a rock in order to placate the Gods and rescued by Perseus. He lay there in bed recounting those heroic tales wondering where his goddesses would fit into the legends.

Outside, there was perfect silence. In London, the sound of a city, sirens, cars and motorcycles and at weekends the rowdy behaviour of party-goers, was always invading the peace. In the countryside no such distractions existed, except for the nocturnal calls of wildlife, lullabies that could envelop the mind in sleep.

Then some owls flew into the peace. They were nearby, three he could make out, each one cooing after the other, vying for vocal supremacy and the chance to mate. They were a soothing melody to his tumult and as Robert listened to their assignations, he fell asleep into a deep sleep which awoke his memories once more, not of myths, but something altogether different.

The images were blurred. He could see himself standing outside the cottage, which one he could not tell, facing a fierce storm and a raging sea. Spindrift whipped from the white crests of breakers and in the distance a ship was battling its way towards him. As it came closer, he could see it wasn't a modern ship but a galleon in full sail and standing on the bowsprit was a demonic man, a pirate pointing with long fingers to Robert, cursing him and vowing revenge, and as he did so the spindrift turned to tiny arrows that flew into the wind, piercing Robert's heart.

He turned away in pain and looked back at the cottage. Now it had no windows and the entrance porch was transformed into a portico supported by two Doric columns. He moved to go within, and as he passed through the doorway he was inside a shell, a blank space, an antechamber to a temple, a Greek temple with massive Caryatid columns and a central doorway of monumental size, carrying the weight of his turmoil. He walked up to the entrance and opened the heavy doors revealing a cavernous empty space, in which the gods themselves could reside. He looked up to a thousand pinpricks of light, stars which adorned the heavens. From one of them came a shooting star, falling to the ground in a flash of light. In front of him arose a figure, a goddess. It was Madeleine. Then a second meteorite fell to ground, and again a flash of light and another goddess. This time it was Caroline who arose from the light. And then a third meteorite, a flash of light, another goddess, and the estate agent, Tara, stood before him.

Each one was wearing a long chiton, a flowing gown, and their heads were adorned with a crown of narcissi. They looked at Robert and held out their arms, wanting him to make love to them. They came closer and closer, each one trying to beguile him as they lost their robes, enticing their pleasures for him to adorn their bodies. And as they did so, he looked at himself and saw he was the god Apollo watching his Graces running their hands up and down their naked figures, wanting their god to take them.

Then Madeleine approached him, writhing like a snake about to strike, entrancing him, and as she neared him she said, 'I am the goddess Happiness, come to me,' and she stretched out her arms as though luring him to her breasts. But he didn't go with Happiness. Then came Caroline performing the same ritual, and she whispered, 'I am the goddess Beauty, come to me.' But neither did he go with Beauty. And then came Tara and she said, 'I am the goddess Charm, come to me.' Nor did he go with Charm. And with that they encircled him, each Grace holding one another on the shoulder, and began dancing a seductive rhythm all the time looking longingly into his eyes. He followed them. He desired them. He wanted each one of them. And as he circled with them, his head began to spin into a vortex until he could no longer see his Graces, no stars, not even the temple, just an empty void from which eternal torment would spring forth.

Robert sat up in bed. He was sweating and the dream, which in the end had been so vivid, was losing its potency. The images of the demonic sailor had melted in perspiration, their meaning lost to his thoughts about his Graces. He got up and looked out of the window. The owls were no longer audible for they had flown away, metaphors of a mind that was wrestling with guilt. He asked himself, who would he choose? It was between Beauty and Happiness, Charm had no place in his heart. But in the reality of the night, Happiness was dead, taken from him by an avenging God and Beauty was a forsaken love.

And as he thought about his lost Happiness, the twin antagonists of fate and destiny swelled up and that even if he could not have children, nor grow old with Madeleine, if he could change the past then he would trade his remaining years for one more day with her, one more hour, one more minute, to say he loved her and watch her die in his arms, their love sealed on the mountain she adored, on the edge of heaven where she would rest.

But fate had brought him to this point in time and destiny had created the dilemma he now faced; seek a lost Happiness or choose Beauty. But as events were to unfold, it would be Charm that was to beguile Robert.

6

Webbs Hotel was a splendid Georgian building in the centre of Liskeard, not far from the old cattle market where Robert had parked his car. As he stood outside, wondering if what he was about to undertake was the right thing to do, his gaze was attracted to the entrance portico, with its two Doric columns standing proudly in the centre of the façade. Sash windows were evident either side, stretching up three stories, with a street-level basement below, probably the kitchens and servants quarters when it was the home to local gentry. The architecture reminded him of his nightmare and the choice he was about to make, as he took the portentous step into the unknown, having forsaken Beauty in favour of Happiness.

Inside the hotel, the auction room had been laid out with rows of cushioned chairs from the doorway to the front, where there was a long table and two grey-suited gentlemen in conversation. Scattered amongst the seats were the buyers, not as many as he had thought there would be, but still with enough time for more to arrive. Sitting down at the table on her own and studying some documents, was Charm. She looked up and espied Robert entering the room and smiled, flicking her red hair to one side as though gesturing him. He smiled back at the friendly face and the flash of her hair, realising that he had rejected her in his nightmare but was somewhat buoyed by her presence. She though, had been making a clandestine signal to a young man seated at the back, who looked at Robert as though noting an intruder and one who needed to be pacified.

Unaware of this telegraph, Robert walked up to Tara. 'Good morning

Tara. Well, I've come to register for the auction,' he said in a cheerful and positive tone, attenuated by the prospect of buying the cottage.

'Good to see you, Mr Colliver,' she replied in a raised voice, which seemed to resonate around the room as everybody stopped and looked at them. Then in a much lower voice she continued, 'I can see you've read the auction pack. I just need to take a few details and give you a bidding card.'

Tara took the details and then beckoned him to one side of the room so as not to be overheard. In a whisper she announced her plan, one that would secure the cottage for Robert and provide her with the opportunity she desired.

'I shouldn't be telling you this, but in auctions the vendor sets a reserve price on the house. If that isn't reached then it's withdrawn from any further bidding and no sale occurs. I've persuaded the vendor to set a high reserve, because of the interest in the property. But it's unrealistic. Few, if any, are likely to bid beyond it, let alone anywhere near.'

Robert was listening intently but wasn't sure where her tack was going.

She continued. 'The house will be withdrawn, and with that you can make a private offer on the property which I will put to the vendor and advise him to accept. Do you follow me?'

Robert now understood. He was going to be part of an illegal sale. He was honest and such activity abhorred him. Normally he would walk away from such an underhand deal, but he wanted the cottage, and was prepared to do almost anything to secure it. Tara knew that and gambled that he would play the game.

'Yes, but isn't it dangerous?'

'Not if you follow the rules. Make a few early bids and then withdraw as though the bidding has gone too high. Wait for the sale to be withdrawn and come and see me.'

'What if the bidding carries on? What then?'

'Unlikely. But if it does, watch for my signal. I will cough and that will indicate for you to bid again.'

'Okay,' Robert said in an unsure tone.

He sat down near the back not wanting to be noticed, although everybody in the room had observed him with Tara. He wondered why she was doing this. She didn't know him and had nothing to gain and everything to lose if her game was uncovered. Some people like digging around for dirt, and this was a muddy deal.

Using the auction pack details as a decoy, he surreptitiously looked at all his fellow bidders but couldn't decide if they were for his cottage or one of the other three properties up for auction that day. There was a middle-aged man, perhaps in his forties, near the front who had turned around and was chatting to a man whom Robert couldn't see properly. Next to him, in the same row but a few places along, were a young couple, but they didn't seem serious contenders for the cottage as they had details about another property. There were two men in working clothes, as though they were in the building trade, three rows down from him who could be possibilities and hence may make a bid. But nobody else fitted, not that there was a stereotype. Robert was testimony to that.

The man, to whom Tara had gestured, was sitting behind Robert and looked as though he had some facial infection, although Robert didn't want to stare at him. Another man sitting in the row in front of him, boyish in appearance, was clearly a reporter, with notebook and camera by his side. Why a newspaper man would be at an insignificant auction, Robert could not guess.

After about fifteen minutes another couple and a single woman had joined the congregation. Rather than a house sale, it seemed to Robert like a sparse religious meeting, where an evangelical minister was to give a rousing sermon to convert the disparate scattered and unrepentant heathens onto a righteous path. As it turned out the auctioneer introduced himself in a rather placid and restrained manner explaining the procedure, lest anybody bid accidentally.

There were four properties up for auction, the first of which was a detached house in need of renovation. It sounded lovely, set in five acres with many outbuildings and a stream running through the land and Robert was almost tempted to bid for it. The auctioneer asked for bids starting at the advertised sale price, but no one came in. He dropped the price and the middle-aged man volunteered a slightly lower bid. After that the bidding went up steadily and was finally sold to the young couple. The next property followed a similar pattern and was sold considerably higher than its reserve, which concerned Robert. The third one though was unsold, it not having reached its reserve, the auctioneer declared. Lammana was the last property for auction.

By now the participating audience had dwindled and there were only a few people left, the middle-aged man, whom Robert had by now deduced was some sort of property developer, the late arriving couple and the reporter. Robert thought it strange that a detached cottage with no near neighbours, in a sequestered position with fantastic views out to sea and along the coast, could generate so little interest. But he was glad it didn't.

Just as the auctioneer was about to start another person, an elderly man perhaps in his sixties and well-dressed, hurriedly arrived in the room, in somewhat of a panic that he was too late. He apologised, obtained a bidding card and the auction began.

The opening bid came from the couple and then Robert entered with his own, continuing for a few more bids until he declared himself out, as Tara had instructed. The bidding continued with the old man joining in. Contrary to Tara's expectation, it didn't stop: it went up and up. Robert was getting worried, Tara's plan seemed to be unravelling and there was no audible cough from her. He looked at her, but she had her head down, engaged in some papers. The price was still within his budget, but he could see the cottage slipping from his grasp. The only consolation was that there were only two rival bidders now, the middle-aged man and the new arrival, and he was just about to become the third when Tara coughed. She looked apologetic. Robert, sensing it would be incriminating to bid immediately, waited a few moments and joined the bidding. The middle-aged man now dropped out and it was now a combat between ages, the weapons being money, and the winner would claim the prize of Lammana.

In the end there was no slugging match as Robert put in a pre-emptive bid close to his maximum budget, gambling that it would throw his opponent, making him realise that he couldn't win. And it was a knockout bid as the gavel went down without his contestant recovering, or so it seemed to Robert. He was jubilant, having just bought Lammana. The auctioneer congratulated him and Tara smiled a broad smile as though she had engineered the auction to her satisfaction. She had.

Robert went up to the front table and handed over a deposit to Tara.

'Congratulations Robert,' she said with another smile.

'Thank you Tara, but I was getting a bit worried at one point.'

'Yes, not according to plan,' she whispered, 'but the result is what counts.'

Robert agreed in his mind, but it was his money that had secured the victory, not hers. But he had the cottage and all he wanted to do was to go to Looe and view it again.

'Can I arrange a viewing this afternoon?' he asked Tara.

'Of course. I shall come myself with the keys. Say about two o'clock?'

'That's perfect. See you then.'

'Most definitely,' she said and as Robert walked away, she repeated it to herself with satisfaction, 'most definitely.'

Robert left the hotel and was about to make his way to the cattle market, when the reporter from the sale room stopped him.

'My name is Malcolm Thomas from the South East Cornwall Gazette. I wonder if you have anything to say on the purchase you've just made of Lammana?'

'Sorry?' Robert replied with a quizzed look.

'Let me rephrase. I'm researching an article on Cornish smuggling and the cottage has some history attached to it, although most of it is myth and legend. I wonder if you have any information on the cottage yourself?'

'No. As far as I'm aware I've purchased a cottage in need of renovation.'

'What made you buy it?' he asked.

'Well, it's none of your business really, but if you must know it's because I like it.'

'You are aware of its history, I suppose?'

'No?'

'It was the birthplace of a notorious pirate.'

'I'm not aware of that fact. Anything else?'

'Well, as I've suggested it's all myth and legend. But one thing is for sure, those that have purchased the cottage either don't live long enough to enjoy it, go mad in it or never sleep in it.'

'Perhaps they have over-active minds. Ghosts and phantoms are conjured by such thoughts.'

The reporter could see that Robert knew little or nothing at all, and he wasn't going to get anything he didn't know already. But he wanted to see his reaction to the legend of the cottage.

'You do know...' he began.

But Robert stopped him from continuing. 'Please, I'm rather busy, so if you don't mind I must be getting on.'

'Sorry to have troubled you. Thanks for your time,' replied the reporter, thinking that this man did not know anything of its provenance. With that he went on his way.

Robert was somewhat perplexed by his comments. A place with history? Something to do with smuggling? He shrugged his shoulders and continued on his way. But walking back to the car park he felt that history following him, whatever it was, and as soon as he reached his car, history had caught him up. It was the old man from the auction room.

'That cottage was mine. It belongs to me,' he protested in a hoarse voice.

'I'm sorry, but I've just bought it. It's a legal purchase.'

'You think so?'

'Yes, and I'm not about to argue it in public. Excuse me.'

But the old man was insistent.

'You know the place is haunted. Oh yes, haunted all right. I've seen the ghost myself,' he added, hoping to frighten Robert.

'Really? Ghosts are a figment of an imaginative mind and one that usually wants to see such things,' he replied, rather annoyed by now.

The man grabbed Robert by the arm and uttered to his face, 'they are real enough. You mark my words. He will come for you. You are cursed you are, and he will come for you.'

7

The drive from Liskeard to the coast along the East Looe valley, through the villages of St. Keyne and Duloe, is an agreeable exploration of a hidden Cornwall. The road snakes its way along, sometimes high above the valley floor affording beautiful panoramas, before descending to narrow bridges that cross the river itself, eventually emerging into the wide estuary near Looe.

But the drive for Robert had been tainted with the disclosures of the reporter and the old man. He was beginning to wonder what he had purchased. A cottage with history? The birthplace of a notorious pirate? A haunted cottage? And worse, that he was cursed? He tried to clear his mind of such thoughts, but like his demons, they were beginning to be indelible images.

He looked out of the window at the stunning valley, heavily wooded in deciduous trees that were waiting to spring forth their verdure canopy but for now were providing light for carpets of wood anemones to exploit. With virtually no traffic on the road he could afford to let his mind wander, in complete contrast to London where vigilance and full wits were required behind the wheel. Passing through the village of Duloe, he noticed a sign for a stone circle and decided to take a quick look. He had always been interested in archaeology and ancient history and had often found that by perambulating around a stone circle, somehow anxieties were addressed as though he were praying for answers, much like Tibetan Buddhists do with their prayer-wheels on which mantras are decorated.

The megalith was located near to a delightful church, in a field where a flock of sheep were grazing, they looking somewhat bemused at a stranger invading their privacy. Approaching the structure, Robert could see that it was nothing like Avebury, or the Rollright Stones, nor even the Neolithic stone circle of Callanish on the Isle of Lewis in the Outer Hebrides, not that he was expecting so. Yet its size was disappointing, being approximately forty feet across and confined to a hedge, which further added to his dismay. Nevertheless, he thought it had an unpretentious charm, particularly as several of the crystal-white granite menhirs were quite substantial, the tallest of which was a good foot taller than he. There were seven of them positioned in an oval, not the usual circular configuration, the major axis seemingly aligned to north-south indicating an astronomical connection. But Robert was more interested in its spiritual feel, and touched each menhir, feeling their connectivity with the elements that seemed to provide a conduit for his pessimistic thoughts concerning the cottage, so that they had dissipated by the end of his clockwise circumnavigation of the standing stones. He paused to admire the view and noticed a ruined manor house in the distance with no roof and crumbling walls, but set within a beautiful wooded valley, and wondered why such a building had been left to the vagaries of time.

With his mind refreshed, Robert continued on to Looe. He now began to focus on the logistics of renovating the cottage and how long it might take. Accommodation would be needed, he thought, somewhere to stay for the first couple of months. He had already decided to have some lunch in the café and ask John, the proprietor, if he might know of a place he could rent. Then he would have to arrange finance. That would mean a train journey to London and an overnight stay. Perhaps he could avail himself for a night in Caroline's flat, but he hadn't spoken to her in over three months. Come to think of it, he thought, she hadn't contacted him either. He would ring her tonight.

It had barely been an hour since the gavel went down and here he was already mapping out his future in a new idyll. Not the one with Madeleine, he thought, but she would be watching him from her heavenly rest and following him all the way. That was what he would like to think, although he naturally had no faith in such an afterlife. Every culture, every civilisation has this in one form or another: a necessity for man to believe that death is not the final act, that our mortal coil will live on forever and we will be united with the ones we love and stand alongside our maker. Robert was ambivalent about this. He held no credence in resurrection or the human body being transmuted to some spectral form, although he did accept the faiths of other people and their belief in such a destiny. And so it was with Madeleine. He would think she was in her paradise waiting for him to join her, although he wasn't sure if the Lord, should such an existence prevail, would admit him to His exclusive club.

Robert reached the bridge spanning Looe harbour as though it were a familiar place, one which he had crossed many a time. It was only twenty-four hours ago that he had been standing there in the bitter cold, wondering whether to stay or go. Destiny then had controlled his actions, his mind determined to accept whatever fate awaited him, and as he drove over the bridge, it was as though he were crossing a threshold into a domain of uncertainty.

He drove on to the car park. It was huge, probably accommodating about five-hundred vehicles, he estimated, but in March, with winter still proffering and no hint of spring warmth, it was virtually empty. As he was getting out, Robert noticed a builder's merchant truck coming from the far end and wondered if there was a yard there. It would be useful, he thought, and proceeded to go in that direction, passing some recycling bins and a small boating lake. Opposite was the heronry he had spotted yesterday with some birds already nesting. Further on, the car park gave way to a gated entrance to a wooded valley. An information board declared it to be Kilminorth Wood, containing ancient oak and beech trees, some coppiced, with an abundance of wildlife from kingfishers to butterflies, wild flowers to mosses and ferns, and with pictures showing the common species likely to be found within. To the left of the woodland was a small trading estate where he found the builder's merchant and a car repair garage with the name 'Trevellick' announcing its trade. With his curiosity satisfied, he returned to walk back across the vast expanse of tarmac and to the bridge once more.

Standing there, thinking about the café proprietor's words, he wondered why there was antagonism between the two towns. As far as he was aware, it was just one community. But now he had bought

Lammana, was he too going to be prejudiced? He counted the arches again. There were still seven. He was not expecting otherwise. However, on closer inspection he could see there was an eighth arch, smaller and not spanning the harbour, under which ran a footpath from the car park to the West Looe quayside. Perhaps it meant something he thought as he made his way along the quayside towards the café.

Without the biting wind of yesterday the walk felt more comfortable. The tide was out once more and the man who had his vessel careened was now working on the port side. Patrolling the muddy basin were the usual avian suspects, mainly herring gulls with the greater black back gulls bullying their cousins. Amongst the sea birds Robert noticed an interloper, a lone phalarope, which had probably been blown in on the northerly winds from the past few days. Their usual wintering grounds are predominantly in Scotland, and he wouldn't be surprised if local twitchers arrived soon to see this vagrant amongst all the ubiquitous gulls. He deduced from its plumage it was a grey species, but wasn't entirely sure if it was a phalarope at all. He would look it up when he got back home. Home, he thought, is now here, and that made him feel anxious, suddenly realising that he had nailed his colours well and truly to the West Looe mast.

Inside the café the old sea dog was at the same table by the door and acknowledged Robert with a sort of grunt, which he considered must be another condemnation. It couldn't be his new status because nobody knew, and Robert wanted it to stay that way, at least until he was the legal owner of the cottage. John, the proprietor, was surprised to see him, but pleased that he had chosen his establishment for lunch again, obviously unaware of Robert's ulterior motive.

Like the old man he sat at the same table, but this time ordered a cappuccino and a panini and sat back to enjoy the baroque music, Corelli, Robert could tell, being quietly played as a background accompaniment to his Italian *pranzo*. How civilized, he thought, and remembered a restaurant in Dharamsala, an old English hill station in northern India and home to the Dalai Lama, where the owner, a lovely Nepalese woman, played nothing but baroque music and where Robert used to have the most delicious omelettes for breakfast on a veranda overlooking the foothills of the Himalayas. 'It was Nirvana,' he muttered to himself with a pleasing smile bringing back so contented a time, and as he looked up, unaware of his public utterance, he saw the old man and the proprietor staring at him as though he were a mad *sadhu*.

Robert got up, still perplexed by the look of astonishment on the two men, and went over to pay his bill. As he did so, he enquired about renting some accommodation. He estimated it would take about two months to renovate inside the cottage and if it took longer, with the warmer weather coming it should at least be habitable by then. The proprietor suggested a couple of places but said his best bet would be with Harbour View, since the clients who were supposed to arrive yesterday had, in fact, cancelled, and he believed there were no more bookings for the foreseeable future. He gave Robert the number and told him to mention his name, implying that he knew Robert and would be some sort of character reference. Robert thanked him and left the café with the old man still at his table who muttered under his breath, but loud enough for Robert to hear, 'another bloody foreigner in Looe.'

*   *   *

The cottage looked even more idyllic, despite the continuing overcast weather. But there wasn't the wind of yesterday and looking out across the bay the sea had a more benevolent look, no white crests to the waves and even a couple of sailing yachts racing the ocean. The navy had made an appearance too, with three frigates and a Royal Fleet Auxiliary vessel on some manoeuvres far out towards the horizon.

At two o'clock Tara arrived, catching Robert in a daydream sitting on an old bench looking out to sea.

'Penny for them,' she said, making him jump in surprise.

'Oh, it would cost you more than that for me to divulge them,' he replied. He was being facetious because his mind was quite empty in semi-meditation at the sheer beauty of the scene that soon would be his.

'How much more?' she enquired, wanting to engage with Robert and so gain his confidence.

'Oh, a pirate's ransom,' he said. He wasn't quite sure why he had said that as he meant to say King's ransom, but it seemed natural and quite appropriate. Tara though was shocked and felt unnerved by this remark as though the words were an invocation. She quickly changed the subject.

'I have the keys here. Expect you're keen to see inside?'

'Yes. I've been wondering what work needs to be done.'

Tara opened the front door and invited Robert inside. There was a narrow hallway which had two doors leading off into the two rooms either side, which he had previously peered into from the outside. They were about the same size, containing dated wallpaper peeling away from years of neglect and damp, yet despite the shabby appearance of both rooms, he liked the feel already. At the rear of the property, the kitchen needed most work, containing just a stand-alone sink unit with taps that didn't work and the table and chairs he spied before were fit for only firewood. Next to the kitchen, off a small vestibule which led to the side extension, was the bathroom, comprising a bathroom suite in avocado green, a throwback to the seventies Robert thought, when perhaps the cottage was last updated. Off the hallway was a staircase leading to the upstairs which gave access to a main bedroom above the lounge and a second bedroom the opposite side. Robert wondered if the second bedroom could be split to accommodate a new bathroom, leaving the one downstairs as a cloakroom. The plumbing seemed to fit and he was sure that there would be no problem, other than doing it.

Whilst he went around from room to room, Tara followed him, making suggestions as though she herself were moving in as well. In her mind, she was. But Robert appreciated her involvement, and was beginning to like her presence.

'So what do you think Robert?' enquired Tara, as they stepped outside.

'Not as bad as I feared.'

'I know its early days, but if you need any help then I would be pleased to assist. The agency has several tradesmen that it uses, plumbers, electricians and so on, and I'm sure they can be made available, should you require.'

'Thanks, that may be useful,' he replied in a grateful tone. 'Is this your normal level of service?' he then added.

'Well, only to clients we like,' she said in a somewhat suggestive tone. For we, Robert read I, and enquired, 'is this a personal service then?'

'You could say that. I felt that Lammana cottage was meant for you. As I said before, it was fate that you got it.'

After the morning auction Robert wasn't so sure, but said, 'well fate and a pirate's ransom.'

Again, Tara felt uneasy and made her excuse to leave. 'I've got another viewing shortly, so I'll have to go now. Drop the keys into the office later on and let me know when you're down here next.'

'Will do, and thanks once again.'

'My pleasure,' she parted with, and went on her way, not to a viewing as she had intimated, but to an important rendezvous that had as its agenda the cottage and Robert Colliver.

Robert looked around outside again, but this time taking greater note of things. Whereas yesterday it had been a viewing of the heart, he could now see that the guttering needed replacing, a few tiles were missing and one of the chimney stacks required re-rendering, particularly as he had seen signs of damp in the bedroom it served. But like yesterday, he was in awe of the stunning sea view and the prospect of sitting outside on a hot summer's day in his new idyll.

He sat down on the bench again and sank back into his meditation. He was suddenly disturbed by a rustling noise quite nearby, the same noise he had heard on the path. It came from behind the cottage, and with a slight trepidation he quietly stepped around the back to investigate. It was now louder and coming from up the bank. Something darted from a thick shrub and disappeared out of sight, a fox perhaps, he thought, although it seemed larger, perhaps the size of a sheep.

Disturbed by this happening, Robert went back inside the cottage and into what would be the lounge. He wanted to get on with the task of renovation now and so decided to peel off the wallpaper. No one would mind, he thought, after all it was his cottage, but for legal formalities. The paper came off easily, and as he removed one strip after the other something began to reveal itself, painted on the plaster.

At first Robert couldn't make it out, but the more he peeled away, the clearer it became: an old galleon with three masts and in full sail. He peeled some more wallpaper and was suddenly shocked, almost stupefied, to see the image of a figure standing on the bowsprit, a demonic pirate pointing forward with long fingers, venting rage. It seemed as though it was Robert himself who was the recipient of his ire. The image triggered his memory of the dream. The dream he had last night, only this was real. What force was at work here, he wondered, that he could dream such an image and with the same demented figure? He felt a little uneasy, and remembered the old man's words from the car park. Surely the cottage could not be haunted. 'It's nonsense,' he said in a determined voice, as though to exorcise any demons that might be stalking him. And as a sign of bravado, he continued to remove more wallpaper. But as he did so, some writing appeared which sent a cold shiver right through him, for next to the painted galleon, were the words:

I CURSE YOU. I WILL COME FOR YOU.

And below that was the demented writing of a previous owner:

I HAVE SEEN HIM.

8

London is a metropolis that radiates wealth from its core. It's an inverse law of economic prosperity, proportional to the distance from its centre. In Cornwall that gravitational wealth is weak and the City feels light years away, so much so, that planet Cornwall might drift off into its own orbit of independence. The Cornish have always felt like that, ever since Doniert, the last King of Cornwall, died in AD875 and the region became part of the burgeoning kingdom of England.

When in Cornwall do as the Cornish do, forget London, forget the City. That is what Robert thought as he looked out of the window of a Great Western Railway train bound for Paddington, watching it approach the Albert Bridge that spanned the Tamar. But he couldn't forget London. He'd once had a symbiotic relationship with it, where a love blossomed and where he had found happiness. That was, it seemed, a lifetime ago, and now, rather than optimism the city held apprehension within its walls, at the forthcoming encounter with another love that had recently faltered.

For the following couple of days he just had to tolerate London, a place he knew well when devouring its cultural menu. Yet his appetite for such institutions had diminished in favour of organic cravings, where the soul is nourished simply by admiring natural beauty as though it were a masterpiece in a gallery or a magnificent stone edifice. Enrichment was to be found in watching waves of ripened corn dance in the wind, or listening to the dawn chorus, or the sound of the sea as waves break on a sandy cove, or simply silence, or any number of notes that the inherent world plays in such captivating form.

Recent events had overlaid that score by uncertainty, where

supernatural forces were at play and he was the object of a game in which he knew nothing of its rules. But as the train crossed the Tamar Robert sensed he was leaving that envelope, and beyond the divide he could sit back and let emptiness take control, watch the countryside slide by, and with the horizon of Cornwall becoming ever distant, his concerns would evaporate and the invisible force of the capital fill his mind with its energy.

Yet, no matter how distant that horizon became, Robert couldn't get Looe and the cottage out of his astronomical telescope. Its aperture was wide and he could still see clearly the wall painting, a *fresco* to a forgotten antihero, a man possessed, a man who wanted to find him, curse him. Was a demented pirate playing with him? It was preposterous, yet his mind could not liberate the thought.

He had told himself that no such phantoms existed. His philosophy told him that. As he tried to blur the image it would refocus again, only sharper, more vivid. The pirate's long fingers were accusing him, cursing him. Was he cursed? He thought love may be a curse upon him. Perhaps it was his own judgement upon himself? Or was he fated to confront his spiritual accuser in a cottage where his life would collapse into a dense cloud of gaseous vapour, to be consumed in a black hole from which no life can escape, and where an eternity of torment awaited him? His nightmare had foretold that.

Robert awoke from this dark matter, particles of a hallucinogen that had clouded his journey. With the train pulling into Paddington, he had been overwhelmed by unearthly apparitions and now faced the very real presence of negotiating the London Underground at rush hour, making his way to Pimlico where Caroline lived. He had telephoned her after the auction, requesting that he might avail himself for a couple of days in the flat they used to share, having explained the circumstances. He was expecting a terse response and would not have blamed her, but she was quite accommodating and by her cheerful note, even looking forward to his return.

He emerged from Pimlico tube station with dusk enveloping the city. He was glad to be out of the claustrophobia, where humanity was reduced to the absurd, sardines within a shoal, where kinematics dictated their movement, not the individual consciousness. Over the last few months life in the West Country had liberated him from such irrational behaviour. Within the confines of the Tube he had felt like a fish about to be trawled, unable to escape the suffocation, with release from the geometrics of motion only coming when surfacing into the fresh air of the urban environment. Having escaped the net, Robert took a deep breath and then another, and life finally returned to his being, sanity to his mind.

He was early. Six o'clock, Caroline had said. He had an hour to wait and so with light fading, he walked down to the Embankment and looked across the Thames. It was in this twilight hour that the city was at its best, particularly by the river, with lights reflecting in the rippling water, a shimmer of brightness and a sense of expectancy for the night ahead.

Looking at the reflections, he wondered what tonight would hold, being back in the flat he had shared for four years, but now no longer his home. How had it come to this? It felt as if they were two strangers meeting for the first time again. That was five years ago, when they were in a small group travelling around North West Africa, taking in the sights of Morocco and the Atlas Mountains.

The first words he heard her say were, 'Pisces is my least compatible star sign.' As a way of an introduction, each group member had to say a few words about themselves. Robert had said he was like his star sign, 'easy-going, fond of water and a dreamer, trying to attain the unattainable.' Caroline had replied, 'I have a strong will, hate water and love a challenge in life.' It was obviously a direct assault on his character, but as he watched her talk, he fixed his gaze on her beauty, her slim figure, and as he fell entranced by her presence, he found himself undressing her and making love to her on that evening.

It was the first time, since Madeleine, that he felt so intensely passionate about somebody and he knew, despite the poor omens, she was the one for him. But as she finished speaking, his trance, his spell, was broken and the dream of attaining the unattainable was as real as ever. She had told him they were not compatible, yet beneath the layer of words Robert sensed there was a spark of emotion, an intangible fusion of two connected minds.

Over the following few days, as they travelled around the country, that spark would not ignite. He tried to engage with her but she would rebuff him and seek the company of fellow travellers. But as the week progressed they found themselves drawn together out of a mutual disdain for group travel and even agreed on a preference for independent travel, not the irritating constraint of a group which seemed to be a platform for hedonistic pleasure. But they were on different wavelengths of that common spectrum: whereas Robert would mention Nepal and the Himalayas, Caroline would say India and the Mughal culture. She was using Robert as a shield, he thought, and had given up hope of attaining his dream as they ended their Moroccan adventure in the cosmopolitan city of Tangier.

It was a very hot day and the group had decided to party on the beach. Robert had found the notion quite acceptable, considering the heat and that he had seen enough Moorish art to fill his curiosity. However, he changed his mind after overhearing Caroline say she was going to the local museum and would join them later. He guessed it was the Kasbah Museum just outside the *medina*, and hatched a plan to be there pretending to be absorbed in the exhibits, as she stumbled across him.

Before Caroline left, Robert made his move. But plans require conviction. The reticence, which had dogged his attempted courting of Madeleine, now surfaced again. He considered abandoning the hair-brained scheme for the enticing cool waters of the Atlantic, even trying to convince himself that he had the wrong museum, or that she probably wouldn't turn up, or if she did turn up he would back out. He told himself to be bold and seize the moment. So, spurred on by the thought of conquest, he made his way through the narrow streets of the *medina*, filled with its unfamiliar sights, sounds and smells, a sensory overload that seemed to distract his uncertainty. Soon, sweating from the heat, he found himself outside the museum, a former Sultan's Palace that was gleaming white in the midday sun.

He had anticipated the air-conditioned rooms inside, but to his dismay found it even more stifling with only ceiling fans to cool the sultry air. The main display rooms were empty except for seated attendants, half asleep in the oppressive atmosphere as though they were exhibits themselves, ones that could testify to time, unlike the artefacts that frequented the display cases which seemed to be lost in time as well as space. Many of them were of African origin and didn't interest Robert although a magnificent Roman mosaic from the ancient city of Volubilis was impressive. But all the placards next to displays were written in either French or Arabic, which were naturally lost on his tempered enthusiasm. So Robert found himself strangely attracted to those exhibits below strategically placed fans and rather than trying to decipher the meaning of Roman tools, pottery shards or a reconstructed pot, he revelled in the delight of a welcome breeze.

He had been moving from one fan to another for over half an hour with no sign of Caroline, and was about to abandon the affair when he entered another room that contained not another sterile cabinet of lifeless art, but to his surprise, a cartographic exposition that seemed to leap out at him and touch his imagination. Maps had always fascinated him, ever since an early age when he had been taught by his father to interpret the Ordnance Survey maps that graced the family home. But it had been an atlas on the history of world exploration that triggered his obsession with old maps and the explorers who plotted them, risking everything to chart beyond the known world. He realised then, that maps had a language of their own and those that master the script of latitude and longitude and the symbolism of the cartographer, are able to read much more than the written word itself, thus providing a unique view of the world, where geographical knowledge was power.

If Robert's mission was to captivate Caroline, then the array of charts before him temporarily extinguished that quest. For adorning the walls were maps of Europe and Africa depicting trade routes and other unknown facets, some dating back to the sixteenth century, others more recent. But it was one particular display that had focused his attention. Alongside a display case containing coins and jewellery were old maps of England and the South West and in particular, a Tudor map of the Cornish coast seemed to have pride of place. On it he could make out Plymouth and the town of Looe, with an island showing a chapel, a bridge spanning a river and a fortified barbican on the east side of the town. He tried to read some of the explanatory text, but his French wasn't good enough although he did decipher 'Barbary

Pirates' and the year 1660. He became absorbed in the cartographic displays, so much so, that he failed to notice Caroline standing behind him, her gaze too fixed on the map that Robert was admiring.

'Didn't expect to find you here and so engrossed in an exhibit it seems,' she said with an air of confident surprise and loud enough to wake the attendant who was dozing on a chair at the far end of the room.

She startled Robert causing him to turn around quickly almost colliding with the display cabinet.

'Caroline!' he exclaimed in a restrained tone of amazement, 'what are you doing here?'

'Evidently doing the same thing as you,' she replied, with a slightly sardonic smile on her face. 'I expected you to be at the beach with the others.'

Robert hesitated. He had forgotten about the explanation which had melted in the heat of the moment. He had to think quickly and dredge up a reason for being at the museum. 'Well, it was tempting, but I wanted to find out about the Barbary Pirates and their connection with England,' he said having regained his composure, and breathed an inner sigh of relief that he had come up with a plausible explanation.

Caroline glanced at the cabinet. 'Can you understand French?' she quizzed, but didn't wait for his answer. 'Do you want me to translate?'

He declined. His curiosity for the exhibits was now supplanted by the exquisite display in front of him. She was the reason he was there. The maps could wait; Caroline was an altogether richer prize. He stood rooted to the spot, his eyes gazing longingly into her eyes and she into his. He could sense she hadn't fallen for his deception, yet her eyes told an altogether different story: one of anticipation. Anticipation for what, he thought. To admit his deception? No, it wasn't that. She was waiting for him to seize the moment. He edged closer, all the time looking at those beautiful eyes, then her lips, moistened by the tip of her tongue, which he wanted to taste, to explore, to love. She was telling him to kiss her.

Yes. No. *Carpe Diem,* he told himself. His heart was pounding. He wanted to kiss her, kiss those lovely soft lips and taste her passion, entwine their tongues like snakes in an act of love. Yet he couldn't seize the moment. His body was frozen, his muscles unable to propel him to his dream. There she was, Caroline, her aura enveloping his mind so that he could only see a heavenly goddess offering him her spiritual soul, willing him to take her, and with the desire of a thousand nights to come he finally moved to kiss her. But he had waited too long.

'It's hot in here,' she declared in a soporific tone.

He had hesitated and the moment had evaporated into the charged heat of the museum. Was she playing with him, wondering if he would take that final leap of faith and attain the unattainable? Chart the unknown? He felt sure of the electricity, but the spell had been broken and he could feel the charge drain from his body, drawn to earth from the bolt of her comment. All he could do was agree with her.

But Caroline was still a positively charged particle, unmoved by his negative display and was still excited, wanting a current of passion to flow through her body, for Robert to satisfy her desire. 'I know where it will be cool and where we will be more comfortable,' she softly spoke.

Robert looked into her eyes, eyes that were luring him with her beauty only to reject him as his dream foretold.

'Back at the Riad,' she continued, 'in my room.'

She touched Robert on the cheek and moved her fingers across his lips and said, with a flutter of excitement, 'what better way to cool off than to strip naked.'

Robert looked at her and smiled. It was a half-smile. Did he hear her correctly? She was offering herself to him. He went to kiss her, but she put a finger to his lips and said, 'wait 'til we get back'.

*   *   *

As Robert leaned against the Embankment wall looking across the river, watching the shimmering light reflected in the water, he remembered those first few moments in the Riad.

They stood facing each other as though back at the museum, but this time Caroline was removing his shirt to reveal a firm torso that she touched sensuously with her hands, feeling the hard masculine muscles that pleased her imagination, and as she progressed in her exploration of his nakedness she exposed a toned body, taught from the anticipation of the moment. And as Robert slowly unbuttoned

Caroline's dress to reveal the most exquisite body imaginable, he gazed at her nakedness, her sublime breasts and soft nipples, and skin so pure and smooth, tantalising his senses, waiting for him to caress and anoint.

They kissed and enveloped each other with their passion, enraptured as though they were heavenly deities taken to a higher plane, a level above consciousness, a mystical experience exploring beyond the horizon in an act of tantric love, where two minds are fused together and explode in a climatic supernova. Within a nebula, new stars are born, new life created, created from nothing but their individual lust.

*   *   *

Robert sat down on a bench elated by his memories of that afternoon in the Riad. But it was the creation of life that had sowed the seeds of their separation. 'You are a man. You can walk away. I'll have the scars of the abortion for life. It was your fault. You didn't want the baby. It would prevent travel. It would interfere with my career, you told me,' she would say, even though it was she who wanted to travel and she who secretly wanted to further her career.

The reasons would surface every time there was an argument between them. But they were taciturn arguments creating a malignant impasse, the result of which would be a cancerous deadlock that thrived in the deafening silence. At first, they were isolated, but over the years they had become more frequent, until one day, a few months ago, the stalemate had lasted for over a week with only the perfunctory acknowledgements of one another's company, so that Robert thought it best to have time apart. Caroline had readily agreed. He had left for his sister's the following day.

9

Twilight had given way to a moonless night which was glowing from the multitude of lights that London throws into the atmosphere. Sparkling reflections in the river from offices and street lights on the opposite bank created the effect of a substitute heaven, as though the Thames were the Milky Way snaking its way across the sky.

In those reflections were constellations and other galaxies. In Robert's imagination he could see, in the river of stars, the red giant of Betelgeuse in the constellation of Orion and a flashing neon sign on a tall building, mirrored in the water was a pulsar from a distant galaxy, signalling a place to eat in the galactic array of restaurants lining the river bank. This was a London he liked, hidden in the shadows of a cosmos where everybody was anonymous, an insignificant point in an infinite space.

But night-time London was transitory, not enough to sustain his need for permanence. He heard Big Ben strike six, looked towards Parliament and the clock tower, collected his thoughts, and made his way to Caroline's flat.

The building was a red-bricked Edwardian tenement block, converted into flats and home to the predominantly professional. He stood outside the building for some time, wondering if it was a good idea staying with her. He felt as though he was back at the museum again, unable to make that move, only this time it wasn't so much as seizing the moment, more a case of delaying the awkward encounter. He rang the bell for her flat.

Over an intercom Caroline's voice barked, 'Who is it?'

'Hi, it's me.'

'Who's me?' she queried.

She knew only too well who it was, but was playing games yet again.

'You know who. Me, Robert.'

'Oh yes,' came the reply.

The door clicked open and he made his way up a flight of stairs to the top floor. The door to her flat was open and Robert entered into a familiar space unchanged since he left.

Caroline was in the kitchen, a glass of wine in hand, reading a magazine. She was dressed for a night out.

'Hi Caroline, good to see you.'

She looked up, smiled, and said, 'Good to see you too, Robert.'

'Hope you don't mind me imposing myself upon you like this and at such short notice.'

Realizing that she was not going to be able to finish reading the article, Caroline put the magazine down and finally took notice of Robert's presence in the flat.

'Not at all. After all, it's not as though you're a stranger to me or the flat. Would you like something to drink?'

'Tea would be nice.'

'After six and you want tea? Have you gone dry?'

'No, it's just that I've been getting used to it more over the past few weeks. Guess it's become a habit.'

'Sticksville is softening you,' she retorted in an ironic tone.

'On the contrary, I'm finding the countryside rather to my liking.'

'You'll be voting Tory next,' she said in a teasing voice. She knew that would touch a nerve.

'Never,' he replied vehemently.

There was a pause and a moment's awkward silence which Caroline broke.

'Look Robert, I'm going out tonight so you'll have to look after yourself. A friend is picking me up shortly. We're going to the opera,' she cagily explained. 'And before you ask, it's a male friend who is on a course I'm giving at the Library.'

Robert detected a tone of pathos in her voice, or was he deluding himself and wished to hear it. He had only himself to blame, having left thinking that time apart might heal their wounds. Instead, they had become septic and now amputation of their lives seemed inevitable.

'Isn't that a conflict of interest?' he said.

'No, it's an adult course. And in any event, it's not your concern.'

Robert knew when to stop pursuing Caroline. She would and invariably could be dangerous when backed into a corner. She always won arguments or wanted the last word.

'What opera?' he asked with a touch of melancholy.

'Don't be angry, Robert, but its Madam Butterfly. It's a new production at the Coliseum.'

It was scant consolation that the venue wasn't Covent Garden. It was where they used to go and Robert looked rather dejected at the prospect of her with another man, especially since Madam Butterfly was their special opera, a Puccini masterpiece of heartfelt sorrow and despair, with no happy ending. Perhaps it was an allegory for their relationship, he thought, chosen especially to tell him that theirs is all over, without actually having to say it.

He had introduced Caroline to opera and Madam Butterfly was special because it was the only time he had seen her weep real tears of emotion; the doomed heroine and the music must have struck a chord at her heartstrings, because he never saw such an outburst of emotion again. As for Robert, she would often see him with tears in his eyes listening to music from composers who could reach deep down into the soul, such as Mahler or Beethoven with Wagner at the pinnacle of the elite group, where every note was a motif to life itself. Caroline would say it's just music, not real life, whereupon Robert would argue that music is a metaphor for life, providing a gateway into the human soul and that, anyway, she had no heart.

Robert wanted to show his disapproval of the choice, but in a civil voice hoped she had a good time. He continued though, 'I've never thought English versions capture the true emotions of a production, particularly Puccini. Better take a supply of tissues though, in case I'm wrong.'

Caroline acknowledged his sentiments and dismissed them immediately as she changed the subject.

'What brings you to London then? Something about a house in Looe is it?'

'Yes, I've bought a cottage on the cliffs overlooking the sea in the town. It was at an auction and I need to arrange the finance for it.'

'Oh Robert, you didn't bid on yourself again I hope,' she said with a laugh. 'I remember that debacle at the saleroom with the fireplace, when you bid on yourself.'

'Not this time,' he said and turned around to look at the fire surround and remembered the happier times and the fun they had refurbishing the flat. Indeed, at every turn there seemed to be a reminder of those days and he somehow wanted to rewind time and relive them once more. He turned to face Caroline who was watching him scan the room and knew exactly what he was thinking, for she faced those same dilemmas every day.

He was about to describe the cottage when the doorbell rang. Caroline answered and shortly after in strode the adversary to her affections. He could have been a character in a Wagnerian music-drama itself, displaying a blond mane and a stature that defines confidence, almost arrogance, not the sort of man Caroline would go for, he thought. She introduced the two combatants and they greeted one another, his handshake gripping Robert's hand, declaring his male ego and pronouncing he was now the alpha male in her flat, and Robert would have to fight him for the territory that was once his.

There was an atmosphere of tension as both men sized each other up. Jock, for that was the name he gave, was a good few inches taller than Robert and probably a good few stone heavier in weight too, and in any fight he would have no problem in defeating his challenger, let alone Robert. Not that he wanted a physical contest, and so playing to his intellectual strengths, opened up with a verbal jab.

'Where do you come from? I detected a slight Scottish accent,' he enquired.

'You're right. My name's a giveaway. I was born in the Highlands, but have lived in and around London for some years now although my work takes me all over the place.'

Robert wasn't really interested in where he lived or in him at all, but thought he ought to show some civil courtesy with Caroline present.

She, sensing a rut for supremacy, retreated to the bathroom, leaving the two stags to fight it out. In an act of self-preservation Robert too retreated, but to the kitchen to find something to eat. Food was more on his mind than the spoils of battle and he knew that victory in any conflict would not be his.

In the refrigerator was fresh pasta and a jar of pesto, together with some salad items. Whilst Robert started to prepare the meal, Jock was master of the lounge and proceeded to demonstrate his ownership by pacing around in such a way that it resembled a Scottish lek, a circular arena where competing male birds display and fight for domination. Finding that his only contender was more interested in food, he manoeuvred himself into an armchair, Robert's armchair, and opened a bottle of beer and a packet of crisps to declare victory and consume the spoils.

There was an imposed silence between the two men. Every so often, Robert looked up to see the Wagnerian Scot seemingly assured of his domain, yet with arms outstretched and fists clenched he looked ready and waiting for a move. That move, when it came, was an innocuous enquiry to break the tension which, after a couple of minutes, was too much for Robert.

'Do you like Puccini?' he said.

'No, not that keen on pasta,' replied Jock.

Robert chuckled to himself at the misconstruction. Jock remained deadpan without betraying any emotion. Robert wondered if he was an imbecile or so confident that he could afford to be seen as such, but unbeknown to him, Jock was a child of suffering. Neither laughter nor tears revealed themselves, for he was born into a theocratic family that forbade such frivolities, where abstinence and obedience was the law, the commandments of a harsh and judgemental childhood.

'What about travel?' he enquired, having decided not to pursue his conjecture. 'Caroline has a passion for it and we've been to many places together around the world.'

'Yes, I know, she's told me. She said you met in Morocco, in a museum of all places.'

Robert couldn't believe she would be so forthcoming with their personal life and guessed he had coaxed it out of her.

'What about you, Jock. Do you like to travel?'

'Oh yes, who doesn't? So long as it's five-star hotels, luxury air-conditioned transport, and there's good food on the menu.'

For Robert, that was confirmation that Jock and Caroline were not compatible. He certainly couldn't see them travelling together, staying in a hut in a remote village on the Andean Altiplano where the only luxury was an outside hole in the ground as a toilet, and on the limited menu was guinea pig with either rice or chips. Or hitching a ride in a truck across the Himalayas, snaking its way along a single-track mountain pass with a thousand foot drop to one side and sharing the cabin with a convict in chains, his guard complete with Kalashnikov alongside a mad co-driver, cooking food on a kerosene stove which would burst into flames as the vehicle hit a rut in the road. Such travel would be an anathema to Jock. Was Caroline blind to this, or was it sex that was the interest? Perhaps she wanted rough carnal sex, the opposite of their relationship and now that he had left she was in need of a real man, a Siegfried from the Scottish Highlands

Robert was about to ask him what he did, knowing already that Caroline would have described himself as a retired lay-about who did nothing, when she reappeared ready to make a move. He wished them a good evening and was glad when the flat was his. Siegfried had left his mark though, with a half-finished bottle of beer and crumbs from the crisps, a scent marking to let him know he was still the alpha male even though he had left the arena.

Over the following few hours, Robert had his supper, went through the auction pack again, this time knowing he had secured the cottage, and decided on a course of action. He would arrange the finance tomorrow, stay one more night with Caroline and then head back to Cornwall. He didn't want a second round with Siegfried fearing what might happen if things got out of control. He abhorred violence, preferring diplomacy, where either logic or intelligence wins the fight and the only casualty is self-esteem. That was not Siegfried's *modus operandi*, he thought. There was something not right about him, but he couldn't pin anything on him. He was the complete opposite to Caroline and Robert thought he would rather be tossing the caber than attending the opera.

Robert went to bed early in the spare room. Caroline had made an effort. The bed was made, there was a clean towel and she had left him something to eat as well. Despite it feeling strange to be back in the flat, he was tired and fell asleep quite quickly thinking of her and Siegfried at the opera. He passed into a dreamlike slumber soon overtaken by a nightmare, made in Valhalla and of Wagnerian proportions.

He was a dragon guarding the stolen Rheingold, forged into a ring of magic and power that men would kill for. And into the nightmare came his nemesis, Siegfried, with sword in hand to slay him and steal the gold. The dragon fought him but Siegfried was too strong and thrust steel into the heart of the beast, and as the dragon lay dying he could see Caroline by the side of the victor and they sang a song of love and victory. Then she went over to the dying dragon and looked at the creature that had lost. There wasn't victory in her eyes now, but loss, for they were shedding tears, tears for a forgotten world where she was free to wander the skies, a world that had now gone forever. It was so vivid that Robert imagined she was there by the bed looking at him asleep, with tears in her eyes. Was it the dream? He was half asleep, half awake, a transient state between reality and fantasy. He could sense she was there, somebody was there, but he dare not open his eyes for fear it was all a chimera.

10

The day dawned over London with the now unfamiliar sounds of traffic, sirens and a low drone that pervades an urban environment that were clamouring inside Robert's mind, more used to the natural tones of the countryside. He had slept well since his apparition and woke a little after seven-thirty. Caroline was already up and dressed for work, sipping a mug of tea and now reading a book instead of the magazine.

'Some Earl Grey?' she said, knowing full well he disliked the concoction.

Robert politely declined and made his usual breakfast tea as Caroline continued to be immersed in the book she was reading.

'Still reading,' he ironically remarked.

'Food for the soul,' was her reply.

'Food for the body is more important. Have you had breakfast?'

'No time.'

He decided to make her some toast as she continued to read. He gazed at her. Even early in the morning she looked beautiful. If only things had been different, he thought, and was about to say something to that effect but was interrupted by the toast popping up. Having buttered two slices and spread them with marmalade, he gestured to Caroline that she might like to eat and returned to his private recriminations.

'Thank you Robert,' she said, looking up and smiling at him. She picked up one of the slices and took a careful bite.

'Did you sleep well? I could hear you muttering something when I got in, so I took a look. You were murmuring something about treasure and tossing about as though battling the bed sheets,' she said continuing to eat her way through the piece of toast.

Robert was pleased. He did sense her in the room.

'Must have been dreaming, but I can't remember.' He paused to think about his dream and then continued, 'How was the opera?'

'You were right. It's not the same in English, but good nonetheless.'

'And Siegfried,' he said realising instantly his mistake. 'I mean Jock. Did he enjoy it?'

Caroline looked at Robert with a stern face as though the nickname had insulted her, not her companion.

'What's this with Siegfried?' she intoned in a rather abrupt manner.

'Sorry, just my musing. He reminds me of the character in The Ring, the one that goes off with Brunnhilde.'

'So I'm Brunnhilde now, a warrior maiden who falls in love with a hair-brained Arian thug?'

'No, it's not like that,' protested Robert.

But he was digging himself into a hole this time, one that he probably couldn't escape from and he didn't want to upset Caroline any further. To restore calm he changed the subject.

'What does he do?'

She looked at Robert for a few moments, deciding whether to pursue the indignation, but thought better of it.

'He owns a company investigating inheritance and unclaimed estates. He's on a course I'm giving on medieval and post-medieval boundaries. He's a nice chap when you get to know him. He asked me out a few weeks ago. I like him and he makes me feel wanted.'

That was a body blow that hurt Robert. Caroline, he felt, had treated him as though he were expected to provide for her by doing the cooking, cleaning and anything else required, and if anything, it was he who had felt unwanted, as though he were a slave to her ambition. Even though he didn't work, he was financially independent and contributed equally to their relationship and did not, as she often implied, live off her expense.

But rather than arguing his case he just wistfully said, 'I wish you well Caroline.'

She looked at Robert with a forlorn face as though wanting him to utter some other words, words of love and devotion, and was about to say something, hesitated and then sighed. She waited a few moments to see if he would say something, but Robert didn't.

She was disappointed, but was determined not to show it.

'About the cottage you bought. I thought I would see what I can find out about it,' she said. 'I hope you don't mind Robert, but I had a quick look at the auction pack you left out last night and there could be something interesting about its position...'

Robert interrupted. 'Look Caroline, there's no need for...'

But she ignored him and continued. 'Above the cottage is an open area of ground, probably common land, once used for grazing livestock. There's a similar area the other side of the harbour, high up on the cliffs called the Wooldown. It's on the site map. The name suggests it's to do with sheep grazing, which may well have been the case. But I think it could have been an old medieval, perhaps Celtic, field system divided into strips. And the piece of land above the cottage would have been the same, a place to grow crops for the townsfolk back then.'

'Strip lynchets,' he quickly interjected to show off his knowledge.

'No, they're furrows created by ploughing. These are narrow strips of land each farmed by a tenant. They're called stitches and it's a rare form of agriculture only being practiced in a few places, one of which, coincidently, is in Boscastle on the north coast of Cornwall. If this is the case then it would be quite a discovery. That is what I want to find out.'

So that's the reason for the interest, nothing to do with the cottage, he thought. Typical Caroline. But he maintained his outward interest.

'That's fascinating, but I cannot see its relevance.'

'Its relevance is that a chapel is often sited alongside such field systems. There's one in Boscastle and the plot of your cottage is adjacent to an open area of common land. In fact, the boundary protrudes into the area, which makes it possible that it's built upon an ancient Christian place of worship.'

'You mean I could have graves and bodies buried in the garden?'

'I doubt it Robert, they would have been discovered years ago. There may be some records of such.'

Caroline seemed to know more about the cottage than Robert and just from a few maps. He was astounded, despite her professional knowledge of medieval boundaries and field systems.

'How do you know all this?' he quizzed.

'Apart from the fact it's my job, I read,' she said triumphantly, and held up the book in front of her. 'I rest my case,' and with that she got up and went off to work.

Robert was left muddled by the revelations and seriously wondered whether to go ahead with the purchase. Not only could the cottage be on a sacred site, but it may be haunted by a demonic sailor bent on revenge for some ill deed in the past. But he couldn't back out, not without incurring severe financial penalties, and he reconciled that it was all a storm in a teacup.

His appointment with the bank wasn't until late morning so he decided to nourish his soul and picked up the book. It was on Celtic and medieval farming, and the page was open on the *Forrabury stitches of Boscastle*. It was as she described, as he read the text. He also learnt that these stitches were cropped for half a year between Lady Day on 25th March to Michaelmas Day on 29th September, which, it said, were the two quarter days of the medieval calendar. Outside this period the area was grazed as common land, which is what the Wooldown is today, albeit for recreation rather than livestock purposes.

*   *   *

The day seemed to go slowly for Robert. He had successfully transferred the money to secure the property which was now his, apart from the legal formalities. He was pleased, but it seemed to him that it had sealed his fate with Caroline. He had enjoyed the banter at breakfast and even the little gesture of making toast for her. But with him now the owner of a property three hundred miles away, and she following her career path, it was inevitable they would lead separate lives. All Robert had left to fall upon was that it was his destiny, and therefore hers as well.

As a sort of last supper and a thank you, he decided to cook one of Caroline's favourite dishes and spent the afternoon buying the produce and browsing around the streets. He was in the vicinity of Stanford's, the map specialists, and called in to see what they had on the area of Looe. He wanted to impress Caroline but was also curious himself, especially after her disclosure at breakfast. He purchased a large scale ordnance survey map, six inches to the mile, and an aerial photograph taken quite a few years ago before some of the town had been developed. It showed the fields surrounding the cottage and clearly showed how it did indeed project into the nearby land. He hoped she would be as impressed by his investigative efforts as she would be by his culinary cuisine.

* * *

'That was delicious, Robert, despite your usual heavy-handiness in the kitchen and the chaos of pots and pans that is a signature of your cooking. You can certainly cook. That's the one thing I miss,' Caroline said, with a satisfied look.

'A pleasure,' he replied. It was, but he was somewhat deflated that it was the only thing she missed.

Caroline looked at Robert and must have read his expression, for she then added, 'not forgetting "you know what" Robert, your speciality dish,' and smiled a nefarious grin.

It made him feel much better, that there may be still something between them, but for Siegfried and his caber. He smiled again and enquired of her news on the cottage. She explained that she hadn't been able to devote as much time on the investigation as anticipated, but had found a geologists report and map of the area together with an aerial photograph. The latter showed most of Looe and the river valley, but wasn't detailed enough to reveal any markings on the open area of ground above the cottage. Robert showed her the old photograph he had obtained. It was taken at a much lower altitude and showed the ground in much more detail with faint, discernable striations, markings in the vegetation that seemed to show a pattern of stitches. Caroline was impressed, but concluded that only a definitive geophysical survey would determine if the area was a former field system. That though, was beyond their scope.

Unlike Caroline, who appeared disappointed, the provenance of his cottage for the time being was unknown and a matter of conjecture. But she was onto something and her interest was now aroused. She reached down into her bag and pulled out a sheet of paper and was about to tell Robert some further information, when the telephone rang. He expected it be a call from Valhalla. It was her mother. He left her to chat, while he washed-up the dirty crockery.

Robert got on well with Caroline's parents. They lived near to Looe, up on the fringes of Bodmin Moor, in a former mill which they had bought, like him, at auction. Only their idyll had been a complete wreck with no roof and collapsed walls that needed total renovation. It was set in the most beautiful location, in a gently sloping valley with only an old farm complex of buildings as an accompaniment to their isolation. It had a small brook running through the property which supplied a mill race with two water wheels, one an overshot, the other an undershot, used in former times to mill flour. On visits he had made, the setting always reminded him of a forgotten lost valley, a Shangri-La like the one James Hutton imagined in his novel *Lost Horizon*. But Caroline's parents didn't have to cross continents to find such paradise, theirs was self-made. He vowed to go and see them, knowing he would be made welcome, and wondered if Caroline had told them of their predicament. He suspected not, as she could be most secretive at times.

He finished his chores, as he used to refer to all the household duties he undertook, just as Caroline said goodbye.

'Do they know about us?' he asked.

'No, just that things are a bit, well, not right.'

'Do you mind if I go and see them? I shan't say anything.'

He knew he probably would. The tranquil atmosphere and indefinable serenity would open him up and make him confess everything. Caroline knew it too. She had only to look at him with telling eyes for him to confess, even if he had nothing to hide.

'Not at all,' she said in a knowing tone of voice.

Robert picked up the piece of paper from the table left by Caroline in haste to answer the telephone and opened it, revealing a photocopied map of Looe and the west cliff area. It was a geological survey map with the site of the cottage clearly shown, jutting into the Wooldown as Caroline had indicated. Some technical terms explaining the underlying geology could be seen, but what was most astonishing was the name of the high point above the cottage.

'Mount Ararat,' he exclaimed, 'That's in Turkey.'

'Well, there's a Mount Ararat in Cornwall now,' responded Caroline. 'That's the resting place of Noah's Ark after the flood.'

'Yes,' she said in a slow deliberate tone as though emphasising well known scripture.

'What's the relevance of this?' he brusquely added.

'I don't know,' she replied, 'but it's interesting, don't you think?'

'A Christian chapel that may or may not exist and now a biblical Ararat. What next?'

'That's it. That's all I could find out about the cottage. At least if you ever run out of money you could establish the cottage as a site of pilgrimage, grow a white beard to look like Noah and sell model Arks for a living,' at which point they both laughed at such a preposterous thought.

'I tell you what Caroline, this cottage is beginning to become a mystery. I didn't say, but after the auction a man, a complete stranger, warned me that the place is cursed. I dismissed it as sour grapes from a rival bidder. And the other day, I was stripping some wallpaper from a room and discovered a sort of *fresco*, a painted wall with a galleon and a demonic man standing at the bow. Underneath were the words, "I curse you, I'm coming to get you." And some poor soul had written that he had seen him. With all these revelations, I'm not so sure about the place.'

'Curses are just imaginations of believers,' she added with a degree of comfort.

'I know. That's what I said to the man. There's something about this cottage. What, I don't know.'

'Anyway, before I retire, as I'm rather tired,' retorted Caroline, unmoved by his hysteria, 'there's one last piece of information I discerned.'

'What? That witches were once burned at the stake there,' he jokingly added.

'Of course not, although that is perfectly plausible. No, it's to do with pirates.'

'Pirates?'

'Yes, pirates. Looe is the birthplace of a pirate.'

'That's not unexpected or indeed unusual, they have to have been born somewhere, why not Looe?' he said with a sense that something unnerving was about to be revealed.

'No, that's not unexpected nor unusual. But what is, is his name. It's your namesake, a pirate by the name of Colliver. A Captain Robert Colliver!'

11

They left the flat together the following morning, Robert to catch the train from Paddington and Caroline to go to work. It was a lovely morning in the capital. Fair-weather cumulus clouds patterned a blue sky, although it was rather chilly with a hint of frost on some roofs, hailing a spring that had yet to arrive. Mist rose off the Thames as they walked along the Embankment, a slight detour to the tube station, but one which they both were enjoying.

It reminded Robert of times when they would do the very same thing at weekends, stop at a riverside café, have coffee and read the newspaper, he taking the main section whilst she opted for the travel supplement, their lives temporarily suspended by the news of the day and distant lands, resurfacing to connect once more. Today however, they were going to take separate paths, follow their own lives and Robert wondered if reading the newspaper would ever be the same again without the comfort of familiarity.

Pimlico tube station was no better than when he had arrived, with seemingly the entire population of London being devoured by an entrance that was scooping up humanity into a waste receptacle which would disgorge its contents somewhere else. The platform was a sea of bodies. At least he didn't have the prospect of the persistent daily commute to endure, he thought, and the vibrancy of life in the city would soon be a distant memory, replaced by the daily ebb and flow of a relentless tide. Perhaps people are no more than a molecule of water, performing the same laws only on a different stage and in the grand scheme of the universe which stretched out almost fifteen billion years, he thought that was probably the case, especially as man is mainly composed of that most precious of compounds.

As they waited there for the train, an intangible force separating them, he could see all around him the corporeal symbols of love and affection: a couple on the opposite platform kissing and hugging each other, next to them were two people holding hands, and a women of Caroline's years was talking to her husband or boyfriend, discussing the day ahead and that they would meet for lunch at some café in The Strand. Life goes on. Energy is neither created nor destroyed, and the emotional potential of their relationship had been transferred to those lucky individuals Robert was observing.

A poster on the wall of the station caught Robert's gaze. It was enticing people to visit Cornwall, with a picture of a wide sandy beach, a perfectly proportioned family in swimsuits and rugged cliffs with flowering sea thrift, all set against an azure blue sea. He wasn't sure he liked it. Not because of its aesthetics; who wouldn't be enticed by such melodrama. Rather, he thought, it would only encourage more Londoners to seek out the county for their holidays, where peace and solitude would be replaced by mayhem and congestion. The later was the trademark of the capital and any incursion that encouraged such commerce was to be discouraged. Perhaps autonomy was the solution, and that speculation reminded him of the old Ealing comedy, *Passport to Pimlico* and the perverse thought that Cornwall should adopt a similar stance for independence.

He admonished himself for allowing his imagination to wander. He wasn't really concerned about Cornish independence, but instead about Caroline, a distant figure standing beside him, who could have been alone on the platform. He motioned to say something, anything, to break an estranged silence. But his mind was blank of meaningful thoughts even though his heart was beating affection. There seemed to be a mutual distance separating them, much like between strangers. Robert shuffled closer and looked at Caroline. She was staring ahead, seemingly unaware of his presence. He was about to ask her if she would come and visit him in Looe when their train pulled into the station. And, with the multitude that had been waiting on the platform suddenly manoeuvring towards the carriage doors, his palpitating heart and words of connection dissipated in the crush.

The two detached lovers waited until everybody had got on board, wanting to be next to the door, for Robert had to alight at the next station for his connecting line to Paddington. Inside, the carriage was worse than the platform and resembled a factitious vivarium of society where, as in a livestock truck, there was no space between oneself and a complete stranger, where intimacy was an enforced consequence between silent partners. For the first time in the two days he had been in Caroline's company they were now physically close, touching each other, a contact that produced a spark of desire. Robert could detect the scent from her perfume, a heady aphrodisiac that made him want to kiss her and to tell her that he wanted to be with her and not return to Cornwall, and that they should go back to her flat and make love as though they were in the Riad for the first time. Such is fate that as those thoughts raced through him he could not seize the moment, not because he didn't want to this time but because the train arrived at Victoria, his departure point for the Circle line. His moment had, yet again, evaporated, this time with the confusion of people wanting to alight onto the platform.

He hesitated to get off the train, waiting for everybody else to escape the mêlée. With even more of humanity wanting to enter, Caroline kissed him on the cheek and wished him a safe journey. The doors closed and as the train pulled out of the station she waved and tears welled up in Robert's eyes. He watched it disappear into the darkness of the tunnel, into an abyss from which she would never return.

A deep melancholy overwhelmed him, leaving an emptiness that only love could fill. He felt like getting on the next train and declaring his undying devotion for her but he knew he wouldn't. And as the next train pulled in he was hoping, by some divine miracle that Caroline herself would appear, just as in the museum in Morocco, and the magnetism of the hours in her room, the flow of energy that seemed eternal then, would return, never to be discharged again. She didn't appear and as the platform emptied he was left standing as a lone figure in a vacuum, unable to breathe in life.

The journey across to Paddington was a solemn one, with a

symphony of thoughts making it seem like a funeral dirge where darkness could be found in every note. Was he doing the right thing? Was he cursed? Would he see Caroline again? Who was Robert Colliver? This was only the second movement. The first was last night when he was kept awake for what seemed an eternity, thinking about the very same things. His nightmare. Mount Ararat. The demonic sailor. He wondered what the finale would bring; immolation in the flames of a funeral pyre? That would be perfect, he thought: there would be resurrection and he would be a phoenix flying high to his eerie in the sky, alongside his warrior maiden.

*   *   *

The train out of Paddington was late in leaving due to signal failure just outside the station which did not help his lugubrious state. Whilst waiting, he stood watching a moving procession of human beings, each with their own lives, their own loves, come and go, an evanescent scene of places that he didn't know or lives he couldn't discern. He was one of those souls lost in a sea of uncertainty, not knowing where he was going, where the tide was taking him. He could still turn around and wait for Caroline. Planet Cornwall was still a distant horizon, one that had little pull on him other than a cottage on the cliffs overlooking the sea, a place that most people dream about. For Robert, it was reality, and sufficient attraction to lure him to his carriage.

The Great Western service finally left forty minutes late. Its progress out of the capital was slow, which for Robert did not matter as he liked to watch the ever changing world from the carriage window, something which his outward journey had failed to enrapture. Rows of Victorian terrace houses, high-rise flats and tenement blocks presented their faces to him, peoples' homes, although to Robert they looked more like prisons. London was a prison, he thought, where life was governed by its orbit, the diurnal passage of a commute, people chained to its rhythm of work, eat and sleep. He felt sorry for those individuals he didn't know and was thankful that his life was not restrained by such unnatural laws. And as the train picked up speed he could feel the cloud of melancholy lift, his mind clear of its celestial symphony, and the horizon of planet Cornwall become closer and closer.

By the time the train crossed the divide of the Tamar, over Brunel's suspension bridge, he felt a sense of relief that he was finally in the county which was now his home and with the emotional pull of London now waning, he could focus on the cottage. Before he left for London, Robert had secured the holiday home John, the café proprietor, had suggested, and had driven down to leave a few clothes and other items there. He had taken the branch line train from Looe and as the train pulled into the cutting of Liskeard station, Robert had fully recovered. Everything was in place, or so he thought.

Robert alighted from the train at Liskeard, his anticipation growing as he walked the short distance out of the mainline station to another platform for the branch line train. It was a single-track line and the train had yet to arrive from Looe. A bill board on the platform expounded the abundant wildlife of the East Looe river valley which the railway followed. Wildlife and nearby attractions were highlighted such as a clock museum and the ruins of a manor house which, Robert read, used to be the ancestral home of a notorious family, a revered clan to rival the fictional tale of Lorna Doone. Having read the board, he picked up a leaflet on the branch line and sat down to wait the few minutes remaining before the train arrived.

It was still light and the fine weather of London was evident here although there had obviously been a shower of rain for the ground was damp giving a fresh smell to the air, an aroma of the sea with a southerly breeze blowing. He watched a robin building a nest in a discarded and rusty signal lantern, bringing in moss and feathers to line the home, and thought that few people in London, in fact few people at all, would take time to stop and watch such an enchanting spectacle, where life isn't ruled by timetables, but by the necessity of survival. Even some of the ornithologists he had known would dismiss it in favour of driving six hundred miles to look at a rare bird brought in on the wind from its migration, just to add it to a list that propounded their absurd pastime. Such twitchers might as well become train spotters or airplane buffs, for most are not interested in the behaviour of the birds, and could not sit still watching such a common species as a robin build a perfect nest.

The single carriage train, which was little more than a bus on wheels, pulled into the tiny platform. Robert boarded with a handful of other passengers, remembering to sit on the left hand side of the carriage so that he could see the estuary as the train made its way down the valley, even though it is on the right hand side. A strange switch-back occurs along the line where the train enters a terminus one way and, with the driver changing ends, leaves the other way, confusing the tourist to some amusement.

The journey along the Looe valley line is truly picturesque, passing many hidden gems of houses and quaint hamlets which, during the warm summer months, are delightful, almost the exposition of paradise, a place of beauty and tranquillity, untouched by modern life. Every so often, glimpses of the river could be spied, which in the upper reaches was braided with several small channels making it difficult to discern amongst the debris of fallen trees and muddy undergrowth, all of which created the appearance of a primeval swamp.

The train rattled on as though it was a scenic tour, stopping once by request as a passenger alighted at a tiny station in the middle of nowhere, then continuing its slow meandering of the river valley. Finally, the many channels filled in to become a defined narrow river, but wide enough for a small craft like a kayak to paddle. Clusters of cottages bounded the river banks where signs of life could be viewed: a resident stoking a bonfire, a glimpse of a manicured lawn, and further down by a smallholding towards Sandplace, geese were roaming by a pond. This carefree scene of life was in complete contrast to the occasional skeletal remains of half-submerged boats that had fallen victim to time and tide, and the continual decay that could be observed in the abundant coppiced woodland that followed the railway track.

Another passenger alighted at Sandplace, after which the valley opened out to reveal the estuary and extensive mud flats populated by hundreds of gulls, waiting for their evening commute home to Looe Island where they roosted overnight. At the rail terminus by the confluence of the two rivers, small boats were moored, many more than in the harbour itself, those that are able to negotiate the low arches of the bridge or where a mast could be lowered to allow passage beneath. And beyond the bridge, on either side of the harbour, arose the now familiar sprawling towns of East and West Looe.

Robert called in at the estate agents expecting to see Tara, but she was not there. It disappointed him as he wanted to see a familiar face in a town where he knew nobody. Instead a middle-aged man handed him the keys to the cottage, having had confirmation that the funds had been paid to the vendor's solicitor, and wished Robert well in his new home. He made his way to the centre of the bridge and realised he was now well and truly a resident of the west bank with the implication that he had become a sworn enemy of the east. But he was not going to get involved in such political posturing, leaving that to the entrenched attitudes of the locals. Instead he was going to quietly get on with restoring his cottage and, with its seclusion, lead a simple and peaceful existence by the sea.

Light was beginning to fade but dusk was yet to descend upon the town. Robert had decided to take a quick look at his new home before it became too dark. As he walked along the quayside, he could not help but notice a new fishing vessel on the opposite quay, one that he hadn't seen before. Its insignia proclaimed BM for Brixham. It was a monster of a vessel, much larger than the usual fishing boats and was probably moored for an overnight stay before continuing on its journey. The usual suspects of sea birds were in the harbour although no interloper, much to Robert's dismay. And as he passed the café he was surprised to still see a light on but couldn't see anybody inside.

He made his way up the old coast path and the view opened out to show a bright coastal scene lit up by the setting sun. Looe Island was cloaked in shadow, the sun having sunk too low to cast its evening rays. It had now taken on a menacing look as though ghosts that might inhabit its caves and small inlets would come out to haunt the unwary trespassers seeking adventure, who had forgotten that night-time is an altogether different world.

He climbed the switch-back path and came to the wrought iron gate. It was open and the name plate was no longer visible. He searched the ground and nearby undergrowth, but couldn't find it. Trying to think what could have happened to it, he proceeded up the steps to the front of the cottage only to be halted abruptly in his stride. He stood aghast looking at the cottage. He could not believe what was facing him, because hanging from the porch was a doll, an effigy of a pirate, with long fingers and pins embedded in its body! Robert's life, rather than being simple and peaceful, was about to become complicated and tumultuous!

12

The cottage of Lammana was imbued with history. A colourful history. A history that Robert was beginning to experience. It was the birthplace of the Pirate Captain, Robert Colliver, and was once indeed a Christian chapel, as Caroline had conjectured. It was constructed by Benedictine monks as an outlier to both the main monastic chapel that stood on the summit of the Island and a second satellite chapel on the mainland, opposite the Island. Why they should build such a place of worship when there were already two serving chapels, was a mystery. Perhaps it served as a beacon in those dark ages or was used only occasionally, serving the people further inland. Whatever the reason, unlike the two main chapels, it survived the Reformation when Henry VIII dissolved the monasteries and England became a protestant nation.

Whilst the two chapels of the Island and the mainland were stripped of their icons, abandoned, and left to the vagaries of nature and a population that denuded them of stone, Robert's chapel continued to be used over the following centuries. It was a shadow of its former glory, losing its holy emblem and becoming a shed to store tools, fodder and shelter livestock. Neglect though, could not destroy such a pious and solid structure and it was eventually restored to become a home.

But the past would not relinquish its stranglehold and those that chose to inhabit its walls came under its divine spell for defiling its sanctity. The fate for those that lived in sin was damnation and misfortune, even death ensued for the heathens. When William Trevellick burnt the cottage, he sealed his family's destiny by invoking a curse which had lain dormant for years. And now Robert was becoming bewitched by the hallowed building and there was no turning back. He was the latest victim of its defiant past.

There wasn't much that could unnerve Robert, but the hanging effigy had. He felt as though he were caught in a horror film where at every turn the protagonist was confronted by more and more events, each one seemingly more bizarre, more sinister than the last. His nightmare, where a demented pirate came looking for him, cursing him, and where spindrift from waves had turned to arrows that pierced his chest, was now reality. The effigy was his nightmare. How could that be, he asked himself? What evil, supernatural force is at work here? Was he going mad? He had no rational explanation other than that he was suffering a mental breakdown, which he wasn't, he thought, although he wasn't entirely sure of that.

He wished he was with Caroline in her warm flat, cooking a meal and talking about the day, rather than in strange lodgings, cold, hungry and becoming delusional. He had forgotten about food in his haste to catch the Paddington train, and now he was beginning to regret coming back directly to Looe from London. Even his sister's farmhouse seemed a better option; at least she would have something to eat, even though she was a spendthrift when it came to heating. Put on another jumper, leggings or hat and gloves, she would say, rather than burn extra fuel.

He decided to go to the local supermarket just off the little square. He purchased a microwave ready-meal and some other provisions, including a bottle of wine, remembering Caroline's comment and mindful of her sarcasm, and headed back to the house. As he was making his way to the steep path behind the Smugglers Arms, he noticed Jane, the proprietor's wife, or at least he assumed it was her as the only time he had seen her she was dressed for the arctic. She was leaving the café with a man and it wasn't her husband, for the man was thinner and had a head of hair. He thought it odd, especially at this time of the evening, but ignored them in favour of his now rumbling stomach. Food was what he needed, food for his tiring body and confused mind.

Within the hour, having eaten and savoured two mugs of tea, and got the heating working, life seemed tolerable. But he was still agitated by the effigy, especially as his nightmare was now very real. He would investigate in the morning and contact the police as somebody had clearly been trespassing on the property. His property.

He settled down in a chair and switched the television on, scanning the channels for some interesting program to take his mind off events. But all there seemed to be were soaps, reality programmes, US sitcoms and crime dramas and, of course, a football match, a European Champions Cup semi-final tie between Manchester United and Juventus. He left the match on with the commentary a background drone, but wasn't really interested in it, his mind wandering to the image of the effigy.

Still perturbed, he thought about telephoning Tara. After all, she did say if there was anything, give her a call. But he was sure she didn't mean at night. He rang nonetheless. She answered and was concerned to hear about the effigy and immediately volunteered to come round and although Robert declined her offer, she insisted and said she would be there in fifteen minutes. She obviously lives in Looe, Robert thought, and was glad she agreed to come.

Half an hour later the doorbell rang and standing on the threshold was Tara, dressed casually, but looking stunning.

'Come in. It's good of you to come round.'

'Not at all Robert, I'm only glad to help. Not that I can do much, I suspect.'

'Your presence here is help enough. I admit the effigy certainly shook me to the core.'

'I can imagine,' she sympathetically replied. 'I cannot think who'd do such a thing other than youngsters having a prank. The cottage has been empty for some time and they may think of it as their playground.'

'I hadn't thought about that. It sounds as though you could be right,' he said, feeling a little more reassured. But he went on to add, 'That's not the only strange thing that's happened.'

'Oh?' remarked Tara with genuine interest.

'I didn't mention it before, but after the auction a stranger, a man in the auction room, came up to me and said the place was his and that it was cursed.'

'The vendor wasn't at the auction,' she ventured. 'So whoever it was didn't own the cottage. I think it must be one of the bidders, angry that they lost the cottage. I'm sure it's not cursed. That's quite absurd.'

But Tara thought otherwise. She herself had experienced a strange happening one night at the cottage several months ago. It was a new moon and the sky was full of angry clouds with the rumbling of thunder and occasional flash of lightening out to sea. She had been coming from the beach below, up a path which passed near to the deserted cottage. On approaching the building she had witnessed a peculiar light, a ball of white light that seemed to float in space and move and dart around like a sprite. She was rooted to the spot watching it take on the form of a wraith, a ghostly figure that then emitted a spine-chilling moan, a low wail as though it were in torment. Tara was terrified.

Although Tara was knowledgeable in meteorology and recognised the phenomenon as ball lightening, her upbringing convinced her that the Pirate had finally come to take her, just as her forebears had been. But then the light suddenly vanished and the dark night returned, a darkness and silence that left her relieved. But it had shaken her. It was that which had sent a shudder through her when Robert first announced his name. To Tara, he was the Pirate incarnate and she had to propitiate the malevolent spirit.

'Look,' she continued, 'there's nothing that can be done now. Ring the police first thing in the morning and meet them at the cottage. They may know of any local youths who've been hanging around the area recently.'

'You're right, of course. Anyway, I'm not really concerned about the man. It's just the catalogue of mysteries surrounding the cottage.'

'What do you mean?' she enquired with a timbre of interest once again. 'It sounds as though there have been other instances.'

Robert was not inclined to mention anything else as it would mean alluding to Caroline, which he was reluctant to do.

'No, no other events,' he said in an unconvincing voice which Tara immediately perceived. She too was not going to push Robert and left it at that.

Robert offered Tara a glass of wine which she readily accepted. As he was uncorking the bottle, Tara came into the kitchen and put her hand on his shoulder.

'Don't worry about this. You've got a beautiful cottage in a superb location and with a little work, it will be perfect. That's the important thing. You know I'll help you, when my work allows. I would love to,' she reassured Robert.

Robert felt comforted by her words, but more so with that first physical contact. He could feel her warmth transferring to him, radiating down his body, and in that moment he had forgotten about Caroline and her warm flat. He was now glowing from a woman's touch, and it generated a thrill of ardour.

'That's kind of you. I'd appreciate that,' he said with conviction.

'It's the least I can do,' she replied with warmth and held up her glass of wine to toast his new cottage and new life in Looe.

They went back into the lounge and settled down and chatted as though they were on a first date, having just met and eager to impress one another. Robert gave her a brief life story and how he arrived at Looe, omitting to mention Caroline by name. Tara didn't seem to give much away, other than to say she was born in Looe and, but for a few years away at college, had lived there all her life. Robert enquired if she resided in the town itself to which she replied, rather enigmatically, that she was a floating resident. Later she did allude to owning the villa style house on the confluence of the two rivers, but only after Robert had deduced her cryptic reply.

Tara was interested to hear of his travels, destinations which she had only dreamed of, and began to see Robert as the perfect partner, sailing the seven seas with him, dropping anchor in exotic waters, discovering foreign lands untouched by tourism. She admitted to once visiting a Greek island and liked the warm weather and easy-going lifestyle, but found the sea uninteresting. 'No tide,' she said. 'Just the same all the time. And as for the beaches, Cornwall's are far superior.'

She enquired if Robert was interested in the sea, a subtle tack to see if he would be that perfect partner, for she had a desire to sail around the world. Robert, to keep the conversation flowing, replied that the sea was in his blood, to which a pleased Tara thought she had the information she required.

Despite no wedding ring, Robert wondered if she was married or had a partner. Tara was delighted her bait was working and responded by being quite forthcoming on her relationships. She mentioned a couple of failed boyfriends in a rather disconsolate fashion, as though they were inadequate, not meeting her expectations, but was at pains to leave him in no doubt that she was free, single and more than ready for another one.

Tara departed quite late into the evening but left Robert in a much better state of mind, especially with her perfume lingering in the warm atmosphere that she had created. He was glad to have asked her over as he surveyed the empty wine bottle and picked up her glass to finish the wine, tasting her lips on the rim and breathing in her perfume, aphrodisiacs that had found a conduit to his heart, making him feel in an amatory mood.

As he lay in bed thinking of Tara, he fell asleep and into a dream where she was at the cottage and they were making love, on a Greek island, in the warmth of a Mediterranean sun with a refreshing breeze blowing in off the Aegean. She was on top, caressing his chest, running her fingers up and down his naked torso as she rode him in unison with the breaking waves, the crests becoming larger and larger, riding their passion, until both crashed in a crescendo of surf. He awoke in the middle of the night exhausted, sweat on his forehead as though the sea had washed over him cleansing his mind of uncertainty, leaving the emotion of hope. He looked at his watch. Two-thirty. Outside, the night was black but he had a bright glow inside, a glow from a dream that spoke of passion to come and with that he fell back into a deep, contented slumber.

13

Robert awoke with a jolt. Deep contented slumber had turned into a nightmare, conjured by classical mythology and a subconscious that coveted a divine goddess. His Graces had returned. They were beguiling him with their seductive dance, only this time the goddess Charm wanted Robert for herself. She had confided in Artemis that Beauty and Happiness had tried to seduce her brother Apollo, whom being told this was angered and struck the two goddesses down with her deadly bow and quiver. And as Charm won Robert, she danced alone with her conquest, only for him to transmute into an effigy of the Pirate Captain whose fingers accused Charm of treachery.

He looked at his watch. It was six-thirty. Dawn was approaching across the horizon of Rame Head. From the bedroom window he could see a procession of fishing vessels make their way out of the harbour, past the Banjo Pier and out into the bay. Only yesterday he had awoken to the sounds of the city and now he was a world away from the metropolis, a different life, where the tide governs the daily commute, not the deadline of an office clock.

He made himself some tea and sat down in the kitchen to question his new nightmare. But he couldn't make sense of it. The images had now faded and seemed too confused to yield answers. Instead he focused his thoughts on Tara and despite the night time eidetic, he hoped she would call on him today. He could still feel her presence in the flat: the empty wine bottle, her glass with a smudge of pale lipstick coating its rim, and her perfume still lingering in the flat and within his soul.

Her explanation of the effigy seemed quite logical, as against his of a mental breakdown, and as she had suggested he decided to call the local police and report the incident. The officer who answered said he could meet Robert at his cottage in an hour's time. Robert wanted to get there before him and so he had a quick breakfast and left. It was another fine morning, the warmest so far, although he was in no mood to either notice nor enjoy it. All he wanted was to solve this puzzle, but doubted anybody else could do so other than himself.

He arrived at the cottage and looked in amazement to find the name plate back on the gate, even though it was still off its hinges. He hadn't fitted it. Who had? With slow deliberate strides he quietly climbed the steps. Was anybody there, he wondered? He paused before the top, thinking he heard some rustling, only to find it was a blackbird in the undergrowth. He proceeded once more to the front patio area and to his dismay there was no sign of the effigy. It had gone. It was as though he had been dreaming that too. For the first time he seriously thought he had dreamt it all and that perhaps he was suffering some sort of delirium.

The policeman, a PC Trevellick, couldn't explain the disappearance of the effigy. He looked at Robert, a rather abject looking individual, he assessed, and concluded that somehow he was mistaken or had imagined the whole episode. But he said he would record the incident, make some enquiries of local youths and nearby neighbours and let him know of anything that might shed light on the matter. Robert was unconvinced by his attitude but thanked him nonetheless.

He went inside the cottage and was confronted by the wall mural. It was all too much and he decided to strip the remaining wallpaper to reveal any further secrets. Much to his relief, no more were uncovered. He decided to obscure the wall painting with white wash, now realising the enormity of the task he'd undertaken on renovating the cottage, which required a trip to the builder's merchant to purchase the paint and other equipment. That meant walking all the way to the Mill Pool Car Park and back again, carrying a heavy load of material up the steep path to the cottage. Forget the visions of doom, he thought, this was going to be a logistical nightmare of epic proportions.

Rather than face the journey, he sat down on the window seat and looked out across the bay. The morning sun was streaming into the room making it feel warm. He imagined a comfortable armchair by the window where he could look at the bay, with Rame Head framing one side all the way to Looe, and on the other the Island, Portnadler Bay, and a headland beyond. This is what he had purchased, he thought; a beautiful sea view, and with a positive attitude he went outside to the west facing side garden and started to look around to find another entrance, one that had access to the open land at the rear of the cottage.

Behind the summerhouse the vegetation was overgrown with a stunted elder tree, some buddleia shrubs and the ubiquitous ivy, all interlaced with another invader, traveller's joy, the wild clematis often called old man's beard for its fluffy seed heads still adorned the twisted strands. Within the jungle, he found some half hidden steps that led to a barely discernable path with two sharp switch-backs, past the conifer trees to a gate which had barbed wire framing its arch. Some broken fencing to either side was being strangled by more ivy, this time reinforced by thick strands of bramble that already contained green shoots of this year's foliage.

Robert tried to open the gate. It was lodged shut. As he stood there considering his options, he heard the same rustling noise that had alerted him the first time down in the lane. He listened. There was definitely something there. Then it stopped. He waited a few moments, but nothing, and so decided to force his way through one of the fences. It wasn't difficult but he made enough noise to frighten off anything nearby.

Once through he was in a thicket of gorse and blackthorn, which was more of a barrier than the fencing itself. By hacking at the undergrowth with an old machete-shaped implement unearthed in the shed, he managed to make his way up and onto the open ground, a field taken over to a grassy sward. This was the field he and Caroline had looked at on the map, the one which she thought used to be an ancient field system of stitches. There was certainly no evidence on the ground, even though it was well preserved grassland, kept short by grazing, despite the absence of any livestock.

An old track, about four feet wide, skirted its way along the edge of the field bounded by thick hawthorn and blackthorn and home to a family of dunnocks that were flitting in and out of the branches. They are rather drab brown birds with few distinguishing features and even their song is somewhat short and repetitive, almost as though they were trying to emulate their more illustrious cousins, the yellowhammer. Robert momentarily stopped to listen to them singing, taking in the tranquillity of the place, only interrupted by the distant baying of sheep.

It was now that he finally appreciated the lovely day with sun providing some warmth to a chill air that could be felt in the shade. There was a sparkle to the sea below, glistening flashes of light in the gentle swell where Looe Island looked altogether more inviting, uncloaked from its menacing shroud. He noticed a small boat, much like *Lady Jane*, with several people on board making for the far side of the Island, towards a jetty and building where a plume of smoke rose from its chimney stack.

Robert's participation in the timeless scene had improved his perspective. No longer were his delusions a burden, rather they had energised him as he strode his way along the track. To his left, behind a hedge bank, a stone tower structure could be seen above the tops of stunted trees that seemed somewhat incongruous within the natural landscape. He wondered what it was, perhaps a look-out post from Napoleonic times, but he was unable to investigate for the tall thicket. Further on, as he climbed a shallow knoll, another tower gradually appeared in front of him as though it was rising forth from the ground, and as he approached it he realised what it was. Standing in front of the structure the tower loomed above him, about the height of a house, and looked like an obelisk, albeit this one had a metal frame attached on the seaward side, much like a fire escape, with navigation lights set towards the top of the structure. It was a measured mile marker, with the two towers being used for alignment out at sea, and a further two located towards Talland. In the days before modern navigational aids and GPS tracking, they were used by ships to calculate their speed over a nautical mile, measuring the time it took to cover the distance, in both directions, thereby countering the effects of currents and tidal conditions.

Robert felt like scaling the framework, if only to see the view from atop. Ever since Madeleine he had had a fascination with high places, perhaps obsession, whether it was the summit of a mountain which he had to conquer or a strategic hillfort that commanded a gentle chalk escarpment, whose ramparts invited exploration. The tower was tempting but his better judgement restrained such an escapade, continuing instead along the track, now more a road of concrete construction and in somewhat poor repair, before reaching a closed gate, padlocked. He had reached the paved highway from Looe to Talland. It was probably the original turnpike route, for next to an adjacent junction that branched to the tiny hamlet of Portlooe, was an ancient Celtic cross that was clearly an old way-marker for it nestled in a stone bank, clearly visible to passing traffic.

* * *

Back in his lounge, Robert made a note of things to purchase and made his way down to the café. He was going to enquire if the proprietor knew anything about the open land behind his cottage. Inside it was empty, apart from the old sea dog who was at his usual table.

'Hello again,' said the proprietor in a cheerful manner. 'You've become quite a regular. There must be something in Looe that can't keep you away.'

'You're right in a sense. I've just bought a property here.'

'Congratulations,' he said jovially. 'The question is, which side?' he continued in a more serious tone.

And in a cryptic reply Robert declared, 'I've nailed my colours to the starboard side.'

'Well done and welcome to West Looe.'

With that news the old man muttered under his breath, 'another bloody foreigner and here for good now.'

'Might I enquire as to which property you purchased?'

'It was at auction the other day. I bought Lammana.'

With that the proprietor's face went from an enthusiastic smile to the epitome of pity and surprise, whilst the old man who had been listening, dropped his hip flask in astonishment.

'Lammana, you say?' said the proprietor, in a questioning voice.

'Yes, the cottage up on the old coast path. Do you know it?'

'Oh, I know it alright and I guess most of Looe knows it too. It's notorious.'

'Notorious?' questioned Robert.

'Some say it was the birthplace of Captain Robert Colliver, a pirate of some renown and ill-repute.'

Robert was now becoming immune to such revelations, but this injection went deep and he wondered how much more he could take.

'There's more…' the proprietor added and Robert's heart stopped, awaiting the next dose. But just as the proprietor was about to continue, a group of six entered the café and created pandemonium by trying to rearrange tables so that they could all sit together. He apologised to Robert, who said he would call in later when it was less busy.

Yet again, Robert's head was in a spin from this latest revelation. He wondered whether fate was a chain around his neck, with yet another link tightening its grip on reality. He went back to his accommodation to have a drink and try to reconcile everything. He'd forgotten Tara's ghostly look on the first day, but mentioning his name had obviously awoken some fear in her. And the effigy is probably some poor soul who wants to exorcise their own ghosts by leaving it at the cottage with pins in it. It makes sense, he thought, and having drunk his coffee, felt ready to face the omens.

*   *   *

At the builder's merchant, Robert purchased what he needed and as he was leaving the yard he noticed the sign on the garage opposite: it read 'Trevellick Car Repairs.' That's odd, he thought, the same name as the policeman and the family mentioned in the poster at the railway station, but he dared not think more of it for fear of reading conspiracy into a coincidence.

Having already picked up his car from the Mill Pool Car Park and loaded the materials, he drove down the harbour road alongside the dirty Lugger and the array of other vessels, all of which he could see as it was high tide in the harbour. At the café, which now looked empty, he turned right, passed the fire station and Smugglers Arms, around the quaint square with its octagonal building, to make his way up West Looe Hill. It was steep and lined by old fisherman's cottages, making the street look pretty with the sun bouncing off the white-washed walls. Near the top, the road became even steeper and he had to put the car into first gear in order to make progress, but once passed all the residential houses, the road flattened out to a gentle climb, finally arriving at the junction to Portlooe, with the cross at its apex.

Having parked the car, he unloaded and walked across the field carrying his purchases and felt pleased with his positive attitude. But as he strolled with purpose along the dirt path, the delightful bird song and air of tranquillity that had greeted his first foray, had been replaced by a menacing silence as though he were being watched and the wildlife were guarded, respecting this intrusion.

A black cloud had masked the sun, adding to the tension. Robert stopped to inspect the silence. Nothing stirred. Was he imagining nothing? He turned around and looked at the tower. It looked threatening. Was it being used to spy upon him? A bird of prey was perched upon its top, as though it was an accomplice to deceit, except this one, a sparrowhawk, was interested in other prey which had fallen silent to escape its claws. Robert realised the obmutescence was because of its presence, a skilled hunter that would relentlessly chase and devour its victim. Then it flew off and Robert watched it rise on a thermal and glide along the coast, leaving him wondering whether he was a pawn in a game being played between silent protagonists. He was right to be concerned. The accipiter had alerted his instincts, for even though he was unaware and yet to participate, a deadly game had indeed been started.

14

The Quayside Café was part of the game. Which side it was on, how deep it was involved, and who were the participants, had yet to be settled. Robert was standing outside the establishment. The sun was shining once more, and the eerie feel that had greeted him in the field above his cottage had evaporated with the cloud. Yet he felt that same presence, as though the café were an ally in a conspiracy. He admonished himself for thinking such a thought and went inside to partake in a late lunch, having erased the demented wall mural, whitewashing its image from his mind.

He'd expected to see George, the old sea dog, by the door, but to his surprise he wasn't there. Neither was John, the proprietor. Instead his wife was busy clearing away tables.

'Nice to see you again,' she said with a warm smile and a look that suggested familiarity.

'You remember me?' Robert commented with an air of surprise.

'Of course. I never forget a new face in town, especially a handsome one,' she said in a suggestive tone.

Robert ignored the flattery and enquired of John, her husband.

'He's had to go and get some supplies. Won't be back until late afternoon I suspect. Can I help you?'

'Well, I was talking to him this morning, about Lammana, the cottage on the old coast path.'

'Oh yes, that ramshackle old place that's up for sale. You're not thinking of buying it?' she said in a rather derogatory manner, as though he would be a fool to do so. In fact Robert had been wondering the same thing himself, not because of its state, rather the mysterious incidents that seem to be part of its fabric. He was about to tell her he had indeed purchased the place, when she added further thoughts on the property.

'We had a look at the place when we first moved here. Lovely views. But it needed total renovation and inside felt like a morgue. There was a spine-chilling feel about it as though the walls were hiding secrets. Anyway, it was too small for our needs. What really clinched my decision was its history. We learnt that although it hadn't had many previous owners, those that had bought it all seemed to have suffered some misfortune: illness, bereavement, one owner was killed in a car crash, and even a murder was suspected to have been committed in the cottage. Some say the place is cursed, even haunted. That was enough to put me off. It would have been my worst nightmare. John was quite interested in its history and would have bought the place, no doubt. But I vetoed it.'

Again, Robert mentally recoiled from the new revelations having felt more poison enter the mystery. Any more, he thought, and it would be the death of him. Jane could not see any of this inner turmoil. All she saw was a handsome man, calm and desirable. He composed himself to reveal that he had bought her worst nightmare.

'It was at auction the other day,' he announced with conviction that showed he was not concerned by its chequered past.

Jane was taken aback. But in a tone of appeasement or was it sympathy, she was quick to respond.

'I'm sure it will be a fine place once it's done up. As for its history, John is the one to tell you, although he's gleaned most from George; gossip and local stuff you won't find in any book.'

Robert was about to say thank you and take his leave, but she continued on. 'Me, I find it all boring. History, that is. In fact life in Looe is a bit dull. Give me a big city anytime, although there are some things of interest here.'

'Yes,' said Robert in a tone as though he was ending the conversation, but Jane took it he wanted to know more.

'Oh, activities to broaden the mind, if you know what I mean.'

Robert wasn't sure what she meant, although he had an idea based on the secret liaison he noticed last night. Whatever her meaning, he didn't want to stay.

'Thank you. Must be getting on,' he interjected, before she could continue.

But Jane hadn't finished. 'If you want to know anything about Looe, best ask George. Don't think his nibs will know much about the cottage, although judging by the amount of time he spends reading about history, he should do. It's all he does, that and his damn boat. It's enough to drive one to er, well…drink!'

Robert got the picture now and didn't want to know about her problems or activities to broaden the mind. But again she interceded, this time blocking Robert's route to the café door as he tried to edge in that direction.

'You'll find him in the pub now, probably on his second pint.'

He bid her thank you again and this time managed to escape her verbal clutches.

Poor woman, he thought as he left. She was very pretty, too pretty for her husband perhaps, and here she was running a small café in a place far from her family, no doubt, and in a town she evidently doesn't like. Everybody has their problems, he thought, and mine is the cottage at the moment, and he wanted to know more about it. So, he made his way the few paces to the Smugglers Arms to seek George, the old sea dog, in his natural haunt.

The Smugglers Arms was an old whitewashed building, a couple of hundred years old at least Robert thought, if not more, and it looked as though it had witnessed many altercations over the years between free traders and the excise men. A sign at the front invited people to sample their sea shanties and Cornish ballads on Tuesday nights, even sing-along, no doubt washed down with some good ale.

He hesitated whether or not to go in. It was a lovely afternoon and he would rather be outside enjoying the weather. More than that though, he was a coward in situations like this where he would be a stranger in a seemingly foreign place, as though it were a den of iniquity, a retreat for thieves, or even modern day smugglers.

He seldom ventured inside such establishments, partly because he did not drink that much nowadays, but mostly because cigarettes and alcohol seemed to be twin evils that cohabited the same echelon. He hated smoking. He hated inhaling the smoke, lungs convulsing. Most of all, he hated the smoke impregnating his clothes so that he smelt like an ash tray, a walking testament to a deadly vice.

He opened the door and was hit by a cloud of smoke, a fog which enveloped his senses cloaking him in an acrid vapour that would be enough to asphyxiate a giant. He summoned up his courage and stepped inside, looked around, and rested his gaze on the bar where three middle-aged men were sitting, drinking and smoking pipes. Behind the bar was the landlord, a jovial looking man, sporting a beard and looking every bit the bosun's mate.

The three men stopped talking and turned to look at Robert as though he were some alien who had just materialised from another dimension, a place where fishing and the sea were unknown. Someone who would upset the friendly banter and the familiar atmosphere and expunge the age old ritual they were participating in.

Having adjusted to the fog Robert looked around again, but couldn't see George and was about to leave when the landlord bid him welcome. Robert was surprised by the friendly tone which relaxed him somewhat and he advanced to the bar, regaining confidence, but wary the three men were still transfixed on him, an alien life form that had invaded their cosy world.

'I'm looking for George,' he said, 'I was told I might find him in here.'

'Well my lad, you've been told right. He's over there in his usual spot.'

Robert looked and peered around the end of the bar to a small snug where the old sea dog was sitting, supping an almost empty glass. He didn't look up and Robert thought he was in his own world, battling some leviathan sea, challenging Poseidon in a storm-force-ten gale where mere mortals would be swallowed whole by the god himself. But all was peaceful in the snug and Robert turned to the landlord and enquired, 'What will that be?'

'Ale for George, that's all he drinks. And for yourself?'

Robert coughed as a funnel of smoke from the man next to him came seeking a victim of its vapour. He didn't really want any beer but thought he must, if only to prove that he was a man. Half a pint would have sufficed, but he glanced at the men who seemed to be judging his response and realised that only a pint would be admissible.

'Same for me, please.'

The landlord pulled the pints and Robert went over to George. He was ensconced in a small snug, rather weather beaten like its occupant, having, no doubt, witnessed many a stormy night.

'Mind if I join you?' enquired Robert, and put the pints down on the table as George looked at him with an air of displeasure but grateful for a free pint.

'What about the chaser?' he said, making it quite clear that Robert had to provide one.

Back at the bar he ordered a shot of rum. The landlord apologised for his error as though this was a departure for George and smiled a wink at the three men implying, 'there's a gullible one here.' Robert realised he was being used but thought the bribe worth the price for the information he wanted.

Whilst waiting for the rum, the three men exchanged silent words and he caught a glimpse of their conversation and the look of one man eying him as though he hadn't done a day's hard labour in all his years on this earth. The men had faces hewn out of granite and were burly individuals of ample frame who, from Robert's perspective, could carry a lobster pot in each hand. But they also showed signs of spending too many hours at the bar as they all had huge paunches, almost the size of beer barrels. If a man's prowess were measured in girth, he thought, then these fellows would be worthy contenders.

Robert re-joined George in his snug. It was quite intimate, just about able to accommodate four customers on bench seats, which Robert thought rather uncomfortable. Hanging on each opposite wall were photographs of old Looe in the heyday of masted schooners, whilst on the inner wall was a map of Cornwall showing shipwrecks around the coast, above which was a bookshelf containing an eclectic mix of books, which on any other occasion Robert would have gladly perused.

He sat there for a few moments observing the old sea dog and wondering how to start the conversation. George, who had already started on the full glass of ale, put that down and drank the chaser with a cough and splutter as though it disagreed with him. It seemed to be the cue for Robert.

'Expect you miss the sea nowadays,' he opened.

'Me, no. Never liked it,' he said, not looking at Robert but keeping a vigil on his ale. That was certainly a surprise for Robert, because he had the look of an old sailor who had spent too many days in harsh weather conditions that would test the most resolute.

'Haven't been much further than St Georges,' he continued.

Robert wasn't sure where he meant, but wasn't going to show his ignorance.

'Once went out to the Eddystone. Sick as a parrot. Rough, really rough day that was. Can't swim you see, never learnt.'

'Sorry, thought you'd be a seafarer, living in Looe and all that,' Robert said with a touch of commiseration.

'No. Used to work in the quarries up on Bodmin Moor. Hard life that was. Harder than fishing, I can tell you.'

Robert had no doubt and wasn't going to challenge his view with the risks that fishermen undertake each time they leave shore.

'Anyways, you haven't come to ask about me,' he said, finally looking at Robert with soulful eyes that spoke of a sadness to his life.

'You're right. I want to know about Lammana and the land behind the cottage.'

'Guess you do. What do you know about the place?' he asked, bringing up a deep cough.

Robert told him all he knew, omitting the wall mural and his nightmare and George began to reveal the secrets of the cottage.

'Some say it's the birthplace of Robert Colliver, though others say he was born in East Looe near the old church by the sea front. Nobody knows when the original cottage, the one before now, was built, but legend has it that it was on the site of a Christian chapel. The old cottage was burnt down in the mid-eighteenth century by a local landowner, a Revenue Officer charged to catch smugglers. Expect you know about smuggling and how rife it was here in Cornwall. Same in Looe. One night, having received a tip-off, this Revenue Officer caught seven men at the cottage on a smuggling run. During the mêlée one of the revenue men was shot dead. The ring leader and the other six men were tried and hung for their crimes. It was a harsh judgement and one that they didn't deserve.'

He took another sip of his ale and went into a bout of bronchial convulsions, enough to wake the dead. Robert looked at him and could see a lonely old man whose drinking and frequenting a smoke-filled room were taking its toll on his body.

'Excuse me,' continued George. 'If it's not the drink then the smoke will get me,' and took another sup of ale and inhaled another lung full of smoke. He paused to collect his thoughts. 'I said there were seven smugglers that night. Well, there was an eighth man. He escaped. Rather, he was allowed to escape. It was he who had informed on his fellow moonlighters. He was supposed to escape, but instead hid himself and saw the Revenue Officer murder one of his own men in cold blood. He was the one who should have hung, not the ringleader. Not any of the others.'

'How do you know this?' Robert interceded.

'The man who escaped, he was my grandfather so many times removed. Cannot remember how many, five maybe six. That's how.'

George put his hand into his pocket and pulled out a hip flask, the one that Robert had seen him with in the café. George looked at it and sighed. 'The hip flask was his reward for betraying his friends. Solid silver, it is, and has the mark of the devil on it. WT, William Trevellick. He's the one who killed his own officer. But he testified that the ringleader killed the man. The story has been passed down to me along with the flask, a reminder that we are a cursed family, destined to be chained to hard labour. I've only ever told it to one other person and now you. Why I should, I don't really know, but there's something about you that made me tell it.'

'Where does Robert Colliver fit in to all this?' asked Robert.

'Lammana was most probably his birth place. East Looe's claim is probably them trying to steal a pirate's tale for their own end. They even have a Pirate's Day on the Wooldown where they light the beacon and burn an effigy to him, all for the tourist trade, mind you. The cottage wasn't called Lammana then. Doubt if it had a name. Trevellick had the place burnt to the ground and in doing so, a curse, the curse of the Pirate Robert Colliver, a cruel man by all accounts, was put upon him by the ringleader.'

George took another sup of ale.

'You know, the true Lammana is the ruined chapel on the cliffs at the end of Hannafore as you go on the coast path to Polperro. Some historians say the very first chapel by that name was built on George's Island. There used to be a monastery there.'

Robert was beginning to get confused.

'You mean there's an actual chapel in ruins called Lammana.'

'Yes.'

'And George's Island is the island just off Looe?'

'Yes.'

'And this had a chapel as well called Lammana?'

'Yes, but before the one built on the mainland opposite. That was constructed by the monks as an alternative place when it was impossible to get to the Island.'

Robert was interested in George's disclosure, but he was there to discover the owner of the field.

'The land behind the cottage. Who owns it?'

George began to fidget as though Robert's questioning was becoming tedious. 'Look,' he said with a degree of frustration, 'you'd better go and see old Alfred. He's the friend I talked about and knows more than me about all this. He owns the land at the back of the cottage. He won't mind you using it. But you can ask him yourself. You'll find him at Watergate. Go through Kilminorth Woods and you cannot miss his place. It's called Ararat.'

15

The following day dawned cold and grey, with low clouds covering the cliffs along the coast towards Whitsand Bay and thick enough to obscure Rame Head completely. Even Looe Island was shrouded in a restless mist, the perfect mantle for smuggling, thought Robert, as he looked out upon the scene from his cottage.

From yesterday's pleasant personality, framed in the afternoon sun, the Island had now returned to its menacing character once more. Even the sea, which usually had a benign look in the lee of the Island, beheld an aura of doom as if anybody venturing out of the harbour would be lost to the deep, sucked down to a watery grave. And the cottage itself bore a melancholy spirit, as though remembering its ancient ancestry: a holy trinity of God, the smugglers and the Pirate.

Robert's mood was in tune with the day. Some gulls flew past and looked like spectres in the swirling mist, winged messengers from a world where coincidence and conspiracy are the same. He had dismissed the Trevellick names as a coincidence, but with George's disclosure he was sure of some conspiracy now. What, though, he did not know. The message in his mind was unclear. There must be a link between the past and present and he was determined to find out by visiting this Alfred of Ararat. First though, he was going to the library for any information on Lammana and where it fitted into the web of intrigue.

The library was located in East Looe, in the old quarter near the sea front. This meant crossing the Rubicon. Although it had only been a few days, Robert felt like an old stalwart of the West Looe tribe, especially having survived the initiation ordeal of the Smugglers

Arms, a rite of passage that cemented his place in the hierarchy. That was clearly on the lowest rung and he guessed that he would have to live there for many a year before being accepted; even a lifetime may not be long enough to gain entry within the inner sanctum where only true Cornish men and women were allowed. The bar area in the Smugglers Arms is one such place, an altar where only the chosen few can participate in the daily ritual of drinking from the cup of alcohol and inhaling the incense of tobacco.

As Robert crossed the bridge and ventured down Fore Street to the sea front, he felt as though he were in foreign territory, an invading army of one, exploring the defences and layout of the town in preparation for an assault on the library. He was advancing on unknown ground, his first time in East Looe, and wasn't exactly sure where the Library was located, or even if there was one at all.

The tourist information office was closed, and so he chose to wander up and then down a series of parallel lanes and narrow whitewashed alleyways to look for the building. It was a maze. Old fisherman's cottages faced one another, quaint little places that were the homes to a race of dwarves, for many of the places had small front doors and rooms seemingly no larger than a cupboard, with many having floors below street level, whilst others could only be reached by scaling flights of narrow outside steps.

It was a charming scene, with some alleys bedecked with small shrubs in containers and bistro table and chairs, trying to achieve a Mediterranean atmosphere complete with miniature olive trees. Outside some properties, residents had made an effort to bring spring sunshine to the confined and sometimes claustrophobic thoroughfares, by displaying planters with daffodils and other spring bulbs which had yet to bloom. But for the most part, it was a scene from medieval times and Robert expected to see the old fishermen and their wives come out in smocks and grand skirts to view this stranger in their domain with suspicion, as though he were a revenue man looking for hidden contraband, an enemy within their midst.

All was quiet, since most of the cottages were empty, shuttered holiday homes waiting for the summer season to begin, their doors locked, only to be opened when the warm weather and the owners or guests arrived. He passed an old church where the tower only had one clock, facing away from West Looe, so that the folk there couldn't make use of it, a legacy of former antagonisms. The church no longer served God, but had been converted into flats and now where hymns were once sung and prayers offered, there were the broadcasts of daytime television and popular radio, all wrapped in a reverential worship to interior design.

Along the sea front, was the old life boat station, now a shop selling holiday paraphernalia and down a street where some traffic passed him, he came across a museum, complete with an old cannon standing outside. The museum looked interesting, but it was closed. He cut back in to the narrow alleyways and was once again in a parallel world, where one whitewashed cottage looked like another, a labyrinth from which he would never emerge.

By luck, rather than meritorious reconnoitre, Robert stumbled across the library, a plain building with fine brickwork but few other redeeming features other than it housed the intellectual minds of past and present. He was expecting shelves of interesting volumes on Science, Philosophy and the Arts, but was disappointed to find most of the space taken up to popular fiction with the occasional section on travel, gardening, and a small shelf devoted to biographies of personalities and people he had no interest in knowing about. There was, though, a local interest and reference section where Robert found, to his surprise, a thin book, more a pamphlet, on the *Tale of Two Mediaeval Chapels*. He sat down and began to read and was immediately absorbed by the account of Lammana.

*   *   *

Looe Island had links back to Phoenician seafarers of the Eastern Mediterranean who probably visited the area to trade in tin sometime during the second century BC. It was an important commodity in those days, and there is a legend that Christ, when he was a young boy, visited the Island with his uncle, Joseph of Arimathea, a trader in tin. The first record of a chapel on Looe Island dates to just after the Norman Conquest where there was probably a thriving community of Benedictine monks providing a stronghold of Christianity in a sea of Celtic and pagan worship. The legend of Christ's visit to the Island would be an added attraction for pilgrims travelling further west to the much larger monastery of St Michael's Mount. Although a causeway was originally thought to have linked the Island, much like St Michael's Mount does today, it would still have been a perilous journey and so a second chapel was built on the mainland, as an exact replica of the Island chapel and at the same height above sea level, so that neither could be regarded as superior. Archaeologists believe that such places also served as a beacons in the days before the lighthouse, the only place where light could be seen in a darkened world. By AD1144, both the chapels were known to be owned by the Abbey of Glastonbury and were probably at their most populous, and prospered until they were destroyed in the Reformation.

There was no record of a chapel up on the cliff, the site of the cottage. Not one reference to it. Perhaps it wasn't important enough to mention, Robert concluded, being too small and insignificant. It might have been constructed of timber, since archaeological investigation of the mainland chapel, revealed postholes, suggesting a timber-framed building before the stone construction. A dig was carried out in the mid-1950s and showed that the site had undergone two phases of development: the first, a small rectangular chapel with an altar at one end, with a second phase that added a chancel. The Island chapel may have undergone a similar history, but all that visibly remains today are some decorated stone capitals. It has never been investigated, probably because the Island has been in private ownership since the days of the monastery.

*   *   *

Emerging from the library, having spent the best part of the morning within absorbed in the history of Lammana, the weather had completely changed to match Robert's new mood. Gone were the mist and grey skies of the morning, replaced by sunshine and another lovely afternoon in prospect. Rather than visit Arthur of Ararat, he decided to make use of the fine weather and clear the path that led to the open ground at the back of the cottage. On the way back he called in at the café for some lunch. The proprietor was there and so too was

George. He acknowledged Robert who felt quite privileged, as though he was now accepted as a person and not some 'bloody foreigner.'

'That's the first time I've ever seen him say hello to anybody, let alone a virtual stranger,' John commented in a surprised and hushed tone, as though Robert must have some special status unbeknown to him.

'I spoke to him yesterday in the pub. We got on quite well,' Robert replied.

'The Smugglers Arms?' he asked with equal surprise.

'Yes. Your wife said I would find him in there.'

'She didn't tell me.'

'Well, I was looking for you, but she said George would be able to help. And he did.'

George looked around at the two men and seemed to confirm Robert's assessment of the conversation.

'And did you survive the three wise men? Or should I say three wise monkeys.'

'Let's say they spoke volumes in their silence, and if looks could kill, well...'

'Same for me. Still not allowed to sit at their places by the bar. Quite bizarre really.'

Robert agreed and had some lunch, during which George left with a curt goodbye, saying to seek him in the pub again, when he had seen Arthur. Robert suspected he just wanted more free ale, not forgetting the chaser, but for George himself, he was genuinely interested in Robert, the man who had bought Lammana.

'Now that really is bizarre, two wonders in one day and an invitation,' said the proprietor.

'Pardon?' exclaimed Robert, thinking about what George had said.

'First "Hello", and then "goodbye" and now an offer to join him at the pub. You've either put a spell upon him or there's some special reason that George is interested in you. Whichever, you are a chosen one.'

'I just went to ask him what he knew about the cottage. He told me about the seven smugglers who were caught at the site of the cottage and hung. He said it is reputed to be the birth place of Robert Colliver, the Pirate. That's all.'

'Yes, he's told that story many a time. I think that's all he knows,' the proprietor said with an air of dismissal, as though Robert should have waited for him to tell the story.

He continued, 'Did he tell you about the bridge?'

'No,' said Robert with an interested voice.

'Thought not. Have you counted the number of arches?'

'Yes, seven across the harbour.'

'Aye, that's correct. The tale goes that the builder of the bridge, a Thomas Bond, was asked by a close friend to design it with seven arches to commemorate the seven smugglers and every time one crosses the bridge you are supposed to remember those Looe men who were hanged.'

'Really,' said Robert with an air of scepticism. 'What about the eighth arch, the one on the West Looe side that goes to the car park,' he added, seeing if the proprietor knew of its significance.

'There is an eighth, smaller arch, but I don't think it's relevant to the story. I have heard George refer to it as the Judas arch, but why that, I don't know.'

Robert knew though. George had told him the tale. He didn't really want to be lectured any further by the proprietor and was conscious of time eating into the afternoon, so he made an excuse to leave.

He walked the now familiar route to his cottage. With winter slowly losing its grip, there was some spring warmth to the air by early afternoon and he could see the first signs of the forthcoming season with the occasional wild leek, a lovely little allium with drooping clusters of white bell-flowers, coming into bloom where there was some shelter. With the heady scent of garlic he felt invigorated, wandering slowly up the narrow path. He was in another parallel world, this time where cottages were replaced by the hedgerow, and people by the birds singing, as though they were saying that they've made it through the harsh winter months and now had the bountiful fruits of spring and summer to look forward to in this world of beauty. And as he paused to listen to the coloratura, he was startled to hear a friendly 'Hello' chime above the birdsong.

He surfaced from the recital and turned to see a man, perhaps in his thirties and dressed for a country pursuit, doff his hat which was adorned with a pheasant quill, smile and apologise for startling

Robert. The man was carrying a telescope and tripod over his shoulder and was clearly a serious birdwatcher with a pair of binoculars around his neck and a jacket adorned with logos affiliated to various wildlife organisations. Somewhat over the top, Robert thought, and a walking advertisement to the eccentric.

Robert acknowledged his greeting and two men exchanged pleasantries about the weather and his hobby in the seclusion of the lane just below the cottage. The man explained he had been bird watching a short way along the coast path, observing gulls and other sea birds on the foreshore and across to the Island. Robert enquired, with a genuine interest, what species he had seen to which the man replied, in a rather unconvincing tone, just seagulls and some black sea birds which he was unable to identify. Clearly, this man was a novice, thought Robert, since any serious birdwatcher would not use the term seagull and would know that the black sea birds could only be either cormorants or shags.

He was, Robert thought, not so much an advertisement for the eccentric but for the absurd. The man went on his way and Robert watched to see him make his way down into town, but before he disappeared he turned around and looked, as though assessing Robert, for some unknown reason.

＊　＊　＊

The afternoon was slowly waning with the sun beginning to set below the horizon as Robert looked at the pile of cleared vegetation and the path he had unearthed. He had removed the barbed wire and mended the gate, so that it operated as a gate should, and had even cleared a route through the undergrowth to the field beyond. It was a good afternoon's work, he thought, as he made his way up to the field to catch the last of the sun's rays, before the evening chill reminded him that it was still only early spring.

He watched the sun sink behind a band of floccus clouds and then briefly emerge, only to set below the horizon, signalling the end of the day. But the heavens hadn't finished. An evening show was staged with the clouds cast into dramatic relief, some flamed with reds, orange, and pink hues and others shaded in deep purple with the whole western sky ablaze, not just signalling the end of the day, but the end of time itself, as if the sun had come to claim the earth, as it will one day.

Robert felt the choreographed glow in his heart and wished Caroline was here to witness the spectacle, one which they had once shared on their travels. They had sat, in awe, on the high Tibetan plateau watching such a sunset over the Himalayas and wondered at how a transitory experience can leave such an indelible mark. Their travels had been punctuated by such events: sunrise over the Ganges, meteorite showers in Ladakh, the torrential stair-rods of the monsoon, and an eclipse of the sun in Chile; meteorological and astronomical spectacles that defined their connectivity, a cosmological kinship of spirit.

It was that same spirit for Robert right now, as he imagined Caroline watching the same sunset, their souls connected by a crimson ribbon stretching across the sky, across the country, two minds in empathy with the world. In that moment, he realised fate was playing its hand again. He knew she was going to come. Beauty would come to challenge Charm.

16

Cornwall is dominated by a barrier of cliffs and coves that defy the onslaught of the sea. These cliffs are a battle ground, a theatre of conflict between the elemental forces of the ocean against the solid defiant bastions of the land. In some places, where the cliffs are friable, the sea wins easily, but in others where granite towers prevail, the sea has to win by attrition. Looe is situated between such extremes, its rocks a product of Devonian sedimentation and the subsequent processes of heating and pressure, that has metamorphosed the lithology into purple and grey slates with tongues of intrusive quartz, to make it resistant to all but the most violent of assaults.

Looe is a testament to these battle scars. Landslips and burgeoning coves are a common sight, often causing the coast path to disappear after a winter storm. In the town itself, the land behind the beach has been protected by a concrete barrier whilst nearby, where the cliffs are weak and property is at risk, large angular boulders have been strategically positioned to dissipate further attack by the sea.

The cliffs below the cottage are blessed with the protection of the long concrete sea wall of Hannafore, set behind an extensive wave cut platform of rocks which protrude into the bay towards Looe Island. Behind the sea wall and an access road are two rows of mainly detached mid-war residences, built when the area was developed. Behind these houses is the old cliff, covered with decades of vegetation growth to form a gently sloping friendly face untouched by storms, as though it had won the war of erosion. But just a few yards further along from the concrete defence and the gentile façade of suburbia, the battle wages on with the sea slowly eroding a retreating coastline.

It was there, at the ruined chapel of Lammana, that Robert was standing in the sunshine of another promising day. He had got up early to take a look at the old chapel ruins and had watched the sun rise over the sea with a warm crimson radiance as though it was the afterglow from the previous night's rendition, a spectacular sunset, especially staged for him as a promise from Tibet.

He had first made his way up the old coast path but instead of climbing further to the cottage, at the switch-back, he instead proceeded along and descended down to Hannafore and behind the rear of several hotels, before emerging in the residential part. He could smell bacon being cooked escaping from the large vents above the hotel kitchens, which made him feel hungry for a cooked breakfast, prompting the thought of ordering one at the café.

The sea front was empty apart from a man walking his dog, or rather, so it appeared, the dog walking the man, for he was being pulled by a rather energetic collie which longed to be free of its leash. Further along, approaching a coastguard lookout post, a couple overtook Robert out for an early morning jog. The woman looked familiar and he realised it was Jane from the café. But her partner wasn't John. No, he was a much younger man, slim, who seemed to be enjoying her company for further along when out of sight, or so they thought, Robert could see them in an embrace.

He hid behind the coastguard building waiting for them to continue, not wanting the embarrassment of confrontation. But they didn't resume their run and Robert could only guess at what was so interesting in the shadows of a toilet block. Finally after what seemed like an eternity they carried on, disappearing through a latched gate onto the grassy area of the coastal path. Was she having an illicit affair, Robert thought? It seemed like it. She was certainly attractive and she did say there were activities to broaden the mind and he doubted she meant jogging.

The chapel was a good two hundred yards from the cliff edge which at the Hannafore end was little more than thirty feet high, enough to be classified as a cliff but not like the three hundred and fifty foot one dominating Lantic Bay, further along the coast towards Polruan. Robert climbed the bank to the chapel and could see that it was indeed at the same height as the Island summit, as recounted in the literature he had read about it.

In the early morning sun the chapel, or what was left of it, was peaceful, almost alive with the meditative silence of the Benedictine monks who inhabited the place in the Middle Ages. An information plaque showed a reconstruction of what it would have looked like and Robert could see the attraction of becoming a monk in those days. It looked idyllic. For the monks it would have been far from that, most likely a harsh life and certainly one of devoted prayer and penance.

He wandered around the site tracing out the walls. The south porch was clearly visible as was the nave, the original part of the chapel, and the small chancel, built at a later date, was clearly defined as well. Little else could be discerned from the vegetation growth that covered the ground. He sat down on a wall and looked out towards the Island. It had a mesmerising attraction that draws the observer in as it did so from his cottage, a hypnotic stupor, as though it were spinning a trance, goading him to discover its mystery and luring him into the unknown. He looked at its summit and imagined a chapel perched on high and the monks giving thanks for their sanctuary from a heathen world where life was cheap and expendable. How different today, he thought, and wondered what they would make of a secular world where indifference was endemic and the new religion was consumerism.

It was still early and rather than retrace his steps, Robert decided to make it into a round trip by taking a path which made its way up to the field behind his cottage to the tiny hamlet of Portlooe. He had spotted the path on the Ordnance Survey map which he had consulted to confirm his deduction that the concrete tower was indeed part of a measured mile. His cartographic survey had determined the distance between the two towers which, although rather approximate, measured over 6000 feet, considerably more than a statute mile: empirical deduction was by nature to Robert a scientific necessity for absolute truth.

The path, which had been clearly marked on the map, was rather indistinct in places and contoured around a knoll gradually gaining height until after a couple of hundred yards it disappeared altogether. The map had definitely shown a path, not a right of way though, and he suspected that over the years it had become overgrown with disuse. He was looking for some obvious sign that he was on the right track when a figure came walking towards him, still in the distance, but in the general direction of the path. Robert stopped and waited to see which way he went. As the figure got closer he could see it was a man and a few seconds later realised it was the birdwatcher from the other day. He was still wearing his ridiculous outfit and looked equally as absurd but was not carrying the tripod and telescope this time.

'Good morning to you sir, and what a lovely day it is,' said the man in a convivial manner, not proffering recognition of Robert.

'Good morning,' replied Robert.

'Out for an early morning constitutional?' the man added.

Robert hated that word ever since he was a small boy when his father insisted they take an afternoon walk after Christmas lunch, as though that day were different from all the other days, when no such suggestion was forthcoming.

'Well, it is a lovely morning as you said. Why not take advantage of it. And you? Are you out bird watching, trying to glimpse a chough perhaps, before the twitchers descend upon the scene?'

'No such luck. But I keep trying.'

Robert wasn't convinced of this man previously and yet again his knowledge of birds was not compatible with his demeanour. The chough, the emblem of Cornwall, is a member of the crow family but with a distinctive curved red beak. They were once plentiful in the county but the last recorded breeding pair was now over fifty years ago, their demise due to persecution and decline of habitat. As an ornithologist he would certainly have known that they were rare, the nearest breeding area being Wales, and although actually possible it would be most unlikely for him to glimpse one. What was his game, Robert thought?

'Must be off,' he said looking rather anxious as though not to be interrogated further by somebody who knew their ornithology. 'Cheerio,' he said, as he hastily left leaving Robert pondering for a moment.

'Mighty strange,' he commented to himself aloud. Robert wondered what he was up to as he continued his climb upwards and as he did so it dawned upon him that the man could be spying on Jane. That was it, Robert thought, he's a private detective hired by John.

Robert made it to Portlooe, a small cluster of stone-built cottages nestling in a coombe, and although there was no view of the coast its presence close-by was evident by the distant cries of the gulls and the smell of the sea, which gave it a sense of isolation from the constant war that raged only half a mile away. He passed a grand entrance to an estate called Hendersick Hall emanating from which were the familiar calls of peacocks, before emerging at the junction of the old Talland Road and its Celtic cross. At the gate to the field where he had parked the other day was a car but no sign of its occupant. Robert thought it was probably the birdwatcher's vehicle and climbed the gate into the field. It had only been a few days since he was last using the old track but already the grass was beginning to grow, with clumps of wild chives breaking through the sward. He noticed the first signs of blackthorn blossom emerging in the hedgerow alongside some escaped daffodils, the shoots of alexanders and a host of other plants some of which he knew but most would have to wait until they came into flower.

As he approached the cottage the same silence he heard before was deafening him once more. Again he heard some rustling in the hedge and the bolting of an animal as he approached the source of the noise. He tried to see what it was, but it was fleet-footed and escaped him. As he was emerging from the hedge something else caught his eye, a momentary glimpse of a person running away from him. It wasn't the birdwatcher. A few seconds later the familiar roar of an engine and then silence fell upon the field. Robert was beginning to feel paranoid about this field, with the phantom noises and strange sightings, and thought it about time he paid Alfred a visit, if only to alley his fears.

Back in the sanctuary of his garden Robert was pleased to see Tara sitting on the bench in a meditative mood, soaking up the sun. She hadn't noticed nor heard him even though he had tripped on a tangle of bramble and let out an expletive in the undergrowth beyond the garden boundary. He stood there looking at her. She was beautiful. She was slim, her jeans proclaiming long slender legs and her top defining small but well-shaped breasts slightly heaving with every breath she took. He could have stayed there all afternoon watching this angel breathe life into his veins but thought he was taking unfair advantage of the situation.

Tara, on the other hand, had heard Robert swearing and thought it would be to her advantage to pretend not to hear him and see how long he would wait to announce his presence. She could sense his gaze at her body, her sexuality providing the connection between their thoughts.

'Hello Tara,' he said in a quiet tone, as though he didn't want to disturb her.

'Oh, hello Robert, you startled me,' as she opened her eyes and smiled at him.

'Sorry. You looked so angelic there as though meditating.'

'Yes, I was almost floating off to Nirvana.'

'Sorry to interrupt such a mystical experience,' he continued in a placatory tone, 'it's not every day that prospect arises.'

'Don't worry, I'm only kidding.'

'Do you do yoga? You look so lithe.'

'Yes, I do, but not as often as I should. It does keep me supple and is good for all sorts of activities, particularly those which require contortions of the body,' she replied, pleased that he had noticed her slim figure and hoping he might respond to her innuendo.

Robert wasn't quite sure if he had read the subtext correctly, but it reminded him of the famous and resplendent Hindu temples of Khajuraho in India in which tenth century sculptured reliefs of erotic images adorn the walls and where his aesthetic eyes were hypnotised by its unabashed sexuality.

'Have you ever seen photographs of the Khajuraho Temple?' he said with a degree of uncertainty whether it was wise to pursue this avenue, but nevertheless wanting to see where it would lead.

'The Khaj what temple?'

'Khajuraho.'

'No.'

'Never mind.'

'But I do mind.'

'It was just my wandering mind. It doesn't matter.'

'But it does. I insist you reveal your wandering mind.'

Robert could sense he was not going to win the battle of wits.

'It's a temple in India that I've been to. It has images of people contorting their bodies. That's what reminded me of it.'

'What else about it?'

'Nothing,' he replied with no conviction, which Tara latched onto.

'You say nothing, but there is something, I can tell,' she said in a slightly raised and forceful voice that Robert, again, could not ignore.

'It's just my musings but the sculptures depict erotica, frank representations of sex in all sorts of positions.'

She was delighted he had taken the bait and now wanted to reel him in.

'Well I never. Are you trying to corrupt me, you wicked man,' joked Tara, which sent a wave of embarrassment through Robert.

'No, of course not.'

'They seem revealing. Like the Karma Sutra?'

'In a way, but much more enlightening I would say and more real.'

'Well Robert Colliver, you're no ordinary pirate but a latent sex mad pirate who likes kinky erotica. My kind of pirate I must say.'

Robert was flattered and would have made a move but for the fact she had mentioned him as a pirate, which tempered his enthusiasm for the moment.

'So you know about the Pirate?'

Tara realised her mistake. She was annoyed with herself for letting an opportunity slip for she knew that her prey had just slipped the net. All she could do was repair the damage.

'Who doesn't who's lived in Looe for a long time. He's notorious. Not a welcome visitor you could say.'

'Is that why you looked to have seen a ghost in the office that first day?'

'Was it obvious? His curse is as real today as when he was alive. To some folk, at least.'

'And you?'

'Well, let's say I've seen the effect of his reputation.'

'You know this cottage, or at least this site, is thought to be his birthplace.'

'Yes, I've heard such, although others say he was born in the old part of East Looe. Anyway let's leave the subject, it's not one for a lovely day and we were having such an interesting discussion.'

'You're right of course. What brings you here?'

'I have the day off. Thought I'd bring you some lunch.'

She reached down into her bag and retrieved two pasties, still warm from the oven, and they sat together eating the tasty Cornish icon with the midday sun providing a pleasant accompaniment to the meal, together with the waves breaking on the shore below and the sound of gulls above. A small flock of goldfinches injected colour to their meal, twittering amongst themselves as though they were interested in the two humans' behaviour but were really after seed from teasel heads that still stood proud amongst the wild clematis behind them. It was a robin and a couple of chaffinches that braved their territory, eagerly pecking at the discarded crumbs.

Tara asked about the police and apologised for being busy and not enquiring before now. She was equally mystified by the disappearing effigy but since there had been no other incident Robert said he was not unduly concerned. Of more concern, he said, was the lack of progress on the cottage especially as he needed it completed, or at least habitable, within a few weeks when his holiday let would terminate. One of the estate agents maintenance contractors could help, she suggested, to which Robert agreed. After that they sat there absorbing the moment; Robert unable to remove the image of Tara and the erotic statues whilst Tara herself was thinking about her next move, phase one having been completed. That was easy she thought, the second phase would be more of a challenge but one she was anticipating and began to cultivate a plan as to how it would unfold.

17

Estate agents are often viewed with disdain, even ridiculed for their turn of phrases and linguistic ability to transform a house, which is little more than a dilapidated old wreck, into a period property in need of some renovation. Robert felt that was a fair description of his cottage, whichever way one viewed it.

At the moment, with still much to be done, it was the old wreck and he felt overwhelmed by the scale of work. He had only been working piecemeal at it, more interested in the mysteries surrounding its chequered history than turning it into a home, and had made the decision to forget the smugglers and the local pirate for now and concentrate on renovation. But Tara was to change his attitude.

Robert was working outside. He was demolishing the old shed and had spent a couple of hours removing the asbestos sheeting to reveal a timber framework, rotten from years of neglect and emitting an odour of decay. Woodlice infested the shredded wood and even a toad, still in hibernation, had found the damp a welcome refuge, both of which had halted his progress whilst he assisted the inhabitants to escape. It reminded him of Heinrich Harrer's experience in Tibet when the Buddhist monks were alarmed at his digging for fear of killing worms and would carefully remove the creatures to a safe place much to the consternation of the author. Even Robert had the same issues when gardening, his ethics preventing the mass destruction of living creatures that were innocent victims simply trying to live.

An early morning chill had evaporated into a hot day and with the sun now quite high in the sky and a very gentle breeze, it was radiating warmth like a summer's day. Robert had stripped down to just his jeans and heavy work boots. Sweat was cascading off his forehead, he was covered in a film of dirt and his lungs were heaving from the physical effort of the morning. With the sun penetrating his naked torso he was invigorated and the pulse of living felt like a narcotic enveloping his senses. He stopped to look at the cottage. It was an idyll with its whitewashed walls gleaming in the sun, too much for his eyes to take and so he turned to focus them across the bay. The sea was a perfect azure blue speckled with ripples of turquoise and by now, beyond midday, the tide was well out just about on slack and the thought of a first venture into the still cold waters was an inviting distraction.

Robert was engrossed in the view, watching a bright yellow canoe making its way through the narrow channel between the mainland and the Island which now was revealing its rocky coastline at low tide. Then a dolphin caught his gaze, jumping out of the water in an arc of delight, and he became mesmerised by its antics at play in the bay. He was enraptured by the whole scene, lost in a world so delightful, when a voice from beyond interrupted the theatricals.

'Lovely view,' the voice said with the intonation of a familiar female.

Robert turned around to see Tara standing above him with the sun shining brilliant on her slim figure, a seraphim within the heavens of a blue sky.

'It is,' he replied, 'I don't tire of it.'

'No, I wouldn't. Cannot think of a more pleasing sight to wake up to,' she said in a seductive voice and looking at Robert with a decisive longing.

'I don't. Each morning...' It was at this point he realised she wasn't talking about the view and changed the subject. 'You must excuse the lack of attire. I've just spent all morning taking down this old shed. I sweat so easily.'

'Don't apologise, it's every girls' dream to see a naked man, well near naked, displaying his prowess.'

She was now standing in front of him focusing first on his eyes and then darting up and down upon his nakedness, making him feel her penetrating gaze. He was now beginning to blush and felt self-conscience as she began to visually play with him, for although he did have a good physique he didn't think of himself as every girl's dream.

In his youth, whilst still at school, he realised that most girls wanted a good time; to go clubbing, have a laugh and listen to popular music. This was the antithesis of his aspiration. He was interested in learning and did not participate in popular culture finding it too facile, preferring the urbane pleasures of classical music and the acquisition of knowledge, wanting to know about the world he lived in, how it worked, its history, its geography, its art and culture, the solar system and cosmos. Consequently, he never had a girlfriend until he met Madeleine. And then it was her who had made the first move. And now he was being seduced once more, although this time he had the confidence of age and experience to repel Tara's advances.

He motioned to put on his shirt.

'Oh, don't on my account,' as she manoeuvred herself to prevent him.

'Would you like me to take my top off too?' she said in a cheeky tone, not giving any indication whether she was serious or not.

'Now you're playing with me, aren't you?'

'Perhaps. But it is such fun and the sight of your naked torso is most appealing, especially since it is glistening from hard labour.'

'And how long had you been standing there watching me?'

'Oh, long enough to assess your qualities,' she said in a playful tone.

'And what did you deduce?'

He was beginning to feel a little more confident even though she still had him at a disadvantage standing so close to him, her body radiating an electromagnetic force that was beginning to make his heart beat faster and faster.

He had watched her come down the steps from the gate above into the garden, slowly and deliberately making her entrance, transfixed on her pulchritude form, a vision of beauty that in those moments he wanted. She wasn't wearing much more than him, flaunting a thigh length skirt and a body-hugging top which emphasised a delicate form through the diaphanous material. If anything, she was every man's desire, her eyes penetrating into his soul, seducing him with verbal foreplay, reducing him to basic carnal thoughts. He was falling for her charm.

'Well, I haven't had a chance to see them all yet, but from what I've observed, so far, they're very promising.'

He stood there, his chest sweating in the intense heat of the moment. His heart was thudding, his pulse racing along guilty with anticipation from this temptress standing before him, wanting him to submit. He looked at her lips. They were full and soft. He looked at her breasts. They were gently heaving. He looked into her eyes. She was, without any effort, luring him in, baiting him with her sexuality and slowly reeling in her victim, enslaving him for her own pleasure as she put her hand up to his forehead and wiped away the dripping sweat with her forefinger.

'Such a heady mixture, sweat and testosterone,' she said, and proceeded to lick her finger seductively.

'And those toned muscles, hard from a mornings labour,' and ran her hands down his upper arms, feeling his biceps. Robert stood there feeling the electricity flow from her hands into his body, a charge that had him helpless. Tara then motioned to kiss him and as their lips met she had finally landed her man in an embrace that he could not escape, a net that had him writhing with pleasure, intoxicated at the hands of his seductress.

*　　*　　*

'That was some yoga session,' he sighed with exhaustion, spent like a fish gasping for air, unable to comprehend its fate.

'I didn't come here to demonstrate the shakti position,' she responded with a smile, the smile of a satisfied Machiavellian.

She lay there soaking up the sun next to her catch, a man whom she had baited, reeled and landed so easily. The opportunity was too good to miss and her judgement of him was perfect and her performance impeccable from the situation that she had skilfully manoeuvred. She had the effigy hung outside the cottage to effect some reaction and hoped he would seek advice and comfort from her. It worked and she was pleased and satisfied with her scheming. Robert too was a satisfied man as he looked at Tara next to him, her recumbent form radiating a lascivious glow.

Robert felt good. He felt more than good. He felt that this was the beginning, although the beginning of what he wasn't quite sure. He had witnessed a completely different side to Tara the Estate Agent, one that he couldn't have imagined. She had awoken some deep-seated desire within him and had found the experience both pleasurable and irresistible, not least her sublime body which he wanted more of, wanted the pleasure of worshiping her exquisite body as though she were a deity, an exalted goddess to be anointed with his passion.

There they lay in the sun, two naked bodies entwined, each thinking their own thoughts, absorbed in the moment of ecstasy. For Robert it was anticipation, excitement, adventure of the unknown. For Tara it was satisfaction. Both musings were interrupted by a distant rumble.

'Can't be thunder, surely,' Robert remarked with surprise.

'Navy on firing practice,' Tara replied, with a tone of disapproval.

'Not your favourite service, I gather.'

'No, not exactly.'

'Any particular reason?'

'Several reasons. Perhaps the most culpable is their responsibility for mass killings of dolphins. A few months ago a large pod of dolphins stranded themselves on a beach further down the Cornish coast. Why would they do that? It must be the Navy's sonar interfering with the dolphins' natural communication that caused them to go inland, into the shallow waters of a bay and so become beached. They all died despite rescue attempts to float them again. Of course, the naval authorities deny it is their fault, yet it is the only plausible explanation other than mass suicide.'

Tara seemed passionate about the incident and Robert didn't want to be drawn into a discussion on the subject even though he would have liked to defend the Royal Navy for its important role in the defence of the realm. Instead, he was intrigued by Tara's intense stare at the Island the whole time she recounted the dolphin tragedy, as though the place held a magnetic attraction, one which she couldn't govern.

'Have you been over there?' he enquired.

'Where? To where the dolphins were drowned?'

'No. Over to the Island. You look at it as though it has some hold upon you.'

Tara immediately returned to Robert unaware that she had been so engrossed in it, its polarity creating a field of ambiguity in her mind.

'Yes, I've been there on many occasions. I know it quite well.'

Tara then explained how the Island was owned by two sisters who purchased it in the sixties. The Carter sisters, Annie and Madge as they were known, had a celebrity status back then. Two women living alone on an island that could be, and indeed was, cut off for weeks on end in bad weather, without mains electricity or any other service. It was a hard life. Tara's father used to go out there and help out with ferrying of goods and general maintenance and on many occasions Tara would go with him. Consequently, she got to know the sisters and the Island very well, almost a second home for her.

When the elder sister died two years ago Tara took it upon herself to console Madge, the younger sister, and help her through bereavement. She herself had suffered the sudden loss of her father when he was drowned at sea in a fishing accident involving a frigate at night time, something else she blamed the Navy for.

'So you see I have my reasons for disliking the Navy. The frigate was blacked-out for some manoeuvre and the trawler my father was in was rammed and sank in minutes. The crew and skipper, my father, were all drowned.'

'I'm sorry to hear that. If I'd known I would never have mentioned it.'

'That's alright,' she said in a doleful tone, wanting Robert to feel guilty and so make him feel for her.

He put his arm over Tara to comfort her and in doing so her sorrow seeped into his veins and he kissed her, he kissed her lips, her neck, her breasts, and she responded to his intimacy, his desire and they made love once more, their bodies entwined again in an ecstasy of pleasure. They forgot the distant rumble of gun fire, the scream of the gulls, the waves breaking on the rocks below. They were in their own world of passion where time is stretched, stretched to infinity and beyond, where energy invades the space that their desires inhabit, a union of two bodies, two stars that have collided in a cataclysmic explosion.

Robert stood up and went inside the cottage leaving Tara outside to cool in the sun. He returned with two bottles of beer and some food, only to find her laid outstretched as though time was a dimension that she had forgotten, soaking up the sun's rays, unaware of the offerings laid out for her.

The beer quenched Robert's thirst but not his desire for flesh as he looked at his conquest who laid there before him, naked, willing him to another session before the sun started to lose its potency. And so, like a moth to a flame, Robert proceeded to anoint Tara once more, exploring her curves with hands that caressed her body with the touch of innocence. She lay there letting the sun god worship her, penetrate her until he lost his power to provide any more warmth from his rays and they both fell into an embrace of satisfaction, he euphorically satiated as only a man can be and she pleased with her machinations.

With the sun now low in the sky and a chill beginning to envelop the two lovers, they dressed and sat outside watching the light fade, a red glow lining the horizon.

'Red sky at night,' he uttered. 'Should be another nice day tomorrow.'

'Do you believe in those country tales?'

'Generally, yes. They're usually based on years of observations and there is generally good scientific evidence to back them up in many cases.'

He explained how the two instances of dust in the upper atmosphere, usually from southerly winds, and the low rays of the sun being bent in the atmosphere scatters light so that only the red end of the spectrum is visible, thereby creating the typical sunset phenomenon. He wasn't sure if Tara was listening or even if she was really interested. She seemed to be meditating, her face expressionless, her gaze looking out towards the Island once more and her thoughts focused on something else, something else much more important.

18

The following few weeks were taken up in a blissful whirlwind of sex interposed by work on the cottage. Except for the kitchen, which was his final job, enough had been done for Robert to move in. Since that providential day, when Tara had seduced him, their passion had become hotter and hotter, matching the weather which had given way to a month of glorious spring sunshine, each day seemingly better than the previous one.

It couldn't last, everybody had said. Robert wanted it to go on for eternity, so enraptured in his dichotomous existence. Tara would organise his day, where work would be rewarded with the promise of her divine body as though she were using Robert as a slave for her own amusement, which of course she was. Was he a slave? It seemed like it, but if this was his kismet then he would gladly submit to her will and her corporeal delights.

The weather didn't last. It broke one night with a violent thunderstorm that blew in from the continent, from across the Bay of Biscay hitting Cornwall and the South West with lightening, and unleashing wind and rain that the gods themselves would be impressed with. However, it had blown through by the following morning leaving a calm atmosphere, as though it were a mirage on the imagination.

It had left its mark. Debris was scattered everywhere. The sea front was piled with seaweed, enough to fill several truck loads, whilst the road to and from Hannafore was closed because of a landslide leaving one house only yards away from collapse. Several cottages in the low lying older part of the town, Robert's parallel world, had been flooded due to drains unable to cope with the deluge. Thankfully, there wasn't a high tide that night, otherwise the flooding would have been considerably worse.

The cottage had not escaped the maelstrom. A tree branch had broken and landed on the pitched roof of the kitchen but fortunately only doing minor damage to the roof slates. The branch was from an old apple tree that had seen better days and had been uprooted to reveal stone slabs that, on closer inspection, Robert was concerned to see were gravestones.

He could decipher some writing rather weathered from many a year but still discernible in places, revealing on one headstone a John Vening but no date and on another the year 1742 with no readable name. He thought back to the conversation with Caroline and how he had jested about a graveyard and now here was one, unearthed in a storm. It seemed to confirm her suspicion that the cottage was once the site of a Christian chapel and Robert wondered what other revelations were awaiting him, although he was glad he hadn't found any bones.

Rather than dwell on the implications of the unearthing, Robert decided to get on with the task he was there for. Tara had gone away for a few days, on a conference she had said, and had left instructions for the kitchen floor to be taken up and re-laid as it was uneven and dipping in the centre. Robert was well aware of its state and had already prepared a delivery of sand and cement to the gated entrance of the field. He had spent the morning transporting heavy bags in a wheelbarrow across the field, having to make umpteen trips which, by the last one, had finally exhausted him. It had been a mammoth task.

He sat down outside with a cup of coffee to recover. He glanced at the gravestones. Something caught his eye. It looked odd, as though it shouldn't be there. He went over to investigate and to his horror, a bone was protruding from the soil. Using a trowel, he carefully scraped away to reveal the whole bone which, to his untrained eye, looked ominously like a human femur. He was now anxious lest he unearthed more and was reluctant to continue. His reticence was well placed as he soon had another bone and with increasing apprehension another and then another, until it seemed he had a complete skeleton, minus its skull. Then, to his utter panic, the skull appeared. He was face to face with death. This was his worst nightmare.

As a young child, he had been taken by his father to a church on the south coast near to the town of Rye. The church, as he recalled, was unremarkable except for a crypt. His father had asked him if he wanted to go down and see some bones. Being a boy, fascinated by animals, he had agreed, only to be confronted by row upon row of human bones, stacked in their hundreds behind a wire cage. It was a macabre sight. Whilst his father continued exploring the crypt Robert remained behind, mesmerised by the sight, a childish fascination with the supernatural. Unaware that he was alone, a freak electrical power surge had switched off all lighting in the church leaving Robert in total darkness. He called out in panic but only heard his echo superimposed upon his fathers concerned call. He could not tell which way to go. He had tried to make his way out but it was too dark to see and in that black void he felt alone, as though this was the end of him and that he would never see daylight again. In reality, the lights were only out for a few seconds but it was an eternity for the young Robert, leaving an indelible impression upon his mind. When the lights returned they blinded him, making him think he was in heaven but instead he found himself in hell, for into his vision, after the blackness of space, were hundreds of skulls, their empty eye sockets piercing him, giving him the fright of his life, one that was to remain with him for the rest of his life.

* * *

Empty eye sockets were staring at Robert once again. He shuddered. This was a real nightmare with the body of some poor soul now a pile of bones in Robert's garden. With some hesitation he removed the skull from its earthly tomb. Together with the rest of the bones, he carefully placed them in a box and stored them in the sea shack, an old table cloth draping the box as some sort of memorial shroud to the unknown dead.

The skeleton had unnerved him. He didn't know what to do. By rights, he should report it to the police but something told him not to, not just yet at least. He didn't want forensic pathologists digging up his garden nor other strangers in and out of his cottage. To block out his responsibility he decided to take a walk down to the chapel of Lammana and seek its solitude, a place where thoughts are more lucid. He would make a decision there.

Afternoon sun shone through a break in the cloud, its corpuscular beam spotlighting the Island, a bright halo that encapsulated the summit as though pronouncing its pious past. Was the Island holy, a Benedictine place of worship all those centuries ago? And his cottage, was it the site of a chapel? Were there more graves to be unearthed? He sat down on a bench looking at the Island, the spotlight gradually dimming as more cloud obscured the sun, returning it to shadows and its questioning past.

He wanted to switch the thoughts off, but his mind wouldn't let him. What should he do with the skeleton? He did not know. He looked down and focused on some ants emerging from the edge of the concrete base, a procession of emmets towards a discarded apple core which they were busily devouring. He watched the ordered operation to purge his mind of its deliberations. An inspection flap, much like a manhole cover but slightly bigger which was hinged on one side with a recessed handle on the other, was set within the concrete structure. He tried to lift it, but it would not move. Subconsciously, he was hoping it was a secret key to answers, but concluded that it was just an inspection flap, no more, no less, and that his answers would remain locked up.

It began to rain. It was only light drizzle but nevertheless he got up and headed for some shelter along the sea front of Hannafore. A café was open near to some tennis courts and he went inside and ordered tea. Whilst drinking the hot and comforting beverage, he noticed the birdwatcher on the foreshore, tripod out and looking through his telescope at the Island. He must be keen, thought Robert, to be out in this rain which by now had become persistent enough to soak the individual. He couldn't see much bird activity, at least nothing that would induce him to be outside getting drenched, he being more of a fair weather birdwatcher. Before he had finished his tea the bird man had packed up and gone, walking off below the cliffs towards Talland.

Robert waited for the rain to ease before continuing to West Looe quay and the café. He would have a late lunch. Inside, George was at his usual table and said hello in a friendly tone, even enquiring as to whether Robert had seen Alfred. He told him he hadn't. George seemed dismayed. John looked at the two men in amazement at how George, a man who had barely spoken any words to him, was in conversation with Robert.

'Whatever it is you're taking, I want some of it,' he said.

'There's nothing, just my charm!'

'There's got to be something. George is a secretive man. Even those that have known him for a long time don't get that sort of acknowledgement.'

'As I said, it's pure charm.'

John left it at that and took Robert's order. Whilst waiting and looking out the window across the harbour, he noticed some activity on the far quayside. A fishing boat had started its engines producing a cloud of smoke that drifted upstream towards the fish market and a group of anglers waiting for their hire boat. He thought he saw Tara. It looked like her, with her red hair. But it was only a fleeting glimpse, as the figure climbed down onto the fishing boat and disappeared from view into a cabin. He looked for any further sign of the person, a woman he was sure, but there was none. After five minutes the vessel left the harbour, making for the open sea.

It was a red, Newlyn registered, fishing boat with its NN insignia, a small trawler with winches at the rear and heavy iron otter boards positioned on the side of the hull, used to keep the net open and on the sea bed. It was an effective form of fishing but did damage to the fragile ecosystem and was indiscriminate in the catch. With each vessel having strict quotas any fish caught that exceeded a prescribed limit were thrown overboard. Robert had watched many times the iconic spectacle of a fishing vessel returning to port, the deck hands gutting the legal catch and disgorging unwanted fish, with the inevitable flock of gulls trailing in its wake.

Robert was thinking about Tara and their blossoming relationship, how he knew little about her whilst she knew so much about him. Was it her on the vessel? She was at a conference, she had told him. Away for three days. Why lie? John served his lunch and Robert took the opportunity to enquire about the fishing vessel.

'Do you know anything about the Newlyn fishing vessel in the harbour?'

The proprietor looked puzzled. 'Don't know of any such vessel.'

'You must do. It's red and the only one with an NN insignia.'

'Oh, you mean *SeaQuest*. It's not a Newlyn vessel. In fact I don't think there is a registration for that port. NN refers to Newhaven.'

'I thought it was Newlyn, being in Cornwall.'

'An easy mistake.'

'Do you know who owns it?'

'My friends, the Trevellicks.'

'Your friends? You know them?'

'I was being facetious. No, I don't know them. They are the Looe institution that I referred to when we first arrived in Looe. Sooner or later anybody who lives here long enough encounters the family, one way or another. And that's a fact.'

The name was beginning to become familiar to Robert too and he wondered if they were involved in his mysterious happenings. And he felt sure it was Tara he saw board the trawler. Was she a Trevellick?

Robert ate his lunch but the questions in his mind soured the gastronomy and rather than stay any longer he decided to go back to the cottage and make a start on the kitchen floor. He had decided to leave the boxed skeleton for now.

Before he left George grabbed his arm. He could see John looking on, even more in awe of his esteem.

'Them Trevellicks. You don't want to cross paths with their likes,' he uttered in a tone that sounded like an ominous warning. Robert was about to respond but George continued more cheerfully, 'Come and see me in the Smugglers. There's something I want to ask you. But not here. And don't forget to see Alfred,' said George looking at the proprietor, either to make sure he was out of earshot, or wanting him to see his interest in Robert.

'I will,' he replied, and left the café, with John in complete bemusement and George with a wry smile on his face, a smile which was to change Roberts outlook in Looe.

He proceeded up the coastal path which, with the recent rain, was muddy and although he was no detective there were obvious footprints in the mud. They were not from a shoe but a hiking boot, a large size, and fresh, coming from the direction of Talland towards town. At the gate to his cottage there was a confusion of them suggesting somebody had paced around outside, perhaps even entered the property, although he could see no sign of entry.

As he climbed the steps up to the cottage a cigarette butt caught his gaze. Whoever it was, they had trespassed. He felt uneasy. Robert followed what looked to be a trail of prints to the gravestones, where there were more. From feeling uneasy he was now concerned. Whoever it was may still be inside. The front door had been left unlocked as he always did when going out during the day. He picked up a crowbar that he had been using to free the headstones and quietly, with deliberate steps, edged his way to the porch.

There were signs of ash from a cigarette and the tell-tale sign of a boot print on the slate. He opened the door very slowly. It yielded a creek, much to Robert's chagrin. Inside was quiet. No sound of an intruder. Perhaps they had heard the door and were themselves standing motionless, their heart beating a little faster as Robert's was. Whoever it was didn't care about leaving an obvious trace of their presence because he detected some faint prints in the hallway. Somebody had most definitely been inside.

He called out, 'anyone there?' No answer. It was a foolish thing to do, reprimanding himself. What sane intruder would answer? Maybe he's insane, a madman. All sorts of scenarios were now entering his mind as he carefully inched towards the lounge, crowbar ready to strike. He peered around the door to find the room empty. It was the same with the sitting room, which was serving as a kitchen for the moment. There was no sign of an intruder in the makeshift kitchen, nor the side porch. Robert was beginning to think he had fled. But he hadn't inspected upstairs and any real man would investigate.

The thought of encountering a complete stranger, a burglar, terrified him. He wasn't a violent man and doubted whether he could defend himself with real conviction, especially against a seasoned campaigner. He had to go upstairs, he told himself. Perhaps if he remained downstairs and made a cup of tea it might fool the intruder into fleeing the cottage, leaving him alone. That's cowardly. Be a man and go upstairs.

Robert obeyed his conscience. Step by step, he climbed the rungs. They creaked. He hadn't really noticed that before but now, in the dead silence of a confrontation, where stealth and quietude were essential, they echoed throughout the cottage, informing anybody concerned that he was coming. At the top of the staircase on the small landing he stopped and listened. Listened for some sound, a creak of a floorboard, the sound of breathing, that would tell him of an intruder. Nothing. Not a sound. He opened the bedroom door. From the doorway it looked empty. He peered into the small box room. It too was empty except for some tools. The bathroom door was open but he couldn't see behind the door where the bath was located. With some trepidation, he peered around and to his delight found nobody there. The cottage was empty. He sighed with relief. But just as he did so he sensed a body loom large from the landing behind him and before he could turn around, a blunt instrument struck him on the shoulder and he crumpled to the floor. His assailant, who had been hiding behind the door of the main bedroom, then made his escape, leaving Robert dazed and crumpled in pain on the bedroom floor unable and unwilling to pursue his attacker.

19

It rained overnight. Not the deluge from the previous day, but a mizzle that soaked everything, creating a sense of rejuvenation in the morning shadows of daylight. Hedgerow foliage, grass and the emerging wild garlic, gave off an aroma that touched the senses and cleared the air, a natural cure for the heavy head. Robert breathed in the medicinal bouquet, his head still feeling the blow that had felled him. He felt slightly better although it was probably the painkillers that were really having a beneficial effect.

He was walking up to the cottage inspecting the muddy ground for further signs of the mystery attacker. No sign of an intruder today, his were virgin footprints. After the encounter, and having recovered sufficiently from concussion, he had locked the front door, as he normally did every night, but had fitted a padlock to the outside, a crude attempt at some deterrent. Yet despite the extra security he still felt wary. Why would anybody want to burgle him? There was nothing of value inside, although an opportune thief would not know that.

His first task, as it was most days when he arrived at the cottage, was to make tea. Forget the natural remedies of the hedgerow and the prophylaxis, tea was the panacea for all ills. He sat on a stool in the window of the lounge and drank the reviving brew, a true elixir of life, watching a fleet of naval warships and a carrier out for daily manoeuvres before heading back for tea themselves. It reminded him of the old adage that Britain conquered the world and forged an Empire because of the Navy, with tea as its secret weapon.

Through the window, the day was clearing with blue sky breaking through the high-level cloud. Shafts of light were being projected onto the ocean, silvery patches sparkling in the ripples of waves, diamante reflections as though the sea was the fabric of earthly existence, a mesmeric force that clears the mind of the onlooker. The Island then became momentarily bathed in sunshine, a spotlight of illumination that played to the gallery, Robert's gallery. It was as though the Island was telling him, 'here I am, come and seek me out, learn my secrets, but beware, for I am not what I seem.' Despite the hypnosis, Robert couldn't understand the message. He wasn't dreaming, yet they were in his mind. But why were his thoughts telling him that? Was he delusional? Perhaps it was the concussion. He had no idea.

He returned to the intruder. His cursory inspection of the rooms had revealed nothing taken. That in itself was strange. Or was it the cottage they were interested in? There were footprints all over the garden. What did they want? He couldn't answer his own questions. His head was still spinning with confusion. Mystery and intrigue were surrounding the cottage and the Island began to hang heavy over his mind. Since the auction there had been so many revelations, so many happenings, that it seemed the curse of the Pirate was wrapping its fingers around him, around his neck, a tourniquet that was denying him oxygen, clouding his mind. It was as though the arrows of his wrath were finding their target and he was slowly being poisoned, his mind unable to think coherently. He needed an antidote. He needed to see Tara.

*   *   *

He spent the rest of the morning removing the kitchen slates. It was a poor substitute for Tara but it dulled his mind, emptied it of thoughts. By lunchtime, he felt pleased. Outside the back door was a stack of slates whilst the kitchen floor was now a layer of dry hardcore. In the afternoon he would remove it, lay a damp-proof membrane and a base of sand and level off the hardcore, before cementing the slates back again. Easy? Property renovation though is never that simple and invariably throws up unexpected problems.

As he went to remove the rubble, after what was a brief lunch break albeit garnished with a pasty and sea view, he hit another hard layer. To his dismay he had encountered another floor beneath the one he had just removed. These were flagstones and of some antiquity. But more than that, when he tapped them a hollow sound resonated in the room as though below this older floor lay a void, an empty space that echoed to his shovel. The flagstones were not as accommodating to lift as the slates, being larger and heavier. Using a metal bar as a lever, he managed to prize the first one free and slide it over revealing an open space and, to his amazement, a flight of stone steps leading to darkness, to what Robert imagined was some sort of oubliette, a place of no return.

When illuminated by a torch, he could see that it was a small chamber which looked like an old cellar rather than some dank dungeon. His mind was now racing ahead of him, for he was thinking back to yesterday's events and the unearthing of the skeleton. He was hoping, in fact praying, that nothing like that was lurking in the chamber, for he doubted that he could take any more shocks.

He removed two more flagstones, enough so that he could make his way down and inspect the chamber. It was small, about the size of a large shed, and just tall enough for him to stand up. It was surprisingly dry inside, particularly so for a structure below ground level, and he could see that it was faced with rough stone, held together with lime mortar and supported a shallow cupola in the centre of the roof. It now had the look of a crypt, although at the far end there was an altar which suggested a place of worship. On inspection he could see it was made of stone with carved icons to the front and sides, not overtly detailed, but having an ingenuous style as though the mason were a novice. But what stood out was a decorated Latin inscription that adorned the top, as though it were meant to be seen and read by those that knelt before God. As Robert wiped away years of dust and traced out the stylised script, it revealed an intriguing conundrum:

DEUS IN NOBIS
IN SALUTEM NOBIS CONFIDIMUS

Despite having a little knowledge of the classical language he couldn't decipher its exact meaning other than it referred to God and that presumably, one must have confidence in something or perhaps salute to somebody. But who or what he had no idea.

In the walls of the chapel were small recesses, perhaps for candles Robert thought, and in one of the niches was a small tin box. It looked old, perhaps pre-war from the picture on the lid which advertised its contents to be lozenges. He tried to prize it open. It was rusted shut. He shook it but nothing rattled inside. It felt too light to contain anything at all but he was, nevertheless, intrigued to ascertain if it was empty.

He climbed out of the crypt into the kitchen, picked up a knife and went into the sitting room to examine the box more closely. In the bright light that was streaming into the room he could now see that the lid was advertising cough sweets, with a man obviously cured of the affliction, since he was smiling with obvious relief. Robert though, was not. He was still having problems trying to open the lid and his expression was of frustration that such an innocuous tin was causing him so much vexation. Finally, using a chisel, he managed to force it open and to his amazement, for he was expecting it to be empty, saw a folded piece of paper inside. He was about to look at it when he heard a knock at the door.

His immediate thought was that it was Tara. He was pleased. But she wouldn't knock, and anyway, she was attending a conference in London. He put the box on the lounge window sill and went to open the door. There on the doorstep, much to his surprise and consternation, was Caroline.

'What are you doing here?' he queried in a rather abrupt tone.

'And nice to see you too,' she responded with equal vehement.

'I mean,' his tone now a little more conciliatory, 'I didn't expect to see you. You've taken me by surprise.'

'Hiding a secret lover? Doing something kinky with that chisel?' she mockingly joked.

'I've been removing a floor in the kitchen.'

'Well, I could see that you weren't having sex, unless that get-up is some sort of role-play.'

This was the familiar Caroline. She hadn't changed, making jokes and innuendo out of ordinary situations. Unless, that is, she had knowledge of Tara, from the bird man or the mysterious intruder, he thought. Perhaps they are one of the same, he a private investigator employed by Caroline to spy on him. No. She wouldn't stoop to that level of deception.

'Well, if that's all you've come for...' he retorted, but was unable to finish as Caroline interjected.

'No, only kidding. Just thought I'd come and see you since I'm at my parents. Make sure you're coping all right on your own. You know how dependent you were upon me to keep you entertained.'

Was she really saying that, Robert thought, although he knew she was the one who organised nights out to the theatre or opera or visits to a new art exhibition. But when he suggested a simple stroll through Regents Park it was met with deaf ears, as though there was no point to it.

'Mind you,' she continued, 'it took quite a bit of finding this place. Had to ask in some café next to the quay. Not exactly Pimlico.'

'That's what I like about it...'

'Aren't you going to invite me in then? Could do with a coffee.'

That's one institution he could thank Caroline for: introducing him to good ground coffee, made fresh, not the bland instant mugs that frequented establishments and which Tara seemed to favour. As he thought about it he was glad she wasn't in town so he could avoid the awkward moment of introductions and then post recriminations from two fronts. The thought of an encounter between Caroline and Tara conjured up a female mud-wrestling contest, one which in a perverse way he would love to witness, as neither would win. It brought a smile to his face, not unnoticed by Caroline.

'Have I amused you?'

'No, just thinking about that time we were crossing the Amazon and our jeep got stuck in mud. We both ended up caked all over in the stuff and looked like, well, demented zombies.'

'What made you think of that?'

'Oh, just that your trousers and boots are covered in mud.'

'Yes, I know,' she said in a brusque tone as though to chide Robert for reminding her. 'I tripped over a tripod of all things, right in the middle of the path. Some clown, and I mean a clown judging by what he was wearing, had put it there. If anything, he looked like a demented zombie, dishevelled and not entirely with it.'

Robert was interested to hear that the bird man was still in the vicinity and active, and even more glad that his supposition was clearly wrong. He was about to ask about Siegfried, but hesitated to collect his thoughts not wanting to cause further upset, but Caroline beat him again.

'We had good times travelling,' she said in a more friendly tone.

They had. But Robert had moved on and so had Caroline. Travel had been a source of cohesion and their memories were a sticking plaster keeping their relationship together. But time cannot always be a healer and his travel memories were fading. They were still visible, but his show-reel only had genuine meaning with her and their separation had tarnished his images as though some corrosive fluid had leaked onto the film and blurred the frames for good.

'Yes, we did have good times and some bad ones. Remember Jaipur?'

'Of course,' she lamented.

But she didn't want to remember the time and nor did Robert.

'Best not, I suppose. In the past. Anyway how are you keeping?'

'Okay,' she said unconvincingly.

Robert knew she wasn't.

'What about Jock?' he asked.

'Haven't seen him for over two weeks and the course hasn't finished yet. I think he was after something, what though, I don't know.'

'Sorry to hear that. He was a bit of a blockhead and you would never have got on travelling together.'

Caroline knew he was right but didn't want to admit it, nor that he had shunned her advances. She went quiet and was summoning courage to say her piece.

'Robert,' she said in a quiet tone, 'I came here today to say something to you.'

'All the way from London?'

'Yes. It's important. I came to say that…I miss you.'

With that one plea, she had stabbed his conscience. She obviously hadn't moved on, or rather Siegfried had moved on and she was left devoid of a punch-bag. He thought that a bit harsh a judgement at this point but that's what he would become again, a release for her failings, her monthly moments. He didn't know what to say.

'That's nice of you to say so,' were all the words he could think of.

'No Robert, I'm not just being nice. I really do miss you.'

Again he was floundering on jagged rocks. He didn't want to stumble, with each pinnacle capable of inflicting a mortal wound in her heart. Perhaps a passive response would signal his predicament.

'Look, I'll go and make a fresh cafeteria. Think I could do with another coffee.'

Robert had converted the living room into a temporary kitchen with a trestle table acting as a worktop containing tea and coffee making facilities, a double-ring stove, microwave oven and a bowl for washing-up that had seen little action for some time. A dining table with two wooden chairs, which occupied the window area so that he could sit and eat whist looking out on the sea view, contained an array of unwashed mugs, plates and opened tins and packets and looked as though the remains of a recent banquet had yet to be cleared, which was becoming a source of exasperation at his domestic inertia.

Despite the disarray the room felt like a place of sanctuary where he could collect his thoughts and decide how to respond. Should he tell her about Tara? He didn't want to drag her into the conversation, not through cowardice, more because he was a gentleman to Caroline's feelings. He made a fresh cafeteria and prepared for his ordeal.

On returning to the lounge ready to confront Caroline with a white lie, he found her examining the paper from the metal box, her professional curiosity having got the better of her emotional outburst. She was engrossed in the discovery.

'I found that...'

'It's interesting,' she replied, not lifting her head from the paper and seemingly not concerned where Robert had found it.

The paper, once unfolded, looked old being ragged at the edges with both the writing and outline of a coastline, fading. It depicted Looe and the Island from, as far as Robert could ascertain, Plaidy to the east of Looe to as far as Portnadler bay, and superimposed on top of the map were dotted lines. They made no sense to Robert.

'What's interesting about it?' he enquired. 'It just shows Looe and the Island.'

'That's true. What's interesting are these lines. They're there for some reason, but what?' she said in a questioning tone, a rhetorical question which she was trying to answer in her mind.

'Just a doodle, perhaps,' he added to feel involved.

'No, I don't think so. Whoever draws a map does so for a reason. These lines are the key, I'm sure. Where did you find it?'

Robert first showed Caroline the gravestones outside which really excited her. 'It confirms my assertion that the cottage was built on an ancient chapel and that the field above must have contained old medieval stitches.'

'That's not the half of it,' he remarked, quite excited himself at showing her the chamber for he knew she would be astounded and speechless.

He led her into the kitchen and as soon as she saw the steps descend down she gave out an elated gasp that left her dumbstruck. She took Robert's torch and edged down, shining the light in every nook and crevice, marvelling at the sight that greeted her. This was, for her, a revelation, something which she could never have imagined to unearth in a lifetime of study. If she had missed Robert she didn't show it. This was her new infatuation.

'It's an undercroft or crypt that has been turned into a small chapel,' she said and went over to the altar.

'What do the inscriptions say?'

'The first says "trust in the Lord". The second line reads "trust in salvation", give or take a few inflexions.'

'What does that mean? Salvation from what?' asked Robert.

'Not sure at the moment. But I have an idea.'

She was looking at the back of the altar, putting her hand near the edge and trying to feel something.

'I think there's something behind this altar,' she slowly expounded feeling right around the edge. 'Help me move it, would you.'

The altar was heavy. No amount of effort could move it. Robert fetched the crowbar to act as a lever. By slowly edging the altar first one way and then another, they soon had it clear of the wall to reveal what was a small definable area, about three feet square, containing modern concrete blocks.

'Wasn't expecting that,' said Robert.

'I had my suspicions. It's obviously an entrance to something,' was Caroline's reply. 'All we need do is break through.'

Robert wasn't sure about the 'we' and didn't want to go headlong into something he knew nothing about, even though Caroline seemed to be on the scent of a discovery. He protested, but was soon chipping away at the concrete blocks.

It was easier than he had thought. The blocks crumbled away readily with a few hammer blows and he realised they were probably mundic brick, having weathered over the years from moisture. Within an hour he had made an entrance big enough to squeeze through. Caroline instructed Robert to enter, declining herself, saying there needed to be someone on the crypt side of the entrance, just in case something happened. That gave Robert confidence!

He entered. A damp musty odour, the smell of death, emanated from the black void as though warning him not to venture any further. But egged on by Caroline, he did. His torch wasn't bright and barely penetrated the dark, although it was enough for him to see that the walls were roughly hewn out of the rock, striated from the mark of tools, whilst on the ground accumulated layers of dust were a testament to its years of isolation. He deduced it was a tunnel that gently sloped downhill, starting a descent into what seemed like hell. The blackness heightened his senses and he felt as though the confined space was crushing him with the weight of time and that a thousand eyes were watching him, his face feeling every nuance as he inched forward, unearthly shapes in the beam of light confusing his mind into believing that skeletal phantoms inhabited every crack in the rock, each one hiding a mask of death.

The torch was beginning to dim and further exploration seemed unwise without proper lighting. He was about to turn around and return to the crypt when he tripped over and fell prostrate to the ground. His torch went out. Only the faint glow of the entrance and Caroline's ghostly form could be seen, a beacon in the blackness of space that would guide him to safety. He fumbled around for the torch but caught hold of something long and smooth and shuddered in fright at what it might be; at least it wasn't alive he told himself. And then he felt another similar object and another, finally grasping the familiar feel of the torch after what seemed like sifting through the debris of a cave dwellers meal. He switched the torch on and to his horror found himself reliving his worst nightmare, staring face to face with a skull and its empty eye sockets. With trust in his thoughts, Robert looked towards the entrance for salvation from the unearthly tomb.

20

Robert looked aghast at the image staring into his eyes, the torchlight shining into the sockets of the skull making the cranium glow like a Halloween mask. It sent a shiver right through him, for he felt that he was facing an accuser who was pronouncing judgement upon him. And that judgement was retribution.

For a moment he was left dumbfounded and only regained his senses on hearing the familiar voice of Caroline.

'Are you alright Robert?' she said with a degree of concern.

He had seen enough and wanted the image to disappear. He switched the torch off, discarded it, and began to crawl back on hands and knees shaken by his unearthly encounter and wanting a good stiff drink, George's rum chaser.

'Yes, yes, I'm okay,' he said emerging from the tunnel.

'You sure? Look as though you've seen the dead.'

'That's exactly what I've seen,' he exclaimed, now standing and dusting himself down, much to the chagrin of Caroline.

'Don't be over dramatic, it's just the dark getting the better of your senses,' she said in her condescending way, as though she would have come out with decorum and not made a fuss.

'No, I really have seen a dead body. Well a skeleton. Well no, a skull. But I'm sure I felt the bones of this dead person.'

'You're joking of course.'

'No I am not,' he said in monosyllabic tones to emphasise the reality of his supposed fantasy.

Caroline was now beginning to believe him. She peered inside the tunnel to see if she could confirm his assertion, but found just blackness.

'Really?' she enquired, still not entirely convinced.

'Yes, really.'

'It's exciting,' she uttered.

'Exciting!' exclaimed Robert, wanting her to know that it was far from exciting for him.

They had retreated to the lounge once more and Robert was sitting in his armchair by the window with Caroline kneeling by his side looking concerned for his welfare but feeling elated by the discovery. She had made some tea and he was clasping the mug for comfort, wondering what to do. Caroline was delighted about the new revelation: gravestones indicated a burial but a skeleton confirmed it.

'Was it a tunnel?' she asked again.

'I think it was. From what I could tell it's been hacked out and was falling away downhill, suggesting it went further. But I couldn't see and then fell over this heap of bones. That skull gave me a fright, I can tell you. Right next to me, its eye sockets staring me in the face and its jaw open as though it were laughing at me for my stupidity.'

'But no harm done,' interjected Caroline.

'No. But I'm left with a big headache. Ancient gravestones in the garden. A hole in the kitchen floor. A chamber, which was probably some sort of crypt, and a probable tunnel. On top of all that, I now have two skeletons!'

'Look, what I meant was you're unharmed and we have unearthed an important discovery that, as far as I'm aware, does not exist anywhere else. It's an academic goldmine.'

Caroline wasn't a business woman but she was an expert on medieval studies and boundaries, with a broad knowledge of archaeology and history, and had soon come up with a working hypothesis to confirm her assessment. The lines on the map showed the route of tunnels from the Island to the chapel on the mainland and hence to the cottage, or rather the old chapel that stood there. For she thought it was an old escape route for the monks who lived and worshipped there in the dark ages of the ninth and tenth centuries, when Christianity was establishing strongholds in the country. Islands were a favoured retreat, with Lindisfarne in Northumberland being the most famous example. St Michael's Mount would be an important one in the South West, and Looe Island would be an ideal place for a satellite monastery.

At this time, England was under siege from Viking raiders. To have a means of escaping any incursion would be wise. Early Christian persecution was widespread and led to ingenious means to escape a premature death. Rome is renowned for its catacombs, a haven beneath the city hewn own of rock and shows the extent that believers would go to, to continue their faith.

'It is not as fantastic as it sounds,' she said, 'and quite plausible to conceive of tunnels here. The blocked up part of the chamber is probably an entrance to one,' she summarised.

Robert was intrigued by her theory and impressed she had hypothesised it so quickly. But a tunnel here, high above the cliff stretching for half a mile to the Island? That did sound too fantastic to be true. It was, he thought, little more than a tunnel for storing smuggled goods, the crypt acting as a cellar would be an ideal camouflage to the operation, easily deceiving the revenue men. Perhaps the Pirate used to be a smuggler and was discovered and had to escape to sea. There, he carried on in the same vein, only with piracy. Robert considered his theory, considerably more plausible than Caroline's. As for the skeleton, he could not explain that.

He expounded his theory but it was met with a cursory nod of approval, which Robert knew meant she had dismissed it. He looked at her. She was thinking.

'Look Robert, I don't want to leave you in this predicament, but I've got to get going shortly to catch the London train.'

'Oh and I thought you were enjoying yourself.'

'That's unfair Robert. I wouldn't go as far as that. It is, though, an interesting discovery. Who knows where it might lead!'

'Indeed,' he said knowing that she had probably already mapped out the future.

Caroline had. She knew the full implication of the discovery and it would cement her place in the academic world. There were a few years work ahead but the rewards could be counted in a professional paper, perhaps even a book, a professorship and maybe even lucrative lecture tours. She didn't want this opportunity to be hijacked by anybody else.

'I must say, you've found a lovely place here and in such a stunning location. I've always dreamt of living by the sea.'

'Really, thought you liked London.'

'I do. But it's just a place to work and an empty place without you.'

Robert thought this the opportune moment to tell him about Tara and how he had moved on.

'Look Caroline...'

She didn't give him a chance.

'What I suggest you do is to still relay the kitchen floor, but cover the entrance to the crypt with a manhole cover. That way you'll still be able to gain access. And as for the skeleton, don't inform anybody. It's probably centuries old and as such is an archaeological find beyond the remit of the police. Put the bones in a sealed box and take them over to my parents' place where they can be stored in one of their outbuildings. I'll arrange for a colleague to come and collect them for forensic investigation. In the meantime, I'll do some research to see what I can dig up, so to speak.'

'You don't have to. This is my problem.'

'Oh but I do,' she said making it clear that he didn't have any option. 'And don't go investigating the tunnel until I return, it may be too dangerous.'

Robert was pleased that she had said that, even though he had no intention of such an investigation, not without backup. Caroline kissed him on the cheek and said goodbye. He followed her to the front door. As she left, she turned around and looked deep into his eyes.

'Before, what I said, I really do mean it.'

'Mean what?' he said, knowing full well what she meant but wanting her to say it again.

'That I miss you. I really do Robert. Jock was just an infatuation. We never slept together.' She paused and then with heart felt intonation said, 'It's you I love. Have done, ever since that day in the Riad.'

He watched her disappear down the steps leaving him in a daze, a state of confusion that had overcome him. Those last few words had plucked a few heartstrings and the melody that played within him was of happy harmonious times together. He still had feelings for her. Admired her. Admired her beauty and intellect, a combination which he found irresistible when they first met and which he still did. He now felt guilty. Guilty that he was having an affair with Tara, even though he didn't love her. Caroline had now produced a few notes of doubt in his mind.

He decided to take a walk to clear his head of claustrophobia. He went back down to Lammana to see if there was any sign of some entrance to a tunnel. He knew there would be none. He sat down on the bench and considered Caroline's thesis. Could there possibly be a tunnel out there, Robert thought as he looked at the Island, built by monks all those centuries ago? It sounded preposterous. Yet Caroline would not venture such a theory unless there was some evidence, which he had to admit there was, at least from his cottage. But from here, from the mainland chapel to the Island? Surely not?

He walked on along the coast path towards Talland Bay. At first it was a wide grassy sward in which a few cattle were grazing, but after a gate it gave way to a flat, well-worn path, bounded on both sides by high hedgerow. It was short lived for a stream had cut a declivity through the landscape and as it reached the cliff, tumbled over creating a mini waterfall. A wooden footbridge spanned the gully and a side path took him down onto an enclosed beach which, after the previous night's storm, contained large deposits of seaweed already beginning to exude the familiar odour of the sea. The tide was out and the limited expanse of grey sand and rock was a tonic of tranquillity for a mind that was wrestling with its conscience.

It was now late in the day. Even so, the beach wasn't entirely his own with a family engaged in playing with their daughter, building a sandcastle in a clearing amongst the rocks and decorating it with seaweed and shells. They looked happy and content in their world of family life. Robert conjured an image of such a scene with Caroline, but could not see her reduced to the level of filling a bucket with sand. He thought perhaps he was being too harsh on her and that motherhood would bring changes, but as much as he tried to reconcile it his overwhelming thought was that they had had the chance themselves and she had vetoed it. But for all her faults she had come to see him, which in itself must have been a considerable effort, to admit, albeit without saying so directly, that she was wrong.

Rather than retrace his steps he walked back along the base of the cliff which from the beach where he had just been was about fifty feet tall, gradually decreasing in height as he progressed towards the concrete wall of Hannafore. The cliff face itself was quite friable, with small landslips every so often. This was a place where the sea was winning the battle of erosion. A recent slump contained the remains of a fence, once part of the coastal path, and a large tree that had succumbed to the cliff fall. Debris was everywhere: wood, plastic bottles, rope, an old lobster pot, even the remains of an old refrigerator, the detritus of society. Hannafore had had its fair share of seaweed and washed up flotsam. The concrete promenade was covered in kelp, wrack and all assortments of marine vegetation as well as shingle, making it unpleasant and quite slippery to walk along. The beach was no better. It was a beachcombers paradise and their mantra, 'everything returns' was evident along the foreshore. Much of it would be washed away by the next high tide, but would return once again, probably further up the coast where the effect of long shore drift slowly and inextricably shifts sand, pebbles, and human refuse along a cycle of ocean current. Robert breathed in the sea air. He looked at the debris. His head still felt muddled as though he were on a conveyer-belt of emotion, where one revelation was succeeded by yet another and there was no way of getting off.

21

Several days had passed since the discovery of the crypt and tunnel. In that time Robert had boxed the skeletons, taken the bones to Caroline's parents and had laid a new kitchen floor, complete with a heavy inspection cover so that only the overtly curious, with accompanying levers, would consider lifting it.

He hadn't heeded Caroline's concern about the tunnel and had ventured an exploratory examination, but only as far as light could still be seen from the crypt entrance: he wanted daylight as an accomplice. As she had suggested, it was a tunnel heading towards the old ruined chapel because it descended further, beyond the reach of a more powerful spotlight torch. It would not have been difficult to construct for the slates were heavily bedded and broke away very easily, so that a few men, monks with time to excavate the rock, could make considerable progress. Caroline's theory seemed to be correct. Robert did indeed have a tunnel.

Tara was due back today. Her conference had been quite timely with the unexpected appearance of Caroline and the underground discoveries. He didn't want Tara to know about any of it and so her absence gave him time to conceal Looe's own catacombs. An announcement might have local historians and, most likely, all and sundry making appointments for private viewings. It could even become a tourist attraction if Caroline's thesis was correct. No, he wanted it to be kept quiet and had made sure of such by constructing an antechamber between the two floor levels and packing the space with insulation, easy enough to remove but an effective deterrent muffling the hollow sound to any casual observer.

The day was still early when he awoke, not in the flat but in his own cottage. He had purchased a new bed, mattress and some linen in order to spend his first night there and wake up to a sea view and the sound of the waves breaking on the beach. It was a beautiful morning and he had watched the sun rise over Rame Head, not the horizon of the ocean any more for it was now on its northerly track until the summer solstice.

It had cast a glow across the bay and into the bedroom, as though welcoming him to his idyll. The sea was serenely calm like a mill pond in the bay, yet he could hear the gently lapping waves on the shore from his bed, above which was a delightful heterophony of song from two chaffinches, each one proclaiming their melody to the other until one of them gave in leaving the victor to sing a winning tune. This was accompanied by a virtuoso blackbird, declaring its own territory until the bird song coalesced with the lapping of waves, an indistinct composition of natural tones.

It made a change from the cacophony of noise that the gulls made most mornings in the flat facing the harbour. It bore the full force of their early altercations, shrieking what seemed like raucous insults and behaving as though Looe were a remote rocky outcrop for their own use, which of course it was to them. He didn't dislike the gulls. They were as much a part of the maritime landscape as the cliffs or beaches and were even quite angelic when perched quietly on some roof top or with their heads tucked under some feathers. Rather, it was the mellifluous murmurings of garden and woodland birds that were a preferable emollient to the ears and soul at six o'clock in the morning.

Breakfast was a feast of the English kind. He sat outside and enjoyed the privilege of his endeavours whilst listening to the diminuendo of chords from the dawn chorus being replaced by the crescendo of gulls as they dispersed from the town and harbour to seek feeding opportunities. Only missing at the cottage was good company. But whose? Caroline's surprise visit had ignited a flame of emotion. Tara's was still burning bright, bringing a glow of anticipation at her return. They weren't a couple yet, as neither had expressed their undying love for one another, but there was a burgeoning relationship founded on sexual attraction which for the moment was exciting and enjoyable.

Despite that, Robert wasn't entirely convinced that sex was a basis for a long term relationship, and when he first met both Madeleine and Caroline intellect and mutual desire for travel and culture were the bedrock of their love. There didn't seem that same foundation with Tara. Nevertheless, he was looking forward to seeing her.

Robert was just going back inside when he heard a tentative voice call out 'Hello.' Robert turned to see it was the birdwatcher. 'Good morning sir,' he said as he continued to enter the garden. 'Please excuse me. I hope I'm not disturbing you.'

'No, just having a leisurely breakfast in the sun.'

'Lovely spot for an *al fresco petit déjeuner.*'

'Ah oui. J'aime manger en plein air,' Robert replied wondering if this birdman was a little weird.

'Pardon?' came his reply, in English.

'Yes, I love eating outdoors.'

'Quite. I hope you don't mind me interrupting your breakfast, but I wanted to make an enquiry.'

'Yes,' said Robert as though agreeing to his request and intrigued as to what he could possibly want from him.

'First, let me introduce myself. My name is Ian Gould and I'm an officer with Her Majesty's Revenue and Customs.'

He showed Robert his identification and sat down on the bench. He was still wearing the ridiculous outfit, befitting a person wishing to announce himself as slightly eccentric and not to be taken seriously. Robert offered him some coffee, which he readily accepted, and without his telescope or tripod, he sat there looking at Looe Island through his binoculars.

He was a tall man, not quite as tall as Robert though, but more thick-set with a boyish complexion which denied his age. In one of his multitude of pockets on his jacket he pulled out a packet of cigarettes and proceeded to light up whilst Robert was inside making the coffee. On returning with two mugs of instant coffee it was the first thing he noticed and it somewhat angered him, this disrespectful piece of social etiquette, which was tempered by a glance at the cigarette packet, the same brand as discarded the other day. Was he the intruder?

Robert offered him his coffee, upon which the bird man commented, 'hope you don't mind me smoking,' with an air of confidence that it would be rude to decline.

'Well, so long as the smoke doesn't waft my way.'

The man, sensing Robert's disapproval, stubbed the cigarette out and proceeded to explain his visit.

He was doing some undercover work, which Robert found amusing, investigating an anonymous tip-off that there were some illegal activities taking place on the Island and he was making observations and taking notes and photographic evidence to back this claim. He wasn't able to disclose any further information other than so far he hadn't witnessed anything unusual nor had any evidence to substantiate the allegation. His visit to Robert was to enlist another pair of eyes. His superiors had agreed the action.

'You've just recently purchased the property, haven't you?' he suddenly declared.

'Yes, about six weeks ago.'

'Lovely location and with a good view of the Island. Have you noticed anything unusual?'

'Can't say I have, other than seeing you a couple of times,' replied Robert.

'Oh yes, I see, my disguise. It's based on reverse psychology where stating the obvious deflects from what somebody, especially those you're trying to deceive, might otherwise conclude. In other words, a complete stranger dressed in this absurd outfit must surely be a birdwatcher, standing out like a sore thumb and therefore being regarded as a harmless idiot.'

Robert couldn't agree more.

'What sort of things are you interested in?' he asked with a degree of scepticism as to the whole business.

'Oh, out of the ordinary events such as unusual sightings of fishing boats, people on the Island, night time activity. Things like that.'

'Now that you mention it, I did see a boat full of men go out to the Island the other day.'

'Can you remember how many men and when exactly?'

'No, but it was about a couple of weeks ago. Oh, and there was a canoeist a few days ago paddling round the Island.'

'Yes, I saw him too. A red canoe.'

'No, yellow I think.'

'Good,' replied the man, knowing full well it was yellow, wanting to test Robert's powers of observation and his honesty.

'Well, if you do notice anything else, please let me know. If you could make a note of the event and what time and day that would be most useful. Remember, events like the canoeist may not seem relevant, but put that with other unrelated sightings then patterns can emerge. If you have anything I'll be around for the foreseeable future.'

'Okay,' said Robert, wondering whether he should involve himself further.

'Much obliged to you Mr Colliver.'

Before he left, Robert made an enquiry of his own.

'Were you here the other day?'

'I often pass your cottage, to and from the town,' he replied.

'What I mean is, did you come and knock on the door?'

'No. Why do you ask?'

'Oh, no reason.'

But the bird man, realised there was one.

'Did you find some evidence of somebody here?'

'Well, yes. I did.'

'I can assure you, it was not me. That's the sort of information I'm keen to know about. What day was it?'

Robert told him about the footprints, but not about the assailant or that he had been attacked. He wondered afterwards if he should have been so forthcoming about the intruder and even wondered if the bird man was him. Robert had found a cigarette. He did smoke. But as he glanced at his feet, although he was wearing boots, they looked smaller than the footprints. No, it wasn't the bird man.

He departed, thanking Robert for his help and being most courteous, but leaving him somewhat bemused. He knew my name, he thought. And on top of everything else, was he now to become a government spy? The visit of the bird man had soured his breakfast, although the taste of bacon and eggs still lingered in his mouth. He had one more mug of tea and then made his way down to the quayside to catch the ferry. He needed to get out.

The ferry ride across the harbour lasted little more than a minute but had the feel of an epic sea crossing as the boat, a wooden clad dingy about twenty feet long, much like *Lady Jane* with the helmsman standing at the back steering the tiller with one hand and operating the throttle with the other, arced across the harbour missing a small trawler making its way out on an ebb tide. It was the same red vessel from the other day when he was in the café. A flotilla of swans followed in the wake of the ferry boat, and as Robert alighted the steps on the other quayside they were rewarded with some bread. It attracted a group of juvenile gulls, resulting in a feeding frenzy which only subsided when all the bread had been gobbled up.

Robert couldn't help but think that he was back now on enemy territory, especially after the disclosures of George and John. Since he was there and it was a lovely day and having spent the last two inside up to his neck in concrete and dirt, not to mention the remains of two poor souls, he decided to air his lungs and take a look at the venue for the forthcoming Pirate Day.

First he made his way along the seafront where several people were already enjoying the beach albeit still clothed, although some hardy octogenarians, by the look of them, were about to brave the water. He passed a closed beachside café located just before the concrete blocks that protect the cliff and promenade. Several couples and some retired individuals were making use of the cubist montage using them as seats, some reading newspapers and books whilst others were laying down, worshiping the sun. One old woman, who wouldn't have looked out of place a century ago, with a flowing skirt and shawl, had clearly seen too much sun for her skin was an intense brown and so wrinkled that it looked like the hide from of an elephant. She said hello to Robert and smiled, revealing a perfect set of teeth that any model would be proud to possess.

The steps up from the concrete sea wall to the coast path were steep. He counted over one hundred and it must have been a rise of almost the same height in feet. He rested for a while, looking down on the arc of sand below, the banjo pier and the hotels and houses on the west side of the harbour entrance. He could discern the old coastal path making its way up from the square in West Looe but couldn't see his cottage, it being further around and higher. He was glad. That was one reason why he liked it; isolation from the rest of the town, an island in a sea of conformity where he could be himself and not have to maintain an accepted standard.

Having recovered from the steps, he continued along the coast path, east towards Milendreath before another path branched uphill again to the Wooldown. It was an unremarkable field that was convexly contoured, quite steep in places as it dipped towards the cliff, but did have one redeeming feature: the well preserved remains of a Second World War anti-aircraft gun emplacement. It was a reminder that this stretch of coast, being close to Plymouth and occupied Europe, needed such defences. But as Robert circled it, he was disgusted to find it reduced to an open-air bar containing cigarette stubs and spent beer cans as well a used lighter and other discarded items, despite a litter bin being located nearby. What a testimony to an important artefact of British history with a selfish minority showing little respect, he mumbled to himself, as he picked up the rubbish and deposited it in a nearby bin.

The field he wanted was back towards the town, accessed through a gap in a hedge. It opened to a wide grassy avenue at the end of which was a beacon, a brazier mounted on a metal pole whilst either side were two disused cannons from the age of sailing ships, with concrete blocks acting as their gun carriages. They were pointing out to sea, as though expecting an assault from that direction. Robert looked around but could see nothing else other than, on the distant horizon across the other side of the harbour, the observation tower that was in the field above his cottage.

Robert retraced his steps back to the coast path, carried on for a few hundred yards and then descended down some awkward steps to Plaidy beach. It was deserted. It was perfect. Not for families, for much of it was rocky with little sand for youngsters to enjoy unless they liked rock pools. They were numerous, from small beach-ball size to ones where a swim would be possible, each showcasing a myriad of jewel-like life; pink coralline seaweedand bright green dulse alongside coloured anemones and snails with helical shells, some banded yellow with others displaying nacreous lustres. Darting in the water were rock guppies and a host of unknown invertebrates, each living their lives in a temporary world where the boundary was the vast ocean itself when the sea reclaimed its domain.

Robert sat down to listen to the peace, with only the gentle lapping of the waves, the cries of some oystercatchers and the pee-wit of rock pipits to break the silence. Pied wagtails were darting in and out of the rocks and exposed seaweed looking for food, whilst beyond the expanse of rocks two cormorants flew in synchronisation, low over the water their wings skimming the surface creating a wake, like the vapour trail of two jets.

The sun was warm, quite high in the sky as he squinted in its direction. He removed his shirt and lay back to absorb its energy and feel its vigour, under the branches of a tamarisk tree. It reminded him of the Greek Isles and how he and Madeleine camped under them in the summer heat, talking, kissing, planning and generally living a carefree life in an age when innocence was to be found in such simple pleasures.

A small group of whimbrel interrupted him as they flew in from the town and alighted by the strandline. Their long downward-curved beaks, reminiscent of moorland curlews, soon began to forage amongst the seaweed for sandflies, the flea-like creatures jumping as their cover was disturbed. Suddenly they flew off as a heron came crashing in, landing by the water's edge after bigger prey, crabs and small fish that inhabit the intertidal zone. For Robert, thirty years on from carefree innocence, the simple pleasures in front of him were anything but that. Within the rock pools and for the birds and other animals and beyond his horizon, life was a struggle, a struggle for survival where only the fittest win and pass their genes onto the next generation.

Even the breaking surf dragged his conscious thoughts. Without a soul in sight he could have been sitting on a beach hundred years ago, thousands, perhaps millions of years, before homo sapiens existed to contemplate philosophical conjecture, the same molecules of water producing that familiar noise as a wave reached its tipping point and expounded its fervour in a cascade of released energy. Ever since life existed, even before, the perpetual ocean has been pounding its elemental force, a rhythmic motion where life was created in that primordial soup.

He sat there for almost an hour contemplating life. His life. Where it fitted. What would it have been like with Madeleine? No relationship conflicts. No pirates. No smuggling. No ancient chapels and underground tunnels. No mysterious government agents. He would have children, living a simple life in their idyll, his genes passed onto another generation.

Robert couldn't say that about his present life. It seemed a struggle, not for survival, but to make sense of the bizarre, the unusual events and happenings surrounding his cottage. Was it tainted with an ancient curse? He was beginning to realise that perhaps his destiny, rather than to have offspring, was to solve some long standing feud or riddle that had surfaced when he arrived and by doing so exorcise the curse once and for all. But he didn't really know what was going on. Illegal activities? Smuggling? A pirates curse? He couldn't make sense of anything.

He got up and wandered on further, to where some concrete steps scaled a promontory that separated the beach he was on from the main arc of sand adjacent to the Banjo pier. He looked back and noticed a large fissure in the cliff face at beach level and went over to investigate. It was an entrance to a tunnel. He couldn't see how far it went in but the walls were just like those he had seen before. He needed a torch. He would come back. But as he climbed over the steps and onto the cubist sea wall, he realised that it couldn't possibly lead anywhere being so obvious an entrance and one that would certainly be known. And anyway, he needed a tunnel entrance on his side of Looe.

Robert decided to walk the long way round over the bridge to West Looe and so proceeded down one of the parallel side streets he had so hopelessly got lost in, when searching for the library. No sooner than he was in a narrow alley, hemmed in by houses, he noticed Tara coming out of a cottage. She was some way distant and hadn't spotted him. He was about to call out to her when a young man came out behind her. He withdrew behind a flight of steps that led to a first floor holiday flat hoping that she hadn't seen him. She hadn't. What was she doing? She was supposed to be in London and not back until later. Perhaps she had come back early and was showing a client a property.

They talked for few moment, the man making some hand gestures as though in disagreement with whatever she was saying and then they went their separate ways, she back into town and he towards Robert. He emerged from his hiding place and walked towards the mystery man and as they approached each other Robert could see that the man had a face festooned with macules which masked his age and was sporting a slight limp on his left leg. It was the man from the auction. As they passed each other, their eyes briefly met, revealing an expression of familiarity on the man's face as he bid Robert good day. Robert reciprocated, and they both went their separate ways.

He purchased the few items he needed from a supermarket and bakery along the main street, and then called into the Estate Agents, expecting to see Tara. Instead, there was a young man sitting at her desk.

'Could I speak to Tara please?' Robert asked.

'I'm afraid she's on holiday at this present time. Can I help?' he said in a well-spoken Home Counties voice.

'No. It's personal. How long has she been on holiday?'

'For the past four days, I believe.'

'When is she due back in the office?'

'Oh not until next week. Are you sure I can't help?'

'No, really. Thank you anyway.'

As Robert was walking out the door, the man got up to open it, a chivalrous act as though Robert were a woman.

'I'll let TT know you called in. Whom shall I say?' said the man.

'TT?' queried Robert.

'Oh sorry, Tara Trevellick.'

Robert left in a state of numbness, not giving his name.

22

Robert came out of the estate agents dazed and confused. He stood on the bridge looking down the harbour out to sea. Just as on that first day, the tide was out and the boats were lifeless, without water. He felt their dilemma. He counted the arches again, hoping the bridge had acquired another arch so as to invalidate the tale of the smugglers and thereby rescind the whole story that had been recounted to him. There were still seven.

It was warmer now, much warmer than before, but he felt a chill run through his bones at the name Trevellick. For all he knew Tara was a descendant of William Trevellick, an alleged murderer and a man prepared to see innocent men hang for a crime they didn't commit. And he had encountered the name Trevellick already. It now appeared that there was more to this family and he knew the place to seek answers.

The Smugglers Arms was no different than his last foray. Sitting at the bar were the three amigos, seemingly not having moved from his last visit, in the same positions, each supporting a pint of ale and smoking pipes and once again, clouding the atmosphere. The landlord though, was sporting a different nautical outfit, this time a pirate captain. George was in his snug. Robert ordered ale with rum chaser and a beer for himself. The men looked at him with the same disdain, as though he had invaded their space yet again and that a third time might mean walking the plank or being lynched from a yardarm. Perhaps it was in his imagination, but they were not friendly and murmured amongst themselves as he was waiting for the order, making him feel uncomfortable, self-conscious at his slim, inadequate frame.

Robert was relieved when the landlord had finally served his order and he wasted little time in escaping to George's snug.

'Hello George,' he said as he handed him his ale.

'Here at last,' he mumbled as though Robert was late and that he should have been there days ago.

They sat opposite each other in silence for a few moments, Robert supping his beer and the old man downing his chaser and then coughing as though he had swallowed the wrong way, disguising a bronchial condition which seemed to have got worse. Robert tentatively got onto the question he had come to ask.

'The Trevellicks, what do you know about them?'

'The Trevellicks? They're a rum lot. Quite an odd bunch.'

'What do you mean?'

'Well, they're a family that goes way back. A family with history. You'll find them all buried in the graveyard up at St. Martin's, the church you see as you approach Looe. Can't miss them for falling over their headstones. They've got fingers in all sorts of pies; the fish market, the town council, they own several restaurants and I think a couple of hotels. Oh, and that trawler too. They seem to have the ability to vet any new venture in the town, anything that would compromise their operations. Take the café owner...'

'Yes, he told me about his experience,' interjected Robert.

'He did, did he?' George said, somewhat surprised, and continued, 'You wouldn't think they'd be so successful from the look of them. I don't know them all, but there's a pot-faced chap with a limp. Had that from birth. There's a crazy individual who thinks he's in Hawaii wearing only shorts all year and one of those multi-coloured T-shirts. The clan is headed by a mad old matriarch. Haven't seen her for donkey's years.'

'What about Tara Trevellick?'

'Oh, she's one of the clan, the normal one who manages the estate agents opposite the bridge. They own that too. That's only a side-line I reckon, no doubt so they can control those who want to move into the town. You know the reputation of that profession. And she has a reputation herself.'

'For what?' asked Robert with the utmost interest.

'Apparently, she's quite a man-eater. Not that I have any knowledge of that. Wouldn't be interested in a grizzled old goat like me. Nothing to offer her. She's like those female praying mantis creatures that mates with the male and then eats them after they've served their purpose. Mind you, I don't blame her. Who wouldn't, with such beauty. No man is good enough for her I reckon.'

Robert was shocked to hear this and couldn't believe George was talking about the same person. No, surely not, she seemed so genuine and sincere, not the Tara he knew.

George continued. 'Her father was a smuggler...'

'A smuggler?' questioned Robert in a surprised tone.

'Yes, a smuggler. He was part of a gang smuggling large quantities of cannabis from North Africa, out of Tangiers I believe, into Talland Bay, along the coast from St George's Island. They got caught one night. The father, the skipper of a converted trawler, escaped capture, but was drowned when his craft was sunk by a coastguard vessel. The trawler was blacked out for the operation and didn't see it, not until it was too late. He stood no chance. Some say it was the coastguard's fault, they not displaying their navigation lights. They were though.'

'How can you be sure?' interjected Robert, wanting Tara's explanation of the events to be true.

'I was there. On the church tower, keeping a lookout. Or supposed to be. I clearly saw the coastguard vessel with its lights on.'

'Did you get caught?'

'No, I stayed up on the church tower and escaped the police. Thirteen of the group were not so fortunate. They were tried and convicted in London at The Old Bailey, I think. It was quite an event, modern day Cornish smuggling. That was the last time I did such a thing. Not proud of it, I can tell you.'

George looked into his pint with a sign of resignation that he was indeed a repentant man, and rather than a court of law he had been his own judge and found himself guilty.

'Not much else I can say. You need to speak to Arthur. As I said before, he's the one who knows everything.'

'Thanks George. That was most enlightening. Can I get you another ale?'

'Don't mind if I do. Before you go, there's one thing I forgot to tell you the other day.'

He shuffled about in his seat, as though this piece of information was a new chapter in his tales and that Robert should take note and listen very carefully.

'It's about the Revenue Officer, William Trevellick. I told you it was he who killed one of his own men.'

'Yes,' said Robert.

'Well, it was a man called Joseph Kitt, he killed. He was betrothed to Trevellick's daughter. He discovered that Kitt had raped a girl from the town and that she had a child by him and that he had disowned the girl and child. They were left destitute and without hope, with the consequence that she took her own life and that of the child. Trevellick didn't want this man to marry his daughter. But she was very much in love with him, blinded by his good looks and charm. To Trevellick he was outspoken, perhaps brash, had no real prospects, with a wandering eye for the ladies. He forbade his daughter to marry him but she would not listen. Fearing she would marry in secret he arranged for Kitt to join him on a smuggling raid, which he was only too keen to do. Trevellick killed him in the confusion of the arrests, blaming it on the ringleader. It was one way of ridding himself of Kitt and the smugglers at the same time. He had already organised for them to be tried outside the county and knew they would all hang.'

'Where does that fit in with the Pirate?' asked Robert, not sure of its importance, but nevertheless fascinated by the tale.

George looked towards the bar, making sure the three wise men were not listening. He nodded to Robert. He looked as well and indicated it was alright to continue.

'The girl in question, the one raped, was the Pirate's niece. Her mother and grandmother, Colliver's mother, were dead. They had been evicted from the cottage, driven out, and she was the only one alive, struggling to survive in a community that reviled the family.

They believed her to be a witch and feared harming her, lest they resurrect the wrath of the Pirate. His exploits were well-known and although he was dead, his ghost was very much real, a phantom that could invoke death. So they left her alone. But she took her own life which was salvation for the townsfolk. The day Trevellick burnt the cottage and the Pirate's curse was invoked, they knew he would return to seek revenge. To them, his reputation for cruelty was very real and they feared for their lives, feared that he would smite them all down in retribution. Any unusual death, storm, or even a strange event was attributed to his wrath. That became reality only a few years later when a tsunami hit the town flooding many homes and drowning folk, including children. Happened all over Cornwall. It was a result of an earthquake off the coast of Portugal, in 1755 I think. To the people of Looe it was the curse and so his reputation grew. Still exists today in the minds of some.'

Robert wasn't quite sure why he had been told this tale and how it affected him, although it was intriguing and explained the actions of the men who were the central characters in a miscarriage of justice over two and a half centuries ago.

'How do you know all this? It was a long time ago.'

'It's been the tale passed down in my family, along with the hip flask. I've had the secret for too many years now. Alfred knows of it. But we're both old. Not long for this life. You are to be the keeper of this secret now.'

Robert looked shocked. He wasn't at all enamoured by the honour and was about to protest when George spoke.

'I've told you quite a lot. Now there's something you can tell me.'

'Yes, if I can,' wondering what it may be.

'Oh you can, most certainly you can, Robert Colliver. That is your name is it not?' he proclaimed as though announcing it to the whole establishment and continued, in a slightly louder voice, 'A descendant of the Captain himself.'

Robert was astonished. Nobody knew his name, except Tara. How did he know? But what startled him even more was the stunned silence that befell the bar and then the clatter of glass breaking. Robert could sense a sea change in the atmosphere. George had deliberately announced his name and declared he was a descendant of the Pirate, wanting to see the effect on the three men at the bar. The silence and breaking glass told him all he needed to know.

Robert got up and went back to the bar to buy another beer. The three men now viewed Robert through a different lens as though, like Tara, they were looking at a ghost from the past, a phantom that could curse them, strike them down, and with an act of deference they got off their stools and left the Inn, so as not to fall foul of Robert's wrath. Even the landlord looked at him with astonishment, and offered the ale and chaser on the house.

In the snug, George was a new man. No longer hunched over the table but sitting upright and tapping the table in satisfaction.

'Well, in all my years here, I've never seen anything like that,' remarked George with an air of pleasure, one that seldom visited him. 'You must come again. I'd like to see that once more, just to confirm that my eyes and ears were not deceiving me.'

Robert smiled at him and was pleased that he had brought some pleasure to an old man, even though it meant he had taken on the mantel of a descendant of the notorious Pirate Captain. He left a minute or so later, after watching George down the chaser and then half the ale as though, for the first time in ages, he was enjoying restitution in the Smugglers Arms, free from the shackles of the three wise monkeys.

Robert felt buoyed by the deliverance and that his notoriety might be an advantage, opening doors that otherwise would be firmly shut in a town where longevity of residence was the key. George had even got up from his snug to see him to the door asking him once again to come soon and rather than return to his usual retreat, sat at the hallowed bar as he used to do in the old days.

*   *   *

It was a perfect spring afternoon as Robert stood under the wooden lychgate to St. Martin's Church, looking at the shadow cast by its imposing tower. The clear skies of the morning had filled with fair weather cumulus clouds, shapeless organic bodies creating a humilis patchwork that contrasted with an azure blue background. The afternoon was pleasantly warm. Every so often, a cloud would mask the sun and the temperature would drop, signalling that summer was still some way off, but warmth would return as the sun made an appearance once more.

He liked churches. He liked churchyards. For Robert, they were a window into the past. A window into the past of an individual, a family, a community that had lived their lives and who were now just a name to an unknown life of hopes and dreams, of fears and desires, of births and marriages, and ultimately, death. And from the exuberance of life, they exuded peace and solitude, a testament to those pious souls that had passed through the doors to heaven.

St. Martin's Church was located where George had intimated, on the bend of the Plymouth road, along from the Barbican area of East Looe, high above the town and harbour. It was a pretty church with a squat tower and a double apex wagon roof, set below the road level so that it nestled in a small knoll and seemed to be in a world of its own holiness, a reverent island sanctuary in a sea of profanity. Robert quietly strolled up to the north entrance, taking in the tranquillity of the place and listening to the birds that were singing a choral fugue in keeping with the peaceful atmosphere.

The church itself dated back to Norman times, the only evidence being the north doorway, now hidden behind a Victorian porch with most of the building having been built in the fifteenth century, its windows displaying a rather plain decorated style, characteristic of the middle Gothic. The door to the church was locked, so Robert skirted around the west tower to the main graveyard. Headstones were laid against an old wall, its herring-bone pattern visible between the sentinels to past lives, each one encrusted with green and silver lichen, an indicator of a pure life, free from corruption. He liked the graveyard already and as he walked past the tower, what presented itself before him was pure natural beauty, a vision of heaven befitting such a place of sanctity.

He was looking at a carpet of primroses. Never before had he seen so many. There were thousands. He could hardly walk for treading on them, and, when he accidentally did so, he apologised for desecrating their blooms as though they were markers to the dead. The hot weather had opened these flowers several weeks before they would normally appear and with such an abundant display, it was an unexpected and glorious accompaniment to his quest to find the Trevellick gravestones.

They were located towards the eastern side of the graveyard, across a swathe of yellow that Robert found difficult to negotiate. There were, as George had indicated, quite a few of them in rows, their headstones closely following in chronological order with a few exceptions. He bent down to look at a recent burial for the headstone was showing signs of minimal weathering with only the embryonic growth of lichen beginning to encrust the stone. The inscription was to a Geoffrey William Trevellick, born 1931, died 1979, aged 48, with an epitaph that read, 'He loved the sea and was taken by the deep.' He was about to look at another when he caught sight of somebody walking into the church grounds.

It was Tara. Quite a coincidence and he thought about confronting her but decided this was neither the time nor place. Instead, he quickly retreated behind a stone wall that had a viewing window towards the top and watched as she gracefully danced like a butterfly towards the graves, she too trying to avoid the primroses. She looked angelic skipping across the yellow carpet, arms waving in the air, pulchritude innocence beneath her normal promiscuous exterior. He wasn't sure which one was the true Tara. The one that presented herself today seemed to be an unpretentious woman, empathising with the scene as though she were free of constraint and able to be herself.

She knelt by a rather striking headstone, decorated with a dove. With her hands clasped together, she prayed for a couple of minutes, her head bowed in remembrance. The silence was intense. Robert lay motionless, trying not to breathe, or at least taking slow, deliberate breaths that would melt into the air and not disturb her thoughts.

'What shall I do?' he heard her whisper. 'It wasn't supposed to be like this. I know the family is all important, but I think I'm falling in love with him. Please guide me Mother.'

Unaware of her audience, she remained there in contemplative silence for several minutes before motioning the sign of the cross and departing, leaving Robert even more dazed and confused than before.

23

That night he laid awake in bed thinking about the new revelations of the day and in particular Tara, or should it be Tarara? He had gone over to the headstone that she had be kneeling by, to discover it was dedicated to a Juliet Trevellick, born 1918, died 1955, and to Tarara Constance Trevellick, born 1935, died 1962. Underneath was a single inscription, 'Together at peace'. He surmised that they must be mother and daughter and that Tarara Trevellick was most likely Tara's mother.

Tara was most definitely a member of this notorious family. Was she using him for some reason? Smuggling? The bird man, a government spy, claims there is something illegal happening on the Island. The Trevellicks' had been smugglers until recently. Maybe they still are? It goes on even in today's modern world but under a different guise. Goods brought in across the channel in trucks on the ferries and the Tunnel, people, cigarettes, alcohol, anything where taxes are high and there is a demand for such goods. It was no different in William Trevellick's days. But smuggling here in Looe, within a small community seemed unlikely. What then? Robert couldn't guess. But that was a side show to his main concern; that of Tara. He would confront her with this alleged accusation. Strange, he thought, she said she'd be back today, even though I now know she's been here all the time and I've not heard from her.

His head was in turmoil, spinning from one thought to another, unable to escape his imaginations. But after seeing the time pass midnight and then one o'clock, he finally fell into an agitated slumber where dreams become reality and the fertile mind conjures a tragedy of epic proportions.

He was the Pirate, Robert Colliver, aboard his galleon flying the skull and cross-bones and sailing an ocean of questions, unable to see his way ahead or back or anywhere, draped in a mist of uncertainty. He was alone apart from two sirens by his side, Fate and Destiny, each one leading him first one way and then the other, steering the vessel by their charm and beauty, luring him towards the rocks of an island where a beacon, a sanctuary within the stormy waters, was warning him of his impending doom. As he chose Fate the galleon veered left, clear of the rocks, a salvation from a watery tomb only to be chained by the siren and suffer the torments of a life as her slave. As he chose Destiny, the galleon veered right to safety, only this time for him to be entwined in a continuous shred of seaweed, more and more, suffocating him for eternity. As he got closer and closer, the rocks loomed larger and larger, jagged, knife-edge blades that would tear the vessel apart leaving him impaled on those rocks, and all the time the sirens were competing for his soul, bewitching him with promises of a life of pleasure, a life of fulfilment, but empty promises that only the rocks could rescue him from. And as he looked at the sirens the galleon succumbed to the rocks and he felt the blades pierce his chest as he was taken beneath the waves into an abyss of despair where neither Fate nor Destiny would follow.

He awoke in a sweat from his nightmare, too disturbed by his nemeses to find sleep again. Were Tara and Caroline two sirens luring him towards doom and disaster, to an unknown future? He didn't think so, but his nightmare told him otherwise. He tried to regain sleep once more but his mind was confused, unable to rest, and as the town clock struck two, he got up, put on his dressing gown and went outside.

It was a clear night and quite warm with only patchy cloud sweeping across the starry sky. He looked up into the vastness of space and pondered the infinity of the cosmos, wondering where his nightmare lay within its scheme. It was a futile thought but important to him. Was Fate to be chained to the unknown or Destiny to be lured to the familiar? He wanted answers.

Venus was a bright beacon in the western sky. Its cloud covered surface and retrograde motion seemed in tune with Robert's thoughts as though it too were luring him to uncertainty. Hoping to find some sort of resolution he looked at Orion, still dominant in the night sky but dipping soon to disappear below the summer horizon. But neither the constellation and its stars, nor any of the billions of others out there were revealing any secrets, certainly not to his nightmare.

It was then that a flickering light from the Island caught his gaze. An intermittent random light that wasn't signalling or part of any distress beacon, for it was near the top of the hill and being blotted out every so often by the trees that adorned the east side. It continued for a few minutes and then no more. Strange, he thought, but dismissed it as an aberration in his muddled mind.

A gibbous moon was out, shedding eerie shadows on the ground and in the hedges that surrounded the cottage. The building itself was casting a cloak of darkness upon the side garden from which Robert could hear some rustling in the undergrowth. It seemed to be the same noise he had heard on several occasions and he went over to investigate. There was something in there, a spectre that would not reveal itself, ignoring its stalker but continuing to announce its presence.

Robert stealthily crept further into the thicket not daring to breathe and crouched to give himself a better view. He couldn't see anything in the darkness, but could still hear it, only louder. It was close. He smelt the air and the breath of some evil monster seemed to envelop him, heightening his senses. The noise came closer. It was just the other side of the bush he was hiding behind. A low snort. More rustling. Movement. Robert's heart beat that bit faster. What was it? Some person? Some being? And then, there it was staring at him with large piercing eyes, a long face and horns. It was the devil himself.

* * *

It was the devil incarnate. It was a goat. Robert had found the animal, a mountain goat, grazing on the grass in the garden the following morning, having left him stupefied that night unable to contain his fright. Now he felt doltish, a fool for having considered that Lucifer in the guise of Robert Colliver, the Pirate, had come to take revenge and claim his soul. Trying to reconcile his actions, he concluded it was yet another confusion from his nightmare, half asleep, and was somewhat amused that both he and the goat had bolted at one another's presence. What it was doing in Looe he had no idea, but knew there was a herd of them living wild on the Exmoor coast although that was too far for an escapee.

It was another fine morning although he detected a change in the weather with high-level wispy cirrus clouds, an indication of an approaching Atlantic depression, already visible in the sky. They are a classic indicator of a low pressure system which, by the evening, would be replaced by medium-level cumulus clouds and then strato-cumulus followed by the rain bearing cumulo-nimbus.

Robert knew his meteorology and a seasoned expert can tell when such a weather front is developing without the need for sophisticated technology. Neither weather balloons, a super-computer, nor even the assistance of seaweed was needed, but just good observation, watching the silent performance of clouds as they enter the stage from the west and leave to the east. He always remembered his university lecturer saying that 'a cloudless sky is boring sky' although many would refute that claim, especially those who worship the sun and the deliverance of a tanned body. But today the sun would soon disappear behind thickening cirrostratus blotting out its rays, and by the evening the cloud base would have lowered and the sky filled with dark and heavy nimbostratus leading to prolonged and heavy rain.

With the forecast settled, Robert made for Kilminorth Wood, one of the many ancient types of oak woodland that follow river valleys to the sea in Cornwall. They are an important habitat for both flora and fauna and although he was going to visit Alfred, it was going to be a delight walking to Watergate along the West Looe River.

Make it early, George had told him, although how early he didn't say and so, as he entered the woodland, the time had just passed nine o'clock with the sun still low in the sky, penetrating the leafless trees creating a mosaic of patterns on the woodland floor. The last of the wood anemones were in bloom, a fading swathe giving way to wild garlic. Bluebells would soon appear, but for now their green shoots were clearly visible indicating a future carpet of blue that would produce a glorious display before the leaf canopy enclosed the woodland in shade.

The path skirted the river bank no more than a few yards away and as he progressed at a leisurely pace, the solitude of the place was omnipresent. Only the chorus of bird song broke the silence, a woodland symphony of melodies and intonation, a music drama where every note has meaning, an orchestrated score sheet defining territory, signalling alarm calls or singing a love song complete with a baroque cadenza to rival any composition. He could hear a song thrush declaring its presence and the metronomic call of a great tit above the yaffling of a green woodpecker. Robert felt a palpable thrill in listening to such an exquisite repertoire, a polyphonic performance where the musicians are virtuosos and those that stand and listen are rewarded with one of nature's finest concerti.

The path descended after a while and followed the river bank above the high water mark where a good view of the creek could be seen. Robert stopped and admired the scene. A kingfisher was sitting on an overhanging branch, motionless looking for prey, its iridescent blue plumage catching the sun's rays, whilst on the opposite bank a roe deer had come down to the water's edge, unaware of him hidden in the overhang of the trees, camouflaged by their twisted forms.

He looked up and noticed the cirrus clouds of earlier had already transitioned to a blanket of altostratus making the sun opaque, a watery light, but still with warmth in its rays and hoped his earlier forecast was not misplaced with rain arriving sooner rather than later. Even if it did rain, he thought, it would provide a different experience, enhancing his senses, directing them to some alternative melodrama that hadn't been planned. And before him, was one such pageant. A pair of mute swans, graceful, monogamous birds that mate for life, were arching their necks to form a courtship heart, proclaiming their undying love for each other. He felt privileged to see such intimacy, a window into the world of animals that performed on the same stage and acted the same script as any human did.

Watergate was an idyllic spot set in a small tree-lined valley at the head of a tidal inlet. There were half a dozen cottages vying for the flat valley floor and the limited commodity of sunlight in spring. Two old wooden boats lay in the creek, their hulls half submerged in the mud having been abandoned many years ago, whilst tied to a small jetty, which had seen better days too, was a fibre glass dingy, smug in the knowledge that it would not succumb to the same fate as its neighbours.

Bird song filled the air, bestowing the feel of an amphitheatre whose audience were the ghosts of trees, their longevity having borne witness to such a spectacle on many a spring day. The place had a timeless quality, an enchantment as though each tree, each stone, were hiding a secret that only magic could understand and Robert half expected fairies to come dancing out of the woods, accompanied by Puck, in a spring time celebration to the passing of winter and the mischievous frolicking of the summer to come.

Ararat was the last cottage up the valley, set back from the rest and with garden on all sides. It was a solid looking house constructed of monumental Devonian limestone, grey with reddish veins and containing fossil corals which had been quarried around Plymouth and imported to Looe for local construction, including St. Martin's Church. With stone mullions adorning the windows the cottage formed an imposing façade, somewhat out of character in the quaint surroundings. Robert approached the porch, a stone portico that would befit a house of larger dimensions, but which here presented a grand entrance to a modest residence. The path was overgrown with weeds, although to Robert's natural eye they were plants to cherish rather than destroy, for there were forget-me-nots and daisies sprouting from cracks in the paving and the pervasive dandelion, a beautiful plant in its own right, sprouting everywhere alongside the growing aquilegia and red campion.

He knocked on the door. No answer. Again he knocked and waited. Still no answer. Robert was disappointed, but tempered this with the anticipation of the return walk through the enchanted wood. His last resort was a brass bell with a thin rope attached to the clapper. He rang it and waited. After a few moments he could hear noises from within and seconds later, after the door had been unbolted, standing in front of him and much to his surprise, was the face of the man who had cast curses upon him in the car park after the auction.

24

Robert looked at Alfred who, unlike himself, was not at all surprised to see the man who had purchased his cottage. Indeed, Robert wasn't given the chance to introduce himself, for he was already continuing from where he had left off in the car park.

'I've been expecting you,' he announced.

'Did George tell you I'd be coming?' responded Robert, wondering how he knew.

'No. I've been expecting you ever since the auction.'

Alfred didn't seem quite so incensed now, as then, but Robert still detected a tone of resentment in his voice.

'I must admit, you weren't exactly friendly about it.'

'Sorry, but I was angry. Not at you really, you just bore the brunt of my ire. It was just that the cottage was sold when it had been on the market for so long. I was hoping it would never sell and like its predecessor, fall into ruin through neglect. You see, the cottage has special memories for me. I built it.'

They proceeded to the lounge, a room smaller than its actual dimensions for all the walls, except the fire place, were covered with bookshelves ceiling high, and any spare space was covered with framed pictures, mostly it seemed of travel to distant horizons. Robert could discern the temple of Ankor Wat, the Taj Mahal, Machu Pichu, Mount Kaliash and the enigmatic heads, the moai of Easter Island, testimony to a well-travelled person interested in the unusual.

Towards the back of the room was a large oak table together with several high-backed chairs and stacked with books, magazines and newspapers, whilst adjacent to what was obviously his special armchair at the desk was a typewriter and reading lamp, together with an ornate framed photograph of a young woman. He picked it up. The woman had a familiar look but it was probably just her beauty which conjured Robert's imagination. She was posing in what looked like a 1920s dress, the sort that adorn the socialites of that era and he thought she must be his wife, a reminder to a past life as he sat at his desk.

The rear of the room supported old metal framed French doors that looked out onto a small garden that had little colour other than the green of foliage and ferns, and looked like a grotto where spirits might reside. Towards the front, with a bay window overlooking the creek, was a seated recess and along the exterior wall, two old and thread bare high-backed armchairs were positioned either side of a brick fireplace containing an open grate, ashes still visible from a recent fire and ready for another one with shredded paper and some kindling wood in the hearth.

Books were everywhere. They were, Robert surmised, his passion, his life. The room felt alive as though all the words in the library, for it seemed more noteworthy than Looe's own compendium, were opening up their pages to another devotee of literature and learning, somebody who would love and cherish them just as Alfred had done and his father and grandfather before. With no photographs of any offspring in the room, Robert thought that the books were Alfred's children, that spoke of history, of geography, of philosophy, of politics, of a life that had travelled the world, which only conversed with him when he wanted to, that would not judge him nor lie to him, but neither would they love him.

In this hallowed room, full of knowledge, Robert felt humbled. He had expected to find a man like George, rough, hewn out of granite, a man etched by hard labour, but instead he was erudite, learned and, despite being in his seventies, looked much younger, not aged by a life at sea or in the mines but by scholarly endeavours, academia and the spires of Oxford. He had the appearance of a professor, being slight of frame with a goatee beard and wearing a light casual jacket and bowtie that would not look out of place at a rowing regatta.

Alfred had gone to make a pot of tea which gave Robert the opportunity to indulge himself in perusing the shelves. He could scarcely believe the books he was looking at, an eclectic mix arranged haphazardly with no methodical connection between volumes, with botany next to a text on classical Greece alongside a novel by Dickens. It gave the collection an authenticity, of being used. A book taken and then replaced, not in its original location but somewhere else, where it could connect with its neighbour in a new association, each assimilating their knowledge, their spoken words, into its volumes as though by some osmotic process.

Robert had only scanned a fraction of the shelves when he came across a book on smuggling. He opened it to the first page to find a quote by Rudyard Kipling entitled *The Smugglers' Song*. He read it:

If you wake at midnight and hear a horse's feet,
Don't go drawing back the blind, or looking in the street;
Them that ask no questions isn't told a lie,
Watch the wall, my darling, while the gentlemen go by.

Five and twenty ponies;
Trotting through the dark,
Brandy for the parson;
'Baccy for the clerk;
Laces for a Lady;
Letters for a spy,
And watch the wall, my darling, while the gentlemen go by.

It seemed to resonate with him as though he knew all about the activity, one which was still going on but under different skies. He continued to read and discovered that 'free trading', as smuggling was euphemistically called, although illegal was nevertheless a highly organised industry involving all levels of society, and those that carried out this trade were almost universally admired by everyone or at least turned a blind eye to it. They were popular amongst local people simply because they brought goods to those who couldn't otherwise afford them, particularly when the government introduced taxes on such goods. Cornwall was one of the most notorious counties where smuggling was rife, particularly during its heyday of the eighteenth century when taxes on spirits, tea and other luxury goods were raised again and again in order to finance European and Colonial wars.

Robert looked up to see Alfred come in with a tray of tea. He had been engrossed in the narrative of the book and could have continued reading, but returned the book to its original slot so as not to disturb the harmony of space it occupied next to books on the crusades and an old travel almanac on Italy, and hoped that he hadn't violated any local custom.

Alfred noticed Robert's concern but said nothing, putting the tray on a side table. The tray itself was plain which only enhanced the beautifully decorated teapot of roses and honeysuckle with matching cups and saucers and a jug of milk, together with the expected accoutrements. He would have been content with a simple mug of tea, but this was as felicitous a display as he had seen in a long time.

'It was my mother's,' Alfred commented, noticing Robert's surprised look as though this was a dying art form only to be found in exclusive tea shops or high class restaurants.

'We would have high tea every afternoon with bread and jam, homemade of course, not the stuff you get nowadays.'

'It looks, well, charming,' replied Robert.

'Charming,' retorted Alfred as if offended. 'It's antique and quite valuable.'

Robert apologised for his ignorance and was secretly honoured that he should trust him with such finery, although it didn't look it, he thought. But then he was no expert on the subject of bone china tea-sets, whereas Alfred probably was; he had spotted Miller's antiques trade bible on the book shelf, albeit many years out of date, sitting next to a volume on course fishing which was probably even older judging by its threadbare spine.

Robert watched Alfred fiddle with the teapot as he drunk his expensive beverage. It was a nervous action as though he might be trying to communicate with his mother, a séance to a past life where the rattle of a spoon or the tea leaves themselves would indicate some message unknown, a perceived link to a childhood tea-time ritual, to the good old days when bread was bread and tea a luxury to be enjoyed, savoured, not drunk as though it were an antique institution at odds with modern life.

Whilst sipping his tea, for he dare not gulp it down, he scanned the room, his gaze settling on the picture of the moai heads. He and Caroline had visited Easter Island during a three-month long visit to South America and had been captivated by its remoteness, being the most isolated inhabited place on the planet. It was home to a unique culture which evolved on the island, culminating in the huge stone carved heads, icons of the ancient world, that adorn many locations around the island and which strangely almost always look inland and not out towards the ocean. Caroline had insisted they make the detour and he was glad, for of all their peregrinations it was there, on Easter Island, that Robert found his special place, one where he felt time had drawn him there all along.

Alfred, having finished his tea and no longer rattling his cup and saucer, noticed Robert looking at the photograph.

'Rapa Nui,' he said, doubting whether Robert would know its Polynesian name.

'Yes I know, the local name for Easter Island. Quite an extraordinary place.'

Alfred was impressed and Robert had now gone up one notch in his estimation.

'As you say, quite extraordinary. An allegory, one might say, to man's capacity for self-destruction.'

Although Robert had secured a notch in his esteem, Alfred felt sure there would be no further progress confident he would not know of its history, the subject being an anathema to most young people these days, with little relevance to modern day life.

'Indeed,' said Robert realising he was being tested by Alfred, and proceeded to tell of how the people, skilled seafarers from Polynesia who first settled there over fifteen hundred years ago, found an island covered in palm trees, a rich soil perfect for agriculture and seas teaming in fish and other resources. Over the next few centuries they prospered and the population grew dividing into tribal groups but unified in this island paradise. To give thanks for their bounty, they began to build the statues and as one group tried to out-compete another, they became ever larger, devoting more and more time to their ancestral deities. They cut down the trees, so that within a few generations the landscape was denuded of its timber and without the binding effect it gave to the soil, it was soon washed away by rain. It left the island without its two most important natural resources. So began a period of conflict with the inhabitants galvanising into their tribal groups and attacking their neighbours for their meagre resources. The statues became a symbol of strength and power to each tribal group, embodied in their eyes, and when one tribe defeated another, they would topple the vanquished heads over, face down, so that power would drain away making them and the tribe impotent. The inhabitants of a paradise on earth, a Garden of Eden, had destroyed themselves through greed and conflict, without any regard for the environment on which they depended. They were stranded, in the middle of an unforgiving ocean with nowhere to go and no means of escape.

'A truly earth island, one might say,' finished Robert.

Alfred was amazed at his knowledge. Impressed. He had secured several notches in his esteem and was beginning to take a liking to this young man, a man who would be a fitting beneficiary to his life's work, a custodian to his library. Alfred knew all the books in his collection, each one having a history of its own and a unique place in his thoughts to a particular event or time that was catalogued in his mind. Ask him about a subject and he would go around the room selecting books at random, yet collectively they all pertained to the chosen topic.

He got up and went straight to a book on Easter Island and then over to his desk and started rummaging through a pile of magazines, finally selecting a particular one.

'That is the accepted scenario,' he said, 'but recent research has cast doubt upon that. Rather than the Islander's self-destructing by destroying their environment, they tried to be harmonious with it. True, they did cause deforestation, but realised, perhaps too late, that they needed to work with nature and not against it. The demise of the people themselves is now attributed to the first western explorers bringing diseases to the indigenous population who had no resistance to them. Exploitation by outsiders put further pressure on the people, but they survived and now flourish with tourism as their main industry.'

It was now Robert who was impressed. Alfred showed him the magazine, opening the page to the article he had only recently been reading.

'It's in this latest publication. You can take it. There's more to read about it. I must confess, I've never been to Easter Island. Would love to have done. In fact, all the photographs are of places that I would have visited had I had the opportunity. Travel before the war was difficult, especially to remote places like Easter Island. You had to have either wealth or connections, neither of which I possessed, nor was I able to travel due to personal circumstances at the time. And now I'm too old.'

Alfred looked doleful and Robert didn't know what to say. He was about to add some comfort to the old man by suggesting it wasn't too late, when Alfred intervened.

'Have you been there Robert? You certainly know a good deal about the culture.'

'Yes. And to almost all of the places you have on display.'

'I envy you Robert. Travel does broaden the mind, much better than reading about it in a book.'

'But the next best thing,' interjected Robert, to offer the crumb of solace which he had been denied, to an old man who would never see these wonders of the world.

A silence befell them both, Robert wondering what to say next and Alfred reminiscing on a life of regrets, of one mistake in particular which had cost him. It was his penance, he would tell himself, a sentence every bit as deserving as one behind bars, although there he could repent and get on with a life, as such, rather than regretting one morning on a hot summer's day sixty-three years ago. Yes, it had been a life sentence.

The silence was broken with the chime of a pendulum clock in the hallway. It was midday. Alfred looked up from the melancholy and noticed Robert sitting opposite him seemingly with a vacant expression waiting for something to happen.

'Well young man, you came to enquire about your namesake. Did you find him in that book you were looking at?'

'I doubt it,' replied Robert.

'You doubt whether he existed?'

'Well, I don't really know. Probably not.'

'I can tell you that Robert Colliver most certainly did exist. He was born in Looe, exactly where is uncertain, but most likely on the site of the cottage.'

Robert noticed he had not said his cottage, as though Alfred still considered the place to be his own.

'We don't know exactly when he was born but he was baptised at St. Martin's Church sometime in March 1666, with the parish records clearly showing his parents as Pascho and Agnes Colliver. Little is known of the family. They were not wealthy nor owned land, but were probably merchants in Looe since Robert appears to have been educated, being able to read and write which was not the rule for the poorer people of the land. The first reference to him dates from 1690 when he is recorded as being aboard a privateer brigantine, captained by William Kidd.'

'The pirate William Kidd?' exclaimed Robert.

'Yes, the very same. A privateer was an armed vessel owned by a private individual holding a commission from the authorities, a legal authorisation to plunder ships, especially those who they were at war with or any hostile ship, such as pirates.'

'Then it wasn't a pirate ship he was on?'

'No. Neither he nor Kidd were pirates at that time.'

Alfred explained that they were involved in a legal activity sanctioned by the then Whig government under the monarchs William and Mary. However, Captain Kidd was not well liked amongst his crew and there is an account of him killing a man, albeit accidentally, which would later come to haunt him. As a consequence, Colliver is known to have taken a leading part in a mutiny against him, abandoning Kidd ashore whilst sailing on to New York, gaining another commission and attacking ships on the eastern seaboard of America. At some time in the following years he sailed to the Indian Ocean, where it is believed he turned to piracy; capturing ships, plundering, burning villages and slaughtering the native people and generally acting in a way far removed from the swash-buckling heroes of fiction. He was, by all accounts, a brutal and cruel man without compassion. His fortunes almost changed when he was captured and tried for piracy but escaped death because it was his first conviction, a benefit of all who could read. Colliver's education saved his life.

This setback didn't deter him and again he returned to the high seas where his reputation grew, his acts of piracy increased and he committed many crimes including the murder of passengers and crew from a plundered ship who were battened down in the hatches when the ship was set ablaze. He encountered Kidd for the second time on an island off the coast of Madagascar and commandeered his crew leaving Kidd marooned, unable to leave, and although he did make it back to New York, he was arrested for piracy and taken to London for trial. Meanwhile, Colliver continued his attacks on ships culminating in the plunder of a large merchantman, a great prize that was worth a fortune to Colliver, but not before they killed many of the crew and passengers on board, putting the rest into long boats without oars, sails or even water, casting them adrift to their fate.

With this one ship Colliver was a wealthy man, and there was no need for him to risk his life with further exploits and with the timely offer of a pardon for all pirates who surrendered, Colliver took the opportunity. But it was a trick. Many who had surrendered were hung for piracy, but not Colliver who turned King's evidence against his fellow shipmates and survived. He was still sent back to England to stand trial alongside Kidd. They were interred at the infamous Newgate Prison. Kidd was convicted of piracy, partly because Colliver turned King's evidence again, and was condemned to be hung, which was carried out at Execution Dock in Wapping in May 1701, his body left to hang in chains. Colliver was more fortunate. He was reprieved, having given evidence against other pirates but was still kept in jail, only being released over a year later on a royal warrant of pardon from the new Queen Anne.

Robert was spellbound by the account of his namesake and having heard of his cruel and brutal deeds, he now hoped that he was not a descendant of the this evil man, a man it seemed without compassion. As for Alfred, he was in his element, a teacher imparting his years of scholarly knowledge to an eager audience, soaking up the details and looking increasingly awestruck as the tale unfolded. He felt like an ancient philosopher telling the tale of the Trojan War, how Agamemnon set sail with a thousand galleons to bring back Helen of Troy. Only his tale was not heroic like the Greek legend, but the harsh world of eighteenth century piracy where life was cheap and the rewards were gold, not honour. In telling his tale, Robert wanted to know more.

'So Captain Colliver wasn't a Caribbean pirate then?'

'No, Pirates operated where there were rich pickings and the Indian Ocean, with the lucrative trade of the Dutch East India Company, provided pirates with just that. Even Cornwall has fallen prey to pirates, the so called Barbary pirates of the West Coast of Africa based around the port of Salee in modern day Morocco. They raided the southern coast of the county seizing fishermen at sea and even raiding towns. Looe suffered at the hands of these pirates and their captives were taken back as slaves or hostages, with two Looe men escaping to tell of their tales. As for Colliver, after his release he disappears from any known records. No one knows what he did or where he went or even when he died. But I have my own theory.'

And with that Alfred fell silent, thinking about his research and the real possibility of finding Colliver's long lost treasure. He wasn't interested for its monetary value, he wanted the prestige of solving a mystery and the recognition of fellow academics who had dismissed his assertion that the treasure was cached somewhere in Looe. William Kidd had previously done a similar deed, hiding his treasure of gold, silver, diamonds, rubies, candlesticks and porringers on Gardiner's Island off New York, paying the proprietors in gold and threatening them with death should they steal the haul. So it is possible that Colliver did a similar act, hiding his treasure on Looe Island.

Much to Alfred's chagrin, Robert didn't seem interested in his theory. He wanted to know about Lamanna and the cottage.

'You said you built the cottage?' he asked, breaking the silence.

'Yes, back in 1935. I bought the old ruin and land behind and built the cottage as you see it today, except for a few minor additions. I say I built it, but it was George who did most of the work.'

'So that's how you know him?'

'Yes. He was the only person I could find to help restore the old ruin. We've been close ever since. Don't see much of him these days though. How is he? What did he tell you about Lamanna?'

Robert told him everything that George had related and as he did so Alfred started to fiddle with the teapot again.

'Did George not say he helped rebuild the place?' asked Alfred.

'No, nor did he say you once owned it.'

'Wiley old George. A true friend.'

Robert was wondering how he might tackle Alfred's knowledge of the crypt.

'Was there anything unusual about the cottage?' he tentatively enquired.

Alfred thought this an odd question to ask and wondered if he might have found the crypt and the tunnel with its interned bodies.

'What do you mean unusual?'

'Well, anything out of the ordinary.'

'No, nothing other than a well. Have you found anything?'

'No, but just wondering.'

Both men were now looking at each other disguising their secret, or in the case of Robert trying to, but Alfred could see that he wasn't exactly honest with his answer.

'How did you come to lose the cottage, if I may ask?' said Robert trying to deflect his lack of composure.

'Soon after it was completed, about a year later I think, I had to sell it to pay off a debt. I sold the cottage but kept the land as it wasn't worth much. There's a right for West Looe residents to graze livestock for half the year. It was originally farmed by the people of Looe...'

'Yes, divided into stitches,' Robert was keen to interject to impress Alfred.

'That's right. How did you know?'

'I've a friend who's done some research about them. She's an expert on medieval history.'

'She sounds interesting,' remarked Alfred, 'your girlfriend perhaps?'

'Not exactly.'

Alfred sensed a disconnection between them and did not want to pry, and although he was keen to meet a fellow academic interested in his passion for history, he wanted to give some advice to Robert.

'I know it's not my place, but I sense that you and your lady friend were lovers. If that is the case and you do still love her and she loves you, then do not let complacency drive a wedge between you. Take it from me, love is the most precious of emotions. Without it, we are nothing but an empty shell that has no life, no meaning.'

Robert was taken by surprise at the sentiment. He was right, of course. Complacency was the catalyst for their separation. And their love? It was still potent. And it was certainly most precious.

Alfred was about to ask to meet her when Robert got up quite suddenly.

'It's been nice to meet you Alfred and thank you for all that you've told me. It's much appreciated. But I think I've taken up enough of your time.'

'It's been my pleasure. And as for taking up my time, well, let's say that I've plenty of that. You're most welcome to come again. Next time, bring your lady friend. I should very much like to meet her.'

'Until next time,' replied Robert.

He left Alfred standing in the porch, a sad figure that looked lonely, empty of life, a life without love, and he watched Robert wave and then take the high-level path back to Looe, with the first few spots of rain beginning to fall.

Alfred returned to his desk and looked at the photograph of the young woman, the woman he had loved over half a century ago. His mind wandered back to the cottage. They were standing outside looking towards the ocean, heads touching, embraced in affection, each feeling the others love. That was a long time ago, he thought. A lifetime. Tears ran down his cheek. Tears for his lost love. A love taken from him one fateful day. He had forsaken that love when young and foolhardy, before he had discovered the sanctity of the written word, a wisdom that had converted him, much like the monks of Lammana, not of the scriptures but of a penance, a penance to a deed, a deadly deed that had haunted him for so long and one which would come to judge him quite soon.

25

With George's unmasking of Robert's identity, his notoriety had spread around the town. It was a revelation to many that there was a living descendent of the Pirate in Looe itself. Of course, most considered the proclamation as pure coincidence, even dismissed it completely, but despite these reservations he was asked by the Town Council to be their guest of honour at the Pirate Day pageant. He accepted reluctantly, not wanting to offend, but loathe to be drawn into the bandwagon of Captain Colliver, which was liable to descent into farce with him being asked to dress up like the Pirate and promote the town tourist trade. At least he was glad that he hadn't revealed the underground crypt and tunnel, for who knows where that would have led. And as he thought about that fact, he realised that he still hadn't heard from Tara.

Tara was on Looe Island. She had been there all day, trying to fix a faulty generator which had broken down at the most inopportune moment. A shipment was due within the next few days and they needed it operational. She had planned to see Robert and was looking forward to taking her game to a new level, but for the moment, the emergency took priority.

She had gone out the previous day on a fishing boat to be transferred to a waiting dingy on the far side of the Island and out of sight of the mainland: she had become aware of a customs man snooping around and didn't want to attract his, or anybody else's attention. As it was, just as the vessel was leaving its moorings in Looe harbour she had almost been spied by Robert as he was taking the ferry across from

West Looe. She had managed, but only just in time, to duck beneath the gunwale and was sure he hadn't noticed her. But it was close.

Tara was being helped by two men on the Island. They were family. They were Trevellicks. By late afternoon, the generator was still not functional and Tara was beginning to be concerned, not just for the shipment but because of the weather, for it had deteriorated since her arrival. The south easterly breeze that had accompanied her out on a calm sea had now veered to a south westerly and increased to a strong wind, force five or six she estimated, and with it a heavy swell that made any escape hazardous. And to make matters worse, it was dusk with low clouds hanging heavy in the sky, threatening rain.

She would have to spend another night on the Island with her two cousins, who wouldn't be her chosen company in such a situation. But tonight she would have the pleasure of a guest who had come across with her. He was most certainly not family, being tall, strong and blessed with good looks that would be a welcome distraction, and by morning she would have tamed this giant and the gale would have blown through. 'Could be worse,' she muttered to herself.

Tara and her two cousins, Tom and Jake, were in a purpose-made hut the size of a small shed, where the generator was located. Between her and the two men and an assortment of machinery, not forgetting the generator, space was limited and with the pungent odour of diesel oil and sweat pervading the air, Tara was becoming increasingly irritable.

'Tom, don't just stand there, be useful and go make me and Jake a coffee.'

'Okay Tara,' he replied with an accent of resignation. Tara didn't think much of him, she considered him useless and capable of only the menial tasks, to which he had become accustomed to be given. He could see she was becoming agitated and was glad to be away from her company and in his own world where he was left alone.

'And before I forget, that business with the goat was stupid. I told you to keep a watchful eye on Robert, not create a scene.'

He responded with some pride at his initiative. 'But it worked, and I think…'

'Look,' retorted Tara with mounting irritation, 'you are not required to think, but just carry out my instructions. Is that clear?'

'Yes,' he replied in a child-like manner.

'And I thought I told you to dress in something plain,' she added.

Tom had been warned to wear something appropriate and so he had come in his trademark colourful shirt, albeit rather more muted than his usual attire, more like a camouflage outfit, but nevertheless it had annoyed Tara. And as he left she turned to Jake and commented, 'at least I can rely on you.'

That pleased Jake. Tara didn't think much of him either, with his grotesque corpuscular looks, something which had been reinforced over the years, so much so, that even he could not look at himself in the mirror without flinching in shame. He was the mechanic, the fixer of machines, and despite her abhorrence at his physical appearance she knew he would sort the problem.

Both Tom and Jake were not the ideal people to have, but in the business of smuggling, secrecy is the corporate strategy and loyalty the bottom line. Keeping the illegal activity in the family was important. It made sense. And they had proved themselves over the previous two years of operation, in which Tara had seen the trade increase and her wealth accordingly. She would continue until she had enough to establish a life more befitting her talents and ambitions, aware that greed was the foe, not the policing authorities. For now though, her two cousins were a necessary burden that she had to tolerate.

'How much longer do you think Jake?' she said, anticipating a negative answer.

'Not much longer. Almost there, I'd say.'

'Good work Jake.'

Again, he was grateful for the recognition and thought that perhaps she valued him after all.

'I can finish myself. If you'd like to go back to base and tend to our guest...'

But before he could finish, she had got up and was out, breathing fresh air into her lungs and feeling alive once more. Jake had taken an instant dislike to the stranger, partly because of his handsome face and muscular body, something which he knew Tara would admire.

'He's an outsider, not to be trusted,' he had told her, but the man had presented Tara with some credentials that she found intriguing and despite the risk, he might prove useful.

Base was Smuggler's Cottage, located a short distance away, nestled amongst trees that populate the eastern slope of the Island. It was not Tara's idea of a perfect abode being small and damp and having limited natural light. But it was perfect as a base of operations, as was the Island itself, for apart from exposure at low spring tides, it was effectively a fortress with treacherous rocks surrounding most of the coastline.

Entering the cottage, Tara felt a cold shudder down her spine as though the ghosts of long dead smugglers were sending her a warning, a coded message to be wary of this stranger she had admitted to the shrine. He was ensconced in an armchair in the parlour perusing over a map of the Island. Unbeknown to Tara, he had hired a helicopter from Plymouth and flown over the Island a few days ago taking aerial photographs, and had downloaded them onto the latest computer technology, a portable laptop, which had produced a three-dimensional image. Tara was impressed.

'Could have done with that myself a few years ago,' she commented and went on to say, 'You and me would make a good partnership.'

He didn't think so. He liked to work alone. His motto of 'one's company, two's a crowd' had served him well to date and although Tara was very attractive and clearly an ambitious woman, one he would not hesitate to have, this was business and it was business before pleasure for this man.

'Yes, I guess we would,' he replied as he smiled, wanting to keep her on his side for as long as necessary.

For Tara, it was a serious consideration. She could do with an intelligent partner to compliment her two imbeciles and she was sure that, given time and her skills, she could tame and control this man, as she could all the men she had so far encountered. No man, she considered, was superior to her. Perhaps in physical strength but not in mental fortitude. A man has muscles but a woman has the more powerful leverage of her body which can beguile any man whose primitive desire to perpetuate his genes, leaves him a helpless slave.

In some way she felt sorry for them simply because they cannot help themselves, their desire being an innate part of the male psyche, a desire for sex. And sex was what Tara offered. Apart from Robert, whom she had found required a more unconventional approach, but nevertheless had been won over, she had not yet really met her match. But his demeanour revealed that here was a man who would take all her considerable talents and skill to conquer. And it was her intention to win him over.

Jock picked up a map. It was a treasure map of Looe Island and on it was a cross marking the spot to something, perhaps treasure. It was the reason he was on the Island with Tara. He had acquired the map and had approached Tara with a proposition to split any proceeds should it be genuine. Tara was sceptical, as too was Jock, but the map was old-looking and seemed authentic. It was too simple. But as Jock knew only too well, sometimes things are just that.

'I don't think this map is going to be much help really. It's too obvious when X marks the spot of buried treasure,' he wryly sighed.

'But it needs investigating, nevertheless,' replied Tara, surprised at his lack of enthusiasm.

'Oh indeed. Leave no stone unturned, even if it seems futile. I've brought an instrument that may be able to help us,' as he got up to fetch a bright silver metal case from the corner of the parlour.

'I was wondering what was in that case you brought with you.'

'Have you used a metal detector on the island?' he enquired.

Tara's hopes sank as she thought that was all he'd got, a metal detector, which she, herself, had already used, only to unearth just a couple of old Victorian coins. She replied with a sense of disappointment, having thought he had more acumen. 'Well, yes I have, but it didn't produce anything.'

'Thought you'd have used one, so that's why I've brought a magnetometer. It measures magnetic anomalies and can detect buried objects, even changes in soil composition, to some depth. Archaeologists use them to discern the outline of buildings from buried foundations which cannot be ascertained on the ground or by ordinary observations, although crop markings can sometimes give clues. I've used the device on a couple of occasions with some good results.'

Tara had to retract her misgivings and now considered Jock was certainly going to be of use. She was right to agree to the venture, although somehow he had known about her smuggling operation, yet she wasn't about to divulge all its secrets.

Jock had approached Tara with the lure of the map, which he considered a fake, secure in the knowledge she wouldn't want to compromise her venture. He had an ulterior motive. As for splitting any proceeds, he had no intention of doing so and whatever the outcome, he would move in on her operation and take it over. He was certain the two men would support him, especially if he could expand the smuggling, and if she resisted then he would threaten her with exposure. He was in a win-win situation.

'You must think we're a bit backward down here in Cornwall,' she somewhat meekly replied.

'On the contrary, you've got a perfect operation here. I admire your ingenuity, although I'm still mystified how you manage to get goods ashore covertly.'

'That's the benefit of local knowledge,' she replied with a renewed conviction.

Jock opened the case and proceeded to assemble the contraption, which after a few minutes resembled little more than a bar with two prongs at either end replicating an upturned U-shape.

'This is a recent innovation in the field of archaeology and I'm fortunate to have a contact who can supply me with the latest technology.'

'And the computer?' asked Tara.

'That's different,' he replied. 'There's a whole lot of things that are about to revolutionise society, and these laptops are one of them. Have you heard of the World Wide Web?' he enquired.

'No,' said Tara feeling slightly overawed by the technical knowledge of Jock, but reconciled that she could belittle his ego with the age-old guile of a sensuous body.

'It's a means of accessing information and communicating. Computers have been around for fifty years now, but recent advances have meant they are getting smaller, cheaper and more powerful. Forget the telephone. Forget books. Forget the old ways. It's the future of the world. Soon, everybody will be leading a virtual life, a life inside its core, where the World Wide Web, or the internet as it is now euphemistically referred to, will rule. It will be the new messiah, a silicon god, and the people will pray to this omnipresent deity, not with piety, but with devotion to its promise of a panacea, a drug which will chain people to its altar of addiction. It's going to be a behemoth that will inherit the earth. It will change everything. Those that do not convert or choose to ignore it will become dinosaurs. And they're extinct.'

Tara felt as though he were giving a sermon where this instrument he had resurrected was his pulpit, and with his arms animated he looked every bit a preacher delivering a eulogy for a brave new world where technology would be the new religion and those that tried to defy the doctrine would perish.

By now, Tom had joined the congregation and was spellbound by Jock's convictions. He would have converted there and then to the Messianic message that offered a far more rewarding life, one which he might be able to participate in, but for his beholder, Tara. He knew she considered him useless and had come to accept it, even play to it on occasions when it suited him, but even he knew about the World Wide Web.

Tom had brought tea in for Tara and Jock who was now demonstrating the machine having hidden a couple of objects under a rug. He had simply passed the device over the rug and was connecting it to his laptop using a wire lead.

'Device not found,' he exclaimed in frustration as he read out an error message being displayed on the screen. 'Sometimes these computers are more hassle than they're worth.'

He tried again, but still the laptop was not recognising the magnetometer and was about to abandon the exercise when Tom intervened.

'Let me have a look,' he said in a timid voice as though he were a child wanting to help in an adult world.

Tara looked at him in complete astonishment, firstly for the temerity that he could help and secondly for interrupting Jock. She was about to admonish Tom, when Jock turned to him.

'Do you know about computers?' he asked.

'Oh yes. I have my own. It's a 300 megahertz Intel Pentium II processor with 64 megabytes of SD RAM, 8 megabytes graphics card and a 10 gigabyte hard drive, all running windows 98, although I often prefer to use the underlying MS DOS commands,' he proudly declared.

'Some machine. The latest specification if I'm not mistaken,' asserted Jock, impressed by Tom's sagacity. 'Here, see if you find the problem.'

Tom took the laptop and keyed in instructions with a deft touch and muttering technical jargon which even Jock did not understand. After a few minutes Tom paused and announced that he needed the machine's device driver, to which both Jock and Tara looked blankly at each other as though he was talking in a foreign language. He was. He was now in the internal world of the computer, where everything is a matter of binary codes, and communicating with this silicon titan required the skills of a surgeon to detect a faulty device or a psycho-analyst to determine whether the memory really had no knowledge of a program.

'It's the handshake protocol that controls the flow of data between the magnetometer and the computer,' he said in simplified terms, at least as simple as he could make it, although Tara was still bemused. But Jock realised what he was talking about.

'You mean the device control program?' he queried.

'Yes. It'll be on some floppy disk I expect.'

Jock searched in the case, pulling out the disk, to which Tom acknowledged that it was what he wanted and proceeded to load it into its drive.

After a few more minutes on the laptop, Tom triumphantly declared that the two machines were now talking with each other and showed the screen displaying the scan of the rug. Tara could just see a random display of black and white dots, which confirmed her mistrust, but to the trained eye there were two clear anomalies which indicated the hidden items. Tom went over to the rug to point them out. He was pleased with himself. He had found the buried treasure. But as he turned to Tara expecting a smile of approval, only a glare of displeasure greeted him. Jock though was nodding and smiling.

'That's some lad you have Tara. I'm impressed,' he said with conviction.

Tara though, was not impressed. She was concerned. For she could see that Tom had been converted by this preacher of technology and she was now wondering if it had been a good idea collaborating with him, allowing him on the Island. She now realised that a usurper had invaded her domain.

26

ooe Island is small. It's just over twenty acres in area and takes only a quarter hour or so to circumvent its coastline. But for all of its size it has a long history, dating back to the early days of Christianity in Cornwall when a chapel and small monastic community was established on the high point of the island. The original chapel was probably constructed of timber, but by late Norman times when the chapel is first documented in records, it had been rebuilt in stone.

The chapel is little more than a meagre collection of carved tracery now, but there is evidence of the building in the grass which covers the summit, giving a clue as to the size of the chapel. An early Tudor map shows the Island with a prominent chapel at the top, but it was almost certainly deserted by the time of the dissolution of the monasteries and left to ruin over the years, the stone probably being used for the construction of the Island buildings.

Today there are three main cottages on the Island, constructed about two centuries ago. The main residence is called Island House, located towards the south east tip of the Island it was originally built for Revenue Officers to combat smuggling and contains a distinctive square extension that has a squat spire-like roof that was probably their lookout post. Nearby is Jetty Cottage, aptly named because of its proximity to a landing stage, whilst further back towards a small beach that faces the mainland is Smuggler's Cottage.

Tara was still fuming when she left Jock and his new disciple within the smugglers base, going out into the evening air to seek space for a claustrophobic mind. She needed to think. Jake, for all his faults, was right not to trust this usurper and she was annoyed. Annoyed with herself for allowing him onto the Island. She had been tempted by the prospect of finding some buried treasure and it was that lure that had hooked her into the current predicament, as easy as she had landed Robert. Perhaps Jock had guessed about the smuggling, she thought, and pursed her lips in bitter contemplation, realising that she needed all her guile to outwit him.

It took less than a minute to walk the short distance to Island House and see Madge. Tara loved Madge. She was like a mother to her. Yet despite her devotion, Tara had an ulterior motive which had manifest itself when she was perusing her deceased father's personal papers. Amongst them she found a document that related to an archaeological excavation of the old chapel of Lammana on the mainland in the 1950's which her grandfather had funded. The document was a revelation. During the excavation, it mentioned they had found an ancient tunnel, from an undercroft in the mainland chapel out towards the island that was possible to traverse for some three hundred yards at low tide, before it became completely flooded.

The discovery was never revealed, kept secret by the Trevellick family. The entrance to the undercroft still remained hidden in the undergrowth of the ruined site, but the tunnel entrance on the Island was never discovered. However, about three years ago Tara had stumbled across, quite by accident, an extensive ramification of caves many feet below the ground. They appeared to be ancient, perhaps prehistoric, but she hadn't been able to find the tunnel entrance and didn't want to cause any undue conflict with Madge. Over the following months she explored the cave system, mapping it until she eventually found the Island entrance to the tunnel, deep under the centre of the Island.

Tara realised the potential of a secret tunnel to the mainland. She didn't want to compromise Madge and advised her to relocate to the mainland, saying it wasn't suitable for her to be on the Island any more, particularly with her advancing years. But Madge wanted to stay, no matter how much persuasion there was from Tara, thinking that she only had her welfare at heart. With Madge still on the Island, and with the help of Jake, they began to assemble the equipment needed to pump out the water. Using the Island generator and on a low tide, the water was slowly drained from the tunnel for the first time in centuries and she was able to make her way, underground, to the mainland chapel.

Since that day, she had successfully used the tunnel to bring ashore many shipments from France in a modern day free trade where all the goods were exempt of tax, albeit illegally. Her uncle had previously been involved in a similar activity some twenty years ago operating out of Talland Bay and so he organised the continental part of the smuggling ring. He brought the cargo, a variety of goods but mainly cigarettes, tobacco, spirits, and cannabis from the continent, across the Channel in his fishing trawler which was then transferred to a smaller craft off the Island, usually at night, and stored awaiting transfer to the mainland distribution network. That was the weak link in the chain of operation, carrying the goods up the cliff passing close to the cottage of Lammana and across the common land to a waiting vehicle. Now that the cottage was occupied, it created an extra concern as well as the reason for Tara's interest in Robert.

Tara opened the back door to Island Cottage. Madge was sitting in her favourite chair in the parlour dozing, waiting for the electricity to come back on.

'Almost finished, Madge,' she said, 'won't be long.'

Although she had endured many years with such a situation, she was always glad when the lights were on, especially nowadays as she got older and less able to cope with island life.

'Thank you so very much Tara. You're a good girl. I don't know what I'd do without you.'

This is what Tara wanted. She was hoping that through her kindness Madge might bequeath the Island to her. But Madge had other plans. Although she thought a great deal of Tara, even considered her the daughter she did not have, she was not, like herself, interested in wildlife and keeping the Island a sanctuary for the birds and marine life that inhabited the shores. She was sure Tara would develop the Island and turn it into an exclusive holiday retreat just like Bigbury Island in Devon, home to a famous Art Deco hotel which had entertained many fashionable people over the years, including Agatha Christie. No, she was going to leave the Island to the Cornwall Wildlife Trust to manage it as a reserve and maintain it for the benefit of the wildlife and create an observatory for all things natural.

'Looks like we're in for a storm tonight,' said Tara, looking out the window.

'Well I've seen many of those over the years,' replied Madge, with a dismissive tone, not against Tara but as defiance against the heavens as though they could produce anything to frighten her.

'Expect you have. Even I remember the hurricane of '87. The one they didn't forecast.'

'Aye, I remember that one. Mind you, there was a storm in 1974 which coincided with the highest tides for three hundred years, due to the alignment of some planets I think, that caused more damage. Huge seas crashed over this house. A Victorian boathouse behind the beach was washed away and a large barge, which we used for transporting goods, was torn from its moorings.'

'Well, I doubt if we will see the likes of those storms tonight.'

'You can never tell,' responded Madge, looking at the barometer and realising that the pressure was already quite low and the weather front had only just begun to approach the south west peninsula.

Tara went outside and walked to the promontory and crossed the little bridge to Trelawney's Isle, a small parcel of land at the end of the south-east corner.

She stood and faced the oncoming weather. She loved the elemental forces of a storm, especially on an island where they are more dramatic and where the awe-inspiring spectacle of waves crashing on the rocks would transmit their energy to her. She would feel alive, just like on her uncle's trawler in a force ten gale, or what seemed like a storm to a young girl. The elements then didn't frighten her and nor did the approaching storm. She turned and looked towards Looe. It was well protected, unlike the Wooldown above where she could see preparations for the forthcoming pageant. Was the Pirate a curse upon the people, or was it just her family? Was Robert a curse upon her, she thought?

She looked at his cottage on the cliff top and could see a figure standing there and wondered where he fitted into the grand scheme. Did she love him? She did like him. She liked the control, the thrill, the pleasure of him submitting to her, worshipping her body with reverence as though she were a deity to be anointed with his devotion. It was an elixir for her and she was becoming intoxicated by his presence, unable to detach herself from the drug.

She could see the irony. She, who supplied mind altering drugs to the addicts, was one herself; but addicted to sex. Not the conventional sex of a loving relationship. No, this was the dependency of a hard drug where the user is unable to escape their habit, finding themselves in an endless circle of euphoria and despair. It was a polarised existence in which she had no control. Did she want to be cleansed of her addiction? Not when she was having a high. But today, standing on what seemed like the edge of the world, waiting to be judged by the forces of nature, she felt alone and vulnerable. She wanted love. She wanted Robert's love.

*   *   *

Robert was standing outside his cottage looking at the Island and the approaching storm. He still hadn't seen Tara. He could see a lonely figure standing towards the end of the Island and could sense a connection. Was it Tara? The silhouette, like a matchstick figure, looked like her as he peered through his binoculars. And if it was her, what was she doing out there with a storm brewing and night time about to envelop the skies.

Her secretive movements had sown a seed of doubt in his mind and he wanted answers, answers to a tangle of questions that were slowly strangling him. More than anything, if he was honest, he just wanted to be with her, to experience the electrifying power of the storm together, make love to the shadows of light and feel the energy, that pure energy of life which she would bestow with equal potency to the elemental forces raging outside.

He looked at the figure again. It was her, he was sure of it. This time it wasn't a matchstick he saw, but the unmistakable curves of a woman, her long legs, slim figure and long hair blowing in the strong breeze were recognisable. It could only be Tara. He watched her. That connection was now tangible. She too, he imagined, was thinking the same as him. The lonely figure on the edge of the Island wanting, needing, the comfort of love, except her love was false, a detached love that would blow away as easily as the storm would do.

And then a flock of gulls, perhaps one hundred or more, too many to count, glided past Robert, a procession carried on the current of air towards their roosting ground on the Island. They flew tantalisingly close to the cottage, so close that he could almost reach out and touch them and fly with them to see this lonely figure, a sentry standing firm, a gatekeeper intent on defying the meteorological onslaught, and seek entry into her thoughts and so assuage his doubts.

The gulls seemed anxious, making excessive squeals, communicating that bad weather was approaching, their evolutionary radar detecting the drop in air pressure together with the scent of an Atlantic depression approaching, forcing them to head for the beach which, in the lee of the island, was a safe haven to ride out the storm. Robert though would have to face its full force and went inside the cottage, shut the door and immediately felt alone and vulnerable. He wanted love. He wanted Caroline's love.

27

The day of the Pirate Pageant loomed with grey skies, low clouds and the threat of rain in the air, but above all, with near gale force winds. Robert's forecast that the weather front would have blown through overnight was wrong. Instead, it had developed out in the Atlantic from three separate frontal systems, merged and was now tracking its way towards South West England to unleash its wrath on the peninsula and the town of Looe.

Such developments way out in the ocean cannot be detected by cloud spotting alone and Robert was obviously unaware of this meteorological mix when he had made his forecast. It was to be the perfect storm, an event that would enter local folklore and cement Robert as a harbinger of doom.

The town folk said it happened every year. The Pirate Pageant was always beset by bad weather and that every year he brought disaster to the town in some form or another. If it wasn't flooding then it was a poor summer season. This year it was to be the approaching storm. But people had short memories. Either that or they believed in his curse, a legacy they didn't or couldn't ignore, and forgot that the last two years had been blessed with benign weather, even unusually hot and dry for late spring.

Experts amongst the population declared such diverse weather patterns as a sign of global warming. Others dismissed such random events as the cycle of life, where what goes around comes around, and sooner or later his curse will come true, just as it did nearly twelve years ago when the '87 hurricane wrought havoc to the community.

The fact that it was six months after the Pirate Day did not seem to matter. It was his wrath then, as it was to be now.

As preparations were being made on the Wooldown, stalls set up, a marquee erected, music, food and all the essential amenities associated with an outdoor fair, the wind had already strengthened making it increasingly difficult, often nigh impossible, to keep the infrastructure from blowing away. It was too late to cancel came the cry from the optimists' camp. Come what may, and much to the concern of many, the burning of Robert Colliver's effigy, the climax of the pageant, would go ahead as though to defy his curse. Abandon the event was the pessimists' rally. They were concerned for the safety of the crowd and that his curse would lead to death and destruction.

And just as their cause was winning support, with the worsening situation and the forecast of storm force winds, the buffeting abated and a benign air of calm bestowed the ground. It was surreal. In just a matter of minutes the wind had subsided which persuaded the authorities to continue preparations. But like the eye of a hurricane, where calm precedes a violent sting in the tail, such a decision would prove to be a misjudgement of titanic proportions.

* * *

The pageant started in East Looe by the bridge, where the effigy was carried through the streets, up and along the coastal path, and then finally onto the Wooldown. The effigy, a generic pirate, was dressed in a flamboyant open calf-length coat with large side pockets and turned-up cuffs on its sleeves together with britches and knee high boots. Beneath the coat was a similar length tunic tied at the waist with a band, in which were two pistols, and supporting these was a belt with large buckle. A sash was looped over one shoulder which contained a scabbard for his cutlass which he was holding. His face was bearded, covered in flaming cannon fuses. He had an eye patch and covering his head was a jaunty tricorne. He looked every bit a pirate and as evil as Captain Colliver himself.

By tradition, the effigy was the work of a local school and was deemed more important than the national symbol of contempt, Guy Fawkes. He had tried to destroy Parliament, a meaningless establishment to the Cornish, then as now, and one which, if he had succeeded, would have been applauded by the populous of the county. Robert Colliver, the Pirate, was the hated figure of Looe. Now, almost three hundred years later, he had been turned into an icon, a figurehead of commerce and enterprise, ignoring the fact that he plundered ships and killed innocent people in the name of piracy. For most, it just represented an event not to be missed, just like the New Year celebrations in the town, and his burning, was a symbol of renewed hope for a prosperous season ahead and to pronounce that Looe is open and wanting tourists to visit once more.

Whilst the effigy was being carried through the town, Robert was up on the Wooldown taking in the festivities on offer. As guest celebrity he was given the freedom of the pageant which meant he could ask for anything and not be charged. This suited his spendthrift ethos and so he was gorging himself on local produce glad that he had forgone lunch that day, not through abstemious economy, but because he had to collect kitchen units and other equipment from the builders' merchant and ferry them across the field, which had been a challenge in the wind.

But now, up on the Wooldown, it was still eerily calm with just a moderate north westerly blowing. He wandered over to the beacon, the brazier crammed full of wood, ready to be adorned with his namesake's effigy. He looked up and beyond into the sky but could not detect any sign of a break in the thick cloud base which was heavy with nimbostratus and he doubted if the front had cleared through. If not, he thought, then we are in for an interesting time unless the current window of weather holds long enough. But of course, it wouldn't.

Robert was standing by the cannons which guard the beacon, sentinels to a condemned effigy, looking out towards the Island, wondering if Tara was still marooned there. A familiar figure approached him. It was John, the proprietor.

'Hello Robert,' he cheerily announced, and with a slight uneasiness continued, 'I gather you're the guest of honour to light the effigy and burn yourself - so to speak.'

'I guess so,' replied Robert.

John stood there with Robert and gazed with him at the Island.

'It looks rather foreboding today. More like an island fortress than the pious place it once was, although the two are not always mutually exclusive of one another.'

'No,' said Robert in a deadpan tone, taking a few seconds to reply, not wanting a history lesson.

John took the hint.

'Have you been out there?' he enquired.

'Not yet. But I would like to.'

'Unfortunately, it's a private island and not possible. It was bought by two sisters some years ago now. One of them died recently and the other, quite old, still lives there apparently.'

'Must be a lonely existence.'

'Guess so, although she has supplies ferried across and a friend who visits her regularly. The estate agent from town, I think.'

It was Tara, he thought. But why hide it from me and make it into some mystery? He immediately felt better and was viewing the Island not as a fortress, even though it still looked foreboding in the gloom, but rather as a place of enlightenment which explained everything, the flickering light, the bird man's misplaced interest and the connection he had felt last night with the figure, the matchstick who was Tara communicating her love for him.

John could see a change in Robert's demeanour and sensed an interest, which pleased him.

'I could take you round the Island in my boat, if you like,' he said.

'Would you? That'd be good. Every time I look at it, I always wonder what the dark side of the Island looks like.'

'Well, I could tell you, but its best left for you to see for yourself.'

'When?' Robert quickly added, eager to go as soon as possible, not thinking that there was a storm approaching and its consequential aftermath.

'When the weather improves and the tides are right. Say the day after tomorrow. Come and see me at the café. Let's see, high tide will be about late morning then. That should be okay. Come about mid-morning. Haven't done the Island trip for ages myself. Look forward to it.'

Robert felt good and was prepared to engage with John. But he was now looking anxious, fearing his wife was chatting up some handsome young man and setting folk talking. He didn't mind his wife's wandering eye but he didn't want it public knowledge even though, unbeknown to him, it was.

John left Robert still staring at Looe Island but with a smile on his face and the thought of Tara and how he might get to see the Island. From his cottage the Island was a constant focus, one that had now become an obsession, so that he now believed it held the key to his destiny. Somehow, this tiny speck of rock was going to secure his fate.

As he thought about life and how it had brought him here, the wind veered and backed to the familiar south westerly and increased in strength. The crowd were too engrossed in the festivities, witnessing the arrival of the procession and the effigy, to notice this change, but with a gust of wind blowing away a gazebo and blowing over a stand there was no mistaking the sudden change in the weather.

Most took it to be an aberration and took little notice, apart from a few people chasing after lost hats and embarrassing moments as skirts rode high revealing undergarments to the giggles of onlookers. The effigy was paraded around the ground to the beacon where it was placed on top of the pyre by two men climbing ladders, much to the cheer of the crowd. The men fiddled around for a few moments as though making the pirate more comfortable, but in reality making sure it didn't burn too quickly, wanting the spectacle to last for as long as possible. And it certainly was to be a spectacle.

It was now Robert's moment. He was ushered to the beacon and asked to say a few words before lighting the pyre. He was unprepared for a speech and in that moment, as he scanned the crowd and they looked expectantly at him, their eyes focused on this legend, a phantom from the past, the words that he spoke would reverberate long after Robert Colliver, the Pirate Captain, had been reduced to ashes.

'In my namesake Captain Robert Colliver, I light this funeral pyre.'

The crowd gasped, not in anticipation as Robert took a long pole containing a burning torch and lit the beacon, but in the words he had uttered. For in mentioning the Pirate's name he had invoked an ill-omen, summoned the forces of evil, and just as the flames took hold, the sky turned dark, the wind increased, and a ferocious tempest was discharged upon the Wooldown. An apocalyptic scene ensued, for within seconds lightening had struck the pyre, a thunderbolt from the devil himself that left the crowd apoplectic as the beacon erupted in flames. Hell was being unleashed from a slumber, as if the predictions of his return had become a self-fulfilling prophecy.

The effigy was burning brighter and brighter with bursts of fire radiating from its body and in those flames the transfixed Robert could see apparitions of his nightmares, the Pirate Captain coming to seek revenge, spitting arrows of fire and cursing the descendants who violated his home and family. He was rising, like a phoenix from the conflagration, rising up in the gusts of wind that were by now reaching gale force, his effigy flying off into the wind as though symbolising a rebirth of his spirit. Only this spirit wanted revenge and duly landed on the marquee setting it ablaze. Screams came from within as people ran out to escape what would have been certain death. And as the marquee burned, shards of flames reached out all around the ground, setting alight stalls and small tents and then a caravan, even the portable toilets, so that in the end the Wooldown was surrounded by fire encircling the crowd who could not escape. It was as though the god Wotan had invoked Loki and he were at play and would not abate until everything had been destroyed. Captain Colliver's apocryphal curse was real. He had finally had his revenge.

28

Superstitions can persist in a community, particularly if it is an insular one where families can be traced back through generations. And within a family those superstitions can run deep, embedded in their psyche, in their veins, passed on from one person to the next, embellished with time, so that eventually they become real, as real as the tale itself.

The Trevellicks were such a family. Beneath their veneer of respectability, they were no better than the smugglers William Trevellick had condemned. They were obsessed by the past deeds of their forefather and the curse that was put upon him and his subsequent prodigy by the smuggler, Josiah Thomas. The events of the pageant had affirmed their superstition and the curse of Captain Robert Colliver, the ghost who they believed in, had now finally been exorcised. For the Trevellicks that should have been the end. But the culture of superstition had trickled down through the years, distilled so that it had become a potent cocktail of suspicion and fear, and the Pirate's curse had spilled over and found a new vessel in the shape of Robert Colliver, the mortal.

The Trevellicks had good reason to be superstitious. Since that fateful night in 1749 they had been bedevilled with bad luck which the family had construed as the curse. The first calamity was the death of William Trevellick's eldest child, son and heir to his estate, which in itself was not unusual in those times except that his was the most bizarre and gruesome accident that it could only have been the work of the devil, so they believed.

It happened whilst the son was out riding. He had wandered into a dense and remote copse, one which was known to be treacherous, thick with vine. At some point his horse must have bolted because he was found hanging from a vine branch which had twisted around his neck. How it happened was unclear, but it appeared his head must have got caught in the twist of the vine, a ready-made noose, and without being able to release himself the more he struggled the tighter it became. He would have hung there for days before dying, a death that haunted his father who witnessed his son's contorted death mask.

Successive generations had their fair share of the Trevellick luck with many miscarriages, babies dying in infancy, sons dying before their parents, and suicides, all of which could be explained by life's rich tapestry of inheritance but was interpreted as the curse striking them, not leaving them alone. The final tragedy occurred over sixty years ago with the disappearance of a young daughter of Henry Trevellick in mysterious circumstances, which at the time could not be explained.

Juliet was a beautiful woman who was due to marry a local man from another wealthy family, an arranged marriage to suit both parties. He was older and quite a plain man afflicted with gout and was most certainly a bad match for the daughter. They never married for he disappeared too, one summer's day in 1935. Six months later, and out of wedlock, Juliet gave birth to a baby daughter. It was after the birth that the mother disappeared, presumed dead, for no body was ever found. Suicide was the verdict although some said she was sent to a convent to maintain the Trevellick family pride, the child having been born out of wedlock. Whatever the reason, she was never seen again.

Tara was a Trevellick. She too was wedded to the family. It had been instilled in her from an early age, as though the Trevellicks were a Cornish institution that had to be preserved at all cost. They had spread far and wide over the years but Looe was their base, their ancestral home, even though they no longer had the magnificent mansion that William Trevellick had once owned. That had been lost by Tara's great grandfather, Henry Trevellick, to settle debts he had accrued due to poor investments in London, the moneymen of that city taking advantage of a country gentleman who knew nothing of their world but had been lured into the certainty that he could make a fortune. He committed suicide rather than face ignominy of failure.

Tara never knew her mother. She had died during childbirth. Tara's father died when she was only ten and so without parents, she was raised by her great aunt Constance, the elder daughter of Henry Trevellick. She was still alive and at the grand old age of eighty-nine had the honour of being the matriarch of the family.

Tara loved her Aunt Constance. She was a maverick, in the days when it was difficult for a woman to assert her independence, and had been married and divorced many times, too many for Tara to remember. Her aunt would tell tales of her liaisons, her infatuations with the rich nobility of the county who all seemed too pompous and self-opinionated to interest her for long, and how she finally fell in love with a handsome man who was witty and intellectual and who loved her eccentric behaviour and who never demanded her to conform, as she had to within the social stratosphere of the landed gentry. They married after the death of her father, and had a son, Tara's uncle.

Although Aunt Constance was the head of the family, her advanced years meant that she delegated most of her duties to Tara who became the matriarch-in-waiting. Tara wasn't the direct heir to the family. That position, being on the male descendant line, fell to Jake, but his and Tom's lack of leadership coupled with Tara's strong personality had made her the natural successor, one which Aunt Constance sponsored and then supported.

It had many privileges but most notably respect amongst fellow dignitaries of East Looe and the all-important council seat which had an historic veto, secured by William Trevellick after his successful capture and subsequent conviction of the smugglers, and which still stands today solely for the head of the Trevellick family. She was, therefore, a powerful and influential member of the town council who used her position and talents to promote her own agenda. The family owned many establishments in Looe, from shops to restaurants, an estate agency as well a hotel, most of which had been secured in the past few years from proceeds of smuggling.

*   *   *

It was two days after the pageant and Tara had just left an emergency town council meeting in which the events of that fateful day had been discussed. The pageant was a disaster and the only consolation was that nobody had been killed. Several people and young children had been hospitalised but none seriously and now the recriminations were beginning to take root.

The main county newspapers had missed a scoop, but the local press had reported the whole story as told by a young reporter at the pageant. His account made it to the regional newspaper and even had national tabloids interested in the curse of the Pirate Captain. Tara was concerned. Concerned that Robert would be dragged into a whirlwind of reporters whose only interest was in selling a story, even if the truth was stretched beyond common sense. She was also concerned for her operation and the forthcoming shipment. It couldn't be stopped. So, she had informed the meeting that she personally would see Robert Colliver and offer him assistance and protection from the wolves of Fleet Street who would surely hound him until they had torn every scrap of sordid information from him, whether it was relevant or not.

The tumultuous events of the pageant had, in fact, been witnessed first-hand by Tara. She had managed to escape the Island during the lull in the weather and had been in the crowd, unnoticed by Robert yet close enough to have seen everything: the sudden awakening of the storm, the thunderbolt from nowhere, the deluge of rain that couldn't douse the pyre or the fireball. She had witnessed all of that, yet it was the image of a thousand sparks of fire that had fountained over Robert which lodged in her mind the most. He was untouched by that pyrotechnic burst and in his eyes had been the transfixed glare of the devil, a paralysis as though he were being possessed by the Captain's soul and had been chosen to continue the torment of their family in his name. She no longer saw Robert as a lover to be enslaved but one to be tamed and pacified.

* * *

Tara climbed the cliff path towards Robert's cottage, a now familiar trail but one she hadn't traipsed in many a day since she left instructions for the kitchen floor to be re-laid. This time her usual confidence had deserted her and she was a little apprehensive about the encounter, not because of the time lapse since their last liaison but due to her new vision of Robert as a harbinger of doom for the Trevellick family.

Those images of Robert standing beneath the pyre had tainted her perspective and she now had to adopt a new approach. So she was no longer going to rekindle the fiery relationship, but to placate him, so that he was not an anonymous enemy who could inflict a fatal wound on her.

Just before the entrance to the cottage she paused and gazed at the Island through a gap in the hedge. A small craft was heading out mid-channel, between the Island and the mainland, one which she didn't quite recognise being a small inshore vessel, of which there were many in the harbour. Two people were on board.

She had left Jock and Jake on the Island and had come back with Tom, not trusting to leave the new protégé for fear of a conspiracy, or worse still, a *coup d'etat*. She had told Jock to lie low and not do anything until her return, but was sure she could see movement towards the back of the beach heading for the western tip of the Island. At least they were avoiding Madge, she thought, but didn't like their insubordination or the fact that they were so exposed to the houses on Hannafore.

Voyeurism is a pastime for many with a view in Looe, a lens on the distant world behind the camouflage of anonymity. People talk, and gossip spreads rumours which ultimately become lodged in the conscious and become fact. Soon authorities would start investigating which could become awkward. At least Alex, the local police officer and family member, would stifle any concerns, but if they got to Liskeard then outsiders would be on the scene and beyond her control. She watched the two figures climb onto a cliff path and disappear out of view.

Tara walked the few steps to the cottage gate and looked up. Was she entering into a spider's web where Robert, the Pirate's descendant, had spun a trap to seek final revenge on the Trevellicks? She opened the gate and slowly climbed the thread of steps, still unsure of herself, the curse overwhelming her sense that he was just another man whom she herself had trapped with her own curse, the guile of a temptress who could lure any mortal man with her charm.

She knew Robert's weakness but her mindset today was not to enslave him but to entice him, lead him to her lair but not let him enter, leaving him empty, unfulfilled and eager to enter at his own will and so enslave his mind, his desires, his will. But those devilled eyes she had seen were etched in her own eyes, in her very being, eyes that she couldn't rub out and escape from, no matter how hard she tried to erase them. She felt as though she was playing with the devil and those that play with him are themselves enslaved. With that thought she almost turned around. But pride and a papering of those images took control and rather than retreating to the sanctuary of the town she found herself advancing towards the porch and the entrance to his web.

The front door was closed but unlocked. She opened it and called out. No answer. Robert left the door unlocked, not because he was lax or ambivalent about security but owing to his failure, so far, to install a decent lock. His obtuse thinking was that a thief who wanted to break in could do so easily, even with a lock fitted, and if they did there was nothing valuable inside to steal and hence they would leave the property empty handed, having done little or no damage to the door or the cottage in the process.

He was quite laid-back when it came to many things, Tara thought, as she made her way, first to the parlour and then to the lounge, taking in the heady aroma of a male den. His easy-going attitude was a refreshing change from the closed mindsets of most men she knew, they being paranoid about something or other, some trivial aspect of their psyche, a child-like trait or an obsession with sport or drinking or toy soldiers, that made her wonder at the absurdity of them.

Robert though, was open minded and not constrained by social *faux pas* or conventions, or even a need to assert his masculinity in her presence, although he did do so, much to her pleasure. Perhaps he was bisexual, she suddenly thought. Captain Colliver was reported to have been a homosexual, having had a close relationship with a fellow shipmate. Maybe his sexuality had been inherited by Robert, not that she was sure such a trait could be passed through the genetic code. Surely not, she muttered to herself as though rebuking her own stupidity.

But it had set in motion a train of thought that intrigued her, made her forget her current place. It even pleased her and made some sense, explained why he had such an empathy with her, understood her sexual needs and was able to arouse her like no other man. Subtle nuances as though he were aware of his own sexuality and that her pleasure was his pleasure. With that thought and his musky scent, she now wanted Robert. She could feel a need for him to anoint her naked body, for him to submit to her once again. She called out once more, only this time with a seductive tone hoping that he had already sensed her longing and would come down the stairs, naked, ready to be a slave to her body. But no answer, just impotent silence.

He was definitely not at home. Disappointment overcame Tara, an anti-climax to what she had just anticipated. She went into the kitchen to find it finished, not with fitted cupboards like so many nowadays, but with a rustic look, albeit new, and perfect with the floor now level and a rug covering the slate flags.

'He's done a good job here,' she told herself with a smile coming to her face and her mind becoming cross-wired as she thought how good he was with his hands. With that lurid thought Tara was about to leave when she caught her shoe on the rug and in doing so revealed the corner of something strange, certainly not a slate. As she lifted the rug it was plain to see that in the centre of the kitchen was a manhole cover.

Robert had obviously come across something, perhaps an underground drain or water supply she surmised and was curious to find out what lay beneath. She tried to lift the cover with her bare hands. It was too heavy. She needed special levers and searched the kitchen to no avail and was just about to give up when she realised that they would be in the small under-stairs cupboard.

They were. With some difficulty she lifted the cover to reveal an empty space with polystyrene insulation at the bottom. That was strange, she thought, for having been versed in her youth about the mysteries of a man's world of construction, electrical circuitry and plumbing and having forsaken the noble female arts of dressmaking, needlework and other domestic pastimes because it was deemed necessary by Aunt Constance in order to compete on a level playing field, she could immediately sense something not quite right. On removing the insulation and a second inspection cover below, which was easier to lift being of lighter material, steps leading to the antechamber were revealed, confirming her initial suspicion.

Tara was now anxious again, this time hoping Robert wouldn't return and catch her unearthing his hidden secret. Perhaps it's the entrance to Hades, she thought, a place to bring the victims of his curse. But she was being inane, her thoughts conjuring up illusion where there was none. She gingerly made her way down into the chamber and at the bottom, with just enough light from the kitchen, she could discern a small chapel with what looked like an altar at the far end.

She knew the legend of the Colliver family building a cottage from a ruined chapel, one that the folk at the time said would come to haunt them, curse them as the prophecy said. She had also been told about a tunnel that linked it to the old chapel of Lammana down below by the shore. Could it be true? Was this the entrance to that tunnel? She would have to find out. But not now. Her mind raced with permutations as to how she could manage this delicate operation. She would need a decoy to lure Robert from the cottage for a few hours, and immediately knew who to call upon to provide such a service.

29

Lady Jane had a sweet purr to her as she cut through the waves on the short passage to Looe Island. She was indeed a fine craft being sleek and elegant, a vessel which would endure all sorts of situations and come out looking perfect.

'Much like my wife,' said John, the café proprietor, with a chuckle.

Robert looked at this portly man, a man who had seemingly just read his mind, and couldn't quite equate him to his wife.

'I saw her the other day,' he remarked and was about to explain he saw her out jogging, alone and not with another man, but was immediately interrupted by John.

'Expect she was with a man,' he announced in a tone bordering on animosity, as he steered the boat starboard to avoid some buoys marking sunken lobster pots.

This surprised Robert. Did he know of his wife's infidelity? Perhaps he suspected himself and had lured him alone on his craft to commit murder and throw his body over the side, to which he was most definitely going to quell any such thought John might have.

'No, she was out jogging. Along Hannafore.'

'Did she try to seduce you?'

'No!' exclaimed Robert, quite surprised by the forthright enquiry. 'She didn't even see me.'

'Sorry,' came an apology.

'I don't follow. Why would she try to seduce me?' queried Robert, knowing full well why she might try.

'No, perhaps you don't follow. You see, our marriage is not quite the harmonious relationship it seems to be. In fact it's a sham. She has affairs. Has done for some time. Ever since we've been married. She doesn't know that I know and I don't want her to. She might want to leave me. Take the kids. I would have to sell the house and business which would leave me with nothing. Then where would I be? Least this way I have an income, I see my kids every day and I have a beautiful wife that is the envy of my friends.'

John was now pouring out his troubles to Robert as though he were a therapist, a punch-bag to take all the blows he had endured during his marriage. He explained how he was first told about her affairs by the so-called friends he worked with, who would taunt him for being too feeble to stand up, like a real man, and confront his wife. When he later discovered that a couple of his work mates were involved, it sent him into depression which further compounded the matrimonial relationship.

'I'm sorry to hear all this, John,' replied Robert, trying to assuage him.

'Don't feel sorry for me. It's not your fault. And I'm sorry to think that you might be involved with her. I can see you're a man of integrity. I've come to accept the situation. I'm to blame, if there is blame to apportion. You see, when we first met I was working as a fisherman on trawlers out of Hull. I was the skipper. I loved the life. Back then I was a lean strong man and Jane admired me for that. But I was away for sometimes several weeks up in Icelandic waters, fishing for cod. Do you remember the Cod War?'

'Yes,' answered Robert.

'Well, I was fishing during that time. When we got married Jane wanted me to give up fishing. I couldn't. I wouldn't. If I had of done, then who knows? Maybe it would still be the same. She's always had a high libido, one that no one man can satisfy, I reckon. So when I was away, she started having flings. I didn't know about it at first, but when I did find out I left fishing. I wanted a fresh start away from Hull. So we moved to London and I worked in Billingsgate. I thought everything would be alright, but she continued to have affairs.'

By now, Robert did genuinely feel sorry for John, an honest man who deserved better from life.

'I should have left her then, but I loved my wife and have two lovely children, so there's something to be grateful for. Now I tolerate her infidelities, so long as the children aren't affected and I'm not ridiculed. My life now is the café. Next year I've plans to start an Island boat trip, like we're doing now except with a glass-bottom vessel, so the tourists can see the wonders of the deep.'

'That's a really good idea. I'm sure it'll be popular,' said Robert, hoping that was the end of his confessions. A moments silence befell the craft as they passed close to a marker beacon.

'That one has three flashes,' he said pointing to the beacon and taking Robert by surprise, not at the sudden announcement, but at the change of tack. 'The one at the end of the Island has seven, the last flash being long,' he continued.

From his cottage, Robert could see these two marker buoys and knew their flash sequence, but didn't say anything. He was glad that John's diatribe about his circumstances was over.

But it wasn't. 'I've let myself go in recent years,' he continued. 'I used to be a slim and fit man, like yourself. But I love cooking and eating too much, which has led to my oversized frame. Jane must look at me with revulsion. I would. It's a wonder we still sleep together. We don't have sex, mind you.'

Another brief silence greeted Robert with a thankful sigh, as John slowed the boat to a sluggish pace near to some rocks. All he could hear, apart from the gulls, was the mesmerising chug of the engine and the gentle lapping of water against the hull. He looked down over the side into the wonders of the deep. The water was crystal clear and he could see a mass of kelp swaying in the current, a forest of green that becomes beached at low tide denying the observer the full majesty of this humble seaweed. It was the savannah of the sea, and darting in and out of the fronds were small fish, and where the sea bed became visible a spider crab as large as a man's torso could be seen.

He looked up and across to the Island. It was quite close now and on the beach he could see two figures, men by the look of their gait, pass a sign, which he couldn't read being too far out, and climb up onto the cliff path that follows the shore. He wondered what they were doing and as he pondered the thought, *Lady Jane* entered into clear water once more and John opened up the throttle.

'Look at this,' said John, passing Robert a compass.

Robert watched the compass, the needle pointing towards the general direction of the town. He was wondering what he was supposed to see when suddenly the needle started spinning round as though magnetic north had vanished. After a short distance, the needle returned to its normal state, leaving Robert bemused.

'Quite bizarre, isn't it?' suggested John.

'What causes that?'

'Does that every time. Not exactly sure why, but I reckon there's some lode with magnetic properties protruding out from the cliff and under the seabed, making the compass go haywire.'

For Robert, this was indeed a strange phenomenon. He realised it may not be a lode but Caroline's tunnel. He looked towards the shore, to the old chapel, and immediately saw that it was on a direct path from there to the centre of the Island. Could the magnetic anomaly be a tunnel? Was it a tunnel, he thought?

The craft was passing the sheltered beach which was just a few yards away. Robert could now read the sign at the rear which informed visitors that this was a private island and landing was forbidden. John slowed the boat down once again and began an anticlockwise traverse past the beach and parallel to a rising cliff. This part of the shore was visible from Robert's cottage and although he had looked at it through binoculars, being so close now he could see that it was quite rocky, all the way to the western tip of the Island. They were now approaching the north-western point of the Island.

'That's Dunker Point,' John said. 'Quite a treacherous part. The tides can easily draw a boat in onto those rocks. There's no hope if that happens.'

Robert was now beginning to enjoy the trip, free from John's marital problems, when he duly continued his confessional.

'I know she's seeing someone,' he said breaking the tranquillity. 'I hoped moving down here might change things. She goes out early in the morning for a run now which she's never done before. It's a sign of a new interest. Who, I've no idea. Don't care anyway. She used to go out in the evenings, for some fresh air she would say, but now it's the mornings. On a diet and fitness regime, apparently. I can guess what the fitness is. Not for me at any rate.'

Robert knew who it was for, of course, but wasn't going to say. By now he was beginning to regret this offer of the Island circumnavigation which was turning out to be an exercise in counselling, not that he had given any advice. He needed to get John out of his melancholy and was just about to ask him about the Island, when he continued speaking.

'Anyway, enough about my problems. It seems you have a young lady in your life, if I'm not mistaken. She came into the café the other day asking after you, well directions to your cottage.'

'You are mistaken. She used to be a girlfriend but we have drifted apart. We're good friends and who knows we may get back together again, although she lives in London and me, well here in Looe.'

'I sincerely hope you do Robert. She seems a lovely person and very beautiful. Love is precious. That's the one thing I miss nowadays.'

From Dunker Point, the boat was charting new waters for Robert, and to mark the watershed the craft began to pitch in a heavy swell reminding him of the trip out to the Eddystone lighthouse all those years ago.

'Not sea sick are you?' came a concerned John.

'No, not at all. Been in worse conditions.'

'Good man.'

The south west face of the Island was altogether more different, being wilder and having high cliffs with deep coves cutting into the rock. Breakers crashed relentlessly against jagged outcrops and a white foam lathered the sea before it dissipated on the next incoming wave. Above the splash zone, Robert could hear the unmistakeable honking of nesting cormorants and shags, their guttural cries piercing the noise of the surf. As the boat approached the shore, he could see some adults with young already, whilst others were standing motionless on strategic pinnacles, wings outstretched, drying them in the westerly breeze.

'They're cormorants,' announced John. 'They do that with their wings to dry them out, since their feathers, unlike other aquatic birds, are not waterproof.'

Robert knew this, but didn't challenge his identification. John had been pointing to some shags. They are a strange sea bird, an ancient warrior of the sea, with an almost prehistoric mien and their adamantine green eyes portrayed an air of menace as though they were the guardians of the Island, and those who ventured too close would feel their wrath with their bright yellow gape spearheading demonic anger.

By now John had steered the boat on its easterly track towards the south east point of the Island known as Trelawney Isle, beyond which is a channel and then a cluster of rocks called the Rannays. At low tide it is impossible to negotiate the channel by boat, but at high tide, as now, it was safe, but required careful navigation and nautical skill in the ebb and flow of the current.

'This is the interesting part of the Island,' came John, turning around as though to check that nothing was following in their wake.

Robert could see that there were several caves dotted along the shore line, some embryonic, but others had grown into large chasms projecting a black void that could accommodate a small vessel like *Lady Jane* but would be difficult to enter, even in the moderate swell that was buffeting the boat.

'You know it's been used for smuggling,' came John again, his voice becoming drowned by the crashing surf on the hull.

'What, the caves?'

'No, the Island.'

'Yes, I've read a little about it.'

'Well let me elucidate you,' not taking any notice of Robert's reply and considering that what he had read was probably guide book gloss and not the historical fact.

John told him much of what Robert had read himself, that during the eighteenth and nineteenth centuries, Cornwall was a major centre for smuggling. Commodities such as brandy, gin, tea and tobacco were the mainstay of the trade, particularly from the Channel Islands where they were exempt from taxes imposed by Parliament, although France and the port of Roscoff were also exploited by the free traders.

Although Polperro was the main centre for smuggling in the region, Looe Island was an ideal staging post for contraband where it could be concealed until safe to transport onto the mainland. The eighteenth century was perhaps the heyday of smuggling and it has been estimated that by the end of the century, over half of the spirit consumed in the country had no duty paid. After the Napoleonic Wars, the tide changed for the smugglers. A Parliamentary Act made it illegal for gatherings of three or more men and the preventive service saw an influx of recruits from the armed forces, culminating in the formation of the Coast Guard.

For Looe, this increased risk in smuggling was highlighted in a raid, where the preventive boats seized over one hundred ankers of spirit off Looe Island in the early nineteenth century. Smugglers became more ingenious in deception, concealing goods behind false bulkheads, building boats with hollow masts or false sides, even disguising tobacco as rope. This meant making smaller runs and gradually smuggling decreased in scale, but has never stopped. It is not the enterprise it used to be and perhaps more lucrative nowadays are drugs.

All this was relayed to Robert who, with increasing alarm, had been watching *Lady Jane* head towards the Rannays, the rocks revealing themselves every time a wave broke over them. John was becoming more engrossed in telling the tale rather than steering the craft, which he seemed to be ignoring, or at least not concerned that they were heading for disaster. Just when it seemed that all was lost, he turned the tiller and the boat entered the channel with, as it turned out, plenty of room to spare.

'That's Trelawney Isle, just there,' said John.

Robert recognised it as the place Tara had been standing the night before the storm hit the coast.

'The Trelawney of twenty thousand Cornishmen who marched on London?' asked Robert.

'Yes, the very same. He used to own the Island. Well, his descendant did, but sold it in the 1920s and his estate manor too, near Pelynt,' continued John. 'It's a caravan park now,' he added with an ironic tone. 'You know he never marched on London and there certainly weren't twenty thousand Cornish men...' continued John, who was suddenly interrupted.

'But I thought...'

'Lots of people think that, from the song. I admit it does suggest it, but it never happened. Jonathan Trelawney was one of seven bishops imprisoned in the Tower of London in 1688 by the then King, James II. It was a time of religious intolerance, a legacy of the reformation, and the Catholic monarch wanted to challenge the protestant Church of England and did so by issuing two Declarations of Indulgence towards Catholics. To cut a long story short, the bishops petitioned the King who had them tried for seditious libel, to dare speak out against his will. There was a popular outpouring of disapproval from the people and when they were acquitted, the church bells in his home town of Pelynt were peeled in celebration.'

Robert was now looking out to sea, half-listening to John's latest monologue. A feeding frenzy in the distance had caught his eye. They were unmistakably gannets, about a dozen or so, diving into the water beyond the Rannay rocks, whilst others were gliding high above the waves waiting to dive for fish. They were huge birds, all white except for a yellow tinge to their necks, and yet despite their size they were perfectly adapted, with sleek bodies and narrow wings which are folded into the body as they are about to enter the water, a final twisting motion giving them extra momentum into the dive.

He was surprised to see them as there are no close breeding colonies, the nearest being in Pembrokeshire in Wales or across the channel in Brittany. He had watched gulls follow fishing boats coming into harbour many a time, the men on board gutting the fish and discarding the entrails, but seeing the gannets was a privilege and worth the ride alone.

John, in the meantime, was concentrating on steering *Lady Jane* through the channel before emerging unscathed into calmer waters beyond the Rannays.

'Have you heard of An Gof?' he suddenly asked.

'No.'

'He's the one that should be remembered for marching on London with twenty thousand men. An Gof is Cornish for 'the smith'. His actual name was Michael Joseph, a blacksmith who, with many in the county, indeed the country, protested against the excessive taxation levied by Henry VII in order to fund wars against the Scots. That was in 1497. On the twenty-seventh of June that year, having challenged the superior King's forces and been defeated, he was executed. Hung, drawn and quartered: the penalty for treason.'

John was in his element, talking history with a captive audience that couldn't walk away, as his wife did. He had become quite animated, making head movements and arm gestures as though giving a seminar to an important dignitary. And Robert, he realised, was indeed that, for he showed him respect and listened to him which had provided a prophylaxis to his earlier outpouring of troubles. He was now enjoying himself, something which he hadn't done for a long time, and with that he continued his lecture.

'Today that date is celebrated in Cornwall as An Gof day. It's rather low-key, unlike St. Piran's Day. That's on fifth of March. He's the patron saint of Cornwall. Should be An Gof. His epitaph is *I would have a name perpetual and a fame permanent and immortal*. It's ironic that very few have heard of him, whilst Trelawney lives on, even though he did little for the common folk of this land.'

John fell silent once more and steered *Lady Jane* along the Island's coastline. He pointed out Island Cottage where the remaining sister lived and Jetty Cottage close to the foreshore with a landing stage close by.

'There's a third house called Smuggler's Cottage, but you can't see it. It's hidden by those trees,' he added.

Robert looked and could just make out a building through the developing foliage.

'It used to be the home to an infamous brother and sister, an Amram and Jochabed Hooper, formidable smugglers by all accounts. They adopted the nicknames of Fyn and Black Joan, stealth and cunning being the trademark of the profession. They would have used many ploys to conceal contraband. By Jetty Cottage there's a sinking stone, which smugglers used to weigh down casks strung together underwater. It's just a stone but with a hole for the rope to be tied. It was probably used as an anchor as well.'

By now, Robert was in a trance, his mind wandering between listening to John's monotone voice, a counterpoint to the sound of the boats engine, and the lap of waves that had hypnotised him. He was now mesmerised by the surface currents and the world beneath, watching colours merge and then scatter, prismatic light that distorted his view.

John, seeing Robert gaze into the fathoms, stopped the engine and let the boat drift in silence. Now he could see the depths. There was no kelp here to obscure the sea bed, which seemed to project a burnished glow from the sand crystals that were reflecting filtered sunlight. And in this jewelled kingdom, fish and other marine life were displaying patterns to match many a tropical reef. The pearl lustre of a discarded scallop shell caught Robert's eye and he tried to reach down and pick it up, but the water was too deep. And as *Lady Jane* drifted, into his vision floated the occasional flotsam and jetsam, intruders into this aquatic world, the detritus of a society that had no respect for its environment, to linger for years perhaps centuries with no respite, the ocean becoming a depository for progress, a place plundered for its bounty as though it were an indestructible resource.

Robert was still too engrossed in the aquatic inhabitants to notice the two figures he had spotted on the beach, now heading back from their circuit. Jolted by John switching on the engine, he surfaced from his thoughts and looked up just as the two men were skirting below Jetty Cottage, trying to avoid the main residence.

They were closer now than before. But both men were still strangers. The taller figure had a familiar gait about him, one that Robert couldn't quite place. He asked John if he had any binoculars on board and to his amazement, he opened a locker next to the tiller and produced a large pair, the sort that a ships commander might use to identify other vessels on the horizon.

They were heavy and in the pitching boat it was not easy to focus on the two figures, but eventually Robert had them in his sight and as soon as he did so immediately removed them from view, stupefied by what he had observed. He looked again. It can't be, he said to himself. What's he doing here? Because what Robert could see was the tall, arrogant, alpha male that he had met in Caroline's flat: it was Siegfried.

30

Smuggling is an occupation as old as time itself, whatever guise it takes. It's probably as old as that most ancient of professions, prostitution. At first sight the two enterprises may seem poles apart, but examine their core principle and similarities can be discerned. As any good business in keen exploit, they are surely out to satisfy a demand, a demand on the one hand for cheap contraband free from oppressive government taxation whilst on the other, a desire for a personal service. Yet while both are openly illegal, they persist because of that demand.

Tara was a smuggler. She was not a prostitute although she did use her femininity and sexuality to advance her business interests. Jane, the proprietor's wife, however, was a prostitute. At least she used to be.

Being the wife of a fisherman who worked on board trawlers, meant Jane was alone for days, sometimes weeks and during that time she had found, or rather cultivated, her own entertainment to pass the lonely days and nights. She had become a call-girl. She didn't like the term prostitute which sounded degrading, a sordid title for an anonymous service which had no allure whatsoever to her. Rather, she dealt with wealthy professional clients, the businessmen, lawyers and doctors, who were intelligent and wanted more than just sex; to be wanted, listened to, to be understood. She almost saw herself as a therapist where sex was only part of the package, with sympathy to their problems being as much a part of the service, be it an escape from work or home or some problem that they had. Men, she realised, were adults with a child's mentality, needing the comfort of a surrogate mother.

It seemed only natural to her that she should follow this vocation, having always been promiscuous. When her husband was at home she played the role of a dutiful and loving wife, devoted to her family, but when he was away and the children were at school, she metamorphosed into a sexual predator. She liked the ritual of dressing for her clients, the meeting at a top-class hotel, the posturing as the man lavished attention and complements upon her, something which was a rarity at home, and the expectation of the chase with the final kill that sated her voracious appetite. Until the next time, that was.

Jane did not want the move from London. She had protested quite vehemently when John had proposed they move, almost insisting against it, but when he suggested Looe would be the perfect place, she had readily agreed. John's bid to open a restaurant floundered at the local council. They refused a licence. However, Jane was approached by Tara who offered a proposition, in confidence and without her husband's knowledge. Tara had recognised a compatriot in Jane, a woman who wanted to assert her authority particularly over men, and Jane was asked, in return for the approval of a café licence, that she used her good looks and skills to Tara's advantage and obtain information and gossip whenever required. Jane agreed. She was quite excited about this new role, different from what she had known but still offering opportunities, whilst for Tara she was the perfect lure to bait chosen victims, to disclose secrets that she would otherwise be denied.

Over the four years since her arrival Jane had proved useful on many occasions and recently had passed on information about the birdwatcher, whom she very soon realised wasn't one at all but a government official, when he had inadvertently left his identity details open for Jane to see whilst in the café one day. Tara had then tasked her with finding out the reason for his presence in Looe and so Jane had arranged an accidental meeting on the cliff top a couple of days later.

She had used her charm to engage him in conversation, even when he seemed reluctant to do so, occupying his attention to contrive a scene whereby she managed to nudge his telescope down a section of cliff. Whilst he retrieved it, she searched his bags and pockets to discover his identity and from his notes found that he was interested in the Island and that he had made a visit to Robert Colliver. Tara was pleased with the report and paid well for a job which Jane found all too easy.

However, her following assignment was more challenging as it involved forming a relationship with a man who Tara discovered had been asking too many questions about Robert and the cottage. It was the reporter. It wasn't difficult though, not for an expert like Jane. She had followed him one day along the coastal path making for Polperro, and had got as far as Talland where he had made for the tiny church perched above the bay, its distinctive detached tower looking out to sea like a lighthouse, a signal tower for smugglers in years gone by. He had spent almost an hour in there, much to Jane's consternation as she wondered what there was inside to occupy so much time. She had waited at the beachside café outside, sunning herself whilst partaking in a refreshing iced tea.

It was a hot spring day and by late morning the sun was high enough in the sky to cast some welcoming rays to a worshiper like Jane. She had decided to decamp to the beach, to a sunny but strategic spot, where she could see the coastal path heading back to Looe or onwards to Polperro. As she lay there, stripped to just a bikini swimsuit, soaking up the sun's rays, she suddenly realised that he could return to Looe via the back road which was beyond her view. Having considered the alternative option of moving location, she appeased her sense of duty and continued her vigil on the beach in hope he didn't choose the alternative route. Her tan was more important.

Talland Bay is a sleepy sort of place situated two to three miles from Looe. It has a natural open cove and used to be a prime spot during the heyday of smuggling in the eighteenth century and even as recently as twenty years ago, when a gang were caught and convicted of bringing a large quantity of cannabis from North Africa ashore one September night.

Today it is a quiet retreat with few visitors, and those who do venture there are rewarded with a sheltered bay and a beach consisting of a smooth, wave-cut platform of grey and pink rocks, interlaced with beads of glittering quartz veins. As the tide retreats, a small sandy shore is revealed, which soon becomes larger, giving way to a fine arc of shallow water, ideal for swimming.

Jane was stationed in a sandy inlet keeping a watchful eye through the tinted lenses of her sunglasses. There was no sign of the reporter after a further twenty minutes or so and she thought that he must have backtracked on the road. But good fortune was with her, for quite unexpectedly, and much to Jane's relief, he made an appearance and sat down to take some lunch on the beach, close to where she was sunbathing. She observed a surreptitious glimpse from the onlooker, which encouraged her to change position and provide an alternative prospective for him. As he ate his lunch, making the occasional choreographed side-glances, Jane got up and slowly, and with a deliberate and a provocative walk, made her way to the water's edge and felt the numbing sensation of the Atlantic. The sea was cold. Nine degrees Celsius cold. Only the warm Mediterranean or Caribbean waters would normally entice her. She was going to have a convincing swim in this sub-arctic ocean where hypothermia can insidiously set in after only a few minutes, and then act as though she were drowning and so draw the reporter into a rescue bid. She was sure he would respond. What man wouldn't? Anyway, there was nobody else to rescue her.

Those first few steps into the icy waters are the worst, sending a sensation of pain, a message from the brain to go no further. But Jane ignored the warning and tentatively edged more and more into the water up to her waist, pausing and then, after what seemed an eternity, making that final plunge, the leap of faith into the awaiting agony. She was swimming but couldn't feel her body. Her limbs seemed detached with the cold already penetrating deep into her core. Her legs abandoned any coordination with her arms. She began to flounder. Then scream. This was no act but real panic. She shouted for help, her hands waving in a desperate struggle for air, her lungs gulping the saline water. She was drowning, she could feel it, and the more she struggled, the worse it got and under she went.

He waded in, fully clothed, and lifted her out. To her saviour she looked visibly shaken. She was, but like a professional, quickly regained her composure and sense of reason, ready to cement the physical bond that now existed between them. She held him tight for warmth, her body clinging to his wet shirt, arms around his neck, and she kissed him on the cheek in act of felicitous satisfaction.

For the young reporter, this was a moment to behold. A pretty woman, half naked in his arms, seeking life-giving warmth, her tanned skin glistening with water droplets clinging to her like jewels bedecking a mermaid. In that moment, as he looked at his conquest of the sea, a beauty beyond his imagination and with the latent scent of pheromones that this delightful vision was exuding, he had been won over, his reserve had been uncloaked no longer covering his emotions.

'Are you alright?' he said with concern.

'Yes, but I'm so glad you were there to rescue me,' came Jane in a tone of gratitude.

'It was nothing. I'm sure you'd have been fine. You weren't out of your depth.'

'But I panicked and anything can happen then. I felt myself drowning. Think I reacted to the cold water.'

'Yes probably. It's still cold, even at this time of year.'

'I'm Jane, by the way.'

'I'm Malcolm.'

'Well Malcolm, you were so commanding, a natural life-saver and one so handsome.'

With that compliment, one that had never been paid to him in his twenty-two years and certainly not from someone so beautiful, he felt a retreat back into his shell, to the safety of his own person, whom he was happy to be with. He looked at her. She was older than him, he could tell, but that didn't matter. Her beauty was her youth. Too beautiful for him. Dare he consider that she would want him, a shy, inexperienced man who knew nothing of love, except the love of his mother? And yet here he was, next to his dreams, and that dream was now reality and it spoke of valour and of attraction.

'I'm certainly no life-saver. I'm not a particularly good swimmer and if you had been further out, well, I don't know.'

'You would Malcolm. I know you would have still come to rescue me.'

'I guess so, when it comes to it.'

'Anyway Malcolm, what do you do when you're not saving damsels in distress?'

'I'm a reporter.'

'That's interesting. What paper?'

'Oh, I'm freelance at the moment.'

Malcolm felt more at ease now with Jane, yet still reverential at her imposing beauty. He would have liked to ask her out but he was too timid to pursue that avenue, the rejection a confirmation of his own inadequacies and ordinary stature. Jane knew this. She had already seduced him. It was in his mannerisms, his shyness not to be seen looking at her, his constant fingering as though he were playing with imaginary worry beads and in his eyes, the desire for her. She knew the look well.

Naturally Jane took the lead in their relationship, which progressed from a secret liaison at Webbs Hotel in Liskeard and early morning runs, meeting at the fisherman's shelter by the quay, to meeting in the ruins of Lammana where they had sex, not the leisurely act of love making, but the unfulfilling act of a prostitute. Yet despite her apparent decline in standards, she found the slow pace of entrapping her client a challenging and exciting prospect, where the subtleties of a marathon, the twists and turns of the chase, provided a more satisfying victory. And she was victorious with Malcolm. With her guidance, he grew in confidence and with that confidence divulged all the information to Jane that Tara required.

Jane discovered, much to her surprise, that he was the son of a Frederick Thomas, whom she knew was the owner of a Tudor manor not far from Looe. She informed Tara of this and, what was more, in his notebook were references to her and the Island with question marks indicating some association. She also discovered that he had been on the Island, having canoed out there one day and landed, not on the beach, but in a cave on the far side where he had found evidence of contraband. According to his notebook scribbling, he had gone there out of curiosity but now realised the Island was being used for smuggling.

31

After Tara's discovery of the crypt beneath Robert's kitchen floor, she had quickly sought out Jane and tasked her with luring him away from the cottage, for a couple of hours at least. She had not disclosed the reason for the subterfuge and Jane, on her part, had not enquired, although she was naturally intrigued. Jane had already provided some information about Robert, or rather Caroline, when on her fleeting visit she had been in the café to ask for directions to the cottage.

It was a few days later, when both Jane and John were serving in the cafe, busy with late breakfasts and morning coffee, that she had taken the opportunity to ask Robert about Caroline. On the occasion in question, Robert had ordered a latte and saffron cake, which he said was his favourite and particularly delicious being home-made. She had, much to John's annoyance, paid undue attention to him at the expense of other customers in a crowed café and had interrupted him whilst reading, she noticed, a book on smuggling.

'Not thinking of taking it up, are you?' she suddenly asked, having just served the table next to him.

'What?' responded Robert, looking up, somewhat perplexed.

'Smuggling.'

'Oh. No. Just curious about it.'

'It goes on, even today,' she added.

'It most certainly does. Did you know that smuggling used to occur on Looe Island? It's quite fascinating…'

'Quite,' interrupted Jane, not really interested in a history lesson. She was on a mission to seek some information.

She noticed her husband, with a look of anger in his face, gesturing to her at the full café with customers to be served and tables cleared. She ignored him.

'Did the young lady find you the other day?' she enquired.

'Young lady?' he queried.

'She came into the café asking about you, or rather your cottage.'

'Oh yes,' now realising whom she was talking about, 'she found the place eventually.'

'Good.'

Jane hesitated, not quite sure how to proceed. She needed a name and if not a name then some small snippet of information that could lead to it.

'Is she your wife? Girlfriend, perhaps?'

'No, just a good friend.'

'She seemed quite lost down here.'

'Yes, Caroline lives in London, but her parents have a converted mill up on the moor, near...'

Robert stopped, realising he was divulging more than he intended or should, and that it was none of Jane's concern. She sensed the retreat and left it at that, realising that she had acquired sufficient information for Tara to trace the mysterious woman. For Jane she had procured her own information, that the beautiful woman, Caroline, was not attached to him and that Robert was a free agent, except for Tara.

That was two weeks ago. The latest mission was different as it involved more direct action and was the opportunity Jane was looking for. Ever since that first, brief encounter in the cafe when she was dressed in some ski suit on a cold winters day, she had lusted after Robert, a handsome man with a physique which she would like to know intimately. Tara was aware of this. She had previously warned her not to pursue Robert as he was her concern and had repeated the threat again, after delivering the latest objective. She had done so quite emphatically, instructing her that under no circumstances was she to seduce him or do anything that would interfere with her on-going plans, and as she put it, 'he was her prerogative.' But Jane had decided to ignore Tara, and play the situation to her advantage.

She had left a note at Robert's cottage which requested that they meet at the old chapel the following evening at about six o'clock as she had some information which he may find revealing. It was a ruse, of course. She was going to suggest that there was more to Tara than he might think and that she was using him for her own selfish interests. By doing so, she hoped he might see her as a friend, a confidant, and so establish a more intimate relationship. That was the plan, but even for an expert like Jane, the best laid plans can often unravel.

∗   ∗   ∗

Robert was early. A full hour too early. Not because he had misjudged the time but because he wanted to explore the old chapel once more, something he hadn't done since Caroline's visit. He had received a package from her in which she had enclosed the result of the forensic tests on the crypt skeleton and the one unearthed in the garden. They were both male. The one in the crypt was probably in his twenties, according to bone development, and was dated to around sixty years ago give or take a few years. The other one was a little older, perhaps in his early thirties and dated to the fifteenth century, which makes it one of the original Chapel burials, most likely associated with one of the unearthed headstones. She had also done some research about the tunnel and had discovered that they were more common than one would imagine.

A tunnel over half a mile long is known to have been excavated on the north Cornish coast at a secluded cove a few miles north of Newquay. It would have been an ideal location for smuggling and the tunnel was no doubt used to hide contraband, maybe bringing it ashore inland. And in the early nineteenth century, coastguards discovered a tunnel cut through chalk for a distance of two hundred yards from the cliff to a house in the town of Margate in Kent.

Caroline was sure that their find was a tunnel, but more ancient and nothing to do with smuggling but a lifeline between the Island monastery and the mainland at a time when overseas raiders, particularly the Vikings, were making incursions on the kingdom. Robert was still not convinced and hadn't ventured far into the tunnel in order to refute her assertion. But he was intrigued and wanted to explore the old chapel site to unearth a tunnel entrance or at the very least see if one was physically possible.

His search was in vain. As with his first attempt he couldn't find anything remotely like a tunnel entrance. He had expected so, but nevertheless was disappointed. He sat down on the ruined wall and looked out over to the Island. The tide was out. The expanse of rocks and kelp beds could be seen, creating in some way more of a barrier to the Island than the sea itself, the boat trip the other day taking only a few minutes to reach the beach. It was a delightful excursion he thought, soured by the presence of Siegfried. He could not imagine what he was doing on the Island but thought it must have something to do with Tara.

Jane's note had come at an opportune moment, for both of them. At any other time Robert would have ignored her request for a clandestine meeting, knowing that she was unfaithful and that her real motive was to seduce him, as John had suspected. Robert was sure there was more to Tara and Jane might be able to provide that information, whilst for Jane, she had the opportunity she was looking for, a secret meeting with her infatuation.

As Robert sat there contemplating the bizarre events of recent weeks, he noticed the moon rise slowly above the horizon. It was not yet full and it was still daylight, but the moon glided above the peak of the Island an imperfect halo above the location of the ruined chapel. A cold wind danced passed him, its unearthly moan an echo to a distant past where unheard pious chants would fill the air, being blown by the wind, reaching out to an unknown universe. He imagined those monks and what their insular lives would make of today's secular world, where devotion is not an incantation to God but the superficial words of a pop song whose message is love and sex in a material world.

It was now past their arranged meeting time and Robert was about to depart when he could see Jane running towards the chapel from the gate that led to Hannafore. She was jogging, and wearing tight shorts and a vest top which was intended to accentuate her slim, desirable, tanned and toned body and provide a distraction that Robert couldn't ignore. And try as he might he certainly couldn't ignore her, for she was a distraction, a distraction from his mind and the reason he was there.

'Sorry I'm late. Hope you haven't been waiting too long,' she announced after coming to a stop and bending over, hands on knees to regain her breath and composure.

'No, not long,' replied Robert, still fixated on her pulsating form.

'You obviously got my note. Trust it wasn't too enigmatic and that this secret rendezvous isn't too mysterious.'

'No, not at all.' But it was and he felt a little uneasy that her presence was now so close, yet so unreachable.

'It's about Tara. I know you two have been seeing each other, professionally or otherwise is not my business. But I feel obliged to say something about her, especially as you are new to the town and she is a leading light, and as such has influence. It has come to my attention that she is, I believe, involved in, how shall I put it, underhand, perhaps illegal activity and that activity involves the Island.'

She paused to look at Robert's reaction, for she was hoping for some raised eyebrow or nod of disapproval even surprise, but there was none to be observed which somewhat worried her.

'I realise this may seem outrageous, but I have your interests at heart and I certainly don't want you to be hurt by her.'

Robert was still silent, looking out to the island, watching the moon rise further in the sky with a hint of dusk descending upon Rame Head.

'Robert, do you understand what I'm trying to say?'

He did. She wanted to drive a wedge between him and Tara and so seduce him, just as Tara had done. They were two pertinacious women cast from the same mould, who wanted to assert their dominance to satisfy a sexual need and he had fallen into a trap with one temptress, which he had to admit he had enjoyed, but not a second and certainly not with Jane, the wife of poor John.

'Yes, I do. You think Tara is involved in smuggling,' he quietly spoke.

She didn't. But she had fabricated the tale after observing Robert read about it, without actually mentioning smuggling. Robert had done so and her ruse had worked. Jane was pleased with herself.

As she sat next to Robert and moved a fraction closer to him, it made sense. Robert was reading about smuggling in the café. Tara frequently goes out to the Island. The Island used to be a place for the activity. Robert had said that. She could now feel her heart throbbing, not from the cardiovascular activity of jogging, but from being close to Robert, almost touching him and finally, with her heart pumping adrenalin through her veins, she made that connection by putting her arms around him in an act of comfort.

'I suspect so, I'm sorry to say. I do hope you're not too shocked.'

Robert wasn't. He had expected some move and the arm lock, for that was how it felt to him, was that first move. He could almost predict the next.

'If there's anything I can do, and I mean anything, then don't hesitate to ask. I want to be there for you. As a supportive friend.'

For the first time Robert looked into her eyes and Jane felt an immediate elation that she had won him, for in his eyes, she could tell, was the language of passion, a passion which she was about to enjoy. Robert did have passion in his eyes but it was the passion of truth which he was about to discharge upon Jane, to tell her she was a manipulative and condescending woman whom he had no desire to know, let alone be with, and that she should respect her family by refraining from extra-marital affairs.

But before he could expound his ire, a low hum pierced his thoughts. From which direction was difficult to tell, but it gradually grew louder and louder until suddenly from behind them, into view came a yellow rescue helicopter, its rotor blades shattering the silent sky. It circled around and hovered just a few hundred yards away on a steep section of cliff, not far from Robert's cottage.

By the time Robert reached the incident, with Jane trailing behind him and quite annoyed by the untimely interruption, there were already several coastguard operatives directing operations. He was told that a man had been discovered part way down the cliff, his condition unknown, but because of the heavy vegetation cover the helicopter, all the way from RNAS Culdrose on the Lizard, had been called to winch him to safety.

The backdraught from the helicopter, which was only a few hundred feet above them, was ferocious, causing Robert to shield his face and Jane to turn away, her hair being blown about much to her exasperation as she had just had it professionally done at the local salon and at great expense.

With the winch man having secured the casualty, the helicopter moved to clear the cliff and lowered the stretcher to the waiting crew below. One of the coastguards transmitted an all clear signal and the helicopter turned, headed out to sea over Looe Island, and veered south west to make for base and refuelling. A medic was by now attending the casualty, but the man was not moving. The surrounding helpers were looking at each other with horrified nods. The rescued man looked like a scarecrow, stiff and lifeless. Robert then caught sight of his jacket and instantly recognised the attached insignia. He edged closer. There was no mistake. It was the bird man's jacket. Just as the medic got up, Robert could see the face of this man, or what was left of it, for his eyes had been gouged out and his skin pecked and what he observed was the ghost of his nightmare, a faceless man who was most certainly dead.

32

Tara, Jock and Tom were making their way up the coastal path towards Robert's cottage. They were late.

'Hurry up Tom, there's no time to stop,' berated Tara, infuriated at his sloth-like speed.

'Sorry,' came a meek and contrite reply, some yards behind her and unable to keep up, having paused momentarily to catch his breath, unaccustomed as he was to walking uphill and at such a quick pace. His thighs were aching and his heart was bursting, yet he never felt better, pleased, overjoyed, that he had been asked to help, succeeding Jake in the hierarchy of the business.

Jock suggested he come, when Tara couldn't locate Jake. He would have been the preferred choice, the only choice, and because Jake was not available Tara had requested Jock join her, much against her better judgement. Jock seemed to think that Tom would be of some use but Tara knew, despite his technological skills, he would be useless and most likely a liability. And at this early stage in the operation to explore the hidden tunnel in Robert's cottage, he was proving all too predictable. And when secrecy was the watchword, he was wearing his trademark multi-coloured shirt and shorts which even Jock found perplexing.

Tara and Jock didn't wait for Tom but strode on, reaching the cottage front door later than the pre-arranged time of six o'clock. Tara went to open the door. It was locked.

'He never locks the door,' she said, turning to Jock with an expression of surprise and exasperation.

'Clearly he has on this occasion. Perhaps he was expecting an intruder,' replied Jock in a sarcastic tone.

'Now what?' she shouted, more in response to Jock's reply.

'What about the back door?' came another jibe.

Jock's attitude was beginning to annoy her and she privately chided Jake for not being available when she needed him. But she had no alternative really, especially after Jock had told her that he had some evidence that a secret tunnel may exist between the cottage and the ruined chapel. How he knew, she was unsure, but he pre-emptied her move when he suggested that they provide some means of luring Robert away from the cottage and investigate themselves. And so, here she was, with a rival to her domain who was displaying equanimity like a well-oiled machine, whilst Tara was slowly becoming a rusty coiled spring.

This was part of Jock's stratagem. He was already conspiring to depose Tara, and unhinging her, making her make mistakes, infuriating her, was all part of the process. Whilst what he had in mind for her was not quite as drastic as the idea of her dead body, he had already removed one threat, the birdwatcher. It was an accident, but an accident waiting to happen at the hands of a killer, a former soldier and mercenary who had seen action in Africa where brutality was a weapon used by militants, intent on overthrowing a regime.

Jock had confronted the birdwatcher on the coastal path, near to the cottage. He was a goliath to the diminutive man, a Scottish heathen who would leave him bruised and senseless should he see him again in Looe, and in threatening the birdwatcher Jock had pushed him to the ground as a warning, only for him to fall down and crack open his head on a sharp rock. It killed him. Jock took all his belongings and rolled him over the edge of the cliff where he tumbled down to come to a rest on a shallow shelf, head facing to the heavens, inert eyes staring into space. For he wasn't dead, but lay there unable to move for an eternity, until loss of blood dulled his senses and he passed from a cruel world where evil can be found in such a beautiful place, into one of eternal blackness.

* * *

Tara came around from the back door having found it too was bolted, only to find the front door open.

'How on earth!' she exclaimed.

'Oh, Tom looked under the flower pots. That's where he keeps his key,' said Jock, pleased that Tom had made a vital contribution to the mission. Of course, he was going to look under them anyway, since years of contact with people had taught him that they exhibit obvious behaviour, a contradiction of actions, which he found always made his job easier.

Once inside, they quickly set about the task. Tom was assigned to keep vigil at the foot of the gate, whilst Tara and Jock gained access to the tunnel. He didn't need any special lever to remove the first manhole cover, lifting it with consummate ease, much to Tara's pique. Perhaps he was of use, she thought. With the insulation and second cover soon following, Jock descended into the crypt followed by Tara. With increasing indignation, she watched him move the stone altar with insouciance, whistling while he moved the heavy object as though it were constructed of wood. With the altar to one side, they could see that there was a tunnel and with Tara remaining in the crypt, Jock ventured into the unknown, down into the bowls of the earth.

He was no stranger to situations like this, having once explored an underground cave system in Yorkshire, alone, to recover a Neolithic artefact, an earth goddess with prodigious, almost grotesque, breasts which had recently been discovered by some potholers. They had returned, quite fortuitously, to the local inn where Jock was staying with tales of their find. He had befriended them and gained enough information to ascertain the cave system it was in. It was a gamble, for their tale may just have been that and he would have been risking his life for nothing. But it paid off, both in terms of the find and the reward it brought. So, the small rock-cut tunnel facing Jock, which could be no more than a few hundred yards long, posed no problem for him.

The first few yards sloped down gently but then became steeper, and to compensate for the drop, rock-cut steps had been roughly chiselled out, each one about a yard in length before a step to another level. Some were steeper than others, requiring careful placement of the feet in order not to fall, particularly as he had to bend over, making progress rather slow in the light of a torch. He had descended several tens of feet, he guessed, and was about to investigate further when a faint call, an echo from a distant Tara, told him to get out and be quick about it. He didn't know what the panic was about but in his usual measured style he retreated back to the tunnel entrance to see Tara peering through the hole in front of the altar, anxiously saying that Robert was returning.

'We'd better get out quick,' she ended, which was stating the obvious to Jock.

Tom had just rushed into the kitchen, shaking with fright, informing Tara that Robert and some woman were on the coastal path making their way back. Ignoring his vigil, he had gone part way down the path to watch the helicopter rescue when he spotted them already half way up the cliff. They had yet to reach the rescue crew, but were only a matter of minutes away from the cottage.

With lightning speed and perspicacity, Tara retrieved the front door key, put it under the nearest flower pot and closed the door. She then unbolted the back door and told Tom to make his escape out the back and over the top field to the marker tower, where he would find her pickup truck. She had, despite not wanting any complications, anticipated an unexpected return and so had driven the vehicle there in case of such an outcome. Tara, having made sure Jock had got out of the crypt, made her escape leaving him to shut the rear door. Whilst Tara was acting, Jock had reinstated the covers, replaced the rug and was making his exit, just as Robert and Jane reached the front porch.

* * *

The rescue incident had brought the intruders time. PC Trevellick had taken a statement from Robert, remembering him from the complaint about the hanging effigy. Whereas Robert's incident had gone no further, with the death of a man, the Officer knew the Liskeard Constabulary would have to be informed, resulting in a detective being assigned and the inevitable questions and unwanted attention that would ensue. He knew Tara would not be pleased, but it was beyond his control. If the death was deemed suspicious, then all hell would break loose.

Robert bent down to recover the key. He was perplexed, trying to recollect which pot he had left the key under. He was sure it wasn't under the one where he had just found it, having left it under a turquoise-coloured pot, not a plain terracotta one. He shrugged his shoulders and put it down to the incident he'd just witnessed.

With Robert visibly shaken from seeing the dead bird man whom he had spoken to only a few days ago, Jane had insisted on accompanying him to the cottage to comfort him, to connect with him and was now even more pleased, realising she had a key to his heart, a key that he had deliberately shown to her, revealing the way.

As Robert opened the front door, Jane motioned to enter as well. He was in no mood nor did he want her attention and gave an excuse that he wanted to lie down, feeling tired and faint. Jane said she would make him some tea but he insisted otherwise, and after another attempt Robert waved her off, glad to see her disappear down the steps, although not without a last look by Jane back at Robert with a smile and wave.

He was genuinely tired and faint. Seeing the dead bird man had given him a shock. Somehow it connected with him and he realised that the strange events that had befallen him so far now included death. He made a mug of tea and took a sip. He needed it, to calm his thoughts concerning mortality. Yet his mind was still active and it returned to the key. He was now convinced that it was under the patterned pot. There were three pots and he had selected the wrong one. Was his mind confusing him, conjuring tricks as though by some magic force? Yet another conundrum. Had somebody been in the cottage yet again? Perhaps the same intruder returning to the scene of the crime? Then he noticed the back door unbolted. Was his mind turning reality into imagination, just as his nightmares had turned into reality? He couldn't tell. He was confused. Perhaps he had left without locking up, he thought, and was about to bolt the door when he spotted the rug was the wrong way round. He had purposely placed it with the floral pattern facing the hallway. But now it was upside down. It had been moved. This, he was absolutely sure of. His initial suspicions had been confirmed. Somebody had been inside the cottage and there could be only one reason why.

Everything looked normal as he lifted the facing cover. The insulation sheets were in place. These he removed, and having pulled the second cover away he climbed cautiously down into the crypt. It was there that he found the altar had been moved, ever so slightly, but enough to reveal the tunnel entrance. If the other incidents had been in his imagination, this most certainly was not, because he knew that the altar had been left firmly against the wall. Somebody had discovered his secret. It's not Caroline, he thought. But who? Tara? Siegfried?

He prised open the tunnel with a crowbar and peered inside. Blackness. He edged forward into the empty space, thinking he heard something. He shouted out. Silence. Perhaps he was imagining again, that some phantom was lurking below, a poltergeist haunting the cottage, trying to turn him insane and drive him out, just like the previous occupants. He even imagined, in that dark tomb, he could hear it, noises, some shuffling as though the dead bones of the man had come to life, to accompany him in death. And just as Robert was about to retreat from the underworld and return to safety, the altar was suddenly slammed shut behind him. He scrambled to the entrance and shouted out. No answer. He tried to move the altar. He could not shift it. Try as he might, the altar would not move. Robert was trapped inside a pitch black void that was now his sarcophagus.

33

No man is an island. But Tara was. Looe Island was her destiny and that destiny was entwined, like the tree of life, with Robert. She knew it since that first encounter in the estate agents that now seemed a lifetime ago. It had been foretold, recounted by the three Norn's of her family, the three generations that had passed the folklore down through time, of Captain Colliver and how he cursed the family and how he would return to seek revenge.

It all fitted. Everything fitted perfectly, even though logic and reason would tell her otherwise. She had been bewitched by the poisonous concoction of a curse and a dead pirate, and now a pirate incarnate had fuelled the mixture, which she had drunk. Its effect was seeping through her very being, spreading its pernicious cocktail and enveloping her mind, so that she could no longer separate reality from fantasy. She was entranced by his legend and no matter what she thought or what was rational, she was convinced that Robert and her were fated to the end.

Whatever she did would make no difference. She could abandon everything and seek salvation at the ends of the earth and he would find her to play out the final scene. Whatever fate awaited her, she had already been judged. And so, with her destiny decided and events spiralling beyond her control, she was once again on the Island to oversee the latest shipment of contraband. It was a large consignment, not in terms of size but in value, the largest so far which posed an increased threat from investigating excise officers.

Jock was now involved. How he had become so, she could not really say, other than he had a unique gift of infiltrating an operation by stealth, before anybody realised it. Until it was too late. She reconciled her misgivings by convincing herself that he would be useful and may even be a scapegoat if things went awry. Yet she didn't really want him there on the Island, as he was the catalyst to her problems, her solecism.

Before Jock appeared from out of the ether, even before Robert, she had a compact and quiet smuggling operation with just her, her uncle and the two cousins, with small quantities of goods being offloaded to a grateful, if anonymous, public. It wasn't anything amoral. No lethal hard drugs or trafficking of people, although she had been offered the rich rewards of such smuggling. No, she was a moral smuggler in the spirit of the free-traders of old, supplying goods that were in demand, often considered the luxuries of life that many low income people in Cornwall could not afford. Besides, she would often tell herself to persuade her sceptical mind, the leeches of the City with their insider deals and corporate tax evasion made millions and all she was doing was making peanuts from a harmless bit of business.

That was until now. This shipment, with Jock's financial backing, was to include heroin and cocaine, drugs which can destroy lives and ultimately kill and she did not want to be a part of such evil. But her edification had been vetoed, everybody having been seduced by the prospect of vast profits, profit in the millions, not the thousands which they had been used to. The coup was now happening and the insurrection had side-lined her. She was becoming redundant. The only way was to fight back and take charge of the operation.

She countenanced her decision by wrestling with her conscience. It was just another supply and demand, the economics of a society that had broken down where the dispossessed were thrown on the scrap heap of social inequality and where one person's success was at the expense of another's demise. It's the law of the jungle where survival means kill or be killed, eat or be eaten, and drug users were at the bottom of the food chain, a socio-economic class to be exploited like any other in the hierarchy. Tara didn't really agree with herself, but she was powerless to change anything and if this was her destiny the thought of being a millionaire added to the argument.

The shipment was coming in that night. Her small trawler would rendezvous mid-channel with a French counterpart where they would transfer the goods and then make their way to Looe Island. Their trawler would wait half-mile offshore, and under cover of darkness and unnoticed from the mainland, transfer the goods to a small craft that could enter the large cave on the far side of the Island. There, they could be unloaded and stored in an underground chamber for later transfer: that would complete the first phase of the operation. The only dangerous part of the operation was being challenged by coastguard vessels on patrol, but since night fishing was a common practise from Looe, there was little to worry about.

Tara was with Jock, waiting in the cave entrance for a signal from her trawler, a double flash to mimic the Eddystone lighthouse. If it were seen, then it would probably be construed as a reflection in the water and so be ignored. There had been no problems in the many operations she had undertaken so far and she didn't see anything going wrong tonight, especially as there was a new moon and a moderate swell which would deter casual yachtsmen. It would be tricky to land, but the sea state added to security.

After the encounter at the cottage she wanted this operation to run like clockwork. Jock had informed her that the tunnel was blocked and led nowhere, although he hadn't had time to investigate fully. She reminded him that if he hadn't insisted on bringing Tom, then they would have had more time, and in doing so implied that he had made a fundamental management error which in this game could prove fatal. There was no love-lost between them and a smouldering tension was brewing beneath the surface of their partnership.

She and Jock were silent partners. Neither were conversing with one another whilst waiting for the signal out at sea, Tara being wary of Jock and Jock keeping his own counsel. He had been told to observe the operation, take orders from Tara, and not lead in any way, and had reluctantly succumbed to the directive, not wanting to arouse mistrust. He needed to witness the operation. But the silence was too much for Tara. His compliance, which normally would be pleasing, was gnawing at her and she needed an outlet for her frustrations.

'Trust you left everything as it was in the cottage?' she said in an authoritative tone.

'Naturally,' came a terse reply.

'He didn't see you?'

'Of course not.'

'What took you so long then?'

'I wanted to see if he suspected anything.'

'You didn't confront him?'

'No. Why would I?'

He was being cagy, she felt it. And she was sure he had something to do with the death of the customs officer.

'Did you have anything to do with that dead man they found on the cliff?'

'Not at all.'

She didn't believe him.

'You didn't do anything to Robert Colliver, did you?' she asked with a determined voice, as though that would be a violation of some ancient pact. Jock had had enough of the interrogation and responded accordingly.

'Look, I don't go around just assaulting people. As for Robert Colliver, I don't know the guy and have no reason to do anything to him, as you put it. I can assure you that I just observed him, never spoke to him and never laid a finger on him. He went into the kitchen to make a drink and that was the last I saw of him.'

Tara fell silent once again, not satisfied with his demeanour which revealed not just a modicum of mistruth, but a blatant lie. She would have to satisfy herself when tonight was over and pay Robert a visit.

Jock gestured at the signal from the trawler and they set off in the open boat, much like the proprietor's craft but not as elegant, for it bore the marks of many a landing in the cave where the hull had been battered against jagged rocks in the swell of the surf. The moderate swell was like a mountainous sea to Jock and within minutes he put his head over the side and wrenched vomit, much to the amusement of Tara. Here was the mighty clansman, a man apparently ready to overthrow her kingdom, reduced to a nervous wreck by a sea that was, in her eyes, practically calm. For the rest of the trip he lay on the bottom of the deck, looking at Tara with her smug smile. He would wipe it away, he thought.

The small craft approached the trawler and drew alongside with the skipper, her uncle, greeting as though this were a Sunday afternoon stroll, which in a way it was for them.

'There's not the usual haul this run,' he commented, in a way that required some explanation. But Tara wasn't going to tell him the change of cargo for she knew he'd disapprove, having already been involved in such activity and only just having escaped capture by the authorities.

'What's up with him?' he asked looking at the seal-like body that occupied the bow deck of the boat.

'Oh, just a sprat that I've hooked,' she shouted, knowing that it would enrage Jock into some action.

It worked, for he got up and helped with the transfer of the goods which didn't take long, much quicker than normal with no heavy crates of wine and beer. The return was a repeat of the outward journey for Jock and he was pleased to be back on firm ground after two abortive attempts to enter the cave, not through poor seamanship but Tara wanting to prolong his suffering, each time making a wide arc, broadside to the swell, which added to his discomfort. Jock was sentient to this with renewed determination for payback.

Unloading was again straightforward and having stored the goods, Jock was eager to know the second phase. Tara was not going to reveal that, not just yet, and said that they needed to wait for a low tide. He had assumed they would be transferring the goods that night, which by now was the early hours of the following day, but it was still Tara's operation and so a frustrated Jock vented his anger by kicking the boat and almost holing it, forgetting it was their lifeline to the mainland. Tara now felt more in control and with a successful night's work she and Jock set off for the harbour, their renewed silence a simmering volcano that would erupt very soon.

34

It was pitch black. Not a photon of light penetrated the darkness. Robert was in the tunnel, his eyes trying to seek out a pinprick of light. But he may as well have been in the middle of a black hole where no light can escape its gravitational pull, for he could find no solace from the immense weight of nothing. And gravity was exerting its force, making him feel that the void was pressing against him, crushing him into a dense mass. He imagined unseen particles, neutrinos, quarks and other dark matter, bombarding his flesh so that they would leave just his skeleton as evidence that he had occupied the space, just like the victim he had discovered there a few days ago, only this time it would be his bones that were unearthed, another man, unknown, who had succumbed to oblivion.

He shouted. Nothing. Nothing, but penetrating silence. Yet in that silence he could hear the rocks buckling and folding, heating and cooling, expanding and contracting as though he were listening to the birth of a continent beneath his feet, an echo of eons of time that had created the rock from the depths of the mantle and that now entombed him. And over that time, he himself may end up a fossil, a living record that a future palaeontologist would discover and wonder at this creature who had lived a life and died in such total isolation.

The black void, the silence, the sense of hopelessness was clouding his mind with dark thoughts. He needed to think rationally. Nobody knew he was there except the person who closed the tunnel. It couldn't be Jane, returning to seek revenge for his rejection. No, she alone couldn't move the altar, it was far too heavy. Only a strong man could do so, and so quickly. It must have been Siegfried. But why? Robert didn't know but now guessed he may have had something to do with the death of the bird man. It was too much of a coincidence.

It now seemed Siegfried had finally won their duel, started in Caroline's flat and concluded here on his own territory, where he should have been the victor. He had lost and in losing he now faced death. As he sat there, with no solution in sight, no prospect of immediate rescue, the reality of the situation filled him with a deep sense of panic and horror that he was not going to make it, that he was going to die a lingering and agonising death.

He prayed. He prayed to God, any god or deity that would listen to him. He prayed for salvation, to see daylight once more, any light, but not this complete and utter darkness. He didn't want to die. Not like this. He was supposed to live a happy life, in an idyll with Madeleine, until fate snatched her away, and with that thought he could feel his demons return to haunt him once more. Perhaps this was his fate, a fate worse than death itself, to slowly die in an anonymous void where only death would be salvation.

He remembered the inscription on the altar. He could sit there and trust in salvation. Those monks, he thought, hacked out the tunnel to determine their own fate and so would he. Crawling on all four limbs he slowly made his way down, down to as far as fate would let him go. Only then would he accept its edict. Until then, he was going to fight for existence in this black world which hadn't been touched by divine spirits. This was his world now and his alone and he was the master of it and its destiny and whilst he had a breath of life in him, he would rule with determination that escape was possible no matter how dark his demons became.

After just a couple of yards he felt something. It was a bone. Was this a premonition, he thought, of his own fate? It was, he assumed, the missing bone from the skeleton, the ulna which he had obviously failed to collect. What he would have given for a torch. And then he realised, a moment of divine realisation, that he had discarded it that day in the tunnel and had never recovered it, never found it. It was still there, somewhere in the blackness. He methodically began to search, sweeping from side to side with his hands, praying his memory was right. And it was. His prayers had been answered. In his hand was the torch, a symbol of hope in the black world. For a moment he hesitated. Would it work? He dare not try for fate was in his own hands, a finger flick away from eternity. He switched it on and to his absolute and unimaginable relief, one that he didn't want to experience again, there was light. Not the bright light of a fully charged torch, but light nevertheless. He was no longer blind. He could see. His prayers had been answered and he said thank you to his saviour.

He used the torch sparingly, shining it ahead to see the lie of the tunnel and then switching it off. He didn't know how long it would last and suspected, judging by its dimness, that it wasn't long. Down he went, down over rock cut steps as though he were entering into Hades itself, and with every step down it seemed to get warmer and warmer, an oppressive heat as though it was a burning hell and he was its next guest.

He seemed to descend for a long time, sometimes getting steeper and other times levelling off, but all the time down. Down was good, he thought. It meant he might break through out on the cliff face, maybe even the old chapel if Caroline was correct. He hoped she was. She always was.

This was her ultimate test. Be right, he thought, and I shall live. Wrong and I will die. If only she knew the life giving importance of her assertion, he thought, and he felt he would give anything to see her once more, to hold her in his arms, make love, and even listen to her innuendo and condescending chatter, anything but this torture. Then he remembered his last vision of her as she kissed him goodbye and realised he hadn't returned her love and by not doing so he was forevermore to be dammed, and to appease his conscience he instinctively said, 'Caroline, I love you.' And as he uttered his love for her, he heard his words echo, 'I love you, I love you, I love you,' getting fainter each time, only it wasn't his voice he heard in the echo but Caroline's. He didn't want her words to end and felt alone once more when silence befell the tunnel. But she was with him and her spirit now carried him along to his awaiting fate. Whatever it was, he would no longer be alone.

It took, it seemed, an age to negotiate the tunnel and reach the end by which time he was exhausted with sweat. It came out of the gloom of the torch light, a blank wall of rock, a solid granite face where there was no way forward, and with a terrifying realisation he slumped to the ground in despair. After all his efforts, he was thwarted. How could this be, he thought? He was supposed to live and see Caroline again. She was there. She'd said everything was going to be alright. She was wrong. He was one of those many thousands, probably millions, throughout history who had a tale to tell, yet they, he, were not allowed to live to tell it.

The torch light could not penetrate the darkness any longer, its faint glow like a setting sun, its precious light slowly dimming, a star losing its power never to shine again, until just a pinprick of light remained, a beacon of life in an infinite void. He watched it disappear and once more he was in total darkness, only this time without any means of rescue, without any means of escape, without any hope at all. And in that infinite void, within a vast and ever expanding universe, which ultimately would expand to nothing but a black void, his world had contracted, shrunk to nothing, to his mind, his own thoughts, to the imaginations that the mind can conjure and where time stood still.

He still had Caroline. She was going to be with him to the end and that thought comforted him, made his pain feel bearable. He talked to her and she put her hand on his, their fingers interlocking, a fusion of beating hearts. She kissed him, not on the cheek but on his lips, a sublime kiss like it was the first. But it was his last. She told him again, everything will be alright. But he didn't believe her now. He told her she was always wrong and with this admonishment she began to creep away. He said he was sorry. He didn't mean it. But she still faded from him. Don't leave me, he begged her. You're my light, my life. Don't leave me to die here alone. But his mind couldn't hold on to her, couldn't recall her. She had gone.

He began to weep and then sob, a desperate, lonely cry for resurrection. He cried for Caroline, for Madeleine, for his mother. 'Don't leave me,' he howled. The ululation was a release, a primordial cry to summon his ghosts. But as the reverberation subsided all that remained was silence and total blackness. Ever since his ordeal in the church crypt he had struggled to defeat the dark. It underpinned his subconscious. And now it invoked the Grim Reaper and Robert began to dance with death.

35

Tara stood at Robert's front door. She knocked and turned to look at the Island. Over there is a fortune, she thought. One more phase and it would be hers. It may have been Jock's finance that secured the shipment, but it was her operation, she had the contacts and hence controlled the money. Jock was not going to get a penny, not even his own money back.

She knocked again but harder, louder.

She would run him out of town. She abhorred violence but could engage a trio of heavies, men who would be a match for Jock, men who could lift lobster pots in each hand, to persuade him to leave and never return. And if he refused, which he probably would, there was the threat of his involvement with the dead man.

She wasn't entirely sure it was Jock but sure enough that the threat would suffice, especially as there would be evidence of his complicity with fingerprints and maybe even blood splashes. And should he respond with his own accusations of smuggling, then where would the evidence be? Certainly not on the Island. The contraband would have long gone and she had a good reason to be over there, helping out with Madge. She was in a win, win situation and it was good, she considered, to be back on top once again.

There was no sign of Robert. The door remained closed and there was no sign of life from within. She went to get the key but it was not there. Not under any of the pots. She tried the door. It opened. She called out. No answer. She went inside and looked first in the lounge and then the sitting room. Everything was as it should be. So too was the kitchen, although she found Robert's front door key on the worktop next to the kettle. It was full of water and a used teabag and carton of milk beside it. A half-drunk mug of tea was also on the side. She felt it. It was cold. Strange, she thought, Robert's never one to let tea go cold. It was as though he were at home and had just popped out in the midst of his tea-time ritual.

She went upstairs. The spare bedroom was empty as was the bathroom. His bedroom too. The bed was in a mess as though he'd been sleeping in it, although from experience, as she recalled, she knew he rarely made it until he went to bed, much to her annoyance. They had had good times in that bed and she felt a pang of emotion and a welling of desire to be there with him right now, he tied to the bed and she legs abreast him, teasing him with her naked form, to arouse him, so as to satisfy her primeval lust. She knew how to control him, she thought with a smile to her lips, a masochistic role that would leave him helpless, make him beg for mercy and to announce his devotion to her, that he loved her and that he was her slave.

That seemed ages ago and a lot had happened since, she lamented to herself, resigned to her memories of their intimacy that she knew were never to return. For a brief period in her life she had felt normal with Robert, helping him renovate the cottage, choosing colour schemes, furniture, and working together, sitting outside after a day's work watching the sun's rays disappear from the Island. Happy days that fate and a Pirate's curse had interrupted.

She went over to the window, not just to look at the Island, but to linger longer in the room, to feel his presence, a tangible link to joyous days. She looked at the Island. It was their destiny, that she was convinced of. But how? What events would play out over there? She need not ever go to the Island again, she could remove it from the scene. But she knew she had to, if only to discover what script had been written for them.

As she looked out to the Island, to her consternation she could see Jock on the beach having just alighted from a canoe, which he was now dragging up to the high tide mark. And in that moment, his image had severed Tara's memories of Robert and now she was back in reality. He's obviously up to something, she pondered, but what? She would have to get out there and find out.

She went back downstairs and called out once more. Still no answer. Strange, she thought, that his keys are on the side and yet no sign of him. Then she looked at the rug. Surely Jock didn't trap him down there? But she considered it a distinct possibility and so proceeded to open up the crypt and peer inside. Empty. She called out and waited a few moments for a reply. Nothing. Good, she thought, at least Jock didn't do anything stupid, and she closed the entrance, replaced the rug, and left the cottage to make her way back down to the Quayside Café. She would have a word with Jane.

Fortunately Jane was alone in the café. It was fairly busy with several groups having mid-morning coffees and George, whom she was aware of but had never spoken to, nor he to her, was at his usual table by the door. She beckoned Jane to one side.

'Have you seen Robert?' she said in a quiet voice, looking around the café at the assembled audience, half of whom seemed to be looking at the two women as though they were about to duet together. Not a love duet, but one where jealousy and lies are the motifs, and music from a Puccini aria playing in the background would provide the score.

'No,' she replied, 'not since yesterday at the cottage. Did you get out okay? I saw you leave out the back.'

'Yes. I was just preparing a surprise welcome for him to celebrate his completing the renovation of the cottage,' she explained, knowing that Jane was eager to know her reason for being involved.

'And was he surprised?' asked Jane.

'That's the thing. When I went back, he wasn't there. I've just been there now, and still no sign.'

'Perhaps he thought it was from his girlfriend. The surprise that is.'

This was an underhand comment from Jane, designed to annoy her. It worked. Tara though, was not going to let it show, much to Jane's dismay.

'If so, he immediately went out and has not been seen since,' replied Tara.

'Perhaps he packed a few things and has gone to see her.'

The ire, which was brewing inside Tara, was now showing outward signs, in that whereas before she was standing motionless, now a twitching movement could be discerned by Jane. She was about to strike a reactionary blow.

'When we were together, he talked about her as though he was still in love with her. That's why I mention it.'

'What did he say?'

'Oh, now that the cottage is finished, she will come down and live with him and that he was looking forward to that time.'

Tara knew this was a lie but it still hit a nerve and she was beginning to seethe beneath the surface. Unlike her, Jane was the model of composure, a skilled tactician who had many years of deception without exposure. She could see the visible signs of Tara becoming enraged and it just needed one more jab to make her react.

'He said that he couldn't have done it without your help, and although he enjoyed your company, you were just a friend, nothing more.'

Tara looked at Jane with venom, an anger that would have reduced anybody, other than her, to beg for forgiveness.

'You bitch,' yelled Tara in a constrained tone, realising that there was now an audience awaiting the final scene.

And with impeccable timing the aria was complete and the duet parted company with Tara slamming the door, leaving everybody in the café staring in amazement. For the customers, those that had bothered to listen, they had been treated to a fine performance, worthy of the accompanying music which, as luck or fate would have it, came to a crescendo as Tara left the stage, leaving Jane with a triumphant smile.

* * *

Tara was in a rage. She commanded Jake to take her out to the Island immediately, after he had refused because it was not time yet and he would have to hang around out there for ages. She rebuked him for his insolence and naturally he acquiesced to her demand.

Once on the Island she ordered Jake to remain in Smuggler's Cottage until she returned. She was going on a patrol. First, she called in to see Madge. As usual she was in the parlour, in her favourite chair which had a view along the coast to Rame Head and out to the endless horizon of sea.

'You alright Madge?' she asked, having calmed down, her demeanour now matching the sea.

'Yes. Quiet isn't it. Nothing much happening. Been reading about this chap who was bequeathed an island in the Hebrides by his father. Beautifully written. Almost poetic. Wish I could write like that.'

'Well, your book is pretty good, I must say.'

'Maybe, but his Island, or rather Islands, the Shiant's, are far more interesting than here. So much marine wildlife. So remote. Full of puffins, razorbills, guillemots and a host of other sea birds. Wish I'd had an island like the one in the book. It seems idyllic, not like this place which seems, nowadays, like an appendage to Looe.'

'Well maybe. But most people would think that you are lucky to have your very own island and still be living there.'

'You're right, of course. But it's not the same since Annie died. I get the feeling that it has changed. Something is going on.'

'How do you mean?' asked Tara, now listening with intent.

'Can't put my finger on it, but there have been noises recently.'

'What sort of noises?'

'At night. Not all the time mind you. The cottage seems to reverberate with them at times. You know there is a cave system underground, which may be acting like a sounding board.'

'No. I didn't know there were caves.'

'And then I think I can hear the sound of some machine.'

'Expect that's the generator.'

'Never used to be able to hear it. And all night?'

'It does come on occasionally. Expect it's become noisier over the years. It's getting old. Jake said he thinks you need a new one.'

'As long as it's working, then it'll do.'

Tara liked talking to Madge and that was reciprocated. But she wanted to get on with her patrol, concerned as to what Jock might be doing.

'I brought you some provisions. They're in the kitchen.'

'Thank you Tara.'

'Just going to walk round the Island.'

'Okay. Don't get lost.'

Madge chuckled to herself and watched Tara leave, thinking that she was lucky to have such a wonderful, caring, person, make a special journey to see her.

Tara's walk round the cliff path revealed nothing of Jock and so she made her way to the summit via the path from Island Cottage, doubting he would chose to go that way. That way, she could surprise him. Nearing the top she heard a voice. It was Jock talking to somebody. Quietly, she crept closer until he was just visible.

He was talking on a mobile phone, pacing around in a circle as though marking some boundary, a lek, a caperchaille display ground, where the protagonists were not these grouse-like birds, but the Trevellicks.

'Yes, I've sorted him,' he half shouted into the phone, as though he were talking to somebody on the mainland.

. . .

'Just the Trevellick gang left.'

. . .

'Tom, he's rather stupid but good with computers. He'll be useful.'

. . .

'Got him in my pocket.'

. . .

'No, no trouble.'

. . .

'Can't say that with Jake. He's loyal to Tara.'

. . .

'Tara, well, I'll be pleased to deal with her.'

. . .

'Think it might be on for tonight. Haven't been told. She was very cagy about it.'

. . .

'Not sure exactly, but think there may be some tunnel which they use.'

. . .

'Did a geophys' the other day and found some interesting anomalies. My guess is there are some underground caves from which runs a tunnel.'

. . .

'Geophys' anomaly was too regular to be natural. So probably man-made. Can't be sure, but that's my best guess. Also, there's a tunnel from the cottage, but it appears to go nowhere.'

...

'Sorry, can't hear you. Signal breaking up.'

...

'What?'

...

'Hello. Hello.'

Jock looked at his mobile as though the loss of signal was its fault. He switched it off and proceeded down the path, towards Dunker point. Tara, meanwhile, retreated back the way she came to Smuggler's Cottage which she would easily reach before Jock. Jake was sitting reading the newspaper with a hot mug of tea and a sandwich, ensconced for the evening, quite at home and quite content.

'Tea's just been made. It's in the pot,' he said, not looking up from page three which he had been admiring for some time.

'Never mind about the tea, we've got trouble.'

Now Jake looked up and was about to enquire as to what trouble there was, for he could see none on the Island, when Tara interjected.

'Throw that tea down the sink, and the pot too,' she ordered.

'What?'

'Just do as I say,' she shouted.

Jake knew Tara sometimes had a short temper, particularly when things weren't going her way, and realised this was one of those moments. Without questioning, he did as she said and then waited for further instructions, rather aggrieved that what he pertained was going to be peaceful, quiet evening before removing the goods was now going to be anything but that.

'Look, Jock will walk through that door any minute now. If he asks anything, say we've only just arrived and that we had to bring provisions over for Madge. Is that clear?'

'Perfectly.'

'Good. I'm going over to Madge, as though we've just arrived.'

'Okay.'

Tara made her way over to the cottage just as Jock was approaching. He saw her and immediately stopped in his tracks. What's she doing here, he asked himself? He stepped back out of sight and pondered the situation. He didn't think she saw him. Should he stay and have to explain himself or go? His intention was to observe Tara's next phase of the smuggling operation incognito, but that element had now gone. He decided to return to the mainland and so slipped back to the beach and launched his canoe.

Tara returned after about half an hour. Jake was sitting in the same chair, waiting. Waiting for what, he had no idea and wished whatever was going to happen would happen.

'Where's Jock?' she asked, looking around.

'Haven't seen him.'

'You must have. He would have come back here.'

'Well, he hasn't.'

Tara considered the possibilities and concluded he had spotted her and so had gone back to the mainland. He didn't want to explain himself, she thought, which meant he had not seen her when he was on the phone. With that conclusion, she asked Jake to make a pot of tea and said he could finally settle down for the evening.

Tara, though, was far from settled. The conversation she had overheard was still resonating in her mind, the meaning of it all, the consequences. She went outside and made her way to the end of the Island, across the little bridge onto Trelawney's Isle where she had stood the other day, defying the storm. She looked up at the cottage, to an empty sentinel on the cliff top, hoping to see his figure, a connection like before. But he was not there. Could he be her salvation, she thought. Probably not, if anything he was her nemesis, and yet she believed that she was genuinely concerned for him, especially with Jock out of control.

There was no storm today, it was calm. But she felt like a raging tempest. She had to tame the turmoil that was inside her. Defy Jock. But the turbulence of his conversation and the fact that he had been on the Island, without her knowledge, was battering her, with no respite in sight. He clearly had his own agenda which appeared to be taking over her operation. But above all, she now knew he had an accomplice.

36

It was still pitch black. Not a photon of light penetrated the darkness. Robert's inner-most fears and torments surfaced in the vacuum of the tunnel, a psychological torture of the soul, where a hellish solipsism was experienced. Only this was no theory, it was reality. He was in his own world. No living creature existed alongside him. No life, but his own.

A curious paralysis had overcome him in that void, a sense of clarity that penetrated the dark. A clarity that comes through meditation, where all external distractions, sounds and vision are removed from reality leaving just the physical being and the mind, the unreality of the self. In that black hole Robert had found enlightenment. All his delusions, as Buddhists would describe them, his problems, anxieties, nightmares, even the burden of his cottage, now seemed irrelevant for he was in a trance, in a state of total absorption detached from the external world having stultified reason, and now he felt a sense of freedom and tranquillity. He had attained Nirvana.

He had experienced such a state, although only transitory, once before, when he had spent a month in a Buddhist monastery in the remote region of Ladakh, deep in the Indian Himalayas. It is known as Little Tibet, for in this place there were many Tibetan monasteries, free and away from the constraints of Chinese intransigence, where monks could practice their ancient religion and provide guidance and learning to others.

Robert was one such soul searching for answers to a life that had no meaning. There he had felt happy and contented, a simple life where the pressures of a western society were removed and where the daily ritual of chant and meditation awakened his mind from his sleep of ignorance, to the true nature of things.

In his enlightened world of the tunnel he had now achieved omniscient consciousness, the release from everyday concerns and the extinction of individual passions and he understood that the true path to Nirvana, the ultimate state of spiritual tranquillity, a place of perfect bliss, could only be attained through pain and suffering and by overcoming that paradox.

During his journey to self-awareness he had passed through many states, suffered many setbacks. He had wept, shouted, cursed, dreamt, reasoned, loved and had talked to himself. Any outsider looking into Robert's emotions would think he was insane, and insanity, he thought, was the only way to live his life in the void. He had even imagined he heard Caroline's voice, some distant call, an echo from another world from which he was fading. In that void it was his Buddhist teachings that saved him, a mixture of divine and spiritual intervention, a fusion of beliefs that was the path to his enlightenment.

He felt a propinquity to his thoughts in the totality of existence, a warmth towards his memories of Buddhist teachings and with that comfort, he had come to accept his fate. And so there he was, in his own world, sitting cross-legged waiting to die. How long he had been like it he couldn't say. Time had no meaning in the void. It could be minutes since his encounter with destiny or it could be days, weeks, months, years. It did not matter. Salvation wasn't going to be found in death. He had already found it in life. He had found its meaning. And as he sat there he chanted the Buddhists mantra, *Om mani padme hum*, 'Oh jewel in the lotus flower', taught to him by a monk who told him to recite it whenever he needed guidance or help. Robert didn't need any guidance now, nor help. He was waiting for reincarnation.

As he chanted those sacred words a realisation overcame him, an enlightened clarity as though his mind was shining a corpuscular beam of light at the blocked rock face. He could see. See everything; the tunnel beyond, the outside world, the Island, and the ocean. He could see that the blockage was not solid rock but a fabrication, a man-made construction of brick, weathered over the years so that it looked like granite and an apparent impenetrable barrier. He went over to the wall and ran his hands over it and as he did so some fragments crumbled in his fingers. It was a wall of mundic brick, the blocks which his cottage was constructed of, only here it had been attacked by moisture and it would be possible to chisel it away, if only he had one.

He did, of a fashion. There was the bone. Not a chisel, but it would work, given time. Time is what he had. But after the exertion of climbing back up the tunnel and down again to retrieve it he was thirsty and without water he would not last long, and there was no knowing how long it would take to break through. But despite that, he knew he was going to make it. He had to make it. In the darkest recesses of the void of his mind he had been granted a vision of his future.

How long it took to him to break through to soil Robert did not know. It felt like a lifetime, by which time the bone had been eroded to a fine point which dug into the turf as he thrust it forward. He released the bone and there was light. Not bright daylight, but the background glow of night time, a luminescence from the light of Looe.

To anybody out that night it would have seemed too dark to see anything. But to Robert, it was like the sun itself, a bright shaft of light penetrating his black void, and with that light was the welcome taste of fresh air as he widened the gap to a hole he could push his head through. He could hear the waves breaking in the distance, the cackles of gulls roosting somewhere and far away a siren, the low bass tone of the foghorn for the night was shrouded in mist. Within a few minutes he emerged from the bank like an apparition from some tomb, an unearthly figure that did not belong in this world but lived in the underworld, the world of eternal darkness. Even as he staggered free of his ordeal he still wasn't convinced of his escape but the physical sensation of a damp ground told him otherwise and he gave thanks for his release.

He laid there for quite a while unable to comprehend his salvation. How did he know about the mundic brick? Did he really attain enlightenment in there? Whatever, he was grateful for his redemption, to live once more, to breathe, to love, and he knew he was a better person for his experience. He laid there peering into the night sky, only he couldn't see the stars. But his mind could. He could see through the fog and see the universe in all its glory and the blackness of space seemed a companion, not the mysterious emptiness that he had viewed it many a time before. And he looked at the ground and saw beauty in the grass and even in a snail that was slowly creeping towards him, a creature that was part of his world, a meeting of two beings. He picked it up and put it aside to let the snail continue on its path, both souls in their own world within the infinite vastness of the cosmos.

With some brush and bracken Robert blocked the hole he had made in escaping his tomb and began to make his way back to the cottage. But he had to wait. He had proceeded only a few yards and had yet to get his bearings when he heard voices, not imaginary ones but the low banter of two people somewhere in the mist.

Robert crouched low behind a thicket and waited. They were coming in his direction, their voices getting louder until out of the swirling mist two spectres appeared carrying boxes, blurred visions for he couldn't see their faces, but he recognised one by a limp to his walk whilst the other had a familiarity about him, wearing a colourful shirt that punctured the grey night.

'Thank god this is the last of the shipment,' he said.

'Couldn't agree more. Been a long night having to take the slow route up top and not via the cottage as usual,' came the reply.

'Not sure why she insisted on this way,' the first man continued.

'No, but I bet it's got something to do with him.'

'Jock?'

'Yes, him. Don't trust him.'

'Oh, he's okay.'

And with that the voices faded and the spectres dissolved into the mist.

Robert was about to continue, when more movement caught his ear, now highly sensitive to the faintest of noises the lightest of feet. He waited and out of the mist came another phantom. This time it was a tall, sleek woman with crimson flowing hair which seemed like a beacon of light, illuminating his mind. She was still a blur in the fog, but he knew it was Tara. He wanted to announce his reunion with life to her, but restrained himself for he had the dreadful thought that she might have something to do with his ordeal. So he let her pass and just like the two men, she too merged into the night.

What was going on? Was he witnessing an illusion, a delusion, dreaming it all, death dancing with his mind conjuring the events and he was still back in his dark void and not in the real world. But he knew reality. He could feel the cold mist on his face, on his feet wet from dew, and the continuous low pitch groan of the foghorn playing its warning tune, sending out its message to Robert that he was alive, but to beware. And in this world of impugnment he wanted answers. Who was Jock? What were the two men up to? Was Tara involved in smuggling?

He couldn't make sense of anything right now or begin to answer those questions. He was too tired, too exhausted, too thirsty. All he wanted was his bed, but only after a much needed reality check of his armchair and the mug of tea, which by now had gone cold.

37

$\mathfrak{I}$n one of life's ironies it is often the case that the poacher turns gamekeeper, thief becomes police officer and even a smuggler can change to become a crown prosecutor, a magistrate, a defender of the law. And the latter was no better illustrated than with the Thomas family who metamorphosed from villains to respected pillars of society.

That used to be the Trevellicks' domain. But one act of treachery on that night in 1749 turned them into smugglers. Not immediately, but the slow decay of time worked its insidious tentacles into the fabric of the family through Captain Colliver's curse, slowly eroding their respectability into rotten strands, reaching into the inner recesses of their hearts and minds and turning them into outlaws.

Yet, from that treachery a new order arose. A family whose lives had been embedded in free trade, to that of magistrate, part of the judicial system that they once tried to defy. Just as decay had eaten away at the moral fibre of the Trevellicks, so the Thomas family had fed on that rich harvest and had grown a desire to see justice, to witness the collapse of the Trevellick dynasty and so rid Looe of a disease that had festered for close on two and a half centuries, ever since William Trevellick had become Lord of the Manor, magistrate, entrepreneur and then murderer.

Frederick Thomas was a wealthy man who had made his money in the City. He had now retired to his home in Cornwall, Hendersick Hall, which he had purchased a few years ago. It was located a couple of miles west of Looe in a quiet coombe that gently meandered its way to the coast, near to Portnadler Bay, on the way to Polperro.

Hendersick Hall was an old Tudor mansion of red brick with impressive chimney stacks and crenulated walls, typical of the period, and elegant leaded windows, which were protected by thick variegated ivy all the way up to the roof line. The house resided in its own estate stretching all the way to the coastal path, which gave it private access to the beach. Immediately surrounding the Tudor hall were manicured lawns, edged with Himalayan shrubs and interlaced with a mixture of trees, some young and others mature, but mostly of oriental origin, casting their shadows across the green grass, giving the appearance of an exotic arboretum, a colonial retreat complete with wandering peafowl.

The Hall had a chequered history. Frederick Thomas bought it, partly because of its history, as he was a historian as well as an art collector and connoisseur of antiquities from all around the world. He had been educated at Eton and Oxford, studying history and classics, and despite his years in the City, history was his passion alongside collecting paintings and artefacts from around the world.

He was a cultured man who excelled in whatever he did. Yet he could be scathing about the banal, the humdrum lives of the populous, whom he considered beneath him in social standing and intellect. He would mock their propensity to abbreviate names and adulterate the Queen's English, watch soap operas as if they were reality and worship sport as some sort of tribal cohesion, shamanic dances to an inanimate deity that reduced humanity to a ninety-minute life and where success would bring euphoria, whilst defeat, the melancholy realisation of their pathetic existence.

Frederick Thomas was in his study, a private domain in which he kept his possessions, his acquisitions, as he called them. They had been collected over a period of time when he was a merchant banker during the boom times of the 1980s, the so called Thatcher years, where a new breed of financial predator had evolved. Whereas his colleagues would flaunt and spend their wealth on hedonistic pursuits, lavish holidays, even Porsches; he invested his in historic art, works that represented an era, a fashion or a culture. For all around the wall of his study were paintings, some by obscure artists but others most definitely by the famous including Picasso, Klimt, Manet and his most prized, by the pre-Raphaelite Dante Gabriel Rossetti. As well as these masterpieces, there were art objects and artefacts representing different cultures ranging from a Neolithic figurine to African tribal carvings. The furniture which supported this array of art was equally impressive and the whole room would be an auctioneer's delight.

Money was no object to Frederick Thomas. He was dressed, like his gallery, in the finest clothes and looked as though he were about to spend another day, albeit a little more casual, at the bank. He was a tall man, slight of build, certainly not corpulent like many of his colleagues used to be, considering the many lunches and banquets he used to attend. He was balding, but with hair that had turned grey at an early age, attributed to the stress of the job, he believed, for his father had neither gone bald nor grey until he was into seventies.

He was sitting at his huge desk, which like many a top executive desk was practically empty, devoid of the burdens of work, except for a writing pad on which were a pair of spectacles, paper and a fountain pen. Accompanying the stationary was an elegant Art Nouveau lamp together with a rather odd looking figurine with oversized breasts and an enormous stomach. She was rather ugly, but to Frederick she represented beauty and more besides. He was attracted to the naked female form in all its fascinating variety and to the casual observer, his study would appear to be an eclectic collection of erotic images, perhaps pornographic, but to Frederick it was pure art.

He was speaking to somebody on the telephone, or rather a mobile phone, which to his approval had progressed from the brick-like structure he used to carry around with him to an acceptable size, which he wished he had during those heady days of insider trading and investment banking. His cavalier approach had earned him a reputation not only as a risk taker, but also a person who would let nothing stand in his way to achieve his goal.

'What about the snooper? Have you warned him off?'

...

'Good.'

...

'How do you see it?'

...

'Will he cooperate?'

...

'You sure he'll be no trouble?'

...

'Okay.'

...

'Yes, she can be commanding.'

...

'Well make sure you leave no trail. What about the second phase?'

...

'How do you think it's to be done?'

...

'What makes you think that?'

...

'Are you sure about that? It seems a bit unlikely to me.'

...

'A tunnel from the cottage...Hello. Jock, are you there? Hello.'

The signal had gone leaving Frederick not only frustrated at the poor reception he had to endure but also curious about the tunnel. He left the mobile on hoping Jock would call again. He didn't.

Frederick sat back his chair, a departing gift from his office colleagues, the very same chair he had made, and occasionally lost, millions in a few minutes trading. The later, he considered, were the acceptable risks involved in his job and when describing such instances to friends he took perverse pleasure in telling them that it wasn't his money he had gambled with, but theirs.

He was considering this tunnel. Could there be one? If so it was interesting, not only from the operational angle but historically. He knew of the existence of many tunnels related to religious monuments but not one in this country and it was here in Cornwall, on his doorstep and he could be the one to reveal it to the establishment.

He went over to a large bookshelf and pulled out a book on the history of the two chapels of Lammana and began reading. After an hour of perusing this book and a couple of other volumes, he was frustrated. Nothing, not a hint of a tunnel. He had even looked at the archaeological dig report which would almost certainly, he considered, have found some evidence of a tunnel entrance at the very least. But nothing there either. He rang a bell and after a few moments a man servant entered.

Frederick looked up. 'Christian, do you remember the dig in the 1950s, down at the old chapel of Lammana?' he asked in a quiet and calm voice.

Christian wasn't born in Looe but in nearby Polperro, where he used to live. Even though he was younger than Frederick he was old enough to have remembered such an event, especially as he used to walk the five miles to work as an apprentice shipwright in Looe and would pass the dig every day. It would have been a prominent excavation, perhaps unusual for the area at that time, and Christian had become friendly with some of the workers.

'I do remember the dig FT.'

Rather than calling him Sir, Christian referred to Frederick as FT which he took to be a mark of respect to his working days when colleagues would address him as such. For Christian, it was no deference but rather a mark of displeasure due to his penchant for the Financial Times. It was the newspaper of choice for Frederick, which he used to religiously consult every morning when in the City. He still did, but it meant a requisite journey every day for Christian to collect the offending publication from Looe, even on his days off. But it wasn't that exercise that caused antipathy, but the fact he invariably had to settle the account out of his own pocket, for which Frederick had conveniently, or otherwise, forgotten to reimburse him for.

But he was grateful for Frederick employing him, when so many others had turned him down because of his age. The benefit meant he was allowed to reside at Hendersick Hall, albeit in a rather small garret, after he had been forced to vacate his iconic quaint fisherman's cottage overlooking Polperro harbour in which he had been born and raised, so that it could be renovated and converted into a second home for some wealthy family from London.

Frederick tolerated Christian, not due to some philanthropic gesture but due to a direct request from Christian's granddaughter, an attractive girl in her late twenties who had been seduced by Frederick when he had worked in the City. She had been allured by his wealth, for he was over forty years her senior and looked quite a lot older than his age. She lived in London but Frederick would avail himself for a night or two at his London penthouse suit in Canary Warf, whenever he had business there, and for the rest of the time she was able to live rent-free in luxury she would otherwise be unable to afford. She had asked Frederick, as a favour to her, to employ her grandfather, without his knowledge, and he had agreed.

Working at Hendersick Hall did not agree with Christian. He did not like FT, especially as he paid him a low wage even though he seemed to be working above and beyond his duty. He also felt uneasy entering Frederick's study, surrounded by such unabashed images, reducing the whole estate, he considered, to a place of debauchery. But most of all he detested wearing a suit, since most of his working life he had dressed in manual clothes, the attire of an honest working man, and he felt constrained in the black uniform, a straightjacket which mirrored his demeanour.

'Can you remember who was involved?'

'Well it's a long time ago now, but apart from the director, who I believe died a few years ago, nobody else save George.'

'George?' he queried.

'George Topham.'

'Where can I find this George Topham?'

'He lives in West Looe but seems to frequent the Smugglers Arms, more so than his abode. You can usually find him there most days.'

'Thank you Christian.'

Christian turned to make his exit, but then paused.

'You may also find him in the Quayside Café,' he added, knowing it would touch a nerve.

'Thank you Christian. Oh whilst you're here, some coffee would be most welcome.'

'Yes FT.'

He left leaving Frederick to consider his options.

He would most certainly not enter the Café. Such a place was below his standards, but more significantly Jane served there and he didn't want a meeting in such a degrading looking place with her.

Frederick was acquainted to Jane. She was his mistress and confidant and he had known her since London, when she frequently entertained him in his Mayfair apartment. After his move to Cornwall, he had forgotten about her until one day she had quite unexpectedly turned up at the Hall, announcing herself to Christian as though she were family.

Frederick had been pleased, as too was Jane, to rekindle their routine once more, only this time in the splendid surroundings of his estate. It was the reason Jane had readily agreed to the move to Looe, knowing Frederick had purchased a mansion nearby and thereby she hoped to find a route into his home and affections once more. For Frederick, she would be useful as his eyes and ears in Looe and in particular to his adversary, the Trevellick family. Jane had told him that she was working for Tara Trevellick and would pass on all information that she ascertained and more. Frederick was most certainly pleased.

Meeting this George in the café would compromise their relationship, bring it down to a sordid level, which he had no intention of allowing. So it would be the Smugglers Arms. He had a magistrates hearing late in the afternoon so would seek out this George at lunchtime in the Smugglers, a place which he had never been to, more used to the ambiance of hotel receptions and the food of *haute cuisine* to that of the pub lunch. Still, needs must, he thought, and this could certainly be worth it, not in terms of monetary value, he had enough of that, but the prestige and credibility such a discovery would give him.

Christian brought the coffee in on a silver tray, accompanied with a plate of chocolate biscuits and today's post, the latter of which was late. Frederick cursed what he considered the ineffective way business and commerce operated in Cornwall, as though its remoteness from London was an excuse for unpunctuality or a slow postal delivery. The county wouldn't have been his first choice for retirement, being so far from London, but he had purchased the Tudor mansion because of its history and that it was once the ancestral home of the Thomas family.

During Tudor times, at the height of the reformation, Hendersick Hall was a refuge for catholic sympathisers, the house retaining its original priest hole as well as other places of hiding. Later, when the English Civil War was raging, it was a command post for the Royalists until they abandoned it to defend Plymouth and was promptly taken over by the ragged army of Cromwell's roundheads, before he reorganised it into the New Model Army. It had also served as hospital and officers' mess during the first and second world wars, but more recently it was reduced to a hippy commune until they were forced to vacate by the council for refusing to pay any taxes. Frederick stepped in and purchased the entire estate and had spent most of his liquid assets in repairing the building.

Despite his ambivalence about Cornwall, recent events had proved that it was an auspicious move. He had discovered, via his accomplice, the perfect operation for his passion in art and antiquities and in particular the illegal trade in such valuables, the smuggling operation which he was certain was carrying on through the hands of his arch enemy, the Trevellicks. He intended to grab it in a hostile takeover, worthy of his days in the City. There was to be no asset stripping here, save a few employees, but the simple transfer of operations, and when the dust had settled he would have the perfect undercover route to move art and artefacts in and out of the country.

Jock Stewart was his accomplice. He had known him for a long time and it was he who had secured many of the pieces of art work and antiquities which adorned his study. A few were legitimately purchased and some acquired from dubious sources, but most were there having been stolen, some from museums and art galleries, but the majority from private collectors from around the world and smuggled into the country to end up in Frederick's study.

They were a source of pride, a passion which he could not otherwise afford, for much of his wealth was tied up in stocks, shares and bonds, which he still dealt in, the adrenalin rush of watching a fortune rise was as strong today as it was back in his prime. The habit of a lifetime of work was too embedded to forget and so it was, it seemed, the lifetime of the family's past. The old adage, once a thief always a thief still holds for some as it did for the Thomas family. Except for them, it was once a smuggler, always a smuggler.

38

haze had risen from the sea obscuring the horizon which, up until then, had been clear, gilded in silver, a boundary between two planes that formed the backdrop to Robert's cottage. With the haze the sea and sky merged, an alchemy of elements now forming an indistinct portrait. Sailing craft and other boats floated in an ethereal ocean of a blue and grey palate, spectres, ghostly craft suspended in space, where mass defied gravity and logic was confused by a parallax of slowly moving objects. And in this picture was Looe Island, framed like a giant whale surfacing, a spiritual hump from the depths of the ocean, breathing life to the canvas, a focus for the observer in this impressionistic surreal world.

It was afternoon on a warm sunny day and Robert had just surfaced himself from the depths of a slumber that had consumed his being for over twenty-four hours. He was sitting outside, still somnolent from his rest, but having recovered enough to appreciate the beauty of the day, a wonderful feeling of being alive and a sense of majesty at witnessing this masterpiece of nature where the world was a homogenous wash interjected by the focus of destiny.

And flying into this frame, from the continent beyond were hundreds of butterflies, painted lady butterflies that had wintered in warmer climes and were now on their annual spring migration, to find a mate and produce the next generation. The cottage garden was awash with these beauties and together with native tortoiseshell, peacock and red admiral butterflies they were dancing in the air, aerial acrobatics on the wing, ballerinas, creating a kaleidoscope of colour, a tempera to this canvas signalling that the bright colours of summer were here and life was a beautiful romance.

It was a mesmerising scene and Robert was enchanted by such delicate, perfect creatures that chose his garden to dance their courtship and mate before their short lives came to an end. He wondered if his own life were like these winged beauties, never to be truly fulfilled, never to live a long and happy life, but just experience fleeting moments of pleasure followed by nothing but a vacuum that needed to be filled with meaning. He had travelled half way around the world to seek an answer to that conjecture, yet all the time it was there in front of him, in nature, had he looked, had he taken time, as now, to free his mind of delusions.

Robert looked at his cottage, looked at his garden and looked out to sea. He was living in a perfect picture, an idyll, yet there was something missing, some brush stroke that would complete the scene. It was love, true love. He had found it all those years ago and just as life would be taken away from those butterflies, so his life was snatched from him as though he were not worthy of happiness. Perhaps, he thought, he was a descendant of Captain Colliver and this was his penance, to drift through the eddies of life never to find love again for the Pirate himself took it away from so many.

Caroline had come close to fulfilling his passions since Ireland, but there was something missing from their relationship, an intangible essence that binds two lives together. Was it a shared commitment? Perhaps, he thought. One thing he did know, there was still the spark of desire, a synapse of connection between them which had not been extinguished. Their last encounter had confirmed that, and her declaration of love was one which could only have been heartfelt. And in his tomb, that spark had illuminated his dark world and he knew then that he loved her, had always loved her. It was her love that had kept him alive in his darkest moment, and as he thought that, still somniferous from his ordeal he drifted off into an unworldly sleep, a contented repose in which his mind played snapshots from their adventures, and she was with him, close to him.

Robert was in two worlds. He was conscious of the sea and the cries of the gulls but his mind was in a dream-like state, where reality and the imagined are a mixed blur. With the sun warming his soul he was with Caroline, back in the museum, in the Riad, making love to a sublime goddess once again, a vivid love whose presence seemed real. He heard a susurration, a quiet greeting, an enquiry which seemed like an echo from his dream. Robert half opened his eyes. There she was, still in his dreams, only more real, the vague outline of her body now more focused, sharper than in his mind. Only she was different. She wasn't dressed in her usual conservative attire befitting a professional, one who wished to portray an aura of respectability, but instead before him was a woman announcing her sexuality. He blinked, wondering whether this vision was a figment of his mind, having wandered too far from reality into his world, the world of his mind.

'Hello Robert,' came the whisper.

For a brief moment he was back in the museum once more, only this time she was bathed in sunshine, her beautiful face adorned with a glowing smile that spoke of desire, of finding a lost love in the sea of white haze that framed her sublime figure.

'Hello Caroline,' he uttered, unsure whether he was still in his dreams.

'Hope I haven't disturbed you,' she said, still quietly as though she wasn't sure if he was indeed with her.

'For a while I thought you were in my dreams.'

'You were dreaming about me?'

'Yes. I was in the Riad, in your room.'

He didn't need to go on for she knew exactly what he was dreaming, the same dreams she had been having all these months apart. She sat down next to Robert on the bench and kissed him on the cheek. He responded by holding her hand and gently kissed her on the lips, a passionate kiss as though he were in the Riad, in her room, kissing one another for the first time.

'Strange isn't it,' said Robert, 'how if you think about something, someone, it seems to happen.'

'Strange indeed. Strange how two people can be connected, their minds fused to the same frequency such that their thoughts can transmit between them.'

'You mean some sort of telepathy?'

'Something like that. But more an emotional energy, an indefinable force that connects two people. Remember how when one of us thought something, the other would be thinking exactly the same thought at the same time?'

'Yes. It is strange. One might call it love.'

'That's what I would call it,' replied Caroline, looking at Robert, knowing what he was thinking.

They sat together in silence absorbing the moment, the picture they were viewing, appreciating its beauty its subtle composition, ever changing but remaining constant. They both sat thinking about the Riad, her room, both of them naked on her bed making passionate love, the transcendental love of two people who were connected by a life force that had bound them together for eternity, until the universe itself had expanded beyond their imagination, each one wanting the other yet unable to move, rooted to a belief that time had somehow changed things.

For Robert time had indeed changed things, for in that time he had been having an affair with Tara. Should he say anything? He should. The silence, which was now judging his morality, was broken by him.

'I have a confession to make,' he said looking at Caroline with soulful eyes that portrayed guilt.

'I know,' she replied as though she were waiting for his confessional.

'You know?'

'I know what you're going to confess.'

'You do?'

'That you've had an affair with a woman called Tara.'

'How on earth do you know?'

'Apart from my all-seeing mind,' she joked, 'Siegfried came to see me. He told me about the affair. I must admit that I was a bit shocked, angry even, but I realised we had unintentionally become free agents. I guess you thought I was having some fling with him. I wasn't. So I don't blame you.'

She fell silent, for she herself had a confession to make, but needed a moment of reflection, a moment of composure. She had rehearsed the speech many times, but now, when it was to be performed, she found it difficult to articulate.

'I know it was my fault you left,' she finally opened. 'I realise what a fool I've been, taking you for granted, my work seemingly more important than our relationship. I thought it was unbreakable.'

She paused once more, but then continued.

'A few weeks ago, I had had a busy day and came home feeling very tired. Normally I would just stay in and relax, but that evening I felt a need, a compulsion even, to go out for a walk. Why I don't know. Perhaps just to clear my mind of the delusions of work. Anyway, I was out walking. It was dusk and I saw that same sunset we had sat and watched over the Tibetan plateau, the one where we pledged our undying love no matter what came between us, even if we might be thousands of miles apart we would be together in spirit for eternity. At that moment, I felt your heart in mine, a fusion of love between us that nothing could tear apart. If I hadn't gone out then I'd never had seen that sunset, not from my flat. Was it just chance? Logic tells me it was, but my heart says it was fate, fate that I should choose to go out and witness that sunset, feel the connectivity between us over time and space. It was a message from Tibet delivered in the wind from their prayer flags, from those monks we befriended and who told us that we had a special karma that transcends time, transcends distance, and that when the time is right enlightenment would descend from the heavens to envelop us, welding our minds and our souls together, stronger than ever before, never again to be corroded by indifference.'

Caroline paused again.

'I want us to make a new life together. A new life here. I want it to be our idyll where we have children and grow old together. It was written in those clouds, in the wind, in my heart, and nothing can now erase those lines.'

Caroline was looking out to sea, tears rolling down her cheeks a symbol of her deep love for Robert, who himself had watery eyes and an epiphany of emotion, having been touched by a divine spirit from a place thousands of miles away and yet sitting right next to him. The words, he thought, were like an aria worthy of Isolde herself, a declaration of her undying love to her Tristan, words that were accompanied by the haunting Wagnerian music which played in Robert's mind as he listened to Caroline's recitation.

'I too saw that sunset,' he said. 'I too thought the same.'

And with that, the singing stopped, the music ended and they looked at each other and knew what the other was thinking. It was a physical emotion that needed to be embodied, just as in the Riad, in an act of tantric passion that was theirs and theirs alone. Their naked bodies entwined, energy flowing between their souls, their minds fused, enveloped in orgasmic ecstasy as though they had found their lost horizon, an amour that will now transcend time, transcend distance itself, where only destiny can intervene to destroy their new found love.

•

39

ara had spent the last two days organising the distribution of the contraband and planning the demise of Jock. The mobile phone conversation she had overheard on the Island between him and some unknown conspirator had unnerved her, made her realise how vulnerable her operation was, especially from people she didn't know. It was a family trade and needed to remain so. She would go back to her original scheme of only goods that the people wanted, not the hard drugs of the criminal world where life was cheap and tended to be inhabited by ruthless gangs with no moral justice. The one shipment of cocaine and heroin had brought in a fortune and in the world of illegal trade, greed was the enemy, not the law.

She was on her way up to Robert's cottage. She wanted to see him. She wanted to make love to him and feel his naked body next to hers. To be part of his world again where normality was the backbone to his life, where everyday chores were a pleasure to be savoured rather than endured, as it seemed her life was right now.

It was another lovely day and as she approached the path which ascended to his cottage in the warm sun, the scent of honeysuckle out in full bloom caught Tara and she breathed in the heady aroma and felt an erotic vigour flowing through her, a renewed determination to win Robert all over again.

She knocked at the door. No answer. She tried the door. It wouldn't open. She knocked again. Still no answer. She hoped he was in. He must be in after his unexpected disappearance the other day, she thought, and knocked again. This time she heard footsteps descend the stairs and her hopes were filled with anticipation but were immediately chastened as the door was opened, because there standing in front of her was Caroline, with nothing on save one of Robert's shirts which was enough to cover her from feeling embarrassed.

'Hello,' she said, 'you must be Tara.'

Tara had been floored in one blow and Caroline hadn't even touched her. It was bad enough seeing her in Robert's cottage, but without any clothes on, so to speak, this was too much. All her hopes and feelings had been scattered on the floor and she was left with only the fragments of her desires.

'I haven't had the pleasure.'

'No, but I have,' said Caroline in a satisfying tone which left Tara with no doubt as to what she meant.

'And you are?' asked Tara, still composed but beginning to whelm up inside.

'I'm Caroline. Robert's partner.'

'I'm sorry, but I didn't realise he had one. He told me he had moved down here on his own.'

'Well, we did have a period of separation but that's now in the past. We are very much together once again and for good.'

Caroline was taking pleasure from jabbing Tara, stripping her bare, making her more and more uncomfortable with each word she spoke and enjoying her advantage, something which she had never done before. But Tara was a determined adversary, a seasoned veteran of such sparring, and she could take the attacks, the jibes, in her stride. She wanted to hear from Robert himself, hear that he had chosen this woman, who was as beautiful and as cunning as herself. She looked passed Caroline into the hallway, silently asking to be admitted, which Caroline had no intention of doing.

After hearing the knocking on the door and peering out of the window to see this woman standing by the porch, she had decided to be steadfast and not let her steal any advantage. She assumed it was Tara and since Robert was still asleep, still resting, she had undertaken to evict her from Robert's life without his knowledge.

'May I speak to Robert?' asked Tara, very politely and with a restrained smile.

'I'm afraid not, he's fast asleep. I don't want to disturb him.'

'It's important,' she said. But it was unconvincing and in any case Caroline was going to ignore the request.

'I'll tell him you called, but I don't think he wants anything to do with you anymore.'

She was about to close the door in Tara's face when Robert came stumbling down the stairs, wondering what was going on, only to see the two women in verbal combat. To his innocent eye, in female mud-wrestling there was no winner between the combatants, only the delight in watching two perfect bodies reduced to a frenzied spectacle of mud-slinging. So he decided to stop half way down and sat on a rung to watch the outcome. But Caroline had heard him and turned around to announce it was Tara, but that she was just leaving. Tara had spotted him too and seized her chance.

'Hello Robert,' she said, brushing passed Caroline before she had realised her mistake in leaving a gap, which Tara had just exploited.

'Hello Tara,' replied Robert, seemingly disappointed to see her, which he was, but more aggrieved that he was denied an opportunity to see these two adversaries in action.

'Cup of coffee would be most welcome,' declared Tara, 'as usual,' with emphasis, so that Caroline knew she was in a fight.

'I'll make it,' she said, and left Robert and Tara to an uneasy posturing towards the lounge, Robert sitting in his window armchair opposite Tara.

She looked at Robert. His gaze was out the window, detached from her not knowing how to proceed. But he needn't have been circumspect for it was Tara who was concerned, concerned that she hadn't seen him for some time and in that time this woman had taken her place in his bed.

'Sorry I've not been to see you for some time but work has been a bit hectic recently.'

'Thought you were on holiday. That's what the chap in the estate agents said.'

'Yes I was,' thinking she might have escaped a full explanation.

'How did the London trip go?'

'London trip?'

'Yes, your conference.'

'Oh boring.'

'So you attended?'

'Yes,' she said with a questioning tone, as to why he had asked.

'Then how come I saw you, here in Looe?'

'Think I got back early.'

She could tell by the frankness of Robert's questions that he was angry and she needed to placate him somehow.

'I called the other day but you were out. In fact, I've called on a several occasions in the past few days with no answer. I've been concerned. At least I can see you're alright.'

'Yes, I'm okay.'

He was still looking out the window. Not once did he look at Tara. She, though, was looking at Robert, watching the nuances in his facial expression for any sign of an ease in his intransigence. She was deciding whether to play her trump card, the affair they had, when Caroline came in with a tray of coffee.

She had been eavesdropping from the kitchen and could see Tara was making no headway against Robert, with a tangible tension between them.

'Good to see you two are getting on so well,' she said, breaking the silence in a cheerful tone so as to emphasise their estrangement.

'Just reminiscing,' said Tara.

'Reminiscing on five months work here?' queried Caroline. 'Robert and me have had five years of happy memories,' she added.

Tara had now had enough. She had lost one argument today with Jane, but wasn't about to let it happen twice. She was now going to strike a decisive blow towards Caroline.

'We've had a happy five months, haven't we Robert? Plenty of good memories.'

Robert was still looking out the window, his mind seemingly outside somewhere, a model of equanimity. He had been listening intently to the verbal sparring and wondering who was winning. Caroline was well in the lead on points, he thought, but that last comment of Tara's disguised a fight back. He now looked at her, determination written on her face and he knew what she was about to say.

'It has been good getting the cottage renovated,' he said stoically, hoping that he was wrong.

'I meant,' added Tara, 'we've had a happy, no delightful, no, more, satisfying I would say, five months in your bed.'

Caroline looked at Tara, not with surprise or even anger as expected by her, but with a resigned air that it was yesterday's news. Tara's knockout punch hadn't even winded Caroline.

'I know,' she triumphantly declared.

'You think you know all about it,' replied Tara with venom, knowing full well, she probably didn't. 'You know all about how I would tie Robert to the bed and make him proclaim his undying love and devotion to me. Not you.'

This was now a body blow to Caroline. She hadn't expected such a fierce assault, and one so candid.

'Yes I know. Not every sordid detail, but I know about your bondage sessions.'

Robert now looked at Caroline with surprise, somewhat embarrassed. How did she know?

'I found the rope in the bedroom and imagined she hadn't been showing you how to tie a bowline.'

Up until that point Robert had been a spectator in the bout, listening to the two beautiful women fight over him, something he could never have expected twenty-five years ago as a teenager, shy and hopeless with the female sex. Here in front of him were two perfect goddesses who were engaged in combat, the spoils of which would be him and his desire to worship them, as though he were an irrelevant mortal in a clash of Titans.

He had had enough of the insults and decided to referee the match.

'Stop you two,' he forcefully demanded. 'You're like two thick-skinned mud-wrestlers. Let's call it a draw. And I think you had better take your leave, Tara, before things get out of hand.'

Tara agreed. She had been defeated once again by another adversary who was better than her, had more in her armoury, and had won by tactics rather than crude insults. She had lost and left to lick her wounds, having made an excuse of an appointment at the Estate Agents.

Robert felt sorry for Tara, for she had helped him in the renovation of the cottage and had been there to help when Caroline was not. His ambivalence was tempered by the conclusion that there were indeed no winners in female mud-wrestling, only the audience, and he smiled a perverse smile that he would really like to see them partaking in the real thing, and that given the opposing talents Tara would probably win that contest.

'What is it?' asked Caroline.

'Nothing.'

'It's not nothing. I can tell. You've got a lurid smile, one that suggests something - immoral.'

'You could say. Just amused by you two.'

'How so?'

'Well, your verbal sparring reminded me of mud wrestling.'

'Female mud wrestling I assume?'

'I know it's rather sexist, but that's what made me smile.'

In the past, Caroline would have erupted into a tirade of insults at Robert for thinking such a chauvinistic expression. But she had changed and wanted him to know it, even though she was somewhat hurt by his thought that she, an intelligent woman, would stoop to such a basic level to satisfy a primordial male lust.

'It is. But I guess you're just a normal man beneath that sensitive exterior.'

Caroline pulled Robert towards her by his dressing gown belt, undid the cord and slid the robe off. She proceeded to repeatedly run her hands over his chest and down to his groin several times as he stood there, naked, exposed to her desires. She had read his mind, for she then began to run her fingers over his nipples and then squeezed them, digging her nails in gently, applying the pain for which he craved. She could see the effect it was having. Each time he would respond to her, would submit to her in a way he would never have done before, for the pain found a conduit to his desires and he begged for more. She found it stimulating, arousing her own passion and they went back upstairs to explore a new dimension to their tantric love where he would worship her naked body in a spiritual arousal, where the pain was an aphrodisiac, a drug that Robert was addicted to and now, so too Caroline.

*　　*　　*

It was late morning, almost midday, when they surfaced once more, having spent an eternity in carnal pleasure. They were in the parlour having a late breakfast when Caroline spoke of her previous visit.

'I see you've put an inspection cover over the crypt.'

'Yes, a double one.'

'And have you explored the tunnel yet?'

'In a way, yes.'

'How do you mean?'

'Well, I went right to the end and it was blocked.'

Caroline was disappointed to hear that, but then Robert explained the circumstances. She listened with increasing incredulity at his imprisonment in the black void, as he put it, and how his Buddhist teachings helped him survive the ordeal. And his vision of the granite wall was a miracle to match any such Christian saints, remarked Caroline. He then explained how he got out using the bone of the skeleton, a fate that he described as fortuitous, for had he not missed it he may still be entombed in his underworld.

'You poor soul, Robert. I cannot begin to imagine what it was like,' said Caroline, taking him in her arms and comforting him.

'I think I experienced every emotion, every nightmare known to man in there,' he said with conviction. 'If it wasn't for you Caroline, the thought of never seeing you again, then I'd be dead by now. You saved me.'

Caroline was touched by this gesture of faith in her ability to keep him alive. She hugged him even tighter.

'When I broke through it was night time and quite by chance, I caught sight of Tara and two men carrying boxes up the cliff, I assume to some van parked in the field up top.'

'What do you think they were doing?' she asked.

'Well, I'm not entirely certain, but I think they were involved in some smuggling from the Island.'

'Surely not. Old fashioned smuggling like that, in this day and age?'

'What else could it be? And speaking of the Island, guess who I spotted out there.'

'Cannot say,' replied Caroline, although she had a feeling who he was going to mention.

'Siegfried.'

'I'm not surprised. You know I said he visited me. Why, he never said, although I was led to believe he was just informing me about you and Tara. The thing is whilst he was in my flat, I think he saw my research into Lammana.'

Caroline explained how, when she returned to London the previous time, she dug out an old map purchased in the bazaar in Tangiers. That was a copy. She wanted to see the original, the one in the museum. Using her contacts, she managed to obtain a copy of that map, which the authorities were only too glad to help, especially the prestigious British Library. Her copy was identical, except for one important part: on the reverse of the original was a verse, a cryptic message to treasure. Robert read her transcribed text.

To Lammana thou must go
Across t'sea a verdant Isle
There you'll find a place next the sea
And treasure there be found

'What do you make of the verse?' she asked, noticing Robert ponder its contents for a few moments.

'Clearly, it refers to the Island and suggests that there is treasure to be found over there.'

'The reference to an island could be anywhere, although that is the obvious conclusion. That's what Siegfried wanted to find out, I think, whether I knew anything about the Island and treasure. And I handed it on a plate to him,' she said with a sigh.

Caroline now paused to think for a few moments, before continuing her exposition.

'There's something else about the map. Something which Siegfried would not have seen. In fact, neither have I. Next to the text is the faint trace of another map. It's too faint to discern any outline. I've had it sent for x-ray analysis. It may be nothing, but it could be important. I should receive it in the next few of days.'

She paused again.

'One last piece of information. After Siegfried's visit I phoned my dad. You know he's a retired police inspector. I told him about Siegfried and asked if he'd be able to find anything out about him. Well he certainly did. A few days later he rang me to say that apparently he is on the police radar. His real name is John McNeish but he uses several aliases: Jock McNab, Jock McKenzie and McCallum Stewart, to name but a few. He has been convicted for handling stolen goods and is currently under investigation for a possible connection to illegal trade of works of art.'

'It must be him who shut me in the tunnel. He is the only person strong enough who could move the altar so quickly. I'm sure it was him.'

'If so, then he's got something to do with Tara and the smuggling,' concluded Caroline.

'That's the conclusion I've arrived at. Whatever is going on, be it smuggling or something else, the answers are to be found over there,' as he pointed to Looe Island. 'I'm going to go over there and find out. I'm determined to get to the bottom of this intrigue.'

'Don't you think it would be wise to go to the police?' she responded, now concerned that they may become involved in something beyond their depth.

Robert looked at the Island which was bathed in sunshine and seemed inviting, a place where adventure could be found. If Tara was involved, which he somehow doubted, he didn't want her to be associated with Siegfried. He seemed to be several leagues above her in the criminal world. He was going to ignore Caroline's request, even though she was right.

But he would have done well to remember its aspect yesterday, when it looked ghostly, a place of portent, for he was going to enter a place shrouded in mystery and encumbered with its past, a place where his and Tara's destiny would finally be played out, deep in the bowls of the Island.

40

Clouds are nature's poetry. Without them, there would be no drama. They communicate her moods as a moving stanza of emotion. Fair-weather cumulus clouds often confer well-being, a sense of contentment at their amorphous shapes, whilst towering cumulonimbus are menacing, a warning of turbulent times. Even for the most optimistic meteorologist, a prolonged heavy blanket of stratus with its persistent drizzle and dull conditions can induce a morose pessimism, forcing the affected individual to seek relief in clear-blue skies.

The day had started out saturnine as dawn proclaimed its presence over the mainland beyond Rame Head, just after five o'clock in the morning. Yet two hours later the overcast conditions had all but cleared Hendersick Hall, leaving the residence bathed in a photogenic light. Shadows were reaching out across the lawn, rays bringing to life the fading wisteria that covered the south façade and stone features that soon would be hidden by the midday sun, silhouetted, providing a brief glimpse of unnoticed forms. Even in summer the mornings are often chilly and with the mercury having dropped in the small hours of the morning, dew now bedecked the estate grass, creating coloured reflection in the droplets, from a low penetrating sun.

Inside the Elizabethan Hall, despite the warm morning outside, a fire was alight in the study. Facing the front of the building it was always cold, its French doors having a northerly aspect, receiving little sun. There were plenty of rooms that Frederick could have chosen with sunny dispositions and better views of the gardens, but he had selected the room specifically because it seldom saw any sunlight, except at dawn and dusk during the summer months. Perhaps it reflected his antipathy of people, a self-induced dissonance to his embedded pessimism, where sunlight could cure the disorder and provide harmony to his life. But he didn't want that. Rather, he would prefer to suffer the isolation of reason than conform to normality. He wanted to be different.

He was different. Friends were not his wanting. As a youngster he was slight of frame with a timid and detached trait which manifested itself in seeking his own company. It was an ingrained trait, that other children had misunderstood, considering the peculiarity as aloofness, that resulted in him being bullied, not only by his peers but by his father too, who ridiculed him, considering him lacking ambition and altogether an unworthy heir. Naturally, Frederick retreated into his own shell where people were despised and if he was unhappy, so too should others be. He would relish when the weather was gloomy, particularly if it lasted for weeks, for it seemed to dampen enthusiasm and induce melancholy in his persecutors.

Frederick had selected the study room, not because of his lugubrious personage, but because it was capacious and ideal to display his treasured art and antiquities. To preserve their fabric the collection needed to be away from the damaging ultra-violet rays of the sun. That was of paramount importance. Of secondary concern was his comfort, and so Christian was tasked with lighting a fire on most mornings when FT was in residence, even though well-favoured weather had been forecast. Christian considered it not only unnecessary and somewhat of a luxury, especially when many folk could ill-afford heating during the cold winter months, but also with the attendant ash and fumes of a wood-burning stove, a hazard to the integrity of Frederick's beloved possessions.

Nobody else was in the room as he started the fire. He could hear voices in the hallway and shortly after that, Frederick and Jock came into the study. They had been eating breakfast in the morning room, which benefited from the early warmth of the sun, and had lingered there discussing plans, which even Frederick had enjoyed, more used to partaking meals in his study by a fire which provided comfort and familiarity to the old man.

'That's settled then. You'll go out to the Island tomorrow and carry out the plan as discussed,' announced Frederick in a commanding tone, sitting back in his chair at the desk.

'I'll make sure they are all out there before I take over. That way, I know there will be no surprise visits,' countered Jock, as he shuddered from the cold atmosphere. He glanced at the fire which had yet to emit any heat. 'You should consider some other form of heating this room,' he quipped.

'The wood burner is good enough, thank you very much.'

'Yes, but I was thinking of your acquisitions, particularly the paintings.'

'They're far enough away from the heat.'

'But what about the dust and fumes?'

'They can be cleaned. In any case, I like a real fire and the stove does provide some protection.'

Frederick got up and went over to the fireplace to inspect the embryonic fire that Christian had started and who was now kneeling down and adding larger pieces of wood to the burgeoning flames. He looked up at FT, expecting him to comment that the blaze was too fierce or not enough wood had been used, as he often did in his condescending style, but today he just ignored him, perhaps because of an audience.

'When you've done Christian, some coffee.'

'Yes FT. For one or two?'

'For two.'

Christian was well used to FT's brusque nature but was naturally unaware of its history. It was ironic, he thought, that it seemed to coincide with good weather, when he himself felt uplifted as though all his woes were endurable. Normally, FT would offer polite indifference wanting to project a polished sedate character, an image in contrast to his ruthless streak, one that he must have in his line of work. He shrugged his shoulders, closed the stove door and finished tidying the hearth, unnoticed by the two men looking at a new acquisition Jock had secured.

It was a birdman carving from Easter Island. Jock had purchased the carving from a private source, very cheaply, claiming it to be a modern copy which had been poorly disguised to look old.

'At the time, I wasn't entirely sure myself whether it was a fake or not. I've had it authenticated by radio-carbon dating, and it has been found to be an original. It dates from the mid to late eighteenth century, about the time the cult first appeared on the Island.'

Frederick explained the birdman cult to Jock, and how an annual race to an island rock two miles off the main coast to obtain an egg from nesting sooty terns and back again, resulted in the winner claiming the title of birdman for the coming year, and with it privileges in a society where resources were scarce. The birdman carving, therefore, was a symbol of prowess and triumph, qualities which he appreciated and accordingly he placed the object on the mantelpiece in full view, as a reminder to his success in the City. Jock knew all this, of course. He needed to if he was to obtain all these objects of art, but he didn't want to spoil FT's moment in espousing his knowledge.

'Talking of the birdman,' said Frederick, 'I gather that the disguised ornithologist come revenue man was found dead the other day.'

'Yes, I heard it too.'

'Anything to do with you?' enquired Frederick.

'Well, the last time I saw him he was still alive. I admit that we had an altercation and I pushed him and he fell down the cliff, but I thought he was unhurt.'

'Hmm,' considered Frederick. 'Be careful Jock, I don't want such pernicious actions done in my name. Is that clear?'

'Yes FT. I'll be more careful.'

'So how will you deal with the Trevellick girl?'

'Not entirely sure yet. It often depends upon the immediate circumstances, but rest assured I will be careful, if that's what you were thinking.'

'It had crossed my mind. Remember Jock, not in my name.'

Jock was only too aware of FT's feelings about violence, more concerned for his own welfare, than that of Tara, who he knew represented a longstanding grudge held by the Thomas family against his adversary. For Jock, his concern was for the mission, getting a result, because that meant he would be paid and if there was collateral damage, then it was a price worth paying.

He was used to such circumstances in his world and contrary to what Frederick said, he was doing all this in FT's name, as he looked around the room at the art work, most of which he had secured. He bid him good day, just as Christian came into the study with coffee, who stood stupefied, watching Jock as he strode through the hallway and stepped out into the mid-morning sunshine, a welcome radiance from the oppressive gloom of the study.

*   *   *

The sun was radiating more than warmth upon Robert and Caroline. They were still in bed, oblivious to a world that was revolving, moving on, making plans, sadness and sorrow, joy and happiness, new life and death. They were in a carefree world of love, where there are no problems, no anxieties, where life itself is pure bliss, where reality is side-lined in favour of amorous lust, where nothing matters except the other person, their body, their soul, their love.

They were lying there, on the bed, infused with warmth from the sun's rays that were streaming through the bedroom window, providing a life-giving force to two people who were lost in their own passion. They were sated and entwined from making love. Not the masochistic seduction that Caroline so expertly manoeuvred yesterday, when she had enjoyed delighting in Robert exalting her body, controlling his desires, and watching him succumb to her domination, so that he would, as he was only too desirous to do, worship her as a goddess. No, not that, but the gentle and slow touches of sensuous love, where fulfilment comes from enlightenment of the mind and body, where the energy between two bodies melts and merges to create a spiritual communion of deep intimacy, culminating in a wave of euphoria of two minds in union, two hearts locked together and two souls lifting consciousness beyond the physical plane of reality.

Robert was the first to make a move back into the real world. He got up and looked out into the bright scene. The sky was a perfect blue. Without a cloud to be seen, there was no focus in its limpidity until a profiled horizon. The sea, however, was glistening like diamonds from a radiant sun, creating patterns which constantly changed with the current, a moving composition studded by jewel-like craft in an ocean of opulence. He watched a luxury cruiser, the one which had a berth near the bridge and was adorned with netting, make its way out of the harbour and past a sleek schooner anchored in the bay. It was an impressive craft and in Robert's current libertine mind, he wondered which of the two vessels would befit Caroline.

He glanced back at her. She lay there asleep, her naked body radiating in the sun from his adoration, a sublime figure whose sensual curves and smooth skin were a delight to his senses, and were a mimesis of the moored craft. She opened her eyes and smiled. It was a smile of contentment, of love. He smiled back, a smile of devotion and fulfilment, thinking that she was a divine spirit of the sea that had to be worshiped. She closed her eyes and drifted back into her contented world.

Robert looked out to the Island. He could see a forlorn looking figure standing at the edge of the world and knew it was Tara. In that moment, he felt a pang of sorrow for her. In his mind he said sorry, sorry that it was not different – for her. His mind wandered back to the storm. There had been a brief affinity between them. They had been two lonely figures united by a desire, a need for love. He had found his. She though, was still a solitary soul in a world of six billion people and her world, her destiny, was to be alone on the Island, an island that once sang of brotherhood, unity and the holy spirit of mankind.

* * *

For Tara, the radiance of the morning sun was lost on her. She could not feel its warmth, for she was in a world of no meaning, standing in her favoured place on the Island, at the extreme tip on Trelawney's Isle, seeking solace in its remoteness, its sense of space where solitude can be washed away by the tide. She wanted it to happen. She wanted absolution. But unlike the storm, where the crashing waves would have obliged her, today the sea was calm, a benign spirit that was to continue her torment.

She had been in a state of desolation since her enforced retreat from Robert's cottage. Melancholy was consuming her, eating her away, for she was, despite the situation, still in love with Robert. She reproached herself for not realising it sooner or making a move earlier, before Caroline appeared to claim him. She was sure of his infatuation.

She would have won him, but for a woman who had outflanked and outfought her. The Island was all that she had left.

With all her misgivings, she felt alone. To accompany her sense of emptiness she was on the edge of an extreme, a place where land meets sea, a no-mans-land of rock, and the forces that play out are ones of defiance against destruction. In her mind's eye storm clouds were gathering, enveloping her mood, and despite the uncertainty she relished the challenge of defying its onslaught. This was her destiny, she thought. Her and Robert's destiny? She was unsure. Whatever, there was an instinctive ambiance that it was about to be played out soon: she felt it in her bones, in her sinews, in her heart. They were tense from expectation as though a fall in barometric pressure had conditioned her attitude. She needed to prepare her defence against an assault that was surely to come from Jock. He was her enemy and that enemy would kill to achieve its aim: the destruction of her and the Trevellick family. Where Robert fitted into this battle, she didn't know, but he was going to play an important part, one which would decide both their fates.

41

$\mathcal{A}$nybody who lives by the sea is in some way influenced by its tidal rhythms. Fishermen certainly are. The visitor to the coast, unaccustomed to the daily ebb and flow, will be aware of the tides if they stay long enough. Even the wildlife, birds such as Sanderling, Dunlin, Knot and a host of other waders, their feeding habits are governed by the tides. At low water, they will be on the inter-tidal mudflats of estuaries or on the shoreline feeding on invertebrates, constantly following the water's edge, only to be evicted when the tide finally reclaims its territory.

Tides, though, are not what they seem. To the casual observer, the sea appears to rise and then fall, flow in and out along a static coast. It is an illusion. As a body of water, it is the sea that remains static against a backdrop of a rotating earth during its twenty-four hour cycle.

The moon is the driving force for tides. The sun does have an effect, albeit weaker, and together with bathymetry, the geography of the coastline and oceanic currents, all combine to create tides that vary with location. It is the gravitational force of the moon that exerts an elliptical bulge in the oceans and when a point on the earth, such as Looe, is in direct alignment along its major axis, it creates a high 'spring' tide. This has nothing to do with seasonality, since there are two spring tides each month as the moon orbits the earth, but rather a term to describe a tide springing forth. As the earth rotates, after about six hours or so, that point becomes orthogonal to the moon and is correspondingly on the minor axis of the ellipse, so that a low-tide is the result. Move on another six hours and Looe is back onto the major axis again and another high tide, with a final low tide forward another six hours, resulting in the familiar diurnal pattern.

During the moon's elliptical orbit of the earth, these spring tides are particularly high or low when it is either a new or full moon, when it is more or less in alignment with the sun which reinforces the gravitational effect of the moon, a period known as syzygy. At other times of this orbit, during the quarterly phases of the moon when the sun and moon are orthogonal to one another, the gravitational influence of the sun counters that of the moon, reducing the tidal range to a minimum and lower 'neap' tides are observed.

On the equinoxes, when the sun and moon are in alignment and the moon is at perigee, it's closest to the earth, these tides are exceptionally high and exceptionally low and account for a large tidal range in Looe of almost twenty feet. And if a strong southerly gale is blowing on a very high spring tide, it is not uncommon for the town to flood from the tidal surge, particularly in the old quarter where many of the properties lie below the harbour wall. In comparison on the corresponding low spring tide it is possible to walk out to the Island, albeit getting slightly wet feet since the water does not disappear completely, but leaves a channel of thirty feet or so to negotiate by wading through water ankle high.

The vernal equinox had long passed, when the tides are at their most extreme and when, by tradition, folk would wade out to the Island and be greeted by the Carter sisters and presented with a daffodil by Annie, grown in the walled garden next to the Island Cottage. Since her death Tara had tried to stop the practice, but visitors still wade across the channel fascinated by the fact that it is possible to walk to the Island as those early monks once did, albeit then along a causeway. To discourage unwanted visitors she had erected a sign to remind them that the Island was private and that no landing was allowed. She didn't want casual strangers wandering around, although that was highly unlikely since anybody who attempts the crossing has but a few minutes on the beach before they have to return, lest they wish to swim. And an incoming tide can cause a strong current through the channel which only a confident swimmer would be wise to attempt.

Robert had been observing the tidal paradox, watching the sea recede from the rocky shoreline and the kelp field slowly reveal its fronds. Robert knew of the tidal illusion and was now beginning to wonder if Tara was casting a similar deception upon him. He had to find out.

It was late July and just over a month to the Autumnal equinox, when the tides would be at their lowest again. Even now they were still quite low and Robert was going to wade across the channel to the Island. A low spring tide was due; one in the early afternoon, the other in the early hours of the following morning when a new moon would create the perfect cover for his adventure.

Caroline wanted to accompany him but Robert said he needed her on the mainland, just in case anything went wrong.

'What could go wrong?' she queried looking rather concerned.

'Don't know, but I'd feel happier if one of us were here, looking out,' replied Robert.

'I suppose you're right. But promise you'll be careful.'

'Of course I will. If there's any sign of trouble, I'll lie low until daybreak and you can ask John, the café proprietor, to pick me up from the jetty.'

Robert had thought of asking John to take him out there, but he didn't really want to involve him unless absolutely necessary. And a rescue would be one of those situations.

'All right,' said Caroline, resigned that she was to be a spectator in his adventure, one that she wanted to be a part of.

July and August is the high season for Looe, as it is for the rest of Cornwall. With the schools on their summer break and visitors on their annual holiday, crowds of people were thronging into the town, a steady stream of mankind all heading for the sea front.

The last few days had been hot and sunny and the beach had been packed, so much so that when Robert and Caroline had seen it from the old coastal path as they made their way into town, they could hardly believe their eyes for the sea of bodies. They were exhibiting all degrees of shades from lily-white to lobster-red, with each family group having staked out their territory with wind breaks or towels, some with pushchairs and others with inflatable dinghies and tents, a circular encampment separating them from their neighbours, creating a coloured mosaic in-filled with a sandy matrix. The sight both bemused and amused them, the effect being that they turned around and headed back to the peace and seclusion of the cottage.

Today was another hot day and low tide was due at about two o'clock in the afternoon. It was still an hour away but the rock platform and mass of kelp were already exposed and a crowd of people were now making their way out to the Island. Within half an hour that crowd had been transformed into a multitude, Robert estimated about one hundred, all wading through the shallow water trying to avoid patches of slippery seaweed, many treading carefully, gingerly, as though the shallows might hide some deadly creature that would pierce the unsuspecting skin of anybody brave enough to cross with bare feet.

It was a sight to behold, and if not a march into the unknown then it was an adventure where blue starfish and strange sea cucumbers, scallops and the occasional stranded guppy could be hunted and friends made with the natives next to them, laughing and joking in the absurdity of the expedition because they had forgotten their hat or sunglasses and were now beginning to suffer the hardships of life without the comforts of their camp.

And in that phalanx were Robert and Caroline. She was not happy, hating the crowd, exasperated by the bawdy banter and the stubborn cries from children who refused to go any further, and the stupidity of one parent who had brought a pushchair. Robert pointed out, despite her reservations, that there was safety in numbers and it was unlikely they would be spotted with the mass of humanity alongside them. They were there, of course, to research the crossing, for Robert was naturally going to attempt it at night and a crossing during the day would give him an idea of where to go and what places to avoid.

As they approached the beach Robert could see the two men he had seen the night he escaped the tunnel, one stationed at the entrance to a track on the left hand side of the upper beach, and the other man on the right leading to the low coastal path around the Island. Both men were pointing to the sign and directing people back the way they had come. They were definitely not allowing anybody to set foot on the Island itself, although some hardy and foolish men were trying to negotiate the jagged rocks, presumably to find an alternative route.

There was no sign of Tara but she must be somewhere, thought Robert, and he scanned the place to see if he could spot her. Why he wanted to see her, he wasn't sure, but felt that she and the Island were one, that there was some sort of symbiotic relationship between them and without the sight of Tara, the Island was a deserted shell without a soul.

Within an hour of low tide the Island was indeed deserted. Everybody had made their way back in a mass exodus from the beach as though fleeing from some disaster; a sinking ship or an island that was about to erupt. With the last few stragglers wading chest deep, the sea reclaimed its rocky platform once more only to have to relinquish it again twelve hours later.

After their foray, Robert and Caroline went back to the cottage and sat outside under a parasol. Robert was studying the Island, psyching himself up for the night crossing, but still searching for a glimpse of Tara through his binoculars. Caroline was reading his book on smuggling.

'Did you know that women often feigned pregnancy so that they could hide bladders of brandy under their voluminous skirts, taking the contraband to be sold secretly away from the Revenue Officers,' she said, thinking that Robert would be interested in this surreptitious activity. 'And that…' she continued turning to Robert, who had not heard a word, having dozed off.

She was glad he was asleep. She continued to read, absorbed by the tales of smugglers and the excise men, a battle of wits, each one trying counter the other and, in particular, the resourceful and extraordinary lengths the free traders would go to hide contraband from the preventive officers. But after a while, she too succumbed to the soporific influence of a lazy afternoon.

By early evening, the lazy afternoon had metamorphosed into an al fresco dinner followed by an evening watching the dusk settle over the Island, preceded by a setting sun, a red orb that seemed to float downwards beneath the horizon behind the cottage until its presence was no more than just a glow, which then faded to a western radiance. Robert tried to catch a bit more sleep but was wide awake, thinking about what he had let himself in for. He was having second thoughts.

Maybe it's better to go tomorrow, he questioned himself. Why do something now when you can do it tomorrow, used to be Caroline's rhetoric at his inertia? He'd like to think it wasn't true, but knew there was a grain of truth in the mantra.

The intense afternoon heat had given way to a sultry evening. Crickets could be heard, their familiar stridulations an evocation of the cicadas of the Mediterranean countries. The night felt like one too, unusual for Cornwall with its maritime influence. With global warming becoming a real possibility, according to the prophets of doom, Robert thought it would be rather fortuitous that Cornwall would become the favoured place for holidays. That would be fifty, perhaps one hundred, years in the future and he, like most people alive, would not benefit from such speculation.

Time was going slowly for Robert as he considered all the permutations that could go wrong with the venture. He looked at his watch and tried to distract his mind from the task ahead, the delusions of failure, or worse capture by Siegfried. It was only ten minutes ago that he had checked the time and the minute hand had barely moved, or so it seemed.

Low tide that night was at two thirty in the morning which would give him about three hours before dawn, plenty of time to make it across and seek a hiding place. First he was to signal to Caroline that he'd made it and was alright. Three flashes on his torch, after which he was going to make for the cottages and various other buildings, hoping that nobody would be up at that unearthly hour. He wanted to see if there was anything unusual and from there go to the far side of the Island to the caves he had seen from *Lady Jane*, particularly the larger one, and see where it led to. After that he had no idea, but by then the tide would be on its way out and he would have to wait for low tide and make his way back across the channel.

As the time finally approached, Robert began packing a small rucksack with a few items; a torch, camera, spare plimsolls, some sandwiches, chocolate and a bottle of water. Having finished that, it was then time to depart. There was nobody about at two o'clock in the morning, although there were a couple of houses with lights on displaying evidence of habitation, but they were towards the town end and didn't pose any sort of risk. In any case, Robert was going for a night-time wade, which might seem strange to most people, but not unusual. Caroline gave him a hug and wished him luck to which Robert responded with a kiss, said that he would be alright, and with a parting glance set off into the dark.

The moonless sky was ablaze with stars as Robert looked up into the heavens. The amber glow from the town obscured some constellations but above him and out towards the Island and the sea, it was a perfect stargazing night. He looked back to see Caroline wave and spied the pole star above her head, high in the sky, a guiding light to steer by.

The route was obvious at first, following a concrete causeway that had been constructed to be a storm-water outfall some one hundred yards from the sea wall. The causeway then doglegged to the right, towards the Island, and soon petered out leaving him to tread slowly and carefully between rocks and exposed seaweed. Every so often he switched the torch on to illuminate the next section to be traversed and after about fifty yards or so he felt the first signs of the cold water flow over his feet. Soon he was ankle deep and then up to his knees.

The water seemed colder without the warm sun of the day countering its effect and numbness crept up his legs as he got deeper. He stopped mid-channel when he heard a noise, but it was only a stray oystercatcher startled by his presence. He continued, ploughing through the water, becoming shallower with each step, until the dry shingle of the beach welcomed him. The crunching under his feet of the pebbles and dried seaweed seemed to echo in the night sky, causing some roosting gulls to start cackling and then, as he got closer, to fly off in a mass making the most terrible din that would surely wake the dead, he thought. Quickly he made for the top of the beach and the safety of cover and waited for five minutes before concluding that the dead were not going to intrude. Phase one was over. He was now on the Island.

Phase two began with Robert signalling Caroline, who responded with the same three flashes and who then made her way back to the cottage to continue observation when dawn broke. Robert headed up a grassy track for the cottages, using only the minimal light that seemed to radiate from a thin veil of cloud that had now invaded the night sky, it being the reflected glow from the urban lights of Plymouth and the lights of Looe itself.

After a short distance he encountered his first contact, a shed with double doors like a garage. Peering through a dirty widow and shining his torch he could see a small tractor and some garden equipment, which must have been the Island's maintenance machinery. Next to this shed was another, this time with a single door entry. He quietly opened it and a strong odour of fuel hit his senses, for this was the generator house and he realised, of course, the Island hadn't mains electricity.

He continued his progress up the track and came to Smuggler's Cottage on the right, a building he was expecting to see cloaked in darkness, certainly not with a light glowing in a downstairs room. It concerned Robert. He wasn't expecting anybody to be awake. He paused to listen for any sign of life. After a couple of anxious minutes he walked on, confident that he was alone, slowly and carefully making sure he made no noise or as little as possible. Waves were swashing on the rocks nearby and he hoped they would drown any excessive disturbance he made. But he had progressed only a few yards when he heard a door open from Smuggler's Cottage. A few seconds later a dark, unidentifiable figure appeared on the track and in the meagre light Robert could discern a man of considerable stature that could only be Siegfried.

Robert quickly ducked into a bush. Siegfried shone his powerful torch up the track in Robert's direction and then down towards the beach. If he comes this way, Robert thought, he'll be sure to spot me. Go to the beach, he said to himself as his heart started pounding, knowing that he could not escape this man if spotted, and as he prayed for divine intervention, Siegfried headed for the beach.

Robert sighed with relief, waited for him to disappear and now with some urgency, made for Jetty Cottage and the path that led to the caves. He needed to be careful, but just as he had that thought he fell over a stone by the cottage and gave out a muffled yell as his head hit the stone wall of the building. He momentarily shone his torch at the offending object to glimpse the sinking stone that John had mentioned, its distinctive hole clearly visible in the light. Adjacent to the stone was the door to Jetty Cottage. Robert slowly opened it and peered inside. He couldn't see anything. He dare not shine his torch inside, but judging by the combination of distinctive odours of gasoline and tar and the smell of the sea, he concluded it was a storage-shed and shut the door. The caves were the most likely place where evidence of activity would reveal itself, that is, if there's any to be found. So far, his nocturnal escapade was proving to be unproductive.

The entrance to the cave was difficult to reach, having to climb down rocks which he couldn't quite see. But he made it and still with the tide low, although it was now on its way in, he walked inside and shone his torch to reveal a cavernous space much larger than it seemed when he last saw it from *Lady Jane*, partly because it was now empty of water.

He could discern a sort of landing stage and made for that, but on approaching it, found it was more than his height above him. With no visible sign of access he was thwarted. Then he spotted a metal ladder fixed to the rocks towards the back and was able to scale the rungs and reach the platform. He heard a noise and looked down to see the cave floor being inundated with the incoming tide and immediately realised that soon he would be trapped inside unless he found an alternative means of escape, which he thought there must be, or else he abandon his search and leave now before the water became too deep.

He decided to press on into a cave network that was at first natural but then increasingly became clearly man-made, constructed of some sort of ancient brick with some caves having collapsed, and as Robert progressed further in he realised it was an extensive ramification which seemed to be leading into the heart of the Island and where, if he was not careful, he could get lost. He decided to retrace his steps, partly because he didn't think they were going to lead to anything significant, but mainly because he suspected that he had missed the exit route.

On returning, he explored some of the side caves. Each one was empty. But then, as he shone his torch inside yet another, in a far corner he could see some boxes and adjacent, a tarpaulin covering something. The boxes had clearly come from the continent with writing in French and one in Dutch, and inside he found what he was looking for, evidence of smuggling in the form of contraband:

cigarettes, spirits and perfume, all labelled for an English market. He replaced the goods he had removed but retained a packet of the cigarettes for evidence. He went to lift the green tarpaulin, expecting to find further contraband, but to his horror under the cover laid out as though in a coffin was a man whom he recognised. He was wearing the mask of death.

42

Death is the final act in the life of a living being. The death of a loved one can be traumatic, an emotional deliverance that the person is never going to walk this earth again. For most people, any death is a tragic event, especially if that death comes before our three score years and ten. But for Robert, the death of a human being is no different from that of an animal, no matter how insignificant, for every creature has a life, an intrinsic will to live a natural lifespan.

When his father died he had shed no tears for him, even though he was present when the last breath of life was exhaled from his body. Yet a few months later, he poured tears of genuine grief for the death of his cat, an animal that he had loved with all his heart, for it had not judged him, scolded him or even ignored him, but had shown unconditional love and devotion even when he himself had chided and slighted his feline friend.

In his adult years, Robert's manifest love of all animals, creatures that he believed had an innate right to an existence, would cause him a dilemma. He certainly could not deliberately kill. Even an accidental death invariably wounded his conscience. When gardening, he would have to be vigilant and extremely careful and any life that succumbed to his spade would be apologised to, as though giving it the final rites, a recognition that it had lived this earth and he had extinguished its existence.

Animals have no intrinsic desire to kill unless it is for food or self-preservation. The human race, however, is essentially amoral, where life is seen as a commodity and where philosophical superiority gives it a divine right to control the kingdom, to be judge and executioner.

Robert looked at the dead man. Somebody was his judge and executioner, he thought, looking at the blood stained head that had received some blunt instrument. He recognised the man as the one he had seen in the old part of East Looe talking to Tara, who had passed close to him, had smiled and whose face was riddled with corpuscular warts. He didn't know his name. He didn't need to. He was just another dead human being in the thousands that would die that day, from a population where his death is of no consequence in the grand scheme of life. Yet this man had a life, his life. He had hopes, dreams, a desire to live, and some evil being snatched all that from him and Robert knew who that was likely to be.

He replaced the tarpaulin in a dignified fashion and left the chamber to make his way back to the main cave, now realising that Siegfried was somebody to be wary of, a man to avoid at all costs. Approaching the main cave Robert could see flashing lights, not directly, but in the walls of the caves, an aurora of reflected colour that told him somebody was ahead in the main cave and it was likely to be Siegfried. He edged forward slowly, with his own torch switched off and crept along to a point where he could see some of the landing platform, but where he could not be observed himself.

It was still dark although there was greyness in its light that suggested dawn was approaching. And approaching the cave, for the tide was now well in, was a small craft and as Robert watched it get closer and enter the cave he could see it was Tara. Disappointment ran down his face. He didn't want her to be involved and although he had suspected it, this was proof, proof that she was a smuggler and that he would have to expose her operation and in so doing, ruin her. He didn't want that. But his morals told him he had to, especially as she seemed to be in collaboration with Siegfried. With him though, he would have no compunction whatsoever in reporting him to the police and he wondered what exactly his involvement was.

'Have you got the goods?' he asked of Tara brusquely, as he secured the boat to a metal ring.

'Yes, I have it,' she replied not looking at Jock and looking herself rather perturbed.

'Good. Then let's go.'

Robert waited for the two to disappear up a passage that he hadn't explored. From a safe distance, he followed them. It led to a small room, a sort of antechamber, off of which was a door. He opened it and climbed a flight of steps that led into Jetty Cottage, for it smelt of the same maritime odour as before. Surrounding him were cans of fuel, fishing equipment, nets and a couple of lobster pots, a sail and various items of furniture and garden implements, all of which looked to be the remnants of a house clearance. He had seen enough. He was going to get off this Island, not by walking back across the channel, for he couldn't, but escape by using the boat.

Dawn was by now fast approaching as he looked at the craft, similar to *Lady Jane*, and then looked at the cave entrance and the swell, amplified by the current as it hit the rocks. Could he do it, he wondered? He had to. It was a challenge for a skilled seafarer and Robert had never steered a boat before, except a small rowing dinghy on a lake when he was young. This was going to test all his skill, nerves and a lot more besides.

Clambering into the craft he managed to rock it and almost lost balance. A dunking in the swirling water would have been fatal, he thought. He looked at the controls, searching for an ignition switch or something and wished he had taken more notice when out with John. He found the ignition with the key still there and proceeded to start the engine. His first attempt failed. He tried again. Still no luck. On the third, the engine fired and he gave a stifled 'yes' to himself. But as he said that, his world went suddenly blank from a blow to the head. He collapsed to the bottom of the boat and lay there, out cold.

*   *   *

Robert was once again in a black void. Only this time, as he gained consciousness from his cerebral blow he was chained to a wall by his wrists, unable to move, not knowing what had happened, except that something heavy had struck him senseless.

His head was throbbing, pounding with pain from concussion. As he regained some vision he could see it wasn't the total blackness of the tunnel, for a few photons of light were visible, a glimmer of daylight from the cave which gave him a blurred, gloomy view of his imprisonment. It was a brick constructed space which contained nothing, other than himself and some hooks on the far wall, from which hung a grapnel and some rope. It was the antechamber.

The swell of the sea and the breaking waves were echoing into his world, a reminder that he had almost escaped and that if he had done so, would be with Caroline by now, enjoying the warmth of her body and the comfort of her soul. He wondered how long he had been there and looked at his watch. It was broken, stopped at five thirty-eight. What time it was now he had no idea and hoped that Caroline was sending a rescue party. His predicament seemed more hopeless than before, probably deadly, for this man, Siegfried, dealt in death and he may be his next victim. He tried to escape his bonds. It was a vain attempt. The shackles were padlocked to a ring which was well embedded in the wall and unlikely to be worked free, even if he had enough time to do so. He was definitely going nowhere and waited for his jailer to appear.

Robert awoke to the sound of footsteps coming down from the cottage above. He had been asleep, his forehead pulsating, making him feel drowsy where slumber was the only anodyne to his pain. He must have been out for some time for the chamber was now dark. Gone was any semblance of daylight and gone was his pounding head, although it still felt delicate as though another blow would severe it completely from his aching body. The footsteps came closer. More than one person was coming down and it seemed one of them was complaining, or at least making some muffled noise of protest. The door swung open and there standing in its entrance was Siegfried who was holding onto some rope attached to which was a captive, a companion for Robert. It was Tara.

Tara was shocked to see Robert but conversely Robert was somehow glad to see Tara, his countenance providing some solace to her. It meant she was not involved in the smuggling, as he had thought, and that it was Siegfried alone who was the dragon that had to be slain. Tara was gagged. She acknowledged her surprise with eyes that told of her astonishment and head gestures, along with muffled sounds that spoke of disappointment. His gratifying sight of Tara was somewhat tempered by the fact that they were both bound, incapable of escape and at the mercy of this man.

Siegfried tied Tara to a ring on the opposite wall, checked her bonds and looked at Robert.

'You have a companion to talk to,' he said, knowing that it would be a one way conversation.

'Why is she here and bound?' asked Robert.

'Because she is no longer needed. What you don't need, you throw away,' and he laughed as he left the chamber, locking the door behind him before Robert had the chance to argue for her release.

Robert looked at Tara, an abject ghostly figure in the dim light of the chamber, a pale shadow of her ebullient self who stared at him, the stare of a broken-hearted and defeated soul.

'Are you okay?' he said, realising that she probably wasn't.

She nodded in the approval, even though she felt far from alright, more disgusted with herself for letting Jock take advantage of her.

'Is there anybody else on the Island?' he asked.

She nodded yes.

'Your two colleagues?'

Yes, she nodded again. Robert realised that Tara didn't know about the body. He pondered for a few moments, whether or not to tell her. Would it push her over the edge? If he didn't say anything, then she may have false hope of rescue. He looked at Tara. She looked at Robert. In his mind, he could tell she was asking for the truth.

'I have some bad news Tara. One of them is dead. I found his body in a cave below.'

Tara looked as though she had seen a vision of hell, for her eyes were staring wide into an abyss of darkness as she lashed at her shackles, trying to free herself in a fit of rage. Robert could see she was distraught and that she had no idea. Tara gave a muffled sound, her anxious intonations indicating she was asking who it was.

'He had warts over his face,' he said.

She closed her eyes and seemed to be praying, for she did not open them until Robert spoke again.

'I'm so sorry, Tara.'

She nodded an appreciative head gesture, grateful for his sympathy, which she felt was sincere.

'Is there anybody else here that can help?' enquired Robert.

Tara hesitated and then shook her head. Their predicament, Robert thought, didn't just seem hopeless, it was now desperate. Their only prospect of survival lay with Caroline and, so far, nothing was forthcoming from her.

Throughout his deepest despair in the tunnel he had relied upon Caroline, meditation, and his Buddhist teaching in that black void, but this time was different. There were other forces at play: a dark, evil force, the yin of Siegfried against the yang of hope, the yang that represented Robert and somewhere in between was the counterbalance of Tara, a force which could sway things either way. He had to remain positive, postpone hopeless thoughts and rely on hope, hope that something would happen. He looked at Tara who returned his gaze only with eyes that were penetrating into his soul, speaking volumes in the silence, telling him that she loved him, that even though their predicament was hopeless, it was their destiny to die together.

43

Caroline stared at the Island, her eyes darting from one point to another, focused each time on a single spot, expecting to see Robert, hoping to see Robert. But for all her searching, he did not show himself. Only a flock of sheep were visible that had decided to frequent the beach where he had landed.

She wondered what they were doing there. On the beach. On the Island. She knew that there was a species living on the Shetland Isles, or was it Orkney, she couldn't quite recall, that had adapted to eating seaweed, but these sheep just seemed to be congregating in a circular group seemingly doing nothing. Perhaps Robert was using them as cover, she speculated with some amusement, not really convincing herself, more in hope that he was on his way back and not in any trouble.

It was still early, just gone eight o'clock in the morning. The clear blue skies of the previous few days had given way to high-level cloud where breaks in the stratus created spotlights of sun on the water, a moving beam of brightness within a grey stage, where later participants would add to the backdrop of this theatre. The tide was still flowing, not yet at its high point, but the Island had already shrunk from the wide expanse at low water, the sea having covered the wave-cut platform and now lapping onto the cliff and reducing the beach to a small arc of sand that the sheep were now occupying.

It was captivating viewing for Caroline, more used to a brick façade and the soulless windows of other flats, softened only by a plane tree growing from a garden quadrangle below her flat. From the amphitheatre overlooking the stage in front of her she felt a sense of freedom, space to breath, the perfect place to be with Robert. In Looe, she considered, life is not to be found in museums and art galleries or cafes and restaurants, but in the ebb and flow of the tide, in the raw power of nature and the gentle sway of time, the nuances that being in contact with the earth brings; looking at the butterflies dancing gracefully in their courtship, dew drops on leaves, a robin singing in the trees, the acts of time in a scene that is forever changing, matching the rhythms of the play that is the natural world.

Such a world was not natural to Caroline's persuasion. She would readily immerse herself in a historical muse where manuscripts and maps were her sensory instruments to the past, a past which often was the source of conflict in the present day world. History was important because it reconciled many unexplainable truths. Without knowledge of the past there would be no future, no reference point from which to move forward.

Such a dichotomy was the foundation of her relationship with Robert. She would learn from her mistakes and be a better person for it. She would still be independent, she told herself, but would understand his needs, his desires and not just her own and by doing so they would bind their relationship beyond the ties of complacency into a future symbiosis where she would need him and he would need her.

Caroline surfaced from her thoughts, not realising that a stranger, an old man, was standing at the foot of the garden path that led to the front door, admiring the natural beauty that confronted him.

'I'm sorry to disturb you, my dear,' said the old man as he doffed his hat in deference, indeed reverence, at the beautiful creature he was addressing. 'Did I startle you?'

Caroline looked at the stranger and saw no threat or malice in the man, whose face portrayed a person of learning, a venerable scholar who's only vice was to admire sublime beauty as a reminder of the past, when he was young and able to advance such lustful thoughts.

'Not at all. May I help you?'

'I'm looking for Robert, Robert Colliver. I believe he lives here.'

'He does, but I'm afraid he's not here at the moment.'

'Is he due back soon?'

'I'm not entirely sure when he'll be back.'

The old man stood looking at Caroline, she expecting him to say more, or at least that is what she surmised. But he was inspecting this vision of beauty as though he were fifty years younger, a hot-blooded male wanting to know her, explore her and discover the delights that lay beneath her exterior as though he were examining an illuminated manuscript for the first time, the *Lindisfarne Gospels*, whose magnificence could be found in every page, whose detail to perfection was a testament to the creator of such beauty.

'Forgive me for asking, but you are not by any chance Robert's partner?'

'Yes I am,' she replied with some circumspect and continued, 'Why, may I ask?'

'He came to see me several weeks ago and mentioned you were, like me, a historian. I said I would very much like to meet you, but he failed to tell me that, how shall I say…that you were such an attractive historical philosopher where all too often such academics are the epitome of their profession, relics of the past.'

Caroline took no offence to his comment and considered it to be a complement from an old man in his dotage and was even amused by his articulation, which only a learned individual would aspire to verbalise.

'That's kind of you to say so,' she responded. 'Robert also neglected to tell me of his visit to such a scholar, knowing I would be interested.'

'Permit me to introduce myself. My name is Alfred Thomas.'

'I'm Caroline. And now that formalities have been accorded, perhaps you would like some tea or coffee.'

Alfred hesitated. Tea was his predilection, although not the beverage of builders, but the distinctive flavours only a connoisseur would consider drinking.

'Have you Earl Grey tea?' he tentatively enquired, not expecting a favourable reply.

'Robert doesn't appreciate the finer flavours of gastronomy, having the palate of a Neanderthal, but you're in luck since I have purchased some especially for myself.'

Caroline retreated indoors to the kitchen and Alfred followed, hesitant to step inside the cottage once more after almost six decades.

It was within its now silent walls that he had found both love and betrayal, and where he had committed an act of treachery that had haunted him all his life.

As he crossed the threshold he immediately felt the walls awaken from their repose, telling him he was not welcome, that he had violated the sanctity of time. And as he glanced from side to side, faces of the dead would appear, familiar faces that had loved him, had hated him, and had judged him as he had judged himself, only they were mere shadows of their former selves, ghosts, whose tormented souls wanted revenge, revenge for a crime that had remained unpunished.

The kitchen was worse. Here, close to his nemeses, he was being taken by their vituperation, sucked into an underworld of eternal damnation where the floor would open up and take what had been denied them for so long. His mind, so used to contemplative serenity, was in turmoil and a state of iniquity, where every clatter of cups and saucers were now a peremptory of guilt, a path to perdition in the vaults of hell and as the percussion grew louder he could withstand the torment no more and sank to the floor in an act of penance.

'Forgive me,' he cried, 'Forgive me.'

Caroline, who had been making the tea and unaware of Alfred's ferment, turned around in amazement and saw him on his knees as though praying to the underworld.

'Are you alright?' she questioned with a perplexed tone, wondering what he was doing, semi-prostrate on the kitchen rug over where the inspection chamber was located.

Alfred returned from his incubus, embarrassed that he found himself seemingly in a position of prayer, but with a mind that had been to hell.

'Please forgive me,' he said with piety.

'Forgive you for what?' replied Caroline.

'You must think I'm some sort of schizophrenic mad old man,' he said, 'but I was having a panic attack.'

She looked intently at Alfred, not convinced of his explanation. His words had sounded like they were coming from his very being, uttered in desperation, as though he were trying to exorcise his soul from some deed that was consuming him.

'That's alright, but I think you should go and sit down.'

Alfred went into the sitting room and sat down in Robert's chair by the window. How could he have let himself be overwhelmed so, he told himself, and looked out to the Island wishing he were a postulant a millennium ago, living a life of piety in the monastery of Lammana where he could absolve his sin and so redeem himself. The Island was his salvation, a sanctuary from his demons, an answer to his postulations on the treasure of Robert Colliver.

Caroline came in with the tea and sat opposite him. She poured Alfred a cup who, like herself, had it unsullied by milk or sugar. They sat there drinking the weak tea, Caroline thinking about the extraordinary outburst by Alfred which she was now beginning to link with the crypt, especially as he seemed to be directing his absolution at the hidden chamber, and Alfred still perplexed by his uncharacteristic paroxysm.

'Now, you must tell me, whom should forgive you?' she said, breaking the silence.

Alfred was startled by this unexpected enquiry. He continued to look out of the window, hoping that Caroline's question might melt in the atmosphere of uncertainty. But he hadn't met suspicion before in the shape of beauty.

'There is something that is concerning you and I feel it has something to do with this cottage.'

'You're quite right, my dear,' he replied with an air of resignation.

He realised that in Caroline he had met a superior intellect, an inquisitive mind that could delve beneath the surface and trowel the horizons of time to reveal the secrets of the past. She was to be his inquisitor, his judge, for he saw a fellow historian who would not play to fickle emotions or preconceived perspectives, but be percipient and interpret the facts and reach a reasoned verdict.

Alfred looked at Caroline, but rather than being a historian she was now his judge and jury, his route to absolution or damnation. Caroline, though, was not viewing Alfred as accused, for she did not know what the indictment was, but rather she was anticipating a historical conundrum, a puzzle which he wanted her to solve, and as events were to unfold, that is exactly what was to happen.

44

*E*arly afternoon saw a dramatic change in the weather. The morning high cloud had descended to a thick blanket of nimbostratus coinciding with an increase in the wind speed. It had veered to a south easterly, bringing with it a deep swell and large waves crashing onto the beach, unusual for Looe, protected by the Island from the prevailing winds.

Surfers were taking advantage of the conditions. A dozen were paddling out to meet the incoming swell and then wait for the big one that would propel them in an arc of surf before it dissipated, leaving them to repeat the process once more. But with the strong winds, many of the waves were blown out before their prime leaving the surfers frustrated that they were not on the north coast where, with an off-shore wind and an Atlantic swell, the waves would be clean and huge, probably up to ten feet or more, making for perfect surfing conditions.

Caroline had watched the surfers on the beach as she made her way into town, unable to comprehend their sport where waiting was the watchword, waiting for the right wave that only came along every so often, ten seconds of action in ten minutes of vigil. Surfers would say it was worth it for the adrenalin rush, the feeling of taming a wave, if only briefly, that could destroy them, but for their technical skill.

She too had been waiting. Waiting for Robert to return. But, unlike the surfers, she had been denied the euphoria of success. She was now anxious for Robert's safety and so was making her way into town, walking as quickly as possible to the local Police Station. She had waited until the ebb tide had started to flow and still with no sign of

Robert had decided to report his absence to the local Constabulary, having already tried to ring them without success.

At the reception desk, a Police Constable Trevellick had taken her report and logged it as a missing person case. He had assured her that he would investigate immediately, since it was to do with the Island, and report back to her in due course, but that she was not to worry as these incidents were so often false alarms, the person in question having been delayed and turning up wondering what the concern was about.

It was now late afternoon and Caroline had heard nothing from the officer. She was not convinced by his dismissive attitude as though this was a false alarm, having impressed upon him that he was marooned on the Island. She had not mentioned the exact circumstances but implied he had gone over there at low tide and had not returned. The tide was now well in, the channel too deep to negotiate, and with the weather worsening she was now very concerned and decided to seek alternative help from the café proprietor, as Robert had suggested.

She found the café half full with customers mostly partaking in afternoon tea, although a few were clearly having either a late lunch or early supper, for there was the pleasant smell of home cooking pervading the establishment. It made Caroline feel hungry, especially so as she had not eaten since breakfast, being too embroiled in Robert's predicament and the confabulations with Alfred. They were still reverberating in her mind, his tale being so similar to Robert's experience that history seemed to have repeated itself, which as she well knew, often did.

The proprietor and his wife were both in the café, he in the kitchen and she serving the customers. Caroline entered and made her way to the counter where a selection of pastries and gateaux looked tempting, despite her aversion to such food as superfluous to her nutritional needs. As she eyed the delicacies, Jane came back from attending a family that had ordered tea and cakes, holiday folk from the Midlands she could tell by their broad accents, seemingly out-competing the rest of the congregation that were emitting a discordant low drone.

'Can I help you?' enquired Jane, looking intently into Caroline's eyes, determining whether this contender for her crown of beauty was a threat and deciding to feign indifference.

'I'm looking for John, the proprietor.'

Instantly, Jane was on the defensive, a trait which was embedded in her psyche, where competition was to be guarded.

'May I ask what for? He's my husband.'

'Oh. Please excuse me. I'm a friend of Robert Colliver and he told me if I needed help, to enquire at the café for him.'

This was now different. For Jane, Caroline was an adversary and one that she was more than capable of handling.

'And the nature of this assistance?'

'Perhaps I may explain that to your husband.'

'He's detained in the kitchen at the moment. As you can see we are rather busy right now. Perhaps if you explain what help you require, I can pass it on to him.'

Caroline was about to leave the café, realising that she had met a stone wall that would only give way with heavy hammer blows, when John emerged from the kitchen having overheard the conversation.

'I'm John, the proprietor. How can I help?'

'Can we speak privately please?' looking first at John and then his wife and observing a note of disapproval in her manner, not directed at her, but at her husband.

'Certainly,' he replied and added, administering the comment to his wife, 'I'm just popping outside for a moment, dear.'

His remark was forceful. She was fuming with rage at him for leaving his post to accompany this beautiful woman for a secret discussion that she would not be a party to. He would pay for it later on, that he knew, but for the moment he was going to enjoy the moment.

Outside, in the Fisherman's Berth, she explained the situation and her concern for Robert. John understood only too well and was sympathetic to her misgivings. But as they spoke, he could see that the weather was not conducive to a rescue mission, with even the harbour water, rather choppy. Out in the bay it would be worse and a landing on the Island, neigh impossible.

He conveyed this to Caroline which she reluctantly accepted, judging that his maritime experience was more on the cautionary side, especially considering the circumstances. As soon as the sea state improves he would go out there, he said, and tried to console her with the fact that Robert was probably nice and cosy inside Island Cottage where Madge, the owner, lived. Caroline was unaware of this and with that comforting knowledge she bid him goodbye and hoped he wasn't in too much trouble with his wife.

* * *

Alfred was still at the cottage, immersing himself in the research documents and the map of the Island that Caroline had brought with her from London. He didn't need food to keep him going, just the nourishment of history and the prospect he might be close to proving his theory.

The cryptic verse pointed to the Island as the place where the Pirate's treasure was buried. It seemed obvious, but where? On the summit, within the walls of the old chapel? It would be the favoured spot. By the time of Captain Robert Colliver, it would most certainly have been deserted, most likely have started to deteriorate, even collapse, being at the mercy of storms. If he himself, Alfred thought, were to bury treasure that is the place he would select. The perfect hiding place. In a dilapidated chapel would have been a reliquary, a small chamber under the floor in front of the altar. How apt he considered: once a place for priceless holy relics and now, if he was correct, the resting place of priceless treasure.

When Caroline returned to the cottage she found Alfred sitting in Robert's chair as she left him, only now he was dozing, a wheezy sound emanating from him as he breathed in and out. On his lap was the map which had interested him, so much so that Caroline could detect the eager anticipation of a young boy about to be given a present, a long awaited present that had been lodged in his mind for years.

She made herself a mug of tea and went into the parlour, not wanting to disturb this man who was, by now, a fixture in the household. Even though it had only been a few hours since Alfred had entered Caroline's world, she had already taken to him, indeed, liked him. It was not because he was a fellow academic and historian, rather his mannerisms: the elegant way he had introduced himself, the polite gesture of removing his hat, his quiet voice, almost hypnotic as though words were his route to the heart, a thesaurus-like seduction which only a learned recipient would appreciate. Caroline did.

She sat down and considered what Alfred had told her. It was a remarkable account worthy of any crime novel where fiction borders on reality, except in this instance, reality was more chimerical than fiction. She could almost recount his tale verbatim and even his exordium, if somewhat exaggerated, was a masterpiece of suspense.

'What I am about to tell you,' he quietly and slowly deliberated, 'is a tale of romance, betrayal, and damnation, the likes of which you will not have heard in a long time. A story so bizarre, that you will think it the work of fiction, of a mind that has gone beyond reality into a world of fantasy, a fable that would bestow its author immortality in the pantheon of literary giants.'

So began Alfred's secret, a secret that nobody had heard before. Caroline was to be the privileged individual who was to hear his confession and to judge him and then deliver a verdict, which he would abide by.

'Where shall I begin?' He looked at Caroline, anticipation carved in her expression. 'The beginning is my birth and the parents I never saw. I was born just before the end of the Great War. It was out of wedlock, so I've been told. In those days it was a sin that no mother wanted to be accused of, for it meant a lifetime of ignominy. As fate turned out, she was to be spared public shame since she died a few days after giving birth to me, a consequence of complications of my birth which I know nothing about. I also know nothing about my father, other than that he was an officer in the army and died serving in France, blown apart by a shell during the bloody offensive of Passchendaele. I was brought up by my adopted parents, Henry and Edna Thomas. Henry was my mother's brother. They were not rich but of sufficient means that I had an education and attended Oxford where I studied history and the classics. My life was being mapped out for me but I was an impetuous youth, like so many then and since, and thought I knew better. On graduating, rather than continue with scholarly studies, I returned home to Cornwall and became infatuated with the most beautiful creature I have ever met and being a confident individual and one who had prospects, we fell in love. I wanted Alice more than anything and to prove my devotion to her I bought this cottage in 1935, which then was a wreck, and rebuilt it to serve as a family home for us. We would sit outside on the warm summer evenings and talk about our future, how we would have children and grow old together, how I would write and be a famous author and she would be by my side and we would be happy in our idyll. I remember well one day she told me that life could never be as joyous as then and that we would be together for eternity, in life or death, and she said to me "when you look up there I shall be and when I look up there you shall be." We were going to marry and live the perfect life.'

Alfred paused, his now watery eyes staring into the past, belying there was a future, a future that was denied to him. Caroline gazed out of the window, as she had done every so often as Alfred recounted the tale, hoping to see Robert come up the path towards the cottage. Her disappointment was tempered by the enthralling account, which Alfred had not yet finished.

'We were in love,' he continued. 'But love is a capricious passion, especially when more than two people are involved. My father forbade me to marry Alice. He did not explain why, just that it would be sinful, a sacrilege against God. I naturally ignored him and planned to marry Alice secretly. We arranged a liaison at the cottage one morning, to go into Liskeard and be married at the church there. When she arrived I could sense something was amiss. Gone was the joyous enthusiasm, replaced by a solemnity that told of a lost love, a love snatched away by events beyond our control. She said it was impossible for us to marry, that we would be living in sin for the rest of our lives and that we were never to see each other again. I was heartbroken. I could not believe she was the same Alice that had mapped our future together. I pleaded with her to change her mind but she said it was impossible. I wanted to know why, but she did not say. And then I discovered the reason, for into the cottage came another man, the man she was to marry. Did she love him, I asked? She did not answer. I became enraged by his presence and snatched Alice in an act of possession, of desperation that he might leave if he could see our love. But she spurned me. I could not believe what was happening and in a fit of anger pushed Alice towards the man she had chosen, only to see her loose her balance and fall lifeless to the ground. She was dead. The man, in an act of revenge, hit and felled me: blood was running from my nose and mouth. By now I was fuming that Alice's death was the fault of this man and in an uncontrolled fury I retaliated and soon found myself standing over his dead body.'

Caroline looked aghast. Alfred looked demonic. His gaze was fixed on Caroline's face as though she were Alice, his long lost love, and he was staring into her soul and asking for forgiveness. He sighed.

'I did not know what to do. The only thing I could do was to confess my crime. That's what any decent and upstanding person would have done. I would have been hung for that deed, but it would have been justice, justice for Alice, at least. I killed her. But my friend George, who was to be my best man and witness and who had helped me renovate the cottage, then arrived. He advised me otherwise. Put them in the crypt, he said. Seal the entrance. Why sacrifice your life for a crime of passion? I protested. But his cool and calculated argument won me over.'

Alfred paused once more. Caroline was enraptured. She now had a name, if not a face, to the bones that Robert had unearthed and was about to disclose her knowledge of the crypt when he continued his confession.

'You're going to ask about the crypt. What crypt, you may well ask?'

'Yes,' she quickly interrupted. 'But I was going to say that I know about it.'

Alfred's eyes popped out in amazement.

'You know about the crypt?'

'Yes. Robert discovered it when relaying the kitchen floor.'

'Have you been in there?'

'Naturally. Such a find.'

'Indeed it is. Did you discover anything else?'

'You mean the tunnel?'

'So you moved the altar too. And found two bodies, well skeletons by now I would say.'

'Well, no. We found the bones of one person. A man.'

'You must be mistaken. There should be two bodies.'

'That may well be the case, but there were definitely only the bones of one body.'

At this point Alfred, who had been sitting forward in the chair eager to hear of Robert and Caroline's discovery, slumped back and looked out of the window into space, where seemingly his beloved Alice had gone.

'It's impossible. She was dead.'

'She may not have been. Sometimes it is possible for a body to appear dead yet there is still life within its frame.'

'Yes, that's true. But the tunnel was sealed. At one end the altar and the other George bricked up. If she was still alive, and I pray she was not, then escape was impossible.'

'Then her body was resurrected,' said Caroline, as though that's the only other possible explanation.

'Don't be ridiculous.'

'Of course it wasn't resurrected. Then the only conclusion is that she was alive and managed to escape, or that she was indeed dead and the body removed.'

Alfred nodded in agreement, though still not quite believing what he was agreeing to. Caroline though, was sure of her deduction.

'You mentioned a George, your friend who presumably helped you move the bodies.'

'Yes. He was a stalwart. Without him I doubt I could have managed.'

'Is he still alive?'

'Very much so.'

'And where might we find him?'

'Well, he usually frequents the Smugglers Arms from lunchtime onwards for much of the day.'

'Then we shall pay him a visit. I'm certain he will have the answer.'

*　*　*

Caroline looked out of the parlour window. Still no sign of Robert. Perhaps he was nice and cosy, ensconced in Island Cottage drinking tea and having a delightful time. She hoped he was.

She sat back in the chair and considered Alfred's tale. She had shown him the crypt, which he knew only too well, but they both had failed to move the altar, despite their effort with a crowbar. He'd had another panic attack down there but this time it was more controlled, as though the calm historian was defeating his inner demons, his professional curiosity overcoming any display of weakness. Nevertheless, he was glad to be free of the heavy weight of personal history and return to the lounge armchair.

Caroline was now eager to discover what happened to the body, having been enthralled by Alfred's tale. It may have been Robert who discovered the crypt and tunnel and she that had dated the bones, but that was all they knew. Everything else was a mystery, an empty supposition that needed to be filled. Alfred had added substance: a name to the bones, even a face, and most important of all, the circumstances of the find. All too often, especially in archaeology, such information is conjecture. But now, it was real history, history that had come alive, and there was more to be told.

She got up from her chair and went into the lounge. Alfred was awake.

'Oh, hello, Caroline. I thought you were still out.'

'I've been back about half an hour. You were asleep.'

'Me asleep? Never. I may have been thinking with my eyes shut. But not asleep.'

'Well, now that you are…alert, shall we go and see George?'

'Good idea. It would be good to catch up. Haven't seen him for some time.'

Alfred put the map and papers that he had been studying on the chair and the two of them made a move for the hallway. The ghosts of earlier did not materialise for Alfred as he retrieved his hat and looked in a mirror to see a man who now appeared younger, revitalised by recounting his ordeal, as though he had found absolution from Caroline. She had listened with grace, hadn't interrupted him, and her silent judgement was propitious.

He thanked her. She understood his gratitude and could see in his mirrored reflection a face which revealed a burden lifted, and she smiled at him and felt that his comfort was her comfort, that Robert was blessed with good fortune. But that comfort, that good fortune, was abruptly turned to distress and shock as she opened the front door, because standing in the porch, looming tall and menacing, was a blonde Arian thug.

45

Jock, Siegfried, even the blonde Arian thug, was a man whose stature demanded authority and whose demeanour meant compliance. As he stood in the porch, with a slightly surprised look upon him, his presence was all encompassing, a man whose slight movement of the arm or a blink of the eye spoke volumes, a man with supreme awareness of his captive audience, for they could not escape the magnetic pull of his huge bulk.

He had come to Robert's cottage expecting it to be empty and so was slightly astonished to see two figures in the doorway, one familiar, the other a complete stranger. For a moment he just stood there looking at them, and they at him, Caroline and Alfred unable to move for Siegfried's broad frame blocked the porch preventing them from leaving the cottage.

'Caroline. What a surprise. Come to think of it, perhaps it's not such a surprise after all, considering the map you had on display the last time I saw you.'

'You know this…this…man?' quivered Alfred, looking at the towering figure in front of him, a giant of a man that the gods could have sired.

'Unfortunately, I do.'

'You do?'

'It's a long story, best explained later.'

Siegfried had inched a step closer and was now within arms-length of them, an intimidating distance which both of them felt.

'Perhaps I may be able to help you,' he said in a dead voice.

'No, I don't think so,' responded Caroline.

'What I meant was, I think I can provide you with the time for you to explain our relationship.'

'That's kind of you, but we were just on our way out.'

'So I can see. But I'm afraid you will have to cancel any engagement you have.'

He now stepped over the threshold and grabbed the two rag dolls, for that was how they seemed to him, and ushered them to the kitchen.

'I came here to see how your friend Robert Colliver escaped from the tunnel that I cleverly entombed him in. But now I can see how. You obviously knew of the chamber and let him out.'

'How did you guess? There are some sparks in that head of yours. And there I thought that all Scots were brainless barbarian Picts.'

'Don't mock me. I can make life very uncomfortable for you.'

'What have you done with Robert? Is he alright?' spoke Caroline in a more conciliatory tone.

'He's alright, if a little tied up on the Island.'

'What's your game Jock? What do you want?'

'Let's say that I have some interests here and me finding you and this old man has presented me with a dilemma.'

'Please, not on our account,' said Alfred.

'But I cannot let you go free, so I must detain you. But where?'

He flung the rug away and lifted the first inspection cover, a heavy metal object that Siegfried removed as though it were plastic. As he was engaged in repeating the process on the second cover, Caroline seized her chance and made for the back door. It was locked and wouldn't open on the first attempt, but as the key engaged and the door opened, in that instant of delay, Siegfried had responded like a coiled constrictor and was clasping her shoulders in a vice-like grip, which had her yelling with pain.

'A pathetic attempt, I must say. Remember, I can make life very uncomfortable for you both and I will if there are any more such foolish antics.'

He returned to the crypt entrance, removed the second cover and gestured the two defeated individuals to enter the black hole.

'At least let us have some light. I beg of you. There's a torch in the drawer over there by the sink.'

Siegfried looked at Caroline, a figure in a pose of servitude, somebody who knew they had been beaten into submission, and considered her request. He opened the drawer and removed the torch and then filled a bottle with water and gave them to her.

'Don't let it be said that I do not have compassion. I shall return and free you when my work is done.'

'When will that be?' asked Alfred.

'Soon.'

'What if something happens to you?' asked Caroline.

'Then pray that nothing does,' he replied with conviction and a smile that left the two captives far from comforted by his supposed humanity.

He gestured the two victims into the crypt as though they were being invited as special guests to an exclusive venue, except this one descended into darkness. As they climbed down, Alfred realised that they were entering, not a crypt, but an oubliette, a sort of dungeon from which no egress was possible and that their fate was in the hands of this obdurate jailer. Siegfried was indeed considering their fate, wondering whether he should return or not. He had not yet decided. It would depend upon how successful the operation went and how great the reward was and with that final thought, he sealed them inside.

Caroline switched on the torch to reveal an eerie atmosphere, as though the dead of centuries were touching the void, electrifying the atoms and creating a conduit to the past. She now knew how Robert must have felt, only his imprisonment was much worse, almost unbearable without the comfort of light, a blind person in an alien world where deep unholy images are resurrected to torment the soul.

Considering his earlier outburst, Alfred seemed immune from such unnatural delirium, but with the knowledge that his beloved was no longer an interned corpse, he had felt the weight of his deed lift and with it the demons that had haunted him so resolutely earlier.

'Are you alright, Alfred?' enquired Caroline, pointing the torch in his general direction but avoiding his face.

'Surprisingly so, considering our predicament,' he replied.

'Well, we cannot wait for Siegfried to come and let us out.'

'Siegfried?' said Alfred in a rather questioning tone.

'Oh, it's Robert's epithet for him and I've taken to calling him it too. He reminds him of the antihero in Wagner's Ring Cycle, with his blonde hair and somewhat arrogant personality.'

'I see. Let's hope he doesn't end up dead like his namesake. It will be our funeral march that will be playing, as well as his.'

'Not if I have anything to do with it. We've got to get that altar open.'

'I don't see how that will help. And in any case, we couldn't move it before.'

'We have to. Trust in salvation is the watchword.'

'You've translated the inscription?'

'Naturally. It seems rather apt that we should heed the same sentiment as those monks all those years ago.'

'Indeed, except there is no exit from the tunnel.'

'Oh, but there is.'

Alfred looked puzzled as Caroline went over to the corner by the altar and picked up the crowbar that had been left there earlier when trying to move the stone edifice. She wedged the crowbar into the narrow gap behind the altar and pushed hard. No good. It remained anchored to the ground.

'Here Alfred, if you hold the crowbar then I will push on it with my feet.'

'Alright, but be careful. We don't want to damage the altar.'

Careful was the last thought in Caroline's mind. She wanted to escape their prison and the only way to do it was by brute force. She laid on her back and with her legs bent, uncoiled a blow on the crowbar with such force that it sprang from the Alfred's grip clattering to the floor. Still the stone alter remained stationary. She tried again with the same result, only this time a fragment of the altar broke off which Alfred picked up and examined as though he were a geologist inspecting its mineral composition.

'Strange,' he said, 'it doesn't seem like stone, although it's difficult to ascertain in this light.'

'We need to concentrate on getting out of here, Alfred,' retorted Caroline, in a slightly annoyed voice, which she attenuated.

'You're right. Perhaps I may suggest using the crowbar lower down on the altar, nearer its centre of gravity where it can exert more of a force.'

'Okay. But hold on tight.'

Caroline positioned the lever as Alfred suggested and hit it with one almighty thrust of her legs. It worked. The altar moved, not much, but enough to push the crowbar in further and gain a better purchase. A second foot blow moved the stone edifice further, and within ten minutes or so, it had moved enough for them to squeeze their tiny frames through, into the tunnel and into the burial place of Alfred's nightmares. Yet he was still calm. Caroline, though, sensed Robert's ordeal, his black void, only she had the torch and it shone a bright light into the distance, into his void, an enlightened world which had saved him.

The two of them slowly made their way down the passage, their heads bowed for the tunnel was too low to stand fully erect. Every few yards a rock-cut step appeared which became more frequent as they made progress and as the passage became steeper, each step showing the striated marks of a pickaxe or some similar tool, an indelible testimony to the monks who carved out this tunnel with only basic tools and their bare hands and who had braved the claustrophobia with only a candle to provide light. It was a supreme sacrifice for them and they must have thought it worthwhile to provide a safe passage from the shore to the top of the cliff.

It reminded Caroline of caves in the Dordogne in France, where early man must have endured similar hardships to decorate the walls with symbolic paintings of antelope, horses and other wild animals. Whilst they are of the Upper Palaeolithic period, over eighteen thousand years ago, the tunnel was certainly not of that antiquity, but as she shone the torch from wall to wall she was hoping to find some evidence that monks had once been inside.

'When do you think this tunnel was made?' asked Caroline.

'Your guess is as good as mine. Perhaps during the ninth or tenth century, is my thought. It would be good to come across an engraving on the wall, to confirm that.'

'It would. The ninth or tenth century is my guess too. During the Viking raids on England. They were known to have targeted Island sanctuaries like Lindisfarne and Lamanna would have been no different, a place where wealth could be found and pillaged as they made their way around the coast.'

'Yes, exactly my thesis as well. It then follows that there must have been a tunnel from the Island to the mainland, as your map suggests.'

'That's what I think, but I expect it is flooded by now, if not collapsed.'

'Maybe not,' exclaimed Alfred as he rubbed his hands against the tunnel. 'Look at the walls here. They are remarkably dry, don't you think? This rock must be impermeable.'

'Maybe they are, but we're not under the sea.'

'True, but I think a second tunnel may exist.'

By now they were close to the end when Alfred stumbled and fell over, just managing to catch himself from falling completely on his head. As he did so, a blunt metallic object caught his grasp. Caroline stopped and looked back to see if he was alright only to find him hold up something as though he had found treasure.

'Shine the torch on this my dear.'

She pointed the beam of light at the object, but her gaze caught sight of a glint in Alfred's eyes.

'I do believe I'm holding an old coin and one of some antiquity. Judging by the engravings and the insignia, it's a Spanish piece-of-eight.'

'You're right. It looks silver and is of the right type.'

'Plundered treasure I reckon. You know what this means?'

'Well, not exactly,' came Caroline.

'That the Pirate Captain Robert Colliver was once here, standing as we are standing, in this tunnel.'

46

$\mathfrak{I}$slands hold a magnetic attraction in the population of a country surrounded by sea. Since the dawn of mankind, they have been a sanctuary, a special place where people dedicated to a life of contemplation could find peace and solitude, cut off from the mainland and from the hardship and endeavours of medieval life.

Looe Island was no exception. The Benedictine monks, who built a community on the summit of the Island, carved a niche for themselves in an uncertain world, a Celtic world of mystery and potent magic. Life was on a precarious *arête* where, on one side, bad weather coupled with poor harvests could result in a fall to starvation whilst, on the other, raiders from the sea would end their pious existence hastening their ascent to heaven.

To combat the later, these few redoubtable souls sought a route to salvation, a secret tunnel that would deliver them from evil and allow them to continue their dedication to a God, a God that provided redemption in a savage and fickle transient world. It took years to construct and whilst many never witnessed the final breakthrough, those that did gave thanks to the Lord for it was His work, a holy devotion that they undertook and in doing so they earned their place in a heavenly afterlife.

Centuries later, the tunnel was now being used for an unholy practice. It was as if the devil had taken over the realm of the good and pious, corrupting the people who came into contact with it, turning them into his slaves where damnation was their unknowing reward.

Siegfried was one such convert. He had already killed for the right to be master of the tunnels and had imprisoned two others, shackled them in the catacombs beneath the Island to be dispatched when his work was done. For the moment though, whilst they were alive, there was hope and in the antechamber where they were being held Tara was their hope.

It had taken hours, but Tara had managed to free herself from the cloth gag by chewing through its fibres, gradually weakening them so that they eventually shredded in her mouth. Robert, in the meantime, had descended into an insular world, a nascent melancholy where this latest episode of imprisonment was one too many and where there seemed no hope of salvation.

'Are you alright, Robert?' enquired Tara, spitting out the remains of the gag and not quite articulating the sentence correctly as her jaw still ached from its bounds.

Robert looked up, totally surprised by the words that echoed in the chamber as though he were already hallucinating his end at the hands of his tormentor.

'You're able to talk,' was all he could say, still not quite believing his mind.

'Evidently.'

'How did you do it?'

'Patience and determination.'

'It doesn't help in the grand scheme of our predicament. But at least we can now converse before he comes back to kill us.'

'I'm surprised. You give up too easily.'

'You would be surprised if I told you of another impossible situation I found myself in at the hands of that man.'

'Well, then surprise me.'

'There's no point. Whatever I say, the outcome will be no different.'

Tara looked at Robert, a man she admired, but right now a man who looked defeated and in need of inspiration.

'Let me tell you, then, of an impossible situation that my Great Aunt Constance used to tell me when I was young and when I couldn't face life. It concerns my grandmother. I never knew her, though I wish I had for she was, according to what I was told, a remarkable woman, a woman who if she was alive today would shame you for such a defeatist attitude. She was a beautiful woman who fell in love with an equally handsome man, a local lad who was educated and had recently returned to Looe having studied at Oxford. They were made for each other. Two perfect people, but unfortunately in an imperfect world. They wanted to be married, but their respective fathers forbade them. Try as they might, if they couldn't get married with their families blessings, then they would do so secretly. My grandmother's father, a Henry Trevellick, had already found a suitor for her and told her that she could not marry her desired sweetheart because he was her half-brother from an illicit liaison he had ashamedly had, and that an incestuous marriage was socially unacceptable as well as being morally wrong. She protested, but to no avail, for he threatened to disown her if she pursued this unholy matrimony. She agreed to marry the suitor, even though she did not love him. She agreed because of the family. But she did not agree to never seeing her true love and would take herself off to meet up with him. One day her betrothed had followed her to your cottage, for it was there that they used to meet, her lover having bought it and who was rebuilding it for them. The betrothed discovered their secret and confronted the two lovers in an act of passion which enraged him. He lashed out at her, for she had repelled all his advances, and in doing so she fell to the ground and hit her head. She lay lifeless on the ground.'

By now, Robert knew this man, this lover, was Alfred. But he failed to comprehend how her situation was impossible. He was about to ask, when Tara had more to say.

'My grandmother didn't know what happened after that. All she knew was that when she regained consciousness, she found herself in a black hole, a tomb for the dead. She had assumed that she had been mistaken for dead and placed in a vault, for next to her was her betrothed who most definitely was dead for his body was icy cold. She shouted to be let out, but got no answer. She was condemned to damnation in hell for all she knew, without light or hope, to die slowly as a punishment from God for daring to defy His commandment. But she felt sure the imprisonment was a test, a test of her devotion, and so she prayed for salvation, for forgiveness, and promised Him that she would lead a chastised life in His presence until the day she died. She prayed for days, but without any sign of that salvation. And then finally, God was merciful. He must have heard her for she found out later, having spent three days in that black void, a man, a servant of God, came and rescued her, released her from her torment. Not once did she doubt her salvation. She knew that God was with her and true to her word she entered holy orders and lived and died in the service of her Saviour.'

Robert listened with incredulity that Tara's grandmother had suffered like him, days of torment in a black void and that it was spiritual enlightenment that had saved them both: for the grandmother, a Christian belief, for Robert, a Buddhist philosophy.

'So when was your mother born?' asked Robert.

'I wondered if you'd ask that. She was born about six months after the ordeal. She was already pregnant with her and it was her lover who was the father.'

This was becoming a revelation. It was now obvious that Alfred was Tara's grandfather, neither of whom knew, as far as he was aware, of the other's existence.

'Did you ever meet your grandfather?'

'No. To this day I don't know who he was. My grandmother fulfilled her promise and entered a nunnery, but only after the birth of my mother. On occasions, my Great Aunt Constance would take her to see her in the convent, but was sworn to secrecy. She was never told anything of her father, other than that he was a kind man, a man of learning and he would be proud of her. This is what my Aunt told me. My grandmother never saw him again.'

Robert wondered if she should tell her. He would, but not in the antechamber. He now knew they had to escape, if only for Tara to finally meet the grandfather she had never known and for Alfred to meet the granddaughter he knew nothing about.

'It is certainly a remarkable and inspirational tale. And you're right, she would shame me but for the fact we have shared a common demon and we have both had the determination to face that demon and find enlightenment.'

'How do you mean?' asked Tara, rather perplexed by the ambiguity of Robert's comment.

'Another time. For now, we must do something positive.'

'Like free ourselves from our bonds,' declared Tara, as she brought her hands from behind her back, free from the rope which had, until that moment, held her to the wall chain.

'How on earth?' exclaimed Robert.

'Simple. Well not so simple. But there are few knots which I do not know and that I cannot undo. With a little time and patience and the fact that I have a unique ability to dislocate my thumb and so slip through a narrow gap, it was easy.'

'Remarkable. You certainly are a woman of many talents, I must say.'

'You may, although you should already know that by now.'

Robert felt a little uneasy at that innuendo as he stared into Tara's eyes and she into his, realising that she was back in his cottage and they were making love, she enjoying him as she seemed to be right now. As with his present predicament, he felt his vulnerability once more.

'I think my bonds may be a little more of a problem,' he said wanting the moment to go away, not that it wasn't the right moment, but he could see himself being lured, once again, by her sexuality.

Tara could sense Robert's restraint, that the connectivity they once shared had been severed and that she had lost him, lost the only man she had truly loved, just like her grandmother had lost her lover. She got up and took the grapnel off the hook and forced one point into the loop of the lock, wedged it against a stone and tugged it with a quick action, and in one blow, the lock was broken and Robert was free.

'Not a problem,' was Tara's reply.

They were both unencumbered now, but not yet out of danger. They decided to make their way round the south side of the Island to the beach and hold up there, waiting for either Siegfried to leave or the tide to retreat sufficiently enough to wade across. But just as they were about to execute their plan, footsteps could be heard coming down from the cottage above. No sooner than they were free from their bonds, then Siegfried was on his way back to dispatch his captives.

47

It was two against one. But even those odds were stacked against Robert and Tara. The only place they could go, their only escape was down to the cave entrance.

'We can escape in the boat,' suggested Robert.

'No, we haven't enough time to get it started and out before he gets here. Our best bet is to hide in the caves back there. They're like a catacomb and I know them well. We can hide. He'll never find us there, if he dares enter.'

'He could do a Theseus,' said Robert, not in jest, but thinking it was a real possibility.

'A what?'

'A Theseus.'

Robert could see that Tara was not up to speed on her Greek mythology and so decided to abandon that notion, thinking in any case, that it was an idiotic suggestion.

'Never mind,' he said, 'ignore me.'

Tara had indeed ignored him. She had dashed onto the boat moored in the cave, opened a locker, removing a flashlight, and was already on her way into the cave system, to which Robert thought it wise to follow suit.

Once deep into the cave system Robert could see why they were safe. It was a maze, a true catacomb of labyrinthine passages and cave-like chambers from which ran other passageways to yet more caves. He had only scratched the surface before and was glad he had done so, for he may still be wandering in perpetuity.

After about five minutes, Tara stopped.

'This should be far enough,' she said, looking at Robert's bewildered expression, as though he had entered a true underworld. He had. This was the route to the tunnel under the channel, linking the Island to the mainland, which Tara had negotiated many times and so knew its path well. But for a novice, it must have seemed like the entrance to the Minataur's lair itself.

They sat down and waited keeping their voices low, for sound in the cave system echoed and magnified as though it were a giant musical instrument, a sounding board where each word was a chord and a phrase a whole ensemble.

'Hopefully Siegfried will think we have already made it across to the mainland,' whispered Robert, thinking that he ought to say something.

'Siegfried who?' asked Tara, looking at Robert as though the caves were dulling his mind.

'Oh, it's my nickname for him, a character from a Wagner opera.'

'And what's this Theseus, you said back there?'

'Oh, it's a chap from Greek mythology who goes into a labyrinth to kill a monster, half man and half beast, a bull. In order to find his way back out he ties a thread at the entrance and uncoils it as he goes along, so that he won't get lost.'

'That's ingenious. Expect you think I'm a bit stupid, not knowing about opera and Greek mythology.'

'Not at all. On the contrary, who but you could have escaped their bonds back in the antechamber. Few could resist your charm.'

'Except you?'

'We did have a good time together but I think we have both moved on,' was Roberts reply, not really knowing what to say to ease Tara's anguished words.

'You have. And I can understand that. She is very beautiful, your partner. And clever too. But I haven't moved on. I still remember that first time you walked into the Estate Agents. I saw your look. I knew then that we were destined to be together, but I thought it would be in love, not as captives and now fugitives from our very own monster.'

'I know. Any other time, any other life and things might be different Tara.'

'I never said it before, Robert, perhaps because it wasn't until Caroline arrived that I realised it. But I love you.'

Tara's mood fell into a lugubrious reflection and for the first time in many a year her eyes watered and tiny drops of tears ran down her cheek.

'I love you Robert,' she quietly spoke to herself.

For all her scheming and guile to lure this man to her, it was Robert who had finally won the game. Tara had lost. She had lost her love and she knew that nobody else like him would ever enter her life again.

In some perverse way she wanted Jock to find them, to kill them, so that she could die in his arms, her love sealed in their death, for she did not want to go on living without him. He had become part of her. He was her destiny, their destiny, entwined together in a fate which they would share. That is what she wanted.

She looked at Robert. His face was a shadow in the torchlight, in the outline of his features and with his stare into space, she sensed the detachment. She knew it was too late now, too late to rekindle a lost love. But not too late to do the right thing and with that thought she realised what she must do.

'Let's go. I think he should have gone by now.'

'Okay. Just one thing Tara. I know our destinies have been linked, I've felt that for some time, but whatever happens, please look after yourself.'

'Don't worry on that account. I will.'

They retraced their steps back to the main cave expecting the boat to have been taken but it was still moored there, much to their relief.

'Don't think he fancied taking it out of here with that swell,' commented Tara.

Robert agreed, 'Only a fool would attempt it.'

'Not exactly a fool, only one who couldn't handle the sea well. As for the fool that's to be you, Robert. You need to escape this Island and seek some help.'

'No way. Not without you.'

'I need to stay. Somebody needs to keep him on radar and besides, there's Madge to look out for. I have a responsibility towards her.'

'But you don't expect me to steer the boat out of this cave and to the harbour on my own?'

'That's exactly what you must do.'

'But look at the weather. And the swell out there.'

'It's worse than it looks. Getting out is easier than you imagine. Once out, you must steer the boat starboard, that's right, in a clockwise route around the Island. You don't want to be negotiating the Rannay's. That would be foolish. When you enter the channel between the Island and the mainland just keep to the middle and to the right of the marker beacon. It's then plain sailing to the harbour.'

It sounded easy enough to Robert, but he knew it would be anything but that. He boarded the boat with Tara who started the engine and gave him a crash course in the operation of the controls.

'Just steer well clear of Dunker Point, the rocks at the end of the western shore, closest to the mainland. And remember, to steer left move the tiller right and converse. Okay?'

'Okay.'

Tara stepped off onto the small rocky jetty and looked at Robert as though it would be for the last time, a desolate love that would dissolve in the murky sea. She really wanted to go with him, her impulse telling her that she should, but pragmatism making her stay. She watched as he opened the throttle and edged forward.

'Good luck,' she shouted.

Robert turned and looked at Tara. It was like that moment on the cliff top by his cottage when he saw her on the end of the Island, defying the elements. There was a connection then, as now, and he wanted to stay with her, to be by her side, defying, not the elements, but Siegfried, a duet in defence of the Island. But she was now an isolated forlorn figure, left on her Island to face the unknown. He waved and returned to steer the boat clear of the cave entrance and into the open water, into the dark and murky unknown.

At first it wasn't too arduous, with the Rannay's giving some protection from the strong south easterly, but soon the small vessel was pitching and rolling in the deep swell. He was drenched with spray and feeling cold, even though it was a mild night, but he was gaining confidence and the boat was becoming easier to handle with more protection from the wind on the western side of the Island. He heard the cormorant colony cackling, a hyena-like laugh as though he were a fool to be traversing the Island in such weather. By now, the craft was fast approaching Dunker Point, the crashing surf indicating where the rocks protruded into his path. Despite an easier sea, the undercurrents had forced the vessel too close to the shore and to avoid the rocks he swung the tiller hard to port. Just as he did so, the engine spluttered and then cut out. He tried to start it. It wouldn't. Without power the boat started to drift, not away from Dunker Point, but directly towards a certain clash with the rocks.

Robert didn't know what to do. There were no oars. He could hear the crashing surf of Dunker Point. He tried the engine again. Still it wouldn't start. Then he heard a wail from the shore and imagined a siren standing on the rocks luring him to his death. Within seconds, the boat had struck the jagged spines, ripping through the hull as though it were matchwood, breaking it up into splinters with the sea engulfing the boat and sinking immediately. Not waiting to confront the sea-nymph, Robert had dived into the water moments before the vessel sunk, just enough to be clear of the rocks that would surely have torn him apart. He was now at the mercy of the current, which rather than taking him towards the nearby shore was soon casting him adrift in a stormy sea and away from safety.

Drowning is not an immediate death. There is time for the victim to consider the manner of their fate and if they are a good swimmer, perhaps avoid the watery grave of a cruel, unforgiving ocean. Robert was a good swimmer, yet without any buoyancy, he was being dragged down by the waves, each time taking in more water as he desperately tried to breathe. After just a couple of minutes the cold was beginning to reach his core and he could feel life leaving him. And as another wave sucked him under, filling his lungs with more salty brine, gradually asphyxiating him, he wanted it to end. The next plunge would be his last. Death would be a release. And so, with another huge wave sucking him under once more, that final descent into oblivion had begun.

48

Hendersick Hall was an island of calm in a sea that was foaming trouble. That's how it seemed to Jock as he approached the front of the building in his jeep, along the gravel driveway which snaked its way to the elegant façade of the grand entrance. The sound of peafowl could be heard, a throwback to its days as the retreat of a former high commissioner for India, a gift bequeathed to the estate from a maharajah. Frederick Thomas had been obliged to continue their upkeep and was glad to do so, for they added a sense of serenity to the place, despite the courtship vocals.

Jock was not enamoured by them even when they extended their fan-trains, displaying the exquisite pattern so characteristic of the male bird. He preferred the wildfowl of the Scottish Highlands; the ptarmigan, the black grouse and his favourite, the capercaille. They were hardy birds, able to survive the harsh winters of the Cairngorms where he was brought up, not the fancy frivolity of these imports which did nothing but lounge around and parade themselves as though they were the aristocracy of the avian world, where all other species were inferior and beneath their contempt.

The roar of the jeep, as it negotiated the gravel drive, seemed to be a signal for one peacock to attack the metal intruder and vent its credentials by pecking at his feet and legs as he made the gauntlet between his vehicle and the front door. For some reason this particular bird, a maverick amongst the timid and gentile flock, did not like this man who would happily bear a loaded shotgun on the peacock and blast it all the way back to Rajasthan.

Frederick was amused, as was Christian, by the peacock's bravado at this giant of a man who could, so it seemed, tear one apart by his bare teeth. It was a thought that had often passed Jock's mind, in a bilious act, but one nevertheless out of curiosity as to their taste, slow roasted with a dram of single malt.

He had managed to outflank the bird on this occasion, making it to the steps without incident. He opened the front door, not ringing the bell nor waiting for Christian to announce him, and walked straight into the rear study where he knew with the utmost certainty that Frederick would be. He was right. Of course he was right. Frederick was sitting in his high back seat, away from the doorway so that Jock couldn't actually see him, he being so slight that the chair appeared to be several sizes too big for him, or rather that he was a child in an adult's repose.

It was the later, for on swivelling around expecting to see Frederick, presenting himself was a young man, almost a boy by his appearance, who was no fitter to sit in the seat. It was a man's chair and this boy, whom he had not seen before, was certainly not a man by Jock's standard.

'And who are you?' demanded Jock.

'I might ask the same of you, since this in my home and you have not been announced,' replied Malcolm with an air of authority which surprised Jock.

'I've come to see the master of Hendersick Hall,' retorted Jock, not willing to give into this young upstart, who at least could hold his own in verbal combat.

'I'm afraid he's indisposed right now. Can I be of assistance?' came another jibe from the upstart.

'No. I need to speak to Frederick Thomas. It's urgent. Most urgent.'

'As I said, he's indisposed. I'm his son, Malcolm. Perhaps if you tell me the nature of this urgent matter...'

Jock had had enough. He had been polite, as polite as he could be, faced with such intransigence and from a fresh-faced lad who said he was Frederick's son, and who was clearly enjoying his position.

'Look. I'll indispose you if you don't get up out of that chair and go and find your father. Now!' he said with force and with both hands leaning on the desk, staring eyeball to eyeball, his face etched in a quiver as though he were about to explode.

And Jock would have done so, but Malcolm considered retreat the better part of valour and made a move for the door, which before he had reached it, opened, and in walked his father.

'Ah, I see you two have already met. This is my son Malcolm,' he said turning to Jock. 'And this is Jock, an associate of mine,' turning to Malcolm.

'Yes we have already been acquainted with each other, you might say,' replied Jock.

'Would you mind leaving us for the moment Malcolm? I've some private business with Jock,' said Frederick, making it plain that it was not a request.

Malcolm left and Jock felt the weight of his anger lift and return to normal. Frederick could see there was some antagonism between the two and tried to placate Jock, for he knew of his short temper and how easily he could become unhinged or simply ignore his immense strength.

'Please forgive the impetuousness of youth. He's a good lad, if a little shy.'

Shy was not a word Jock would have used to describe Frederick's son's character, more impolite, perhaps disrespectful, certainly not having acquired the grace of his father.

'We may have a problem. Tara's entourage have been dealt with and she and the man, Robert Colliver, had been imprisoned. I said had been, but they have escaped and hence our problem.'

'Your problem. Not mine, unless they know about me.'

'No, they don't. That I am sure of.'

'There was also a need to restrain two other individuals at Colliver's cottage. They are securely out of the way, but I think some assistance would be useful.'

Frederick pondered his request. There was none available, except for his son. He didn't want to involve Malcolm in the operation since he had no idea what was going on. But if Jock asked for help, which he never did, then he must need it.

Jock put a map on the desk in front of Frederick. It was the map Caroline had copied from the museum in Tangiers.

'I recovered this from Colliver's cottage. It's a copy. But I think a copy of a genuine map. It shows Looe Island and the immediate coastline with a cross here,' as he pointed to a spot on the Island.

'But it's almost identical to the one you acquired,' said Frederick with disappointment. 'There's nothing new here.'

'What I was about to show you,' declared Jock with a somewhat condescending voice, as he turned the map over 'is this,' pointing to some writing.

Frederick now became interested. He read the cryptic verse.

To Lammana thou must go
Across t'sea a verdant Isle
There you'll find a place next the sea
And treasure there be found

'Now that is most interesting. Clearly, the Island is the place where the Pirate buried his treasure. He knew of the legend. He also knew that the pirate, William Kidd, hid treasure on an island near New York and that he and Captain Colliver were known to each other, having sailed together. It makes sense that he would hide his booty on an Island, the Island opposite his place of birth, an Island that he would probably have known well.'

Frederick was excited. He congratulated Jock for his good work and was now prepared to reciprocate, especially as he just asked for help.

'The help you asked for? My son can help, so long as he's not put in any danger and does not discover the true nature of the operation. Is that clear?'

It was to Jock. He was getting no help at all. What use would his son be other than a burden, a weak individual whom he would have to nursemaid and protect from danger? Still, his extra pair of eyes would be of some use and he could chaperone Tom who was in Smuggler's Cottage awaiting his return.

'Okay, so long as he's willing to come. I don't want any reluctant tantrums.'

Frederick called for Malcolm who wasn't to be found anywhere. Even Christian couldn't locate him. Malcolm, though, had been listening to the conversation between his father and Jock and was pleased to be part of the operation. It gave him a chance to uncover the smuggling, which he had suspected was happening on the Island, and so provide a scoop to his journalistic aspirations, to be part of a national newspaper and be an investigative journalist.

He had listened, in hiding, from behind a panel in the study. It was Christian who had discovered it one day whilst cleaning the kitchen panelling, a secret passage that led to the study. In fact, there was more than one passage, for they festooned the Elizabethan hall, a veritable labyrinth of hideaways and secret spy holes in almost every room, including in the upstairs bedrooms. Malcolm, on hearing his call, could have simply opened a doorway into the room but that would have given him away, for he believed that his father knew nothing of the passages. So he retreated back to the kitchen where Christian was preparing the evening meal and made his way along a narrow corridor to the entrance hallway and hence the study.

Frederick and Jock were still in discussion and turned to look at Malcolm enter the study as though nothing had happened.

'We've been looking for you,' said his father in a slightly raised voice, an indication of some inconvenience that his son had caused.

'Sorry, I've been outside.'

'How would you like to accompany Jock here to the Island to give him a hand?' asked Malcolm's father

'What sort of hand?'

'Just keep an eye on the place, while I perform a few tasks that need doing,' said Jock

'Alright. I've never been over there and it would be good to see the Island.'

'Good. That's settled then,' said his father.

'We'll leave at once,' said Jock.

'Now?!' exclaimed Malcolm. 'But it's getting dark.'

'How observant of you. Are you afraid of the dark?' retorted Jock.

'Well, of course not. But go across now?'

'It's urgent as I told to you earlier. Are you coming or do you wish your father to tuck you up in bed?'

'Alright,' protested Malcolm, unsure now whether it was a good idea to be going with this man. But at least he could do some investigation over on the Island and maybe discover what was going on there.

The two antagonists left Frederick in his study and went outside to the jeep. The peacock was waiting for Jock, or so it appeared, because as soon as he set foot on the steps leading down from the front door, it came from behind the vehicle and was making its way to intercept him. He could not escape the ambush, and was soon being pecked, leaving Malcolm unscathed, much to Jock's vexation.

'It seems to have a liking for you,' remarked Malcolm, as he got into the jeep.

'I'll kill it one day,' came Jock's reply, which Malcolm took to mean he would, given half the chance.

*   *   *

A canoe was not the mode of transport he was expecting, rather a proper craft, one with an engine and one which had better stability and certainly more comfort. It was a two-seater, sea-going type, open with no watertight seal that river canoeists tend to use and Malcolm looked at it as though it were not seaworthy enough for one person, let alone two, especially one who was built like a tank.

The canoe had been beached up beyond the cliff top about half a mile from Hannafore, just below the Hendersick estate lands, which meant it had to be hauled back down to the water's edge. With Jock, it was no problem, he lifting it as though it were a toy boat whilst Malcolm was given the arduous task of carrying the paddles and a flash light. The tide was half in and fortunately there was a small inlet of sand between a rock platform, which made the task easier, otherwise a launch off rocks would have been hazardous. Even so, it took a supreme effort to battle the incoming surf and with Malcolm in the front he naturally bore the worst of the waves, drenching him in spray. But soon they were in clear water and paddled hard to the

Island making the landing on the pebble beach. Jock hauled the canoe up above high water and ushered Malcolm to Smuggler's Cottage.

Inside, Tom was on his computer, playing some sort of game where strange figures were in a world of castles and caverns and where danger seemed to be lurking around every corner. But in the magical world he inhabited it did not matter if you were killed by a dragon, you just got up and started again, only next time you were ready for the fire-breather. He looked up and said hello to Jock and acknowledged Malcolm before returning to his game.

'Look, I've got to go and check a couple of things. Make yourself some tea or whatever and I'll be back soon,' declared Jock, realising he now had two useless helpers.

He left the two in the parlour and walked down the track towards Jetty Cottage. Malcolm followed him outside, but from a safe distance, and saw him enter the cottage but decided to return to the parlour and see what the computer wizard had to say.

He was still engrossed in his game, but this time he turned and introduced himself.

'I'm Tom.'

'Malcolm. What's your role in all this?'

'Oh easy. I'm to find the treasure before anyone else does and not get myself killed by some monster.'

Malcolm could see he was talking to a child, one who had not yet found the concrete world of adults.

'I mean, what are you doing here, on the Island?'

'Just keeping an eye on things. That's what I've been told to do.'

It now seemed there were two of them doing just that and whatever was going on, he was not going to discover it from Tom. Malcolm decided to make some tea and sat watching Tom mutter to himself as some unknown troll or a familiar adversary caused him to change his game plan because they had escaped his imprisonment. He was in a world of his own where fantasy was being matched by reality, for no sooner had Malcolm finished his tea, then in rushed Jock in some state as though his game plan had also gone awry.

'Look, I've got to go back to the mainland right now.'

'We've only just got here.'

'You're staying with Tom to keep an eye on things. Report anything unusual.'

'Such as what?' asked Malcolm.

'How do I know? Anything that does not seem to be normal.'

Malcolm was going to ask what was considered not normal, but thought better of it and just acknowledged the command.

With Jock out of the way it would give him the chance to explore the place, even though it was dark. He had the flashlight and time was on his side. To make sure Jock was indeed heading back across the water, he followed him to the beach and watched him paddle his way back to the shoreline below the Hendersick Estate, his bulky figure melting into the gloom as though a cloud of uncertainty had descended upon his plans.

49

After Robert's departure, Tara had watched him disappear into the gloom before racing around to the western part of the Island to chart his progress. Dusk had given way to a dark evening, with a half-moon illuminating her vantage point as it appeared from clouds that were scurrying across the sky. She could only just make out the shape of the craft in the water, perilously close to the shore and certainly not far enough out to clear Dunker Point.

She shouted, but Robert could not hear her above the raging sea. The boat continued on its perilous course and her concern was attested when she watched, with horror, the small craft hit the rocks and break up in the pounding surf. She thought Robert was dead, torn to shreds on the rocks, but was relieved to see him in the water, a bright yellow speck appearing and then lost in the heavy swell. But her relief was short-lived as he was carried out to sea only to dissolve into the maelstrom of chaotic waves, a small figure in an unforgiving sea.

Tara was distraught. She should have gone with him. Surely he wouldn't perish, not now after all that he'd been through, and her only crumb of comfort was that she had insisted he wear a lifejacket. She scrambled down to the rocks of Dunker Point, not in hope of a rescue, but to be closer to the man she loved, to be part of his suffering and will him to safety.

She remained there for some time looking into the darkness. If anybody was to drown at sea it should be her, she thought. It was her right.

'Take me,' she shouted to the gods. But they didn't. All that happened was a large wave crashed onto the rocks dousing her in spray.

'More,' she shouted.

And so the gods obliged. Before long she was drenched, not caring, because she was drowning in her sorrow and didn't want to surface. There was nothing she could do but surface. She surfaced to seek revenge and kill the man whom had been responsible for Jake's and now possibly Robert's death. And in that ferment, she planed his demise.

* * *

Tara's plan was to sabotage Jock's canoe, so denying him his escape route, and then lure him into the tunnel just after low tide, with the pump making it passable. She would lead him to the mainland exit and there, somehow, render him incapacitated. How, at this moment in time, she didn't know, but she was sure that something would come to her. That would give her time rush back down the tunnel onto the Island and switch off the pump, which would result in a rapid rise in the water level, hopefully too much for even Jock to cross. He would be marooned within the tunnel, unable to go back or force an exit, for the exit was a heavy reinforced concrete slab that could only be moved from the surface, using special lifting irons. That was the plan, but as soon as she reached the beach it had already faltered. The canoe was gone and presumably Jock with it.

Tara considered her two options. She could lie low until low tide and wade across to the mainland. But by doing that she would have abandoned her Island and effectively left it for Jock to reign supreme, his *coup d'etat* having been won without much resistance.

No, she wasn't going to retreat, instead she would hold fast, resist the attack and would wait for his return and carry out the plan on the next low tide. So she set off for Smuggler's Cottage hoping to see Tom, Jock's new recruit into his army, and try and persuade him to become a turncoat to her cause, if not for the Trevellick family.

Smuggler's Cottage was devoid of light, except for a strange and eerie flicker that emanated from the parlour window as though ghostly apparitions were invading the room with evil intent, seeking out victims to haunt or even kill. Tara approached the back door with caution, not knowing what to expect. Surely Tom wouldn't be inside with such an unearthly, spectral phenomenon.

But as Tara slowly opened the door she could see the familiar chubby figure sitting at a computer screen, and in the light show his trademark shirt took on a new dimension with a kaleidoscope of colours making him look like a wizard on amphetamines. Indeed he was a wizard for he was in middle earth, battling phantoms and monsters, using his supernatural powers to win his maiden, a beautiful flaxen-haired princess who would provide a substitute to stimulants, where he was handsome and heroic and would live happily ever after in his world of dungeon and dragons.

He was so engrossed in his fantasy that he failed to notice Tara standing behind him, peering at the screen and wondering what on earth he was doing, watching him dodge a troll and then kill it. She could see he was happy, for a smile could be seen in the reflection of the screen, a contented smile from a man who found life and love in a computer game. Perhaps that was the only time he was ever happy, she thought, and in that moment felt a pang of guilt for all the times she castigated him. He was family, after all, and she decided that a friendly and sympathetic approach was required.

'Hello Tom,' she said, forcing a smile as he turned to see her standing over him.

'Oh Tara, you startled me. I thought you were on the mainland. That's what Jock told me.'

'As you can see, he was not telling you the truth. I've been here on the Island, all along.'

'I'm not sure I like him much. He shouted at me earlier today.'

'I don't like him either. He's dangerous.'

'Where's Jake? Haven't seen him for a couple of days.'

'Me neither.'

'Probably somewhere else. Expect he'll be better off there than here.'

'I think he'll be at peace, wherever he is.'

Tom looked at Tara and, for the first time in a long time, saw a friend, somebody who took time to talk to him, not dismiss him as an idiot, which so often was the case. He had few friends in life. In fact, only one friend and that was Jake. But now he could add Tara to his list. He felt happy about that and returned to his game with renewed confidence to win his princess.

Tara made Tom a mug of tea and one for herself and sat down to rest for a few moments to decide on a strategy to placate Jock and lure him into the tunnel. He wouldn't need much persuasion, since that was the very reason she was tied and gagged by him in the first place, for refusing to show him the underground route to the mainland. How, though, could she convince him of her change of heart, especially as he knew she and Robert had escaped his clutches?

As she sat there thinking what to do, she heard Tom shout 'yes' in a restrained manner and fling his arms up in triumph and she knew he had found his silicon love, perhaps the only love he would feel in his life, and she thought that the two of them were alike in some way, two souls who will never have the contentment of true love.

She went over to see Tom's spoils and found him already starting on the next game level and watched him avoid an evil looking creature, what, she had no idea, by deploying some sort of phosphorus flare which apparently blinded the protagonist allowing Tom to escape his deadly foe.

'Of course!' exclaimed Tara and patted him on the back saying, 'thanks Tom, you've been a great help.'

Tom looked perplexed. He pondered the complement wondering if he had heard right, concluded that he must be mistaken and carried on with his quest.

Jetty Cottage was a conglomeration of the forgotten. Items which were once considered useful but now just fit for disposal, littered the space. In amongst the broken lobster pots, torn netting, rusting garden equipment, boxes containing the assorted and the redundant and two canoes that were clearly not seaworthy for they had holes in their hulls, there was the most useful, a flare gun and cartridges. Tara peered inside a dusty old chest which contained more netting but no flare gun and rummaged amongst a shelf system supporting half used paint pots, brushes and other paraphernalia used to repair and maintain craft, all held together by threads of cobwebs. It was hopeless, she thought.

Her last hope was an antique chiffonier, or at least it looked antique to Tara, with twisted finials, ornate carvings to the shelving and brass handles in the *fleur de lis* design that spoke of French craftwork, except it now showed its age with faded colours and marks that bore testament to its demise. She looked inside the drawers but found an assortment of crockery and kitchen utensils, some of which she had no idea what they were for and for all she knew they looked like medieval instruments of torture from a castle kitchen. She did, however, recognise carving knives and picked one up, which although blunt had a lethal point and shuddered at the thought of thrusting the blade into human flesh. She doubted her conviction to use it, but nevertheless took it, for Jock was a dangerous adversary and anything that could save her own skin would be useful.

Finally, the bottom drawer to the cabinet yielded what she was searching for. Inside were two flare guns and a box of cartridges. She only needed the one gun and took three cartridges. This was an indemnity, just in case one of them was a dud.

Several years ago she was out alone fishing off the Eddystone lighthouse, when the engine on her vessel had stopped. It wouldn't start and she found herself drifting to the rocks. With no radio she deployed the flare, only it didn't ignite, nor the second. It was only the last flare that signalled her emergency and she was rescued by the Plymouth lifeboat as her boat was about to hit the Eddystone reef. Since that incident, she had always had a back-up and so three flares would be needed.

With the flare gun, her plan was complete. She would leave the gun and cartridges hidden by the generator which was positioned near to the tunnel entrance. She would lure Jock down, start the generator, retrieve the primed weapon and then follow Jock into the tunnel, with the gun hidden. On the other side, she would deploy the flare, make her escape and flood the tunnel. It was a simple plan that had many uncertainties, but it was the best she could formulate, given the situation. With that thought, she proceeded down to the cave system.

It was ominously dark, like her thoughts which were out there in the sea, hoping against all hope that Robert had made it ashore, still alive. She looked out through the cave entrance and could see Robert wave, a cipher to his impending doom. In that wave she perceived a touch of anxiety, that he would rather stay with her and defeat Jock alongside her, as their destiny foretold. Why did she let him go? She wanted so much to be with him, and yet, when their lives were interlaced in a common cause, she sent him away. Perhaps it was because his heart was given to another that she did so and with that thought, picked up the flashlight and entered the labyrinth.

She didn't really need the light. Darkness was now her companion. She progressed through the passages like a firefly, generating her own light, seeing beyond her senses into the black, anticipating every turn, every cave. But even for Tara, within the familiar, sometimes the unknown touches the void and as she made her way deep into the caves she felt something pass through her hand. It was thread-like, taught, as though some giant spider was waiting for a vibration, before it sprang to inject its hapless victim, caught in an unseen web. She switched on the flashlight and discovered a length of fishing line, which most certainly was alien to this world. It was vibrating, as though somebody, something was tugging on it and could see it trail off into the dark, into an unknown lair. She followed it around a bend in the honeycomb of rock and then detected a faint flash of light illuminating the chamber beyond. There was somebody in her domain and they were waiting for her.

Now the cave network became a place of uncertainty. The familiar became unknown and several times she bumped into rocks that normally she would have avoided. Her heart began to race. Who was this person? It couldn't be Jock, could it? Maybe he had anticipated her move and had hidden his canoe and was now luring her into his web, to be trapped and consumed by his deception. She took out a flare cartridge and inserted it into the gun, hoping it was not a dud and just in case she had the knife handy, tucked into her belt behind her back.

She edged forward in the gloom. The flashes of light grew brighter creating a surreal atmosphere as though the aurora borealis was shimmering above, hues of green and yellow reflecting from the rocks in the ions of light. Now faint noises could be heard. She peered around a corner and saw the spectral figure of a man standing at the entrance to the tunnel. She watched as the man shone his torch into the black hole, illuminating it for a few yards. It was not Jock. But who? She had to challenge him. It was her domain and she was going to defend it. She very carefully put the flare gun down and took out her knife. Then slowly, stealthily, she crept up behind him, until she was within reach. She grabbed his arm, twisted it behind his back and had the knife at his throat, ready to strike should he resist.

'Who are you? What are you doing here?' she shouted.

The man cowered. He had never been compromised like this, ever.

'Please, don't do anything. I won't harm you.'

'No you won't. But I may, if you don't answer me.'

He told her everything. He dare not lie, although he didn't tell Tara that he was on the Island to investigate smuggling. When he had finished, he looked at his attacker, a beautiful woman, and felt ashamed at his cowardly act. She would think him such a timorous man, who couldn't even defend himself, let alone another person, having acted so pusillanimously. Tara, however, did not see that. She saw a young man, a lad, out of his depth, and could see he posed no threat, and that he had been coerced into involvement with Jock.

Knowing that he would not be back for some time, she decided to return to base and leave Malcolm with Tom.

'Ingenious of you to do a Theseus,' she said with a wry smile, winding the line as they retraced their steps back to the cave entrance.

'Sometimes it pays to know your Greek mythology,' he responded, now feeling considerably better knowing that the woman was a friend and not the enemy. In fact, he now viewed Tara as a compatriot, a woman who knew her mythology and she was Persephone, goddess of her caves, an underworld where she had been roaming and where she had, without any intention, enraptured him. For Tara, they were indeed her caves. She was queen of her domain. But for how long, as a fierce and cruel Hades was about to challenge that crown and both she and Malcolm were soon to confront his wrath.

50

iracles can happen. Miracles do happen. One in the form of a lifejacket saved Robert from a watery grave. Not the lifejacket itself, although that was what ultimately saved him. No, it was the spontaneous inflation of the yellow vest that was the miracle, because Robert could not recollect having pulled the release cord, certainly not as he was sinking beneath the waves.

He coughed and choked as he surfaced, not knowing how he had escaped death but relieved he had for he wanted more to life, to see Caroline, to have a family and grow old. And he wanted to see Tara once more and thank her for saving his life, for insisting he wear a lifejacket, when he was prepared to face the ocean with nothing but his foolish courage.

He was by no means safe but heading in the right direction. The current was now taking him towards the shore, but ominously close to rocks that would tear him apart, even if those of Dunker Point had failed. He began to swim and between the crests of the waves could see a break, an inlet where he could swim to safety. But his state of lassitude was overcoming him and as much as he tried to make for the tiny beach, the current was forcing him ever further away. It was no use. He would have to let the sea determine his fate and hope landfall would be a benign part of the coast, for he had no energy left to fight the relentless sea. And so he drifted, a piece of flotsam treading water, heading towards a headland and a wall of rock that would surely, one way or another, seal his fate.

His fate, though, was not the rocks beneath a towering cliff, but the welcoming shallows of a cove and as his feet touched the seabed, rather than a rough irregular outcrop of rock, he felt the smooth, pleasant deposits of sand, a fitting outcome to his prayers of deliverance. He hauled himself closer and closer to the beach and in the crashing surf sank to his knees exhausted. In one last supreme effort he dragged himself clear of the water that had almost taken another soul to its locker.

Robert lay on the beach not wanting to move. Unable to move. All he could do was stare at the sky watching skittish clouds race across his vision, giving a glimpse behind its veil into the cosmos, and he thanked his protector for yet another chance at life. He was enervated by his ordeal, yet elated by his deliverance. Trust in salvation, he thought, as he continued to look into the vastness of the universe and wondered if he had been a cat in a past life and that its fortune had transmigrated to his being, and with his mind hallucinating, he could see his beloved tabby look at him with satisfaction that its soul had found a worthy champion.

How long he lay there he could not tell. Only the retreat of the sea, now several yards away from where he had beached himself, told of the time. With another effort, he rose onto two weak legs, stood still for a few moments and regained some balance and sense to his surroundings. The tall cliffs to his right looked foreboding in the dark, bastions of doom had he not been fortuitous and been cast into the cove. Out at sea and quite far to the left, above the waves, he could make out the familiar shape of the Island and estimated he must have drifted about a mile from his demise in the boat.

'A miracle,' he told himself.

But he spoke too soon, for it was then that he felt a dull pain in his thigh. He was bleeding and as he tried to move a sharp pain grabbed his senses and he buckled in agony. He needed help, but as he looked around for assistance he realised that there was none. He had replaced one prison for another and now was alone once more, this time trapped in a cove with no escape and no relief from his pain.

The beach was a perfect arc but not completely of sand. To the far end, towards the Island and Looe itself, were rocks, whilst in front of him at the top of the beach were more cliffs, not of resistant rock but unstable shale where landslips could be discerned, with trees lying on slumps at the top of high water. Robert staggered along the beach, trying to spot an exit. A high promontory blocked his path. The sea was washing against it and if salvation was to be found, he would have to negotiate the surf once more. Just when he thought it would be safe to attempt a traverse, a huge wave came crashing in, which would have surely taken him. He could wait for the tide to retreat further, but his pain was stabbing him, telling him to risk another such wave.

Robert stood there, watching first one swell and then another hit the rocks. He remembered his father's assertion that every seventh wave was the big one. He doubted it was true, just maritime lore, but nevertheless started to count them. When a large wave crashed yet again on the promontory, he decided to chance the following one. After the sixth wave hit the rocks with some ferocity, he made his move. Progress was good and he was half way round when a rogue surge hit him, propelling him towards a buttress which, fortunately for Robert, had been worn smooth by wave action. He survived the impact and found himself prostrate, viewing the heavens once more, recovering from his latest battering and wondering how many more lives he had left. As the sea washed around him, he felt like some piece of littoral debris left for some beachcomber to find, a stranded seal or dead dolphin that had succumbed to inertia. He summoned his depleted energy, raised himself upright, and surveyed the cove. He was still cut off with no escape, for looming in the murky night was a headland that, most definitely, he was not going to negotiate. It looked foreboding, a black wall of rock that proclaimed doom should he attempt another traverse.

Robert was not so much marooned in a cove this time, more of a bay, and to his relief the cliffs seemed much friendlier, thick with vegetation almost down to beach itself. There were also signs of human life. Debris from a camp fire and some scattered beer cans could be seen and he now felt some advancement in his circumstances, because it meant there must be some access point. And as he staggered along the foreshore, his injury still reminding him of urgency, he found some concrete steps half hidden by a tamarisk tree, ascending the cliff face. He thanked his feline luck.

He climbed steadily, one step at a time, not wanting to aggravate his wound and at the top reached the coastal path. It would be an easy walk back to Looe and his cottage, but for his anguish. As he clumsily walked along the path he soon realised that he might not make it and to make matters worse, the path descended in a series of steep steps to a wide ravine where a bridge crossed a small stream. It was there, as he climbed over a wooden style that Robert succumbed to his pain and collapsed to the ground.

For a few seconds he felt light headed, not sure of his condition and whether he was about to slip into unconsciousness. He breathed heavily, almost hyperventilating. The cold night air seemed to revive him although his thigh was still painful. But as he regained his cognition there seemed to be salvation from his suffering, for in the distance, beyond a shallow wooded coombe, was the glow of some lights from a house and a plume of smoke from a chimney stack, indicating there was somebody at home. It was only a short distance away, considerably closer than Looe, and with a clear path leading to the residence he decided to make for civilisation.

Despite being a short distance it was uphill and took considerable effort for Robert to reach the building. And as he entered, what appeared to be an estate garden, the house transformed into a manorial residence of some grandeur with lights from garden lanterns illuminating the façade. He was at the back, with no discernable place of entry other than French doors which all looked locked and deserted.

By now his side was constantly aching with a dull pain and every so often, especially as he forgot about his wound, a sharp reminder would register his attention, causing him to emit a muffled cry of anguish. As quickly as possible he made his way around to the front and to a grand portico that spoke of wealth. He rang the bell. He had no idea what time it was, other than night. Perhaps everybody was asleep, he thought, as he waited for the door to open. It seemed an eternity, but eventually the door opened and standing there looking quite shocked at Robert's state, was an old man dressed in a smoking jacket. Robert stumbled and finally collapsed at the entrance to the lair of Hendersick Hall.

* * *

The next thing Robert knew he was sitting in an armchair by a blazing fire, wrapped in a soft blanket with nothing on but his modesty. The man, who stood before him as he lost consciousness, was sitting in a chair behind a large desk smoking a pipe, the tobacco smoke creating a haze which clouded Robert's mind.

'Ah, I see you are now with us,' spoke the old man.

Robert looked at him wondering who this man was, an unlikely saviour, but one who seemed pleasant and certainly educated judging by the surroundings he was in, a room covered in art and antiquities and oozing culture.

'Just about,' was all he could manage.

'Well, you look a good deal better than when I found you. Permit me to introduce myself. My name is Frederick Thomas, at your service.'

'I thank you for your kind assistance,' replied Robert and then added, 'and I'm Robert Colliver.'

With his announcement Frederick recoiled in his seat, quite astounded that the man Jock had been on about, who was a potential adversary to his ambitions, was not only in his house but sitting in his study, where strategy was played against him. Yet despite this, he could not be anything other than courteous, a trait that had served him well in the world of finance, where business dealings were conducted in friendly negotiations to appear conciliatory, only for the final transaction to be a ruthless takeover without regard to any human suffering. Business was business and in his world any sign of weakness was seized upon by the opposition. It wasn't going to be him.

'Well, Robert Colliver, it is a pleasure to meet you.'

'Forgive me for asking, but I must use your telephone.'

'I don't think you are in any fit state at the moment to talk to anybody. Perhaps I can help.'

'I need to telephone the police. A friend of mine is in grave danger.'

'I'm a magistrate and have connections with the Constabulary. Allow me to telephone on your behalf.'

Robert agreed and with Frederick now sitting opposite him by the fire, explained the situation to him on the Island. He listened with interest for he never received such a detailed account from Jock and he was becoming increasingly concerned at the reckless attitude Jock was taking, evidenced by this man in front of him. He went over to his desk and dialled a number.

'Hello, is that Inspector Adams?'

It was the Inspector. Frederick explained the situation to him, every so often adding a nod of confirmation or a look of disapproval, as Robert half listened to him, making sure the facts were relayed correctly. As he did so, he glanced around the room, looking at the paintings decorating the walls and objects bedecking bookcases and occasional tables. He recognised some miniatures of Indian origin, depicting peafowl in Mogul gardens on a nearby wall alongside a variety of etchings and sketches of nude females. There were paintings by artists he knew and others unfamiliar whilst the art objects were clearly valuable antiquities ranging from Chinese figurines, maybe from the Ming dynasty with its distinctive green hue, to a wooden carving of an African woman, a shamanic figurine with nubile breasts that seemed to catch the prurient eye.

Robert thought he had entered into the anteroom of a brothel, not that he had ever been in one himself, for there were nude females everywhere, albeit in the guises of art. He had to admit they were tasteful, even alluring, except for a grotesque looking object of an earth mother goddess which seemed to have pride of place on his desk.

But his gaze finally settled on an object to one side of the desk, a table lamp identical to the one his mother had, and that he had coveted so much as an innocent youth. Now, in middle-age, he had tasted the delights it had beheld back then, yet its exquisite form still captivated him. He went to get up but a sharp pain attacked his side and he now recalled the injury which had temporarily left him. He sat back down and waited for Frederick to finish the conversation, but now fixing his gaze solely on the lamp, looking questioningly at the naked form he knew so well.

After what seemed an interminable length of time, with Frederick asking after the Inspector's family and inviting them for a meal sometime, he finally finished the call.

'That's settled,' said Frederick putting the telephone down. 'The police will mount an investigation and go out to the Island immediately. A launch, I understand, will be deployed from Plymouth.'

'Thank you,' replied Robert, grateful that something was now being done.

But it wasn't. Frederick had indeed been speaking to an Inspector Adams of the Devon and Cornwall Constabulary, but his coded words were not acted upon for the officer was a friend and benefactor of the Thomas family, and as such was in Frederick's debt. And the launch, which Robert assumed was a police boat, was remaining very much in Plymouth.

Frederick went back over to the fireplace and sat down. He looked into Robert's eyes who glanced away, not comfortable with his gaze which seemed to penetrate his thoughts, as though he were trying to influence him. It was his old trick of putting opponents off their guard, making them reveal some small secret or piece of information that would make all the difference to a deal. In this case, the deal was much more valuable, the stakes higher and Frederick wanted a further advantage over the one he already had. Robert, though, was interested in the table lamp.

'I was admiring your table lamp. It looks a genuine antique. Art Nouveau?'

'Indeed it is. Are you in the trade?'

'Oh no, just an admirer of exquisite forms.'

'That she is. I obtained it from a friend who acquired it from a private individual, so I gather.'

Robert wanted to take a closer look. Could it be the lost lamp of his mother's? Surely not. But there was something familiar about it, the curves of the naked idol which he knew so well and its tarnished appearance, even the dirty hue to the opaque glass ball. He got up again, but this time enduring the pain for his curiosity. He went over to the desk.

'May I take a closer look?' he asked.

'By all means. But be careful, it's worth a fortune.'

Robert lifted the lamp up and examined it with minute detail. He knew the lamp as though it were his own hand and was sure it was the one. Only one way to confirm it. He tipped it carefully on its side and there, underneath were the initials RC, although they were his father's initials, a wedding gift from his wife. It was most definitely his lamp. The coveted lamp of his childhood.

'Quite exquisite and solid silver,' he commented and looked down, wondering how it had ended up in this man's room.

'Indeed,' said Frederick, his suspicious nature coming out in his tone. He knew only too well the mannerisms of a man locked in his own thoughts, thoughts in this case related to the lamp. What was the connection, he wondered? It must be Jock. He would have the answer.

Robert put the lamp back down on the desk. As he made his way back to his armchair, he noticed a familiar carving on the mantelpiece. It was small, about twelve inches in length and depicted a figure, half man and half bird. The man's body was elongated with an emaciated appearance and appeared to have wings for arms. The head was of a bird with a long curved beak, the upper bill curled at the end, unmistakeably that of the frigate bird. Frederick could see Robert focused on his latest acquisition and was somewhat relieved at his new interest and pleased that here was somebody taking an interest in his art collection.

'It's from Easter Island,' he announced.

'Yes, I know. It's a birdman totem.'

'Would you like to take a look?' he said, quite surprised at Robert's knowledge.

He picked it up and studied it in detail, as though he were inspecting its authenticity. He was. Frederick could see a puzzled look gradually evolve in Robert's expression as he turned the birdman around and upside down and then rubbed it with his finger.

'Is there a problem?' he enquired.

'I'm not sure. Is it genuine?'

'Of course,' replied Frederick, with an indignant tone.

Robert replaced the carving back on the mantelpiece and sat back down in the armchair, relieved to take the weight off his hip. He looked at the old man opposite him, trying to judge what his reaction would be to his reply.

'I'm not an expert, but I think you may have a fake. A good one, but nevertheless a fake.'

'And what, prey, makes you think that? Do you know anything about Easter Island culture?'

'As I said, I'm no expert, but if the birdman you have was genuine then it would have been carved from the wood of the Toromiro Pine, a tree that used to be indigenous to the Island. It's now extinct there and can only be found in a couple of botanical institutions. The wood has a distinctive reddish colour. But if you scratch at the carving it is only skin deep. Underneath is a lighter coloured wood, which means it is a copy.'

Frederick was astonished by Robert's dismissal of his genuine piece of antiquity and amazed at his knowledge of so obscure a subject, although still sceptical about his assertion, particularly as it meant a considerable loss on his investment. More than that, it was that he had a fake when he was in the market for the genuine article.

'I have been assured it is genuine. It is, I know, rare and as such is worth a considerable sum,' he responded.

'I doubt it.' He looked at Frederick, this man who had admitted him into his home and had been kind to him, was now viewed through tainted lens. Robert now saw a man who had his lamp and who had a fake artefact, one that he thought was genuine. He was not all he seemed to be and Robert decided that even if he was unfit to move, nevertheless, to leave the house and make for Looe.

'I thank you for your hospitality, but I think I've outstayed my welcome,' he announced.

'Nonsense,' said Frederick. 'In any case, you are in no fit state to leave. You haven't even any clothes on,' he added with a gentle laugh of amusement.

Robert looked at himself with embarrassment at the stupidity of his decision.

'I insist you stay. My man-servant will take you to wherever you want in the morning.'

Robert couldn't argue, not without some clothes, and sat back in the armchair, which was, at least, a comfortable seat of repose, by the fire and with his glass of wine.

Frederick left the room, making his excuse, but bade Robert to help himself to more wine, in fact insisted he should for medicinal purposes.

But he would rather have tea, and in any case the wine tasted corked, or something, he couldn't quite tell. He poured the remainder into a pot containing an exotic plant and hoped it wouldn't kill it off. He rested back in the armchair once more and looked around the room again scanning the array of erotic art, and now noticed a set of three more Indian miniatures, depicting the Karma Sutra. His mind reeled back to that day at the cottage, the day that Tara was going to seduce him. He smiled. She did in the end, he thought, as he played that scene again in the warm intimacy of his mind. He wondered what she was doing now. He should have stayed. He should be doing something to help her, to protect her, he said to himself and tried to get up. But his whole body felt like lead and he slumped back down again.

The room was silent except for the crackling wood of the fire, its warmth creating a soporific ambiance as he felt his eyes become heavy, his exploits now overcoming him with exhaustion. He was half asleep. He glanced around the room and felt a sensation of being watched, voyeurs looking at him from their frames.

It was then he saw her. She was staring at him with her penetrating eyes transfixed on him. She was half naked and holding a crystal orb, her breasts inviting his senses, willing him to become her victim, to sacrifice his heart and soul to her. He was now drifting off into a shamanic world where reality and fantasy are one, where the boundaries are blurred and images are mistaken. He felt a presence. Was it real or imagined? He could not tell. He opened his analeptic eyes. There she was, standing in front of him, her eyes bewitching him with a lascivious intent.

51

J ane looked at Robert. She had him where she wanted him. She had been watching him fall asleep, not because he was exhausted, but from a sleeping draught he had unwittingly been drinking in the wine. But she looked anxious. He was not in a deep sleep, as expected, but was tossing his head and mumbling as though in a trance. He verbalised some words but they were confused, indistinguishable from the head gestures he was animating. Then he opened his eyes, not fully, but she could feel his stare. In that moment he recognised her.

His eyes returned to slumber once more and his body relaxed into a state of torpor, no longer exhibiting agitated convulsions, as though some demon had been playing with him like a puppet. She looked longingly at Robert, a man who had invaded her mind and one that, try as she might, would not retreat from her thoughts. He was no use to her like that. She knelt down by his feet and rested her head on his lap and could feel the warmth of his body, and the slow rhythmic pulsation of his heart.

It was Jane who had undressed him, removed his wet clothes, and in doing so gazed upon his naked form, a voyeur into privacy. She stretched up to kiss him. She wanted to go further, to satisfy her desires, and would have done, would have become a succubus in that moment of weakness, but for Frederick making an entrance into her fantasy.

'Is he out yet?' he enquired.

'I think so,' she responded, quickly hiding her intentions.

'Well, he doesn't look as though he'll be going anywhere now,' he commented with a wry grin, as he looked at Robert. 'Tie him up, just to be on the safe side. Jock can deal with him later.'

As she bound Robert's hands she could feel an erotic rapture overwhelm her, that after all her scheming she had finally enslaved her infatuation. She tied the knots as though wanting him to escape, so that he could exert his masculinity upon her, but only after she had had her pleasure. Frederick could see the delight in Jane's face and the sensuous way she was tying the rope and found the scene alluring to his masochistic tendencies.

When he first met Jane she was a high-class call girl. He paid for her services. Not just for sex, but for her to tie him up and whip him; whip him forcefully until he begged for mercy. The pain was like an aphrodisiac, inducing pleasure from the suffering, penitence in the cut-throat world of hostile take-overs and bankruptcy. It was a dichotomy that reflected his status as a man who would inflict pain and misery upon others, especially when his investment bank took control of a company and broke it up, making people redundant and bankrupting creditors. He needed to feel their pain, a surrogacy that provided succour, and Jane obliged, taking pleasure in providing the domination that he craved.

For Frederick, in his retirement, they were now unwanted fantasies, no longer needing absolution from the pressures of work. He had seen enough. He liked having Jane around as a trophy, much like his art collection, and he would delight in watching her undress and pose as though she were a statuesque beauty, another acquisition he could adore.

She was more of an informer nowadays, rather than a sexual companion, and although she had divulged many useful items of information, she had neglected to tell him that the man who had sought sanctuary in his home was Robert Colliver. She would have known. She had her own agenda, one that involved seducing him no doubt, and he felt betrayed and nauseated by it, that she would commit such an act in his home.

'I think it's time you left,' he said.

'Really? Don't you want me tonight?' replied Jane, with an air of disappointment, not at departing from Frederick, but leaving Robert in such a compromising situation.

'No. I've some important business to attend to,' replied Frederick.

'Alright. Don't let that brute harm him.' She looked at Robert and said, 'Sleep well,' and in her mind she added, 'I'll have you tomorrow.'

*   *   *

After half an hour or so of silence in which Robert, still asleep, murmured to himself, Frederick returned to his desk and inspected the birdman carving that had been dismissed as a fake. Perhaps he was right, he thought, and after looking at the lamp with a suspicious consideration, turned his attention to the map that Jock had secured. Then, the door to the study opened and Christian entered.

'Excuse me sir, but the gentleman's clothes are now dry. Perhaps if he cares to come with me.'

'Thank you Christian. He's sleeping at the moment. Leave them in the kitchen for now. That will be all for tonight,' said Frederick.

Christian turned to leave and was shocked to see the gentleman with his hands bound. He took a quick glance at FT who was still immersed in the map, failing to notice his man servant's concern. He left FT musing over the map and returned to the kitchen. There was certainly something amiss. Who was this person? A man bound in the study. Quite bizarre, he thought. He opened the door to the secret passageway and crept along to the study spy hole. FT was now sitting by the fire, a glass tumbler in hand.

'Well my friend, you have certainly been a nuisance, although you have provided some very useful information. Soon I will have the Island and the treasure. You will be no more, a curse extinguished, just as you namesake was, Robert Colliver, Pirate Captain.' He raised his glass towards Robert, toasted him and drank the glass of malt whisky.

Christian was astounded. He knew of the legend. Was this man actually Robert Colliver? And was he going to be killed? The hulk, Jock, would no doubt do the deed, which FT would wash his hands of. He needed to rescue this man. He could wait for FT to retire, but he often stayed up all night, dozing in his armchair by the fire. He needed to lure him away. But how? Christian returned to the kitchen to consider how he might achieve that aim.

Events though, were to overtake his empty thoughts. A commotion was developing outside, loud enough to force Frederick to investigate.

Christian could hear footsteps coming towards the kitchen and quickly entered the passage way, not before collecting the man's clothes and shutting the panelled door just in time, as Frederick came into the kitchen. He could hear FT call out for him and then open the rear door.

Christian made haste to the study spy hole, opened the panel door, and was soon untying the bonds, trying to wake Robert, but to no avail. Christian slapped him on the face and Robert awoke, feeling groggy and wondering what was going on. With some urgency, and imploring Robert to move, Christian explained the situation which a bemused patient still found confusing.

But then Robert remembered he was in Hendersick Hall, a place of mendacity, where nothing was quite as it appeared; where fake art could be found, stolen artefacts, and now, a prostitute. He had remembered eying Jane, a glimpse of a femme fatale, who had plunged to new depths of deception and degradation. And when Christian elucidated that a large blonde-haired man, a hulk of a man by all accounts, Robert knew he was in danger. It was only then that he arose from the comfortable armchair, aching pain enveloping his whole being, and followed the stranger, staggering on his feet into the passageway and another dark void in his life.

Christian told Robert to remain there until it was safe to leave, handed him his clothes, implored him to be quiet for the passageways resonated to the smallest of sound and returned to the kitchen just as FT was coming in from the garden.

'There's something going on beyond the lawn, Christian. Go and see what it is,' he commanded.

Christian ventured outside and crossed over to where a battle was raging between a peacock and a blonde haired hulk. Who was winning was hard to say, and so he left them to conclude their encounter, hoping that the peacock was victorious.

On returning to the kitchen Christian now faced another assault. FT had returned from the study looking angry, almost apoplectic.

'Where's our guest?' he demanded.

'I don't know. Last I saw him, he was with you in the study.'

'He's not there now.'

'I guess he woke up and left. His clothes are gone,' as Christian pointed to where he had left them.

'And you didn't see anything?'

'No. I was upstairs. I came down when I heard the noise outside.'

Frederick was unconvinced but before he could continue the interrogation, in burst Jock in a state of rage, about to erupt.

'That pesky bird. One day I'll get...'

'That pesky bird, as you put it, and all the rest are a sacred symbol of India and were a gift to the estate, and as such have diplomatic immunity,' intervened Frederick.

'Diplomatic protection or not...' added Jock.

But Frederick had the last word, 'they are to be left in peace. Anyway, you have come at an opportune moment.'

For Christian, the peacock had decided to attack Jock at indeed the most opportune moment, for it had given him the time to rescue Robert, who was now listening to the conversation taking place from within the walls of Hendersick Hall.

'For all your contrivances Jock, it seems that your foe, Robert Colliver, has eluded you yet again. Unfortunately, he was here in my study, his hands bound, but I've just discovered he's escaped me as well.'

'That man, I'll do the same to him as that bird. I'd better get after him. He cannot have gone far.'

'Please refrain from including my peafowl in your machinations. As for chasing after him, I suspect he may still be within these walls. He did not escape through the study French-doors, for they are locked, as is the front door. He cannot have left by the kitchen back door, unless he passed you whilst battling my peacock.'

'No, I'm certain of that.'

'Then he is still in the house, somewhere.'

'I'll find him,' retorted Jock, 'If it's the last thing I ever do. Then he'll wish he'd been born a peacock!'

52

Caroline and Alfred had escaped the tunnel emerging, as Robert had done so, into another world where normality was the keynote. But whereas a night time mist and foghorn had greeted his awakening, they found themselves in the gloom of dusk which was leaving a westerly glow to the horizon. Unbeknown to the two captives the afternoon had been gradually deteriorating, with a fresh southerly blowing in off the sea, and the balmy evening of the night before had been replaced by the threat of inclement weather.

Fortunately, they were not spotted emerging from the thicket which obscured the tunnel itself, even though a few tourists below the ruined chapel were making their way back to hotels and guest houses after an evening perambulation. Both Caroline and Alfred looked dishevelled. They dusted themselves down making themselves look as though they hadn't been scrambling in a rabbit hole, which of course they had of sorts, and sat on the nearby bench to consider their next move.

Without regard to the worsening weather conditions, it was there looking at the Island descend into shadow, that Caroline decided to wade across on the early morning low tide, as Robert had done only twenty four hours earlier. She was now even more concerned for him. She should have vetoed his insistence on her remaining behind and gone with him, and whatever he was facing, it would be together and not him alone.

She informed Alfred of her intentions and suggested that they go and see George, as that was what they were going to do when so rudely interrupted.

'Good idea. Expect he will still be ensconced in the Smugglers

Arms, having notched up double figures in pints of ale, no doubt,' declared Alfred.

'Could do with a drink myself,' replied Caroline.

'Even I, a teetotaller, would welcome a dram of whisky. For medicinal purposes, mind you.'

'Of course, to aid recovery,' said Caroline, thinking that's what Robert would say.

The Smugglers was busy with locals and tourists listening to sea shanties from the local Polperro Fishermen's choir, singing and clapping along to a ballad, whilst in a back room several youngsters were playing pool lounging around with their girlfriends. This was an alien world to Caroline, more used to refined bistros of wine and tapas in London, not the bawdy banter of coarse working men and women and the pints of ale and packets of crisps, all enveloped in thick acrid smoke that was a contender for a Victorian pea-souper. Under any other circumstances she would have walked straight out, and was about to when Alfred pointed to a man sitting alone in a small snug tucked along from the bar.

George was half way through a pint of ale and outwardly in his own company, for he showed no sign of listening to the music nor of engaging with the loud banter within the public house. He was, though, contributing to the atmosphere, smoking a pipe which was producing enough fumes to asphyxiate anybody sitting next to him which Caroline and Alfred, much to their consternation, had no option but to do.

'Hello George,' said Alfred.

George looked up and a spark of light ignited within him at seeing his old friend once again.

'Hello, Alfred. Good to see you. How long has it been?'

'Too long.'

'Chosen a right old night to come visiting,' remarked George, which Alfred, a little deaf in his dotage, could hardly hear.

'Happened to be in town. Anyway, how are you?'

'Can't complain,' he said taking a sup from his glass and then inhaling another lung full of tobacco, before exhaling in the direction of Caroline who was sitting opposite him as far from his chimney as possible without being overtly rude, but still receiving a plume of smoke, which made her cough. 'Sorry, my dear,' he apologised, noticing Caroline wince and recoil at the smoke. 'It's what keeps me alive, this and the ale,' and looked at Alfred as if to ask who she was.

'Oh this is Caroline, a friend of Robert Colliver. You know him.'

'Yes, I know him. Have you come about the Pirate Captain? You know more than I do, Alfred.'

'No, not the Captain but about the two bodies in the tunnel.'

George, in the process of supping another draught of ale, spilt a mouthful at the surprise and direct enquiry.

'You were there,' he said looking at Alfred and indicating whether it was alright to speak of the episode in their lives, over fifty years ago.

'It's alright, Caroline knows. She and Robert discovered the crypt and tunnel, but found only the bones of one body. How do you account for that?'

'Must have miscounted,' he said dismissively.

'Not likely, is it George? The other body just didn't disappear. You know what happened. Tell me. It's alright to say. Too many years have elapsed for there to be any recriminations.'

George looked at his two inquisitors and thought.

'I swore an oath,' he protested. 'An oath until death.'

'But she's not alive now to judge you. And it is important. Important to me, your lifelong friend George, to know the truth.'

He knew he had to tell Alfred of how he went back to the cottage two days later to make sure everything was as they left it, and that the floor had dried out to leave no trace of the crypt entrance. As he stood there, in the silence of a cemetery, he detected the sound of the dead in his mind, the two bodies wanting resurrection, wanting justice. He thought it was his imagination but the sound, a dull thud and distant wail, was real, too real to be the dead and he realised that perhaps one of the bodies may not have been dead after all and it was buried alive in a tomb from which no escape was possible. He uncovered all his work and as he entered the crypt the sound was only too real, the cry for help from a female voice that could hear her saviour. She thanked him for her release from hell and prayed thanks for salvation and vowed a life of devotion to the glory of His mercy.

Alfred had already made his escape and she made George swear that he never tell him of that day, that she would name the child she was carrying, for she knew it was a girl having had a premonition during her ordeal underground, Tarara, after the place where she was conceived and where her father once had their dreams encapsulated, in a place that God had sanctified. She would give birth to her daughter and enter holy orders and give service to the Lord until He claimed her for His kingdom.

He told this to Alfred who was overcome with grief that had he known she was alive, he would never have abandoned her and that he, they, would have had a life together, instead of apart, separated by dogma and an act of jealous temper that had haunted him to this day.

'She told me that she forgave you,' declared George. 'She said that it wasn't your fault, that she was to blame and that she should never have given in to her father and her family.'

'If only…If only,' sighed Alfred.

'What's the significance of the name Tarara? She wouldn't have told you unless it had some meaning,' interjected Caroline.

Alfred knew. He knew as soon as George mentioned the name.

'Can't you see Caroline?' said Alfred.

'No.'

'It's a sort of palindrome.'

And then Caroline could see. The daughter was named after the hill that the cottage was built upon; Ararat. But Caroline could see further than just that horizon. She now realised that the woman she had met the other day, the infatuation of Robert, was Alfred's granddaughter and he didn't have any knowledge of her, let alone her existence. She would tell him later on, in more appropriate surroundings, not the ferment of a public bar, and now felt they had gained as much information as they needed to explain the missing body.

But Alfred needed some more answers.

'Do you know where Alice is buried?' he asked.

'In the grounds of Sclerder Abbey, where she died.'

'And did the daughter, Tarara, have any children herself?'

'As far as I'm aware, no,' he said.

Alfred detected a hesitation in his answer, a hesitation that told him that maybe she did have a child or children, but that he was not going to say and decided to wait for a quieter time and confront him alone.

Caroline looked at George with her piercing eyes, eyes that could penetrate the guilty conscience and force a confession. George noticed her gaze. Only momentarily, for he quickly looked away, knowing she knew of Tara. He didn't tell Alfred because he didn't want him to know the truth. He was ashamed of her, ashamed for he knew both her mother and grandmother, who were righteous people. He knew about Tara's reputation and her involvement in smuggling, which would, he thought, grieve Alfred more than not knowing.

Caroline and Alfred left George to finish his ale and were glad to be out of the fumes, breathing fresh air into their lungs, detoxifying themselves of nicotine and tar vapours. The deadly mixture had impregnated their clothes and anybody wishing to follow them need only to have followed the noxious trail left in their wake. And that was what George was doing, as he rushed as quickly as he could up the hill, coughing loudly, which his two quarries could not help but hear. They stopped and waited. He reached them breathless and convulsed a terrible cough as though he were about to be asphyxiated. Having gained his composure, such as it was, he told them there was something he needed to show them at the cottage, not now, for it had waited fifty years and one more day would not matter, but that it would explain everything.

53

$\mathcal{E}$xpect the unexpected was Siegfried's motto. It was usually a good dictum in his line of work. Unfortunately, he had neither expected the two prisoners to escape their shackles, nor for Robert to survive the rocks, let alone swim ashore and make it to Hendersick Hall.

He had deliberately left the boat untouched or, at least, seaworthy in the cave but had sabotaged the engine so that it would stall only after a few minutes at sea by untightening a pipe connection thereby cutting off the water cooling supply. That plan had worked, but some unknown force or guardian angel must be protecting Robert, he thought, for he had escaped yet again. He now needed to instigate an alternative plan to combat his misjudgement.

He suspected the two fugitives had hidden in the cave system, but dared not enter a lair that Tara knew well and where he would be at a disadvantage. That was not good practice. So he had left them to make their escape by the boat and watched, quite surprised, as only Robert took to the waves, emerging from the cave entrance into the raging sea and taking the course he had anticipated. He watched the boat disappear round the southerly tip of the Island before he made his own escape, realising that there would be little chance of survival on the rocks off Dunker Point. With Tara remaining on the Island, presumably to defend her territory, he set another plan in motion, this time where, converse to his motto, he would do the unexpected.

He had gone to the mainland to locate the entrance to the tunnel. It had to be obvious. And as he looked for likely places the entrance could be, it was indeed conspicuous to his trained eye. It was under a seat which had been installed only a couple of years ago in dedication to one of the Carter sisters, Annie, who used teach in Looe and who would signal her sister from the mainland, from the old chapel of Lammana, whenever the weather prevented her from returning to the Island. When she died, Tara had suggested a memorial bench to her which Madge had found most agreeable, a fitting tribute to her sister, who found Island life a touch more arduous than her more resilient sibling. For Tara, it provided the perfect opportunity to gain access to the undersea tunnel and deflect questioning eyes from the necessary building work.

Beneath the seat Jock had observed a concrete block, which, on close inspection and by tracing the edges, was clearly the place. With a little persuasion he had lifted the trap door, which was much lighter than anticipated, being constructed with a spring loaded hinge. Quite ingenious, he thought. Jock's new plan was to swim along the flooded tunnel, which he estimated to be no more than one hundred yards and which he knew he could manage, to emerge on the Island and mount an ambush from a direction Tara would not anticipate.

In order to swim the tunnel he needed a wetsuit, goggles and snorkel and so headed for Hendersick Hall where his diving equipment was stored. It was now in the early hours of the morning and although the peafowl were roosting in a stand of trees Jock, nevertheless, was still wary of them in case a brave or foolish male cock bird should challenge him.

He was ready this time though. He had his commando knife at hand and would use it with pleasure should one of the wretched fowl come his way and was almost wishing one to challenge him. And one did. It didn't go for the ankles, rather it flew down from a nearby tree and in an instance had caught Jock on the head with its beak creating a wound and a loud commotion as he tried to catch it. He almost succeeded. But the peacock had flown out of reach and gave out a cry of triumph leaving Jock defeated, yet again, by those pesky birds.

*   *   *

For all his searching, Jock couldn't locate Robert. He had found an upstairs window open and concluded he may have climbed down the outside of the house, using the ivy for hand-holds. It was Christian who had slipped upstairs and opened the window of a bedroom, hoping that the hulk would make that conclusion. But Jock wasn't convinced, not a man who was bound. He retreated to the study where a glass of malt awaited his efforts.

'No sign of him,' remarked Jock.

'I'm sure he is here,' replied Frederick. 'The Hall is a veritable labyrinth of passages and rooms, so he may still be hiding somewhere. Anyway, for the moment there is something I want to ask you.'

Robert had heard Siegfried enter the kitchen and utter his words of consternation at the peacock. Robert was back in a black void once more, only this time it seemed even more claustrophobic, where the walls were closing in on him, brushing his two shoulders with barely enough room to move in. He had managed, with some difficulty in the confined space of a narrow passageway, just about two feet wide, to dress himself, or at least make himself half decent. He had dare not switch the torch on whilst Frederick and Siegfried were in the kitchen and he now knew that they were in some alliance and that this old man, who had seemingly been kind to him, was involved in some fraudulent activity.

As the two men left, he switched the torch on to reveal a narrow passage which was just wide enough for him to negotiate. It went off in the direction of the corridor towards the study. He followed its path and was surprised at how clean it was, with few cobwebs and little sign of a forgotten past. It was, he thought, well used. After about twenty feet was a junction which turned towards the direction of the study before coming to a dead end. He could hear voices. It was Frederick and Siegfried. He switched the torch on, concealing its glare with his hand, and guessed it was the study for the panelling had given way to a solid stone wall which was warm to the touch and most likely the back of the large inglenook fireplace. He moved back to the wood panelling and could make out a small opening, a spy hole into the world of subterfuge.

The hole was cleverly concealed from the room itself and offered the voyeur an opportunity for espionage and the secrets that could make the difference between success and failure or life and death, without the need for sophisticated electronics or satellite surveillance, so long as the protagonist was quiet. Frederick was sitting at his desk whilst Siegfried was in one of the fireside armchairs, hidden from Robert's view and drinking his whisky.

'This Colliver chap. He told me that this birdman carving was not genuine, that it was just a tourist fake,' as he picked up the offending object.

'What does he know,' retorted Siegfried.

'Quite a lot I gather. He was very specific about the wood. That it was carved from Toromiro pine which used to grow on Easter Island. He stated it was a reddish wood which clearly this is not,' showing Jock the scratched surface.

Jock had to be careful. This was the first time he had been questioned on one of his acquisitions which he knew to be a fake. In fact, many of the objects of art he had secured for Frederick were indeed fakes. Good fakes, but fakes nonetheless, for which he had made a substantial profit at his benefactor's expense.

'I'll look into it when this current business is finished,' he said, hoping that would placate Frederick.

'Alright, but I'll want some evidence of providence. And this lamp. He was interested in it. Why would that be?'

'You haven't questioned my methods before. Why now?' he said with some irritation.

'Perhaps because it's now relevant, especially as he now knows about me, no thanks to your incompetence.'

This was a provocative attack on his ability which Jock took very personally. He got up and stood large over the desk with an intimidating glare that Frederick found alarming, not used to violence or even the pretence of its action.

'I obtained it from his mother. I had spent weeks contacting people with the name of Colliver and had finally struck lucky with her. She had alluded to a link with Cornwall, albeit on holiday, but that was all I needed for a follow-up visit which yielded the map you have. I told her that I was a historian seeking any information about pirates and seafaring in general, and she was kind enough to show me a Spanish coin and the map. Naturally, I didn't want to take them there and then, but later broke into the house and stole the map and to make it look like a burglary, took the lamp which I spotted to be genuine Art Nouveau that would appeal to you as well as add value to your collection. Does that satisfy you?'

'It was indeed a good acquisition, Jock. But he must have recognised it somehow.'

Siegfried picked up the lamp and looked at the base.

'Perhaps the initials RC caught his interest.'

'Yes, that's it. I can see that they are not part of the silver mark as I had thought, but a later addition.'

'What do you want me to do?' asked Jock, becoming a little anxious that his time was being wasted by such trivia.

'He's a threat to me,' replied Frederick, not wanting to say the words he meant.

But Jock knew what they were and said, 'I understand.'

Time was pressing for Jock, but he remembered an envelope he had found with a postmark from London and franked by the British Library. It contained a copy of a map. He pulled it out of a pocket from his cargo trousers.

'I came across this in Colliver's cottage. It's postmarked from the British Library where his girlfriend works,' he said, removing the map from the envelope.

Frederick opened it and immediately scrutinised the outline map that had been revealed by x-ray analysis.

'It depicts a coastline, I think. And there's yet another cross marking a spot on the map,' added Jock. 'And there are two more verses to the one we know about on the map I obtained from his mother's.'

Frederick looked amazed at the map. It had no features other than two crosses. It seemed useless. Instead, he turned his attention to the two new verses, his anticipation matched only by his excitement. He read the complete text.

To Lammana thou must go
Across t'sea, a verdant Isle
There you'll find a place next the sea
And treasure there be found.

Above the waves that judge a soul
And a stairway to a heavenly Isle
There you'll find a place across the sea
And treasure be yours to keep.

To Lammana thou must go
And seek the pious dead
Deliver thou self to a sacred shrine
And treasure be mine to tell.

He looked up.

'What do you make of the second verse, Jock? The last one seems to reiterate the first verse.'

'Not sure. A stairway to a heavenly Isle? I doubt it refers to Looe Island. But where?'

'They don't seem to add anything. We must be missing something,' an exasperated Frederick said in frustration.

'But the coastline may do, if only we could decipher where it's meant to be,' commented Jock.

He went over to a bookshelf and retrieved an atlas of the British Isles. They looked at the coastline of Cornwall. Nothing matched the profile. And then they compared the rest of England and Scotland. Nothing.

'Perhaps it has no meaning at all,' remarked Frederick in a consoling mood.

Jock then turned to the page showing Ireland. 'Colliver spent a year in County Kerry, I believe. Perhaps the verdant isle refers to the Ireland.'

'You may be right Jock,' exclaimed Frederick.

They studied the southern part of the country, but still a match foiled them. Frederick sighed.

'It appears Ireland is not the place. In any event, there's no evidence of the Pirate Captain having ever been there.'

Jock sat back down in the armchair, frustrated, and finished his whisky. He was glad that he had gone back to the cottage after locating the mainland entrance to the tunnel, to check on his two prisoners. Had he not done so, then this vital piece of evidence would have eluded them. He had spotted the envelope on the floor by the front door and thought it may be important, especially having seen the postmark for the British Library.

So far, that importance had eluded them. Jock tried to reconcile the riddle, but he was still too agitated to concentrate. Perhaps it required some more information, he thought, some unique knowledge that only somebody who has lived there would know.

Robert, having listened to the conversation with incredulity from his void, was now in a state of shock. This man was becoming an ever increasing menace, his tentacles having even touched his mother. And the map, the map that should have accompanied the coin, the pieces-of-eight that his father had bequeathed him, was in his hands.

But what concerned him even more, was the fact he had the map that Caroline had mentioned. He must have been at the cottage. He would have confronted her. He dare not consider what he had done. He had to get out. But in his angered and agitated state, Robert forgot about the words of caution from Christian and dropped the torch. Fortunately, it struck his foot and so only made a dull thud but enough to catch Siegfried's attention.

'What was that?' said Jock, interrupting Frederick.

'What was what?' he replied.

'That sound.'

'Didn't hear anything. Probably the fire.'

'No. It sounded hollow as though it came from behind that panel.'

Siegfried got up and approached the panelling. Robert stopped breathing. Even his breath may give his position away. Siegfried put his ear to the wall. Frederick looked at him as though he had finally cracked, the peacock having tipped his sanity. Siegfried tapped the panelling. To him it sounded hollow.

'Do you know of any secret passages in the Hall?' he asked Frederick.

'None, although I've suspected there may well be. But I haven't had the opportunity to investigate.'

Siegfried strode out of the study, with intent, to the kitchen where Christian was sitting drinking some cocoa.

Robert followed the sound of footsteps and heard Siegfried talking to Christian about the manor and in particular whether he had come across any secret passageways.

'Don't know if I have,' he said, to which Siegfried looked at him with a puzzled frown trying to determine his meaning and deducing that this old man would be incapable of knowing anything.

He went over to the far side of the kitchen, away from the outer wall, and started tapping. A hollow echo resonated in his ear and he immediately began to look for an obvious place where a concealed door might be. His hands fell upon the rose finial, the key to the door. He pulled and twisted it. Nothing. He stood back and as though admiring the Tudor decoration, looked again and began to feel the wooden panelling.

Robert, by now, was in panic mode. If he found the door then his time was most certainly up. He retreated back down the passage but instead of a left he took the right turn which came to a false stairway that led up to the first floor. He went up only to find that this had been blocked at some point leaving him trapped and at the mercy of discovery. Trapped, except here a voracious beast was onto his scent.

He waited for the sound of footsteps, but heard none. Perhaps Siegfried had gone, given up, he thought. But he was still in the kitchen, determined to find the secret doorway which, by now, he was convinced existed. He tried the decorated Tudor rose finial again, twisting it, but it remained unmoved. He glanced at Christian catching a look of anxiety in his face as he watched Siegfried prowl up and down the panelling, sniffing as though on the scent of prey.

Siegfried was about to go outside to the tool shed and get an axe, when suddenly he thought of something. He had once before been in an old Tudor Hall, in Cheshire, not to acquire anything that day, but as a tourist looking over the mansion, noting objects which took his interest. His attention had been drawn to a curator showing some visitors a secret priest hole. It was almost impossible to detect, yet with the twist of a concealed knob as part of a decoration, it was opened. It was explained that the door handle, for effectively that is what it was, had to be simultaneously pressed and turned for the secret hole to be revealed and with that knowledge he went over to the panel again, with Christian now looking anxious once more having sighed with relief when he had abandoned his first attempt. Siegfried applied the same principle to the rose finial, and the door opened.

Although it was dark inside, light from the kitchen shone into the passage which Siegfried could see had been used recently. On the floor were a few small patches of wet which could only come from within, from somebody or something, the passage being well inside the building away from outside rain penetration. He removed a small torch from a pocket and proceeded along the slender passageway which, because of his ample frame, required him to twist from side to side as though swimming in a sea of darkness, descending into the bowels of the manor, like a bathysphere into the depths, with only his torch giving light to reveal his prey.

At the junction he went left and came to the study spy hole which still showed Frederick at his desk, pondering over the map. Back now and straight on, his torch lighting the unknown, where spiders and other invertebrates lived each one waiting for prey to enter their world. Siegfried was another predator only his prey was larger. He could smell fear, it pervaded the depths and as he progressed along the passage that scent became stronger so that he could now taste his quarry, taste the fear that was being released from its pores. He knew it was close.

Up the staircase he trod towards to where Robert was standing, his rigid body, his mind, unable to seek escape from the slow inextricable echo of footsteps. He wondered what to do, sweat now exuding from fear for his life, a helpless prey being hunted by a stealthy monster. He desperately tried to find a catch or release mechanism to a door but could find none. The footsteps got nearer and nearer, the light brighter and brighter, and Robert's heart beat faster and faster as the sea monster, the giant squid from the depths of the ocean with its tentacles slowly feeling its prey, tasting its prey, got closer and closer. He was but a few breaths away from being devoured by a leviathan of the deep.

54

The crossing on low tide was not the benign paddle that Robert had faced the previous night, when the weather was calm, but a struggle to wade through a surge of water brought in on the now strong southerly wind. It was causing low water to be a good foot higher than predicted and, coupled with the swell, the water was lapping up to Caroline's thighs in places.

She had been wise enough to remove her jeans and wear a pair of sandals for the trek across to the Island, leaving Alfred rather bemused that she should show no modesty in his presence. He wanted to go, but just as Robert had prevented Caroline so she dissuaded Alfred from attempting the crossing which, she thought as she paused mid-channel, was the right decision, for she was having trouble in keeping her balance, particularly so, when a large wave hit her broadside.

Once across, and with her jeans back on, there was no turning back as the water, even after only a few minutes, was too treacherous to risk. She summoned her resolve and made for the track to find Robert. Before he had left on his exploration, Caroline had insisted he draw a rudimentary map of the key landmarks from his circumnavigation of the Island with John, and show the salient places and the route he intended to search. Armed with the route, she passed two small buildings not on his map but soon came to the first cottage he had marked.

It was dark, but a faint flickering aurora was coming from one of the ground floor windows, manifest in a ghostly whine from the conifers that cloaked the cottage and made it look a foreboding residence, a natural home to thieves and smugglers. Caroline crept up to the wall and inched along until she could just peer inside. Nothing, except a coloured luminescence and the shadow of the man on a wall, a glow that announced life was within. But what life was it, for the shadow looked like an alien life form that had materialised from the eerie drone of the wind.

She ducked beneath the window and peered in again, but this time saw a man sitting at a computer which was discharging its particles of light, an unearthly apparition of ionic power, a solar wind, creating an ethereal tableau, reminding her of a visit to the Shetland Islands during the winter months where the Northern Lights had enraptured her and Robert.

Caroline pulled away from the window and wondered whether to go in and announce herself, explain why she was there and ask about Robert. It sounded sensible but she could not tell if this person was friend or foe. He looked harmless in his bright shirt, but appearances can be deceptive. She decided to explore a bit further and resort to him if she found nothing and turned to leave only to be faced by a figure looming over her and about to strike with some instrument in her right hand. The blow missed, not because the assailant misjudged the trajectory, but Tara recognised Caroline and at the last second and pulled away from her target.

'What an earth are you doing here?' remarked Tara.

'I might say the same thing, especially as you were about to knock me down.'

'I didn't know who you were. And this is my Island.'

'Your Island? You own it.'

'I don't own it. But I do manage it.'

'Well, I guess I owe you an explanation for one snooping around on your Island.'

But before Caroline could expound her reason for being on the Island at night, Tara had interceded.

'I think I know why you're here. Come inside.'

The sitting room inside Smuggler's Cottage where Tom was ensconced felt like a freezer, being warmer outside than in, and Caroline wondered what form of antifreeze the portly young man was using, clothed in shorts and a shirt and wearing only sandals. Her feet were no better protected, but at least she had a warm fleece to repel the cold. The kitchen was much warmer. A range was emitting some warmth with a pot of tea brewing on its hot plate, and sitting by the Aga was another young man, looking shy and bewildered at the presence of two beautiful women. He remained silent, apart from reciprocating when Caroline bid him hello, whilst Tara was engaged in preparing a welcome beverage.

'Such a contrast to yesterday,' she said, 'but that's what I like about our weather. No two days are the same. An Atlantic storm can blow in at any time clearing the air, changing the atmosphere.'

She was being courteous, indeed friendly with a hint of metaphor, knowing what she was about to tell Caroline concerning Robert's demise. As Tara poured the tea she looked at her adversary to Robert's affections and realised she was different, not in appearance, but different in their lives. For her, it was the sea. For Caroline, academia. Yet right now as she looked Caroline up and down, that difference had coalesced into a common cause. Not Robert, but the defeat of Jock, for she was no longer an adversary but an ally who would almost certainly respond to her battle cry. But before she could say anything, Caroline had intervened first.

'Have you seen Robert?'

'Yes, he was on the Island held prisoner by Jock, the man you call Siegfried. Robert told me the story.'

'He did, did he?' queried Caroline.

'We were both bound and chained in an underground chamber.'

'Bound and chained!' exclaimed Caroline.

'Yes. We escaped though.'

'You said he was on the Island.'

'Robert took a boat for the mainland.'

'So he's over there now?'

'I'm not sure. You see, the boat drifted onto the rocks off the Island and he had to jump into the water.'

Caroline was now concerned. 'Was he alright? Did he drown?'

'I don't know. He had a lifejacket on, so hopefully he made it ashore, but the sea can be unforgiving.'

'He's a good swimmer,' said Caroline more in hope than expectation.

'Then he stands a good chance of making it ashore.'

'I pray that is the case.'

'Me too,' echoed Tara, knowing that a miracle was needed for him to survive.

She paused and left Caroline to her thoughts, a moment's reflection before she was to sound her bugle.

'I think Jock, Siegfried I mean, had something to do with it.'

'With what?' responded Caroline as though she had been interrupted.

'With the accident to the boat. Well perhaps not an accident, for I'm sure the engine cut out as he was making his way along the coastline, something which could only have happened if Siegfried had sabotaged the vessel.'

'So this man is to blame. He's already imprisoned Robert in a tunnel, and me too. What more is he capable of?'

'Murder,' came the word from Tara.

From the innocent world of excitement, at the thought of uncovering a monument to history in the form of tunnels built in antiquity, to the world of deceit, imprisonment, and now murder. This was now serious to Caroline and fast becoming out of control. She was used to the gentile and passive pursuit of knowledge, where the only exhilaration was the discovery of new texts or artefacts which changed historical perspective, not fictional escapades where villains lurked in every recess, characters falling by the wayside and the heroes or heroines being subjected to untold dangers before triumphing in the end. But when was the end and who were the sacrificial victims who littered the pages along the way?

'Whose murder?' she said, shocked to be saying the word.

'A cousin of mine. Robert found his body in the caves.'

'Caves. What caves?'

'There's a network of them under the Island. They are part natural and part man-made.'

It was man-made that focused Caroline's attention. She was concerned for Robert, but was powerless to do anything whilst on the Island and so for the time being her mind changed gear into her academic mode and the possibility that, as she had theorised, they were connected to a tunnel under the sea.

'Is it possible to see these caves?'

'Indeed it is. I am going there myself to confront your Siegfried and end his evil intentions.'

This was not exactly what Caroline had in mind, more a scientific exploration of the network to determine its age and significance, not a confrontation with their arch enemy.

'You don't intend to take this man on?' she said with an incredulous tone.

'I do indeed.'

'But he's a monster. He could swipe you down like a fly.'

'He could, but then I know those caves and he doesn't. Therefore I have home advantage. And in any case, I've got my secret weapon.'

'And that is?' enquired Caroline, expecting a revolver or some weapon of mass destruction to fell a monster.

'A flare gun.'

'A flare gun?' questioned Caroline.

'Have you seen one ignite. Expect not. Let's just say that he will be like an effigy on a bonfire, a fitting end, don't you think? Will you come?'

Caroline didn't exactly think it was a fitting end for any human being, even one like Siegfried, but she was not going to intervene and was more interested in the construction of the caves that were to be his tomb than to recommend an alternative course of action: namely wait for the authorities to deal with him.

'I'll come, but don't expect me to pull the trigger.'

'I shan't. That will be my pleasure.'

All the time the two were speaking Malcolm had been silent, listening to the unfolding narrative of the two women. He now realised the enormity of the situation and that this Siegfried was in fact Jock, and that his father was involved in something. What, he could only guess, but he suspected it was smuggling of some description. There was a story here. A story of smuggling, sabotage, death defying heroics and murder, that would cement his position as a journalist and he wanted to be part of the action.

'Might I help?' he asked, in a somewhat timid voice as though he were not worthy of these two goddesses.

They both stopped talking and looked at him. Caroline had been wondering if he was, in fact, mute, for these were the first real words he had uttered. Tara though, was astounded that he had made such a request, considering his reaction in the cave.

'No,' ordered Tara, as though that was her final edict, but then added in a more affable tone, 'I would like you to look after Tom.'

The two collaborators went into the parlour where Tom was still on the computer but no longer playing a game. Instead, he had something interesting to tell Tara.

'Come and have a look at this, Tara,' he said in a meek voice, not wanting to seem demanding.

'What is it Tom?'

'There's something interesting on Jock's computer I've found. Something which I don't quite understand.'

Tara went over and looked at the screen. It was a list of files, most of which had names she hadn't heard of, but two were recognisable, that of Trevellick and Colliver. Tom opened the one labelled by their name to reveal text about dates and comments on activities that he had undertaken. There was confirmation of his intention to take over the Island, contain any threat and remove Tara. But what concerned Tom was a note from a couple of days ago which alluded to Jake being taken care of after he had tried to attack Jock.

'What do you think it means?' he asked.

'Perhaps he's been locked away somewhere,' she said, looking at Caroline as if to tell her to be quiet and not say anything.

'I do hope so, because here he says he pushed some man over the cliff.'

'Why would he incriminate himself like this?' asked Caroline.

'I don't know,' replied Tara. 'Maybe he wants to relive his actions and does so by typing them out. He certainly seems to derive pleasure from them. I can vouch for that.'

Caroline remembered her father's words of caution. There are many sick and often clever minds out there, he had warned, and Siegfried was one of them. Be careful, he had said, and stay clear of him. He is dangerous. She had tried to heed his warning, but Siegfried's egocentric selfhood had already invaded her world and he was about to enter it again, only with more dangerous and ultimately deadly consequences.

55

$\mathbf{\mathcal{F}}$ortune is a gift. It's a gift bestowed to those that find and pick a four-leaf clover. So said Madeleine. He didn't believe it then but embraced the folklore as inflective Irish luck. But when she tragically died that fateful day on the mountain, he abandoned the tradition in favour of fate and destiny, two protagonists that seem to define his life more accurately. But now he was beginning to see otherwise. A pattern was emerging.

He had been fortunate many times in the past few weeks; first from escaping the tunnel and then imprisonment, drowning, and the noise from the peacock that had contrived an escape plan. And now it was there again. Just when he thought that Siegfried would have his quarry, just when those tentacles were tightening their grip around him, strangling him of hope, a door opened and there, standing in the entrance was Christian, giving him another escape route. A lucky escape route to safety from the monster of the deep.

But this was the last of his nine lives and he wasn't yet safe. Siegfried would break the secret door down, that was for sure. So Christian ushered him along the first floor landing corridor, past several rooms, to a door which, when he opened it, had two flights of narrow steps, one up to the next floor and another down to the kitchen. It was the maids and servants route, not the grand staircase for them, but a confined exit from the landing.

Christian was not going down, nor up. Instead, he opened a trap door in the floor and beckoned for Robert to enter. It was a priest hole. Hole didn't quite do it justice, nor describe its function, because there was quite a surprising amount of space for Robert to move in and sit down, even enough for him to lie down and sleep if he so wished. For a Catholic sympathiser a priest hole was a lifeline and they would have had to live in such a place for many days to escape the Protestant inquisition, and who knew how long Siegfried would stay in search of his prey. Christian closed the trap door and went down the stairs to the kitchen.

Siegfried did indeed break open the door, a loud noise echoing throughout the house which even Frederick could not fail to hear. He came up to see what the commotion was about, to find Jock opening doors to rooms in search of his prey.

'What on earth are you doing, Jock?' he demanded.

'Searching for that Colliver man,' he replied not looking at Frederick but continuing his search.

'You've already searched once.'

'Well, I'm searching again. He was here, just now, that I am certain of.'

He opened the servant's door to the staircase. He looked up. Then down. Robert was only a few feet away, lying still, holding his breath, lest he reveal his hidden world. He feared even his heartbeat might catch those tentacles that could taste fear.

'Quiet,' Jock commanded.

Jock stood motionless listening to the sounds of the Hall, sounds of the past where even the tiniest of movement, as Frederick shuffled a foot, could be heard in the wood panelling. The very fabric of the building, its timber frame and wooden pegs that over time had shrunk and cracked, was alive with sounds. But even for Jock's acute hearing, he could detect no living creature.

Even the most persistent hunters give up on their prey when realisation sets in that they are not going to succeed. But Jock didn't. He tried a different approach, one that came naturally to him, and descended the servants' staircase to find Christian sitting at the centre table, still drinking cocoa. He looked up but didn't show any surprise, which Jock took to be guilt.

'Where is he?' he demanded.

'In the study where he normally is,' he calmly replied, although within he was petrified.

'Don't play games with me. Where's Colliver?'

'I don't know. I said so to FT.'

'He was here. I can sense him. I can smell him.'

'Then I believe your senses are misguided.'

Jock went over to the table where Christian was sitting, hauled him out of the chair and put him in an arm lock, his arm twisted behind his back whilst his neck was grasped by Jock's strong forearm so that he was completely immobile, simultaneously choking and in pain. He tried to wriggle free but Jock had hold of him like a vice, continuing the agonising pain, and as he increased the tension on his neck and twisted Christians arm even more, the pain became unbearable for Christian, so much so, that he screamed for relief. But none was coming.

'Where is he?' demanded Jock once more.

'I don't know.'

Jock was going to do worse but was prevented by Frederick coming down the steps to see the scene of an inquisition.

'Let him go,' he shouted.

But Jock ignored him.

'Where is he?'

'Jock, I will not ask again. Let him go.'

This time Jock released Christian who immediately bent double on the floor, gasping for air and trying to rub life into his arm that felt as though it had been severed. Frederick first looked at Jock to inform him of his displeasure and then attended his man servant as best he could. Frederick, for all his guile and mental intimidation in the cut-throat world of corporate enterprise, was appalled by physical violence. He had witnessed it during the conflict in Italy when the allies became entrenched at Monte Cassino. There, he had to watch as another officer, senior to him, interrogated prisoners who were subjected to physical abuse, even torture, in order to extract information. It was abhorrent then, despite the situation of war, and it was more so now.

For Frederick, Jock had shown him his true colours and he didn't like what he had witnessed. Despite his usefulness in the past, he decided in that moment to severe his ties with this ruthless man, but only after the current business had been concluded.

Jock retreated to a store room just off the kitchen to collect his diving equipment and left the two men, and Hendersick Hall, for good. He too was going to severe his links with Frederick, an association which he had thought, for several months now, had run its course. He had the information he needed to continue his quest for the pirate treasure, a lead that was to be found in Ireland. But first there was the business on the Island and he was determined that nobody, not even the cunning Tara nor the irritant Colliver, would get the better of him.

For Robert, still in the priest hole, he was oblivious to these events. He could hear the screams and shouting and knew it had something to do with Siegfried, but what exactly, he had no idea. All he wanted was to be released from yet another enforced imprisonment. After the noise had died down, his world went frustratingly quiet again. Not a sound, except for the creaking of wood as though the building was talking to him, saying that he was not the first person to escape persecution and that in time he would see daylight once more so long as he was patient.

Patience was beginning to wane for Robert. He wanted release. But the Tudor Hall continued to speak its history and in so doing he found his mind wandering through time and space, back to Ireland, back to Madeleine, and the map that he heard Siegfried and Frederick talking about. They mentioned Ireland and County Kerry. Could destiny be beckoning him back to the place of so many memories? In the study he had seen a vision of Madeleine in the pastel half-nude figure, enclosed in a guilt frame and hanging on the far wall. He had thought it was Tara. But it was Madeleine. The same Pre-Raphaelite features he knew so well: her full lips and searching eyes, her long red hair and thick fringe. It could have been Tara seducing him, but with the echo of Kerry in his mind he realised it was Madeleine calling him from the edge of heaven.

Just then, his present world was restored as Christian opened the trap door. The two of them went down to the kitchen where Christian assumed Robert would leave before any other incident befell him.

'I need to get into the study,' he informed Christian, who thought that his stay in the priest hole had affected his mind.

He believed that the manor was haunted, haunted by its past deeds, and that anybody who could connect with those spirits would surely be hypnotised by them. And Robert, he thought, had been bewitched.

'You need to go,' he replied.

'Yes, I know, but not before I get into the study,' he insisted. 'Is there a secret door in the panelling from the passage?'

'Yes, but it's too risky now, especially after all the commotion. Come back later in the day and I'll create an excuse for FT to leave the study.'

'Alright. But I will be back.'

*   *   *

Dawn was approaching as he finally escaped into the night air and away from the confines of Hendersick Hall. Do the unexpected, he had told himself. He realised that Siegfried may be waiting for him and if he was, that he would be somewhere out the front, the back being too obvious. So he was going to use the bird man's reverse psychology and leave by the back, make for the tool shed and the cover of some shrubs and then skirt around the front to pick up the driveway and then the road back to Looe. That was Christian's suggestion, since Robert had no idea which way to go other than back down to the beach he had found himself on only a few hours ago.

Robert looked at his watch. It was broken. He now remembered that. No matter, because he could tell it was about five o'clock, since sunrise in early August was around that time. A whispering chilly wind brought with it the smell of the sea, of fresh seaweed deposited on the beach and a salty air from a breeze that evaporated in the now gentle south westerly wind. It was invigorating Robert as he made his way across the estate grounds to the Talland road and the way back to his cottage.

The peafowl were still roosting in the trees, although a few early risers were already parading the grounds marking their territory for the day's rituals and contests. An owl swooped low over the lawn on its last hunting foray before retiring until the following night and a fox darted out of Robert's way, stunned to find another creature following his run, which Robert was using to prevent his shoes from getting too wet in the damp grass.

The blanket of cloud from the overnight storm had cleared away and, with pressure rising, it signalled a return to the anti-cyclonic high of the previous days and the promise of more fine weather. Robert, though, was more concerned to get back as quickly as possible to the cottage rather than linger to appreciate the morning, which under normal circumstances he would gladly do. There is no better time, when most people are still entertaining a duvet, and the world seems to be an isolated place, to value life, where only the wildlife are one's companions, already busy in the business of surviving another day.

Robert thought that. Survive another day. He sensed he was not alone. Somebody was following him. He stopped. Quiet, except for the ever present cries of gulls and the sound of a tractor in a distant field breaking through a muted dawn chorus. It was now that he appreciated the beautiful day for what it was: a glow in the east heralding the rising sun, a magical light that cast shadows in the lane that seemed to enhance his instincts. He continued, but was wary and felt vulnerable in the uninhabited world. Was Siegfried following him, to ambush him and end his life this day?

Siegfried was most certainly following Robert. He had waited in a large shrubbery out the front of the Hall anticipating his move, expecting the unexpected, for to leave out the back was too obvious, too dangerous, and so it was natural he would escape down the drive. He had been surprised, though, to see Robert come out from around the side of the Hall and realised that he too was thinking of strategy, trying to avoid his clutches.

After about twenty minutes, Robert came to the track that led to his cottage, the back way in past the navigation tower and the field that Alfred owned. A flock of sheep were in occupation, neither eating nor sitting as is their wont, but alert, and as he climbed the gate, an eerie presence befell the field with all the sheep now wary of the new intruder as though he was the enemy, a fox that had come to devour a lamb. As they watched Robert walk quietly along the track, they looking at him and he looking perplexed at them, they were not concerned about any fox, for lurking behind a gated recess in the boundary hedge, within striking distance of the path and in full view of the flock, was the real enemy. And its prey was duly heading towards him, unaware that in a few moments those tentacles, which had so nearly caught him in the Hall, were about to finally have their man.

Siegfried had cut through to the coastal path further up the Talland road and made his way to the adjacent field intent on springing a surprise on his quarry, to confront him face to face so that there was no chance of escape. But Robert sensed there was something wrong. The sheep were not looking at him now, but ahead, as though the danger was there and not with him. He looked back. It was clear, but too far to make a run for it. The tower offered a chance, especially if he climbed it and hid behind the signal lights. If it were a false alarm then no harm done and it would be a good vantage point for any sight of Siegfried. It was a chance worth taking. So, rather than carry on, he stealthily crept to its base and began a nimble scramble to safety.

Siegfried didn't hear the manoeuvre, yet he could tell that something was amiss for some of the sheep looked towards Robert, whilst a few bolted at his sudden movement up the tower. He responded, not with the same urgency, but with the knowledge his prey was trapped for he saw him reach the top of the tower before hiding from view. And, as Robert peered out to see if it was all clear, he could see his plan had rebounded leaving him trapped and at the mercy of the blonde Arian thug.

Robert scanned the horizon for a rescuer, a farmer perhaps, but all was quiet, not a soul to be seen. He looked down. It was a long way. Too far to jump. He looked for any means of escape, but nothing. And all the time he could hear the relentless steps of Siegfried get closer and closer until finally, there he was, standing at the base of the tower looking up.

'Yet again our paths cross,' said Siegfried, with a smile that announced victory. 'Did you really think you could escape me?'

'Well, yes,' replied Robert, unconvinced by his own ability. 'I've managed to on several occasions already,' he added.

This time there was no escape and Robert stood on the edge of death to accept whatever fate awaited him. Siegfried was ecstatic. He was going to enjoy the moment. He started to climb the framework, not once taking his gaze off this man who had eluded him, wanting to see the fear in his eyes, the knowledge that his end had come, that he could jump or face his dagger. Robert was on the precipice, but he didn't show fear, for he was not going to give this man the nourishment that he obviously craved. But as Siegfried reached the top platform, pulling his dagger from its scabbard, that fear was now palpable. He was terrified inside, not of this man, but of never seeing Caroline again, wishing he could say farewell, kiss her goodbye and tell her he loved her. He had cheated that mortal coil many times and death would take him to Madeleine, and if God denied him His Kingdom then he could see her and wave to her from the edge of heaven.

Siegfried was standing but a few paces away, his eyes still fixed on Robert.

'They were battles. It is the war I've won.'

Robert couldn't disagree. 'What is it you want?' he asked.

'It's not what I want, it's what you have.'

'And what is that?'

'Ever since that day in Caroline's flat, you have been the key to my quest. I expect you know that I visited your mother and stole the map you saw in the study, from the secret passageway where you overheard me talking with Frederick. Well, your mother told me about you. She was proud to talk about you. It took me a long time to track you down in London, to Caroline whom I befriended. She is a beautiful woman and so very intelligent. Why she should like you I don't know. Perhaps she's after the same thing as me. But you have something I want.'

'I have nothing to give you,' said Robert.

'But you have.'

'I still don't know. Perhaps you can enlighten me.'

'Your life. That's what I want.'

Siegfried edged closer towards his helpless victim, until the point of his dagger was but a thrust away. There was nowhere for Robert to go. He looked down. It was still a long way, but his last chance of escape. He jumped over a scaffold pole, a controlled leap of faith to grab the lower railing of the next level down, when his foot snagged causing him to lose balance and sense weightlessness. And as he realised that death was but a moment away, as he was about to free-fall to earth, a hand grabbed his ankle, leaving him dangling, where one single action would uncoil the thread.

Siegfried had saved him and he wasn't going to let go. With a single pull, he had Robert back from the brink, standing on the platform, dazed, looking out to sea with the Island within its frame as though some force from there had counterbalanced his fall. He didn't understand. He couldn't understand why he was alive. All he knew was that there must be a reason.

* * *

Standing in the kitchen of his cottage, he realised what the reason was. He was going to kill them both. Make one watch, as the other was extinguished of life. He would entomb Robert in the crypt and find Caroline. He was relieved that she was not at home. Where she was, he could only guess, and hoped that wherever it was, she would not come back. This man, this monster, could be cruel, he thought, as Siegfried removed the inspection covers, only to be greeted with an empty crypt.

Siegfried gave out a muffled yell as though all his well-planned schemes were unravelling before his eyes, by two people who should be no match for his skills. Robert was expecting to be left in the chamber but was surprised when he was escorted from the cottage, out onto the coastal path, and then shepherded towards the old chapel, like a lamb to the slaughter.

'What are you doing?' he asked.

'You'll see soon enough.'

At the old chapel, Robert had his legs bound. He sat and watched Siegfried move the bench and lift two concrete blocks to reveal an entrance to another dark place. Robert knew what it was: it was the entrance to a tunnel that traversed its way across to the Island. He looked at it. Tara was over there. Fate was returning him to her, to share their destinies, together, as she had known. Whatever that fate was, it seemed it would be soon. Siegfried had said so.

Robert took what he thought might be a last look at the world before he descended into hell. It was a glorious morning. The low morning sun was by now framing the Island in a magnificent hue, a glow that appeared as a halo, ornamenting its mien as though its monastic past had come to offer salvation.

A robin, his favourite passerine, much more melodic than any other, sang to him in a stunted juniper tree, an exquisite cadenza that left him with welling tears. He had told Caroline, that whenever she heard a robin sing that it was he, soliloquising, telling her that he loved her, that she was always in his thoughts and that they would be together forever, even in death. And now that death was close.

He wiped his moist eyes and focused on the tunnel entrance. Siegfried beckoned him down. Just as he was descending the steps, he looked up to see the robin still eulogising his message. He smiled. But then into his vision flew a flock of rooks, their black forms rising up and down on the breeze and their harsh bass caw drowning the euphonious robin as though it was a sign or portent of an impending catastrophe that was to befall this beautiful day.

56

The cave system fascinated Caroline. Tara, however, was concerned about executing her plan and wanted to move on as swiftly as possible, but Caroline halted her progress by stopping every few yards to examine the brick work that encased the catacombs. At one particular stop, Tara looked around to find she had disappeared, only to discover her in a branch cave looking in wonder at an arched chamber that resembled, she thought, the celebrated Etruscan Caves of Clusia in central Italy.

She explained to Tara that the Etruscan's were the predecessors to the Romans, their culture based in modern day Tuscany and dating back to the eighth century BC. They were a maritime civilisation and traded all throughout the Mediterranean, with their pottery having been discovered off the coast of Cornwall. They were trading within the area, probably wanting the local tin, and therefore it was distinctly possible that some of them were responsible for, or at the very least influenced, the construction they were looking at in the cave.

Tara was not impressed nor concerned for a group of people who lived over two and a half thousand years ago, but for the fact, like herself, that they were seafarers, for they were not going to help with the present situation and the threat of Siegfried. She tried to instil a sense of urgency in Caroline, but, unlike Tara, historical discoveries were the catalyst for her ego, not the thought of some showdown with an evil villain. But rather than be left in the almost endless network of caves to wander in perpetuity, despite being a prospect she would relish, she decided to follow Tara.

They reached the large chamber which was the entrance to the tunnel under the seabed and Caroline was immediately fascinated by the prospect of exploring it, to determine if it was the same date or constructed later, as she had hypothesised, by Christian monks of the early middle ages.

'Can we go down there?' she enquired.

'It's possible, but not now.'

'Why not now?'

'Because,' Tara replied with some resignation, 'there is too much water in there, unless you have some scuba diving equipment.'

Caroline was disappointed. She looked around. The chamber was natural although there was evidence of it having been enlarged with marks on the walls indicating some working of the rock. In the gloom, away from Tara's torch, she stumbled over a piece of machinery which, on closer inspection, Caroline took to be a pump, for leading off of it was a discharge pipe heading back down the cave system from where they had come.

'What about this, it looks like a pump?' she enquired.

'There's probably too much water. It can only be used at low tide and that's not for some time now.'

'Have you tried to see if it would cope now?'

'Not exactly.'

'Well, why not give it a go? I believe the tunnel to be watertight. Clearly it isn't, but the pump may remove the water faster than it can be filled.'

'That's possible, but I'd rather leave it to another time.'

But Caroline wasn't going to give up. She decided to appeal to Tara's emotional nature and her obvious love of Robert.

'I need to get off the Island and search for Robert. He may be hurt, washed ashore somewhere in need of help. Surely you wouldn't want to think that you could have saved him if anything has happened, would you Tara?'

She could see Caroline was tugging at her heart and rather than be responsible for anything worse occurring, since she already blamed herself for the tragedy that had befallen him, she agreed. The pump was diesel operated and several cans of fuel were stacked nearby, so Tara filled the tank and started the pump. It sprang into action after a splutter, making a noise which would have woken Looe itself, but calmed down when it had warmed up and was pumping water which Caroline could see from the bulge in the discharge pipe.

Slowly the water level receded in the tunnel until, after about half an hour, it couldn't be seen. Caroline was anxious to explore but Tara made her wait, not wanting to take any risk should the pump fail, which it sometimes did. There was no longer Jake to monitor the machine, nor repair it.

Finally, Tara indicated it was safe to proceed and the two of them began, very cautiously, for the base of the tunnel was still wet and slippery, to enter the chasm on a shallow descent. Tara was leading, holding the torch, swinging it from side to side in order to illuminate as much of the tunnel as possible, whilst Caroline followed close behind in the shadows, glancing at the walls. Every now and then she could see something interesting. Tara wasn't stopping: this was no archaeological investigation, it was a rescue mission. But she had to stop in her tracks when Caroline insisted she do so to take a close look at an inscription she had glimpsed in the reflected light.

'Just this once,' she insisted.

'Shine the light just there,' requested Caroline, not really taking any notice of Tara.

'I've seen that before,' said Tara.

Caroline looked at the text. It was in Latin.

IN NOBIS OPERARI POENTENTIUM
DEUS IN NOBIS
PSALLAM IN GLORIA
IN SALUTEM NOBIS CONFIDIMUS

Within the confines of the tunnel she didn't try to translate the script, but below the inscriptions was a date, AD MXVII, which she could immediately deduce.

'There's a date. It's 1017. That must be when it was excavated,' she declared.

Caroline took out a small notebook from her back pocket and began making a note of the translated Latin text. It was not clear and she could not interpret every letter, but after a couple of minutes had transcribed it to paper. She was about to try and decipher it there and then in the tunnel, when Tara, rather annoyingly, intervened.

'No time for that now. Do it later.'

Caroline was excited as they pressed on, for she had recognised the final line as the same on the altar. This meant they were linked. It was an escape route for the monks. She was now convinced, and with her mind wandering from the task of their rescue, she suddenly felt water.

'From now on we'll have to wade,' said Tara. 'Don't know how deep it'll get.'

As the ground descended on a shallow incline, so the water became deeper, until at the lowest point of the tunnel it was only up to their knees. Tara was pleased because it meant she could operate at any time of the month, although she very much doubted whether her lucrative free trade would continue now that it had been discovered. Perhaps the tunnel and cave system, she thought, could be turned into some archaeological museum where people would pay to see the wonders below the Island, especially as Caroline seemed to be sure of its antiquity. But Madge would, no doubt, veto the idea and so she would have to return to her mundane business and the Estate Agency.

At the half-way point, Tara stopped. She could still hear the pump, it being amplified in the tunnel. This was the point of no return should it fail and she turned to Caroline to explain the significance.

'Do you still want to carry on?' she then added.

'Of course, it makes no difference. If the pump fails now, we either head back towards the Island or on to the mainland.'

'Yes, but what I mean is that the exit is via a concrete trap door. Usually, I get one of the boys to check that there is no obstruction. Naturally, I haven't done that.'

'So what you're saying, is that if we continue and cannot open this trap door and the pump fails, then we're stuck.'

'That's about it.'

'But it's still going. Let's go on.'

So they continued, with Tara keeping an ear on the pump whilst directing the torch and Caroline still looking at the tunnel walls for further markings. But they had only gone a few paces when the tunnel seemed to vibrate. They stopped. It was only momentary, but both of them felt the movement.

'Probably the Navy,' said Tara.

'How so?' enquired Caroline, wondering how they could cause such a phenomenon.

'Firing. They practice it not far away. Expect it was some sort of shock wave from an explosive. There have been unconfirmed reports of whole pods of dolphins being killed and washed up on beaches because of their activity. I've experienced such vibrations many a time. There's no problem.'

Caroline wasn't entirely convinced by Tara's explanation and thought it more like a mini earthquake, hundreds of which hit the country every day, nevertheless too weak to be noticed. But underground, where shock waves are amplified, even a small one would be felt. From being excited she was now concerned, for there would be only a thin crust of rock above the tunnel and with the weight of water, the 'quake may compromise its integrity.

But Tara continued, and as they progressed the water became shallower until they had cleared it and were approaching the trap door and the exit to the mainland. The chamber was small, not like the cavernous space on the Island, and had signs of recent work with concrete reinforcement by the exit. Caroline spotted a date, 1955, etched into the rock and the initial GA alongside it. Not exactly early middle ages, she thought, but knew an excavation had taken place sometime after the Second World War. It proved that they had discovered the tunnel, yet there had been no mention of it in official records and certainly not in the archaeological report.

Whilst Caroline was musing over the inscription, Tara had been trying to open the trap door but without success and was about to ask for help when noises could be heard above, the sound of something being moved, which Tara knew to be the bench, followed by the trap door slowly being opened. Quickly, the two women retreated to a safe distance down the tunnel where they could still see the chamber. Tara switched off her torch. They waited. The door was swung open and daylight penetrated the darkness with the sight of a man climbing down, first his legs, then his torso, and finally the head, and to their horror they could now see the familiar blonde mane of Siegfried.

They retreated further and quietly turned to head back to the main chamber but with the torch light now off it was not as easy and in their haste, Caroline slipped and gave out a personal expletive, not out of pain, but that she was now drenched. The tunnel acted like a resonance chamber where any tiny sound is amplified and so her discrete alarm call echoed all the way to where Siegfried and his prisoner had entered. The trap door had just been closed, sealing Robert and everybody else into another dark void, a world like no other, because in a few moments a cataclysm would turn the place upside down.

57

atural catastrophes are a part of geological history. They can be seen in the rocks that are exposed along the cliffs of Looe and beyond, folding, faulting and even igneous activity in the form of granite intrusions. But the cataclysm that was about to happen in the tunnel that Tara, Caroline, Siegfried and Robert were now in, was certainly not natural. It wasn't an earthquake, although it felt like one to them. It was the result of the tunnel having being emptied of water and above them, on the sea bed, water pressure was beginning to bear upon the structure at a weak point right in the middle of the tunnel, where the group were now to be found.

None of them were anywhere near safety. Siegfried had all but caught up with the two women when a sudden vibration, much more violent than the previous one, caused them all to stop and look up to the roof of the tunnel and witness a crack develop. It slowly got wider and as it increased, so water began to seep from it, first a trickle, then a fountain, and before they knew it a torrent was pouring from the fissure. The inundation was threatening to engulf them all.

They were all in danger of drowning from the deluge that finally poured into the tunnel, no longer wading through water but swimming, swimming for their lives. Within a few seconds they were all submerged as the water continued to fill the tunnel with such a force, that it propelled them along to the large chamber.

Miraculously, they had all survived as they emerged from the wash, one by one, gasping for air. It was Tara who took the initiative and positioned herself at the exit, next to the pump where she had hidden the flare gun. Robert was the final body to emerge from the watery tunnel, drenched, as were the others, although Siegfried was better off, wearing a wet suit and with his huge frame it made him look like a performing seal about to do a trick.

The water that had engulfed the chamber from the tidal surge began to dissipate and as it did so, Robert slowly got up and looked around to see first Tara and then Caroline, both looking astonished but glad to see him.

'You're alive!' they said in unison.

'Naturally. That was some swim.'

The women laughed, but Siegfried was not amused. He had his own interminable way of expressing things.

'It seems we have a full house.'

Robert, who was still on some adrenalin rush from his swim, could not resist the chance to make fun of Siegfried again.

'We have a king and two queens. You must be the jack. The jack of...'

'Robert, don't,' intervened Caroline, realising that their situation was bad enough already.

'Wise words,' responded Siegfried to Caroline.

The four of them stood in the chamber, a circular quartet wondering who would make the first move, as though the chamber were now a gladiatorial arena where supremacy was the prize for the victor and death awaited the losers. Robert was the first, but just as he stepped one pace forward, Tara put her hand up, that told him to wait.

'This is my Island. This is my fight,' she said looking at Siegfried, beckoning him to make a move, and then added, 'You shall not pass,' words that were intended to challenge him.

Siegfried did not need encouragement.

'We shall see,' he said and from his belt removed a large knife, a commando knife with a serrated blade that looked ominous and considerably more lethal than the kitchen knife Tara had at her disposal, hidden from Siegfried's view.

He approached her. She stood her ground, terrified at the thought of that blade piercing her body. Slowly, Siegfried crept nearer and Tara, still rooted to the spot, looked at death. And as he got to within a few feet of her she glanced, first at Caroline and then Robert, hoping to distract Siegfried, enough for her to make a move. It worked. She pulled out her knife and lunged at him. He managed to parry her from the full thrust but her blade caught his arm and blood began to ooze from a wound which, even for the infallible man himself, made him wince. Momentarily, she had another chance to strike. But hesitation was her downfall, for in that split second he had regained his vision and awareness and had Tara in an arm lock with his blade, its sharp edge at her throat about to dispatch her like a sacrificial lamb.

Faced with certain death, Tara accepted her fate for there was nothing she could do but wait for the inevitable. But it didn't come.

'That manoeuvre was quite pathetic. Did you really think you could overpower me?'

Tara was in no position to argue or negotiate and she was but one hand movement away from death. But she was defiant.

'Go on. Do it. But let the others go. It's not their Island. It's yours now. You've won.'

In his younger days, particularly when he was a mercenary, Jock would not have hesitated to strike a death cut. But he didn't, and in not doing so exhibited weakness according to the rules of his game. Perhaps it was because she was so beautiful, that to disfigure, to extinguish such a perfect form, would be sacrilege and whilst he had no emotional attachment, he did recognise beauty when he saw it. Whatever the reason, Tara had a second chance and she still had the flare gun.

'What is it you want of me?' she said choking from the strangle hold.

'You have nothing to give me. But your friend over there has,' and Siegfried looked at Robert who in turn wondered what it was. His life? But he had that before and didn't take it.

'You can save her, my good friend, if you will tell me where that mark on the map is.'

Caroline was lost, as was Tara, but clearly this map and the mark, whatever it was, were very important to Siegfried, important enough to threaten to kill Tara. But Robert knew what he was talking about, having overheard his conversation with Frederick, although he hadn't actually seen the map.

'I've no idea,' he said.

'Don't play games. This is not the time,' sinking the blade into Tara's throat enough to draw some blood.

'I heard you talking, but I never saw the map. And that's the truth,' replied Robert with anxiety, now realising the enormity of the situation.

Siegfried unzipped a thigh pocket and removed a plastic bag, which on opening it revealed a copy of the map in question.

'You have precisely five minutes to work it out, otherwise Tara, despite her beautiful looks, will be no more.'

Siegfried threw the map to the floor and Robert opened it. It looked like a map showing some coastline. But not in Ireland, at least, not in Kerry, and with no landmarks, no towns and no roads or rivers, nor even any scale, he really didn't know where it depicted. As for the mark, it may as well be anywhere. He swivelled the map, one way then another, but still could not tell where it was. Time was fast running out. Caroline was looking at him, urging him on to solve the puzzle. He caught Tara's gaze, her eyes trying to tell him something about the pump but it was no good, he could see nothing to help the situation.

Siegfried could see his hesitation. Exasperated, he offered Robert some advice.

'First, I know you spent some time living in County Kerry and I'm sure you know what the map depicts and hence I'm sure you know where the mark is and what it represents. And second, should you fail, I will kill her and then I will do the same to your girlfriend. You have just two minutes left.'

Robert was mortified. Two minutes and Tara would die, he thought. He read the new cryptic verses. They meant nothing. He was floundering. He looked at the map again.

Then he had an idea. Siegfried obviously thought the map had something to do with his time in Kerry. What if he spun a tale to confirm it? He would say the map was irrelevant and hope he would fall for it. He had no other option.

'Okay, I'll tell you. But first let Tara free. That's the condition. I swear that I will tell you.'

'I'm afraid you're in no position to set conditions. However, I accept your word.'

He let Tara go who took a few side steps and sighed with relief at her release, holding her hand to her throat and looking at the blood on her fingers. Robert told Siegfried about Madeleine and the cottage and its location, spinning the tale so that it drew his attention, giving Tara a chance to slowly edge towards the pump and the flare gun. But as she bent down to reach for it, to her dismay it was gone and with it any hope they now had, for she felt sure that he would kill them all now.

Siegfried picked up the map and looked at it. He gazed at it, almost into it, as though he were processing it with a second sight. He turned it all ways and then he smiled.

'Good,' he declared.

Siegfried had what he wanted. He didn't need Robert any more, nor any of the others. He would dispatch them one by one and decided it would be Tara first, since he had already tasted her blood, his blade stained red from the small cut he had given her. She was bending down scrabbling for something and so he pulled her up and raised his knife to strike her, when a voice from the shadows, from the bowls of the caves, stopped him.

'Put down the knife,' it howled, an echo from the dark.

Siegfried was astounded. What devil of a thing was lurking beyond the light that could command him so? And as he thought that, into the light came the devilish thing, in the shape of a meek and mild mannered person who never in his life had hit a living person, let alone try to kill one. It was Malcolm.

He had been lurking in the shadows of a side cave, having followed the two women into the catacombs. He had watched them disappear down the tunnel and had felt the cave shudder and then moments later, faced a wall of water that doused the generator and washed up around his feet. He had picked the flare gun up before it too succumbed to the water and now there he was, poised and ready to use it.

Already he had a dislike, even a loathing, for Jock. He was a man the total antithesis of his persona, one who had the look of a killer. He had made the fateful decision to side with the enemy and help Tara, the beautiful woman whom he thought was a goddess of the caves, an earth goddess that could enchant men, for she had enchanted him without her even realising it.

Only a few days ago he had been wondering how he might get onto the Island and, once there, what he would find, for his research and investigations had unearthed a smuggling ring, one that involved his father and this man Jock. Using the secret passages in Hendersick Hall, which Christian had told him about one day when he was chatting to him in the parlour, he had overheard discussions between his father and Jock about a shipment of paintings from the continent. Jock was to collect them at a rendezvous mid-channel, a mile off the Eddystone lighthouse, and bring them ashore without the authorities knowing, for they were stolen paintings and as such were not destined for any gallery, but to be sold to private collectors. Tara, he thought, was involved too, having been alerted by Jane when he disclosed his interest in the Island and smuggling. But the incident just now, clearly demonstrated that she was not party to this operation. He was glad.

He had first known of Jane some six months earlier when he had seen her with his father and wasn't entirely sure of her motives, although he could see what his father wanted from their relationship. And seeing her naked, incognito from a spy hole in the bedroom, he had wanted her too, wanted that sublime body to make love to him, not his father. So it had been quite fortuitous that he had encountered her on Talland Beach and had been invited into her affections as some kind of reward for saving her life.

He had soon realised her open affection was a subterfuge for information. Malcolm was working on the smuggling story, hoping to write a definitive piece, sell the story, and so make a name for himself and become an investigative journalist for a national newspaper. He had been working on the story with a friend, a photographer, who had ambitions of his own. He had posed as a customs officer but had accidentally fallen to his death a few weeks ago, a death which Malcolm had thought too coincidental. He had his suspicions, but there was no proof until he heard Jock admit his involvement and, by association, his father's, who was now an accessory to murder.

He didn't love his father. He didn't even respect him, because his world was contrary to his own: he dealt in truth as opposed to his father's secrecy and deceit. More than that, he had cheated on his mother, his only love in life, who had been cast adrift to fend for herself when he had millions in the bank. Malcolm had returned recently to investigate the smuggling and expose his father for what he was. And now he found himself on the Island, in the underground caves, facing the man responsible for his friend's death, and he himself was about to commit a crime, a crime of retribution.

The dark cave with its flickering light mirrored his thoughts as he maintained a discrete distance from Jock. His thoughts were focused on the deed, with doubts about his ability clouding its clarity. Could he do it? He had to. If not, another death would happen and this time he would be responsible. It was now or never. It was time to act.

He moved forward out of the shadows, his heart now beating so fast that he was sure he was going into cardiac arrest, sweat perspiring from his forehead even though the cave was cool. He held up the flare gun and pointed it at Jock. The two of them stood motionless staring at each other, Jock with a determined and calculated look and Malcolm, his heart beating even faster, his hands shaking, not knowing what to do.

'So it's you,' said Jock, surprised to see his benefactor's son, but not showing it.

'Release the girl,' he commanded.

'Who'd have thought you'd turn out to be a knight in shining armour? Or rather, a joker with a flare gun.'

'This is no joke,' he replied, his voice incised with a quiver that betrayed his fear.

Tara, who at this point was slowly edging away from Siegfried, could see what he was seeing, a scared young man out of his depth and unable to carry out his threat.

'Use it,' she shouted. 'Don't mind me, just kill him.'

But of course he couldn't. He was there to save her, not kill her. And Siegfried knew it as well. He, with one deliberate step at a time, started to move towards his executioner.

'Use it,' Jock said, 'Like the girl said.'

Malcolm was now paralysed with terror. His threats had been hollow. He had no intention of using the flare gun. With each step, Jock got nearer. Eleven yards, ten, nine. Malcolm looked at Tara for some courage, for some way out. Eight yards. Seven.

'Fire man, for God's sake, fire,' she shouted again.

But still he stood motionless, entrenched and unable to respond, drowning in his own hesitation, to the closing threat of Jock's advance whose knife was poised ready to take its next victim. It would, but not before Malcolm, that meek and mild-mannered young man who had never hurt anybody in his life and who really wanted to impress Tara with his own initiative, pulled the trigger and unleashed an inferno.

58

Miracles can happen. Miracles do happen. They happen not only to those that deserve such divine intervention, but to anybody that conforms to prescribed convention rather than trust to the vagaries of fate or foolish bravado. And so, in the fireball that was propelled through the tunnel, Siegfried survived, just as he survived the fire dragon Fasholt and had thrust his sword into its body, felling it and so capturing the prized ring, the Ring of the Niblung. Real life often follows fiction, or a Wagnerian music drama, and so Siegfried, or was it Jock, picked himself up and thrust his knife into the dragon that was staggering around not aware that death was his reward for love and loyalty, or was it hatred and stupidity. It was a sweet death for Siegfried. It was an agonising death for Malcolm.

What a brave fool Malcolm was. It shows what latent love can do to a naïve young man who had not tasted real love in his life and who thought that he had been sent to rescue a maiden in distress, save her, fall in love and live a happy life, she devoted to him and he dedicated to his work. That's how life works in a world of fantasy. No it doesn't. If he had known his Wagner, then he would have realised that the hero dies because of that love: he found his maiden, his warrior maiden, they fell in love and he was killed because of that love.

It was Tara's courage that made Malcolm pull the trigger. Her defiance in the face of death. A bright flash had emanated in the chamber, a super nova of an explosion that felled Siegfried and engulfed Malcolm in the shock wave. It reverberated from wall to wall with the fireball, a fireball forged by the god Loge, gaining intensity until it filled the chamber with white heat.

Siegfried survived because of the miracle of his wetsuit, a thin skin protecting his own which would surely have fried him. But even so, his face was burnt and the goggles melted, but they had protected him so he could live and fight another day, to see Malcolm and end his torment and to seek the cooling ointment of the water from which he had just emerged and make for Hendersick Hall to perform some damage limitation.

Robert and Caroline had already plunged themselves into the water when they realised that hell was about to be released. They didn't see Siegfried escape, assuming that he had perished in the devouring fire, alongside Tara and the unfortunate man. They couldn't have survived. She couldn't have survived. She had died defending her own Island, a destiny that she must have known in those final few seconds, encouraging and goading the young man to pull the trigger and unleash a fire ball that would ignite the fuel cans. She had seen her love, Robert, and his lover dive into the water moments before, and she died with the satisfaction that he was safe. She loved him, had loved him, and had paid the ultimate price for that love.

When the inferno had subsided, Robert and Caroline emerged from the water to a scene of complete desolation. The chamber was wiped clean. The walls were charred black. The pump was a melted tangle of metal. There was no sign that life once stood there facing each other, tempting death. Their bodies had been cremated in the intense heat and all that remained were ashes that were indistinguishable from the fallout of vaporisation.

For Robert and Caroline it was a real nightmare made in hell. They didn't want to remain in the tomb, and so made their way back to the main cave and the welcome relief of daylight and the life-giving force of the sun. They felt numb. They felt euphoric. But it was a pyrrhic euphoria for in life there is death, Tara's death and the death of the young man, Malcolm. Had they been dreaming it all? No. It was a paradigm for a nightmare which only reality could have created. And they had survived it.

Outside in the early morning daylight, a thin blanket of cloud had now obscured the sun and a light shower was washing away their sorrows. Both proclaimed their thanks to the heavens with outstretched arms and drank the rain, an elixir that breathed life back into their souls. They put their arms around each other, for comfort, for warmth, for thanks that they shared the nightmare, had cheated death, and emerged unscathed. It seemed the end of a journey that had taken them to the ends of the earth and back again, a journey like no other they had been on before. Now, in the dawn of a another day, it was a new beginning, a rebirth of their love that had blossomed in the heat of a museum, which seemed like a thousand and one nights ago, which had forged a new beginning then, as it had now.

They walked to the end of the Island, to Trelawney Point, and sat down to seek restitution for their salvation from their underground incubus. The light shower had now subsided and with a break in the clouds the sun shone upon them, its rays illuminating them as though they had just given a performance on the stage of life.

Robert looked out to sea and imagined Tara sailing the seven oceans, seeking her forlorn love, never finding it, to sail an endless passage forever, not ever knowing true love. Caroline could see him stare out into the distance, beyond the horizon, as though searching for something, somebody. She knew who that somebody was. She hadn't known Tara, but she was a special person to have sacrificed herself for Robert and would like to think she would have done the same. That is true love, she thought, and Tara must have loved Robert. She put her arms around him and kissed him on the cheek and smiled at him to say that it was alright to think about her, to mourn her, for she deserved that for such an unselfish act.

The two of them must have sat there for some time, holding hands and in their own thoughts. Robert was still at sea, searching for Tara. Caroline, though, had returned to earth and was now thinking about the inscription that she had transcribed in the tunnel. Her notebook had gone, washed away in the deluge, but its text still remained vivid in her mind and she now tried to translate it. But even for her trenchant mind, with the memory of the narrow escape fading but still refusing to depart, she could not concentrate enough to make any progress. She had to write the text down before it too faded.

She arose from beside Robert and made her way to Jetty Cottage, hoping to find paper and pen to write the text down. Robert didn't really notice her leave. He sensed that he was alone, just as he was the day up on the cliff at his cottage, looking at the lone figure where he was now, the figure of Tara facing the elements, defying the forces of nature. That day she had won. Today she had succumbed to brimstone and had met her maker. She had died the way she lived, he thought, remembering their time together and her lascivious persona that had charmed and lured him. For a time she was his Grace. She was not Happiness for she never found that. She was not Beauty either, although she was certainly that in life. She was, though, Charm and she had beguiled him like his dream had foretold and he was glad she had, for ultimately it had brought him together with Beauty.

Caroline had searched Jetty Cottage and had found some paper and a pencil. She had forgotten a few letters, but had remembered most, enough to guess the missing Latin script. Her mind was still confused and muddled and so she decided to wait until they were back at the cottage, off the Island that had almost killed them both. As she was making her way back to Robert, a launch approached the jetty below, with a man on board, waving, beckoning her attention.

'Ahoy there,' he shouted as though on a rescue mission.

He was. It was John, the proprietor, who had gone to the cottage to find Caroline and take her out to the Island. Alfred, who had just arrived, had told him of her walk across at low tide and so here he was, mounting a rescue of the survivors of an Island in distress. He manoeuvred *Lady Jane* alongside the jetty, moored her to a post and jumped ashore whilst Caroline watched, thankful he had remembered his promise.

'Everything okay?' he enquired.

Caroline wasn't sure what to say, what to tell him. She thought it best, for now, not to mention anything and leave it to Robert. If he wanted this to go further then she would agree, if not then it would remain their secret.

'Yes, everything is fine. I found Robert. He's over there at the moment,' as she pointed towards Trelawney Point.

'I'm so glad. Told you that it would be. Storm in a teacup.'

Caroline thought it was more like a cyclone in a vat, but she didn't want to have to explain herself.

'You were right. But I was worried.'

'Shows you care.'

She nodded in agreement and went to fetch Robert while John remained behind to keep a watch on the boat. It was still a little rough and he was mindful of a rogue wave forcing the vessel from its mooring. He watched Caroline walk toward the end of the Island and in doing so saw some smoke, he thought, coming from the southern part, from where the caves were located. It was then that he noticed Madge coming towards him.

'Have you brought some provisions?' she asked on reaching John.

'No. Come to rescue a friend.'

'Rescue?' she said rather perplexed.

'Yes, he got stranded here yesterday when walking across at low tide. His partner was worried and came to me. Because of the weather, I've only just been able to make it across.' He pointed to the couple. 'There they are.'

Madge waited for them. She was annoyed they were on her Island but relieved that they were unharmed.

'Are you two alright? I gather you got stuck here yesterday.'

Robert wondered if she had heard anything and was now investigating. He didn't want to disclose the events unless it became absolutely necessary.

'Yes, we're fine. Just a little tired and in need of a good cup of tea. I should say that we're friends of Tara.'

'You should have called on me. I'd have seen you alright.'

'That's kind of you to say. Hope we didn't disturb you last night.'

'Oh me, no. Slept like a log. Not even an invasion of the Island would wake me.'

Robert was relieved, as rather than an invasion, a cataclysm had happened beneath her feet and she had slept through it. No wonder Tara had used the Island for her smuggling operation. Madge was the perfect foil. She could come out here at any time without arising suspicion and her nocturnal activity would not be heard by Madge.

Robert and Caroline bid Madge good morning and apologised for the intrusion upon her Island.

'No problem,' she said. 'Perhaps you would like to come again, but by more conventional means. Tara, could give you a tour of the Island and the caves. They're Etruscan, so I'm led to believe. Would you be interested?'

'We would,' replied Caroline.

'That reminds me,' continued Madge, 'have you seen Tara? She was supposed to bring me some more provisions.'

'No we haven't,' said Robert.

'Hope she hasn't forgotten. She's a good girl to me.'

Robert and Caroline were a little concerned for Madge now. Her lifeline had been severed.

'Perhaps John here could fetch some over later on,' said Robert looking expectantly at the proprietor.

He was delighted to be of help and agreed. Madge told him that her shopping list was held at the local supermarket next to the Smugglers Arms, added a few extra items and thanked him for his kind assistance. The three of them boarded the boat and John manoeuvred the craft around, opened the throttle and headed back to the mainland, back to reality. As *Lady Jane* made her way back to the harbour, Robert turned and looked at the Island for the last time. It was as though the cataclysm that had befallen its core was now manifest in its diminishing size, that something had been lost within its caves and without Tara, Looe Island would never be the same again.

*   *   *

For the rest of the day, both Robert and Caroline lived in a stupor, wondering if the Island was a figment of their imaginations, wondering whether they really had survived the inferno. Of course they knew they had, but as the fire had spread across the surface of the water they were submerged under its skin, holding their breath in fear of their lives. It seemed an experience only fictional characters had to endure as they fought evil, ordinary people caught in an extraordinary scenario that had been conjured by the devil. The fire was a fitting end to Robert's nemesis and now they could get some rest, take stock and continue with the rest of their lives.

Alfred had gone back home after Robert and Caroline's return from the Island. They didn't recount everything, but enough for him to be amazed. Not so much at their escape, but at the tunnel. When Caroline had described the inscription he was even more excited, realising that the Island was indeed the most likely place where the Pirate Captain had cached his treasure. She gave him the copy of the Latin text and, being a scholar of the Classics, asked him to translate the text, even though she could do so herself. He left them on that afternoon hoping that it would reveal the proof to his theory and thereby vindicate years of academic ridicule, that X does mark the spot of buried treasure.

For Robert and Caroline, as they stood watching the night descend upon the Island, it was a place that would forever be etched in their memories, a place that defined a moment in their lives. They had confronted evil within its bowels, one that they would rather forget. But this maleficence had not yet finished with them and despite their profound desire, they were not about to continue with the rest of their lives, not just yet.

59

The following day Alfred arrived early, too early for Robert, still in a deep slumber and not willing to vacate a lovely warm bed and a beautiful, salacious woman, about to have her wicked way with him. She slowly removed her robe, teasing him with her svelte body, inviting him, but denying him his passion. And with his body naked for her pleasure, her fingernails inducing pain so that he responded as she wanted him to, to provide her with a phallus to engorge her senses and penetrate her soul.

And as he grew more excited, instead of ecstasy he found torment, for the seductress had turned into a ghost with long flowing red hair and the phallus was now a flare gun which he was holding, pointing at a blonde wraith, a figure of immense stature who had been watching the two lovers. 'Use it. Don't mind me, just kill him,' wailed the ghost. But he was paralysed with guilt, unable to fire. So he pointed it at the ghost. 'Use it,' responded the wraith, 'like the ghost said.' But he still could not fire. He pointed it back again to the wraith and as it approached Robert, the ghost shouted, 'Fire man, for God's sake, fire.' And he looked at the ghost and the wraith and fired, not at the two phantoms but at immortality, and in the brilliant inferno that engulfed him he awoke from his nightmare to an empty bed and the sun streaming in through the window, blinding his thoughts.

He sat up looking at the dishevelled sheets, a bed that had witnessed a catastrophe, and wondered if his conscience was rebuking him for not doing anything, for not helping Tara. He should have perished in the inferno, not her. It was his destiny to burn like the effigy and absolve everybody of the Pirate's curse. He should have done that.

Challenged evil to a duel. It was his fate, ever since that first encounter in Caroline's flat. It was there that the duel had started, had continued with his ordeals, and should have ended with just the two of them in the chamber, a gladiatorial lek where survival of the fittest is the rule and as an outcome, the morally strong would have defeated the amoral weak. His demons were back, returning to haunt him for another death which he believed was his fault, one that he could have prevented.

Downstairs, Caroline was oblivious to turmoil. She was talking history with Alfred, he showing her the translated Latin text, which he described as childishly easy:

In penance we work
In god we pray
In glory we sing
In salvation we trust.

In his excitement yesterday, he had failed to realise that the Pirate Captain would not have used Latin. Indeed, much of the country would then be reading and writing in Old English, different from today's idiom.

'The date was probably the year the tunnel was completed, proving that there was a monastic settlement on the Island before the known recorded date and well before that, I suspect, for it would have taken years, maybe decades, to complete,' said Alfred.

'I agree, but it doesn't help in your theory about the cache of treasure,' replied Caroline, not really thinking it was a sound hypothesis anyway, with no hard evidence.

'I know.'

'I think Robert may be able to help. He was shown a map. It was of the Irish coast in County Kerry. It had a mark on it, just like the map of Lammana. There was also an inscription, a cryptic verse, in addition to the one we've seen.'

Alfred was intrigued and asked Caroline to wake him from his rest. She was averse to disturbing him, but just when she was about to tell

Alfred of her reluctance, she heard heavy footsteps descend the stairs, as though the half-dead had made the decision for her.

Robert didn't immediately go into the lounge, but made himself a cup of tea and went outside through the side porch and looked towards Rame Head. He had thought about this moment on his first viewing of the cottage, waking up to see the sun rise across the bay, although today he was rather late and had missed it by several hours. Would he have bought the cottage if he had known what misadventure was to befall him, he thought? Of course he would. It was still his idyll, even if it had been tarnished with guilt. He turned towards the Island. It looked serene and peaceful in the morning sun, hiding behind a veil of innocence, a place where piety was once euphoniously chanted but where yesterday, violence and destruction had sung a discordant note.

Back in the sitting room, the two historians were engaged in some conversation about the field above the cottage and how a geophysical survey might confirm it had previously been farmed as stitches. Robert entered and they stopped talking, as though he were some stranger entering a coterie, where his presence was an intrusion and where he would upset the balance of arguments or decisions. He sat down on a two-seater sofa, positioned along the wall opposite the fireplace, and took a sip from his tea. He was still in a trance.

'How are you feeling today?' said Caroline, not having had a chance to enquire with Alfred's early arrival.

'Oh, alright,' he replied with a deadpan voice, looking into the fire hearth, expecting it to spontaneously ignite into a fireball.

'Robert,' said Caroline in a quiet, yet determined, questioning tone. 'The map you mentioned, where did you say it was?'

'County Kerry in Ireland. As you know, I used to live there for a time.'

'And this mark on this outline map? You know where it is?'

'Yes. Well, I think so.'

'Where?' added Caroline expecting Robert to have explained it.

'It's difficult to say without the map. I know where it is. It's a cottage, exactly like this one, in a remote valley going down to the sea on the west coast of the Ring of Kerry. I think it was built by the Pirate Captain. He must have gone there for some reason or perhaps no reason at all. But he built the cottage as a reminder of his family home. A homage to his parent's maybe. Who knows?'

'I think you may be right,' said Alfred, excited by this new information.

'There was some text on the map. More verses,' added Robert

'Can you remember them?' enquired Alfred.

'No. Didn't really take note of it. My mind was on other matters.'

'We need to see that map,' said Alfred.

'How?' asked Caroline.

'Simple. We go to Hendersick Hall and ask,' courted Alfred, as though the suggestion would not go down to well.

It didn't. At least not with Robert, for his ordeal there was still vivid, and although Siegfried was no more, it was a place in his mind that he didn't want to return to so soon. Caroline, though, was all for it.

'I think Alfred and me should go. You stay here Robert.'

Robert, now ensconced in the sofa, his legs tucked in on the cushion and his dressing gown covering him, suddenly woke up.

'I don't want you going there.'

'I appreciate your experience there Robert, but I don't think an old man, a frail one at that, as you describe him, will pose any threat.'

He couldn't disagree.

'I know. All the same I don't want you to go there.'

The negative, for Caroline, meant the opposite. She did not like anybody telling her what she could or couldn't do, especially twice. She was a free spirit, and Robert knew it.

'Look. I'll take your car. It will take no more than ten minutes to get there and another ten to get back. If we're not back within the hour, then come and rescue us,' suggested Caroline, knowing that Robert was going to agree.

'Alright. But no more than an hour.'

'Better make that two,' echoed Alfred, as Caroline got up from one of the armchairs and left the room with Alfred trailing behind, she looking at Robert as though to say it wasn't her fault.

By the time the pair had reached the car, parked just beyond the tower, half an hour had already passed, mainly because they had stopped a couple of times to study the lie of the land in the field, trying to see if there was any evidence of the stitches. They hadn't found any discernable banks, but one low hump which stretched for most of the width of the field seemed promising. Yet despite his interest, it was Alfred who was aware of the time slipping by, having to urge Caroline along, lest Robert's wrath was provoked.

They drove up to Hendersick Hall along the gravel driveway, having to negotiate several peafowl that decided to cross their path, whilst in the distance was the unmistakeable call of the cock bird creating an aristocratic, almost colonial, feel to their entrance. They could be approaching the Viceroys residence in Calcutta, but for the Tudor architecture and the sight of a gardener sitting on a motorised lawn mower.

'When Robert and I visited the Taj Mahal, they were cutting the grass with two oxen and what looked like some medieval threshing machine,' she said to Alfred.

'Such a magnificent mausoleum,' he replied, not quite understanding where this fitted into their quest.

'Indeed,' she said, taking in the heady aroma of freshly cut grass, a very British phenomenon.

They pulled up outside the main entrance and alighted to a gaggle of peafowl, interested in somebody new who might feed them some forbidden fruits. They were not treated to their favourite snack, for the two immediately climbed the steps and rang the bell and less than thirty seconds later, the door was opened by Christian.

They announced themselves and explained to the manservant that they were historians on the trail of a Captain Robert Colliver and his long lost treasure. They had made enquiries in the town and had been directed to the Hall. As a piece of bait, they said they were working on a theory that he had visited Ireland once, having seen a map in Tangiers that alluded to the coast of County Kerry, and on that map was the name of Lammana.

It worked. They were invited in and shown to the study where Frederick was sitting at his desk, intrigued by the mysterious visitors who seemed to know quite a bit about the Pirate Captain.

'Welcome to Hendersick Hall. My name is Frederick Thomas.'

Alfred went ashen. Was it coincidence? It must be. We cannot be related, he thought. Caroline noticed Alfred's pallor and made the introductions.

'I am Caroline Davies and this is Alfred...'

'...Smith,' interjected Alfred.

Frederick looked at Alfred more closely now and could see something in his eyes, an enquiring gaze that spoke of learning, and despite the intervening years, something familiar in his comportment, in the way he stood and the way he seemed to look disdainfully, almost dismissively, at him. In that moment he saw through Alfred's disguise. He knew him. He knew him only too well.

'We are historians. I work at the British Library and Alfred is a former Oxford Academic. I expect your butler to have explained the purpose of our visit.'

'Yes, he did, although I'm not quite clear how I may be of assistance,' replied Frederick.

'We are on the trail of a pirate, a Captain Robert Colliver, who, as legend has it, buried his treasure. We believe, from a map we've acquired, that his cache may be in Ireland. In County Kerry, to be precise. We happened to be talking about it in a café, when the woman serving us mentioned that you were some expert and may be of help,' explained Caroline.

Frederick listened to the absurd fabrication and realised that they knew nothing.

'Quite a tale. I'm sorry. As I said before, I cannot help you. I know nothing of a pirate captain, nor buried treasure.'

They were disappointed. He was not taking the bait. Caroline then decided she would call his bluff.

'We seem to have been misinformed. We're very sorry to have disturbed you. Thank you for your time.'

Frederick had encountered such strategies many a time in his professional life and could sense when a person was genuine. And these two were certainly not.

'Not at all,' he said, 'I'm sorry I haven't been of any help.'

Caroline had backed them into a corner with no way out. They had to leave and try an alternative tack, but as they were leaving, Alfred turned towards Frederick, who was still sitting at his desk.

'May I ask you a question? A personal question,' enquired Alfred.

'By all means,' replied Frederick expecting such an enquiry.

'Are you the son of Henry and Edna Thomas?'

'I am indeed. And you are not Alfred Smith, but Alfred Thomas, if I'm not mistaken.'

'You are not,' replied Alfred, slightly embarrassed at his attempt of a disguise.

'It's been a long time.'

'Almost fifty years.'

Caroline was lost. Clearly these two men knew each other and the connection must be with their surname. She looked at Alfred.

'It seems your friend is in need of an explanation,' said Frederick, noticing Caroline's puzzled look.

'This is my half-brother. I was brought up by his parents who treated me as their own son.'

'Yes they did, at the expense of me. They showered you with love and saw in you the son they had always wanted. You went to Oxford, whilst I had to find my own way in life.'

'I'm sorry you feel like that, Frederick.'

'I do. It may be almost fifty years but I've never forgotten, as though it were yesterday. And then you just left, leaving me to pick up the pieces.'

'It's a long story,' replied Alfred in defence.

'Maybe, but I know enough of it. How you were banned from marrying your sweetheart and the mysterious disappearance of a suitor. No wonder you ran away. You didn't have the decency to face the music or even say goodbye. My parents were distraught.'

'It isn't something I'm proud of.'

'But it's something I would expect of you. Expect of a family that brought untold pain and misery to mine for a deed committed by your ancestors.'

Alfred looked at Frederick, wondering what he was talking about. It seemed to be the ramblings of an old man still living in the past which, judging by his art collection, was exactly that.

'I know. For the treacherous betrayal of Josiah Thomas at the hands of William Trevellick in 1749. But how is that related to me?'

'Because you are a Trevellick,' announced Frederick with satisfaction that he had mortally wounded the enemy. 'Your father was none other than Henry Trevellick, the father of your sweetheart. That's why you couldn't marry her. She was your half-sister. You are a Trevellick, through and through.'

60

Robert sat outside on the bench in his dressing gown, looking out towards the Island. It hadn't changed. It was still the same with its three cottages, the copse of trees surmounting its summit cascading down its sheltered slopes, and the rugged coastline, frequented by gulls and cormorants and a flock of alien sheep, all framed in a sky which gave it a benevolent canopy, a place of serenity in a sea of hostility.

Yet the Island had changed. It now leaked malevolence. It was no longer an island that promised adventure that had lured him to discover its secrets. He had found them. Rather, the Island now pronounced concealment, uncertainty, a place that spoke of death. To Robert, the trees were garlands of thorns and the rugged coast a monument to the fallen. Even the birds seemed to frame in his mind, gargoyles guarding the Island's secret and the sheep, which were grazing on Trelawney Isle, were angels of death. It was a mausoleum, a far more exalted place than the Taj Mahal, for in his eyes it embodied a goddess, a goddess of Charm.

He could feel Tara's spirit wandering the caves, trying to find peace and a resting place, to live another life, her spiritual energy for life resurrected once more. He wanted to go over there, to absorb that ebullience and commune with her, to say that she would forever be in his heart, for although he loved Caroline, she had found a special place in the recess of his soul and he didn't want it to diminish.

Tears began to well in his eyes and the Island became a blur. But memories of his terrible ordeal were still acidulous, so sharp that they began to play tricks on him, that Tara had escaped, a body swimming past him in the water, a body that could only have been hers. He dismissed it as an overactive postscript to his mind that had seen her perish, yet could not believe it to be true.

She could not have survived, did not survive the inferno, he told himself and with that his vision began to clear. He now viewed the Island from a past chapter, one that returned to her tale in the antechamber. It was only now that he remembered she told him of her grandmother and how he realised that the grandfather, whom she never knew, was Alfred. He should have told her there and then, that her grandfather was alive and living near Looe. 'Forgive me,' he said, and sank back into melancholy thoughts about Tara, consumed in the fireball.

It was almost the two hours, the time that Alfred had declared when departing for Hendersick Hall, as Robert looked at the two historians climb down the steps into the garden, their faces clearly etched with failure. They may emanate knowledge and learning in abundance, he thought, but they're novices when it comes to the real world.

'How did it go?' he enquired.

'Can't you tell,' replied Caroline.

'Well yes, I can see that you failed in your mission.'

'Not exactly,' came Alfred.

Robert was intrigued. Either they obtained the map or they didn't. He inquisitively asked, 'what do you mean?'

'I have discovered that I am a Trevellick,' announced Alfred, in a disapproving tone to emphasise his displeasure.

'What!' said Robert with an incredulous cry. 'You're joking, surely?'

'I wish I was.'

Alfred recounted the conversation with his adopted brother and how it was a revelation that he was now a Trevellick, and how he had fallen in love with his half-sister, something which he couldn't quite adjust to. Frederick had explained that Henry Trevellick had had an affair with a cousin of the Thomas family and that when Alfred was born, he paid Frederick's parents to bring the child up as their own, for he was not going to compromise his position with such a scandalous liaison.

Apparently, Frederick only discovered this when his father had died, he becoming the head of the family with access to all its secrets.

The payment and subsequent annuity had financially drained the Trevellick family and the Thomas clan were pleased to see their adversaries in ruin. However, they too succumbed to a similar fate, when investments they had, collapsed in the financial turmoil of the Depression, and were forced to sell the ancestral home of Hendersick Hall. With Frederick purchasing the Tudor manor a few years ago, his rise was mirrored by the Trevellicks and their success in becoming Looe's most prominent family and the distrust and loathing of each other, which had waned for a while, surfaced once more with renewed vigour, at least on the Thomas side of the conflict.

If it was a revelation to Alfred, this news created a dilemma for Robert. He had to tell him about Tara. That was the least he could do.

'I've some news of my own to tell you, Alfred,' he opened with a degree of caution.

'Yes,' replied Alfred, sensing some more bad news was about to be divulged.

'Have you heard of Tara Trevellick?'

'I have, but I don't really know her. She must be a niece of mine now.'

'Yes, but there's more. She was killed in the inferno on the Island.'

'I'm sorry for her loss, but I never knew her, apart from the gossip I heard.'

'What gossip was that?'

'That she was the unofficial head of the family and apparently very manipulative. She had a reputation for using people to her advantage, even, so I've been told, using her body to achieve results. There is also rumour that she may have been involved in smuggling. Her uncle was. Also...'

Robert didn't want Alfred to continue Tara's descent into a harlot with little virtue.

'Alfred, there is something you should know, before you condemn Tara completely.'

Alfred waited. Caroline waited, but knew what he was about to say. Robert waited a moment and then pronounced the news. 'Tara was your granddaughter.'

Alfred remained unmoved. He had suspected there may be grandchildren, especially after George had cagily denied that Juliet had had any children. But Tara? He could not have imagined her. He did not know what to think.

'Are you sure?' he asked in a rather questioning tone as to its validity.

'Yes. Absolutely sure.'

Both Robert and Caroline then explained the circumstances and Alfred realised that Tara was indeed his granddaughter. He was astounded by the account and was left speechless. He slumped back on the bench where he was sitting and wandered off, lost to his own regrets.

Robert and Caroline left him alone, to come to terms with the latest revelation, which looked as though it had become one too many as they eyed each other, their facial gestures replacing conversation.

'Look, back to this map. I think I can get hold of it,' Robert suddenly interjected, realising that it might help Alfred in some form of recovery.

'How, when we failed?' questioned Caroline.

'Well, let's just say that I have hidden talents.'

'That you have,' replied Caroline with a suggestive tone to her voice.

Alfred looked at the two and felt embarrassed and raised a half smile to include himself in the private overtones. But his thoughts were really with his lost granddaughter, hoping that the rumours about her were exaggerated by people who envied her looks and success. The last time he saw her was at the auction. She had taken details from him in a courteous and professional manner, but with no hint of kinship or of a family connection. She didn't know him. As he remembered her, he now realised that at the time he was struck by her resemblance to Juliet and her particular mannerism of flicking her hair back, but most of all by her red hair. Very few women have naturally red hair and although he was not a geneticist, he should have investigated the possible connection. He admonished himself for failing to do so, but absolved himself too, by realising that he was then a member of the Thomas family, who he knew were less than friendly to their rivals.

Robert was now ready to leave. Caroline wanted to go with him, but just as with the Island excursion, he refused.

'This time I shall be alright. I know what I'm doing, unlike before. And in any case, I've insider help.'

Caroline was perplexed by his last comment and Robert, noticing her concern, added, 'I will explain on my return.'

'Alright,' said Caroline, now resigned to a dutiful partner, 'but don't do anything stupid.'

'As if I would,' he replied with a smile.

Caroline knew he always acted first without consideration of his actions. Recriminations always followed, much to Robert's annoyance, for she was always right. But this time he had done the preliminary assessment, accounted for all eventualities, had his escape route, and most important of all, Siegfried was no more. As far as he could ascertain, nothing could go wrong.

* * *

And it didn't! He was back within the hour. In his hands he had the map. Caroline was amazed, as was Alfred who had regained his sense of perspective, especially when it was presented to him.

Robert, though, was quite insouciant. He had also recovered the lamp that was rightfully his, stolen by Siegfried from his mother's home. Alfred looked at it with wonder, through the eyes of a beholder to the sublime form it displayed and he could see Robert's desire to own it, to worship it. Caroline now realised what Robert had been talking about when he had told her of the lamp, how her own body reminded him of the beautiful idol he coveted as a young boy. Except, she considered the idol more beautiful, more exquisite than her own imperfect body, even though Robert said there was no real comparison. He put the lamp on the table next to his armchair, switched it on and admired his conquest.

Caroline and Alfred were eager to know, when they had failed, how he managed to retrieve not only the x-ray copied map but also the one that Siegfried had stolen before. He explained how he parked outside the Hendersick estate and walked to the rear kitchen entrance of the Hall where he knew Christian would be. He told him of the theft from his cottage and he was only too willing to help.

Whilst Christian created a diversion, by dropping a tray with Frederick's coffee on it, Robert entered the secret passage and when the commotion began and Frederick went to see what the noise was about, he opened the door into the study and searched the desk. Robert was sure the map would be somewhere there. It didn't take long for him to locate it and he was back in the kitchen within a couple of minutes having picked up the lamp as well and opened the French doors to make out that a burglary had occurred. Frederick would probably guess who it was, but Robert was sure he would be reluctant to call the police.

The two were impressed. Alfred more so at the disclosure that Hendersick Hall had secret passages. Robert then told them about how he had discovered the passages, or rather how Christian had assisted him in his escape from Siegfried. Alfred was ecstatic that there was also a priest hole and Robert had actually used it in earnest to escape the blonde executioner. Having exhausted the tale, Robert sat back in his chair and smiled at Caroline, a smile that spoke of love, that whenever he was in danger he had thought of his love and somehow had escaped death to be with her. It was fate, he thought.

Meanwhile, Alfred was looking at the map and the cryptic verses.

To Lammana thou must go
Across t'sea, a verdant Isle
There you'll find a place next the sea
And treasure there be found.

Above the waves that judge a soul
A stairway to a heavenly Isle
There you'll find a place next the sea
And treasure be yours to keep.

To Lammana thou must go
And seek the pious dead
Deliver thou self to a sacred shrine
And treasure be mine to tell.

He looked baffled.

'I'm not sure that these new lines help solve the problem. If anything, they create even more of a conundrum,' he said. 'I cannot make much sense of them. Waves that judge the soul? That may be referring to him as a seafarer. A pirate maybe? A stairway to a heavenly Isle? But where? Looe Island perhaps. The last two lines are effectively a repeat of the first verse. And the final verse. We're back to Lammana again except we are to seek the pious dead. A graveyard? A sacred shrine? And now the treasure is for him to tell.'

'It is indeed a conundrum,' interjected Caroline.

'And there's still no clue as to where the treasure is,' replied Alfred.

They sighed with frustration.

Robert was aware of the rhetorical conversation taking place but it was washing over him, its contents a glaze in his mind. He wasn't interested in deciphering the riddle, not yet at least. He was still focused on Tara. There was something she had said and he couldn't quite recall it. Something about a treasure map.

Caroline could see he was a distant spectator and realised his musings were for the lamented woman. She herself had, in the end, come to respect and admire her, even if she was a little jealous of her magnetic attraction. It was that thought which had jogged her memory.

She had stumbled across the magnetron when she was at Smuggler's Cottage. Tom had gleefully explained that he had got it working and that Jake and Siegfried had performed a geophysical survey of the Island, not all, but those places which may have been used to bury treasure. It had produced a negative result. It didn't mean that there wasn't a cache there, but it was unlikely. That had implications concerning the riddle, thought Caroline, and proceeded to disappoint Alfred even further. Having explained the circumstances, he was now deflated.

'I guess it's the end of our search,' he dolefully declared.

'For the moment,' replied Caroline. 'Let's sleep on it. Maybe tomorrow will bring fresh ideas.'

It was then that Robert burst out, 'I've solved it!'

* * *

Eureka moments are usually the preserve of the eminent academic or the gifted person. Important discoveries don't just happen though. They are usually the result of years of research and sleepless nights, often ending in dead-ends, but through shear perseverance the breakthrough is made from that spark of genius. Robert didn't think he was an eminent academic nor a gifted person and he certainly didn't spend hours over the riddle trying to decipher its meaning, but he did have that spark of genius.

Caroline and Alfred looked at the outburst in complete surprise, as though he had discovered the secret to alchemy. In some way, he had. Not the distillation of base metals, but the detached lateral thinking, an abstract deconstruction of each line in the verses to produce a concentrate of the thesis, the original thought process of the Pirate Captain who wanted it to remain a mystery to all but the worthy. And as Robert proclaimed his moment of triumph, he did indeed think he was a worthy contender for the crown.

But he had an advantage. He had seen the Pirate's cottage in Ireland. For that is what the riddle was about. The verdant land was Ireland and Lammana was his cottage there, next to the sea, named in honour of the Island he knew. He built it, or had it built, a replica of his family home, probably where he had good memories. What treasure was to be found there, in Ireland, he did not know, but for the person who solved the riddle, the treasure was theirs to keep.

Robert was now viewed through a different lens, a man who could conjure, out of thin air, the solution to a seemingly intractable problem.

'How did you do it?' said Caroline.

'The solution was elementary in the end, worthy of the detective himself, I reckon. I have to admit, though, it was Siegfried who inspired me. But it was my deduction. When I had told Siegfried about the cottage, its location next to the sea on a peninsula, at the very end of the Ring of Kerry, he had looked at the map, quite intently, almost with a second vision. And then he smiled. It was a smile of confirmation, that what I had described was all true and that it fitted. Except, if you look at the outline, it doesn't. But that outline is inverted. Look from the other side and you see the true coastline. The coastline of the

Dingle Peninsula and the Ring of Kerry. Siegfried saw that. That's why he smiled.'

'Quite a deduction indeed,' declared Alfred. He inverted the map and then announced, 'But there's only one problem...'

'I know. The mark now lies out in the sea.'

'A slight problem, I would say,' said Caroline.

'But it's not,' replied Robert. 'Just off the peninsula lies the island of Skellig Michael. And guess what, it used to be the home to a monastic order. The same Benedictine order as on Looe Island. What's striking about the island is that there are over six hundred steps up to the monastic buildings which sit atop a rock pinnacle. A true stairway to a heavenly isle.'

'That is interesting. But what about this stray mark?' interrupted Alfred, pointing to a Christian cross that didn't seem to be part of the map.

'I'm not entirely sure, but nearby is a high mountain well over three thousand feet.'

'Not Carountoohil?' interrupted Caroline with a tone of foreboding, for she knew all about Robert's ordeal.

'Yes, Carountoohil. That's immaterial. What could be significant is that a metal cross stands on its summit. Whether a cross was present in Colliver's day is unknown. But my guess is that the cross refers to the mountain. What the exact significance of it is, I don't know.'

'And from all this, you have concluded that this map refers to a cottage in Ireland?' questioned Alfred.

'Yes, but not any old cottage. It was the riddle, though, that made me think of that. What if it wasn't here, in Looe? What if the Pirate went to Ireland and settled there? The verdant isle refers to Ireland. Across the Irish Sea. Perhaps he had had enough of piracy, especially after the trial of William Kidd. He took his treasure haul with him. For some reason he buried it over there and left, or maybe he died there, unknown, having changed his name. It would have been easy enough in those days.'

'That sounds plausible,' said Alfred, 'but there's no evidence to support your theory, other than conjecture.'

'True, but there again, there is nothing to say he didn't. And nothing is known of his whereabouts after the trial in London, or even when he died. If he had remained here, then I suspect there would be some record of him. And I go back to the identical cottages. What chance is there, that two identical cottages exist so far apart?' replied Robert.

There was a moment's pause while the three of them, with their own private thoughts as to the next move, waited for somebody else to say the obvious. It was Caroline who did so.

'Well, there's only one way to find out,' she said, 'we'll have to go across to Ireland, to County Kerry and to this cottage. You know where it is.'

'I do. I will never forget. But it's been almost twenty years since I was last there and it may not be there anymore.'

'Then let's hope it is, otherwise we may have had a wasted journey. One thing is certain, we have to go,' replied Caroline.

Alfred was now quiet. He didn't feel that the journey was worth the effort. He still believed that the treasure was here, in Looe, not hundreds of miles away in a cottage that was identical to the one here.

'I don't feel up to a road trip,' he remarked. 'I'll stay here and await your return.'

'You must come,' replied Caroline. 'It'll be an adventure.'

'I don't need any more of those in my life. Besides, I'll be a burden to you. You'll be able to travel much faster on your own.'

'Nonsense,' said Robert.

'I've made my decision. You will not alter it.'

Robert and Caroline acquiesced to his stubbornness. They would set out the following day and, all being well, would be in County Kerry within twenty-four hours. It was the first time in four years that they had travelled and they were looking forward to another adventure, only this time there was a mystery to solve and the prospect of riches to be discovered.

Alfred was a little envious and did consider the journey too arduous for him, but in truth, he had his own agenda. He still believed the treasure was hidden in Looe, and he thought he knew where it might be. In fact, if his translation of Caroline's Latin inscription was correct, then he was sure it was in Robert's cottage, underground in the crypt.

61

Ireland is indeed a verdant land. Its position means that it receives the first torrents of rain from Atlantic weather fronts, advancing clouds of water that want to deposit their moisture upon the hills of the emerald Isle and County Kerry is at the vanguard, the first landfall that south westerly storms confront.

It is no accident that the county records some of the highest rainfall totals in the British Isles with the high mountains forcing clouds to ascend, cool and condense, dropping their moisture on the land. Robert and Caroline, as they drove through the weather, could testify to that. Their car was being lashed by torrential wind and rain that must have been ordered especially for them, as a gift from the Heavens to say welcome to this beautiful land where I bestow life in abundance, but beware for those that dare defy my commandments, for I shall have my revenge.

The two treasure hunters had driven in a well organised relay and without a break, save for the ferry crossing from Fishguard to Rosslare, non-stop since their departure. They were exhausted as their destination of Killarney entered the horizon. Caroline was driving the final stretch. She had insisted, realising that it would be traumatic for Robert returning to a place that held deleterious memories. She herself was intrigued to visit the scene of his nightmare which had often woken her, hearing Robert's screams of inconsolable pain and the torture of his soul, so much so, that she often wondered if he were two people, the kind and gentle Robert she knew and the man who had suffered a crucifixion of the mind. Perhaps it was good he was returning. Perhaps he would finally purge the demons. One way or another, she thought, it would either cure him or tip him over into the abyss of despair. Perhaps it wasn't a good idea he was returning, was her final thought.

It was late afternoon as they approached the small town of Killarney. Caroline's thoughts changed gear to the countryside and the looming massif of the Macgillycuddy's Reeks, situated only a few miles south west of the town and which dominated the landscape. It was beautiful. Kerry was beautiful. But she had been disappointed with much of the drive, having expected to see quaint cottages and villages of interest along the way. Instead, the roadside seemed to be populated with modern bungalows and houses with little or no character, which disappointed her preconceived perception, probably accentuated by a romantic notion of a Celtic world where leprechauns lived in hobbit-style dwellings, a throwback to her childhood literature.

There was no such romantic view for Robert. His was the harsh world of a forlorn love. It was a moment if not of dread, then one that Robert had been anxious about, wondering how he would feel back in the heart of his demons, where a God had decided his destiny. The storm seemed to be a prophetic omen. He could feel the tension build within him, a tightening of the sinews, a dryness in the throat, a palpable increase in his heartbeat that seemed to signal an examination of his soul that hadn't been properly exorcised since that fateful day over two decades ago.

He looked at the mountains. They were now beginning to reveal themselves. The weather front, that had battered them since disembarking from the crossing, was now behind them and the sky was clearing, inducing shafts of sunlight through the clouds. The summit of Carountoonhil was still obscured by a blanket of cloud, a curtain that was closed, but in his mind he pulled back the drapes and could see its icon pointing towards the heavens. There was the mountain with its cross visible to all who wanted to make that spiritual journey to the edge of heaven. Only don't defy its sanctity, he thought. Don't make love in the shadow of the cross. He will take you. He will destroy you. He will have His revenge.

Even from the distance of the road, just a few miles from Killarney, the mountain was having its effect, as though its magnetism was disorienting Robert's moral compass, spinning his thoughts in all directions so he was unable to discern a pacified north from a troubled south. Then suddenly the clouds parted, and in the afternoon sun the cross glinted in his eyes, beckoning him to confront his demons, exhorting him to make that journey once more. And although he was in Kerry to solve a treasure mystery, the mountain seemed more important now and knew he must climb Carrantuohill one more time to be close with Madeleine, to commune with her on the edge of heaven and say farewell, the final act in a fateful tragedy.

∗ ∗ ∗

Killarney was a charming town. It was surrounded by mountains and lay approximately at sea level with a large loch to its south western side, the home to Ross Castle and an old Franciscan Abbey. The town itself pleased Caroline, with a mixture of architecture giving it a sense of history and a character lacking in other places they had passed through on the journey from Rosslare. There seemed to be a plethora of public houses all proclaiming the universal elixir of Ireland. Most had live music playing well into the night, as they strolled around the centre of town to stretch their legs and find a place to eat.

Robert spotted Flanagan's Bar, a place he and Madeleine used to frequent, where they would listen to traditional Irish music played by skilled musicians, who had more talent than modern pop stars, and drink pints of Guinness as though it were a life-giving beverage. It was, to their young constitutions, although he now thought that there was some sort of bravado in his youth, as though he had to show that he could take his drink and be a man amongst men. He couldn't. Madeleine was the drinker and she could win any contest, having been breast fed it from birth, she often joked.

It was the height of the tourist season and the town was alive with people. Street buskers were playing impromptu recitals, mainly on fiddles, creating a carnival atmosphere in the town centre, with the torrential rain of early afternoon having given way to clearing skies and late evening sunshine. Families and courting couples were taking rides down to the lakeside in horse-drawn carriages, jaunting cars as they are called, the local jarveys renowned for their storytelling, gesticulating tales of Irish folklore.

Everybody was taking advantage of a lull in the weather, the warm front having moved through. Conditions were due to deteriorate the following day as the cold front made its passage, whilst in its wake was another unusually deep low pressure system for August, tracking fast across the Atlantic. The jet-stream was to blame, said the meteorologists, although that was no consolation for the people who had come for a fortnight of sun, sea and sand. The locals would say, don't come to Ireland if that's what you're looking for, best head south for that.

It was almost like a mini-break for Robert and Caroline, travelling together once more, although under different circumstances and certainly not their usual style of travel. They did once hire a four-wheel Land cruiser and ventured into the Chilean Andes and the Bolivian Altiplano, but their mode of travel was usually local buses often sharing seats with chickens and even a pig on one occasion which, much to the surprise of the owner, gave birth to a litter on the cabin floor. And with seemingly the entire population of a country crammed on the bus, where privacy was no option, it provided a microcosm of humanity and an insight to cultures so very much different from Western society.

The journey to Killarney had been more civilised, if a little boring, according to Caroline and despite the lack of interest, she was enjoying the road trip. Robert though, was still consumed by his demons. They were simmering. Not yet taking him over. But he could sense an eruption of emotions any time and wanted to get the visit to the cottage over with, climb the mountain and return to his own idyll by the sea.

* * *

The following day dawned bright and clear with high level clouds creating an opaque haziness to the sun. It was warm. There was no hint of an approaching weather front, save for the first tendrils of cirrus clouds that loomed on the western horizon. Robert and Caroline had a good breakfast, packed their bags, and headed west towards Killorglin, to pick up the road that was the Ring of Kerry.

It traverses the Iveragh Peninsula that lies between Dingle Bay to the north and the Kenmare Estuary to the south, skirting the coastline, with endless picturesque views around every bend in the road, both out to sea and inland towards the mountains. It is famed for its beauty and can become busy in the summer, so the two set off early to avoid the crowded highways which in places are narrow, creating bottlenecks of traffic and irate drivers used to a faster pace of travel.

The cottage was located at the end of the peninsula close to the small town of Ballinskelligs, down a rough dirt track that had seen little use other than the occasional tractor. That would have been a more suitable mode of transport, for their car almost became grounded in the rutted track and several times they found themselves almost stuck in mud, unable to move but for Robert pushing them free. It was worse than he remembered. Twenty years ago he recalled no such problems. Indeed, the ease of access was one of the advantages, realising that even then vehicular transport was a necessary part of living in such a remote place.

As they got closer and closer to the cottage, Robert felt uneasiness in his mind. Was it wise to revisit a lost life, an idyll that was never fulfilled? How would he react to seeing it again? He felt a presence following him, wanting to see his reaction. He looked around to see if anything was there. Nothing. No Madeleine. Just another vehicle in the distance, a farmer's Landrover, he thought, perhaps curious as to the intruders.

Caroline could sense his anxiety. She herself was on edge, visiting a place from Robert's past. She could feel Madeleine's ghost looking within her, examining her worthiness, judging whether she was the right person for Robert. Madeleine had been put on a pedestal and no amount of reassurance from Robert was going to deflect her own self-judging inadequacies. She wanted Madeleine's approval.

As the cottage came into view, Caroline couldn't immediately see the similarity with Lammana for the roof had collapsed leaving just a shell, a ruin that nature was reclaiming, with ivy and all manner of young saplings and shrubs. Robert's heart sank. It was not the cottage he had last witnessed, had sat outside discussing his and Madeleine's future together, planning and mapping out their lives. Now there was no resemblance to his new idyll, save for the two gable end walls with their prominent chimney stacks and the collapsing side walls, still proudly defying the elements, the window frames having long since rotted away. It was now a skeleton, a lifeless collection of stones in which other life was now seeking an existence. Ferns and wild flowers were colonising crumbling mortar whilst small birds were taking advantage of ready-made holes to make a nest and raise a second brood before autumn set in. Rather than a human idyll, it had now become a natural one, the perfect haven for wildlife, which was not lost on Robert. It was perhaps a fitting end, he thought.

But the view from the front hadn't changed. Looking west, the Skellig Islands were clearly visible, about eight miles off Bolus Head. Not like Looe Island, for they were little more than rock outcrops that had once supported a small community of monks, that were now uninhabited, but visited by tourists to see the place where man used to live in the service of God.

Robert had been there himself. It was a harsh place. Little shelter, but for the stone buildings they had constructed, almost hewn out of the rock itself, high above the ranging tempests below. It reminded him of heaven, where the gods looked down upon the poor souls who had to climb the stairway to salvation, an act of pious pilgrimage from the sea that could swallow a boat into the bowls of hell, even on a calm day, but for the skill of the boatman.

The sea was calm today, although he knew out on the Skelligs it would be anything but that. Caroline was intrigued about the islands and would have liked to have visited them, if only to find that connection Robert was talking about. They both liked wild and remote places, far from the madding crowds, and from the mainland they seemed the personification of that trait. But first they were on a treasure hunt, something which her academic mindset had found difficult to reconcile.

Robert turned and looked at the façade. The porch had gone. All that remained was a wooden front door which was hanging loosely from a single hinge. He pushed it open and ominously it clattered to the ground. Inside, the internal walls were still intact, bare, with evidence of some plaster. He looked up to see the sky, the upper floor having collapsed long ago and the partition walls of the bedrooms decayed as well. Unlike his present cottage there was no lean-to at the rear, the kitchen being to the left of the ground floor and a living room to the right. He peered into what was the living room. It displayed years of neglect, vegetation now growing through the stone flags and lichen and moss inhabiting the walls, a testimony to its decline. A young ash tree was establishing itself in the centre of the room protected, for now, from the prevailing winds. And in a hole in the gable wall a wren was nesting with signs of some fledglings nearby.

If the living room resembled a nature reserve, the kitchen was certainly not. It startled him. He had disturbed a blackbird which, with its characteristic squeal, flew off out through the empty void of the window. But it wasn't the bird that had startled him. It was the obvious signs of somebody having been digging and quite recently. Rubble had been deposited around the room and in the centre was an empty space which, as Robert edged towards it, he could see, much to his disappointment, was not a crypt as in his own cottage, but a small chamber about the size of a chest inside which was a lead box, a reliquary, much like those to be found in chapels. Except here there were no bones or relics to a saint: just an empty space. The box had been opened and whatever was inside, if there was treasure to be found at all, somebody had beaten them to it and removed its contents.

Robert and Caroline looked at each other and thought the same thing.

'It's got to be him,' said Robert.

'But he died in the inferno.'

'Maybe he didn't.'

'Nobody could have survived.'

'But he's not a nobody. He's a hulk of a man, who has no doubt witnessed such annihilation before.'

Robert and Caroline dare not mention his name. They felt by doing so, it would resurrect him, summon him and bring him back from the dead, to haunt them once more.

'Well, whoever it was, they have whatever treasure there was here,' said Caroline, now resigned to a fruitless quest.

'I could curse that man,' Robert said vehemently, kicking the box and only realising it would hurt him after the event. 'I curse you Siegfried.'

Robert slumped to the ground followed by Caroline.

They sat there for a few minutes, heads cowered, dejected, lost in their own thoughts, oblivious to a shadow that had cast across them. It was Caroline who noticed the change, having felt some unearthly presence. She looked up. The sun had been obscured by the hulk of a man standing above them both, looking down at the two figures whom had finally been defeated. Caroline shook Robert's arm, unable to utter a word. He looked up, dumbfounded, to see a resurrected Siegfried.

62

obert and Caroline could make out the silhouette of the broad, tall man. Their nemesis had returned to seek a final revenge. They were in a hopeless position with no means of escape and if there was an end, this was most certainly that time.

'I assume you are referring to me,' came a voice from above, the familiar sonorous voice of a Scottish heathen. He stood there, triumphant. 'Am I to suppose, that I'm a Wagnerian villain...Or perhaps a hero,' he continued.

'Villain,' replied Robert, forcefully. 'And an evil one at that.'

'You do me an injustice.'

'Do I? Didn't you kill that bird man?'

'No. It was an accident. If I had intended to kill him, then I would not have left a body to be discovered half way down the cliff.'

'But you did kill the man in the cave, Tara's relative, Jake,' continued Robert's interrogation.

'Another unfortunate accident. It was he who confronted me. He told me to leave the Island and not return. I refused. The next thing I knew he was wielding a grappling hook, swinging it on a rope, hell bent on impaling me with it. I had to defend myself.'

'So you killed him?'

'I managed to grab the hook and pulled on it. He careered over the side of the landing wall in the cave and hit his head on the rocks below. As I said, an accident. And remember, I could have killed you once, but I didn't.'

'True. But accidents seem to be your trade mark. Was my mother another accident?'

'I admit to breaking into her house to steal the map. Your mother was asleep. I did not wake her nor do anything to her. She must have passed away in her sleep sometime. Surely the doctor would've seen that. It was a coincidence and I'm sorry to have violated your memory. And before you mention it, the lamp was a decoy. Just too good an opportunity. It was quite a magnificent item.'

'At least its back where it belongs.'

'You now have it? I am glad. Truly I am. My business often entails necessary evils, something which I try to avoid. I am not the ogre you think I am.'

'In the cave, you were going to kill Tara, before that man pulled the trigger.'

'I admit, it had occurred to me. She was in my way.'

'And what of the rest of us in the chamber?' interjected Caroline.

'Let's just say the inferno took care of that situation.'

'How did you escape it?'

'I anticipated the situation. Always have an escape route. And mine was the tunnel full of water. That was yours as well.'

Siegfried now stepped closer away from the glare of the sun, so that Robert and Caroline could see his face. It was disfigured with reddish scars, a result of the fireball.

'As you can see, I did not escape unscathed. But I am alive, unlike the callow young boy. He was the son of Frederick Thomas. What he was doing there I don't really know. And why he should defend Tara, is anybody's guess. It's a tragedy that he died. But when you play with fire...'

'Yes, we know about him.'

The arena went silent for a moment, both parties having exhausted their preliminary engagement. Siegfried looked at the open casket.

'I expect you were hoping to find untold riches? Gold or silver, pieces-of-eight? Perhaps diamonds or other precious jewels? If you were, you'd be disappointed. For there were none. I found it empty. But there's more to a treasure haul than gold and gems. This treasure is far richer. In fact, it is priceless. You, Caroline, will appreciate it. An historian seeking truth. Only this treasure tells a tale that has never been told before and I expect, will rewrite history, for I am sure there is more to be discovered.'

Siegfried paused to look at Caroline, her face the embodiment of professional curiosity.

'Do you know of the great storm of November 1703?'

'Yes,' replied Caroline, 'the one which destroyed the newly constructed Eddystone lighthouse and killed an estimated eight thousand people.'

'Yes, that one,' said Siegfried. 'Well apparently during that storm, here, just off the coast, a large galleon founded on the Skellig rocks. Everybody was drowned, save one person, the ship's captain. He was hauled from the raging sea by the few inhabitants of the island, a community of hermit monks. They rescued him and looked after him for many months until he was strong enough to return to the mainland. That man, so the local legend has it, was a pirate captain. He gave his name as Vening, John Vening. Something happened to him on that island for he never returned to the sea. He stayed and became a local notoriety, a man who devoted himself to the good of others. Every year, it is reputed, as an act of penance for his sins he would drag a huge wooden cross up the nearby mountain in bare feet, so that the pain would remind him of his saviour. There he fasted for forty days to mirror Jesus's time in the desert. It's today known as Carrauntoohil, the highest peak in all of Ireland.'

'Is that why there's a cross upon its summit today?' enquired Robert.

'The exact reason is a little obscure, although some believe it is in recognition of the act of piety by this man. Whatever the reason, it has become a personal pilgrimage for many, to follow in his footsteps and be the closest to God in all of Ireland. It's similar to the venerated mountain, Croagh Patrick in County Mayo, where every year pilgrims make the arduous journey, many barefoot, some dragging crosses, to the summit as a celebration of St Patrick, Ireland's patron saint. He fasted for forty days on top of the mountain and it is recorded that this John Vening did the same.'

Siegfried fell silent and the chamber filled with tension, Robert and Caroline wondering what his next move was, a man whose anomie spoke volumes in the silence of the moment.

'I expect you're wondering what I'm going to do,' he declared seeing the two look at one another with apprehension, a mannerism which was all too familiar.

'It had crossed our minds. Arrange another accident, no doubt,' replied Caroline.

'Now there's gratitude.'

'Then why have you come here, if not to kill us?' said Robert.

'I knew you would come. I just had to wait in Killarney until you turned up and then follow you here. It was easy. What wasn't so easy was finding out the information I have just told you.'

'Why have you?' enquired Robert.

'Because I've come to offer you a proposition. Well, not so much a proposition, more of an ultimatum.'

'And there I thought you might have reformed,' answered Robert in a sarcastic tone.

'I have,' said Siegfried.

'Tell that to the judge.'

'You do me another injustice, although I can understand your sentiment. Before I offer you the ultimatum, there is more to tell. It concerns the so-called John Vening. My enquiries have discovered that there was a Vening family in Looe around the turn of the seventeenth century. And in 1727 there is a record of a John Vening having been on Looe Island. Now, according to records, there is no trace of John Vening here in Kerry, after that date. My thesis is that John Vening was none other than Robert Colliver, the Pirate Captain, and that he assumed this pseudonym from his local Looe knowledge, as a man who was invisible, unknown to anybody. It suited his purpose, for he dare not go by his real name for fear of exposure. And, as I've indicated, I think he was now a reformed man, one who wanted to return to his birthplace and be buried there. A skeleton was discovered on the Island which, to this day, has never been identified. It remains a mystery. The Pirate's treasure, if he ever had one, is probably lost beneath the waves off the Skellig Islands. But his story is treasure enough. A pirate, a hated man who murdered innocent people to acquire wealth, only to be touched by some divine spirituality, perhaps finding God, certainly helping his fellow human beings and who wanted to find peace at the end of his life.'

'It's all circumstantial. There's no proof,' said Caroline, interested in his theory.

'True. But let me tell you a tale recounted by my father of another Englishman, a man named John Newton, a seafarer like Colliver. He was, according to his own words, a blasphemous rogue, an infidel and libertine, prone to profanities, gambling and drink. He was involved in the monstrous and wicked slave trade. On one such voyage in May 1748, he was on his way back to these shores when the ship foundered in a storm off the coast of Donegal. As it began to sink, he found himself trapped inside a cabin with no means of escape. All hope was lost. He prayed to the Lord for deliverance and, quite miraculously, a cargo of beeswax and dyers wood broke loose and stopped up the hole in the vessel thereby allowing it to drift to safety. This event changed him. He converted to Evangelical Christianity eventually becoming a respected Anglican priest, who is today remembered for his well-known hymns. He even became an advocate for the abolition of the slave trade, thus completing his conversion from sinner to redeemer.'

Siegfried paused again and looked at his two adversaries. He was feeling piteous, for he had come to a momentous decision and that decision meant that he had to say farewell to them.

'This case contains my investigations, notes and some photocopies of documents that I've made. They are for you.   Make what you will of them.'

'Then you're not going to kill us?' queried Caroline.

'Indeed no. Very few people have got the better of me over the years. You may not believe this, but I have come to respect your abilities to escape my best laid plans. I'm glad. I now realise it is your destiny to find out the truth. For me, the Pirate Captain's reformation is quite inspirational. Something affected him here. On Skellig. That same spirit has touched me.'

'Do you expect us to believe that?' retorted Robert.

Siegfried looked at Robert with a sense of disappointment, almost sadness that he was still vilified.

'Let me tell one more tale then, one that is recounted first hand by its narrator. My father was a Presbyterian Preacher. He was a harsh, tall man, full of anger and conviction. He instilled into me, by any means but usually by frequent beatings, the scriptures and his faith. As a young lad I could not argue with such evangelical hysteria and submitted to his fervour. But later in my youth, particularly as I grew in stature, I started to rebel, so much so that he threw me out of the family home. I had to make my own way in life and chose the army. I served for many years, with distinction I might add, eventually leaving to become a mercenary in Africa. There I was part of a militia overthrowing despot rulers and revolutionary dictators, where life was cheap and where I witnessed humanity at its worst. It suited me and my emotions, for I imagined I was purging my inner hatred, redeeming a soul that had been lost in the bigoted highlands of Scotland. To cut a long story short, I returned to Britain where I secured a job with an investment bank, a sort of fix-it security service where my role was to intimidate and, where necessary, forcibly remove obstacles in the path of their business of asset stripping. It was there that I was approached by Frederick Thomas to secure art objects for him. In doing so, I found myself acting as though I was back in Africa where the mission was the *de-facto* regime. I'm not proud of some things that I have done, not least my actions towards both of you for which I am sorry and I apologise. You may or may not believe me, but I have changed. I have finally found my place in this world and I now know, thanks to your enduring qualities, what I must do.'

Robert and Caroline looked at one another, wondering if they could believe their ears. Had Siegfried found redemption? Was he a changed man, like the Pirate Captain? Both seemed fanciful. Given all that had happened to them at the hands of this man, it was preposterous to think he could metamorphose into a pious individual who would show mercy.

They looked up to confirm their scepticism, to confront him for the last time, but he had gone. Instead, the sun was shining into the chamber, illuminating its interior as though they had found a utopian space in which, once more, to give thanks for salvation. They heard the sound of a vehicle pull away. They looked at one another and hugged in an embrace that described finality to their ordeals.

63

Islands embody an insular emotion. Stay on one for any length of time and that emotion touches the soul with questions. Questions concerning life and our place within it. For the boundary of life is the perceived ocean, the horizon of existence, a clear discontinuity between this world and the next. Add to that turmoil the religious convictions of faith or uncertainty, and the result is either enlightenment or madness.

Those that make the journey to Skellig Michael may be considered mad for challenging the sea to a duel, much like the early pioneers of Trinity House. The lighthouse keepers there had conviction, but some are documented to have become delirious through the isolation, to the extent that murders were committed upon those remote Towers of Hercules.

The early monks challenged the sea. Not in a motorised pleasure launch, but a currach large enough for a few tough individuals to row eight or so miles in an unforgiving ocean. They were not insane. They were redoubtable in their faith. And the reward for deliverance to the rocky crag thrusting its way to heaven was privation, self-deprivation and spiritual suffering, to gain God's favour in a world where greed and lust were the Devil's temptations and a passage to damnation.

Robert and Caroline had emerged from within the cottage and were now sitting on a low dry-stone wall covered in a mosaic of lichen, concealing a herring-bone pattern in the slates that was reminiscent of Cornish stone hedges. In the morning sunshine, they breathed the fresh air of relief. It felt good. They hadn't found any treasure, but as Siegfried himself had proclaimed, the story was treasure enough.

And what a story, if it was true? Only they really hadn't any concrete evidence to support it.

'It doesn't matter that we cannot prove it. At least we can believe that the cruel Pirate Captain found redemption on that Island and became a good man,' said Robert, as he looked towards Skellig Michael.

'And his legacy lives on in the cross on top of the mountain,' replied Caroline, as her gaze fell upon a fallen cross a few yards away. It looked interesting. Why, she could not say, for she had looked at many Celtic crosses in her time, although this one looked out of place, a Christian icon in a secular setting. It seemed to have its own unique pattern of lines and coils, Celtic knot work of interleaving serpents that were a signature to a pagan world and which she found alluring, much like the magnificent artwork in the celebrated *Book of Kells*.

The cross was perhaps about five feet high and recumbent, its obverse side obscured from view. She was disappointed, having to be content with the less decorative reverse side, but as she inspected the stone work some Latin inscription became visible beneath a crust of centuries old coloured lichen.

'Of course it would be in Latin,' she told herself, although she was aware that in this part of Ireland an old script called Ogham was often used, something which she had encountered on a cross in a churchyard in Cornwall. This script was in Latin though. But more than that, it was an inscription which she immediately recognised.

IN SALUTEM NOBIS CONFIDIMUS

'It's the same as on the altar!' she exclaimed with a degree of excitement, realising the significance and looking towards Robert, who was still focused on the Islands.

'What?' replied Robert, still immersed in the Island's foreboding rocks rising abruptly from the sea, thinking what life would have been like there all those centuries ago. They looked close. Close enough to feel their history, a magnetism that attracted the gaze. Two almost perfect pinnacles of rock emerging from the sea, thrusting resolutely towards heaven, projecting a message of divinity for the onlooker.

It must have been the same for the early Christian monks and was perhaps why they felt compelled to make a life upon one of them.

'There's an inscription on this cross, and it's the same as on the altar in the crypt at your cottage,' she emphasised.

'I think you're imagining a connection now,' was his unconvinced reply.

'No really. It's the same. Trust in Salvation.'

Robert got down from the wall and strode the few yards to the fallen cross. He peered at the inscription.

'Can't see it myself,' he calmly added.

'You need to view it at a certain angle.'

He did so, and could see what Caroline meant.

'Too much of a coincidence,' he announced, as he ran his hands across the inscription to feel its outline.

'Indeed. It can only mean one thing. That perhaps Siegfried was right. He was here.'

'Did Siegfried miss it?'

'Maybe? The words are etched so faintly now and covered in lichen. It's the sun which has created shadows to illuminate the inscription. No sun and it would be impossible to see, even by torchlight.'

Now Caroline looked out to the horizon and realised that she must go there. The sun was shining a beacon of light upon the summit of the furthest outcrop, enticing the two disciples to discover its spiritual aura, to explore the place where an evil Pirate Captain may have found redemption and where their nemesis had been converted into a righteous path.

'We need to go out there?' suggested Robert, knowing full well that she was about to request the same thing.

'Yes, we need to see the place. What spirituality exists there to be so powerful that it changed a man?' she replied.

'Apparently two men,' said Robert.

* * *

Skellig Michael is the furthest Island from the mainland, a good half a mile from the inner, uninhabited rock, which must have made the arduous journey even more rewarding in the service of God.

The boat that goes out to the Skelligs leaves from Portmagee, a tiny cluster of houses located on the mainland opposite Valencia Island, a large outlier connected by a bridge a few miles away. It didn't take Robert and Caroline long to get to the quayside of Portmagee but as they pulled into a small car park in front of a jetty they could see a launch, full with passengers, having already left for open water. Their hopes were dashed.

They sat on a nearby bench and considered their options, although they were somewhat limited. A modern fibreglass launch about thirty feet in length with a forward cabin was still moored by the jetty, advertising trips to the Skelligs. There was no sign of anybody on board and so Robert went into a hostelry opposite the quayside and enquired if there were any more trips that day. A bar-tender, in a broad Irish accent which Robert had difficulty in understanding, gave an ambiguous reply that the skipper had cancelled the trip but that there may be one if enough people turned up. Robert took that to mean that just the two of them didn't warrant a trip and left to inform Caroline.

After ten minutes of waiting, another couple, in their sixties arrived and were interested in the boat trip. Robert explained the situation to them, that the trip may or may not occur, to which they all agreed on the easy-going and laid-back disposition of the Irish and how refreshing it was, if a little annoying on this occasion.

Another ten minutes passed and nobody else arrived, to which Robert and Caroline realised that perhaps they were not going to see the island. But as they were about to leave the skipper materialised from the hostelry, the very same man whom Robert had spoken to behind the bar, and they watched him head for the only launch left moored at the quayside.

'You four for the Skelligs?' he bellowed as he clambered aboard the vessel.

As they all boarded and paid the skipper the fare, with a wry smile he commented, 'hope you have your sea legs on today. It may be rough.'

As the launch left the harbour the sea seemed quite calm and all four wondered what the skipper was alluding to. But as it cleared Valencia Island to the north, and the shelter of Bray Head, heading south east to the Skelligs, the swell became increasingly heavy and the vessel began to pitch up and down, each time dowsing the deck in spray causing the other two passengers to seek refuge in the small cabin, whilst Robert and Caroline remained steadfast, taking in the elemental force of the sea.

It took over half an hour to reach the first of the Islands, an uninhabited rock outcrop, precursor to the larger and more imposing Skellig Michael. The skipper circled it so that the four of them could wonder at the spectacle of thousands of sea birds clinging to the cliff face, seemingly impossible to hold an egg or young fledgling. By early August many of the nesting population had left, having raised their young, and were now out at sea, only to return the following spring. Even so, the rock was still a wondrous sight with gannets, fulmars and kittiwakes still clinging to precipitous rock ledges, juvenile birds sitting in their nests waiting for the parents to return with fish and sand eels.

Despite the reduced population, the noise was deafening. The skipper informed his passengers that during the height of the nesting season the rock contained over thirty thousand pairs of gannets, the second largest colony in the world. It was also home to storm petrels, manx shearwaters, guillemots and razorbills, as well as those favourites, puffins. When Robert had visited the Islands it was during the breeding season and he had witnessed that spectacle himself, when such bird populations were even more abundant. For Caroline, it was a revelation and now she realised why such avian creatures could fascinate people, for it was truly a wonder of nature.

Skellig Michael rises majestically from the sea, a pyramid of rock towering over seven hundred feet from the crashing waves, and is composed of the same Devonian sandstone that Looe is blessed with. The two Skellig islands are an outlier of a geological outcrop which forms the backbone of Kerry, from Killarney, along the MacGillycuddy's Reeks, to the south western headland where the ruined cottage is located. Looking back, Robert could just make out the cottage through his binoculars, and could see why such a place left the Pirate Captain bewitched and changed his outlook on life. It had cast its spell upon him and Madeleine, only fate had ripped their idyll apart.

The launch pulled up alongside a stone jetty and what greeted Robert and Caroline was a tier of steps, over six-hundred of them. Some were hewn out of the rock itself, projecting themselves skywards and seemingly so steep that climbing it would be near impossible. In fact, the ascent is the easiest. It's coming back down that tests the nerves of the casual tourist, like climbing the Great Pyramid of Giza where the only way down is on one's backside. As they disembarked, there was a moan and groan from the elderly couple about the Herculean task ahead and no handrails, the wife observed. But the reward is a stupendous view from the summit and the remarkable remains of the sixth century monastery where monks built a life of isolation from a hostile world.

The Island had its own small population of sea birds but much, much fewer and those hoping to see some puffins were disappointed, with all of them having left their burrows two months ago. But what the passengers had come to see was the monastic settlement that mainly consisted of round beehive huts constructed of stone, so well interleaved that even the worst of winter storms could not penetrate the thick walls. They reminded both Robert and Caroline of the stone huts they encountered on Easter Island, except there they were rectangular and spread out along a verdant cliff backed by the lip of an extinct volcanic crater.

But it was the sense of isolation that was omnipresent. For the inhabitants of Rapa Nui, it was an enforced isolation, for the Island is truly on its own in the middle of the Pacific with the nearest landfall thousands of miles away. Here, on Skellig, the monks chose this lifestyle, yet all the time they could see civilisation but ten miles away, even though, at times, it would be impossible to reach. They remained for over five hundred years living their life of isolation, before the Island was abandoned sometime in the thirteenth century for the more urbane life on the mainland near the town of Ballingskelligs where the ruins of their monastery can still be visited, just outside the town, despite the sea beginning to erode its presence.

They went inside one of the slate huts. It felt cosy inside out of the wind, with only the distant noise of breaking waves and screeching gannets penetrating the interior gloom. The walls were like the outside, stone faced and showing the signs of modern-day graffiti telling the casual reader of a visit some time ago or the love between two people. The other huts were the same, some better preserved than others, but each one transmitting its history for those that were tuned to its distant frequency.

'Do you really think that the Pirate Captain was rescued and nursed here?' asked Robert as they ducked below the low entrance doorway, back out into the sunlight.

'I don't know. It's possible.'

'There's something not right,' said Robert as they looked out across the vast expanse of sea, now looking rougher than when they arrived.

'What do you mean?'

'It just seems too much of a coincidence. Maybe Siegfried told a sophisticated tale to create a false trail.'

'You mean he's still after the treasure and knows something we don't and wants us to investigate a dead end.'

'Precisely that. I wouldn't put it past him.'

'If that's the case then why not just kill us in the chamber and be sure of things. There was nobody around. He could have easily done that. Yet somehow, despite his past misdeeds, there was something about the way he spoke, the intonation of his voice as though his sentiments were genuine.'

'I must admit, I detected that too.'

They went into another hut, one of the smallest, as though they were trying to find the proof they required but without any real conviction that such proof would exist. It was in the furthest recess inside that Caroline spotted something. Not graffiti, or at least not any modern day graffiti, but an inscription etched into the slate. Was she seeing something that wasn't there? She beckoned Robert to take a look. He could see the same thing. It was faint and had been over-written with a eulogy to a visit thirteen years ago. Underneath the modern dedication to some persons existence was a Latin inscription. They looked at one another. And both, at the same time, exclaimed disbelief in what they were looking at.

'It just can't be,' reiterated Robert.

But there it was. Not a complete inscription, but definitely the same as in the two cottages.

CONFIDIMUS IN SALUTEM

Caroline realised it wasn't grammatically correct, but the gist was there. It was another coincidence that couldn't be ignored. They looked at one another in astonishment. Siegfried was right. They now had their proof that Robert Colliver, the Pirate Captain, had set foot upon Skellig Michael.

Standing outside the site they could see how and why the Pirate Captain had been touched by some spiritual incantation, even though the monastic order had left long ago. He didn't succumb to madness. The place had touched his soul as it was doing to the two later day pilgrims. It was elemental. It was nature in the raw. They could feel the power of a divine spirit in the dark slates of a solid rock outcrop, in the waves crashing below them, in the buffeting wind and in the gannets hovering on thermals.

And those hermits who rescued the Pirate must have sown the seeds of such a spirit for his soul to have been converted. If the cottage on the mainland had been his sanctuary in the heavens, then Skellig Michael was several levels up the celestial scale, for it infused a sense of mystical aesthetics, other-worldly virtues where piety and penance, faith and contemplation, peace and serenity infected the psyche, altered the mind like an opiate that few places on earth can do. They had borne witness to such an effect. And despite some unanswered questions, it seemed that their adventure had finally come to an end.

64

Climbing a mountain is usually a challenge. It's a test of skill and stamina, the reward being spiritual accomplishment in reaching the summit accompanied by spectacular views, should it be cloud free. But the climb to the top of Carrauntoohil was to be different. It was to be a test of Robert's ability to challenge, not the mountain, but his demons. Challenge them to a combat. It was to be an examination of his conscience and the reward, should he defeat his nightmares, would be peace and absolution with an unexpected and providential test of faith.

The very moment when he and Caroline had made the decision to go to Kerry, he knew that two journeys had started. There was the physical one in reaching County Kerry, but more prominent was the psychological one deep inside his soul to engage the demons that had found a place within the very being of existence and exorcise them from memory. Since leaving Cornwall, he had hidden his demons behind a curtain of antipathy, determined they would not surface. But as they drove towards the mountain the following morning he could palpably feel his body tense, his mind playing images of that fateful day, and the guilt surfaced as he thought about the ordeal ahead.

Robert chose the same route in as before. He wanted to. He needed to. He had to retrace those steps of twenty years ago, a path which had been trod over and over again and etched in his mind, so much so that he could climb the route blindfolded. The western approach provided an easy access to the mountain, climbing steeply at first and levelling off as the path entered a small gully before debouching into a wide, shallow glen revealing two beautiful and serene glacial lakes.

Caroline decided that this would be the perfect spot to wait for Robert, realising this was a personal journey that he must make alone. She had a clear view up to a ridge that led to Carrauntoohil's summit, so could track his progress most of the way. In any case, she was eager to peruse Siegfried's notes that he had left and the arena in which she found herself was the perfect place, an athenaeum for her insatiable appetite for historical truth.

Robert's route to the summit was via Beenkeragh, a secondary peak less than one hundred feet below the highest point, that could only be reached by traversing a grade II listed scramble, which in fine weather was easy for Robert, but if the weather turned, could become a barrier to safety, as it was all those years ago. But the weather was still benign, with a predicted weather front still only showing signs of high-level cloud. He would be up and back with Caroline before any bad weather approached.

Like any good mountaineer, Robert had brought the necessary equipment knowing full well, even back in Cornwall, that he was going to climb the fateful mountain one more time. This time, though, there was no champagne and no love-making to distract him, just a journey to the edge of heaven to say a final farewell to Madeleine.

It was early afternoon by the time Robert had reached the first peak, which although strenuous for a body twenty years older, had been uneventful. Ahead lay the scramble across the arête. It required nerve, sometimes having to descend a few feet to negotiate a tricky section of exposed and smooth rock, before climbing back up onto the knife-edge ridge, before finally emerging to a sloping base below the imposing pinnacle of Carrauntoohil and the cross high above.

He looked back down the sheer wall of the corrie face to the lakes below which were reflecting the light streaks of cirrus clouds in the blue hues of a glassy water surface. Caroline could be seen waving to him and he waved back, a wave to say he was safe and everything would be alright with only a couple of hundred more feet to climb.

The summit, unlike all those years ago, was not deserted. A couple and a family group were eating lunch, the latter more akin to a picnic with a spread that would be worthy of a parkland banquet rather than the top of a high mountain where, as Robert could testify, the weather can change so quickly taking the unwary by surprise. And they seemed to be dressed for such a lowland venue with improper footwear and inadequate clothing.

It reminded him of Tara's brother, Tom, and how he always wore the most inappropriate attire, ignoring the weather. Tom was well padded by layers of insulating fat, but this family were all thin and wiry and he was always amazed at how people can be so ignorant of their surroundings. At least, he thought, the weather was going to be kind for them.

Fortunately, the people were not by the cross itself and so Robert was able to commune with Madeleine in peace and free from the embarrassment of talking aloud to a congregation, which was often his wont, even when fully conscious. He looked west. No longer could he see the lakes below, nor Caroline, but the view to the coast was as spectacular as he remembered. The Skellig Islands, although distant specks on the horizon, were visible, now having more significance since his visit with Caroline yesterday. To the north lay the beautiful Dingle peninsula, with the rugged backbone of mountains rising high above the spits of Inch and Rosbehy Point, impressive sandy intrusions into Dingle Bay.

This was the Kerry he remembered: standing atop Brandon Mountain, a whale-back colossus at over three thousand feet, as it plunges to the sea only a short distance away, or Bantry Bay to the south, witnessing one of the largest tidal ranges in the world. It was a magical time. But that was the past, a distant memory of hope and expectation. And now, he thought, he must finally say farewell to Madeleine and let her rest in peace. He should have done it years ago, but never had the courage to face the mountain which took her from him.

He walked up to the cross and stood in its shadow, the apex framing his chest, piercing his heart as he said his goodbyes. Tears welled up. He began to weep. A weak sobbing of the heart, remembering her as she was on that day. How they laughed and made love, pointed to the headland beyond Ballinskelligs where their idyll could be found, and planned the wedding and subsequent life that was never to happen.

'Goodbye my sweet Maddy. Rest in peace on the edge of your heaven. You shall always be in my heart. I shall never forget you.'

And as he uttered those silent words, the wind began to pick up as though acknowledging him, a breath from the edge of heaven absolving him of responsibility.

That is what Robert thought, but as he looked up from his thoughts he could see a mass of cloud on the horizon, as though time had stood still and that he and Madeleine were there all those years ago and that he would have to relive the nightmare, only more vivid, more real, before any absolution was forthcoming.

It didn't take long. Within half an hour the weather had clouded over and rain was threatening. He had made it to the ridge and began its traverse, but was only just a third of the way along with the most awkward section to still to traverse when the wind increased in strength. It was too strong to risk the exposed arête. But he had no alternative. As he scrambled on hands and knees, the heavens opened up. God was raining scorn upon his attempt to placate Him. Robert moved on, but the rocks, silky smooth when dry, were now lethal weapons to thwart his progress.

And so they did. He slipped and began to lose his balance, the rock face ready to take its next victim, another foolish adventurer who ignored the weather signs. It was only a small lip of rock that halted his slide as he clung on for dear life. He wasn't falling any more, but neither could he haul himself to safety. He tried to gain some purchase with his feet but none was forthcoming. Death was just a hand grip away. And that hand grip was a tenuous life-line which was gradually weakening. He made one almighty attempt to climb back up, but gravity denied his utmost effort. The rain was now lashing against him, weighing him down, his arms numb and about to detach themselves from his shoulder. He could feel life coming to an end.

So he hung, pressed against the rock that at least was denying his maker. Thoughts raced through his mind. Madeleine, Caroline, his mother. But those images were fleeting, for they ultimately rested upon Lammana. Why they should, he could not compute. Perhaps it was his ordeal in the black void, for his present predicament felt like that. Within his tomb he had trusted in Caroline and his Buddhist philosophy. There, the silence had awakened an omnipresent belief where trust in salvation had triumphed. Upon the mountain, the tempest that was raging both within him and outside, could not conjure that truth. But the key was trust, he realised. Trust in the power of the conscience. 'I will survive.' 'I will live.' As he uttered those words he realised it was a delusion, for there was no immediate rescue, not from the thin thread that held him from death.

Trust? Or was it belief? Perhaps faith? He was now arguing, considering, wondering. It was trust: trust in salvation. It was belief: belief in a spiritual force. It was faith: faith that God would deliver him from death. And so, high upon Madeleine's mountain, on the edge of heaven he prayed. 'Please help me,' he shouted as he tried to haul himself to safety once more, his convictions not wanting to utter His name.

God was not listening. God wanted more. God wanted truth.

'Please. Please. Have mercy,' he shouted again.

But his torment continued. How long, he had no idea, for his mind had retreated to its innermost secrets. To Madeleine. He could see her waving to him, from Heaven. She was beckoning him to make that leap from the edge, to join her with God, for he had a place for him. Tara was there too. She told him to be strong. Don't make that leap. Remain beyond the edge of Heaven and live a life with Caroline, have children and grow old, for God has other plans for you. Utter His name and He shall be kind and merciful. And with that image etched in his eyes, he looked up towards the heavens and begged, 'please God, have mercy,' an invocation that came from the depths of his soul.

And God heard his cry for life.

God in the guise of Caroline. She stretched out to grab Robert's arm and with adrenalin pumping through her veins, hauled him back from the abyss and he finally scrambled over the ledge to safety. They both collapsed in a rock hollow, exhausted, yet exalted.

'Are you alright?' she said, breathing heavily between words.

'Yes,' was all he could say as he thanked God and thanked Caroline for salvation.

They sat there in the torrential rain in silence, lost in their own thoughts. God has mercy. Somebody was watching over me, was Robert's thought. Glad I came up here, was Caroline's. They were together.

'How on earth did you find me? And what were you doing up here?' asked Robert.

'I heard a primordial scream, as if you were summoning resurrection. If you hadn't, I'd have never found you. And with the weather closing in, how could I stay down below, knowing the experience you had before. Whatever the outcome, we were going to be together.'

After about twenty minutes, the rain eased enough for them to venture from the safety of the hollow.

'We had better go back towards the summit,' said Robert, now having recovered some feeling in his limbs.

'I think you're right.'

They carefully picked their way amongst the boulders, helping each other, and cleared the ridge, making their way around the base of the summit, towards the long and exposed eastern ridge. The rain had relented but the wind was now gusting, so strong that Caroline was blown over and Robert found it near impossible to stand on occasions.

'We cannot continue. It's too dangerous,' he declared as they reached the fateful gully of Hags Glen. 'We have to go down.'

Caroline looked down. She was not convinced. But then another gust caught her and she nearly slipped down off the ridge.

'Okay. But take it slowly.'

'Slow and careful,' confirmed Robert.

That was their watchword. The initial steep section was successfully negotiated, but as they thought the rest would be easy the rain returned, only this time it was of tropical proportions, causing the gully, which was no more than rivulets of water, to almost instantly fill with torrid gushes. It was then that Caroline slipped. She cascaded down the gully like a rag doll, finally coming to rest by a large boulder, the same boulder, it seemed, that had claimed Madeleine. Robert, terrified, scrambled to Caroline. The scene looked all too familiar. He could not believe that he was re-living his nightmare. Blood was pouring down her face. She was semi-conscious, her eyes looking into Robert's as if saying to him that this was his test. Leave her to get help, or remain by her side.

The rain eased but it didn't relent. The gully was now a ranging torrent. Robert pulled Caroline to one side, away from the gushing water. He assessed her injury. It didn't look too bad, despite the blood. He bandaged it. Of more concern to Robert was her cognitive state?

'Are you alright?' he anxiously asked.

'Think so.'

'Can you move your legs?'

'Yes. They seem okay, except the right ankle feels a little painful.'

'Try getting up.'

Caroline, with the help of Robert, got to her feet, but as she put weight onto her right foot it collapsed in pain.

'I think I've sprained it.'

Robert felt the affected foot. It didn't feel broken, although he was no expert. He then looked into Caroline's eyes, trying to determine if she was up to moving. He tried a rudimentary exercise in cognition.

'How many fingers can you see?' he asked.

'Three'

'How many now?'

'One.'

'And now?'

'Three again.'

'Good. At least you appear alright.'

'I feel okay. Just my ankle. I think you need to get help. It may be broken.'

'That's the last thing I'm doing.'

'Back then was different. This is now. You need to fetch help.'

Robert was indeed being tested. What should he do? Caroline was right. Madeleine was right. He knew that it was the right thing to do. Yet he could not leave Caroline. He looked back up the gully. The water had subsided. The sky seemed to be clearing with the dark grey nimbostratus breaking up to reveal brighter conditions. It was still raining, but had eased to a heavy drizzle. He looked down the gully to where he must go, yet could not. It was about a mile to a farmhouse, the same farmhouse where he had sought rescue all those years ago. It would only take half an hour at the most. He would be back within the hour.

As he was trying to convince himself of the rescue mission he caught a glimpse of the family he had seen on the summit, making their way across rough land that lay beneath the eastern ridge. They must have gone along the ridge. Probably cleared it before the bad weather struck. They were too far away. Nevertheless, he shouted. No response. He waved and shouted again. They couldn't see or hear him. He had to go for help himself.

He looked at Caroline. She had her eyes shut.

'Wake up. Don't sleep,' he said in a raised voice, shaking her to wake her into consciousness.

'I wasn't. Just had my eyes shut.'

But Robert had seen that sign before and remembered the same response Madeleine had given, reassuring him that everything was alright.

'You must stay awake. Think of something, anything. I'm going to get help. I'll be no more than an hour, I promise.'

'Don't worry, I'll be alright.'

'But I shall worry. Promise me you'll stay awake.'

'I promise.'

With that he left, treading carefully along the rest of the gully until it opened out into a wide path that was easier to traverse. He began to walk faster and faster, almost running, until his heart could take no more. He walked briskly for a short distance before breaking out into jogging the final stretch to the farmhouse.

He knocked on the door. No answer. Again. Still no answer. There was no vehicle in the yard. Everybody, it seemed, was out. He looked around, wondering what to do. There was a Landrover in an open shed across from the farmhouse. He prematurely gave thanks, only to discover there wasn't an ignition key. Next to it was a quad bike. He had never been on one before, but considered it to be like riding a motorbike. This time there was a key. It started first time. After stalling it a couple of times, he finally managed to manoeuvre it out from the shed and across the yard to a track.

* * *

Caroline lay in the gully. The rain had thankfully eased. She tried to get up again, but collapsed to the ground in agony and a whorl of dizziness. She closed her eyes, an anodyne to the pain. She felt better, the pain more bearable. Think girl, she told herself, think. Was this to be like Madeleine? No it wasn't. She was going to live.

'I'm not going to die. You will not take me,' she muttered to herself.

She focused her thoughts on the shoulder bag which, despite the circumstances, lay beside her, rather dishevelled from its own trip down the gully. She had clung onto it throughout her traverse of the ridge as though its contents were sacred treasure to be coveted. And they were. The information she had read whilst waiting below the summit for Robert was illuminating. The notes were comprehensive and she was impressed with Siegfried's ability at historical investigation. He would make a formidable associate, she thought, and dismissed the notion immediately as her mind began to wander. The rain had finally eased as she looked down the gully for any sign of life. She was alone. The thought struck her with dread. The pain now seemed to be returning and with it, doubts.

'Think,' she told herself. 'Think.'

But thoughts were hard to come by. She could not formulate them coherently. Her head ached and eyes became heavy. Sleep beckoned. Sleep was what she wanted.

'Think,' she repeated with a jolt. She shook her head and berated herself for almost succumbing to slumber.

'Think woman…The treasure. That's it.'

Caroline now concentrated her thoughts on the perplexing inscriptions. Were they genuine? Assuming they were, she thought, then what does it tell us? Robert Colliver was shipwrecked on Skellig. He built a cottage, a replica of his family home, on the mainland looking towards his saviour, Skellig Michael. The inscriptions are telling us something. What? His treasure? But that was probably lost in the galleon? What if the treasure was not gold or jewels, but something else? What if it was his story? He left sometime around 1707 and seemed to have gone back to Looe. John Vening, his pseudonym, was known to have been on Looe Island many years later. Perhaps he buried something there? Did he die there? A skeleton had been discovered sometime in the nineteenth century on the summit of the Island. Was it him? And there is the cottage. It would still be intact when he returned. Did he live in it? Unlikely. Did he know about the crypt? He must have done, so as to have known about the inscription. It is doubtful he would have been able to read and write Latin. He was an educated man, so could have had the inscription translated. He knew of its meaning. He could have remembered it. So was he trying to tell us something in these three inscriptions? The first inscription in the crypt was the original. It probably meant trust in the Lord to deliver the monks from marauding invaders, down the secret tunnel. The inscription on Skellig Island must be the next in sequence. It was no doubt carved by Colliver when recovering from the shipwreck. It might have been his salvation moment, the realisation that he should trust in the Lord for deliverance from a tempest, when all thought of survival had gone. The third inscription, on the cross, was inscribed under a more calm and collective situation. What was the deliverance from? From this world, when he thought he was dying? From a life...

*　　*　　*

Robert looked horrified as she lay there where he had left her, eyes shut, a blood stained bandage around her head, looking every bit dead. He had rung for assistance having found a bungalow half a mile along the road. The owners had been most understanding, for it was not the first time that the emergency services had been called, knowing full well the vagaries of the mountain that cast a shadow over their abode.

Robert had thanked them and hastily returned to Caroline. Too hasty, for on approaching the farmyard he had lost control of the quad bike and careered into a ditch. He was shaken but thankfully, he thought, unhurt. Within twenty minutes he was climbing the gully, which by now had only a trickle of water cascading down it, scrambling and slipping frantically towards Caroline. He knew he had been too long.

'Caroline,' he shouted as he finally reached her.

She did not respond. He knelt down and shook her.

'Caroline, wake up.'

But Caroline was in another world. A realm where the mind

enters a transcendental state, where all knowledge of physical reality is blacked out and where life is condensed to just abstract thoughts, a manifold of flashing images, the binary pulses of a brain that was processing identity. She was alive. She was solving a conundrum. She opened her eyes to be greeted by the concerned face of a man whom she momentarily did not recognise.

'Where am I,' she announced in a calm voice.

'You're alive. Thank God,' thinking that he had been well over an hour and a half.

'Of course I'm alive. I wasn't about to relinquish my grip on such a story.'

'What are you talking about?' queried Robert, thinking she must be a little delusional.

'The treasure. I've been churning it over in my mind – to keep me awake as you requested. It was quite a conundrum. But I've solved it.'

'Solved what?'

'Solved the mystery of the treasure.'

'But there is none.'

'Oh but there is, and I know where to find it!'

65

It is always pleasing to be heading home, especially after a harrowing and unplanned experience that would test the most resolute of characters. After Caroline's rescue, she had been detained in hospital overnight for observation, suffering from mild concussion, exposure, and a swollen ankle. She was discharged the following day and despite Robert insisting they stay an extra day for recuperation, Caroline wanted an immediate departure for home and confirmation of her deduction.

The journey back was uneventful, although they did encounter heavy traffic approaching the West Country. It seemed unusually busy for the early hours after midnight and although it wasn't a bank holiday, they concluded it was still the holiday season, with many families trying to escape the daytime gridlock that occurs during August. Having disembarked at Pembroke, Robert had telephoned Alfred and left a message to tell him they would arrive back very early in the morning of the eleventh, and that they had some important news to impart; that although they hadn't found any treasure, they knew where it was.

Caroline was excited. Excited because she was convinced that there was treasure to be found, although exactly what she did not know, but reasoned it may be pieces of eight since Alfred had found one in the tunnel. Her deduction was quite logical. Nobody takes the effort to inscribe a Latin inscription, without reason. In the case of Robert's crypt it was to some form of reverence, that beyond the stone altar lay deliverance from danger, and it was probably etched onto the altar during medieval times by a skilled stone mason monk, since the lettering was regular and highly decorated. On Skellig Michael, the script was plain and crude and was the work of the Pirate Captain. It was an acknowledgement that, in the depths of despair when all hope is lost, faith will deliver the soul from damnation, as it did for him during the Great Storm. As for the final inscription on the Celtic cross in the grounds of the ruined cottage, Caroline's thesis was that Colliver was attempting to direct the enquiring mind to the redeemed man he was, not the hated and evil pirate he had been known as. He may have heard tales of himself whilst in Kerry, and was determined to let the world know of his benevolent face, the face of a man who had found salvation in God. He did not want to proclaim his identity and so left clues to whoever could decipher the trail. She did not understand why he had encrypted the clues in verses, but they were his mental map to the treasure and hence the key to unlocking his mind. She had realised, whilst waiting for Robert in the gully, that the final verse referring to the pious dead and sacred shrine referred to the secret crypt and the altar, and that within its structure was the treasure. He trusted that one day the truth would be revealed and only then would he receive deliverance, and that deliverance was his treasure, his story that Siegfried had conjectured.

Robert was unconvinced. He had listened to her argument, but reasoned himself that nobody, especially a megalomaniac pirate, would be so obtuse in his desire to be discovered that he would encode it in some Latin inscription and a cryptic set of verses.

'Why not just say, this is me, here is my life, this is what I am now and this is my treasure, make what you want of it all,' he declared.

There was, however, one convincing strand, which Robert couldn't ignore. Caroline had said that it was the accident that created the conditions for her revelation. Whilst waiting for Robert, she had entered a meditative state where external events were removed and clarity could be found in her mind. Robert empathised with her. He had found the same clarity in the tunnel where he had seen the wall of mundic brick, even though he knew nothing of it. She may be right, he thought. The mind can conjure the unknown, the hidden, the embryo of faith.

They were both quiet during the journey. Caroline was tired and

Robert was still on the mountain, trying to reconcile events that were almost a repeat of twenty years ago. The storm had approached with rapidity. It was ferocious. He had slipped and would have died but for Caroline. What forces were at play to create such a scenario? Was his cry for help, for mercy, an answer from God? That He guided Caroline to him? His analytical mind said no. But there was doubt there, just an atom of doubt, the beginnings of faith, perhaps. He couldn't reconcile his thoughts and so left them on the mountain.

He put the radio on low, for Caroline was sleeping, and listened to some classical music. It was Wagner, the final act of Gotterdammerung: the twilight of the gods.

The music seemed to match his mood. The mountain would not leave him alone. He was now back in the gully. It was exactly the same as before. It was as though he was being tested. Or was he given a second chance? He had to leave Caroline and get help. There was no alternative. Madeleine had died. Caroline had survived. Her injuries were not serious. And then he realised. That was it. Madeleine died, not because he left her on the mountain, but because she had sustained a fatal injury to the head. She slipped, just as Caroline had done, not because of the champagne, but because it was treacherous in the gully. It could have been him. If he had stayed with her she would have died anyway. He wasn't to know. His only regret was that he hadn't remained with her, remained to comfort her and let her die in his arms.

Perhaps it was his reasoning, that he found transparency. Or was it the dying chords of Wagner's epic music drama, the backdrop to his musings, the haunting and yet uplifting immolation scene where Brunnhilde sacrifices herself for the love of Siegfried and mankind, a love which triumphs over the greed for a treasure and a magical ring. And in doing so, the evil of men along with the gods of Valhalla are consumed in flames and a new era of love dawns. Was it his twilight? Not in a funeral pyre. As he saw the first flush of a new dawn appear on the horizon it was his love, he thought, that was important, not the circumstances, for they were beyond his governance. He now felt a heavy weight lift from his encumbrance. He had finally found redemption and although it had taken twenty years, it was always going to be the case.

*   *   *

They arrived back in Looe early in the morning. As they descended the road to the harbour, the welcoming expanse of houses rising in tiers above the familiar harbour greeted their tired bodies. Sleep was what they craved, but the adrenalin rush of discovering the secrets kept them awake as they climbed out of the town towards the back entrance to Robert's cottage.

The morning was overcast, but dry. A muted dawn chorus was singing its final chords as they walked across the open field, occupied by a flock of sheep grazing on fresh grass. The sound of waves breaking below the cliff became louder as they approached the rear gate, and once through, the cottage was now in full view, its gleaming whitewashed walls proclaiming their Valhalla. They both thought of the ruined cottage across the sea in the verdant land of County Kerry, with its vista to the distant Skellig Islands. Looe Island was like a continent, a tectonic shift so close, so accessible by comparison that it looked serene, yet still held the malevolence of death and a cataclysm that had only happened a few days ago. It seemed a lifetime to the two survivors.

Inside the cottage they immediately went to the kitchen. Caroline was surprised to see Robert fill the kettle to make some tea.

'I need it,' he said, realising Caroline's chagrin. 'A few extra minutes won't make any difference. It will either be there or not.'

'You're right,' she admitted in a resigned tone.

'Let's hope your thesis is right.'

'I hope so too. I'm sure it is.'

'One way or another, this will be the end of our quest.'

'I know. It almost seems a surreal moment.'

'Since that day you came and I had just uncovered the crypt?'

'Yes. It's consumed our lives since then. And we've both been close to death. Normality may seem too dull.'

'Normality will be most welcome,' declared Robert.

Having finished tea and eaten some toast, which Robert had also insisted upon, this time requiring nourishment for the soul, they set about uncovering the entrance to the crypt. Within a few minutes, after Robert had rigged up a bright lamp inside the chamber, they were staring at the altar. They dare not touch it, for it did mean the end of the quest, something which they both secretly didn't want, keeping their thoughts to themselves. For it meant separation: Caroline back to her job in London, Robert in his cottage, alone, without any of his Graces. No Madeleine. No Caroline. No Tara. What would the future hold? They looked at one another and then the altar.

'It was here all the time,' said Robert.

'Under our very noses,' echoed Caroline.

'You said that it had some meaning, back then when we first saw it.'

'Yes. But I didn't know what. Neither could I have imagined the journey that we had to take in order to discover it.'

She read aloud the Latin inscription: IN SALUTEM NOBIS CONFIDIMUS. That's what they were about to do, she proclaimed. They slid the altar away from the tunnel entrance and started to examine the sides for any clue as to an opening. None.

'It has to be on the base,' suggested Robert.

With Caroline levering the altar using a crowbar and Robert taking the weight as it was tipped on its side, slowly the base began to reveal itself. Caroline peered underneath. 'I think I can see a recess,' she said in an excited voice. 'Yes, definitely a hole.'

'Lever it some more,' ordered Robert. 'But slowly, this thing is mighty heavy.'

Caroline did as requested, but was too clumsy and the altar reached its tipping point and crashed to the floor, just missing Robert's arm which he removed in the nick of time.

'Well, I guess that's one way of doing it,' he said.

Caroline wasn't paying attention to his near miss. She was probing with her arm inside the altar, like a veterinary surgeon examining a pregnant cow.

'There's a hollow chamber inside,' she relayed, as Robert was looking on in anticipation.

'Anything there?' he asked.

'I can't feel anything. The chamber's quite sizeable, enough for some cache of treasure. But it's empty. There's nothing in there. You have a feel, perhaps there's another secret chamber.'

Robert took his turn. The chamber was empty. There was no other chamber either. He slumped to the ground in appal. Caroline was leaning against the wall, disheartened. After all that they had been through, there was nothing. They both sat there in the chamber in silence, lost in their own thoughts. Robert had switched off the bright light, finding it too illuminating for his despondent mood. Caroline had not objected. Only daylight from the kitchen above lit the crypt, creating an eerie atmosphere as though the Pirate Captain, Robert Colliver, had descended upon them, to taunt them for thinking he had found redemption and left treasure for some ingenuous treasure hunters to find. His metamorphosis had been a ruse. He had been the evil, cunning devil right to the end, and as they sat there, they could sense him laughing at them.

'I cannot believe it was empty. I was sure the treasure would be there,' said Caroline, now looking even more disconsolate.

'It doesn't matter,' replied Robert trying to cheer her up, even though he was equally dejected.

'All that effort. For nothing.'

'But it's the journey that counts. Remember the poem *Ithaca* by C.P. Cavafy.'

Caroline thought about the poem.

'I do. The one about Odysseus's journey home to his island kingdom from the Trojan Wars.'

'Yes. How does it go?' asked Robert, not quite sure of the poem.

'As you set out for Ithaca, hope the voyage is a long one, full of adventure, full of discovery, full of instruction...'

'Ours has been that. And not just this one.'

'All the places we've been.'

'And all the experiences we've had. And this latest journey has been no different. Before we set out, we were two estranged people, living and drifting apart. The quest for the truth has brought us together and made our love for each other stronger. We've discovered that there is a bond between us, a spiritual connection that transcends time and space, just as those monks had said.'

'You're so right, Robert. It doesn't matter that there is no treasure. We have treasure enough in our hearts.'

Robert suddenly felt his heart beat faster. He felt it because, in that moment, he wanted to ask Caroline for her hand in marriage. It was the right moment. But he didn't have a ring, a diamond ring. It had to be a diamond ring. But he could not wait for this seemed to be an auspicious moment. And as he was about to enact his scene of betrothal, the light began to fade as though dusk were falling outside. It was morning on an August day and dusk it was most certainly not. Perhaps some dark clouds were hanging over the cottage, casting a renewed melancholy upon the chamber. But it grew darker and darker, as though the forces of evil were slowly creeping over the chamber, threatening them in the gathering gloom. Unbetrothed, they climbed out of the crypt. And still it got darker as they emerged outside, with night descending upon Looe, as though the curse of the Pirate Captain had one final act to play.

66

An eclipse of the sun is arguably the wonder of planet earth. Some believe it is a miracle of creation that the moon is precisely the right distance from the earth, to produce the aurora of totality and the magical diamond-ring effect as the moon passes from totality during its transit of the sun. Astronomers, however, know that it is simply the result of a clockwork solar system where every single body is governed by Newtonian laws and that it is possible to predict where and when the next eclipse would be and how long it will last, even the path of totality as is transcribes the earth. The ancient Greeks could forecast solar and lunar eclipses and constructed an incredible bronze machine, a mechanical computer to do just that. For them, as it is today, a solar eclipse is a powerful, spiritual happening, that affects the viewer and provides a window into the fickle artifices of the gods or to the majesty of the universe.

Robert and Caroline had emerged from the cottage in the middle of a solar eclipse. Totality was only minutes away. It was Robert who first realised the momentous event.

'It's the eclipse of the sun,' he declared.

'Of course. How stupid of us to forget it.'

'For a moment, I thought the dark forces of the Pirate had descended upon us in one final act of retribution.'

'It did seem like it, I must admit,' said Caroline.

Robert didn't hear Caroline's reply for he had dashed inside the cottage, rummaged through a box of photographic slides and found what he was looking for: blank, unexposed frames that they could view the sun through.

Outside, Caroline looked dismayed. 'Don't think they're going to be much use,' she remarked. Robert looked up and concurred.

The sun was obscured by a cloudy sky. Only the gloom of a darkened earth was evidence of the astronomical event, a path of totality that took in Cornwall and much of Devon. The rest of the country had only a partial view of the eclipse and that's why it was so busy coming back, thought Robert, with half of the country wanting to experience this unique event. Totality could only be viewed in this august location and standing in front of the cottage they had a perfect view, but for the cloud cover.

'Typical,' said Robert. 'It's a once in a lifetime event and we won't see it.'

'But at least we can feel it.'

They could. It was an eerie feeling. Night descending upon day, confusing the mind. Birds began to sing as though it were dusk. Gulls glided silently past them on their way to the Island to roost. The double pulse of the Eddystone lighthouse could be seen on a gilded horizon and a shimmer of light glinted upon the sea, the last vestiges of sunlight far out to sea from an ever diminishing sun. It was surreal. A silence befell the scene as though something was going to happen, something extraordinary. And just as totality was about to occur the clouds parted and the sun became visible, one final portion of its disc still glowing, until that was extinguished by the moon and only a halo of light could be seen, the sun's corona creating the aurora from a sun ninety-three million miles away, yet close enough to touch the soul.

For Robert, it was the auspicious moment. He had his diamond ring. A heavenly diamond ring.

'There's something I want to ask of you, Caroline.'

'Yes,' she said with some anticipation, for she knew what was going to happen.

'Will you marry me?'

*   *   *

Totality lasted eight minutes. It wasn't long enough. Robert and Caroline, along with countless other people observing the spectacle up on the Wooldown, on the beach, along the cliffs, and from every vantage point imaginable, wanted it to last. It was primordial. It was as though one were a witness to the birth of the star itself, a star which had been shining for over four and a half billion years and would continue to do so for another four billion years or so before it consumed the solar system in an expanding giant of red gas. No wonder so many cultures revered the sun, even made human sacrifice to it, for it was a truly remarkable object in the sky, a life-giving ball of hydrogen, a nuclear furnace that could destroy life just as easily as sustain it.

As the last few seconds of totality neared, Robert and Caroline waited for that most magical moment. And as the moon made its pass, the sun re-appeared in a glow so complete, so glorious, that they were lost for words to describe the feeling. They held hands, squeezing each other's fingers in an act of communion, a communion with the infinity of space and a spirit that touched the very core of their souls. They stood there, taking in the majesty of the diamond-ring, a symbol of heavenly love that Robert had waited for.

'Yes,' she said, and they kissed each other in an embrace that sealed their love in the presence of a divine star that would, for them, shine for an eternity.

* * *

They sat down on the bench and watched daylight return, witnessing the outline of the moon vanishing and the sun being restored to its radiant form.

'I think that was put on especially for us,' said Caroline.

'It was auspicious.'

'It's put our disappointment into perspective.'

'It has. You know, watching the eclipse felt like the end of our adventure and a new beginning.'

'The beginning of a new chapter in our lives,' declared Caroline.

'Yes. A new dawn.'

'Do you remember that time in Tangiers, in the Museum?'

'I do. That was the start of our romance.'

'Not quite. There's a chapter you don't know about.'

'There is?' questioned Robert in a tone which belied his intrigue.

Caroline composed herself. She hadn't intended to tell Robert, but their engagement meant she must divulge a secret.

'I've never told you this before. Why, I don't know. It was our last day on the trip and nothing had happened between us. It was my fault for being unresponsive towards you, but I didn't want my infatuation to be obvious. The moment I noticed you, when you stood up to give that absurd talk about yourself at the beginning of the tour, I knew you were the one for me. I could see behind the nervous exterior a mind, a heart, which connected with me. So on that final day, I had to do something. I hatched a plan. I made sure you overheard me talking about going to the museum. I thought if you went, then you were indeed the one for me. So I left early and waited in a café opposite the entrance to the museum. I saw you enter and felt that arrow of desire strike me. I could not wait. But as I was about to leave the cafe, a street vendor accosted me, trying to sell some wares. Normally, I would say no. But he showed me some maps which took my interest. One of them was of Cornwall, of all places. He said it was a treasure map. Naturally, I didn't believe him. But I inspected it and the more I looked, the more I was convinced that he may be right, for it seemed old and genuine and had a cross marked on Looe. I knew that Barbary Pirates from that part of North Africa had plundered the coast of Cornwall, so I bought the map. In the meantime almost half an hour had gone by, and I wondered if you'd still be in there. I rushed inside and to my delight I found you looking at the very same map I had just purchased. I realised I had been sold a copy. But I had secured you, a far more valuable prize.'

Robert was astounded. He thought that it was his prowess that had won Caroline and all along it was her feminine guile that had called the tune. All three women in his life, he thought, had made an advance on him and controlled him to some degree. His dream had told him that, his Graces had tried to beguile him. But unlike his dream, he had not been in control: he had been a helpless pawn in their game. But it was a game he had participated fully in and he would not change a second of it.

He looked at Caroline. She was expecting him to say something. She wanted him to say something. But, ever a man of few words, he remained silent. All he did was to smile at her and kiss her affectionately on the lips, a kiss that told her he didn't mind, that no matter what they would be together, to trace out another chapter in their lives.

Robert was now wondering about the map. It must have been the same map that his father had been given.

'Is that the map you brought back with you, when you returned the second time?' he asked.

'Yes. That's why I had to return to London when you uncovered the crypt. I didn't want to but I realised it might be important, even though it was just a copy. I contacted the museum to ask if they could send the original. They could not, although they did say I could collect it in person, taking responsibility myself for the map. I think they were pleased to be dealing with the prestigious British Library. I managed to persuade the library authorities to pay for a research trip to Tangiers, spinning a tale that the map could provide evidence of a medieval tunnel system.'

'What was it like to be back there?'

'I was only there for one day and didn't go into the gallery. They had already removed the map. I did examine it there and realised that there were faint markings on the reverse and a script that could only be revealed by x-ray analysis.'

'So it seems that Robert Colliver, the Pirate, must have visited Tangiers at some time,' said Robert.

'He must have, or somewhere nearby. The port of Salee further down the coast was a pirate stronghold.'

'He was quite a man of mystery,' declared Robert.

'Talking of mystery, there's something which Siegfried left in the briefcase which I discovered whilst waiting for you on the mountain. With my accident, I had forgotten about it. You'll recognise it. But it's rather inexplicable.'

Caroline went inside to the lounge where she had left the case and noticed an envelope addressed to them both lying on the window ledge. She picked it up. Outside, she delved into the case and retrieved a wooden totem. Robert did indeed recognise it.'

'It's an Easter Island birdman carving. I've already seen it before.'

He examined it expecting it to be a fake, the one from Hendersick

Hall. But this one was genuine, or as far as he could tell without scientific analysis of the wood. It was, indeed, inexplicable. Perplexing. 'What's Siegfried doing with this?'
Caroline showed him the note he had left.

Fellow treasure hunters,

By the time you read this I will be long gone. Don't try to find me. It is a dangerous place where I am heading.

I apologise, but I implied the reliquary was empty. It was not, as is evident by the birdman totem you have. Rest assured, it is not the fake one from Hendersick Hall. I believe this one was meant for you to discover. There is a story to be told, but what, is for you to unearth. It may well turn out to be treasure after all.

I have my own treasure which I will put to good use. One day you may hear about my exploits and then perhaps you may reassess your opinion of me, a man who found redemption in the most unlikely of places. For that, I thank you.

Robert was left speechless. Caroline had already formulated an explanation, but even her hypothesis seemed preposterous. Robert listened as she construed a scenario where the Pirate Captain had visited Easter Island probably on the final journey he had made before being shipwrecked on Skellig Michael.

'He obviously saved the carving, for some reason. Or maybe it was recovered later on, flotsam washed up on the shore of the mainland. It would have been an important symbol of survival to him, a revered object much like any Christian icon, so much so, that he excavated his own reliquary. The cottage must have been like a chapel to him, a sacred place, as this cottage was once.'

'It's all conjecture,' he responded.

'True. But that's what historical reconstruction is based upon, until concrete evidence can be established.'

'Do you think he sailed across the Pacific and back again? And at a time when little was known of the ocean? And would he have had time? We know of his whereabouts in April 1702 and, if Siegfried's theory is correct, he was in Ireland by November 1703, which makes it about eighteen months. Too short a time I reckon.'

'Well, I've no other explanation, unless he made a subsequent sea journey.'

They fell silent, looking out towards the Island, wondering at the possibility. Even now, having found no treasure, his influence was still clinging on, an irritant that would not seem to dissipate. In contrast, the clouds were dissolving, beginning to lift and break up, with blue windows appearing, allowing shafts of sunlight to illuminate them. They soaked up its warmth that provided a welcome balm to their vacillating emotions.

Robert picked up the envelope that Caroline had found. 'What's this?' he enquired.

'I found it on the window sill.'

Robert opened it and pulled out a note.

Caroline looked at his face, an expression of bemusement. 'Who's it from and what does it say?' she asked eagerly.

'It's from Alfred. He says "Wondrous things." That's all. Nothing else. Quite bizarre.'

'If I'm not mistaken, I think he's referring to the treasure. It's what Carter said when he looked inside the tomb of Tutankhamen and was asked what he saw.'

'But there's none here, unless he's found something elsewhere.'

'No, I think he deduced, probably from the inscription, that the treasure was hidden in the altar and recovered it whilst we were away.'

'He could have waited for our return.'

'Perhaps. But if I were him, I doubt I could have waited.'

'Then we had better go and see him.'

However, as they were about to leave the man himself came striding up the path to the front door. He was like a schoolboy, having discovered that the world is not flat as his perception had imagined. He was carrying a briefcase and trailing some distance behind him was George.

'Wondrous things,' exclaimed Alfred. 'It is full of wondrous things.'

He could not contain himself. He paced around, wanting to reveal the secrets of the altar, but Robert and Caroline told him to sit down on the bench and calm himself before explaining things.

Caroline made a pot of Earl Grey tea for the two of them whilst Robert and George had a mug of builder's brew. Robert noticed George add his elixir from the hip-flask and smiled at him. He returned the compliment.

'Did I ever tell you that you are the best thing that's happened to me in a long time,' as he added some elixir to Robert's tea as well. That was it. Robert wasn't going to receive any more flattery although George did add a second dash.

Alfred then apologised profusely for their intrusion into the property, but he just had to confirm his theory, that there was treasure hidden in the altar. He needed George's help to lift the stone, but inside a small chamber he found, not pieces-of-eight or gold or jewels, but a leather-bound diary written by Captain Robert Colliver. He said to a historian this was real treasure. And to whet Robert and Caroline's appetite, he told them what an account it was, a story that could rewrite the history of British maritime exploration.

67

The first circumnavigation of the globe was by the Portuguese explorer, Ferdinand Magellan, whose expedition of five ships set sail from the port of Seville in September 1519. With only one ship and most of the original crew dead, including Magellan himself, it returned in May 1522 having opened up a new route, via the Pacific, to the spice islands of the East and started an international endeavour to map the world and plunder the riches of the Orient.

It took another fifty years, however, before the second circumnavigation was completed in 1580, by Sir Francis Drake in his now famous galleon, *Golden Hind*. Even so, most of the Pacific, including Australia and New Zealand as well as Antarctica, were still unknown, blanks on a map that would only gradually be filled in succeeding centuries. It was left to Captain James Cook, in the latter half of the eighteenth century, arguably the golden age of maritime exploration, on his three scientific voyages, to discover Australia, chart much of the Pacific and circumnavigate Antarctica.

Many, if not most, of these expeditions, particularly in the early years, were commissioned by sovereign countries eager to establish trade and so exploit the resources of distant lands. It fuelled conflict. And out of that conflict arose the buccaneer and eventually, the pirate. During the seventeenth century, piracy became a considerable force, and from this enterprise a notable and controversial pirate and Englishman, William Dampier, circumnavigated the world, no less than three times.

Although his exploits were probably motivated by gain he was, nonetheless, interested in scientific curiosity and discovery and he became famous through his book, *A New Voyage Round the World* published in 1697. It was received to great acclaim, making fascinating observations on a world that was unknown to a population that was eager to know more and probably helped inspire books like *Robinson Crusoe* and *Gulliver's Travels*.

It was to this background, as narrated by Alfred, that he handed to Robert and Caroline the leather diary. It was brown with an embossed cross on the front and rather weather-beaten with age. But the pages inside were in good condition and the text as clear as the day it was written, very neat and elaborate with flowing tails, the sign of an educated man. They started to read, watched by Alfred, whilst George sat indoors in Robert's chair, watching the proceedings from the window.

Heryre in wyth is thee storye of Robert Colliver, Pyrate Captayn and gentlemane to oure Lord, this daye, thee twelvthe daye of Decembere, 1727.

I was borne in thee towne of East Looe, in thee year of oure Lord, 1666, in ye county of Cornwall, Englande. Mye parents, Pascho and Agnes Colliver were goode people, merchants in thee towne and did goode business therye and purchased a house in West Looe up on ye cliffe and named it Ararat for it was hygh above thee flooding of thee town. I did not take to thee family business and so went to sea and soon found myself aboarde a privateer brigantyne captained by William Kidd...

Alfred watched them and guessed they would struggle with the archaic and flamboyant text. He himself did. He reached down inside the briefcase and retrieved a folder of paper.

'It's difficult to follow,' he remarked.

'Slightly,' replied Robert.

'Here, I've transcribed the text and adjusted where appropriate so that it reads more fluently.'

It was indeed easier to read, and they both sat in the sunshine absorbing the fascinating story of Robert Colliver, Pirate Captain and gentleman to our Lord...

J was born in the town of East Looe in the year of our Lord, 1666, in the county of Cornwall, England. My parents, Pascho and Agnes Colliver, were good people, merchants in the town and did good business there and purchased a house in West Looe up on the cliff and named it Ararat for it was high above the flooding of the town. J did not take to the family business and so went to sea and soon found myself aboard a privateer brigantine captained by William Kidd.

Robert and Caroline read how he became involved in piracy and the exploits which earned him loathing and notoriety amongst his fellow crew and seafarers alike. It was his final act of piracy, as Captain of a frigate named *Resolution,* which seemed to encapsulate his reputation. Alongside another pirate ship, he attacked a large merchantman called the *Great Mahomet* which was sailing in the Gulf of Khambhat, north of Bombay. It was a fiercely fought encounter with close on twenty pirates killed but over three hundred of the crew and passengers of the Mahomet, either killed or thrown overboard. The rest were cast adrift in boats without any oars, sails or even water, left to their fate. Fortunately they made it to shore, but many women who remained prisoners on board ship, were not so lucky, being cruelly treated according to Colliver. Some even threw themselves overboard or stabbed themselves rather than endure rape and mistreatment by the crew.

They both realised he was trying to distance his own barbarous acts from those of his men. He may have committed atrocities, but never directly towards women. The fact that he was believed to be gay was never mentioned. But he was honest in his writing, which almost seemed like a confession, a plea for the absolution of his sins.

He went on to describe how he was tricked into accepting a pardon and subsequently taken back to England to stand trial alongside Captain Kidd. Kidd was convicted in May 1701 and hanged, whilst Colliver, in a later trial, gave King's evidence to help convict other pirates, some of whom he had sailed with. He was released later the following year as a result of a petition of clemency to the new Queen Anne.

I was much pleased in being released and vowed to forgo piracy. I was a wealthy man and returned in secret to Looe and to St Georges Island where I hid my cache of treasure in caves beneath the Island. To my anger, whilst I was in prison, I discovered that my father had been killed and my mother and family driven out of the cottage by the people of Looe and had all died, penniless. I cursed the people of Looe and swore revenge upon the town vowing I would return one day to seek retribution for their heinous crime.

I found me a place on a ship, sailing from Plymouth to Cape Town. We set sail, late in 1702, for Africa and first anchored at the port of Tangier where the captain and some of the crew went ashore. I, with some of the remaining crew, took charge of the ship and set sail, making myself captain. We stopped at Salee to take on more crew and sailed down the coast of that continent to Cape Town and hence around the Cape of Good Hope. My passage took me to Madagascar and on to India and down to Java, where I had much success.

Robert and Caroline paused on that comment.

'Did he return to piracy?' wondered Caroline out loud.

'It seems he did. He took control of the galleon and proceeded to India where he had plundered ships before,' replied Alfred.

'Perhaps, after he was released from prison, he wanted to return and live his life in Looe, but the events there changed him, made him angry and he returned to piracy,' added Robert.

They continued to read.

In June 1703 we headed back to England and were almost upon the land when a great storm struck us. We were taken off course and struck rocks on a small isle off the coast of Ireland. All were lost but I, and with our bounty too. I was saved from drowning in the tempest by some monks, living in isolation on a remote rocky island. They plucked me from the water and saved my soul. I have them to thank and the Lord for my salvation. They looked after me and prayed for me and in time I recovered my wits to thank them, for they knew not of my past. They did not judge me as I have been judged. They were kindly people and wanted no reward. Your life is our reward they said.

I was on that island for almost six months, for it was winter and the seas were too rough for passage to the mainland which I could see every day. In time, I found peace within me, from the Lord himself. He had touched me. Why, I do not know, for the deeds of my past must surely anger Him.

In spring 1704 I left the island and vowed to be a reformed person and give thanks for my deliverance. I built a cottage looking out to the island that saved me and every year would carry a cross up on to a high mountain where I would pray for my mother and father and give thanks to the Lord.

He came to me in a dream one day, two years later. He told me to go to sea again. Use my treasure for the good of man. He told me to sail around the world and tell the people of the earth about the Lord and his mercy. That they too can find peace within if they believe in His Kingdom.

Alfred interrupted the two readers.

'I do believe he may have read William Dampier's book, since he was a former buccaneer, come pirate, who sailed around the world. Perhaps Colliver thought he could do the same. Dampier, having become famous and abandoned piracy, joined the Royal Navy and later was commissioned by the Admiralty to chart new lands and find the fabled southern continent.'

'Ptolemy's Terra Australis Incognita,' said Caroline.

'Yes,' replied Alfred.

'His dream, then, was to follow in Dampier's wake,' said Robert.

'Yes. That's what I think. But his was a spiritual journey. Perhaps, the first true missionary.'

I secured a good ship with my fortune and a crew, who had to be of faith in the Lord, for this was a voyage in His name. We sailed from Ireland in July 1706, first heading down the coast of Africa, stopping at Madeira, before picking up the favourable winds to cross the Atlantic for South America. We anchored in Rio de Janeiro for a week and sailed south for the passage to the Pacific, heading west for Tahiti. But poor weather took us off course and we went many weeks without sighting land. Thanks to the Lord, we made land, a small island in the Pacific in March 1707 where the people had never seen a vessel such as ours or skins so white. They were friendly and gave us water and food, even though it seemed scarce to them. The land was without many trees and they carved large stone statues, bigger than any man, to honour their dead.

We stayed there for two weeks before heading north-west and sighted land with high mountains a month later. We were welcomed again by the people and traded goods for food. The women were very well disposed towards the men of the ship and I found it to be a problem with many wanting to stay. Some did, to spread the word of God, after we left two months later.

We sailed west passed many small islands, stopping at some that were uninhabited and others where the people were hostile, coming out to engage us in canoes with strange outriggers. We headed south and came across a large island where the people were also so unfriendly that we had to defend ourselves. They too came out to confront our ship in a large canoe that had one hundred warriors aboard and whose prow was decorated with a frightening figure with a tongue hanging out and the eyes of a demon.

The land was fertile, like England, and for the most part we did not see many inhabitants. We traced the coast south and then west through a channel that separated one land mass from another, and continued our progress for several days until more land was spied. We anchored in an inlet and went ashore inhabited by timid and inoffensive people who adorned themselves with strange markings upon their skin. There, J witnessed the most strange of animals that hopped on large hind legs, some as big as a man and saw plants that the Lord himself could only have created.

From this place, we sailed north, hugging the coast which seemed deserted. As we went further, the sea became shallower and the ship almost ran aground on a great barrier of rock that seemed to follow us for many hundreds of miles. Jt was only through my skill as a mariner that J believe we escaped wreck and an inevitable end to our venture. Jt took us one month, slowly making our way through a labyrinth of channels, to eventually come to the end of the coast and open sea. Jt would seem to me, that because of the length of the coast we had traversed, it may be the southern continent, so many have been trying to discover.

We continued north and landfall was on the New Guinea coast where other navigators had been before us. Then we sailed onto Java and across to Jndia, familiar places to me, but not for piracy, but to spread the word of our Lord. From there our passage took us across to the African coast and down past Madagascar to round the Cape of Good Hope, to anchor in Cape Town before the return to England.

We did not make our shores, for off the coast of Africa we were attacked by Barbary Pirates in three small ships. Jn the fight, we sank one of their vessels and crippled another, but not before we sustained damage to ourselves. We escaped the attack but our ship foundered off the coast of France. We put to our long boats and rowed ashore, but my log book of the voyage was lost and all of our valuables, save a few possessions. Eventually, I made it to England, but without a written record of the voyage, my account was considered the work of my imagination. We took just over two years to circumnavigate the world and the only item that I have as evidence of the voyage is a carving from the remote island in the Pacific.

I returned to Ireland and lived a pious life in the service of the Lord. In the spring of this year I travelled to my home town. Poor health was availing me, and I wished to depart in the place I was born. As I write this account of my life at a once holy sanctuary, I am looking out at my final resting place, a reminder of an island and its inhabitants who saved my soul.

I do not wish to be rewarded for my endeavours. Service of the Lord is reward enough. But I write this as a true account, in sight of God as my witness.

Robert Colliver.

Robert and Caroline looked at one another in disbelief. Was this a true account of the man? Was it written by him? They were the questions in their eyes.

'So what do you think?' said Alfred, intrigued to know their thoughts.

'If it's a true account, then it is quite remarkable,' replied Caroline.

'Quite remarkable,' repeated Robert.

'Indeed. Quite remarkable as it will re-write British maritime exploration,' declared Alfred.

Alfred explained that although Sir Francis Drake was the first Englishman to circumnavigate the world, and Dampier had done so too, Colliver was most certainly the fastest to do so. But the most remarkable fact was that Colliver's route around the globe almost matched exactly that of James Cook nearly sixty years later, whose expedition is regarded as the first true scientific exploration of the Pacific. Although Captain Cook visited Rapa Nui, he wasn't the first man to set foot upon the Island: that is attributed to a Dutch commander called Jacob Roggeveen in April 1722, who named the place Easter Island because he landed there during Easter of that year.

'So, the first known man to set foot on Easter Island is not Roggeveen, but now Captain Robert Colliver,' said Caroline.

'His description of the Island confirms that,' concurred Robert.

'I know the reference to large stone statues bigger than a man suggests that, but it could be anywhere. There are stone carvings on many Polynesian islands. The point is we have no proof it was Easter Island,' responded Alfred.

'But we have,' exclaimed Caroline. She reached down into her shoulder bag and pulled out the small wooden birdman carving. 'This was in a reliquary in Colliver's cottage in Ireland,' she continued.

'Is it original?' asked Alfred.

'As far as I can tell, it is. It's made from the right type of reddish wood, from a tree which used to grow on the Island,' replied Robert.

'Let me have a look at it,' asked Alfred.

He examined the carving, watched intently by the adventurers.

'Radio carbon dating can confirm that, as can analysis of the paper and ink Colliver's account has been written on,' said Caroline.

'Assuming the two artefacts are genuine, don't you think it's remarkable that Colliver's and Cook's voyages were almost identical?' said Alfred.

'Perhaps the Lord was guiding Cook,' said Caroline.

'Or maybe the Lord had been guiding Colliver,' said Robert with an air of scepticism.

'Whatever,' remarked Alfred, 'this means that, rather than Cook, it is Colliver who can lay claim to discovering the continent of Australia and New Zealand. That is one valuable treasure haul.'

They all agreed. It was treasure, but not the gold or silver that many would want or expect. This was historical treasure and the world would be eager to pay for it.

Robert got up from the bench leaving Caroline and Alfred talking about the findings. He wandered over to the sea shack and sat down outside, away from the speculation, wanting his own thoughts to make sense of things. It appeared he was a changed man. It was perhaps the most remarkable part of the story, he thought. The fact that his own family suffered a cruel ignominious end and that he had been rescued by some pious monks who saved him and wanted nothing in return, may have stirred some deep emotion within his soul. He found God and undertook a missionary voyage around the world.

By now it was afternoon and the sunny morning following the eclipse, had given way to cloud cover once more, not a thick blanket, but enough to bring a haze to the sunshine. It was still warm. Robert looked out to the Island. In the end, it didn't hold the key to the mystery. It was his cottage, Lammana, and those monks who inscribed the words, 'Trust in Salvation' on the altar that had solved the puzzle. And Tara? Did she have to die for it? The treasure had cost the lives of three people. It wasn't worth that sacrifice.

Caroline joined him by the sea shack. She could see the conflict in his mind and knew he was thinking about Tara.

'You could not have changed anything,' she said in a reassuring voice.

She was right, thought Robert. Fate, destiny, call it what you will, had propelled him onto a path that was beyond his control. Tara's fate had been sealed the day he saw her in the Estate Agents augmented by her family's obsession with a curse. His and Caroline's renewed love had been forged by Siegfried and sealed by circumstances that were beyond their control. Life is a web spun by events and relationships, and no mortal being can weave the future. And although there are choices, sometimes those choices which appear to be rational, conscious decisions, have, in fact, already been made for us. It is destiny that has already chosen them, as it had done so for the Pirate Captain on a cold spring night in Looe, as it was for Robert Colliver when he had resurrected the past on a cold spring day, two and a half centuries later.

Epilogue

I t was a warm June day, the weekend of the summer solstice. Robert was standing on the bridge that spanned Looe harbour. Throngs of people were passing him, many weighed down by the paraphernalia for a day on the beach and dressed accordingly in brightly coloured attire that spoke of long, hot, halcyon days by the seaside. One such individual, sporting a Hawaiian-style shirt, reminded Robert of his first day on the bridge in the bitter cold of a spring day. He thought he knew the man, but couldn't place him for he was slim and walked with confidence that bestowed a successful entrepreneur.

Many years had passed since that momentous spring day. He looked at the scene before him. Whereas, all those years ago, there was just a monochrome of grey hues, today was entirely different. The harbour basin was full and reflecting a turquoise lustre that was punctuated by rows of orange buoys. They were running from four of the piers and marked out a trace, like the markers in a swimming pool, to which were moored a multivariate of craft that were gently pitching on a slack tide and a warm southerly breeze, that had its origins all the way from Africa. The lugger, which he had mistaken for a piece of art, was gone. So too the luxury cruiser, its berth empty. And the fish quay was deserted, with all the commercial boats fishing out at sea. They would return in a few hours to land their catch, before an ebb tide made it impossible to navigate the shallow river channel.

Robert looked down over the side of the bridge and counted the arches. There were still seven, concrete manifestations to the tale of the condemned smugglers. And the eighth enigmatic arch was still there too, a secret embellishment to the tale, as recounted by George, the old sea dog. Even the bridge itself, after so long a divide between two towns and two families, finally acted as a mediator, uniting disparate forces as though the curse of the Pirate Captain had been purged and no longer bound loyalties.

But amongst the familiar there was something different. Gone were the warning messages that had clouded his thoughts, for all the secrets that had been buried for centuries had been unearthed. Not all of them entered the public consciousness, but remain concealed to a select few who had been central to their discovery. All, that is, except one.

Robert's thoughts flashed back to Tara and the Island. He would occasionally sit outside the cottage, alone, thinking about those few months in the spring and summer of the eclipse year and how life had been superseded by normality. He had wholeheartedly embraced that notion after the momentous events, but now, secretly, yearned for adventure, to sail beyond the horizon.

After Robert and Caroline's marriage in the new millennium, Caroline had left work, sold her flat and moved to Cornwall, she financially secure with lecture tours and the esteem of the academic world. For a couple of years they had lived their idyll in the cottage, but it would not relinquish its enigmatic past and they felt compelled to move. It was a wrench, but they found a more suitable home nearby, not with sea views but close enough so that they could walk down a picturesque private track to a small inlet that had access to the sea shore. It was beautiful, whatever time of year, but winter with its Atlantic storms was their favourite.

Robert would stand on the rocks looking at Tara's mausoleum, gazing at Trelawney Point where she used to stand and watch the crashing surf, imagining her spirit in those waves, her energy pounding the Island which she had loved. After all the years, he still lamented after her and every so often he thought he could hear her beguiling voice, a siren trying to lure him into the sea.

The cottage was never sold. It remained a silent monument to a forgotten past. To the monks who built a chapel and a tunnel system to rival any in the known world, it would be left, untouched, as a testament to their deeds. It was also a shrine to a man who became a hated pirate, yet, later in life, redeemed himself with pious acts and a record of his incredible travels.

The birdman totem that he had left was returned to its rightful place on Easter Island, to a grateful community who welcomed the new discovery that would change its history. Robert and Caroline never revealed the tunnel system nor the crypt in the cottage. It was their secret and that of the Pirate and the monks who had built it. But she did publish a paper on the stitches which received academic acclaim. And the notoriety that followed after the revelations concerning Captain Robert Colliver, pirate turned benevolent humanitarian, secured her position in the hierarchy of the academic world.

It was received with incredulity. There wasn't much evidence, other than the diary which proved to be original, as did the birdman totem. That alone had been radio-carbon dated to the time of the Pirate's circumnavigation, although there was some controversy as to the validity of its antiquity. The fact that it predated Captain Cook's discoveries made headlines around the world, not least in Easter Island and the Antipodes. The two adventurers had been invited to both places, Caroline as an academic and Robert as a celebrity, which produced financial rewards far more than any gold or silver treasure could have done. In the end, Colliver's cache had indeed been treasure and he, as perhaps he had hoped, achieved historical immortality.

Alfred too found fame. His theory about the Pirate was finally vindicated and he received the proper recognition from fellow Oxford academics, although most of his contemporary sceptics were already dead. He decided to let Caroline take most of the accolade and was proud that she was able to carve a place in academia whilst she was young enough to appreciate it. He is now a frail old man who still lives at Watergate, surrounded by his books and memories.

George died within a year of the eclipse of bronchial pneumonia, a result of his drinking and smoking. He was a much-loved Looe institution and accordingly a plaque was unveiled to him, on the wall in his snug, within the Smugglers Arms, inscribed with *ask no questions and you'll be told no lies*, perhaps a fitting epitaph since he took Alfred's secret to his grave. Even John, the proprietor of the Quayside Café, dedicated his table by the door to him, a shrine to a revered man amongst those who knew him, a true friend to Alfred who found his passing difficult to reconcile, his death a severance from a past life.

The proprietor still owns the café but he has staff who serve the customers. John now takes tourists on trips around the Island in his new glass-bottom boat during the holiday season, where the wonders of the deep, or at least the shallow waters surrounding the Island, can be viewed as they listen to his tales of smuggling and the past inhabitants of the Island. Jane moved in with Frederick Thomas for a while, thinking that she would inherit some of his wealth. She didn't. When he died he had a mountain of debts which the sale of Hendersick Hall accounted for, leaving her with nothing. She returned to her husband but it didn't work, he no longer wanting her in the marital home. They are estranged and living apart, but still married, mainly for the sake of the children.

Madge, the owner of Looe Island, died several years later. She bequeathed the Island to the local Wildlife Trust who now manage the place as a nature reserve and observatory. It was what she wanted. She never did accept the mysterious disappearance of Tara, the consensus being that she had been drowned at sea, taken by the ocean as her father had. Madge asserted to everybody that told her Tara was dead, that she was very much alive and would return soon, but as the years passed and Tara didn't return, those people concluded she was suffering from delusion, or worst senility. Those that remained entrenched in the curse of the Pirate maintained that the death of both Tara and the Trevellick matriarch, Constance, within one week of each other, was his doing, the final act in the demise of the family.

Frederick Thomas fared no better. With his son missing he had his police contacts investigate the Island who found no evidence of foul play. After the collapse of the tunnel, the whole system caved in one night, blocking off the route for good, leaving no trace that such a tunnel system existed. Naturally, the remains of Malcolm were buried beyond reach leaving Thomas distraught and guilt-ridden. However, he was even more distraught on discovering that most of his art collection were fakes, with no recompense, not even the satisfaction of seeing his accomplice in crime behind bars. He never recovered from these shocks and died a few years into the new millennium, a broken and bitter man who blamed everybody but himself for his misfortune.

Jock, Siegfried, whatever he was called, was never seen again.

However, one day whilst surfing the internet, Robert came across a web site called *The Wagnerian Hero*. It intrigued him. It contained information about a man called John Vening who was involved in the rehabilitation of orphans in Africa, victims of wars and repression in countries where conflict was always happening. It seemed a strange web title for such a philanthropic act, so that Robert realised it must be him. The fact that he had used the pseudonym, John Vening, Colliver's supposed new name after he was shipwrecked, confirmed his assertion. Siegfried, that Herculean of a man, had been affected by the Pirate's redemption and he too had followed a similar path, if not in the footsteps of piety then in the only way he knew, in a continent that had seen his mercenary activities, mirrored in Colliver's piracy.

*   *   *

Robert surfaced from his recollections, being harangued by two small children who were excited about at a day out on the beach, anticipating building sand castles, eating ice-creams and swimming in the sea. Their mother told them to be patient and turned to her husband and urged him to make a decision.

He was not looking forward to the beach. It would be intolerably crowded, especially as it was high tide and space would be reduced to a small arc of sand. Caroline had suggested the day out, mainly in response to their children blackmailing her that they never did any normal things like the other kids at school. Consequently, she had vetoed Robert's suggestion of a walk along the cliffs and unilaterally declared a beach day. It was now Robert's worst nightmare!

He looked at his two children, Charlotte, the eldest, and Tom, and then to Caroline.

'Okay, let's go. But before we go to the beach there's something I want you two to see,' he said, forcing them to follow him and their mother off the bridge and down the quayside.

'Seagulls,' said Tom, pointing to several that were perched on a boat.

'They're not called seagulls,' said his father in a teacher-like voice. 'They are called herring gulls. The adults have a red spot on their beak. Can you see? And over there are greater black-backed gulls.'

'They live by the sea and both are called gulls, so why aren't they called seagulls?' protested Tom.

'Tell your brother, Charlotte.'

Charlotte proceeded to inform her brother that the description, seagull, is a generic term and that each sea bird, amongst which there are gulls, have a proper name that describes that particular species. She probably elucidated the information far better than her father could have and he knew it. Caroline looked at Robert as though he had engineered the whole exercise, which he had.

'Still the teacher,' she said to her husband.

'Still the teacher,' he replied.

The family wandered along the quay until they reached the place where the Fisherman's Berth was sited, except it was no longer there. It had recently been demolished and a new Fisherman's Berth erected further along. It had an attached glass canopy roof, open at the sides, and looked altogether a more salubrious building than the old bus shelter. Robert took out the photograph of his mother, sister and himself and showed it to the children.

'This is me, when I was your age Tom, standing alongside my mother and my sister, your Aunty Ruth. It was taken at this very spot over forty years ago. Not much has changed, has it?'

'Well all these boats aren't in the picture,' said Tom.

'Those railings in the photo cannot be seen now,' said Charlotte.

'And that building isn't there either,' added their mother.

'True, but it still looks similar,' emphasised their father, indicating that he wouldn't tolerate dissent, not even from his wife.

'Suppose,' the children said rather dolefully in unison.

'Suppose,' echoed Caroline.

'Anyway, Tom, these boats are called luggers. They were used in days gone by, before modern ships and boats. Notice how they all have two masts and the booms, that's the wooden poles supporting the sail at the top and bottom, cross the mast. They are...'

But Robert was now addressing himself, for the two children and their mother had surreptitiously departed to partake in an ice-cream from the café opposite, leaving him to finish the explanation, '... referred to as lug sails, hence the term lugger.'

Every two years Looe holds a lugger regatta and this year was bigger than ever with over twenty of the Cornish vessels moored, making ready to sail for a day's racing in the bay. Over on the east quay a large French three-mast barque, too long to be moored in the main basin, overshadowed the smaller luggers. There was activity everywhere, a throwback to the days when Looe harbour was an important port for the import and export of fish and other commodities.

Robert walked to the front of the moored flotilla, three abreast, sometimes four, and proceeded to take a photograph, framing the vessels so that the effect of a forest of masts and rigging framed the picture. It was whilst taking the shots that he suddenly looked up in disbelief, his face turning pallid as though he'd seen a ghost.

It cannot be, he thought. She's dead. But she looks so much like her. The way she stood and the movement of her body, so distinctive of her persona. But her alluring red hair was now blonde and shorter, not the flowing locks that he had admired. She had her back to Robert so he wasn't entirely sure. Just then she turned around. It was her. It was Tara. A little older, but she still retained the slim body of youth. And her looks hadn't diminished either. Perhaps more mature, but she was still the stunning female he had known. But how had she survived? And why did she disappear? He had to know.

He went over to where the lugger was moored, on the outside adjacent to two other craft. She was busy coiling some rope, humming to herself, a contented murmur that drifted in the breeze. Then she stopped. She stood there motionless, like an animal caught in a headlight, transfixed by a blinding image. She turned around and looked at Robert. Her face went pale as though she too had seen a ghost, a spirit from the past and one that she did not expect to see.

'Tara, it is you,' he exclaimed.

'It is me, Robert.'

'But you died on the Island.'

'Evidently not. I'm not a ghost, if that's what you think.'

'No. That was me, wasn't it?'

'That's a long time ago now,' she replied with a sigh of sorrow.

They both stood there looking at the past, not knowing what to say. Robert had a thousand and one things to ask, but couldn't articulate a single question. Just like that first time her eyes were bewitching him, perhaps seducing him once more, reminding him of a brief hot spring spent together. He was glad to see her, that she was alive. She was pleased to see him, albeit tempered by fate.

'Come aboard. Let's talk,' she said.

'That would be good. I'd better go and tell Caroline. She's over in the café.'

'She's most welcome as well.'

'And two children,' added Robert.

Tara hesitated, with a pang of jealousy. 'Of course.'

The children were delighted to be shown around the lugger, and a crew member took care of them whilst their parents went below deck. Tara had made some tea and they sat in the cramped cabin that smelled of a combination of oil and bilge, looking at each other, assessing how the years had treated each of them.

'Lovely children you have,' remarked Tara.

'Yes,' said Caroline. 'The eldest is Charlotte. She's ten. Tom is seven.'

'How lucky you are,' said Tara with hint of poignancy.

'We've been blessed with two beautiful children,' replied Caroline.

'And what about you?' added Robert.

'What about me?' replied Tara in a tone that spoke of envy.

'What have you been doing? How did you escape the inferno? There are so many questions.'

'I know.'

Tara proceeded to tell Robert and Caroline how she had escaped by quickly darting into a series of passages which snaked from side to side, thus dissipating the energy of the fireball. She had managed to cover her head with an old towel, wet from the deluge, but had not escaped entirely and showed them scars to her arms and legs which had, over the years, thankfully faded.

'After you all left the Island, I remained behind for a couple of days. I told Madge everything that had happened. How I was involved in smuggling, Siegfried, the inferno, the death of Jake, the tunnel. Everything. She was naturally shocked, but forgave me. Why, I don't really know. Perhaps for being honest with her. During those two days, I did a lot of thinking. I realised that I must leave the Island, leave Looe.

I told Madge of my intention. She said I could stay. Pleaded with me to stay. But I couldn't. She accepted my decision. I told her that I would be gone for a while, but would return. That, I think, placated her. I was telling a lie. I had no intention of returning. My life in Looe was over. I had to make a new one, elsewhere. Madge helped me. She secured the funds from my bank account and obtained my passport. I gave her power of attorney over my business interests, with instructions to transfer them all to Tom. And that was it. I left the Island and Looe under cover of darkness, aboard my lugger moored just below the bridge. I had been restoring and converting it for a few years but it wasn't quite finished. I needed radio and navigational equipment as well as stores. I headed to Falmouth to purchase what I required. So as not to be noticed, I dyed my hair and dressed in fatigues, stayed in the port to do some repairs and fittings to the vessel and then headed across the Channel to France.'

'And then what?' interrupted Robert.

'Well, to cut a long story short, I sailed around the world.'

'That sounds romantic,' said Caroline.

'Not exactly romantic. I had a few narrow escapes. The lugger was almost capsized in the Pacific when a huge whale surfaced only feet from the vessel. And we were attacked by Somali pirates off the coast of Africa whilst sailing in the Indian Ocean.'

'What happened?' asked Robert.

'Fortunately, a Royal Navy frigate was nearby and came to our rescue. The first time I was glad to see those boys. And, oh yes, sailing across to Australia, I thought we were going to sink during the most ferocious storm I've ever encountered. Huge waves. The lugger was taking on water and but for the storm blowing through, I wouldn't be here today.'

'So what places did you visit?' asked Caroline.

'Most of the Mediterranean. In fact, I spent three years taking people around. I earned quite a bit and it was enjoyable. I then sailed down the east coast of Africa to Cape Town. Back up to India, Bombay, Madras and other places. Singapore, Indonesia, the Philippines, Australia and New Zealand. I then island-hopped across the Pacific, via Easter Island, to Chile and Valpariso. Before sailing down as far as Tierra del

Fuego. Round Cape Horn. That was some adventure. Up the east coast of the Americas, visiting the Falklands as far up as Nova Scotia. Then across the Atlantic, back into the Med.'

'Quite a journey,' said Caroline.

'I guess. But of all the places I've been to, nothing compares to Cornwall. It is, without exception, the most beautiful place in the world. And I should know.' Tara fell silent with her thoughts and looked wistful, as though she wanted to confide in Robert. He looked at Caroline and made a gesture to her.

'I'd better go and see how the children are getting on. I'll leave you two alone,' she said, getting up.

When she had disappeared on deck, Robert turned to Tara. She was shedding tears, which she was trying to mask.

'Are you alright?' he enquired.

'I am, but I can't help thinking about what could have been. All those places I've seen and they don't really mean anything to me. At the time, perhaps, but not now. I've got nobody to share them with. You see, I miss you Robert. I've missed you ever since that fateful day. I thought I might meet somebody. Oh I've had a few relationships along the way, but they've been ephemeral. No depth to them, so that they dry up after the rush of emotions. None of the men I've met have ever measured up to you. You were different. Those days together renovating the cottage were the happiest of my life.'

Robert didn't know what to feel. He had liked Tara, but had never really loved her. She had become an important part of his life at one time, but deep down he knew Caroline was his soul mate.

'I'm flattered,' he said with some sympathy.

'Are you? You never loved me. I know you didn't. I admit, at the beginning my intentions were to befriend you and so keep you within my sights. The family was all important and the smuggling business came first. But I fell in love with you. And then Caroline turned up and I realised that my chance had gone. I was a fool. She is a lovely person. You are so right for each other. I envy you both. I saw you and me like that, or at least I used to. And now I have nobody.'

'You do,' said Robert.

'Tom. He's just a cousin and one I've never been close to. It's my fault.